DEPARTMENT 19
DARKEST NIGHT

DEPARTMENT 19
DARKEST NIGHT

WILL HILL

HarperCollins *Children's Books*

First published in hardback in Great Britain by HarperCollins *Children's Books* in 2015
This paperback edition published in Great Britain by
HarperCollins Children's Books in 2016
HarperCollins *Children's Books* is a division of HarperCollins*Publishers* Ltd,
1 London Bridge Street, London, SE1 9GF

Follow Will Hill on twitter
@willhillauthor

www.department19exists.com
www.facebook.com/department19exists

1

ISBN 978-00-0-750591-3

Will Hill asserts the moral right to be identified as the author of the work.

Typeset in Berylium by Palimpsest Book Production Limited, Falkirk, Stirlingshire
Printed and bound in England by Clays Ltd, St Ives plc

MIX
Paper from
responsible sources
FSC® C007454

Find out more about HarperCollins and the environment at
www.harpercollins.co.uk/green

For everyone who has come this far.
Just a little further...

The woods are lovely, dark and deep,

But I have promises to keep,

And miles to go before I sleep,

And miles to go before I sleep.

Robert Frost

We have learned to believe, all of us – is it not so? And since so, do we not see our duty? Yes! And do we not promise to go on to the bitter end?

Abraham Van Helsing

MEMORANDUM 1

From: Office of the Director of the Joint Intelligence Committee

Subject: Revised classifications of the British governmental departments

Security: TOP SECRET

DEPARTMENT 1	Office of the Prime Minister
DEPARTMENT 2	Cabinet Office
DEPARTMENT 3	Home Office
DEPARTMENT 4	Foreign and Commonwealth Office
DEPARTMENT 5	Ministry of Defence
DEPARTMENT 6	British Army
DEPARTMENT 7	Royal Navy
DEPARTMENT 8	Her Majesty's Diplomatic Service
DEPARTMENT 9	Her Majesty's Treasury
DEPARTMENT 10	Department for Transport
DEPARTMENT 11	Attorney General's Office
DEPARTMENT 12	Ministry of Justice
DEPARTMENT 13	Military Intelligence, Section 5 (MI5)
DEPARTMENT 14	Secret Intelligence Service (SIS)
DEPARTMENT 15	Royal Air Force
DEPARTMENT 16	Northern Ireland Office
DEPARTMENT 17	Scotland Office
DEPARTMENT 18	Wales Office
DEPARTMENT 19	**CLASSIFIED**
DEPARTMENT 20	Territorial Police Forces
DEPARTMENT 21	Department of Health
DEPARTMENT 22	Government Communication Headquarters (GCHQ)
DEPARTMENT 23	Joint Intelligence Committee (JIC)

MEMORANDUM 2

From: Chief of the General Staff

Subject: Updated lists of the global supernatural departments

Security: MOST SECRET

UNITED STATES OF AMERICA	National Security Division 9 (NS9) Restricted Compound 7C, Nevada Test and Training Range, Nevada, USA
FEDERAL REPUBLIC OF GERMANY	The Office of the Supernatural (FTB) Complex 17, Dortmund, Germany
THE RUSSIAN FEDERATION	Supernatural Protection Commissariat (SPC) Restricted Area A12, Polyarny, Russia
THE PEOPLE'S REPUBLIC OF CHINA	The People's Bureau of the Supernatural (PBS6) Military Centre W, Western Hills, Beijing
THE ARAB REPUBLIC OF EGYPT	Section G (G-Sec) Al-Mazar Precinct, Cairo, Egypt
CANADA	The Office of Supernatural Affairs (OSA) Building 31, Canadian Forces Base Trenton, Trenton, Ontario
THE REPUBLIC OF SOUTH AFRICA	Military Detachment Alpha (MDA) Installation 25, Gauteng Province, South Africa
THE REPUBLIC OF INDIA	National Defence Unit C (N-DUC) Security Complex G341, Gujarat, India

| THE FEDERATIVE REPUBLIC OF BRAZIL | **Federal Security Unit 12 (Fl2)** Basin Airbase, Amazonas, Brazil |
| JAPAN | **Supernatural Self-Defense Force (SSDF)** Intelligence Command, Naha, Okinawa |

PROLOGUE

Jamie Carpenter soared over the battlefield, carrying Frankenstein effortlessly beneath him, marvelling at the scale of the fighting taking place below.

His view of it was fleeting, such was the speed he and the rest of the strike team were travelling, but it was enough to make quite an impression; the battle was already spread out across more than a mile of blasted landscape, the air full of movement and gunfire and screaming, the ground littered with black-clad bodies and soaked with vampire remains. Jamie tore his gaze away and focused on the looming shape of the medieval city, its pale stone darkening in the fading light, and, as he rose over the outer walls, his squad mates close behind him, he saw a distant figure floating near the summit of the hill, high above the raging battle.

Dracula, *he thought, his heart leaping in his chest.* Right where they said he would be.

This is going to be too easy.

Jamie swooped over the walls, rising above the wide cobbled street that led up through the city. He accelerated, the evening air cool as it rushed over his uniformed body, the rooftops passing below him in a blur, and allowed a smile to rise on to his face. As he soared over a wide square, he heard something above him, something that sounded like a flock of birds, and rolled to the side so he could look up and see what it was.

The sky above him was full of vampires.

They dropped silently out of the clouds, a vast dark swarm, and ripped into the strike team like a bolt of lightning, sending them spinning towards the ground. Something connected with the side of his helmet and he saw stars, his vision greying at the edges as his grip on Frankenstein loosened and gave way; the monster slipped from his grasp and fell towards the ancient city. Jamie lunged after him, but was hammered from all sides by heavy blows that drove him back and forth, bellowing with pain. He fought back furiously, but might as well have been trying to punch the wind; there seemed to be vampires all around him, as insubstantial as smoke, apart from when they struck. He ducked under a swinging fist and looked desperately around for his squad mates, but it was like trying to see through a colony of bats that had taken wing at the same time; all around him was darkness and churning movement.

A boot slammed into his stomach. Jamie folded in the air, the breath driven out of him, and sank towards the ground, barely able to even slow his fall. Cobblestones rose up to meet him, and he hit them hard enough to drive his teeth together on his tongue, spilling warm coppery liquid into his mouth. Pain raced through him, before being driven away by the heady taste of his own blood.

He leapt to his feet and scanned the narrow street he had landed in. There was no sign of his squad mates, or the vampires that had attacked them. He looked up, expecting to see them hurtling down towards him, but the sky was clear and empty; it was as though they had never been there at all.

Stupid, he told himself, and felt his eyes blaze with heat. Arrogant. Stupid.

Jamie leapt into the air, determined to locate the rest of the strike team and get their mission back on track.

A hand closed round his ankle and whipped him downwards.

Surprise filled him so completely that he didn't get his hands up until it was too late; his helmet thudded against the ground, and everything went black.

SIX MONTHS EARLIER

ZERO HOUR
PLUS 2 DAYS

1

HOME TRUTHS

CAISTER-ON-SEA, NORFOLK, ENGLAND

Jamie Carpenter stared at his father.

Time seemed to have stopped; there was utter silence, as though even the wind that had been gently rustling the trees around the cottage had paused. Jamie's heart was a solid lump of ice, his limbs frozen in place, his eyes unblinking, his mind stuck on a perpetual loop.

Oh God. Oh God. Oh God. Oh God.

His father looked different than the last time Jamie had seen him; he looked *old.* His face was deeply lined, and pale, as though he had not seen the sun in a long time. There were streaks of grey in his still-thick hair, and he looked worn out, like he was stretched too thin. But his eyes, the bright blue eyes that his son had inherited, still danced in the yellow glow of the light bulb above the door, and it was into them that Jamie found himself staring as his mind tried to process what he was seeing.

The still, silent moment lasted an unknowable length of time. The two men – one young, one old – stood motionless, a distance between them that was far more than merely physical; it contained an ocean of history, of grief and loss and wasted time. Then a noise emerged from Jamie's father's throat, a thick, involuntary sound like a gasp for air, and the spell was broken. The inertia in Jamie's mind spun loose, replaced by outright horror, by disgust so strong it was almost physical. He was suddenly full of the desire to run, to turn and flee from this place, from this apparition from the past, but, before he could force his reeling body to move, his father swept forward and lifted him into a hug so tight the air was trapped in his chest, and the disgust was replaced by a shuddering wave of relief, of something utterly, essentially *right*.

His eyes closed of their own accord, and his face fell against his father's shoulder, his hands dangling at his sides. He could feel his dad's heart pounding, feel the tremble in his arms as they held him tight. Jamie gave himself over to the emotions flooding through him, powerless to resist them; grief, pain, relief and desperate, sharp-edged happiness combining into a sensation he could barely endure.

Then his mind conjured up a single memory: his mother, standing beside him at the funeral of her husband. She was dressed all in black, and her beautiful, dignified face was etched with pain and covered in the shiny tracks of her tears. She was gripping his hand as though it was the only thing keeping her from collapsing to the floor, and she looked utterly lost, as if she had been thrust unwillingly into a world that no longer made sense, that was full only of pain and grief. The memory cleared Jamie's mind in an instant, wiping away the bittersweet cocktail that had momentarily overwhelmed him and replacing it with a single, burning emotion.

Fury.

He raised his arms and pushed his father backwards, breaking the embrace. Julian stumbled, a frown of confusion on his face, then regained his balance and stared at Jamie.

"What's wrong, son?" he asked, his voice low and thick.

"What's wrong?" growled Jamie, fury boiling and raging inside him, the sensation familiar and entirely welcome. "You actually have the nerve to ask me that? Everything's wrong! Everything! And all of it's your fault!"

His father's eyes widened with shock. "Jamie, I—"

"Shut up," said Jamie, his voice trembling with anger. "Just *shut up*. I went to your funeral. I stood next to Mum, next to *your wife*, and watched them bury you. Do you have any idea what that did to her?"

"No," said Julian. "I can't possibly—"

"I'm not done," interrupted Jamie. "Not even close. You let us think you were dead. I watched you die, and that memory has lived with me every single day since. Our entire lives turned to shit after you were dead. You couldn't let us know? Couldn't even get a message to us? Something?"

"It wasn't safe," said Julian. "I was trying to protect you both."

Jamie heard a growl rise from his throat, and felt a momentary surge of savage satisfaction as he saw his father take a frightened half-step backwards.

"That's all right then, is it?" he said. "Everything's cool, because you were trying to protect us. How well do you think that went?"

"I know," said Julian. "I'm sorry, I'm so sorry, Jamie. I made a mistake, I understand that now. But I didn't know what else to do."

"Ask your friends for help?" suggested Jamie. "The ones who'd fought alongside you dozens of times, and who would have done everything they could if you'd just asked them."

Julian nodded, and held his hands up. "You're right, Jamie. You are. And I don't blame you for being angry with me. I'm just trying to explain."

"You can't," said Jamie. "There's nothing you can say to make this OK. Don't you get that? Mum cried herself to sleep every night after you died, and we had to move house every few months because the whole country believed you were a traitor. We had to leave our home, and our friends, and we just barely survived the chaos you left behind. And now you're back, and what? You want me to tell you that I forgive you, that we can just put it all behind us and be a family again? Not a chance. Not a chance in hell."

"I'm sorry," repeated Julian. His face was ashen. "There's nothing else I can say, Jamie. I'm truly sorry."

"I believe you," said Jamie. "But I don't have time to give a shit about how sorry you are. Where did you go?"

"What?"

"When you pretended to die," said Jamie. "Where did you go?"

"America," said Julian. "There was a rumour about a vampire who'd been cured. When I heard about what happened to your mum, I went looking for him."

The fury boiling through Jamie turned as cold as ice.

"You knew?" he asked, his voice low and full of menace. "*You knew about Lindisfarne?*"

Julian nodded. "I knew," he said. "I heard about what you did. I was so proud, son, so proud of—"

"You knew your wife had been turned and your son had joined Blacklight, and still you didn't come in? Even then, you couldn't do the right thing?"

Julian winced, and said nothing.

"How did you know?" asked Jamie. "Who told you?"

"I can't say," said Julian. "I swore."

The answer burst into Jamie's mind like a bolt of lightning, filling him with white-hot clarity. He felt his stomach churn and his legs turn to jelly beneath him.

Oh no. Oh please, no.

He sought another answer, one that wasn't so terrible, but knew instantly that he was wasting his time; there was only one person it could have been.

The one person he wished it wasn't.

"I have to go," he said, and turned towards the door.

"Hey!" shouted Julian. He stepped forward and took hold of his son's arm. Jamie turned his head and stared down at the hand until his father released his grip and stepped back.

"What?" he asked. "What do you want from me?"

"This isn't how I wanted this to go, son," said Julian. "This isn't what I wanted at all."

Jamie laughed, incredulous. "Even now?" he said. "Even now, what *you* want is all you care about."

"That's not what I'm saying," said Julian, his face reddening. "You know it isn't. Why are you making this so hard?"

"And now you're blaming me?" asked Jamie, his voice a low hiss. "You actually have the balls to stand there and blame me for this? *You* did this, Dad. You did it all on your own. I don't know why you've decided to reappear now, and I don't know what you want from me, but I have to go. Now."

Julian stared at him. "Don't you even want to know how I did it?" he asked. "How I faked my death?"

"I couldn't give less of a shit," said Jamie. "And I'll tell you something else, something that you can think about when I'm gone and you're on your own again. I'm ashamed to be your son. Do you hear me? Ashamed."

The red in Julian's face darkened. "That's enough, Jamie," he said, his voice low. "I don't care what's happened, or how angry you're feeling right now. I am still your father and you will not speak to me like that."

Jamie laughed again, a sharp grunt of derision, and turned to the door. Again, his father stepped forward and took hold of his arm, and Jamie felt heat burst into his eyes as his self-control finally failed him. He spun, eyes blazing, fangs gleaming, and shoved his father away, hard. Julian was thrown across the room, slammed against the wall, and landed in a heap on the floor. He stared up at his son with a face full of terror, the expression of a man who is watching his worst nightmare come true before him. Jamie stepped into the air and floated above the carpet, fixing his father with his terrible crimson gaze.

"I never want to see you again," he growled. "Do you hear me? Never."

His father's face crumpled. Tears brimmed in the corners of his eyes.

"You're my son," managed Julian, his voice barely audible.

Jamie's eyes darkened. "Fuck you," he said, then turned and flew through the door of the cottage. He swept down the path, ignoring the sobbing sounds behind him, and flew back towards the idling SUV. He could see Frankenstein behind its wheel; the monster was staring through the windscreen, his face set in a stern line.

He knew, thought Jamie. *He knew what I was going to find out, but he brought me here anyway.*

For a moment, his heart softened towards the man who had sworn to protect him and his family, as he considered the position his father's actions must have put Frankenstein in, particularly once the monster became acquainted with Jamie and his mother. But then the cold reappeared, freezing his heart solid.

He should have told me. I don't care what he swore. He shouldn't have left me in the dark.

Jamie reached the SUV and tapped on the passenger window. Frankenstein looked round, and wound it down.

"Is everything OK?" he asked.

"No," said Jamie, and heard the catch in his voice. "But I think you already knew that, didn't you?"

A grimace crossed the monster's face. "What happened?"

"I know you knew," said Jamie. "Please don't deny it."

"I'm not going to."

"You helped him fake his death."

"Yes."

"And it was you that told him about Lindisfarne. About what happened to me and my mother."

"Yes," said Frankenstein. His face was very still, his grey-green skin paler than usual, his eyes locked on Jamie's.

"So when you rescued me from Alexandru," said Jamie, "you knew my father wasn't dead, even then. You knew I hadn't watched him die, and you never told me. Never told my mum."

A look of immense pain creased the monster's face. "I couldn't, Jamie," he said, his voice a low rumble. "I couldn't do that to you. You have to understand."

Jamie felt the block of ice in his chest crack sharply. Pain bloomed out of it, accompanied by a profound sense of loss, of awful, bitter grief.

"I do," he said, and blinked away sudden tears. "So I want *you* to understand something. You and I are done. I want you to stay away from me."

He tore his gaze away from the monster, leapt off the ground, and accelerated into the sky, desperate to leave everything, and everyone, behind.

2

DIMINISHED RESPONSIBILITY

Kate Randall took a deep breath and pushed open the door to the Security Division, trying to slow her racing heart.

It was ridiculous, she tried to tell herself, to be nervous about entering the wide suite of desks and offices that had essentially become her home in the months since she had accepted the offer to join Blacklight; her office had come to feel like a sanctuary, as chaos and darkness raged around the Department, and the Division contained men and women she would have readily trusted with her life.

But now the Division had changed.

Major Paul Turner, who had for a number of years been the Blacklight Security Officer and Kate's immediate boss, was now Director of the entire Department, having been promoted following the loss of Cal Holmwood on the gravel surrounding Château Dauncy. Paul was unquestionably the right choice and, as a serving Operator, Kate was delighted; she had no doubt that he would lead the Department with the same bravery and dedication that had characterised his entire Blacklight career. But on a personal level, she was far less thrilled; she and Turner had become close over the preceding months, tied together by an unswerving commitment to the Security Division, by the punishing ordeal that had been ISAT, and by red-raw grief over the death of Shaun, who had been both Major Turner's son and Kate's boyfriend.

Inside Blacklight, Kate had found friends, Larissa Kinley, Jamie Carpenter and Matt Browning foremost among them, and she was grateful; she trusted them implicitly. But if she was completely honest with herself, which she always tried to be, it had been Paul Turner she had come to rely on most heavily, and her heart was racing because she was no longer sure that would be possible.

Kate stepped into the familiar hum of voices and activity that always filled the Security Division and made her way through the clusters of desks, nodding to colleagues as she passed, her eyes focused on the door of the office that belonged to the Security Officer. It was next to her own, a proximity that had given rise to a number of unkind comments in the early days of her transfer to Security, in the aftermath of ISAT. She knew that there had been plenty of whispered insults, accusations that she was Paul Turner's pet, that she was given special treatment because she had been his dead son's girlfriend. She had never confronted the charges, and done her best never to show how much they hurt her; she knew that Turner had treated her favourably, that she had become his most trusted Lieutenant in the Division – perhaps even the entire Department – but she did not believe that it had all been about Shaun. She was, all arrogance aside, a damn good Operator, and damn good at her job.

The new Security Officer was Angela Darcy, and Kate would never, even for a moment, have disagreed with her selection – not only was she personally one of Kate's favourite people in the Loop, she was a genuinely outstanding Operator, one whose record more than justified her promotion, and Kate was looking forward to working with her. They had been scheduled to meet the following morning, as part of Angela's first official day as Security Officer, but Kate was eager to get the formalities over with. She reached the door, took a deep breath, and knocked sharply on it.

"Come in," called a familiar voice from inside the office. Kate turned the handle, opened the door, and stepped through it.

The office was no more colourful or full of life than it had been when Paul Turner had occupied it; the walls were the same bare grey, the shelves full only of folders and box files. Behind the desk at the rear of the room, Angela Darcy was leaning back in her chair, a welcoming smile on her face.

"Lieutenant Randall," she said, her voice dripping with fake formality. "It's good to see you."

"You too, Captain Darcy," said Kate, smiling back at her.

"This feels weird," said Angela. "Does it feel weird to you?"

"A bit," said Kate. "Should I call you sir from now on?"

"God, no," said the Security Officer, her face reddening. "Call me Angela, please. Captain, if you absolutely have to."

Kate nodded, her smile still in place. "All right. I'll do that."

"Good," said Angela. "How's everything looking?"

"Fine," said Kate. "There was nothing unusual in the overnight logs, and today's been pretty peaceful so far, all things considered."

"That's good," said Angela. "That's great, to be honest with you. I could really do with a quiet day or two while I get to grips with everything. I'm going to be relying on you a lot in the next few weeks, Kate. Is that all right with you?"

"Of course," said Kate. "Whatever I can do to help."

"Thanks," said Angela, and grinned at her. "I know you think you should be sitting in this chair, so I appreciate you getting on my side."

Kate frowned. "I'm sorry?"

"Come on, Kate," said Angela. "This is me. You don't have to play dumb. I know you wanted to be Security Officer. I know at least part of you thinks you should be, and I'd honestly think less of you if you didn't. But this is the situation we find ourselves in, and I really, really want you on my team, so I hope it's not going to be something we can't get past?"

"No," said Kate, instantly. "It really isn't. You have my word."

Angela nodded. "Good news," she said. "Tell yourself I'm just keeping the seat warm for you, if it helps."

Kate's smile returned. "All right, Captain," she said. "I'll do that."

"Fantastic. In which case, I've got about a million reports to read, and every one of them is apparently the most important thing in the world. So is there anything else right now?"

"Just one thing," said Kate. "Major Turner and I used to meet first thing every morning to go over anything important that had come up overnight. I don't know whether you want to continue with that arrangement?"

"Yes," said Angela. "I do. I think that will be extremely useful. Let's start tomorrow. Nine o'clock?"

Kate nodded. "Nine o'clock."

"Great," said Angela. "Thank you. For now, dismissed."

Kate walked back through the Security Division, a warm wave of relief flowing through her.

She knew it had been stupid to be nervous about meeting Angela Darcy, a woman who was already almost a friend, but she had not been able to help it, for the reason her new Commanding Officer had immediately identified.

Although she would never have admitted it to anyone, Kate *had* been jealous when the new Security Officer had been announced. She knew – objectively, at least – that it could never have been her; she was far too junior, still only a Lieutenant, and her Blacklight experience even now consisted of less than a year's service.

But objective knowledge hadn't stopped it hurting when the decision had been announced.

Now she could feel the pain ebbing away. Angela had instantly seen through her and brought the issue out into the open, which meant they could move past it. And in truth, Kate had to admit that *not* being the new Security Officer would make her life inside the Loop a lot easier; there were plenty of Operators and staff who *already* muttered about how quickly she and her friends had been promoted.

That's not our fault, though, she thought. *None of us ever asked for any of it. And seriously, I don't know why people are so surprised. Jamie is a descendant of the Founders and a natural Operator. Larissa was the first vampire Operator the Department had ever had. And Matt is an honest-to-God genius. How stupid would it have been for Blacklight not to use them? Honestly, how could they not have ended up as important as they are?*

And what about you? whispered an oily voice in the back of her head. *What makes you so special? What have you done? Nothing...*

Bullshit, thought Kate, firmly. *I was on the team that took down Albert Harker. I volunteered for ISAT when nobody else would, even though I knew it would make me unpopular, and I saw it through even after Richard Brennan tried to kill me over it. I've earned everything that's come to me. The people who matter understand that. And Angela Darcy is one of them.*

I'm sure of it.

Kate strode towards the lift at the end of the Level A corridor. She stepped through the metal doors when it arrived, and pressed the button marked 0. Barely ten seconds later the doors opened again, and she walked straight into the dark, floating shape of Larissa Kinley.

"Kate!" exclaimed the vampire Operator. "I was just about to come looking for you. Have you got a minute?"

Kate smiled. "Evening, Larissa," she said. "Of course I have. What's going on?"

"Have you seen Jamie? In the last few hours, I mean?"

She frowned. "Isn't he on Patrol Respond?"

Larissa shook her head. "His squad's off tonight."

"I haven't seen him," said Kate. "Not since yesterday. What's so urgent?"

"He went somewhere with Colonel Frankenstein," said Larissa. "Hours ago. But I've just seen Frankenstein come back through the hangar, and he didn't look very happy. Jamie wasn't with him."

"Maybe he flew back on his own?"

"Maybe," said Larissa, although she didn't sound convinced. Kate took a closer look at her friend and saw the downward curves at the corners of her mouth, the eyes that were slightly wider than usual.

Something's wrong, thought Kate. *She looks worried half to death.*

"Talk to me, Larissa," she said. "What's going on?"

"It's nothing," said Larissa, a little too quickly. "I just really need to find him, Kate. Can you help me?"

"Have you run his chip?"

"I tried," said Larissa. "The function has been locked. Apparently, only Security can access it."

Kate frowned. "That's news to me," she said. "Do you want me to try?"

Larissa nodded. "Please."

Kate pulled her console from her belt, unlocked it, and scrolled to the chip location programme. She searched for Jamie's name, and pressed his ID number with her thumb. The console vibrated in her hand as it worked, then fell still as the results appeared.

"He's somewhere in Kent," said Kate. "A village called Brenchley."

"Shit," said Larissa, and grimaced. "That can't be good."

"Why?" asked Kate. "What's in Brenchley?"

Larissa shook her head. "Don't worry about it," she said. "Thank you, Kate. I'll see you later."

"Larissa, wait—"

But the vampire girl had already turned and flown through the hangar doors at the end of the corridor. Kate momentarily considered following her, but she knew how fast her friend was; Larissa would likely be several miles away already, and accelerating. Instead, she stared at the yellow and black striped doors, her heart suddenly full of worry.

3

RUNNING ON EMPTY

Larissa flew south-east, the wind whipping her hair back, her stomach churning with nervousness that felt increasingly close to panic.

It had been wrong to leave Kate standing in the Level 0 corridor without an explanation, but she had not been able to help it; the news that Jamie was in Brenchley, the location of his childhood home, had sent an awful chill running up her spine. That her boyfriend had left the Loop with Frankenstein without telling her was cause enough for concern; it was clearly a private matter, and private matters involving the monster and the Carpenter family were rarely sources of light and happiness. The fact that Frankenstein had returned home alone had deepened her unease, especially after she had seen the thunderous look on the monster's face as he strode through the hangar, and the results of Kate's chip search had been the final straw; she needed to see her boyfriend immediately. Not least because a voice in the back of her head, the one she hated and tried her hardest to ignore, was whispering that whatever was happening with Jamie was very likely related to the secret that she had made the decision to keep from him.

It's not fair, she thought, as she urged herself ever faster through the night air. *I was going to tell him. I was literally on my way to tell him.*

But the voice in her head was unsympathetic.

You could have told him a hundred times, it whispered. *That you didn't is nobody's fault but your own.*

The dark countryside swept past below, dotted with yellow lights from roads and buildings, from which Larissa's supernaturally powerful ears made out snatches of conversation and the occasional bar of music. Her console was in her hand, and she was following its GPS reader towards the small village where Jamie and his parents had lived before the supernatural had intruded on their lives. Although the truth was that Julian Carpenter had opened the door to it, unbeknownst to his family.

Eighteen miles. Should be there in a couple of minutes.

She shivered. Her altitude and speed were making the climate-control system of her uniform work overtime to keep her warm, but she knew the shudder had nothing to do with the temperature; it was the result of her growing certainty that, no matter how fast she pushed herself towards her boyfriend, it was already too late.

Larissa swooped down until she was barely clearing the tops of the trees, and headed straight towards the red dot at the centre of her console's screen. An empty country road stretched out beneath her and she followed its slowly winding curves, slowing her speed as she banked left and right. Up ahead, a small cluster of houses appeared, set back from the road and surrounded by a dark landscape of fields and woods. The red dot stopped moving, but she would have known she was close to Jamie without its assistance; she had picked up his unmistakable scent floating on the gentle night breeze.

She zeroed in on it, a potent combination of both her boyfriend's distinctive smell and something that bloomed from the centre of her being: familiarity, connection, and love, as clear and bright as a beacon. The road swept away to the right, and just before the bend stood a house, a large, slightly rambling pile of old bricks with an angular tiled roof, a long garden at the back and a front lawn leading down to a towering oak tree that extended far out over the road.

Sitting on one of its highest branches, staring down at the old house, was Jamie.

She brought herself to a halt, floating easily in the air, and stared at her boyfriend. He was pale, which was not unusual, but his skin looked almost grey, apart from around his eyes, where it was red. She felt her heart thump in her chest; she wanted to go to him, to cross the space between them and wrap him in her arms, but she didn't dare.

She was not yet sure exactly what she was dealing with.

"Hey," she said, cautiously.

Jamie forced the tiniest smile she had ever seen him produce. "Hey," he said. "How did you find me?"

"Kate ran your chip for me," said Larissa. "I was worried about you, Jamie."

He nodded his head, and returned his gaze to the house. She floated where she was, unsure of what to do and hating the feeling.

"This was where he was," said Jamie, eventually, his voice low. "Alexandru. The night it happened, he was in this tree with his followers. I heard him laugh, but I couldn't see anything. It was dark and everything was covered in shadows."

"There wasn't anything you could have done," said Larissa. "He'd have killed you without a second thought."

Jamie stretched out an arm and pointed down at the house. "You see that window? The big one?" Larissa followed the path of his finger and nodded. "That's where I was," he continued. "I was looking through that window because I heard Dad's car pull into the drive and I was so excited that he was home. I was always so pleased to see him."

"Of course," she said. "You were just a kid."

Jamie nodded again, and fell silent. After a seemingly endless moment, Larissa forced herself to speak.

"What's going on, Jamie?" she asked. "Where did you and Frankenstein go this afternoon?"

He raised his head, and Larissa felt her stomach lurch at the sight of the empty expression on his face.

"He took me to see my dad," he said, his voice low and halting. "He's still alive. After everything that's happened, after all this *shit*, he's still alive. There's a cottage in Norfolk, where we used to go and visit my nan. That's where Frankenstein took me. That's where he is."

Larissa stared helplessly at her boyfriend. "Jamie…"

"He *hugged* me. Can you believe that? Just hugged me, like nothing had happened. I was nearly sick."

"What happened to him? Where has he been?"

Jamie shook his head. "It doesn't matter. I told him I never want to see him again. Told Frankenstein the same thing."

Larissa grimaced. This was exactly what she had dreaded, every time she closed her eyes at the end of another day in which she had failed to tell her boyfriend what she had overheard.

"Why?" she asked. "What did Frankenstein do?"

"He knew, Larissa," said Jamie. "He knew Dad didn't die, that he was still alive the whole time. He was sending him *emails*, for Christ's sake, giving him updates on me and Mum. How could he do that?"

"I don't know," said Larissa, her voice low. "I presume he thought it was for the best. He would never hurt you, Jamie, not on purpose. You must know that."

"I don't know anything any more," said Jamie. "I can't trust anyone apart from you and Kate and Matt. And my mum. My poor mum, Larissa. What am I supposed to tell her about all this?"

Larissa stared at him. She had no answer to his question.

"She thinks he's dead too," said Jamie. "She mourned him. *We* mourned him. It'll destroy her if I tell her."

"So don't," said Larissa, "if you don't think it'll do any good. Let her be."

"I don't have the right to keep it from her. I can't make that decision on her behalf."

"You can," she said. "If you think it's the right thing to do, if you think you're sparing her pain. Or you just don't know how to tell her."

Jamie stared at her for a long moment, then frowned. His eyes narrowed, and Larissa saw red light flicker into their corners.

"Why aren't you more surprised?" he asked, his voice suddenly low.

"What are you talking about?"

"I just told you that my dad faked his death, that he's been alive this whole time, and that Frankenstein knew about it. So why do you look like I just told you tomorrow's weather forecast?"

"Jamie..."

His face fell, and Larissa felt a shard of ice pierce her heart.

"Oh no," he said, his voice barely more than a whisper, his eyes huge and staring. "Not you too, Larissa. Please. I can't bear it."

"I didn't know," she said, her voice high and unsteady. "Not for certain. You have to believe me, Jamie, I didn't know. I just overheard something I wasn't supposed to."

"What?" he asked. "What did you hear?"

"When I came back from Nevada," she said. "There was a prisoner on the same flight, in handcuffs and a hood. We weren't allowed to even speak to him. When they brought him off the plane at the Loop, Cal Holmwood was waiting in the hangar and I heard him say, 'Welcome back, Julian.' That's all, I swear."

"That's all?" said Jamie. "*That's all?* How many prisoners called

Julian do you think the Director would have made a point of personally welcoming?"

"I see that now, Jamie." She was on the verge of tears, but she ordered herself to stay strong, to get through this without breaking down. "But I didn't know if it would do any good to tell you. What if it wasn't him? Or Cal refused to tell you either way? It would just have made things worse."

"Worse?" said Jamie, his voice rising as his eyes narrowed. "It would've made things *worse*? Are you kidding me?"

Here it comes, thought Larissa. *Here comes the explosion.*

But she was wrong. Jamie stared at her, his face reddening, then let out a long, weary sigh and dropped his eyes.

"Were you ever going to tell me the truth?" he asked, his voice barely audible.

"I was going to tell you this afternoon," said Larissa, realising how pitiful the words sounded. "I was coming to find you when I found out you and Frankenstein had left the Loop."

Jamie let out a grunt of laughter with absolutely no humour in it. "That's convenient," he said.

"It's the truth," she said. "I hope you can believe it."

"No more secrets," he said, and grimaced. "Right? That's what we promised each other."

Larissa didn't respond. There was nothing she could say. She stared silently at her boyfriend, profoundly aware of the chasm that seemed to have yawned open between them. Jamie kept his gaze on the ground, his shoulders hunched, his arms wrapped tightly round himself. He looked so small, as though a strong breeze could have blown him off the branch and sent him tumbling to the lawn below. When he finally spoke again, he didn't look at her.

"I've been thinking," he said. "About everything that's happened since Alexandru arrived in this tree. Blacklight, Dracula, vampires, all of it. And I've realised something. Nothing good has come of any of it."

Larissa felt her heart break in her chest. "Nothing?"

"Nothing."

She tried to ignore the pain his words had sent coursing through her body, and forced her vocal cords into action. "You can trust me," she said, hearing the unsteadiness in her voice. "I know it probably doesn't feel like it right now, and I understand if you find it hard to believe. But *you can trust me*, Jamie. You really can."

He raised his head and looked directly into her eyes. "I've heard that before," he said. "More than once."

Anger burst through Larissa as her vampire side rushed to the fore. She knew she was in the wrong, that Jamie had every right to feel disappointed and let down, but she could not simply float in the cold air and allow herself to be tortured indefinitely.

"What are you saying, Jamie?" she demanded. "No more bullshit. Talk to me."

"I need to think."

"About what?"

"About everything," said Jamie. "About what happens next. It's all coming to an end, Larissa. Everything. Can't you feel it?"

She shook her head, and felt red heat boil into her eyes. She was suddenly furious with him for wallowing in self-pity when there was so much at stake.

My family won't even talk to me, she thought. *They might as well be dead. At least your mum is safe, and your dad still wants you, even if he did lie to you. At least he cares that you're alive.*

"I don't recognise this version of you," she said, her voice little more than a growl. "The Jamie I know, the one that I fell for? *That* Jamie fights to the very end, even when everything seems hopeless. Where the hell is he?"

Jamie stared at her. "I'm tired of fighting," he said.

"So what do we do now? Tell me."

"Go back to the Loop," he said. "I just need some time. I'll see you tomorrow."

Larissa floated in the air, her glowing eyes fixed on his. He held her gaze for a moment, then shifted it to the gravel drive below, where everything had been set in motion by the thunder of machine-gun fire and the apparent death of a man who had been desperate for a way out. She wanted to shake her boyfriend, to scream at him to snap out of it, then wrap her arms round him and tell him that she loved him, couldn't he see that, wasn't that enough for him?

Instead, she turned away without a word and flew back towards the Loop as fast as she could force her body to move. The cold air made her eyes water, hiding tears that she would never have let anybody see, not least the boy she was leaving behind.

ZERO HOUR
PLUS 11 DAYS

4

THE DEFINITION OF INSANITY

Matt Browning's stomach rumbled so aggressively that he immediately looked around to check whether any of his colleagues had heard it, his face reddening with embarrassment. Mercifully, it had either not been as loud as it had seemed or his fellow members of the Lazarus Project were simply too engrossed in their work to have noticed it; there was not so much as a raised eyebrow to be seen.

Matt checked his watch and saw that it was well past noon. He had been at his desk for almost seven hours, and had not eaten since grabbing a sandwich sometime the previous afternoon.

He was absolutely starving.

Matt got to his feet and carefully stretched his arms out above his head until he felt the muscles in his shoulders creak. The doctors had told him he could remove the foam neck brace tomorrow, but for now it was still wrapped round his throat like a thick collar. His back and neck were in constant pain, the result of the car crash he had caused in San Francisco, but a regimen of dizzyingly strong pills was keeping it at bay. The finger that Major Simmons had broken as he gripped the steering wheel was splinted and wrapped in bandages, but mercifully it was the little one, and it didn't interfere with his ability to work.

He lowered his arms and took a look around the lab. At the far end of the long room, Professor Karlsson, the project's Director, was deep in conversation with two of his senior staff. In the corner nearest the door, three of Matt's colleagues were sitting in plastic chairs, staring intently into a slowly rotating holographic model of their best guess at what the genetic structure of a cure for vampirism might look like: a swirling cone of DNA strands, balls of blue and red proteins rotating round grey stretches that represented sections as yet unmapped, of which there were still a frustratingly large number. The rest of the Lazarus staff were huddled at their desks, grinding through the seemingly endless potential formulas that required testing on the project's supercomputer array. Every one would almost certainly turn out to be flawed, at which point the results would be written up and filed away, and the process would begin again.

To Matt's right, her blonde head buried in what looked like a protein recombination equation, sat Natalia Lenski, the girl he no longer knew exactly how to refer to. His friend? His girlfriend?

He had no idea.

Whatever existed between them was fragile, the result of a halting, tentative courtship involving two people to whom confidence did not come naturally, a courtship that had culminated in a kiss that had quite literally taken Matt's breath away. It had been instigated by Natalia as he arrived back from California and been designed to soften the blow of the news he was returning home to: that Jamie Carpenter, his best friend, had been bitten by a vampire, and turned.

There had been two more kisses since. Whereas the first had been full of fire and passion, the second had been gentle, almost chaste, as Matt lay in the infirmary after a scan had confirmed there was no permanent damage to his spine. The third had been frenzied, a stolen moment the previous day when they had run into each other in the Level B corridor, a remarkable coincidence given how much time they both spent in the Lazarus laboratories. The momentarily empty corridor and the possibility of being caught had lent the kiss an urgency that had left Matt dizzy; he still blushed at the memory of it.

But that had been yesterday. Now he was standing two metres away from her without the slightest clue what he should say or do, and the determined way that Natalia was staring at her screen suggested she had no more idea than he did. In moments like this, the ones that other people appeared to navigate with ease but which he found as difficult and confusing as a labyrinth, Matt often asked himself what Jamie would do. The honest answer was usually something reckless and arguably foolhardy, but it was still a helpful exercise. Inaction did not come naturally to Jamie; he would do *something*, even if it turned out to be wrong, and Matt was gradually realising that it was better to try and fail than do nothing.

He took a deep breath, and crouched down beside Natalia's desk.

"Hey," he whispered.

The Russian girl turned her head to look at him, and the smile on her face made his head spin; it was wide, genuine, and utterly beautiful.

"Hello," she said, her voice low. "Are you OK?"

Matt nodded. "I'm good," he said. "Well, not really. I'm hungry. Come to the canteen with me."

Natalia frowned. "Now? I have work to do."

"It'll still be here when you get back," said Matt. "Did you have breakfast this morning?"

"No."

"Then you have no excuse," said Matt. "Come on. I'm buying."

Her frown deepened. "The canteen is free, Matt."

"I know," he replied, and smiled. "It was a figure of... oh, forget it. Just come with me."

"To our canteen? Or the one downstairs."

"Downstairs," he said. "The main one. I want to get out of here for fifteen minutes."

Natalia nodded. "OK," she said, and pushed her chair back from her desk. She got to her feet and blushed a delicate pale pink as Matt stood up and looked at her.

"Is something wrong?" she asked.

"Not a thing," he replied. "Let's go."

They walked along the corridor and into the lift without saying a word.

The silence wasn't awkward, however; it felt safe, and comfortable, and as soon as Natalia pressed the button marked G and the lift began to descend, she turned and kissed him, her body pressed against his. Matt's eyes flew wide with surprise, then closed as he kissed her back, his hands on her waist as her fingers pressed into his shoulders. A flash of pain raced down his back, but he ignored it, concentrating only on not concentrating on anything, allowing himself to sink into a moment that needed no input from his endlessly rational mind.

The lift slowed to a halt with a familiar beep and Matt and Natalia sprang apart as the metal doors slid open, revealing two Operators in full uniform. They nodded as the two teenagers exited the lift, their faces flushed, their skin tingling. Matt momentarily considered taking hold of Natalia's hand, but quickly decided against it; the busy canteen was only a hundred or so metres away, and it was not the time or place for such a wildly extravagant display of public affection.

Natalia smiled as he held open the canteen door for her. The cavernous room was as loud as ever, full of conversation and laughter and the clatter of plates on trays and boots on the tiled floor. As Matt led Natalia to where the long run of metal counters began, she whispered to him in a voice that was barely audible.

"People are looking at me."

He frowned, and glanced around the room. A few heads *were*

turned in their direction, although the expressions on the faces did not appear unkind, or hostile; if anything, they seemed curious. Matt stared back, until understanding hit him and he turned to Natalia with a smile on his face.

"Don't worry," he said. "It's not you. Well, it is, but it's both of us. It's Lazarus. People aren't used to seeing us out of the labs." He tapped the distinctive orange pass that hung from a lanyard around Natalia's neck. "*This* is what they're looking at."

Natalia nodded with apparent relief. "Good," she said. "Although it is not as if we never leave the laboratories."

"Really?" he asked. "When was the last time you were anywhere apart from the labs or your quarters?"

"When I went to the infirmary," she said, instantly. "To see you."

Matt smiled. "Fair enough," he said. "But you know me, and I was here before Lazarus existed. And you know Kate, and Jamie. Most of our colleagues have never spoken to anyone outside the project. I doubt most of them would even know what happened at Château Dauncy if the Professor hadn't briefed them on it."

Natalia picked up a pair of trays and slid them on to the first counter. "Perhaps it is better that way," she said. "Perhaps it is easier."

"What do you mean?"

"Inside the laboratories is science. There are problems that need solutions. Outside there is blood and fear and everything is life or death. Perhaps thinking about that would not help."

Matt nodded; he knew exactly what she was saying. Not thinking about the consequences of Lazarus undoubtedly made it easier to get up and go to work every morning, whereas dwelling on the ramifications of each day that passed without the discovery of a viable cure would likely be crippling.

"How are your friends?" asked Natalia. "I have not seen them since France."

Matt shrugged. "Truthfully?" he said, placing a cheeseburger on his plate and piling the remaining space with fries. "I'm not sure. It was bad when they got back, after what happened to Cal, and so many others. Bad for everyone. I don't know how they keep going, to be honest with you."

"Because they have faith," said Natalia, as she filled a small bowl with salmon salad. "They believe we will win in the end."

"They *did* believe that," said Matt. "And I'm sure some of them still do. Not all of them, though. Not any more. That was their best shot, as far as a lot of the Department is concerned. And they missed it."

"So it is all down to us," said Natalia, and smiled at him.

Matt grinned. "Then I guess we're screwed, aren't we?"

He lifted his tray and led Natalia across to an empty table. He attacked his burger as soon as he sat down, and within three bites half of it had disappeared. Natalia picked delicately at her salad with a fork, a smile on her face as she watched him eat.

"Sorry," he said, wiping his mouth with a paper napkin. "I hadn't realised how hungry I was. It's like you're so deep in work that you manage to forget you're even hungry, then you remember all at once."

Natalia frowned. "Why did you say sorry?"

"When?"

"Just then. You said sorry, then that you hadn't realised how hungry you were. Why were you sorry?"

Matt shrugged. "I saw you smile at how fast I was eating," he said. "It's just what people say."

"Perhaps you apologise too often," said Natalia.

Matt sat back in his chair. "What makes you say that?"

"I hear you say sorry many times. But you are a brilliant scientist, and a good friend, and you have nothing to apologise for. I wonder if you know that."

Matt grimaced. "It's hard for me."

"To do what? Believe in yourself?"

"Yes," he said.

"Why?"

"I don't know," said Matt. "I felt like a disappointment for a long time. It's a hard habit to shake."

"Because of your father?"

His eyes widened with surprise. "I… yeah. Maybe. I think I always felt like I should apologise for not being the kind of son he wanted."

"If you are not what he wanted, he is an idiot," said Natalia, and smiled fiercely at him. "He should have been proud every day to be your father."

Matt felt heat rise into his cheeks. "Thank you," he said. "I think he is now. But I wish we could go back in time and have you tell him that."

"I would tell him."

He smiled. "I know you would."

Natalia smiled back at him, then frowned as a shadow fell across their table. Matt looked up and saw an Operator he didn't recognise standing over them, his helmet under his arm, his face set and solemn.

Oh shit, he thought. *We've been here before. Why are neither of my super-powerful vampire friends ever with me when this type of crap happens?*

"Can we help you?" asked Natalia.

The Operator glanced at her, shook his head, and fixed his gaze on Matt. He put the helmet carefully down on the table and extended his hand towards the teenager. Matt took it, a look of profound confusion on his face, and was almost jerked out of his seat as the Operator pumped his arm up and down.

"I'm Tom Johnson," he said, in a thick American accent. "You're Matt Browning, right?"

Matt nodded; bewilderment had robbed him of the ability to form words.

"Awesome," said Johnson. "I just wanted to tell you that me and the rest of Intelligence heard about what you did in San Francisco. Driving into a brick wall on purpose to take out a double agent? That's insane, dude. Seriously."

Out of the corner of his eye, Matt saw a smile spread across Natalia's face.

"Thanks," he said. "That's good of you to say. I didn't really plan it, to be honest."

Johnson laughed. "Probably a good thing," he said. "You might have had second thoughts. Your neck all right?"

Matt touched his fingers to the foam brace. "Getting there," he said. "This comes off tomorrow."

Johnson nodded. "Glad to hear it. And apologies for the interruption, I just wanted to say hello. You two look after yourselves, all right?"

Matt nodded. "Thanks. We will."

Johnson turned and strode across the room to where a group of Operators were waiting for him. They exited the canteen, and Matt turned to Natalia as the doors swung shut behind them.

"Well," he said. "That was different."

5

FALLOUT

AN HOUR LATER

Jamie walked along Level B, concentrating on keeping his feet on the ground.

He *wanted* to fly down the grey corridor as fast as he was able, but he shared Larissa's instinctive reluctance to demonstrate his vampire abilities inside the Loop. It was not that his colleagues were unused to seeing such powers – the Blacklight base was one of the few places in the world where they might be considered unremarkable – but rather that they felt like something that separated him from the ranks of Operators, a sensation he took no pleasure in.

Jamie had flown back from Brenchley as the eastern sky had begun to purple, reaching the hangar minutes before dawn broke over the horizon. After Larissa had departed, he had spent the rest of the long night deep in thought, his mind churning as it sought answers and explanations. His anger had eventually given way to a profound sense of loneliness, of having everything that he most relied on ripped away from him, and that loneliness had in turn been replaced by self-pity and bitter tears, as he silently raged at the unfairness of it all. He did not deserve the lies he had been told and the betrayals he had suffered; he had always tried to do the right thing, and had received only heartbreak in return. The eventual drying of his tears had been accompanied by a burst of self-loathing at having acted like such a child, like a spoilt brat who believed the entire world revolved around him.

Finally, as the darkness began to soften and lift, determined clarity had settled on him. The intermingled issues of his father and Frankenstein could wait, as could the decision about what, if anything, to tell his mum.

What could *not* wait was Larissa.

As soon as he touched down on the concrete floor of the hangar, he had sent her a message asking if she was awake. He had received no reply by the time the lift had carried him down to Level B, so he had walked quickly along the corridor and knocked on her door. There had been no response, and his supernaturally sharp ears had detected no sounds of movement from inside her quarters, so he had gone reluctantly to his room and slept fitfully, his mind whirring with worry. He had climbed back out of his bed barely two hours later and pulled a clean uniform on, trying all the while to quiet his increasingly frantic brain.

It's fine. It'll be fine. She just didn't want to talk to you last night, and you can't really blame her for that. Go and find her and tell her you're sorry and sort it out. It's not too late.

But there had still been no answer to his repeated knocks on her door or increasingly frequent messages, and no sign of her in the canteen or the Playground or the Briefing Rooms on Level A. He had sat through a routine Operational review with his feet tapping and his fists clenching and as soon as it was finished, after what felt like a thousand hours, he had sent a message to the one person he could ask for help in finding Larissa. To his enormous relief, Kate had replied immediately.

IN MY QUARTERS. WHAT'S UP?

Jamie stopped outside his friend's door, took a deep breath, and knocked on it, hard. A second later it swung open and Kate appeared, a slightly quizzical look on her face; it took all of Jamie's self-control not to hug the breath out of her.

"Morning, Jamie," she said. "Everything all right?"

He shook his head. "I don't think so. Can I come in?"

"Of course," said Kate, and stepped aside.

Jamie walked into the small room and stood beside Kate's desk as she closed the door behind them. "Have you seen Larissa?" he asked. "Today, I mean?"

Kate laughed. "What is it with you two? I had her asking the same thing about you yesterday. Can't you keep in touch with each other without my help?"

"Have you seen her or not?"

Kate frowned. "No," she said. "Not today. What's going on, Jamie?"

He grimaced. "We sort of had a fight."

"I'd worked that much out for myself," said Kate. "What about?"

Jamie hesitated; he didn't want to tell her, didn't want to tell anyone. But he had thrown the promise they had all made to each other in Larissa's face, had deliberately used it to make her feel guilty, and it would be unforgivably cowardly if he did not apply it to himself.

No more secrets.

He lowered himself into Kate's chair and began to talk. To his great relief, his friend listened in silence; she allowed him to plough through the whole story of his trip to Norfolk with Frankenstein, his reunion with his father, and the terrible conversation between himself and Larissa, without interruption or reaction. But as soon as he was finished, she shook her head and stared at him with eyes full of anger.

"You're an idiot, Jamie," she said. "I don't know what's wrong with you sometimes. Do you *like* being unhappy? Are you actively trying to make your life colder and more miserable?"

"Of course not," he said. "I was angry, Kate. I'd just found out that my dad wasn't dead, that he and Frankenstein had lied to me for years. I wasn't really thinking straight."

"I get that," said Kate. "I really, really do. And I'm sorry about what you discovered. But none of it was Larissa's fault."

"Don't you think she should have told me what she heard?"

"What did she hear?" said Kate. "A name? Three words that might easily have been completely meaningless?"

"They weren't, though," said Jamie. "And if she'd told me I could have—"

"You could have what?" interrupted Kate. "Asked Cal if he was keeping your dead dad in a cell? What do you think his answer would have been?"

"I'm not stupid, Kate," said Jamie. "I know Cal would have denied it. But maybe I could have found out some other way, or managed to get in to see him, or…"

"That's all well and good," said Kate, "but you're overlooking the most important thing. She *was* going to tell you, unless you're actively calling her a liar. It's bad timing that Frankenstein decided to come clean on the same day, but that's not Larissa's fault either. *She was going to tell you*, and before you say she had plenty of time to do so, think about what's been going on around here lately, and whether or not she might have had one or two other things on her mind."

Jamie stared at his friend. He knew she was right; everything she was saying was true.

"I need to see her, Kate," he said, his voice low. "I was angry, and I said some stuff I regret. I just... I need to tell her I'm sorry. Can you help me?"

"I'll run her chip," said Kate. She drew her console from her belt and Jamie watched as she tapped the screen with her fingers, silently urging her to hurry. After an agonisingly long wait, the console beeped as the results of the search were returned. Kate grimaced as she read them, and Jamie felt his heart sink.

"What is it?" he asked. "Where is she?"

"I don't know," said Kate, looking up and staring at him. "Her chip stopped transmitting nine hours ago."

"Where?" asked Jamie. "Where was the last position it was tracked?"

"About seven hundred miles off the west coast of Ireland," said Kate. "The middle of the Atlantic Ocean."

Kate pushed the door of her office shut and slid into the chair behind her desk. She turned on her terminal, trying to slow her rising unease as she waited for it to go through its series of security checks.

She had left Jamie in her quarters with strict instructions to stay there until she got back. He had looked thoroughly defeated, as though the life had been drained out of him, but she knew from long experience that it would only be temporary; his despair would rapidly turn to anger, and before she knew it he would be charging through the Loop, demanding a search party be raised for Larissa or, more worryingly, going to look for her himself. He'd agreed to sit tight, but Kate knew she needed information fast; right now, they had nothing to go on, and a response based on nothing was only likely to make an already bad situation worse.

Her monitor bloomed into life and Kate's fingers flew across the keyboard, accessing the Security Division logs and entering Larissa's name into the search field. The terminal worked quickly, bringing up a minute-by-minute record of her locator chip for the last twenty-four hours. Kate scrolled down to the point where Larissa had left Brenchley, and studied the subsequent lines of text and coordinates.

She came back through the hangar. Went to her quarters, then down to the cellblock, where she stayed for eleven minutes. Then back to her quarters, out through the hangar, and in a straight line west until her chip stopped transmitting.

Kate's eyes settled on the line that listed the Level H cellblock. She knew full well that there were only two vampires currently being held down there: Marie Carpenter, who was perhaps the least likely person in the Loop that Larissa would decide to visit, and the third oldest vampire in the world.

Valentin, she thought. *Why did she go and see Valentin? And what the hell did he say to her?*

One floor below, Jamie sat on Kate's bed, his foot tapping incessantly as he waited for his friend to return. He knew that waiting was the right thing to do – they needed to know more before he made the fuss that he was already itching to make – but doing so was frankly killing him.

She's out there somewhere, he thought, as he checked the time on Kate's bedside clock for the hundredth time. *And there's only one reason why her chip would have stopped transmitting.*

Because she doesn't want to be found.

He checked the clock again.

Twenty-six minutes.

That's how long Kate had been gone.

It felt like hours.

Jamie checked his console again, hoping against hope that he would see a message from Larissa glowing on its screen. He knew it was stupid, but he couldn't help himself; it made him feel like he was doing *something*, no matter how insignificant, and distracted him for a brief moment from the onslaught of accusation the guilty part of his brain was currently hurling at him.

Your fault! You drove her away! You ruined everything! Idiot! Loser! Failure!

He tried to ignore the howling voice, but couldn't; it was, after all, absolutely right. He *had* driven her away, of that there could be no doubt; she had come back to the Loop after their fight and within an hour she had been gone. There was simply no way to even begin to pretend that the two events were not connected. It was his fault, plain and simple, and if he got the chance he would apologise to her until he lost his voice.

What if she's gone for good? What if she's never coming back?

Jamie shook his head. He could not allow himself to think like that. It was possible that Larissa was simply blowing off steam, that she had just needed to get away from everything, including him, for a little while. Maybe she had gone back to Nevada, where he knew she had been happy. Maybe a message would arrive from General Allen, telling them that she had gone to visit her friends at NS9 and would be home soon.

Then why would her chip have stopped transmitting?

"Shut up," whispered Jamie. "Shut up, shut up, shut up."

Footsteps echoed down the corridor, a rapid rhythm that would have been inaudible to anyone without his supernatural senses, and Jamie froze, listening for the telltale pause outside the door that would signal Kate's return. The steps stopped, followed a second later by a beep and the whirring sound of locks drawing back. Jamie was on his feet before the door swung open, heat boiling into the corners of his eyes. Kate stepped into her quarters and recoiled.

"Jesus, Jamie," she said. "Have you been standing there the whole time?"

"What did you find out?" he asked. He was aware that his voice was on the verge of becoming a growl, but was helpless to control it.

"I pulled her chip's record," said Kate. "She got back here just after eight thirty last night and left about forty minutes later. Other than her quarters, she only went to one place while she was here."

"Where?" he asked.

"You have to promise me that you're going to stay calm."

"I can't promise you that," he said. "Where did she go, Kate?"

"To the cellblock," said Kate. "She went to see Valentin."

Jamie stared at her for long seconds, then strode across the room, and hauled the door open. His feet left the ground and he was halfway down the corridor before Kate managed to shout, "Wait!"

In his quarters on Level A, Paul Turner opened the message that had appeared on the screen of his console and frowned.

It was from Angela Darcy, announcing that she was back from the cellblock and had ordered the Security Division to officially list Larissa Kinley as AWOL while an investigation was conducted. Turner knew that the formal classification was merely procedural – he had no reason to believe that the vampire Operator represented any kind of threat to the Department – but her disappearance was a body blow nonetheless; with the exception of Valentin Rusmanov, whose loyalties were murky and changeable at best, as the morning's developments were illustrating yet again, Larissa was the most powerful Operator in the Department and her loss would severely diminish Blacklight's ability to respond to Dracula's next move, whatever it was and whenever it came.

The news of Larissa's disappearance had been a bad start to the day. Beyond the tactical problem it presented, Turner was also seriously concerned about the effect her disappearance was going to have on the morale of the Department.

There had been widespread distrust of her when she had accepted the offer to become the first vampire Operator in the Department's long history but, while it had never entirely gone away, it had been dramatically reduced by Larissa's role in repelling Valeri Rusmanov's attack on the Loop and her performance at the Battle of Château Dauncy, in which she and Valentin Rusmanov had fought Dracula to a standstill. He knew there were still people in the Loop who were uneasy at the thought of a vampire Operator, and a small number who would simply never accept her, but he also knew that the majority had come to believe that they were better off with Larissa on their side than without.

Now she was gone, and he suspected that her disappearance would be yet another blow to the already fragile confidence of the Department he now led.

And there's one thing that's absolutely certain, he thought. *Jamie and Kate and Matt are going to be devastated.*

The relationship between Jamie Carpenter and Larissa Kinley – the descendant of the Founders and the vampire girl – was an endless source of whispered curiosity throughout the Loop. Turner had stood in the infirmary barely two weeks earlier as Larissa threatened to murder every Operator in the Department if the medical staff didn't give her boyfriend the transfusion that would stop his turn taking place. Only Jamie's intervention had calmed her down, and Turner knew that her disappearance was going to hit the teenager like a ton of bricks. They had been through so much together that he believed it would be hard, if not impossible, for Jamie to move on if she simply didn't come back.

He wasn't sure the same would go for Jamie's best friend. Matt Browning was buried deeply in the endless grind of the Lazarus Project – *too* deeply in the opinion of most neutral observers – and Turner doubted that even the unexplained absence of his friend would prove anything more than a momentary distraction. It wasn't that he believed that Matt wouldn't care about Larissa being gone, or wouldn't be worried about Jamie, but rather that he was so completely engrossed in his work that his remarkable brain would not be able to justify expending any of its prodigious capacity on something that he could do nothing about.

Kate Randall, on the other hand? On that score, Turner was far from certain. She had first-hand experience in dealing with loss, awful, dreadful experience that had first pushed the two of them together, and he knew how tough she was, how resilient and capable. But she was also devoted to her friends. He was sure there would be a part of her, the part she hid from almost everyone, that would wonder whether there had been anything she could have done, whether there had been signs and signals that she had missed, whether she had somehow failed Larissa when she needed her.

Turner found himself smiling as he thought about Kate, then felt a sharp pang of guilt stab at him. After he became Director, he had made the decision to allow some distance between himself and the teenage girl he had come to rely on. It was for her own good; her rapid rise to a position of influence within the Security Division had caused resentment, and he knew full well that there were many people inside the Loop who believed she had intentionally cultivated a close relationship with him or, even more unkindly, that he had given her special treatment because she had been in a relationship with his son when he died. If he kept her close now that he was Director, as he would have preferred to, the accusations, the belief that she was a teacher's pet, that she was nothing more than his favourite would become ever more insistent.

Accusations which were complete bullshit.

In an ideal world, he would have made her Security Officer, and done so without the slightest hesitation; his job was to ensure that the vital roles inside Blacklight were filled by the best people, and Kate was simply that good. But the world was far from ideal, and it would have been an endless distraction that he, and Kate, did not need.

Especially not now, he thought. *Not if Larissa really is gone.*

The wall screen opposite his desk lit up as a loud tone rang out of the speakers, displaying an INCOMING CALL message. He read Angela Darcy's name in the window and clicked ACCEPT.

"Sir?" asked the Security Officer.

"I'm here, Captain Darcy," he replied. "What is it?"

"I need you to go online, sir. Right now."

Turner frowned, and opened a browser window. "What site?" he asked.

"Any of them, sir," said Angela.

The Director's frown deepened. "Stay on the line," he said, and typed the address for BBC News into the search bar. The site loaded, and a thick black BREAKING NEWS headline filled the screen, twelve words that stopped the breath in his lungs.

VIDEO MESSAGE SHOWS VAMPIRE CLAIMING TO BE DRACULA, ISSUES WARNING TO HUMANITY

Turner clicked on the headline. The page shifted to an article that was only two paragraphs long, with *More to follow* beneath them, but he paid the words no attention; his eye was drawn instantly to the video embedded at the top of the page. The rectangular box was black, with the words A MESSAGE at its centre. With a hand that had begun to almost imperceptibly tremble, Turner clicked PLAY.

The words faded away, replaced by a dimly lit shot of a seated figure. Turner felt his stomach lurch. Little more than the figure's face was visible, but that was more than enough; the pale skin, the narrow features, the piercing eyes, the moustache and the long hair were instantly, awfully recognisable.

Dracula.

"Citizens of the world," said the first vampire, his voice low and smooth. "I am Dracula, and I bring glad tidings for you all. You shall have the privilege of witnessing my rise, which is now at hand. It cannot be stopped, nor given pause. It is certain. It is as inevitable as the setting of the sun. Those of you who kneel may find me merciful. Those of you who oppose me will die. In time, I will speak again."

The footage returned to black, before two words appeared that chilled Turner to his core; he had seen them so many times, in photographs and grainy phone footage, on walls and pavements across the country.

HE RISES

6

ACCELERATION

Turner let out a long, deep breath.

"Are you still there, Angela?" he asked.

"Yes, sir," said the Security Officer.

"Get the Intelligence Division on this immediately," he said. "Every single frame. I want them to find something that tells us where Dracula is. Is that clear?"

"Yes, sir."

"Where did it first appear? The video?"

"Everywhere, sir," said Angela. "It was posted from hundreds of different accounts on hundreds of sites at exactly the same time, twelve minutes ago, and it's spreading faster than Surveillance can track it."

"Assume I don't understand the mechanics of online distribution," said Turner. "Could that have been one person scheduling the release under aliases, or is it hundreds of people acting at the same time?"

"It could have been either, sir," said the Security Officer. "It was highly organised, whichever it was."

"Clearly," he said. "Which makes me wonder what else is being planned that we don't know about."

"Yes, sir," said Angela. "Tell me what you want me to do."

"In terms of the Department, nothing yet," he replied. "I don't want to issue new orders or change the SOPs until we have more information. But I want you to stay in close contact with the police and the Intelligence Services. The public are already scared and paranoid, and this is only going to make things worse."

"Understood, sir."

"All right," said Turner. "Message everyone in the Loop, then play the video on every screen. Let's make sure everyone sees it and try to move past it as quickly as possible. Out."

He reached out and clicked END CALL. There was a low beep as the connection was severed, then silence.

Jamie heard Kate shout for him to wait as he rocketed along the Level B corridor, but ignored her.

He banked to the right, past the metal doors of the lift, and crashed through the door that accessed the emergency staircase, a shaft of concrete and metal that descended all the way to the very bottom of the Loop. The door was ripped off its hinges and clattered to the ground, but Jamie didn't pause; he spun up over the metal banister and shot down the shaft between the spiralling stairs like a bullet from a gun.

Concrete staircases and doors marked with letters flew past in a blur as the distant ground rose up to meet him. At the very last moment, the point at which it seemed that he must surely crash into the unforgiving concrete, Jamie pivoted in the air and slowed his descent, his arms wide, his eyes blazing. He landed silently in front of a door marked with an H and hauled it open.

He emerged in front of the airlock that controlled access to the long supernatural cellblock. He pressed his ID card against the panel beside the airlock door and waited as it slid slowly open. As the billowing cloud of gas passed over him and the inner door opened, he allowed a brief smile to rise on to his face; part of him had suspected that Kate would have already disabled his access, given that there had been no doubt where he was going.

Jamie exited the airlock, took a brief moment to compose himself, and strode towards his destination; the fourth cell on the right, the home of Valentin Rusmanov. Kate's voice shouted in his head as he approached the ultraviolet wall that enclosed it, pleading with him to stay calm, to not do anything stupid, but he barely heard it over the torrent of furious panic that was roaring through him.

What did you do, you old monster? What did you say to her?

He stopped in front of the purple barrier and looked into the cell. Valentin Rusmanov was sitting in a chair near the back of the room, his legs crossed at the ankles, a paperback book in his hands. He was looking directly at Jamie.

"Lieutenant Carpenter," said the old vampire. "What an entirely expected surprise. How are you?"

"What did you say to her?" growled Jamie. "Tell me right now."

Valentin got slowly to his feet, stretched his long arms above his head, and regarded him with a wide smile.

"I assume you are referring to Miss Kinley," he said. "In which case, I'm sorry to have to disappoint you. I don't disclose the content of private conversations."

Jamie took a step forward, his eyes flaming red. "What did you do?"

"I did nothing but listen, and talk," said Valentin. "I assume she has left this charming facility?"

"You know she has," said Jamie.

"Actually, I didn't," said Valentin. "Might I enquire as to why you are so clearly angry with me?"

"Why?" asked Jamie, his voice a low rumble of thunder. "Why the hell do you think? She came down here to talk to you and twenty minutes later she disappeared halfway around the world. *That's* why."

"I see," said Valentin. "You have my sympathies, as I have no doubt you will miss her greatly. But if you are blaming me for her departure, then I'm afraid you are somewhat overestimating my influence. I would suggest you consider why Miss Kinley might have wanted to leave, why she might not have been entirely happy with the status quo. I suspect that will be a more productive use of your time."

"Everyone thought you'd changed," said Jamie. "You've been down here for months like a rat in a cage, telling us to believe you, telling us that you're on our side, but you're not, are you? You don't give a shit about anyone apart from yourself."

"I think Miss Kinley would disagree with that assessment," said Valentin. "Maybe you should ask her. If you ever see her again, that is."

The old vampire's words cut through Jamie like a scalpel. He stared at Valentin, hatred pumping through his veins, filling his body with fire.

"You disgust me," he growled. "I thought you were better than this. I *trusted* you."

Valentin's smile returned. "Silly boy," he said.

The fire inside Jamie flickered and died, replaced by a misery so overwhelming it almost drove him to his knees. He lowered his head and closed his eyes, trying to squeeze shut the chasm of loss that had yawned open in his stomach, to push it closed and down and away.

"Jamie."

He didn't move; he focused only on the pain, on the *grief* that was threatening to paralyse him.

"Jamie. Look at me."

He took a deep breath, raised his head, and opened his eyes. Valentin was standing directly in front of him, the ultraviolet barrier all that separated them.

"What?" he managed.

"I'm not going to tell you what Larissa and I discussed," said Valentin, his tone softer, kinder than it had been. "It was a private conversation, and it's none of your business, to put it bluntly. But if you think I manipulated her in some way, then I don't think you know her very well at all. And if you think this is all about you, then I would suggest you need to get your ego under control. There are things that happen in this world that have nothing to do with you."

"Did you tell her to leave?" asked Jamie, his voice on the verge of cracking. "Just answer me that. Did you tell her to go?"

"I won't tell you what was said, Jamie, no matter how many times you ask."

"I know you have a house in New York," he said. "Larissa's chip stopped transmitting over the Atlantic. Is that where she is? Did you send her there?"

"Please, Jamie," said Valentin. "This desperation is undignified. The Security Officer has the addresses of all of my residences, including the house in Manhattan. I'm sure that will be the first place they look for her."

"You talked to Angela about this?" asked Jamie. "She knew Larissa was gone?"

Valentin nodded. "We spoke about fifteen minutes ago. Do you know what her answer was when I asked her why she was so keen to find Miss Kinley?"

"No," said Jamie. "What did Angela say?"

"Her exact words were, 'She's our most powerful weapon.'"

"So what?"

Valentin smiled softly. "So maybe she didn't want to be," he said.

Jamie grimaced; it felt like he had been punched in the stomach. He stared silently at the old vampire for a long, empty moment, then turned away without a word and walked back down the cellblock.

He stood in the airlock, his shoulders slumped, his head lowered, his eyes closed. When the gas cleared, the outer door slid open, and he stepped out. He stood still, trying to compose himself, to slow his racing mind and think, *think* about what he should do now. In front of him, the metal doors of the lift parted silently and Kate appeared, her eyes wide with worry.

"Jamie?" she said. "Are you all right?"

He shook his lowered head.

"Jamie, look at me," she said, stepping forward and taking hold of his shoulders. He did so, and saw concern in her eyes, saw clear, bright love. "What did you do?"

"Nothing," he said. "He wouldn't tell me what he said to her. Wouldn't tell me where she is. He knows, though. I know he does."

Kate winced. "I'm sorry, Jamie," she said.

He forced a tiny smile. "Everyone's sorry. Me most of all."

"You can't make this all about you," said Kate, her tone suddenly strict and forceful. "She's a grown woman, not a petulant kid. She wouldn't leave the country just because the two of you had a fight."

"That's how it feels," said Jamie.

"I'm sure it does," said Kate. "But you know how she's been since she got back from Nevada. You know she hasn't been happy with Blacklight, with what she was expected to do. She had doubts about it all, Jamie, serious moral objections to this whole thing. Maybe they got too much for her."

"Maybe," he said, as a lump rose into his throat. "But what if our relationship was one of the things that she thought it was worth sticking around for? What if it was why she was still here and I took it away from her?"

Kate stared at him, and said nothing.

"She's gone," he said. "What if she doesn't come back, Kate? Where does that leave us? Where does it leave me?"

Kate stepped forward and wrapped her arms round him. Jamie let his head rest on her shoulder, but as he allowed his eyes to close he was acutely aware that she had not answered his questions.

A deafening crackle of static burst out of the speakers set along the corridor walls; the two friends sprang apart as Angela Darcy's amplified voice replaced it.

"This is a Priority 1 announcement," said the Security Officer. "Please direct your attention to the nearest screen."

The Level H atrium was one of the few places in the entire Loop that didn't contain a single wall screen. Jamie silently screamed at the Department's apparent refusal to allow him even a single uninterrupted minute to himself, and pulled his console from his belt. He accessed the Blacklight network as Kate stood beside him and peered down at the screen, the look on her face suggesting that she was asking herself the same question that was filling his own mind.

What now? For the love of God, what now?

ZERO HOUR
PLUS 13 DAYS

CIVILIAN MEDIA EXTRACT
Ref: 399252/F
Source: *The Manchester Post*
Date: 2nd May

EXTRACT BEGINS

PM CONFIRMS EXISTENCE OF BLACKLIGHT

John Ballance, Political Editor, Westminster

In a specially convened session of the House of Commons yesterday afternoon, the Prime Minister confirmed to packed benches that the secret organisation commonly referred to in the press as Blacklight is real, and enjoys his "full faith and confidence".

Reading from a prepared statement, the Prime Minister confirmed that the clandestine unit is officially named Department 19, and that its operation is overseen directly by his office and the senior hierarchy of the Ministry of Defence, placing it in a similar position to the SAS and SBS – a military organisation with the same levels of secrecy as the Intelligence Services.

Calls by backbenchers for Department 19 to be subject to greater transparency and accountability were given short shrift by the Prime Minister, who stated that the organisation must be allowed to continue unheeded with its remit of protecting the public from threats relating to the supernatural.

The Leader of the Opposition criticised the Prime Minister's statement, claiming that "it raised more questions than it answered", while a senior government backbencher was quoted by the BBC as saying that, in his opinion, "a secret military organisation with an all-too-real licence to kill conducting operations against British citizens is incompatible with a civilised democracy".

EXTRACT ENDS

ZERO HOUR
PLUS 41 DAYS

CIVILIAN MEDIA EXTRACT
Ref: 401132/B
Source: *The London Record*
Date: 30th May

EXTRACT BEGINS

VAMPIRES PETITION EUROPEAN BODIES FOR MINORITY STATUS, CRIMINAL CHARGES

Julian Dawes, Senior Political Correspondent, Strasbourg

A petition was last night presented to the European Court of Human Rights that seeks to have 'vampire' officially recognised as an ethnic minority group. The legal status of the supernatural has been widely debated in recent weeks, following an announcement by the G8 countries in which they confirmed their position that vampires retain the nationalities they held before they were turned, along with any restrictions those nationalities may entail.

A parallel petition to the International Criminal Court at The Hague requested that Department 19 (UK), National Security Division 9 (USA), and similar organisations around the world be investigated for possible charges of genocide and crimes against humanity. Major Paul Turner (UK), General Robert Allen (USA), and Colonel Aleksandr Ovechkin (Russia) were among those named in the petition, although the identities of individuals who work or have worked for any of the listed organisations have never been publicly confirmed.

EXTRACT ENDS

ZERO HOUR
PLUS 67 DAYS

CIVILIAN MEDIA EXTRACT
Ref: 403019/C
Source: *The New York Register*
Date: 25th June

EXTRACT BEGINS

BEIJING BREAKS SILENCE – ADMITS VAMPIRES ARE REAL

Alan Horner, International Affairs Correspondent, New York

The Chinese government in Beijing today issued a statement formally recognising the existence of vampires and reassuring Chinese citizens that their safety remains the regime's highest priority. The statement leaves North Korea as the only nation not to have officially recognised the existence of the supernatural.

The statement, which had been widely expected after a draft document leaked online over the weekend, stopped short of acknowledging the existence of PBS6, heavily rumoured to be the Chinese equivalent of the USA's NS9. Chinese citizens were urged to report all incidents of a supernatural nature to the police.

EXTRACT ENDS

ZERO HOUR
PLUS 91 DAYS

CIVILIAN MEDIA EXTRACT
Ref: 405102/F
Source: *www.newsonline.co.uk*
Date: 19th July

EXTRACT BEGINS

EXCLUSIVE! THE SSL FOUNDERS SPEAK OUT IN THEIR ONLY INTERVIEW

The internet has been buzzing for the last twenty-four hours, following the announcement of the formation of the Supernatural Survivors League, which the mainstream media is already referring to as the Samaritans for the supernatural.

Much of that buzz has been about the two men who founded the organisation, Greg Browning and Pete Randall. Why, you ask? Because both men were already notorious for their rumoured involvement in Kevin McKenna's now infamous posthumous article, widely considered to have been the first crack in the wall of secrecy surrounding the existence of the supernatural.

As regular visitors to this site will be aware, our Features Editor Dan Bennett has shown great bravery in writing about the impact of the supernatural on his own family, in particular his sister Catherine, who is still missing after being attacked by a vampire two years ago in Melbourne. As a result, it came as no surprise to us that Randall and

Browning chose to give their ONLY interview to Dan. We proudly present their conversation in full, unedited and unexpurgated.

DB: Pete, Greg. Thanks for doing this. It's a pleasure to talk to you.
PR: Cheers, Dan. And I'd just like to say how sorry we both are for your loss.
GB: Absolutely.
DB: Thank you. And I guess that's as good a place to start as any. Can you tell me how your personal experiences with the supernatural led to the founding of SSL?
GB: Sure. It involves telling you something that we've thought long and hard about whether we should tell anyone, but here goes. Approximately nine months ago, my son Matt, and Pete's daughter Kate, were brainwashed by the group that calls itself Blacklight, and coerced into joining them. So, for starters, that's why SSL is different from—
DB: Hang on. I'm sorry to interrupt, but are you saying that you both have children who are serving members of Blacklight?
PR: That's right.
DB: How do you know that? My understanding is that Blacklight Operators aren't allowed to tell anyone what they do.
GB: We believe that's the case.
DB: So how do you know?
PR: It's a long story, Dan. Greg and I first met online, when neither of us was in a very good place. I'm a survivor of the vampire attack on Lindisfarne, and at the time I was grieving for Kate. She went missing during the attack,

and the police told me to assume she was dead. I watched them cover it all up and was ordered never to talk about what had happened. So I started searching for other people who were in the same boat as me, and I met Greg on a forum for people who'd survived vampire encounters. Everyone on there was nervous, paranoid even, but it was instantly clear to me that some of them had seen the same things I had. And I knew I wasn't alone.

GB: I was grieving too, although I didn't know whether Matt was alive or dead. I'm still not supposed to talk about any of it, even now, but I don't give a shit any more. A vampire fell out of the sky into my garden, and Blacklight stormed our house, pointed guns at my family, brought scientists in protective suits to collect the vamp. My son got hurt, badly hurt, and they took him with them. Didn't say anything to us, didn't tell us where they were taking him. They just packed him into one of their helicopters and took off.

DB: That's incredible. I mean, that's kidnapping, surely? It's hard to believe something like that can happen in a supposedly civilised country.

GB: Supposedly is right. Anyway. Afterwards, my life fell apart. Matt's mother and I, we'd had some problems, and his disappearance, and what we'd seen, just brought them all to a head, and she left me. Then one day, completely out of the blue, Matt came back. He couldn't tell me where he'd been, but he was safe, and he was home, and that was all that mattered to me. But two days later he was gone again, for good this time.

DB: Gone where?

GB: Back to them. They'd got into his head while they had him, filled it up with God knows what. They let him go, and he went straight back to them. I know that now.

DB: How come?

PR: We saw them with our own eyes. After what happened last year, in Reading. A Blacklight squad arrested us, and Matt and Kate were part of it. I'm sure they weren't supposed to let us know it was them, but they did. We saw them, and actually talked to them for a little while. Then their bosses sent us home, and warned us not to tell anyone what we'd seen.

DB: Jesus. OK, so you mentioned Reading. You're referring to your roles in the publication of Kevin McKenna's final story?

PR: Right. Ever since Greg and I got to know each other, we've looked for ways to make a difference. But we trusted somebody we shouldn't have, and we made a terrible mistake.

GB: We were misled. Afterwards, we both wondered whether we should just keep our heads down, you know? But neither of us could do it. We'd seen so much. And people needed to know the truth.

PR: I don't mind admitting that after McKenna's story came out, I was scared for a long time. Blacklight threatened us with prison when they let us go, and we didn't know whether we were making things harder for Kate and Matt.

GB: But then Gideon went on TV, and everything changed. We saw a chance to do something.

DB: And you definitely took it. So what exactly are the aims of SSL?

PR: We don't have aims as such. This isn't a political movement, it doesn't have a cause. What we hope to provide is a sympathetic ear for people who have been hurt by the supernatural, directly or indirectly.

GB: And I think our own experiences with Blacklight are

what set us apart from the other vampire support groups that are out there—

PR: —although some of them do excellent work—

GB: —right, sure. But SSL is for anyone whose life has been affected by any aspect of the supernatural, including the people who are supposed to protect us from them.

DB: So what can someone who calls SSL expect?

PR: Someone who'll listen to them. And believe them. And won't judge them.

GB: I should make it clear that SSL is more than just a helpline. That's an important part of it, but we also have programmes that will be going live over the next few months that we believe will make a real difference to the public, both humans and vampires. We're going to be offering safe sources of blood, ultraviolet torches and bulbs for people to protect themselves with. The helpline is just the beginning.

DB: SSL is a registered charity.

PR: Right.

DB: But in your statement you announced that you won't be taking donations from the public. Why not?

GB: Because we don't need them. We have a board of directors and a number of private individuals who have been extremely generous in helping us get started. If at some point the financial situation changes, then we'll look at it. But, for now, we don't want people's money. We'd rather they kept it in their pockets.

DB: Let me ask you both a blunt question. Do you hate vampires?

GB: I just told you that we're going to be running programmes designed to make the lives of vampires easier, so let me be very clear. SSL is absolutely not an anti-vampire group. It's a victim-support group.

DB: Right. I hear you. But given what you've been through, I guess a better way to phrase my question would be: how can you *not* hate vampires?

PR: Because we don't believe that they're inherently evil. Many of them are victims themselves, turned against their will.

DB: So if a vampire wanted to volunteer with SSL, he or she would be welcome?

GB: Absolutely.

DB: What about Blacklight? What are your feelings towards them?

PR: SSL doesn't believe that a highly armed military unit operating in secrecy is a good thing for the country.

DB: Come on. Get real. What do the two of you really think?

GB: They kidnapped my son and brainwashed him into a bloody stormtrooper. What do you think I think?

DB: I would assume you're angry with them.

GB: And you'd be right.

DB: So what would you say to those commentators who are calling SSL a personal crusade? Who claim that your motivation for founding it is revenge against Blacklight?

PR: That's completely ridiculous. As we've already said, this is not a lobbying organisation or a pressure group. It's a way for us to reach out to people whose lives have been touched by darkness and let them know they're not alone. It's as simple as that.

DB: And I wish you the very best of luck with it. Thank you both for your time.

EXTRACT ENDS

ZERO HOUR
PLUS 109 DAYS

CIVILIAN MEDIA EXTRACT
Ref: 409043/A
Source: *The London Record*
Date: 6th August

EXTRACT BEGINS

RIOTING BREAKS OUT AS ICC RULES THAT BLACKLIGHT WILL NOT FACE CHARGES

Julian Dawes, Senior Political Correspondent, London

Armed police were called to deal with rioting in more than a dozen European cities overnight, following the International Criminal Court in The Hague's announcement that it would not be pursuing charges against Blacklight, its international equivalents, or any individuals for either genocide or crimes against humanity. The verdict was met with violent protests outside the court, and triggered a wave of unrest across the continent that only ended with the rising of the sun. Professor David Albright, who has campaigned for vampire rights and co-authored the petition that was presented to the ICC, spoke to the media on the steps of the court.

"This is a dark day for European democracy," said Albright. "For more than a century, secret death squads have been carrying out summary executions of men and women guilty of nothing more than being vampires, without affording them due process, or legal counsel. History will view this as the secret holocaust of the twentieth and twenty-first centuries, a holocaust that the International Criminal Court is now a party to."

Authorities in all major European cities have placed police and emergency services on high alert, in anticipation of further unrest as the sun sets this evening.

EXTRACT ENDS

ZERO HOUR
PLUS 140 DAYS

CIVILIAN MEDIA EXTRACT
Ref: 414702/E
Source: *The National Recorder*
Date: 6th September

EXTRACT BEGINS

ALLEGED FORMER HEAD OF BLACKLIGHT RETIRES ON MEDICAL GROUNDS

Kimberley Dennison, News Editor, London

Buried deep in a Ministry of Defence bulletin released online yesterday morning, among the regular schedules of public events and awarded medals, was a small, seemingly innocuous announcement that read as follows:

The Royal Navy announces the medical discharge and retirement of Admiral Henry Seward (GCB(Mil), OM(Mil), DSO) after thirty-four years of distinguished service to his country. Admiral Seward is a recipient of the Military Cross, the Conspicuous Gallantry Cross, and more than two dozen other awards and decorations. Ad perpetuam rei memoriam.

Less than fifteen minutes later, however, the bulletin had been updated, and Admiral Seward's retirement announcement removed. Why? Why would the Royal Navy remove a tribute to such a highly decorated member of their ranks? Was it a premature announcement? Was it removed at the request of the man himself? Or was it because Admiral Henry Seward has been named by multiple witnesses, both human and vampire, as a former Director of Department 19?

Let us consider the facts: firstly, the name. One of the most popular theories to have emerged since V-Day is the belief that the contents of Bram Stoker's *Dracula*, notably its main characters, were real. This has proven problematic as, with the exception of the Hon. Arthur Holmwood, who was a notable public figure of the time, no records have ever been found of Jonathan Harker, Abraham Van Helsing, or any of the other men and women described in the novel. Those inclined towards the conspiratorial insist that all such records were destroyed when Blacklight was founded, although this correspondent finds that explanation somewhat hard to swallow. Nonetheless, if one is inclined to believe, as has been widely claimed, that Blacklight has evolved over the decades and centuries under the stewardship of the descendants of a small group of founding fathers, then the name Seward is clearly of significance.

Secondly, the Admiral's record. The decorations listed include three of the highest honours that this country bestows – the Knight Grand Cross of the Order of Bath, the Order of Merit, and the Distinguished Service Order. These honours make Henry Seward one of *the* most highly decorated Royal Navy officers of the last half a century. But nobody that I have spoken to today, either in Whitehall or at Portsmouth, has been able to provide me with a single detail of the Admiral's career – not a posting, a ship, or even a personal anecdote. To put it bluntly, nobody has ever heard of him.

Could that be because the Admiral spent his career in the shadowy, highly classified world of Blacklight? It's likely that we, the public, will never know, at least not with any certainty. But one thing *is* clear – as Department 19 is dragged, slowly and unwillingly, into the light, Henry Seward's will not be the last name subjected to close scrutiny in relation to this country's defence against the supernatural. In the meantime, all that remains is for this correspondent to wish the Admiral a happy and peaceful retirement, hopefully with nary a vampire to be seen...

EXTRACT ENDS

ZERO HOUR
PLUS 163 DAYS

CIVILIAN MEDIA EXTRACT

Ref: 418905/F
Source: *The South Yorkshire Herald*
Date: 29th September

EXTRACT BEGINS

NEW 'NIGHT STALKER' ATTACK INCREASES TENSION IN MIDLANDS

Robert Viner, Senior Correspondent, Sheffield

A vampire was killed last night on the outskirts of Nottingham in an attack that bears similarities to the so-called 'Night Stalker' killings that have blighted the Midlands over the last month.

The victim was killed in a warehouse in the Trent Bridge area of Nottingham, his remains marked in the same way as the nine previous victims - a wolf's head sprayed on to them with white paint. Previous vampire victims attributed to the 'Night Stalker' have had the front doors of their homes vandalised in the same way, in what has been interpreted by many as a reference to symbols painted on medieval dwellings to mark the presence of plague.

The identity of only a single one of the 'Night Stalker' victims has been released to the public – Albert Matheson, a convicted child molester who had been living in the Kimberley area under an assumed name. Nottinghamshire Police have confirmed that they believe they are looking for a single individual, although they have not ruled out the possibility of copycat attacks. They have appealed for anyone with information regarding last night's incident to contact them immediately.

EXTRACT ENDS

ZERO HOUR PLUS 191 DAYS

7

REDUNDANT

Jamie Carpenter walked along the corridor of Level 0 towards a meeting he no longer saw any point in.

The Zero Hour Task Force had been created specifically to deal with Dracula, and to attempt to prevent the passing of the Intelligence Division's best estimate of when the first vampire would regain his full strength, the implication being that unless he was stopped before then, it would be unlikely he could be stopped at all.

Zero Hour had been six months ago.

Jamie reached the Ops Room, laid a hand on its door, and took a deep breath, steeling himself against the next thirty minutes or so. There had been a time when he had been proud to be a member of the Task Force, working on matters of the very highest priority alongside people he had respected. But Henry Seward was gone, Cal Holmwood was dead, he no longer spoke to Frankenstein, and Richard Brennan had turned out to be a spy who had tried to assassinate Kate and Paul Turner before he too had died. The Zero Hour briefings, once so full of purpose, had become meetings of misery, of decline and failure.

The release of Dracula's video had initially shocked them, then given them momentary hope that it might provide clues to the first vampire's location. But it had led nowhere, despite painstaking analysis of every frame; there had been nothing in the video to suggest where he was or what he might do next, and every other line of enquiry had turned as cold as ice. As a result, Jamie no longer believed there was any chance of finding Dracula before he wanted to be found, and was far from alone in that opinion. And with no updates on the vampire the Task Force had been created to stop, the Zero Hour briefings were now usually full of the terrible things that the public were routinely doing to vampires, and to each other.

The revelation of the existence of the supernatural had unleashed a wave of chaos and violence, one that showed no signs of abating. Patrol Responds, the routine missions that had once seen Operational Squads hunting down and destroying vampires, had become exercises in policing the human population as they hacked and clawed at each other, fear and paranoia hijacking their reason. On a seemingly daily basis, the government called for calm, the supernatural integration groups called for harmony, and those vampires who had been brave enough to put their heads above the parapet tried to explain to the frightened populace that the overwhelming majority of their kind were not dangerous.

But more than six months after V-Day, as the date of Gideon's explosive appearance on *Coffee Break* had become known, the violence continued to escalate, and nobody seemed to have a clue how to stop it.

Jamie pushed open the door and nodded at the men and women already sitting around the Ops Room table. He spotted an empty seat next to Kate, avoided Frankenstein's uneven gaze, and sat down at the same moment as Paul Turner got to his feet and walked to the lectern at the front of the room.

"Zero Hour Task Force now in session," said the Director. "Apologies from Lieutenant Browning and Major Van Thal, good morning to the rest of you."

There was a chorus of muttered greetings and a ripple of nodded heads.

"There's nothing major that needs covering this morning, so I'll keep it quick," continued Turner. "Firstly, I'm—"

"You're pleased to report that Dracula was successfully located and destroyed overnight?" suggested Angela Darcy.

Turner gave her a cold stare, then smiled and shook his head as the rest of the Task Force burst out laughing. And for a brief moment, the dull pain that had taken up residence inside Jamie's chest was replaced by a bittersweet feeling of nostalgia. This was how it had been at the beginning, when he was first introduced into a world full of the fantastic and the terrifying, when the camaraderie of the Department had filled a hole in him that he had believed unfillable. The darkness had always lurked outside, but inside there had been laughter, and light.

Now all that remained was the darkness.

Most of the time, at least.

"Very amusing, Captain," said Turner.

"Thank you, sir," said Angela. "I do my best."

"Clearly," said Turner. "Anyway. As I was about to say, this afternoon I will be circulating the latest collection of statistics and reports that Surveillance and Intelligence have put together. They don't make for particularly pleasant reading, but it is more important than ever that we fully understand what's happening beyond the borders of the Loop. There will be a full briefing tomorrow, but in the meantime it goes without saying that I expect you to keep your teams informed, and maintain morale."

Jamie's good humour disappeared as quickly as it had arrived.

That's a joke, he thought. *Surely it is. There's no morale left to maintain. Most of the time it feels like fear of being court-martialled is the only thing stopping half the Department doing exactly what Larissa did.*

Jamie winced as the pain rushed back to him. Where possible, he tried not to think of her, and had become better and better at not doing so as the months had passed, as it had become ever clearer that she was not coming back. But when someone said her name, or his mind unexpectedly drew her from his memory, the wound that he doubted would ever heal gaped open, raw and bloody. It was another reason that the Zero Hour briefings were always hard: her absence was impossible to ignore.

"As ever," continued Turner, "my advice is that you not dwell unnecessarily on things beyond your control. We do what we can and we keep going, like always. Moving on, I have an update from the Security Division regarding the continuing search for—"

Something came loose inside Jamie, demanding release as heat rose behind his eyes. "What's the point?" he heard himself ask. "Really, just what the hell is the point, sir?"

Turner narrowed his eyes. "I'm sorry, Lieutenant?" he said.

"Dracula's gone," said Jamie. "It doesn't matter how many updates we get from Security, we still don't have a clue where he is or what he's planning. We're only going to know what his move is when he actually makes it, and by then it'll be too late. And while we wait for that to happen, the people out there are tearing each other to pieces and it seems like all we can do is stick our finger in the dam and hope it holds. So I'll ask again, sir. What's the point?"

He stared at the Director, refusing to drop his eyes from Turner's famously glacial gaze, and waited for the explosion. Part of him was looking forward to it; he was hopeful it might make him feel something, even just for a moment.

But it didn't come.

Turner stared at him for a long moment, then nodded. "That's a good question, Jamie," he said. "And I wish I had a good answer for you. For all of you. I wish I had a speech that would make you feel better, that would fill you with fire and fury and send you on your way with nothing but righteous faith in your hearts. But Cal was far better at that sort of thing than I am. All I can tell you is the truth. So yes, things are bad. Despite our best efforts, they're as bad as I've ever known them. Dracula's move will come, sooner or later, and although many of the men and women in this base, perhaps even some of you in this room, believe that it's too late to stop him, I don't. I *can't*. When the day comes, when we're called to fight again, I will expect every member of the Department to be ready. So feel frustrated by all means, feel angry and helpless and like everything is pointless. Then deal with it, put it aside, and do your jobs. For now, that's all we can do."

Jamie stared at the Director as silence fell over the Ops Room.

"I don't know, sir," said Angela Darcy, eventually, a wide grin on her face. "As speeches go, that one wasn't too shabby."

Laughter rippled around the table, and Jamie felt a small smile rise on to his face.

"Thank you," said Turner. "I'm delighted to have your approval. Now if I might be allowed to continue with this briefing?"

NOT FOR PROFIT

LINCOLN, LINCOLNSHIRE, ENGLAND

Pete Randall shoved his chair back from his desk and looked out of the window of his office. The view was an unappetising panorama of industrial units, roads and roundabouts, and low suburban sprawl. In the distance, above the angled roofs of houses and squat grey blocks of shopping malls, rose the spire of Lincoln Cathedral, its beautifully carved stone incongruous against the landscape it overlooked.

More than two months had passed since Pete had accepted Greg Browning's invitation to move south and help him launch SSL, and the view was one of the things he was finding hardest to adjust to. From his study in the house he had once shared with his wife and daughter, Pete had looked out across the shoreline of Lindisfarne to an endlessly churning grey-blue strip of the North Sea and the rugged coastline of Northumberland. He had taken the spectacular vista for granted after long years on the island, but now, faced every day with a grey urban expanse, he realised how much he missed it.

He had not instantly said yes to Greg; in fact, he had made him wait more than a week for his decision. After the nightmarish days the two of them had spent with Albert Harker and Kevin McKenna and the bittersweet relief at seeing his daughter alive – even if she *was* wearing the black uniform of Blacklight – he had returned to Lindisfarne and tried to make sense of everything that had happened. He didn't blame Greg; they had been deceived and manipulated by a monster, and although the method had ultimately veered into madness, he would always believe that the end result of their time with Harker and McKenna had been worthwhile. They had forced the world to open their eyes to vampires, and to the hateful soldiers who policed them, and he would always be proud of that.

It did not, however, mean that he was keen to involve himself again, and he had said as much to Greg when he rang with the proposal that had become SSL.

"Here's the deal," he said. "I'm in, on two conditions. Firstly, I don't want there to be *anything* I don't know. I won't work in the dark again, like we did with Kevin, so, if there's anything you're not telling me, I want to know about it right now, before we go any further. Is that clear?"

"Clear," said Greg. "That's absolutely fair, mate. And there *is* something. The funding for SSL is coming from a series of charitable foundations, backed by private donors who wish to remain anonymous. Which means I can't tell you the names of the people writing the cheques, because I honestly don't know them. If that's going to be a problem for you, I understand, but it's the only thing I can think of that you don't know. There's loads of stuff that still needs working out, but if you come on board you'll be making those decisions with me. You'll be in the loop on absolutely everything, I promise."

"All right," said Pete. "That's fine."

"Great," said Greg. "What's the second condition?"

"I want you to promise me that this has nothing to do with revenge," said Pete. "That it's not about Matt, or how much you hate Blacklight and the way they treated us. Because if it is, you're on your own. I won't say anything to anyone, but I won't be a part of it. I'm done with all that, Greg."

"Me too," said his friend. "I'm not angry any more, mate, I promise you. All I want to do is try and help."

"I believe you," said Pete. "So what's the next move?"

"I'm taking office space in Lincoln," said Greg. "You can work remotely if you want, but to be honest, it would be good to have you down here in person. What do you think?"

"I think I can handle it," said Pete. "Let me sort some things out up here. I'll give you a call in a couple of days."

Pete roused himself from his memories and returned his attention to his computer. He was reviewing the entire log of calls made to their helpline, aware that it was almost time for him to help Greg welcome the latest batch of volunteers. The public response to SSL had so far been beyond their wildest expectations; the projections they had given to their board had predicted three hundred calls a day by this point.

The previous day, they had taken nine hundred and twelve.

The phone operators were working incessantly, starting early and staying late for no reason other than faith in what they were doing. The blood drives, where SSL volunteers took fresh, clean blood from slaughterhouses into communities and made it available to any vampire that wanted it, were also proving massively popular; in Birmingham two nights earlier, they had run out of blood in less than two hours. Pete was in the process of trying to secure more stocks as Greg worked to bring in new volunteers, both for the main Lincoln office and to run the regional projects; after barely three months, SSL already needed every pair of hands it could find.

What struck Pete most as he scanned through the call logs was how often the same names appeared, time and time again. SSL did not record transcripts of the calls it received – they had promised their callers anonymity, and Pete was adamant that they adhere to it – but each call did have a number of acronyms marked against it. Some were obvious – a capital V for vampire, a capital H for human – whereas others were harder to decipher: SI for *suicidal ideation*, TTCH for *threatening to cause harm*, ATHK for *admits to having killed*, and many, many others. Most callers did not identify themselves in any way, but perhaps as many as fifteen per cent gave their names; it seemed to Pete, from the acronyms beside those particular calls, that they were largely men and women who were dealing with crushing guilt, who were searching for absolution. The phone calls he was looking at represented probably the only chance vampires had to speak openly about the things they had done, about the life that had been thrust upon them.

Pete scrolled through the log list, and paused. A name halfway down the fifth page had caught his eye, a name that seemed familiar. He realised why at the same moment Greg Browning knocked on his office door and stepped through it.

"Morning, mate," he said. "Ready?"

"Morning," said Pete. "Come in for a second."

Greg frowned, but closed the door and walked across the office. "What's up?" he asked.

Pete pointed at the name on the screen. "Recognise him?"

"Albert Matheson," read Greg out loud. "Doesn't ring a bell. Should it?"

"Not really," said Pete. "He was the vamp the Night Stalker killed a couple of months ago. I read about him at the time."

"No shit?" said Greg. "ATHK too. I guess he was confessing."

"He was a convicted child molester," said Pete. "He probably had a lot to confess."

Greg shrugged. "Poor bastard," he said. "Does it bother you, mate? That he's dead, I mean? Because given what's going on out there, he probably won't be the last vamp who calls us and ends up getting killed."

"I know that," said Pete. "And no, it doesn't bother me. It was just weird to see his name on the call log."

"Weird," said Greg, and nodded. "Close that down, mate. It's time to meet the new recruits."

Pete rolled his eyes and got up from his desk. He followed Greg out into the open-plan centre of SSL, full of people talking into phones and concentrating intently on computer screens. As they made their way across the space, several of the volunteers looked up and nodded; Pete nodded back, smiled, and stepped through the door in the corner of the office that his friend was holding open for him.

Standing at one end of the small boardroom was the latest group of men and women who had volunteered to be a part of SSL. There were eleven of them; they were mostly young, apart from a couple of middle-aged women and one man who looked to be in his sixties, at least. They all appeared nervous, and Pete moved quickly to calm them down.

"Morning, everyone," he said. "I'm Pete Randall, and you've already met Greg Browning. Thank you all for volunteering to help us out here at SSL. We appreciate it more than you can imagine." He watched smiles rise on to several of the new volunteers' faces and continued. "I'm not going to go over why Greg and I founded SSL, or what we're trying to do here, because I'm going to assume you wouldn't be here unless you already knew what we're about. What I *am* going to tell you is that what we do here is really, really important. The existence of the supernatural is the biggest social issue to hit this country in many decades, quite possibly the biggest there has ever been, and everybody's struggling to keep up with the pace of change. Including us.

"As you know, the second S in our name stands for Survivors.

It's a big word, and to us it means *anyone* who has been adversely affected by an experience with the supernatural. We're not just talking about people who have been attacked, or whose family or friends have been killed. We're also talking about vampires themselves, the majority of whom never wanted to be turned and are simply trying to get through each day without doing any harm. They are survivors too, of a monstrous violation. At SSL, we view everyone equally, we don't prioritise humans over vampires, and we don't judge anyone for the things they might have done. Ever. Is that clear?"

The volunteers nodded as one.

"Good," he said. "Those of you who work the phones are going to hear things that will upset you, that will probably make you angry. You need to be prepared for that. And those of you who work in our outreach teams are going to come face to face with things that are frightening, possibly even terrifying. It's hard work, and it's not always popular, I warn you now. There are plenty of people out there who think that there should be no help or sympathy for any vampire, so be careful who you tell that you work here. 'Vamp sympathiser' can be a dangerous label to be stuck with. So if you decide that SSL isn't for you, we won't think any less of you, I promise. But if you stay, you'll have not only *our* gratitude, but the gratitude of everyone who wants the world to be a better place than it is."

Pete stopped, and surveyed the group. He had given the same speech at least a dozen times in the last fortnight, and was pleased to see it have the same effect it always did; the nervousness on the faces of the volunteers was gone, replaced by clear-eyed determination.

"Any questions?" he asked.

Silence.

"All right then," said Greg, casting a smile in Pete's direction. "There's a six-week probationary period, but I've got a good feeling about you all. You're on the side of the future."

9

THE FAINTEST GLIMMER

Matt Browning looked up from his screen and squeezed his eyes shut. Dots of light whirled and spun across his field of vision as a dull ache pulsed down the back of his head and across his shoulders; he had been in the Lazarus Project labs for almost seventeen hours and he was absolutely spent.

He sat back in his chair, stretched his arms above his head in an attempt to lessen the knots in his neck and upper arms, and checked the time. It was just after 10pm, but the lab was almost full; the Lazarus staff were prone to working until they could no longer keep their eyes open. There were perhaps half a dozen desks unoccupied, but Matt knew they would not remain so for long; they belonged to those men and women who had drifted into nocturnal cycles of working and sleeping, and who would likely arrive any minute to start shifts that would go through the night.

Matt glanced to his right and saw Natalia looking at him; she grinned, before turning her attention back to her screen. He stared at her, marvelling, as he always did, at both her very existence and the impact she had had on his life. The talk had happened almost five months ago now, and there was no longer any doubt: she was his girlfriend.

His first girlfriend.

The first girl he had ever kissed. Or done… anything else with.

Matt blushed at memories that were never far from his mind, feeling heat rise into his face. He doubted he would ever understand why the brilliant, beautiful Russian girl was interested in him, but, for one of the very first times in his life, his prodigiously powerful brain had steered him through the ever-present clouds of self-doubt. Its message had been simple: don't question this, don't overthink it, just hold tight with both hands and refuse to let go. Because relationships tended not to end well for those who had given their lives over to Blacklight, including those he considered his closest friends, and nothing, absolutely *nothing* about the future was certain.

Kate and Shaun.

Jamie and Larissa.

In a display of resilience that Matt could still scarcely comprehend, Kate had managed to move on from the terrible sight of her boyfriend lying dead in front of her, his neck broken, his eyes wide and staring up at nothing. But although she had found the strength to keep getting out of bed each morning, Matt didn't believe for a second that she was really, truly over what had happened to Shaun; he doubted, in all honesty, that she ever would be.

He had similar doubts about his best friend. It was painfully clear to everyone that Jamie still missed Larissa so much that it hurt, despite his protestations to the contrary. Matt had been furious when Kate told him that Larissa was gone, had disappeared into the night without so much as a goodbye, so he could not imagine the depths of anger and misery Jamie must be feeling. In truth, Matt had worried for a while that it might prove the final straw; his friend had been beset by a trio of revelations that would have been hard for anyone to deal with – the truth about his dad, and Frankenstein, and the sudden disappearance of the girl he had relied on far more than he wanted people to know – and it had taken

Matt a number of long weeks to truly believe that Jamie was going to be able to carry on.

Be grateful, he told himself. *For Natalia, and Jamie, and Kate, and for the simple fact that you're still breathing in and out. Because the world could literally end at any moment.*

Matt looked around the long rectangular space that comprised the Lazarus Project's central laboratory. There were three more large labs, sealed behind airlocks and disinfectant showers, along with a twenty-four-hour canteen and two corridors of quarters for those men and women who chose to eat and work and sleep without ever setting foot beyond the project's borders. He briefly considered trying to persuade Natalia to call it a day as well, but saw the lines of data scrolling down her screen and decided not to disturb her. He would send her a message later. With that settled, he reached for his mouse, intending to log out of the Lazarus network, and paused as a window popped open at the bottom of his screen.

He groaned inwardly. The window was an automated notification, informing him that the results of his most recent set of data runs were now available, and for a brief moment he considered pretending he hadn't seen it and leaving as he'd intended. But he knew he couldn't; he knew that wondering about the results would prevent him sleeping, regardless of how tired he was. Instead, he clicked the window open, and double-clicked on the secure link that would load the results. While the computer worked, Matt lowered himself back into his chair and waited.

The data he had brought back from San Francisco had allowed Lazarus to take giant leaps forward; it was no exaggeration to claim that it had saved years of research and development. To best handle the huge amount of new data, the project had subsequently been separated into eight smaller teams, each working independently, each focused entirely on one aspect of the search for the cure. Matt's team had been tasked with analysing the protein coat and envelope of lipids that enclosed the genetic material of the vampire virus itself, and had made rapid progress, to the point that it was widely believed they had learnt all there was to learn.

It was clear that the genetic material inside the virus was responsible for the DNA rewriting that took place in the early stages of the turn, and contained the trigger which began the physical alteration, but Matt had retained a nagging suspicion that the key to undoing the transformation lay in the protein coat rather than what it surrounded, and he had designed structure after structure based on that suspicion. The results that were now loading were the last of what had been officially listed as a dead end, a line of enquiry that the project had moved on from, but which Matt had found himself strangely unwilling to drop.

The screen filled with data, with page after page of equations and genetic analysis. Several lines of text and numbers were purple, and Matt recognised them instantly; they were the protein pairs that had been extracted from the DNA in John Bell's blood, the first reliable building blocks for what would eventually be the genetic blueprint of a cure for vampirism. Matt scanned the rest of the lines, reaquainting himself with the structure he had built, one of literally thousands that he had sent into the supercomputer array for testing over the last year or so. Forty-three per cent of the structure had been confirmed when he sent it in, which was about normal for a test formula; it didn't sound like much, but the percentage had been a lot lower before Matt scraped John Bell's blood and flesh up from the tarmac beneath the wheels of a truck.

Matt tabbed past the structural overview to the preliminary testing results, and sat forward to read them. He skipped the document's first section, which was the Analysis Team's assessment of the design he had submitted, confirming that it met all the criteria to be taken forward for testing. The second section detailed the results of their attempts to physically produce the gene itself, hundreds of lines generated by the sequencers and growth managers showing that this particular gene could be provisionally manufactured with ninety-seven per cent reliability. The third and final section showed what had happened when the gene was introduced into cells infected with the vampire virus, and was always the point at which hopes were dashed. Every set of test results had concluded with the word NEGATIVE, eight letters that every member of the Lazarus Project had come to both hate and expect.

But as Matt looked at the screen, he saw that this report was different; there were two words at the bottom of the document, rather than one, and they were words he had never seen before.

VIABLE REACTION

Matt was suddenly aware that his mouth was incredibly dry. He stared at the screen, trying to comprehend what he was seeing, trying not to let his brain go racing ahead of itself, then picked up the phone on his desk and dialled the number for the testing laboratory.

"Analysis," answered a voice.

"Hey," said Matt, trying to force himself to at least *sound* calm. "I sent a sample through three days ago and I've just got the results back. Can you tell me if these are simulated findings?"

"Which sample?"

"Submission 85403/B."

"Hang on," said the voice. "Let me just bring it up…"

Matt held his breath.

"OK, got it," said the voice. "Those are real-world results. I'm looking at the production vials right now."

Matt felt a shiver race up his spine. "You're sure?" he said. "You're absolutely sure? The computers really built this and this is really what it did?"

"I'm sure," said the voice. "Why? What do the results say?"

Matt looked back at the two words at the bottom of the document, as if he was afraid they might have disappeared in the second he had taken his eye off them.

"Holy shit," he whispered. "Thanks. I have to go."

He hung up the phone, and took a deep breath. There was an unfamiliar feeling spreading slowly through him, one that it took him a moment to identify.

Hope, he realised. *It's hope. My God. This could change everything.*

10

COLLATERAL DAMAGE (1)

WEST BRIDGFORD, NOTTINGHAMSHIRE, ENGLAND
EIGHT HOURS LATER

Max Wellens strolled through quiet streets, whistling a tune he had been trying to place all evening.

It was maddening; he was sure it was a television show theme, most likely from his childhood in the 1980s, but none of his friends had been able to identify it, not even Sam, whose knowledge of popular culture was usually encyclopaedic. It was a simple melody – *duh-duh-duh-da-duh-dum-duh-da-daa* – and it had settled comfortably into Max's brain, with no sign of it leaving any time soon. The only consolation, as far as he was concerned, was that he had successfully managed to pass the earworm on to his friends; both Dan and Barry had left the pub humming it, cursing him as they went.

Max smiled at the memory as he turned off the high street and headed for the park gates. It had been a good night: United had won in the Champions League, the special had been pulled pork burgers, and everyone had been on good form, laughing and joking and mocking each other, as they had been doing for the fifteen years since they met on the first day of senior school. But, as it always did, the walk home from the pub filled Max with pre-emptive nostalgia; he had at least a couple of years before he needed to worry, but he knew there was going to come a time when his youthful appearance was going to raise questions that he could no longer answer with claims of yoga and a balanced diet. When that time came, he would leave Nottingham for somewhere nobody knew him and start again; he knew he would have the strength to do it, but the prospect, unavoidable as it was, nonetheless tightened his chest with sadness.

Part of him believed he should simply tell his friends the truth; he was sure they wouldn't judge him, and it was far from an uncommon problem these days. But he knew it would change things. And he didn't want things to change; he never had.

The sound of the cars and the yellow glow of the street lights on the main road faded away as he walked into the park, his footsteps clicking rapidly across the tarmac of the main path. Trees towered above him on all sides, and Max could hear the movement of animals in the undergrowth and the rustling of branches as they swayed in the gentle night breeze. He followed the path round the lake, past the boats tied up to a small wooden jetty, and out across the football pitches, their rusting goalposts gleaming in the moonlight. On the far side of the field, Max heard voices and laughter coming from the playground. He headed towards it, knowing what he would find: teenagers drinking cheap booze and smoking cheap cigarettes, exactly as he and his friends had done in a dozen similar parks when they were the same age.

"Mate, you got a fag?"

The voice came from the swings at the centre of the park, and Max turned towards it. There were five teenagers clustered round the metal frame and three actually sitting on the seats, as clear a social hierarchy as it was possible to imagine. The boy who had spoken was in the middle, wearing tracksuit bottoms and a thick hoodie, and staring at Max with an expression that he no doubt thought looked hard.

"Don't smoke," said Max. "Sorry."

The teenager looked at him for a long moment. "Prick," he muttered, the volume of his voice clearly intended to be audible to Max. Two of the girls giggled in approval, and one of the standing boys, clearly a member of the lower order of the playground hierarchy, clapped him on the back.

Max stopped. He had no doubt they were harmless, just as he and his friends had been, but he was full of a sudden urge to teach them a lesson, to make them realise that there were things in the night that were far more dangerous than kids full of cider-inflated bravado. And on a gut level, in the base part of himself that he kept hidden from everyone, he was *hungry*.

"What?" asked the teenage boy, getting up from his swing. "You got a problem?"

Max stared at him, feeling the first flush of heat behind his eyes. The boy's acne-ridden face was pale in the moonlight, his mouth curled into an arrogant smile.

Don't rise to it, he told himself. *There's eight of them. Too many.*

"No problem," he said. "Have a good night."

He walked along the path towards the west gate without a backward glance, knowing the boy would stare daggers after him until he was out of sight; it would be no less than his friends would expect. Max strode through the gate and into the quiet estate where he'd lived for the last five years; his house was a square brick box standing behind a paved drive and a small lawn that he only mowed in the evenings. He unlocked the front door, hung his coat on the hook rack in the hall, and walked through to the living room where he flopped down on to the sofa, put the TV on, and was asleep within a minute.

* * *

Thud. Thud thud.

Max's eyes flew open, his heart racing in his chest. He had dreamt of her again, the same dream as always: the trees, the blood, the screams, the freezing water. He sat up on the sofa, rubbed his eyes, and looked at the clock on the mantelpiece, the one that had been his mother's.

Two forty-three, he thought. *Almost three in the morning.*

He got unsteadily to his feet. Something had woken him, something that had managed to penetrate the fabric of his dream and engage his conscious mind. Max went to the window, slid open the curtains that were always closed, and peered out at the dark street.

Thud. Thud thud thud thud.

He jumped. The sound was coming from the front of the house. Someone was knocking on his door.

Max pulled his phone from his pocket and checked its screen. No messages. No missed calls. Slowly, his heart pounding, he walked out into the hallway and turned on the lights. A dark silhouette loomed outside the front door, clearly visible through the pane of frosted glass.

"Who's there?" he shouted, and heard a tremor in his voice.

"Nottinghamshire Police, sir," came the reply. "Open the door, please."

Max frowned. "What's this about?" he asked.

"We've had a complaint of a disturbance at this address, sir."

"There's no disturbance here," said Max. "You must have the wrong house."

"Sir, we're required to follow up on all complaints," said the silhouette. "Please open the door."

Max hesitated, then slid the security chain on the back of the door into place. He unlocked the door and pulled it open a few centimetres. "I'd like to see your identification," he said.

"No problem, sir," said the man. A gloved hand pushed a leather wallet through the gap between the door and the frame. Max opened it and found a plastic warrant card in the name of Sergeant Liam Collins of the Nottinghamshire Police.

He breathed a silent sigh of relief, and pushed the door shut. "I'm sorry, officer," he said, as he slid the chain back. "Can't be too careful, you know?"

"I understand, sir," said the man, as the door swung open. "There are a lot of dangerous people out here."

Max had just enough time to see a circle of glass gleaming in the moonlight. Then a searing beam of purple light blinded him, and his face burst into flames.

He fell backwards, screaming incoherently and beating desperately at the fire erupting from his skin and hair. The pain was unthinkable, far beyond anything he had ever known, enough to drive reason from his mind; all he knew, on an instinctive level, was that he had to put the fire out, had to stop himself burning. His fangs burst involuntarily from his gums, slicing through his tongue and transforming his screams into high-pitched grunts. One of his eyes was empty blackness and awful, sickening pain, like someone had tipped boiling water over it. Through the other, he saw billowing smoke as he clawed at his face and head, and the dreadful sight of two men dressed all in black stepping into his house and shutting the door behind them.

The pain in his head lessened fractionally as his pounding fists finally extinguished the flames. The skin on his hands was charred red and black and peeling away in wide sheets, revealing the pink muscle beneath. Max tried to focus, but felt his reeling body resist him as he rolled over on to his front and crawled towards the kitchen, each agonising centimetre requiring a Herculean effort. He heard voices behind him, but ignored them; his remaining eye was fixed on the fridge, and the bottles of blood he knew were chilling inside it. If he could reach them, perhaps there might still be a chance.

Then he felt a tiny stab of pain in the side of his neck, and realised there was none.

He slumped to the ground as the syringe was drawn out of his flesh, as though the power supply to his muscles had been turned off. His ruined tongue slid limply out of his mouth as one of the black-clad men pressed a boot against his ribs and rolled him over on to his back. Max stared up at him, his diminished vision beginning to blur and darken, and managed a single mangled word.

"Blacklight…"

The man grunted with laughter. "Not us, mate," he said, as Max slipped into unconsciousness. "We're something else."

When he awoke again, he could feel the steady vibration of an engine somewhere beneath him. Max opened one eye and the pain came rushing back to him, deep, searing agony in his face and scalp. He gritted his teeth and let out a low groan; his stomach was spinning, and he was sure he was going to be sick. He tried to roll on to his side, but couldn't move; whatever had been in the syringe was still working on him, paralysing his muscles.

Above him, sitting on a wooden bench and leaning against a metal panel, was one of the dark figures that had burst into his home. He stared up with his good eye and wondered how he had ever mistaken them for Department 19. Max had seen a squad of Blacklight soldiers once, a long time ago, and they had been slick, almost robotic in appearance; the man above him was wearing a black balaclava, a cheap black leather jacket, and a backpack that looked like it had been bought in a sports shop. But then he focused more closely, and felt terror spill through him.

Painted on the man's chest, in crude sprays of white, was a wolf's head, its teeth huge, its jaws open wide. And all of a sudden, Max knew who had him.

"Night... Stalker..." he managed, his tongue barely obeying his brain's commands, his mouth filling with saliva.

The man looked down at him. "Welcome back, mate," he said. "Don't try to talk. It'll just make things worse."

Max stared, his eye wide with fear. He tried to move, felt nothing happen, and bore down with all that remained of his strength. His left hand trembled, but stayed flat against the floor.

"You want me to dose you again?" asked the man. He leant forward and held up a thick black torch. "Stay still or die. It's up to you."

The purple lens seemed huge, as though it was about to swallow Max up. He forced himself to look away, and fixed his gaze on the ceiling above him. It was the roof of a van, moulded metal and plastic, long and wide. Beneath him, the engine rumbled on. He knew what happened to vampires taken by the Night Stalker, had seen the bloody aftermath on the news and online. His only chance was to wait, to not provoke his captors, and hope that enough of his strength returned before they reached wherever they were taking him.

Maybe I'll have a chance then, he thought. *Maybe.*

The van pulled to a halt, and Max was jerked awake. He had drifted back into unconsciousness and dreamt about her again: the blood, the water, the screams. He opened his eye, saw the man with the wolf on his chest still sitting above him, and tried to move the fingers of his hand, silently praying that whatever they had drugged him with had worn off.

Nothing. Not even the tremble it had managed before.

Panic flooded through him; he wondered whether they had given him another shot while he was unconscious, but he couldn't check his neck and he didn't dare ask, providing he could even form the words to do so.

"Are we on?" asked the man, looking towards the front of the van.

"Yep," replied a voice that presumably belonged to the driver.

"All right then," said the man, and looked down at Max. "Let's get you up."

"No," he managed. He tried to force his limbs into action, but felt not even the slightest flicker in response. "Please…"

The man ignored him, opened the rear doors of the vehicle, and disappeared. Max lay on the floor, terror pulsing through him, unable to move, barely able to think. Then hands reached under his armpits, and dragged him backwards out of the van.

His heels scraped uselessly across the ground as, despite the panic that was coursing through him, Max forced himself to look around, to see if there was something, *anything* he might be able to use to save himself from the fate he knew awaited him. He was being hauled across a barren, weed and pebble-strewn patch of wasteland, a place he didn't recognise; he had no idea how long he had been unconscious, and therefore no idea how far he might have been taken from his home. A squat industrial building rose up before him, its windows barred and broken, its bricks crumbling and its paint flaking away; it looked long abandoned. Max strained his supernatural hearing, listening for a human voice, the sound of a car engine, anything that might suggest that help could be nearby.

He heard nothing.

"That's far enough," said a voice from behind him.

The fingers digging into his armpits disappeared, and Max tumbled to the ground, unable to do anything to break his fall. His head connected sharply with the ground, sending a fresh bolt of pain through his battered system, and he let out a gasping sob as he was pushed over on to his back. The two men with the white wolves on their chests crowded over him, torches in their hands, and his vocal cords dragged themselves into life, galvanised by a terror that was almost overwhelming.

"Please," he said, his voice slurred. "Please don't kill me. Please. It isn't fair."

One of the men tilted his head to one side. "What's not fair about it?"

"It's not my fault," said Max. "Being a vampire. It's not fair. Please…"

"What do you drink?" asked the man.

Max stared up at him. "What?"

"You're a vampire," said the man. "So you need to drink blood. Where do you get it?"

"Raw meat," said Max. He felt tears well in his remaining eye. "Butchers. Stray dogs and cats."

"Is that right?" asked the man, and squatted down beside him, his eyes narrow behind his balaclava. "What about Suzanne Fields?"

"Who?" asked Max.

"Surely you remember her?" said the man. "Pretty blonde, nineteen years old. You attacked her when she was walking home through Bridgford Park, then you drank her dry and broke her neck when you were done. Divers found her a week ago, at the bottom of the river half a mile from your house."

"I don't know anything about her," said Max, his voice low. "I never hurt—"

"Don't give me that," said the man. "It's time to come clean, Max. Time to confess your sins. It'll be better for your soul, if you still have one."

The nightmare burst into his mind: the blonde hair, the screams, the taste of blood in his mouth, the freezing water as he pushed her under the surface. He had suppressed it, buried it as deep as it would go, but it bubbled up when he was at his most vulnerable; she had haunted him every night since he killed her.

"I didn't mean it," he whispered, and let out a low sob. "I'm sorry. I'm so sorry. I didn't mean to hurt her."

"That's good," said the man. "Admit what you did. Be a man about it."

"I never wanted to be a vampire," said Max, the combination of pain and misery flooding through his mind threatening to unmoor it. "I didn't want it. I didn't. You have to believe me."

"I do believe you," said the man. "But that doesn't change what you did."

The tears spilled out of Max's eye and rolled down his cheek, burning across the ruined flesh like acid.

"What makes it OK for you to kill me?" he asked. "What gives you the right to sentence me to death?"

"It's got nothing to do with rights," said the man. "This is a war. And in a war you don't show mercy to your enemies."

The black-clad man drew a wooden stake from his belt and held it out; Max stared at it, overcome by horror at the realisation that his life was going to end in this place, far away from his friends and the people he loved.

"Make your peace with whatever you believe in," said the man. "You've outstayed your welcome in this world."

Max closed his eye. He saw the faces of his friends, and felt his heart ache at the thought of never seeing them again. But then, in the depths of his despair, he felt a momentary bloom of relief: he was glad they had never known what he had become, that he had never had to see the disappointment on their faces.

Because he had told the truth to the man who was about to murder him: he did regret the girl in the park, as he regretted the four others he had killed. He had never meant to hurt any of them; he had lost himself in the hunger, and by the time he had remembered himself, they had been dead.

He couldn't change it now.

Couldn't change any of it.

It was too late.

11

THE ENEMY OF MY ENEMY

WEST BRIDGFORD, NOTTINGHAMSHIRE, ENGLAND

Jamie sat back in his seat and stared at the screen that had been folded down from the ceiling of the van. The connection to the Surveillance Division was active; all that remained now was to wait for their first alert of the night to come through.

"What's your bet?" asked Lizzy Ellison, from her seat opposite him. "Domestic disturbance? False alarm?"

"Domestic," said Qiang. "They are always domestic now."

Jamie shrugged. "You never know," he said. "Maybe we'll get lucky and actually see a real vampire tonight."

"Steady on, sir," said Ellison, smiling broadly at him. "Let's not get carried away."

Qiang let out a grunt of laughter, a sound that never failed to amaze his squad leader. When he had first arrived at the Loop, the Chinese Operator had seemed more like a robot than an actual human being: utterly professional, precise, and not given to conversation beyond what was necessary for the Operation at hand. Now, more than six months later and following a concerted campaign by both Jamie and Ellison, Qiang was a markedly different person. He was still unlikely to ever win the award for most light-hearted member of the Department, but he was now capable of making a limited amount of small talk, of telling his squad mates about the family and friends that he had left behind in China, and, on extremely rare and joyous occasions, making small, bone-dry jokes.

As the months after Zero Hour had lumbered slowly past, Jamie had come to see his squad as a lone beacon of stability in a world that was becoming ever more uncertain, and when he had thrown himself into his job in an attempt to escape the misery and chaos that had been threatening to drag him down, his squad mates had been right there beside him. Neither Ellison nor Qiang knew the truth about his father, or why he no longer spoke to Frankenstein, but they knew about Larissa; everyone in the Department did.

Word of her departure had raced through the Loop, causing dismay among those who understood that Blacklight was weaker without her and relief among the many Operators who had never truly been comfortable with a vampire wearing the black uniform. In the first days after her disappearance, dozens of Jamie's colleagues had asked him what had happened, if he had any idea where she might have gone, until his patience began to visibly wear thin and people realised that questioning him further would have been unwise.

The only thing Ellison and Qiang had ever asked was whether he was all right. He had told them that he wasn't, but that he didn't want to talk about it, and they had left it at that. It had been a show of respect for which he remained profoundly grateful.

Ellison had, in fact, been entirely awesome since the day she had joined the Department. Jamie had once told Cal Holmwood that she was going to sit in the Director's chair one day, and nothing had happened since to make him revise that opinion. She was a *brilliant* Operator, smart and agile and fearless, but more than that, she had the uncanny ability to drag him out of himself, to cut through the fog of gloom that hung over him and force him to laugh, usually at himself. Jamie knew he was susceptible to self-pity, and Ellison was the perfect antidote: irreverent, kind, funny, and absolutely unwilling to indulge him. He loved Kate and Matt and relied on them more than anyone, even more than his mum, who, for all her empathy and unconditional love, could never really, truly relate to what his life had become. But Ellison was close behind them on his priority list; when he was on Operations with her and Qiang, he felt accepted and valued and appreciated. He felt at peace. As a result, it was not uncommon for his heart to sink when the time came for them to head back to the Loop.

Jamie was roused from his thoughts by the loud alarm that accompanied a new window opening on the van's screen.

ECHELON INTERCEPT REF. 97607/2R
SOURCE. Emergency call (mobile telephone 07087 904543)
TIME OF INTERCEPT. 23:45

OPERATOR: Hello, emergency service operator, which service do you require?
CALLER: Police.
OPERATOR: What is the nature of your emergency?
CALLER: I just got home from work and something's been painted on my neighbour's front door.
OPERATOR: Does this qualify as an emergency, sir?
CALLER: It's the same thing that's been in the papers, that Night Stalker thing. The wolf's head. It's right on the front door.
OPERATOR: You can call your local police station to report vandalism, sir. This line needs to be kept clear for emergencies.
CALLER: Right. Sorry.

INTERCEPT REFERENCE LOCATION. Violet Road, West Bridgford, Nottinghamshire. 52.933714, -1.122017

RISK ASSESSMENT. Priority Level 2

"All right," said Ellison, rubbing her hands together. "Let's go."

"Have you got the location, Operator?" asked Jamie.

"Yes, sir," replied their driver, his voice sounding through the speakers. "ETA three minutes."

"Very close," said Qiang, as the van accelerated, its engine rumbling beneath them.

"Weapons and kit check," said Jamie. Excitement was crackling through him at the prospect of something that might actually be worth the attention of his squad. Ever since V-Day and Gideon and stupid, reckless Kevin McKenna, Patrol Responds had become purgatory: night after night of false alarms, attacks on suspected vampires who turned out to be every bit as human as their assailants, denouncements and accusations that were usually the malicious result of some minor grudge. This, the call they were now racing towards, had the potential to be different. Everyone inside the Department was following the Night Stalker attacks with great interest, although, for once, Blacklight seemed to know little more than the public and the media.

There had been ten attacks so far, all in the Midlands and East Anglia, all bearing signature similarities, most notably the wolf's head painted on the doors of the victims' homes and across their bloody remains. Public opinion seemed to favour the lone crazy theory, that the Night Stalker was a single individual carrying out vigilante executions, but Jamie, along with the majority of his colleagues, thought otherwise. He knew better than anyone how powerful vampires were, how fast and agile, especially when cornered; even allowing for the element of surprise, he didn't believe that anyone could carry out ten vampire killings on their own, unless they were also a vampire. Which was a possibility, although Jamie subscribed to a simpler solution: that there was no such thing as *the* Night Stalker, but *several* Night Stalkers, at least two, perhaps even four or five.

"Twenty seconds, sir," said their driver.

Jamie fastened his helmet into place, flipped up the visor, and looked at his squad mates. "Ready One as soon as we touch the ground," he said, and felt his eyes bloom with heat. "Non-lethal. Clear?"

"Clear," replied his squad mates.

The van slowed to a halt. Jamie twisted the handle on the rear door and pushed it open. "Go," he said.

Ellison and Qiang leapt down on to the tarmac, their weapons at their shoulders, their visors covering their faces. He was beside them in an instant, floating a millimetre or two above the ground; his vampire side, the part of himself that heightened his senses and kept him sharp, was wide awake, and hungry, as he looked around. They were standing in a quiet suburban estate, a long row of square, two-storey houses with neat lawns and mid-range Japanese cars in their driveways.

"Shall I circle, sir?" asked their driver, his voice loud and clear through the comms plugs in Jamie's ears.

"No," he replied. "We're not going to be here long. Ask Surveillance to bring up the CCTV grid for a ten-mile radius from this location and leave a line open."

"Yes, sir."

Jamie nodded, and looked at the house standing before them. It was identical to all the others on the estate, with one ghoulish exception; sprayed on its front door, in white paint that had dripped all the way down to the step, was a crude wolf's head, its teeth huge, its eyes wide and staring.

"Night Stalker," he said. "Or a good impression, at least. Check the door."

"Yes, sir," said Ellison, and jogged up the driveway, Qiang close behind her. She moved to one side of the door frame, her back against the front wall of the house, and tried the handle. It turned in her hand, and the door swung open.

"Sweep the house," said Jamie. "Both of you. Quick as you can."

His squad mates disappeared inside as he took a closer look at the quiet street. The night air was still and cool; his supernatural ears could pick out the low drone of dozens of televisions from inside the identical homes. Jamie spun slowly in the air, until movement on the other side of the road caught his eye; a curtain had fluttered in the window of the house opposite, as though someone had been peering through it until he looked in their direction.

Nosy neighbour, he thought, and flew slowly towards the house. *What would we do without them?*

Jamie rose over the low wall at the front of the garden, crossed the lawn, and waited in front of the window for the curtain to open again. He had absolutely no doubt that it would; the van and his squad's unusual appearance would prove too tempting. Long seconds passed until the curtains parted, ever so slightly, and the face of an elderly woman peered through them. Her eyes locked with Jamie's, and he smiled widely as they flew open with fright. The curtains snapped shut again; he waited a moment, then flew along the front of the house and knocked hard on the door.

"I didn't do nothing," called a voice from inside. "Get away with you. I won't look no more."

"I'm sorry, ma'am," he said. "I didn't mean to scare you. I need to ask you some questions."

Silence.

"I'm not opening the door," shouted the woman, eventually. "I don't care who you are, I don't open up after dark and that's all there is to it."

"That's fine, ma'am," said Jamie. "That's a sensible policy. I just need to know if you've seen anything unusual in the last hour or so."

"Just you lot," said the woman. "What've you come back for? Can't you leave that poor man alone?"

Jamie frowned. "What do you mean, just you lot?"

"*You lot*," repeated the woman. "All in black, with that big van of yours. Twenty minutes ago it was."

"Thank you, ma'am," said Jamie. He turned away, flew towards the house with the wolf on its door, and touched down on the drive as Ellison and Qiang reappeared.

"Clear," said Ellison. "Nobody home, no remains."

"Signs of a struggle?" asked Jamie.

"There is a burn mark on the hall carpet," said Qiang. "A recent one."

"And a lot of something that looks like blood," said Ellison.

"Shit," said Jamie. "They've taken him, whoever he is. Load up."

The three Operators ran down to the kerb and climbed back into the van. Jamie dropped into his seat and took his helmet off.

"Surveillance?" he said. "Are you there?"

"Go ahead, Lieutenant Carpenter," replied a voice from the speakers.

"We're looking for a black van that left this location within the last twenty minutes. Anything on CCTV that fits that description?"

"Hold, please."

An agonising silence filled the van's hold.

Come on! thought Jamie. *Hurry up, for God's sake!*

"I've got a black 2008 Ford Transit leaving your location seventeen minutes ago," said the Surveillance Operator. "Do you want me to track it?"

"Yes," said Jamie.

"Tracking," said the voice. "OK. The last camera hit was in Bramcote, four minutes ago. Seven miles west of your location."

"Good," he said. "Keep tracking. Operator?"

"Yes, sir," said their driver.

"Get us there as fast as you can," said Jamie. "Don't stop for red lights."

The van raced through winding suburban streets, weaving in and out of traffic and raising a cacophony of angry horns in its wake.

Jamie listened silently to the Surveillance Division updates, trying to ignore the frustration building inside him; he could have got out of the van, leapt into the air, and been on top of their target within a minute, two at the most. But he was the leader of Operational Squad J-5, and they worked as a team; otherwise, he might as well carry out Patrol Responds on his own. The van's external cameras fed the wide screen, and Jamie watched as the landscape they were speeding through changed; the houses and pubs and rows of shops were disappearing, giving way to dilapidated industrial buildings and bridges and yards.

"Thirty seconds," said their driver. "Dead ahead."

"Ready One," said Jamie. "Be prepared for whatever this is."

Ellison and Qiang nodded. This was the highest priority call they had taken in more than two months, and the air in the van's hold was thick with anticipation.

"Ten seconds," said their driver.

Jamie got to his feet, took hold of the door handle, and lowered his visor as calm flooded through him. Then the van screeched to a halt, its brakes squealing, and he flung the door open.

"Go," he bellowed.

Jamie dived out of the vehicle, swooped up into the air, and surveyed the scene. He found himself looking at a patch of wasteland behind a ragged chain-link fence, squeezed in between two warehouse buildings, both of them boarded up and abandoned. Kneeling on the ground was a badly burnt figure, his head lowered, his hands hanging limply at his sides. Standing over him was a figure dressed in black with a wolf's head painted on its chest in white; a second, identically dressed figure was standing off to the side. Both were staring at the Blacklight van with wide eyes.

"Freeze!" yelled Jamie. "Weapons down, hands in the air!"

Without a second's hesitation, the two Night Stalkers moved. One sprinted for the shadows between the buildings as the other darted forward and slammed a stake into the kneeling figure's chest. The vampire exploded with a wet thud, spraying blood and guts in a wide radius. Jamie screamed with fury, and hurtled towards the man as Ellison and Qiang burst through the torn fence, their weapons drawn.

Jamie closed the distance between himself and the man – it *was* a man, he was sure of it, both of them were – at dizzying speed, his eyes roaring with red heat, his fangs filling his mouth, a deadly black bullet fired with unerring accuracy. But when he was still five metres away, the air was suddenly filled with flying lead.

The man spun, pulling an MP5 from his belt, and emptied the submachine gun at Jamie; the speed of the movement took him by surprise, and he had no time to react before the bullets hammered into him. The body armour inside his uniform held, but the impacts were still agony; they drove him backwards through the air, his momentum arrested, his balance gone. The firing continued and Jamie screamed as at least two of the bullets slipped past his armour and pierced his body below the armpit. The scream was cut off, replaced by a rasping wheeze. Jamie tried to draw breath, but felt only the thinnest current of air flow down into his chest.

Punctured lung, he thought. *Oh Christ, that hurts.*

He crumpled to the ground, his back slamming against the hard concrete, and gritted his teeth as he tried to force himself back to his feet. Footsteps rattled around him, seemingly from all sides, until Ellison appeared in front of him and slid to her knees, her visor pushed up to reveal a face contorted with worry.

"Are you all right?" she asked. "Jamie? Are you—"

"Don't worry about me," he growled, his eyes blazing. "Get after them. That's an order."

Ellison stared at him for the briefest of moments, then leapt to her feet and raced away into the darkness, Qiang at her side. Jamie lay where he was, concentrating on taking only the shallowest of breaths. It was hard work, and it *hurt*, but oxygen *was* reaching his lungs; not as much as he needed, he was sure, but enough to keep him alive. He stared up at the night sky, furious with himself.

Underestimated them, he thought. *You had no idea what you were dealing with and you just charged in like a rookie. That guy was so fast, and so calm. He knew what he was doing, and he wasn't remotely scared of me. Military, I'd bet my life on it. Military, or...*

A terrible thought leapt into Jamie's mind, one so huge and awful that the fire in his eyes died instantly as what was left of his breath froze in his chest.

No, he told himself. *No way. It couldn't be.*

He gritted his teeth again, forced the thought from his mind, and pushed himself up to a sitting position. Something moved inside him, sending fresh agony thundering through his body, and glowing light returned to his eyes as sweat broke out on his forehead. It felt like the Night Stalker's bullets had broken at least two or three of his ribs as well as tearing a hole in his lung. He reached down with a trembling hand and twisted the comms dial on his belt.

"Ellison?" he said. "Qiang? Report."

"Lost them," said Ellison, instantly. "It's a bloody rabbit warren back here. Qiang followed one over a fire escape and I chased the

144

other into one of the buildings, but they're gone, sir. No sign of them, and nothing on thermal."

Jamie swore heavily, then broke into a fit of coughing that ripped through his chest like he had swallowed a pack of razor blades. His mouth was suddenly full of liquid, and he spat it on to the ground beside him. The blood was shiny-black in the moonlight, and he felt his stomach lurch at the sight of it.

"What should we do, sir?" asked Qiang.

"Regroup," said Jamie, his voice low and hoarse. "I need blood."

"Yes, sir," said Ellison.

Jamie waited for his squad mates to return, trying to ignore the pain and resist a sudden, overwhelming desire to lie back down. His arms shook with the effort of holding himself up, but he was bleeding from somewhere internal, and he had no desire to choke on his own blood.

His supernatural hearing picked up the sound of footsteps in the distance. Thirty seconds later Ellison and Qiang emerged from the shadows, their weapons in their gloved hands, their visors raised. Qiang peeled away and strode towards their van as Ellison approached Jamie, a deep frown on her face.

"Jesus, Jamie," she said, stopping in front of him. "You look like shit."

He forced a thin smile. "Lucky shot," he grunted. "Got round the edge of my armour."

"Nothing lucky about it," said Ellison. "Don't tell me you didn't think exactly the same thing I did when you saw that guy shoot."

Jamie nodded. "Military."

"Right," said Ellison. "What the hell's going on here?"

"I don't know," said Jamie. "But I think we can conclude that the lone vigilante theory is bullshit."

Qiang appeared beside Ellison, crouched down, and held out

two plastic bottles of blood. Jamie took them, twisted the top off the first, and drank the contents in one go, his head twisted back, the muscles standing out in his neck, his eyes blooming red. Euphoria flooded through him as his body began to repair itself; the pain faded away, and he felt his punctured lung reinflate, filling him with energy. He put the empty bottle down, drained the second, and got to his feet, his body coursing with heat.

"I'm sorry," he said, his voice low. "That was stupid. I let you both down."

Ellison rolled her eyes. "Drama queen," she said, and smiled. Qiang gave one of his short grunts of laughter, then turned towards the black Transit parked by the kerb, his focus instantly returned to business.

"We have their vehicle," he said. "That is good."

Jamie nodded. "Have Security come out here and impound it. I doubt it'll tell us much, but you never know."

Qiang nodded, and stepped back as he twisted his comms dial and established a connection to the Loop. A second later he was giving coordinates in his clear, steady voice. Jamie left him to it, and walked slowly towards the remains of the vampire the Night Stalkers had killed. He looked down at the bloody circle as Ellison joined him.

"I wonder who this one was," he said. "I wonder whether he did anything to deserve this."

"Does anyone deserve to be dragged out of their home and murdered in cold blood?" asked Ellison.

"I've met one or two over the years," said Jamie. "But not many. And this wasn't murder. It was an execution. They were carrying out a sentence."

The two Operators stood in silence, staring at the smear of drying blood that had, until barely five minutes earlier, been a living, breathing human being. Whatever he had been, whatever he might one day have become, was gone, ended in misery and pain at the point of a stranger's stake.

A splash of colour caught Jamie's eye and he dragged his gaze away from the remains. The red-brick side of the warehouse on the opposite side of the road, beyond the wire fence and the two parked vans, was covered in faded graffiti and peeling posters, but what had drawn his attention was fresh and bright at the edge of the yellow glow cast by the street light overhead. It was two familiar words painted in dripping fluorescent green, each letter more than a metre tall.

HE RISES

Jamie grimaced. The words seemed to be everywhere these days, painted on walls and bridges and the shutters of abandoned shops, written in dozens of different colours by dozens of different hands; they were a constant mockery, a colourful reminder of the Department's failure.

Qiang appeared at his side. "Security are on their way," he said. "Forty minutes. We are to stay until they arrive."

Jamie nodded. "Fair enough."

Qiang peered down at the bloody remains. "One less vampire," he said. "Even if we did not destroy him ourselves. It is good."

Jamie smiled. "I used to know someone who would have disagreed with you," he said.

Ellison narrowed her eyes and shot him a look full of sympathy. "You still miss her, don't you?" she said.

Jamie nodded. "Yeah," he said. "I still miss her."

12

HAVEN

THE HUDSON RIVER VALLEY UPSTATE NEW YORK, USA

Larissa Kinley stared at the wide, slowly moving river, felt the night breeze gently tug at her hair, and allowed herself a rare moment of satisfaction.

It was not an emotion she was particularly prone to, at least not since the night she had lost herself in Grey's glowing crimson eyes and woken up changed forever. She had spent her years with Alexandru and his gaggle of violent sycophants, alternately disgusted with herself and genuinely terrified for her own life, and her time with Blacklight wracked with guilt as she again participated in something she could not justify.

She would not dispute that she had done some good in her time as an Operator; she had helped destroy both Alexandru and Valeri Rusmanov, had saved the lives of dozens of innocent men and women, and had fought as hard as anybody to prevent a true monster from entering the world. But did that make up for the harm she had done? For the innocent vampires she had destroyed for no better reason than what they had been turned into, in a great many cases against their will? Jamie, Kate and the majority of her former colleagues clearly believed so, and she did not begrudge them that conclusion.

Sadly, it had not been enough for her.

But now, as she stood in the place she had created and looked out across a river on the other side of the world, she was almost content. A hundred metres out from the bank, one of the river cruise boats chugged slowly south towards the distant lights of New York. The captain sounded his horn, and the tourists on the upper deck waved enthusiastically in her direction; she returned the gesture, a broad smile on her face, and watched until the boat slipped round the bend in the river. When it was out of sight, Larissa turned and walked up the gentle slope; her stomach was rumbling, and she was suddenly keen to see how dinner was coming along.

Spread out before her, extending for several hundred metres in either direction along the riverbank, was the property that Valentin had told her about on that awful night, now more than six months past, when she had stumbled into the cellblock on the verge of tears, desperate for a way out. It was a vast piece of land, running up from the river for almost a mile, so big that many locals believed there were several large estates behind the pale wooden gates that opened on to Highway 9.

The houses that overlooked this section of the riverbank were grand, garish, multimillion-dollar mansions, the rural refuges of Manhattan bankers and actors and rock stars. But when Larissa had arrived on the piece of land that had become known to those who lived on it as Haven, the only standing structures had been a row of sheds and a large antebellum house, two neat storeys fronted with white pillars and a small veranda, surrounded by towering trees, at the centre of the estate.

Now, it was also home to the row of wooden cabins that she was walking alongside as she climbed the slope. They were simple enough, their walls, floors and ceilings constructed of wood from the ash trees that filled the sprawling property, but they were comfortable, and they were warm, thanks to the stoves and metal chimneys that Callum had installed. Most had two occupants, although some had as many as five or even six, family units who had arrived together and refused to be separated. A handful had only one person living in them, which several of the community's earliest residents had suggested was wasteful. Larissa had disagreed, saying that people who wanted to live on their own had every right to do so; they could always build more cabins, which was exactly what they had done.

There were another dozen in the woods surrounding the huge lawn that stood in front of the main house, where the trees were younger and less densely packed together, and another row that followed the route of the felling that had been done, a neat, straight path that reached almost to the highway. All told, there were fifty-three finished cabins on the property, forty-nine of which were occupied, and another twenty under construction. Hidden away from prying eyes, it was rapidly becoming a small town, in much the same way that Valhalla, the commune from where Larissa had drawn inspiration, was a functioning village in the remote Scottish Highlands.

There were now more than a hundred vampires living in Haven, men and women and children who had been on the run when word reached them of a place where they might be safe or who simply wanted no part of what was coming, had no interest in choosing a side when the only two on offer were Dracula or NS9 and Blacklight. For the first ten days after she arrived, Larissa had lived in the big house on her own, suffering loneliness so acute she had begun to wonder whether it might prove fatal, unsure how to go about realising the idea that she could see so clearly in her mind.

In the end, she had come to the conclusion that there was no option other than to simply get on with it.

On the eleventh day, she had flown into town, called the number Valentin had given her, and spoken to a man who seemed, superficially at least, to be some kind of financial advisor to the ancient vampire, although it had quickly become apparent that his remit extended far beyond matters of money. They had spoken for five minutes, in which the man never asked Larissa to identify herself or provide any proof that she was calling with Valentin's permission; the mere mention of the vampire's name had clearly been enough. The following day, workers reconnected the house's gas, water and electricity, installed a new wireless network, cleaned the house from top to bottom, and mowed the wide lawn; Larissa had stood quietly to one side, too bemused to do anything but watch them work. Before they left, one of them handed her an envelope containing a credit card with her name embossed on the front, issued by a bank she had never heard of, and she had said a silent thank you to Valentin.

The following night she had flown down to New York and spent three days searching the towering glass and steel city for vampires, pounding the streets, tracking them down one at a time by scents that only those of her kind could detect. She found them in bars, in subway stations, in houses and apartments, or simply walking the bright streets after dark. They were almost uniformly wary when she approached, and not a single one of those who had listened to her pitch had come with her there and then; in every case, she left them the location, told them they would be welcome, and moved on. Three days later she returned to Haven, and waited to see whether the stone she cast into the water had caused a ripple.

The first vampire had shown up two days later, landing cautiously on the lawn with a bag over his shoulder and a suspicious look on his face; his name was Ryan and he later confessed to Larissa that he had wondered right up until the last minute if he was walking into a trap, whether she was part of some NS9 plot to trick vampires into handing themselves in to be destroyed. She had welcomed him, showed him to the spare bedroom in the big house, and the following morning, the two of them had got to work. They had felled two trees and were about to start the process of sawing their trunks into boards when a second vampire had appeared, a woman from New Jersey called Kimberley who had heard about Haven from an ex-boyfriend of hers and had immediately packed a bag. She wanted no part of any war, and had no desire to spend her life running. A warm feeling had spread slowly through Larissa as Kimberley talked; the woman's arrival was exactly what she had hoped would happen, that vampires would pass the word about Haven among themselves.

Larissa walked towards the big house, remembering those early days of the community's existence with great fondness. The vampires appeared in ones and twos at first, until, almost two weeks after she had been to New York, a group of five – three women, a man and a young boy – arrived from northern California. It had been a hectic time; for the first month, the house had been full to capacity and people had slept in tents on the lawn outside. But then the first cabins had been finished, and Haven had really started to take shape; there was now a network of well-worn paths cutting across the open expanses of grass and through the depths of the woods. Long canopies covered the winding tracks, and gazebos and awnings shaded the junctions from the sun's rays, in a recreation of the system that had allowed Larissa to travel around Area 51 without bursting into flames.

She reached the edge of the lawn and walked towards the house. In front of the old building, a fire had been lit in the stone pit that she and some of the earliest arrivals had dug and lined months before. Grills were positioned around the flames, groaning with meat and foil-wrapped potatoes and sweetcorn, and a plastic barrel of lamb's blood had been placed on two piles of bricks. Two dozen or so vampires were sprawled on the grass around the fire, chatting and eating and drinking. She could see lights in many of the distant cabins, and knew that more of Haven's residents would make their way over to the fire before long. Eating together in the evening had become a widely observed tradition, although it was by no means mandatory; nothing inside Haven was, other than obeying the two central rules upon which the community was founded.

If you wanted to live in Haven, it was strictly forbidden to harm another human being, and you were expected to do whatever work was asked of you.

Beyond that, you were free.

Larissa skirted the cluster of relaxing vampires, strode across the wide strip of gravel in front of the house, then stopped as someone called her name from the darkness. She turned to see Callum stroll round the side of the house, a guitar in one hand, a six-pack of beer in the other, an easy smile on his handsome, bearded face. She returned his smile; the tall, softly spoken Texan had arrived two weeks after her recruitment trip to New York, and they had quickly become close. He had been turned against his will by a girl he met in a bar on the outskirts of Dallas, and was a gentle, hard-working soul who would never hurt a fly; he was exactly the sort of person she had founded Haven for.

"Hey," said Callum. "Beer?"

"Not right now," said Larissa. "How's your day been?"

"Good," said Callum. "I've been helping Pete Conran tar his roof. Messy business. Fun, though."

Larissa's smile widened. "You've got a strange idea of what fun is."

"That's likely true," said Callum. "You coming back out, or are you calling it a night?"

"I'll be back in ten minutes," she said. "I just need to get changed and sort a couple of things out. See you on the grass."

Callum nodded, and strolled towards the fire, the beer bottles gleaming in the moonlight. Larissa watched him for at least a moment or two longer than was necessary, then walked up the stairs and into the house.

She dodged a toy train set that had been carefully laid out on the living-room floor, nodded to Kim, one of Haven's teenagers, who was sprawled on a sofa with headphones in her ears, and floated towards the staircase. Pinned to the wall at the bottom was the rota of jobs that needed doing to keep Haven running smoothly, everything from collecting firewood to stocking up on food at the twenty-four-hour supermarket to felling trees and bleeding the cattle Larissa had installed in a meadow near the riverbank. The rota had originally been written on a single whiteboard; now there were four of them tiled together, with more than a hundred names printed down one side and dozens of tasks listed across the top. Almost half the residents had no job allocated on any given day, as she had never wanted Haven to feel like a work camp; she knew, however, that the majority found some way to help, even on what were supposed to be their days off.

Larissa was constantly amazed at how content she was with the simple life she and the others had built. Everything – the place, the work, the people – simply felt *right*; she believed, with total conviction, that she had done more good in the last six months, had made more of a positive difference, than she ever had at Blacklight. Providing sanctuary and peace for those who craved it sat far more easily with her than ending lives ever had, no matter the justification that had been offered inside the Loop. There was only a single dark cloud on her new horizon, one that she had come to terms with, but which showed no sign of departing anytime soon.

She missed her friends.

And she missed Jamie so much it hurt.

In the first days after her frantic, headlong departure, when the loneliness had been at its worst and she had spent a great many hours wondering if she had made the biggest mistake of her life, Larissa had thought about getting in touch with him, if only to let him know that she was safe. And even as Haven began to take shape, as her days filled up with work and companionship and laughter, the same urge had gripped her at least once a day. She still had her console; it lay at the bottom of a drawer in her bedroom, its batteries removed. She didn't dare turn it on inside Haven, as she had no doubt that Blacklight would be able to trace it, but she could easily have flown to New York or Boston, turned it on, and sent Jamie a message. It would have been easy, the work of no more than an hour at most. But she had not, and she knew why.

She had no idea what she would say to him.

Telling him not to worry would be redundant to the point of insulting; of course he would have worried when she disappeared, and if she knew Jamie, as she believed she did, he would *still* be worrying now. And trying to explain herself would be impossible; she knew there was no way to justify vanishing into the night without even doing him the courtesy of saying goodbye. How could she make him understand that their fight in Brenchley had just been the final straw, the last push she had needed to act on doubts that had been building inside her for months?

She couldn't. She just couldn't. It would make him feel no better, and would only raise more questions, which wasn't fair. It would be easier, as she regularly told herself, if she simply no longer loved him; if that was the case, she could have closed the box containing that part of her life, buried it deep down inside herself, and moved on.

But she *did* still love him. And there was nothing to be gained from lying to herself about it.

Larissa flew slowly along the upstairs landing and turned the handle on her bedroom door. It had a lock, but she had never bothered to use it; it would be useless if any of the vampire residents of Haven was determined to get into her room, and she believed it would have sent a bad message to the rest of the community. She didn't want it to look like she was positioning herself as something special, or that she had anything to hide.

She closed the door behind her and undressed. Her clothes clung to her skin, gummy with sweat and sap from the trees she had helped to pull down; she threw them into the basket in the corner of the room, and flew across to her wardrobe.

Upon her arrival at Haven, she had only possessed a single set of civilian clothes, the same ones she had been wearing when Alexandru Rusmanov had dropped her, broken and unconscious, out of the sky and into Matt Browning's suburban garden. She had rebuilt her wardrobe in the subsequent months, filling drawers and rails with summer dresses and vest tops and checked shirts and jeans, choices made for the practicality of life at Haven rather than for aesthetics. She dragged one of the dresses down and pulled it over her head, shook her hair out, and was about to close the wardrobe and head back downstairs when something at the back caught her eye, something black and smooth.

Larissa reached out and ran her fingers down the fabric of her Blacklight uniform. She had worn it across the Atlantic, with every intention of burning it as soon as she found the place that Valentin had described. And she had almost gone through with it; that first night, which now seemed so long ago, she had put the uniform in a steel bucket she found in one of the outbuildings and stood over it with a bottle of alcohol and a box of matches. But something had stayed her hand. Instead, she had relegated it to the back of her wardrobe, out of sight but not entirely out of mind. She scratched involuntarily at her forearm as she stared at it; there was no scar where she had dug out her locator chip, but the memory of doing so remained, so potent it was almost physical.

Larissa closed the wardrobe and flew quickly back through the house. The smell of barbecuing meat was intoxicating, and she could hear laughter and the gentle rhythm of Callum's guitar over the distant sound of the river as it ran along the edge of the place she now called home.

ZERO HOUR
PLUS 192 DAYS

13

SLEIGHT OF HAND

Jamie was pacing impatiently around his quarters when his console beeped on his belt. He thumbed the rectangular screen into life and read the message that appeared.

FROM: Turner, Director Paul (NS303, 36-A)
TO: Carpenter, Lieutenant Jamie (NS303, 67-J)
Five minutes. Come up Now.

Jamie's eyes flared; a second later he was striding along Level B, resisting the urge to leap into the air and fly down the corridor as fast as he was able.

He had been awake most of the night, turning the Patrol Respond over and over in his mind. His squad had waited for the Security Division to arrive and load the Night Stalkers' van on to a flatbed truck, only to receive a message informing them that the remainder of their Operation had been cancelled, and they were to return to the Loop immediately. But that had been absolutely fine with Jamie; he had been preoccupied by an awful thought as he wheezed on the ground, one that rattled ceaselessly through his brain as they were driven back to base. He had finally slipped into a fitful sleep in the early hours of the morning, and as soon as his eyes reopened he had typed a message to Paul Turner, telling the Director he needed to see him as soon as possible.

He reached the Level B lift, pressed CALL, and shifted impatiently from one foot to the other as he waited. He had not mentioned the thought to Ellison or Qiang; he trusted them completely, but he wanted to keep it to himself, at least for the time being. It was something that went beyond suspicion or theory and, without proof, it could easily be dismissed as paranoia – or wishful thinking – by those who, like his squad mates, were not in full possession of the facts. And there was something else, something simpler, and more pressing.

It was personal.

The lift arrived. Jamie stepped into it and pressed A. When the doors opened again, barely five seconds later, he walked down the corridor, nodded to a pair of Operators heading in the opposite direction, and stopped at the short corridor that led to the Director's quarters. The Security Operator on duty stepped forward.

"Lieutenant Carpenter," she said. "You can go straight in."

"Thanks," said Jamie, and strode forward. The heavy door swung open before he reached it, and he heard the Director's voice emerge through the gap.

"This better be important, Lieutenant. I've got about ten free minutes today and I'm giving half of them to you."

Jamie smiled, and stepped into the room he had come to know so well; he had spent hundreds of hours in it, talking to the men who had sat behind the wide desk on the far side of the room. Paul Turner was the third Director he had served, a turnover that spoke volumes about the turmoil the Department had been through in recent years, and the former Security Officer eyed him carefully as he stopped in front of the desk and stood to attention.

"At ease, for God's sake," said the Director. "What's going on?"

"Morning, sir," said Jamie. "I don't know if you've seen my Patrol Respond report for last night—"

"There are currently forty-nine Operational Squads in this Department," said Turner. "Even now, depleted as we are, if I read every report that every squad filed every night, I would quite literally get nothing else done. So assume I haven't read it."

"Yes, sir," said Jamie. "We got a 999 intercept on a possible Night Stalker incident in a Nottingham suburb. We checked it out, tracked a vehicle that had been seen in the area, and found them, sir."

Turner narrowed his eyes. "You found them?"

"Yes, sir," said Jamie. "We were too late to stop them killing the vampire they'd abducted, and we failed to apprehend them. But I saw them, sir. There were two of them. And I think I might know who one of them was."

The Director sat back in his chair. "Go on."

Jamie took a deep breath. "I think it was my dad, sir."

"Come again?" said Turner.

"My dad, sir. Julian Carpenter."

"What on earth would make you think that?"

"They were carrying MP5s, just like we used to. And the man I saw had military training, I'd bet my life on it. The way he moved, the way he didn't panic, even when I went for him. He wasn't remotely scared of vampires, sir."

"And you think your father is the only person in the country who fits that description?" asked Turner.

Jamie frowned. "Of course not, sir. But it makes sense. Cal wouldn't let my dad back into the Department, but even he knew that it was a waste of time telling him to behave himself. There's no way he would just sit quietly and wait, on the off chance that you decided to reverse Cal's decision. The Night Stalkers are exactly the sort of thing he'd do."

"How would you know that, Jamie?" said Turner. "You never knew the Operator side of him."

"I understand that, sir," said Jamie, aware that his voice was beginning to rise. "But I *do* know how stubborn he was, right up to the point where it cost him everything he cared about. I don't believe he'll just sit on the sidelines, sir. It's not in his nature."

"On that point, you and I are in complete agreement," said Turner. "And I do see why you reached this conclusion. But the man you saw last night wasn't your father."

Jamie frowned. "How can you say that, sir?" he asked. "I was there, and you were behind that desk."

Turner narrowed his eyes. "Be careful, Lieutenant."

Heat rose into Jamie's cheeks, a potent mixture of anger and embarrassment. "I'm sorry, sir," he said. "I just don't get how you can be so sure."

"And I can't believe that you would be arrogant enough to assume that nobody else has considered this," said Turner. "It was my first thought too, as soon as the Night Stalker attacks began. Three months ago."

Jamie stared. "You thought it was him too?"

"Of course I did," said Turner. "As you said, it would be just like him to find a new and different way to cause trouble."

"But now you're sure it's *not* him?"

Turner nodded. "Face the screen, Jamie."

He stared at the Director for a long moment, then did as he was told. He heard fingers tap a keyboard, and a moment later, the Department's network access prompt appeared. Turner logged in, then navigated to an area that Jamie had never seen. A series of menus opened and closed, until a short list of coded entries appeared; Turner clicked on the link beside HTXB/4532MK0, and brought up a grid of video windows. For several long seconds, Jamie didn't realise what he was looking at; then he recognised the front door he had knocked on six months earlier, and understood.

"That's my grandmother's cottage," he said.

"Correct," said Turner. "This is the surveillance web that Julian agreed to as a condition of his release. *This* is how I know."

Jamie examined the wide screen. The windows showed the front of the cottage, high angles of seemingly every room, the driveway at the front, and the garden at the rear. As he watched, the door of the shed opened and his father emerged, brushed off his hands, and walked down the garden towards the cottage. Jamie felt his chest constrict momentarily with a sharp jab of grief, before it was burned away by the anger that flooded him whenever he even *thought* about his father; seeing him live on camera only intensified the emotion.

"We chipped him again before he was released," said Turner. "It's moving now, while we're watching him, and it didn't move last night, not once in seven hours. After he turned out the lights, the audio sensors picked up the sound of his breathing, and thermal showed a constant heat source in his bed. Surveillance checked on him at 3.12am and saw nothing unusual. He was there all night, Jamie."

"Do you record this footage?" he asked, his eyes still locked on the screen. "Can you show me last night?"

"No," said Turner. "We don't record everything. We do live checks at least four times a day."

Jamie turned back to face his Director. "This doesn't prove anything, sir," he said. "My dad's an expert at faking things."

Turner frowned. "If you don't want to listen to me, Jamie, then there's very little point in us continuing this conversation. I'm sorry about what you found out, what Cal and Colonel Frankenstein kept from you, but I'm afraid—"

"I'm not talking about that, sir," interrupted Jamie. "I don't want to talk about it. I'm talking about what I saw last night."

"And I'm telling you you're wrong," said Turner. "Your father has been in your grandmother's cottage in Norfolk, exactly where he's supposed to be, every time there's been a Night Stalker attack. But you're right about one thing. There's a lot more to them than meets the eye. You saw two men, and on the twelfth of last month there were two attacks on the same night, sixty miles apart. Which means there are four of them, at least. Intelligence believes there may be as many as eight or even ten. But your father isn't one of them."

Jamie stared, his mind racing.

Four Night Stalkers? Maybe eight, or ten? What the hell?

"Why hasn't any of this come up in the Zero Hour briefings, sir?" he asked.

"Because the Night Stalkers aren't Blacklight business, Jamie," said Turner. "We're sharing any relevant information with the police, but this is for them to deal with. If you cross paths with them again, by all means bring them into custody if you can. God knows, it might help our standing with the local forces. But unless that eventuality arises, I want you to focus on your own job."

Jamie tried one last time. "How are they finding the vampires they kill, sir? Haven't you wondered about that?"

"Of course I have," said Turner. "What's your point?"

"The Surveillance Division keeps a vampire watch list," said Jamie. "What if my dad has a copy of it, an old one from when he was still an Operator? What if that's what the Night Stalkers are using to pick their targets?"

"Impossible," said Turner.

"Why?" asked Jamie. "Why is that impossible?"

"Because none of the Night Stalker victims so far have been known to this Department," said Turner. "That was the second thing I checked, right after whether or not your father was involved."

Of course he thought of it all before you did. You idiot.

"Right," Jamie said, his voice low and crestfallen. "Would anybody else have a list of vampires?"

"No," said Turner. "And that's more than enough on this subject. Put the Night Stalkers out of your mind unless you're looking at one of them down the sights of your weapon. Clear?"

Jamie nodded. "Yes, sir."

"Fine. Your squad is off rotation tonight, correct?"

"Yes, sir."

"Good," said Turner. "Go and get a drink in the mess." He narrowed his eyes. "You're eighteen now, right?"

Jamie smiled. "Yes, sir," he said. "It was my birthday two months ago."

"All right," said Turner, the corners of his mouth threatening to curl upwards into a small smile of his own. "Go and get a drink. Take Kate with you."

Jamie frowned. "Why Kate, sir?"

The Director shrugged. "She's your friend, isn't she?"

"Yes, sir," he replied. "But why her specifically?"

"No reason, Lieutenant," said Turner, his face once again entirely impassive. "Do whatever you want."

"OK, sir," said Jamie. "Thank you."

"You're welcome. Dismissed."

14

STRANGE BEDFELLOWS

Frankenstein walked down the cellblock and stopped outside the fourth cell on the right. He knew from long experience that the room's occupant would have been aware of his presence since the moment the inner airlock door opened, but he still paused outside the ultraviolet barrier and announced himself; despite the life he had led, the horrors and violence that he had both witnessed and committed, he still set great store on good manners.

"Good afternoon, Valentin," he said. "May I come in?"

The ancient vampire looked up from his chair, set down the book he had been reading, and smiled.

"Of course, my dear Colonel," said Valentin. "I do so look forward to your visits. I don't know how I would cope without the petty insults and unfounded accusations you are kind enough to level at me. I would be so very bored."

Frankenstein rolled his eyes, and stepped through the wall of purple light. He walked across the cell, his huge frame seeming to fill much of the available space, and settled into a plastic chair that groaned audibly beneath him.

"I'm glad to be of service," he said. "How are you, Valentin?"

"What a ridiculous question," replied the vampire, but his smile remained. "I am exactly the same as I was yesterday, and the day before, and every day since I was put back together after our adventure in France. Very little changes inside a cell."

"Courtesy would dictate that you enquire how I am in return," said Frankenstein.

"Courtesy presumably believes that I am even the slightest bit interested," said Valentin. "Tea?"

"Thank you," he said. "You should know how I take it by now."

This opening exchange of insults was by now a well-practised routine between the two men, performed at least once a week, despite an inauspicious start to their relationship; Frankenstein's first visit to the cell he was now sitting in, more than six months earlier, had ended with him threatening to kill Valentin if he didn't stop the private conversations he had been having with Jamie Carpenter, a threat that Valentin had very politely informed him he was in absolutely no position to make good on. But in the aftermath of the dreadful, catastrophic reunion between Jamie and his father, Frankenstein had, for the first time in more than a century, found himself without purpose. Julian was beyond his protection, Marie was safe in her cell, and Jamie, the last Carpenter, no longer wanted anything to do with him.

For a number of weeks, he had drifted through the Loop like a ghost, passing silently among men and women who were risking their lives every night to keep the country from descending into chaos, alone and seemingly useless. His condition, which still required him to be locked into one of the human containment cells for three days of every month, limited his ability to help. Paul Turner had offered him command of an Operational Squad, but he knew it was merely a gesture, albeit one he appreciated. He had thanked the Director as he refused his offer, then resumed his aimless existence. Until one sleepless night, when he had found himself standing outside the cellblock, without really knowing how he had come to be there. He had passed through the airlock and walked down the wide corridor, uncertain of what he was doing, but desperate to talk to someone, *anyone* who might have even the slightest idea of what he was going through.

Valentin walked across the cell and held out a chipped mug of steaming tea. Frankenstein took it, noting the grimace on the old vampire's face; it clearly pained him to present his guest with such an inelegant receptacle.

"Thank you," he said, and took a sip. The tea was excellent, as always.

"You're welcome," replied the vampire. "What news from the world above?"

"Nothing changes," said Frankenstein. "People are scared, and lashing out in every direction. At vampires, at the police and the government, at Blacklight. Dozens die every night, and nobody seems to have the faintest idea how to stop it. At this point, the Operators are little more than glorified police."

"And inside the Department?" asked Valentin. "Is Major Turner continuing to inspire everyone to keep fighting the good fight?"

Frankenstein smiled narrowly. "That is uncalled for," he said. "Paul Turner is doing the best he can, in circumstances that are increasingly trying."

"What circumstances might those be?"

"The public remains grossly misinformed where Blacklight is concerned," said Frankenstein. "So the prevailing narrative has become that we have failed them, that we should have destroyed every vampire by now, or at the very least managed to keep them secret so they don't need to worry. They blame us for a country that appears to be tearing itself apart, despite the many thousands of people who are only alive today because of the work of this Department."

"I'm afraid that's irrelevant," said Valentin.

"In what way?" asked Frankenstein. "In what *world*, for God's sake?"

"People not being killed by vampires was merely evidence of Blacklight doing its job," said the vampire. "People being killed by vampires is evidence of the opposite, at least as far as the public are concerned. Surely you see the distinction?"

Frankenstein nodded. It pained him to agree with the vampire, but he was right; more than a century of silent efficiency meant far less than a single innocent victim splashed across the front page of a tabloid.

"If it makes you feel any better," said Valentin, "my former master will likely rise before public anger reaches the point of revolution, which will resolve the situation one way or the other. You will either defeat him, and be heroes, or you will fail, and nothing will matter any more."

Frankenstein grunted with laughter. "Thank you, Valentin," he said, a lopsided smile on his grey-green face. "I can always rely on you to be the voice of optimism."

"You're welcome," said Valentin. "How's Jamie?"

The smile disappeared. "I don't want to talk about him," he said. "As I have told you so very often. Must we go over it every time I come down here?"

"Why come down here at all if you genuinely don't want to talk about him?" asked Valentin. "You wear your pain like a badge of honour, so proud and strong and stolid, while week after week we play out this little flirtation without ever getting to the meat of anything. So let me ask you again. How is your favourite little vampire? I assume he still can't stand the sight of you?"

Frankenstein shook his head. "You are a petty child, Valentin. Can't you resist the urge to provoke, even this once?"

"It's hardly provocation, my dear Colonel," replied the vampire. "The very purpose to which you have devoted yourself for so long has been removed. One Carpenter out there alone, impotent to influence the events for which he spent his life preparing, the other a central player in what is to come, but who rejects your help. Your situation strikes me as nothing less than an existential crisis, and I am intrigued as to whether you see it in similar terms. But we can continue to talk about banalities, if you prefer? Perhaps you could tell me how the weather has been lately?"

"Mostly cloudy," said Frankenstein.

Valentin didn't respond; he merely stared at the monster with his pale blue eyes, and waited.

"I want to hear about Larissa," said Frankenstein, eventually. "If we are unburdening ourselves, I want to hear about the night she left."

"I will tell you what I feel is mine to tell," said Valentin. "You have my word."

"Fine," he said. "Then no. Jamie still can't stand the sight of me. He can be in the same room as me now, can even acknowledge me in the presence of others, but somehow that seems worse. When he hated me, when anger radiated out of him so thickly I could almost *see* it, it was painful but at least it was real emotion, clear and unchecked. But now? Now he just seems indifferent, and that hurts far more."

"You have lived a long life," said Valentin. "You have known many men, both good and bad and everything in between. Yet despite all that human experience, you were unable to see that this might unfold as it has? I find that hard to believe."

"Of course I knew," said Frankenstein. "Jamie prizes loyalty above everything else. It's one of the very best things about him, even when it prompts him to be reckless and stupid. A long time ago a traitor told him I was there the night he saw his father die, and his anger at what he believed was my betrayal almost got him killed.

I knew that if the truth about Julian came out, he would not be able to forgive me again. But what choice did I have?"

"Tell him the truth?" suggested Valentin.

"Brilliant," said Frankenstein. "Just tell him that he didn't really see his father die, because I helped Julian fake his own execution, and that the man he mourned was probably still alive, despite not even being able to be certain about that. What good would that have done him?"

"I suspect Jamie's argument would be that it was not your decision to make."

"I was trying to protect him," said Frankenstein, his voice low. "As I swore I always would."

"I believe you," said Valentin. "What I do *not* believe is that you have given up any hope of a reconciliation. Surely that is not the case?"

Frankenstein let out a deep sigh. "I don't know," he said. "It's been more than six months, and I feel nothing between us except ever-expanding distance. And in all honesty, why would he waste his time on such a reconciliation? He doesn't need me now, if he ever did."

"Perhaps you should tell him that," said Valentin. "That you understand he doesn't need you. Offer him a friend, rather than a protector."

"I don't know," repeated Frankenstein. "The prudent thing to do is leave him alone. There are bigger things at stake than hurt feelings."

"Honourable," said Valentin, and smiled thinly. "Stupid, but honourable. If the world ends, what will prudence have mattered? All it will have gained you is months of uncertainty and unhappiness."

Frankenstein grimaced. "You've made your point," he said. "And I really don't want to talk about this any more. You're never going to tell anyone where Larissa is, are you?"

Valentin shook his head. "She asked me not to. And I won't betray her, not after France. She could have let me die, but she didn't."

The monster smiled. "Of course, we only have your word for what she said that night," he said. "For all we know, she specifically asked you to tell everyone where she went."

"True," said the vampire. "Is that what you think she said?"

Frankenstein shook his head. "No," he said. "I think she wanted to disappear, I think she asked for your help, and I don't think you agreed because you were grateful for France. I think you agreed because you knew it would cause trouble. Although I suppose I can't prove that either, can I?"

"If that was the case," said Valentin, "the person I would have known it would cause *the most* trouble for, the person it would *upset* the most, is Jamie Carpenter, whom I rather like. In the scenario you describe, my options would have been to either refuse to help someone to whom I owed my life, or do something that would cause pain to someone I respect. Can I assume that even you might find such a decision unpleasant?"

"You did cause Jamie pain," said Frankenstein. "Just as you caused it to yourself."

"How so?" asked Valentin, his eyes narrowing.

"When was the last time Jamie came down here to seek your counsel?" he asked. "It seems that I'm not the only person he's withdrawn from."

A smile rose on to Valentin's narrow face. "Clever, my friend," he said. "And you are quite right, he does seem to have rather tired of my company. I imagine that makes you feel delightfully warm and happy?"

"No," said Frankenstein, his voice low. "It doesn't. I would rather he was talking to you than not talking to anyone."

"How flattering to be considered better than nothing," said Valentin.

"Tell me something," said Frankenstein, ignoring the vampire's rebuke. "Do you think Larissa is ever coming back?"

Valentin shrugged. "I honestly have no idea," he said. "But I'll ask you a question in return. Would you voluntarily throw yourself into this maelstrom?"

"I did," said the monster, a crooked smile on his face. "So did you."

"Correct," said the vampire. "And look where it got us."

"In which case, let me ask you something else," said Frankenstein. "How do you think all this is going to end?"

Valentin smiled widely. "Badly," he said. "More tea?"

15

AT EASE

Jamie watched Kate walk into the officers' mess and smiled as she stopped to talk to a table full of Operators near the door. It had only been thirty-six hours since he had sat beside her in the Zero Hour briefing, but he was genuinely struggling to remember when they had last spent time in each other's company, for no other reason than that they wanted to.

On the other side of the room, Kate laughed loudly at something, and was joined by the men and women sitting at the table. Jamie recognised Mark Schneider and Carrie Burgess, two of the NS9 Operators who had been brought to the Loop by Larissa, what now seemed an impossibly long time ago, and his smile widened. It was good to see Kate chatting happily with her colleagues; there had been a time, barely six months earlier, when she would have struggled to find more than a handful of people in the entire Loop who were willing to speak to her – Kate's involvement in the ISAT investigation and her widely perceived status as Paul Turner's favourite had alienated much of the Department. Now, with Turner promoted and Kate reporting to Angela, Jamie assumed things were getting easier for her, and was glad.

"Hey," she said, arriving at his table and smiling at him. "How's it going, Jamie?"

"All right," he said, and gestured at the empty seat opposite him. "Aren't you sitting down?"

"Not till I've been to the bar," said Kate. "I need a beer. Urgently. You?"

"Sure. Cheers."

Kate nodded and set off towards the bar that ran along one side of the wide room. The Loop, in its current form, was barely thirty years old; it had been almost entirely rebuilt after a research trip Jamie's father had made to Nevada in the 1980s, borrowing heavily from the American designs. The officers' mess, however, had been transplanted intact from the first building it had occupied, one of the cluster of wooden huts and bunkhouses that had been erected under the watchful eyes of the Blacklight founders. The ceilings and walls were panelled with dark wood, the floor was hidden beneath an ancient purple carpet that was now noticeably threadbare, and the furniture that filled the room had been acquired over the course of more than a hundred and twenty years; there were leather sofas and armchairs, like the one that Jamie was now sitting in, alongside wooden benches and velvet chaises longues and clusters of plastic chairs that looked like they had been smuggled out of the Ops Room. Nothing matched, and there was no discernible pattern to anything, giving the place a chaotic charm.

Kate returned and placed four bottles of beer on the table between them.

"Thirsty?" asked Jamie.

Kate shrugged. "No sense in getting up more often than necessary."

"The motto of alcoholics everywhere," said Jamie.

Kate flipped him a lightning-fast V-sign. Jamie grinned, and picked up one of the bottles; she did the same, and clinked hers against his.

"Cheers," he said.

"Cheers."

Jamie took a long swig and set the bottle down.

"How was last night?" asked Kate. "Patrol Respond, right?"

"Bit of a strange one," said Jamie. "I submitted a report."

"I haven't seen it," said Kate. "What happened?"

Jamie took another drink, and launched into the story of his encounter with the Night Stalkers. His friend listened in silence, sipping steadily from her beer, her expression shifting from professional curiosity to genuine intrigue as the tale progressed.

"Jesus," she said, when he was finished. "Are you all right?"

"I'm fine," said Jamie. "Two litres of blood healed the bullet holes."

"Don't try and be all cool about it," said Kate. "You got shot. I don't care if you're a vampire or not, it's still a big deal."

"I know that," he said. "I do."

"I hope so," said Kate. "I worry enough without you starting to think you're invulnerable."

"You worry about me?"

Kate frowned. "Obviously. Why wouldn't I?"

"You don't have to," said Jamie. "Nothing's going to happen to me. I can look after myself."

"Right," said Kate. "The Fallen Gallery is full of people who thought exactly the same thing."

For several minutes, they drank in silence. Jamie was slightly surprised to see that his bottle was almost empty; he could feel faint, fuzzy warmth in the pit of his stomach.

"Do you ever think about after?" he said, eventually.

Kate picked up her second bottle. "After what?"

Jamie looked around the mess. "This," he said. "After all *this*. Assuming we win, and that we don't die in the process, do you ever think about what you'll do afterwards?"

Kate smiled. "You're assuming I don't see myself as career Operator."

"I am."

"I don't know," she said. "I've never really thought about it."

"Bullshit," said Jamie. "I don't believe that for a second."

"Fine," said Kate, and set her bottle down on the table. "Go to university. Spend time with my dad. Try and be normal for a while. How does that sound?"

"It sounds good."

"What about you?"

"I have no idea."

"Bullshit."

Jamie smiled. "That's fair," he said. "To be honest, a lot would depend on my mum. Away from here, if we were out in the world, I'd be pretty much all she had. The only person who knew she was a vampire, at least, and who could understand what that's like. I think she'd want to go somewhere where nobody knew her, and I don't think I could let her go on her own."

"Like where?" asked Kate.

He shrugged. "She always loved Italy when I was growing up. Maybe there. I don't know."

"Do you think you'd look for your dad?"

"No."

"Just no?" said Kate. "You wouldn't even think about it?"

"No."

"What if your mum wanted to see him?"

"That would be up to her," said Jamie. "I wouldn't have to be part of it."

"Have you told her yet?" she asked.

Jamie felt sudden heat behind his eyes. He tried to force it back down, to stop the red glow appearing, but the expression of shock on Kate's face told him he had not been successful.

"Sorry," he said. "I'm really sorry. It's involuntary."

"It just startled me," she said. "It's all right."

"No, it's not," said Jamie. "I know what it looks like. But it was because of my dad, not because of you. OK?"

"I'm sorry too," she said. "I shouldn't have brought him up."

"It's fine," he said. "And to answer your question, no, I haven't told her. If this all comes to an end, I will, and she can do whatever she wants. It won't be any of my business. But I'm done with him, Kate. I told him so, and I meant it."

She nodded.

"How about this?" he said, and raised his second empty bottle. "You think of something else to talk about while I get more drinks. Deal?"

Kate smiled; her face was still paler than it had been a minute earlier, her eyes a fraction wider, but it was a start. "Deal," she said.

Jamie nodded and headed for the bar, silently cursing himself as he went. The red fire in his eyes was an involuntary reaction to certain stimuli: fear, excitement, anger, the presence of fresh blood, to name just a few. But he knew exactly what it looked like, as he had seen it for himself in the eyes of dozens of vampires; it looked like a display of aggression.

It looked like a threat.

"Four beers, please," he said to the barman, and risked a glance over his shoulder. Thankfully, Kate wasn't looking in his direction; she had drawn her console from her belt and her attention was fixed on its screen. He waited patiently for the barman to deliver the second round of drinks, then carried them back to their table. Kate looked up at him and smiled.

"I've got a new subject," she said.

"Oh yeah?" he asked, settling back into his chair. "Let's hear it."

"Our genius friend and his scarily beautiful Russian girlfriend."

Jamie grinned. "Excellent choice," he said. "Let's talk about Matt. When was the last time you even saw him?"

"Maybe three days ago?" she said. "I ran into him in the corridor and managed to persuade him to talk to me for about a minute. What about you?"

"Longer than that," he said. "It must be more than a week. We message most days, although to be honest he hasn't been answering for the last couple of days. I'd say he must be busy, but when is he ever not?"

"Busy kissing Natalia's face off, you mean?"

Jamie's grin widened. "How old are you, thirteen?"

"Piss off," said Kate, smiling mischievously. "I mean, seriously, why wouldn't he be? She's gorgeous, and smart, and nice, and she's totally into him. I'd probably kiss her myself if the chance came along."

"Good to know," said Jamie. "Honestly, I hope he is spending all his time with her. It would be a lot healthier than chaining himself to his desk."

"Agreed," said Kate. "But we both know that won't be what's happening. They're probably in the lab right now while we're sat here drinking beer. It's what they do."

"Probably," said Jamie. "So you think it's real? Matt and Natalia, I mean?"

"I do," said Kate, instantly. "I talked to her about him months ago, just before the bomb in my quarters. She was falling for him then, never mind now. And Matt, thank all the stars in the heavens, seems to have managed not to screw it up. So yeah, I think it's real."

"I hope so," said Jamie. "It would be good for at least one of us to have somebody. Especially if the world really is about to end."

Kate rolled her eyes. "What a cheerful thought," she said. "The world has been about to end ever since you all got back from France, Jamie. It's still here."

"For now," he said. "Part of me just wishes Dracula would get on with it."

"Don't say that."

"Why not?" he said. "We'd either win or we'd lose. At least we'd know. Or we'd be dead."

"Wow," said Kate. "You're really going for the angry nihilist thing these days, aren't you?"

Jamie stared intently at her for a long moment, then smiled. "Am I carrying it off?"

"More or less," said Kate. "I know you really are angry, and I know you feel like you're alone, but you're not. I'm still here, Jamie. So is Matt, and so are Ellison and Qiang, and Angela and Jack and Dominique and Paul and everyone else."

He didn't respond; he merely stared at his friend.

"Talk to me, Jamie," she continued. "Talk to me about Larissa."

He shrugged. "There's nothing to say."

"I don't believe that. Not for a minute."

"It's the truth," said Jamie. "I wish she hadn't gone, I miss her, and I wish she'd come back. That's all there is to it."

"If you say so," said Kate.

"What about you?" he said. "Do you still miss Shaun?"

Kate grimaced, but gave a brief nod. "Every day," she said. "Being here makes it harder, to be honest. When people lose somebody out there, they grieve for as long as it takes and then they get to forget about them. I know that sounds bad, and I don't mean they never think about the person again, but they forget enough to be able to carry on. I get reminded of Shaun every day. *Every single day.* I see his dad, or one of his friends, or I find myself somewhere we had a conversation. It's like I'm not allowed to move on."

Jamie's heart ached for his friend as she spoke, and he was momentarily furious with Shaun Turner for leaving her like this, trapped by his memory, unable to mourn him and let him go. But it wasn't Shaun's fault; he hadn't asked to have his neck broken by Valeri Rusmanov, hadn't done anything to deserve the fate that had befallen him apart from fight bravely against almost overwhelming odds.

"I'm sorry," said Jamie. He picked up his beer, found it empty, and took a long drink from his fourth bottle. "I don't know what else to say. I'm really sorry, Kate."

"It's not your fault," she said, and gave him a fierce smile. "But thank you for saying it."

"No worries," he said. "I was going to ask you about your dad, but maybe we've spent enough time discussing friends and family?"

Kate's smile curdled into a frown. "Oh, on the contrary," she said. "I'm happy to talk about him. I assume you read that stupid website interview?"

"I read it," said Jamie. "I take it you weren't thrilled?"

"That would be putting it very, very mildly," said Kate, a slight edge to her voice. "I mean, I get that SSL is him trying to make a difference, and I suppose I'm proud of him for that, but I'll never understand why he decided to tell the whole world that Matt and I work for the Department. Not only was it a crime, given that they both signed the Official Secrets Act, but it was just such a stupidly dangerous thing to do. If SSL hasn't already made them targets to the people that hate anyone who seems like they're on the side of the vamps, what do they think announcing that they're related to serving Blacklight Operators is going to do? What happens when the next psycho with a grudge against the Department decides they can get to me and Matt by hurting our dads? And what if I can't protect him if that happens? It's ridiculous, Jamie. It's absolutely *ridiculous*. I'm so angry with him."

Jamie leant forward. "That's all fair," he said. "Are Surveillance keeping an eye on him?"

"Yes," she said. The colour that had risen in her cheeks as she spoke was starting to recede. "There's a standing watch on him and Greg. But watching is one thing. Dealing with anything that happens is something else."

"Right."

"Anyway," said Kate, "I'm doing what I can from Security. I just have to trust the two of them not to get themselves into any trouble."

Jamie smiled. "How are you getting on with that?"

Kate laughed. "Pretty badly," she said. "I sometimes forget which one of us is the parent."

Jamie nodded, and drained his beer. His body felt pleasantly loose, his head warm and fuzzy.

"God," said Kate, holding her own empty bottle up to the light. "I'm going to regret this when my alarm goes off tomorrow, but I really don't care right now. This has been nice, Jamie. I think I needed it."

"Me too," said Jamie. "Although what I really need right now is to lie down."

"Good plan," said Kate, and smiled at him. "Let's call it a night."

Jamie got to his feet, and immediately realised that he was quite a bit drunker than he had thought; he felt unsteady on his feet, as though he was swaying gently from side to side. He looked at Kate and grinned; the expression on her face told him that she had made exactly the same discovery as him. She giggled as she noticed him staring at her, and shook her head.

"This isn't fair," she said. "You can just sober up whenever you want. I'm stuck like this."

Jamie recoiled. "I can do what?"

"Your vampire side sobers you up. Larissa found out in Las Vegas. Don't you remember?"

"Shit," said Jamie. "That is seriously tempting. But you're right, it wouldn't be fair. I'll suffer with you."

"Solidarity," said Kate. "I respect that. Let's get out of here."

Jamie followed her across the mess, concentrating hard on walking in a straight line. He nodded at Operators he knew as he passed their tables, forcing what he hoped was a sober-looking expression on to his face, and walked stiffly through the door. Kate was waiting for him in the corridor, her face red with suppressed laughter, and they cracked up as they staggered towards the lift, giggling and loudly shushing each other.

The two Operators got out on Level B and made their way along the curved corridor that, under normal circumstances, housed much of the active roster. Several of the rooms were currently empty; their occupants had been lost during the battle with Dracula at Château Dauncy, and had not yet been replaced, despite the Department's subsequent recruitment drive. The Loop, as a result, did not feel full; the corridors seemed too empty, the canteen too sparsely populated, like a physical reminder of the ultimate price that had been paid by so many.

They stopped outside the door to Kate's quarters. Jamie smiled at his friend, suddenly very aware of how close they were standing to one another. His hands were at his sides, but he would barely have to move them to take hold of her waist. Kate was looking back at him with an even, clear-eyed expression, but there were patches of delicate pink high on her cheeks. Silent seconds passed as they stared at each other, a tension between them that Jamie had never felt before.

"Oh, for God's sake," said Kate. She placed her hands gently on his shoulders, and kissed him. He kissed her back urgently, his eyes closing, his hands sliding up her back and neck and finding her hair, waiting for his stomach to spin, for the same dizzying abandon he had felt whenever he kissed Larissa.

Nothing happened.

After a long, awkward moment, he gently broke the kiss. Kate was looking at him with an expression of great affection, but the colour had faded from her face, and he suspected she was trying not to laugh.

"That didn't really work, did it?" she said.

"No," said Jamie, grinning at her. "It didn't. My mum will be so disappointed."

Kate laughed, and shook her head. "I love you, Jamie," she said. "You're my best friend."

"I love you too," he said. "Get some sleep. I'll see you tomorrow."

ZERO HOUR
PLUS 193 DAYS

16

A BUTTERFLY FLAPS
ITS WINGS

Paul Turner was reading through a requisitions order from the Security Division for fifty new MP7s and fifteen thousand rounds of ammunition when somebody hammered on his door.

He frowned, and pushed the form to one side. An unscheduled knock on his door was highly unusual; anyone who wanted to see him was required to send a message first, and a Security Operator was stationed outside his quarters for the express purpose of preventing people from turning up unannounced. Turner reached out and pressed the TALK button on the intercom that connected him to his protection detail.

"Gregg?" he said. "Report in."

There was a burst of static, and then the Security Operator's voice appeared; the young American sounded out of breath, as though he had just finished a long run.

"I'm sorry, sir," said Gregg. "They pushed past me, but I have the situation under control."

Turner's frown deepened. "Who pushed past you?"

"Karlsson and Browning, sir," said Gregg. "I told them you weren't available, but they wouldn't take no for an answer, and

Browning jumped me from behind, the little shit. I'm waiting for Security to come and collect them, sir."

"For pity's sake, Operator," said Turner, getting up from his desk and walking across the room. "Your enthusiasm is admirable, but do you really think that arresting two senior members of the Lazarus Project is in the best interests of this Department?"

There was a long pause. "I don't know, sir," said Gregg, eventually. "It was a clear breach of protocol."

Turner rolled his eyes. "Call off your alert and go back to your post, Operator. I'll see Karlsson and Browning now."

"Yes, sir," said Gregg, instantly. "I'm sorry, sir."

"It's fine," said Turner, and pressed his ID card against the black panel beside the door. The heavy locks disengaged, and he pulled the thick metal hatch inwards to reveal Matt Browning and Robert Karlsson standing in the corridor outside. Both looked dishevelled, and Browning was bright red in the face. Beyond them, he could see Tom Gregg peering along the corridor, a nervous look on his face.

"Gentlemen," said Turner, "Operator Gregg was right, this *is* a breach of protocol. You couldn't have sent a message telling me you needed to see me?"

Karlsson shook his head. "I didn't want to run the risk of anyone reading it, sir."

Turner smiled. "You've been here less than a year and you're more paranoid than me. I suppose you'd better come in."

"Thank you, Director," said Karlsson, and stepped into the room. Browning followed him, casting one last dagger-eyed stare in Gregg's direction. Turner closed the door behind them and gestured towards the armchairs that sat in front of the wall screen.

"Take a seat, gentlemen," he said. "Let's hear what's so important that it was worth taking on my Security detail to tell me."

"We'll stand, if that's all right with you," said Karlsson. "But I would suggest *you* sit down, sir."

Ten minutes later Turner's mind was spinning, and he was glad he had taken the Professor's advice.

"Does it work?" he said, gripping the arms of his chair. "Does it actually work?"

Karlsson looked at Browning, who took a step forward.

"It works in the computers, sir," said Matt. "And it works in a test tube. We've carried out a thousand data runs in the last two days, using living vampire tissue. Every single sample has been clear of the vampire virus after we introduced our engineered gene."

Turner looked at the young Lieutenant. Matt's face was still flushed from his encounter with Operator Gregg in the hallway, but his eyes were clear, and his mouth was a straight line of determination. The Director had often dreamt of this moment, of a day when his scientists would walk into his quarters and tell him they had found a cure, but, now that it was happening, he found himself unable to fully process it. The scale of the Lazarus Project's discovery – *if it's real*, he reminded himself, *don't get carried away, for God's sake, not yet* – was scarcely comprehensible; if it did prove to be real, it would quite literally change the world forever. He ordered himself to stay calm, when what he really wanted to do was jump up from his desk and wrap Karlsson and Browning in a bear hug of sheer gratitude.

"And you can produce it?" he asked. "On a mass scale?"

Matt nodded. "The genetic structure is stable, sir. We can synthesise it as fast as the labs can churn it out."

"So what's the next step?"

"Under normal circumstances, we would schedule at least two years of rodent and primate testing before we even considered a human trial," said Professor Karlsson. "But these are not normal circumstances, sir."

"Indeed they are not," said Turner. "So what's our alternative?"

"Test it on a vampire," said Karlsson. "A live vampire. But there are ethical—"

"Do it," said Turner. "Immediately. I'll get the Operational Squads to bring you subjects. Test it as soon as there are vampires in the cells."

"Once we have their agreement, sir?" asked Browning.

Turner shook his head. "Test it whether they agree or not, Lieutenant Browning," he said. "My suggestion would be that you don't waste time asking them. Bring the results straight here, whatever time of day it is, whatever my schedule says I'm supposed to be doing. The *very minute* you have them. Is that clear?"

"Yes, sir," said Karlsson.

"Yes, sir," repeated Matt.

"Good," said Turner. "If this works, if this *is* what you say it is, I'll make sure the world knows what you and your colleagues did. I promise you that. I want you to pass my profound gratitude on to every single member of the Lazarus Project. Will you do that for me?"

"Of course," said Karlsson, an expression of pride rising on to his face. "Thank you, sir."

"Thank *you*, Professor," said Turner. "And *you*, Lieutenant Browning. Now get back to the labs. Go and find out whether you really have just saved the world."

17

THE WEIGHT OF THE WORLD

FOUR HOURS LATER

Jamie walked along the cellblock corridor, safe in the knowledge that his mother would already know he was coming.

He could hear her moving about in her cell, even though it was still more than a hundred metres away, and had no doubt that she would be frantically tidying. It was incredibly unlikely that he would notice if the square room was what she considered messy, but she would be mortified nonetheless; as a result, he slowed his pace, giving her time to make the cell immaculate.

Jamie knew that he should be with Ellison and Qiang, getting ready for the Patrol Respond they would be embarking on in less than an hour. The amendment to the Operational SOP – that they were to bring vampires back to the Loop alive from now on – had arrived on their consoles ninety minutes earlier and he should have been discussing such a radical change of policy with his squad mates. In the current climate, with public anger rampant and incidents of violence occurring with dizzying frequency, carrying out the new order was going to be fraught with difficulty; it was, Jamie knew from long experience, extremely difficult to subdue a vampire that didn't want to be subdued.

Killing them was a lot easier.

There had been no explanation for the change in SOP. Jamie had heard the subject being discussed at length as he made his way down through the Loop, thanks to his supernatural hearing, and the prevailing view seemed to be that it was a PR exercise, a way for Blacklight to try and improve their standing among the sections of the population who believed that vampires deserved the same treatment as humans. None of the Operators – or at least, none that he had overheard – had raised the possibility that had immediately occurred to him as he read the new orders, a possibility that he dearly, desperately hoped was the truth.

Matt and his team have made a breakthrough, he thought. *And we're bringing them vampire test subjects. I'm absolutely sure of it.*

Jamie heard his mother stop moving and resumed his usual pace, his boots clicking on the floor beneath him. He wanted to talk to Kate about the change of orders, and he *really* wanted to find Matt and ask him what was going on, but he needed to see his mother first, despite the guilt he felt whenever he did so.

The previous evening, in the officers' mess, he had told Kate the truth about his reasons for not telling his mother that his father was still alive. He knew that Kate – and Matt too, in all likelihood – thought it was a selfish decision, a way for him to get back at his dad and exercise power over a situation in which he had been left in the dark for so long, but that genuinely wasn't the case. He had not told her, and *would not* tell her, because he could see no good that could come from it, and because he had no desire to cause his mother more pain than she had already suffered.

He knew that it was very likely the same rationale that Frankenstein would use for not having told him the truth about his father, and as such placed him dangerously close to hypocrisy, but he was sure, deep down, that it was not the same thing. Had he been told the truth, he could have done something about his father being alive, helped him, or brought him in, or *something*. Whereas there was nothing his mother could do from inside her cell, and it would only be cruel to increase her feelings of helplessness. When this was all over, when Dracula rose or fell and Blacklight survived or was destroyed, he would tell her, and take the consequences of his decision on the chin.

Jamie walked out in front of the UV wall that sealed his mother's cell and smiled. She was sitting on their old sofa with a magazine in her hands, and looking up at him with a ludicrously unconvincing expression of surprise, as if trying to make it clear that she definitely hadn't known he was coming and *definitely* hadn't scrambled to give the cell a quick once-over before he arrived.

"Hello, love," she said, and gave him a wide smile. "It's nice to see you. Are you coming in?"

"Hey, Mum," he said. "I was planning to, if that's all right?"

"Of course," she said.

His mother got up and busied herself with the tea tray as he pressed his ID card against the black panel on the wall. The purple barrier disappeared and he stepped into the cell, leaving the front open behind him; it was a violation of basic security procedures to do so, but he doubted he could find a single person inside the Loop who believed his mother represented any kind of a threat.

"Here you go," said Marie, holding out a steaming mug. He thanked her, took it from her hand, and settled on to the sofa as she lowered herself into the armchair opposite.

"How are you, Jamie?" she asked.

"I'm all right, Mum. Yourself?"

"Oh, I'm fine," she said. "Not a lot really happens down here."

"I suppose not," he said. "Doesn't Valentin visit you any more?"

"He does," said Marie. Her eyes narrowed slightly, as though she wasn't sure whether she had said the right thing. "It's nice to see another person now and again."

"I bet," said Jamie. He had avoided even glancing into the ancient vampire's cell as he passed it, but had still been able to feel Valentin's eyes following him.

"What about you?" she asked. "Still no word from Larissa?"

Jamie grimaced. "No, Mum," he said. "No word from her."

"Oh," said Marie, and forced a smile. "Well, I'm sure there will be soon."

Jamie laughed. "Why would you think that?"

"I'm sorry?"

"Why would you think we'll hear from her soon, Mum? She left in the middle of the night without saying goodbye and she removed her chip so that nobody would know where she'd gone. Does that sound like the behaviour of someone who's about to have a change of heart and come home?"

"I don't know," said Marie. "I'm sure she had her reasons."

"Yeah," said Jamie. "Me. I'm the reason."

His mother shook her head. "That's ridiculous, Jamie. Why would you say something so stupid?"

"We had a huge fight that evening," he said. "You know we did. And three hours later she was gone. You can't tell me to pretend there's no link between the two?"

"I'm not saying that," said Marie. "I just don't like to see you being so hard on yourself. I didn't know Larissa, but I don't believe anyone would throw away their entire life because they had a fight with their boyfriend. What was it about, Jamie? Can you even remember? Because I bet it wasn't anything important."

He bit his tongue. His memory of that evening, of their argument and what it had been about, was crystal clear, but he could not tell his mother that.

"You're right, Mum," he said. "I can't remember."

He sipped his tea as his mother stared at him, a sympathetic expression on her face. He gave her a thin smile, but her gaze didn't change; it was unnerving.

"What?" he asked, eventually. "Why are you looking at me like that?"

"You're a teenager, Jamie," she said, her voice low and gentle. "Only for another couple of years, but you're still one now, and teenagers never believe their parents have ever been through anything that might be relevant to what's happening to them. But I would hope you remember that you're not the only person in this room who knows what it's like to lose someone they love."

Jamie felt his heart lurch in his chest. "I'm really sorry," he said. "It's not the same thing, I know it isn't. I just miss her, Mum. There, I said it. I know you weren't her biggest fan and I know part of you thinks I'm better off without her, but I really miss her."

His mother gave him a fierce smile. "I know you do, Jamie," she said. "Did you know my parents didn't approve of your father when we got together? Did I ever tell you that?"

Good judges of character, thought Jamie, and instantly chastised himself for such unnecessary viciousness.

"No," he said. "I didn't know that. Why didn't Nan and Granddad like him?"

She shrugged. "They were snobs," she said. "Simple as that. They wanted me to marry a lawyer or a banker, someone who could look after me properly, and your dad was just a lowly civil servant at the Ministry of Defence. Well, we all *thought* that's what he was, anyway. Your granddad was so rude the first time I took him home to meet them, and your nan wasn't much better. Years later, after you were born and Julian had won them over, they admitted that they were trying to scare him off, to make him feel so unwelcome that he'd leave me. Isn't that awful?"

"Yeah," said Jamie. "It really is. Why didn't it work?"

"You know what your father was like," she said. "He had a stubborn streak a mile wide. I think it just made him all the more determined."

"And what about you?" he asked. "It can't have been easy, knowing they didn't approve?"

"Oh, I couldn't have cared less," she said, and laughed. "If anything, it just made me even more attracted to him. Which I'm sure isn't something you can relate to."

Jamie smiled. "Definitely not, Mum," he said. "I don't have the slightest idea what you're talking about."

His mother nodded, her grin still in place. "I was young once, Jamie," she said. "I was even a teenager, if you can believe that, and I can still just about remember what it was like. Although to be fair, I didn't spend my adolescence hunting vampires. So that's probably where our experiences diverge a little bit."

Jamie stood up. "Can I have a hug, Mum?" he asked.

His mother flew across the cell, wrapped her arms round him, and squeezed him so tightly that for a moment he couldn't breathe.

"She'll come back," she whispered. "And if she doesn't, it wasn't meant to be."

He squeezed her back. "Thank you," he said. "Any more tea?"

Marie released him. "Of course," she said, and set about refilling his mug. "So what else has been happening upstairs? Anything new?"

"Yeah," he said. "There actually is, for once. The way we go on patrol got changed today. We have to bring vampires in alive now."

"Why?"

"Nobody knows for sure," said Jamie. "Some people think it's a PR thing, that it'll look better if the public sees us locking vampires up instead of destroying them, and that's probably true."

"But you think it's something else?" asked his mother, holding out his mug.

Jamie took it and nodded. "I haven't seen Matt for about a week, and neither has Kate. So yeah, I think it's something else. I think the Lazarus Project has found a cure." His mother's eyes widened, and he moved quickly to clarify what he was saying. "I mean, I think they've made some kind of breakthrough. I think we're being asked to bring them test subjects. But like I said, I don't know."

"You've always said Matt would do it eventually," she said. Her eyes were so full of hope it made him feel guiltier than ever. "You've never doubted it."

"I never have," he said. "But I really don't know, Mum, and I need to be sure you're listening to me. I'm *not* telling you there's a cure. I probably shouldn't have said anything at all."

"Oh, for God's sake, Jamie," she said, and rolled her eyes. "I'm not an idiot."

"I know you're not," he said. "I just don't want you to get your hopes up."

"And I appreciate that," she said.

Jamie sipped his tea. "What do you think you'd do, Mum?" he said. "If this was all over, and you were back out in the world?"

She shrugged. "That would depend on whether or not I was still a vampire."

"Assume not," said Jamie. "Assume you were back to normal. What would you do?"

"I don't know," she said. "I'd like to go somewhere I haven't been before. Somewhere I could read, and sleep, and try my very hardest to never have anything exciting happen to me again." She smiled at him. "I think I've had enough drama for one lifetime."

He smiled back. "Fair enough," he said. "I don't think anyone could blame you for that."

"I'm glad to hear it," she said. "So yes, a bit of peace and quiet would be nice. And I'd like to make some friends. I used to like having friends, before your father died. What about you?"

"What about me?"

"What would you do if you were cured?" she asked.

Jamie narrowed his eyes. "I don't know if I would take a cure."

"I'm sorry?"

"I don't know for certain that I would take a cure, Mum."

"Is that a joke, Jamie?" she said, her tone suddenly sharp. "Because it's not funny."

He shook his head. "No, Mum," he said. "I'm not joking. I know it isn't what you want to hear, but I don't hate being a vampire like you do. And it makes what I do every night a lot easier, and a *lot* safer."

Marie put her tea down, sat forward, and looked him squarely in the eyes. "I want you to make me a promise, Jamie," she said. "Son to mother. Promise me that if Matt and the others really have found a cure, you'll take it. You'll take it straight away."

"I'm sorry, Mum," he said. "I can't do that."

18

HUDDLED MASSES, YEARNING TO BREATHE FREE

PETERBOROUGH, CAMBRIDGESHIRE, ENGLAND
FIVE HOURS LATER

Pete Randall checked his watch, and looked around a community centre that he sincerely hoped had seen better days.

The concrete building, which squatted in a nondescript suburb of Peterborough, was coated in flaking whitewash and floored with peeling linoleum. Plastic tables were lined up at one end of the long room, beneath a fading string of triangular union flags and a handwritten banner announcing that TUESDAY NIGHT IS BINGO NIGHT. Behind the tables stood two large plastic bins, from which a line of SSL volunteers were handing plastic bottles of cattle blood to the vampires queuing quietly along the wall of the community centre and out on to the street.

Several of the volunteers looked nervous, but were getting on with their jobs without complaint. Pete didn't blame them, particularly those who were helping out on their first drive; the blood caused an involuntary reaction in most of the vampires, and the sight of their fangs and the red glow in their eyes was unsettling, no matter how dedicated you were.

The blood drives had fast become a central part of SSL. The first, which Pete had overseen barely a month earlier, had been sparsely attended, and the vampires who *had* shown up had been visibly suspicious, as if they were worried that Blacklight Operators were waiting to jump out from behind the tables and stake them. But attendance had risen rapidly once it had become clear that the drives were safe, and they were now running at least half a dozen every week. Pete had made arrangements with two chains of slaughterhouses to supply blood, but he was already frantically trying to locate more; they had brought two hundred and fifty litres to the community centre, and had already given more than half of it away, barely forty minutes after they had opened the community centre's doors.

"Is this what it means to be the boss?" asked a voice from behind him. "Just standing around and not getting your hands dirty?"

Pete smiled as he turned round. "I'm strategically assessing the situation," he said. "It's vital work. You wouldn't understand."

The girl standing before him grinned and punched him on the arm. The abundance of rings on her fingers meant the blow hurt more than he suspected she intended, but he didn't let it show. Her name was Genevieve, but anyone who called her that was taking their life in their hands. She considered her name evidence of her mother's pathetic obsession with class, her desire to drag their family as far up the social totem pole as was humanly possible; instead, she grudgingly went by Jen. She was twenty, a politics student with a razor-sharp tongue and purple streaks in her hair and a paragraph from George Orwell's *Down and Out in Paris and London* tattooed on her forearm. In the pub around the corner from the SSL office, not long after she joined, one of the other volunteers had suggested that she was a class warrior; her response had lasted for almost twenty minutes, and contained language of such graphic specificity that it could have stripped paint from the walls.

Pete was very, very fond of her.

"All right then," said Jen, narrowing her eyes and grinning at him. "Whenever you're finished being all strategic, the last of the blood needs bringing in. I'm going outside to check on the queue."

"All right," he said. "Give me a shout if there are any problems."

Jen rolled her eyes, tapped the UV torch on her belt, and strode away across the wide room. Pete watched her go, then walked behind the row of tables and out through the community centre's back door, unease momentarily filling him.

They were required to provide their volunteers with at least rudimentary protection against the supernatural; the insurance policy that covered SSL employees explicitly demanded it, and Pete knew many of the volunteers felt better with ultraviolet torches hanging from their belts. But if it *had* been an option, he would have strongly argued for their removal, for two reasons.

Firstly, he didn't like the message that it sent to the queuing vampires. Sales of all things ultraviolet had exploded in the aftermath of V-Day, as the public scrambled to protect themselves from the threat they were now being told was lurking in their midst. Families up and down the country had put UV bulbs into motion-sensor-controlled exterior lights, and men and women – although it was mostly men, Pete had noted – had taken to wearing torches on their belts, like the six-shooters carried by gunslingers in the Old West.

Pete had more reason than most to be suspicious of vampires; he had seen first hand the violence and death left in the wake of Albert Harker's bloody quest for revenge. But he also knew that it had been more the result of Harker's damaged, broken mind than because he was a vampire, and he had agreed to found SSL on that assumption: that vampire was not the same as evil, that the supernatural was not something to be automatically feared. Having his volunteers carry weapons that could only hurt vampires felt uncomfortably close to a betrayal of that principle.

Secondly, and far more pragmatically, Pete knew that the ultraviolet torches were next to useless. He had seen Albert Harker overpower three Blacklight Operators, two of whom had turned out to be his daughter and Greg's son, with apparently minimal effort; if one of the vampires queuing patiently outside the community centre decided to attack someone, he doubted any of the volunteers, or the professional security guards that were also mandated by the insurance policy, would have time to draw their UV torch from their belt, let alone turn it on.

The van that had brought the SSL team from Lincoln was parked outside the back door. Pete pulled the keys out of his pocket, walked round to the rear of the vehicle, and froze solid to the spot, his heart lurching as something huge and full of teeth snarled out of the darkness.

Nothing happened.

Nothing moved.

He dragged in a high, rattling breath, took a closer look at the shadows on the other side of the alleyway, and let out a long sigh of relief.

Jesus, he thought. *Who the hell does something like that?*

Painted across the crumbling brick and cement was a wide mouth, curled open in what could easily have been either a grin or a snarl. Rows of white triangular teeth gleamed in the darkness, and written in the space between them, as though the mouth was about to swallow them whole, were the words **HE RISES**.

Dracula's followers, he thought.

"Pete?"

He jumped round, his heart accelerating, and saw one of the

volunteers, a young man called Rob, standing in the doorway with a curious expression on his face.

"Christ," said Pete, pressing a hand against his chest. "Sneak up on me, why don't you?"

"Sorry," said Rob. "Are you all right?"

"I'm fine," said Pete, blood pounding in his ears. "Give me a hand."

He unlocked the rear doors of the van as Rob walked across to join him. It was a battered white Ford Transit that had belonged to a butcher for almost twenty years, but its engine was solid, and its refrigerated cabinets still worked, most of the time. Pete climbed up into the back, hearing the suspension creak beneath him, and put the last twenty bottles of blood into a heavy plastic sack. He jumped back down to the ground, and held it out to the volunteer.

"Cheers, Pete," said Rob, swinging the sack over his shoulder. "That's the last of it, right?"

He nodded. "How short are we going to be?"

"Maybe a dozen people," said Rob. "We're going to start splitting bottles to try and make them last."

"Good," said Pete. "Give everyone as much as you can. I'm going to check the queue."

Rob nodded, and carried the sack of blood through the open door. As Pete relocked the van, he heard the first cries and shouts from the vampires as they were informed that they were no longer going to be getting an entire bottle to themselves. He walked back into the community centre, past the row of tables and protesting vampires, and headed for the front door, counting the queue as he went. He had reached forty-two when he heard noises from outside that sent a shiver racing up his spine.

Raised voices. A scream.

And something that sounded like the howl of a wild animal.

Pete sprinted through the small atrium, out on to the quiet suburban street, and cut to his left. The queue ran along one side of the building, beneath the large banner that read SSL BLOOD DRIVE – ALL WELCOME and round the corner. Here, the queuing vampires had turned as one, and were staring with glowing eyes at three figures near the end of the line as they grappled and twisted against the wall of the building.

"Hey!" shouted Pete, and accelerated towards them. "Hey! Cut that out!"

He waded into the middle of them without slowing, pushing and shoving until he reached the centre of the commotion and was able to get a good look at who was fighting.

To his right was a vampire in his mid-forties, his eyes blazing, his fangs gleaming, his face contorted with anger. The man was clutching his right hand, as thick smoke rose between his fingers and a low growl rumbled from his throat.

In front of him, standing with his back against the wall, was one of the SSL security guards. He was a giant of a man, barrel-chested and shaven-headed. He had an ultraviolet torch in his hand and a smile on his face so full of arrogance that it filled Pete with the unexpected desire to punch him squarely in the centre of it.

To his left, yelling and thrashing against his outstretched arm, was Jen. Her eyes were wide with shock and fury, her face was pale, and he had to lean into her with both hands and all his strength to keep her swinging fists out of the reach of the security guard.

"Jen!" he shouted. "Calm down, for Christ's sake! What the hell is going on out here?"

"Why don't you ask this dickhead?" shouted Jen, dragging herself out of his grip and pointing at the security guard. "Go on, ask him!"

"Don't point at me, love," said the giant, his voice thick with condescension.

"Shut up," said Pete, keeping his attention fixed on his volunteer. "I'm asking you, Jen. What happened?"

She stared at him for a long moment, and sighed deeply. Some of the colour had returned to her face, and tears appeared in the corners of her eyes as her anger was replaced by shock and upset.

"This guy asked me if he could jump the queue," she said, and nodded at the vampire holding his smoking hand. "I told him he couldn't, and he asked me to check whether he was definitely going to get any blood because he hadn't drunk anything for two days. I told him I would. When I turned away, he grabbed my arm."

"I'm sorry I did that," said the vampire, his voice low. "I really am. I'm just hungry."

"It's all right," said Jen, shooting him a smile before looking back at Pete. "He didn't hurt me. I asked him to let me go, and he did. But then Captain America here waded in and torched his hand."

Pete turned to the security guard. "You did that?"

"The geezer attacked one of your staff," said the guard. "You ought to be thanking me, mate."

"It happened like she said," said the vampire. "You can ask anyone."

Pete turned to the queuing vampires; the entire line was staring at him, their faces full of suspicion. "Anybody got a different version of events?" he asked.

The vampires growled and hissed, and shook their heads.

"Right then," he said. "Jen, take this man to the front of the queue and give him enough blood to heal his hand."

"Come on," she said, and smiled at the vampire. "Let's get you sorted out."

The vampire nodded, the fire in his eyes fading. "Thank you," he said. "I wasn't trying to cause trouble. I'm just hungry."

"It's all right," said Pete. "Go with Jen, she'll look after you."

He watched her lead the vampire away, then faced the security guard, trying his hardest to control the anger threatening to explode inside him.

"Come with me," he said. "I want a word with you."

Pete strode down towards the end of the queue, dozens of vampire eyes watching him as he passed, and round to the rear of the building. He turned back in time to see the security guard stroll round the corner, as casually as if he was walking home from the pub.

"Was that necessary?" asked Pete, as the man came to a halt in front of him. "Do you think setting a man's hand on fire was a reasonable response to the situation?"

The guard shrugged. "He grabbed your girl."

"And then he let her go," said Pete. "Did she ask for your help? Did she scream?"

The guard spat on the ground, and shook his head.

"What would you have done if the whole queue had turned on you?" said Pete.

"I can handle myself," said the guard.

"Against fifty hungry vamps?"

"If I had to. Yeah."

Pete stared at the man. Belligerence and arrogance were radiating from him in waves, but his bravado did not feel fake; he seemed to genuinely believe he could take fifty vampires single-handed if it came to it.

"I don't recognise you," said Pete, eventually. "What's your name?"

"Baker," said the man. "Phil Baker."

"Are you from Dave Calley's agency?"

"Nope," said Baker. "A geezer called Greg Browning hired me direct. Said your usual lot were overbooked."

"Military man, right?"

Baker smiled. "Royal Marines," he said. "Eight years."

Pete nodded; the man's bearing screamed uniform. "OK," he said. "I want you to call it a night. We're almost done and I think you staying is going to do more harm than good."

Baker shrugged. "Whatever you say."

"All right then," said Pete. "Safe journey home."

He walked into the community centre without a backward glance. His head was still pounding with anger, but he was proud of himself for not letting his temper get the better of him; simply removing the arrogant dickhead of a security guard as quickly as possible was the best solution, and further confrontation would have served no useful purpose.

Pete stood behind the tables and watched his volunteers serve the final bottles of blood to the remainder of the queue; they were working quickly and efficiently, and the last of the vampires was now inside the building, lined up against the wall by the front door. He did a quick count.

Thirty-nine more vamps. Fifteen minutes, give or take.

Satisfied that everything was back under control, Pete took his phone out of his pocket, scrolled down his contacts list until he reached Dave Calley's number, and pressed CALL. After barely two rings, the phone was answered.

"Pete?"

"Evening, Dave," he said, walking back out into the alleyway.

"Evening," said Calley. "What's going on? Everything OK?"

"Mostly," he said. "Had a little bit of trouble at tonight's drive. Nothing serious, but something came up that I wanted to ask you about."

"Shoot."

"Have you spoken to Greg this week? I talked to somebody who said you couldn't staff this one because you were fully booked."

"Let me check. Where are you?" asked Calley.

"Peterborough," he said. "All Saints Community Centre."

"Hang on."

Pete waited patiently. Dave Calley ran a security agency in Lincoln that one of the earliest SSL volunteers had recommended, and he had never regretted the decision to take him on; Calley's staff were uniformly large, shaven-headed and monosyllabic, but every one of them was certified and insured and, as Pete had seen for himself on several occasions, capable of staying calm in the face of appalling provocation.

Not like that guy I sent home, he thought. *Baker. Not a bit like him.*

"Still there, Pete?" asked Calley.

"I'm here, Dave."

"I've got my lads booked in for you in Boston on Friday, and in Nottingham and Grimsby on Saturday, but nothing for tonight, and nothing in Peterborough till next month."

"All right," said Pete. "And you haven't talked to Greg?"

"Not about this."

"Could someone else have told him you were booked out tonight?"

"They could have," said Calley. "But if someone did, let me know so I can stick a rocket up their arse, because I know for a fact I've got four lads twiddling their thumbs at home."

Pete grinned. "Will do, Dave. I'll see you soon, all right?"

"Sure thing," said Calley. "See you later."

Pete ended the call. He scrolled straight down to Greg's name and dialled the number.

"Pete?" asked Greg, before his phone had even rung once. "Everything all right at the drive?"

"Everything's fine," he said. "We're nearly done. Had a bit of a security issue, though. A guy I didn't recognise caused a bit of trouble in the queue."

"Shit," said Greg. "That's what I get for trusting people. I'm sorry, mate. Dave Calley's boys were all booked up, so I got a name from a friend of mine. He said they were good people. Did you get rid of him?"

"I sent him home," said Pete. "Phil Baker, his name was. It really wasn't a big deal, but I wouldn't use him again if I were you. He was a bit gung-ho for this kind of work."

"I won't," said Greg. "Cheers for taking care of it."

"No worries," said Pete. "So you talked to Dave?"

"I talked to him yesterday."

"In person?"

"On the phone," said Greg. "Why?"

"No reason," said Pete. "I'll see you in the morning, all right?"

"See you then, mate. Get some sleep."

"Cheers."

Pete slipped the phone back into his pocket. He turned towards the community centre and saw Jen standing in the doorway, looking at him with narrowed eyes.

"Everything cool?" she asked.

"Fine," said Pete, although he wasn't at all convinced that it was. *What's going on, Greg?* he thought. *Why are you lying to me?*

19

RATCATCHERS

Jamie sat in the back of his squad's van, still wondering whether he should have simply told his mother what she wanted to hear. But that would have meant lying to her, *again*, and at this particular moment in time he would rather she was angry with him than placated by dishonesty.

"Everything all right, sir?" asked Ellison.

He nodded. "Fine," he said. "Sorry. I was miles away for a minute there."

"We noticed," said Ellison, and flashed a quick smile. "Thinking about the new SOP?"

He wasn't, but it was much easier just to nod his head.

"The new order is strange," said Qiang. "Although I understand it. We are ratcatchers now."

Ellison frowned. "What are you talking about?"

"In laboratories, they use rats," said Qiang. "For testing. There are no vampire rats, so they must use vampires. We have been ordered to catch them."

"You think this is about Lazarus?" said Ellison.

"Don't you?" asked Qiang.

"I do," said Jamie, pleased that somebody else had reached the same conclusion as him. "I think you're exactly right, Qiang."

"Hang on," said Ellison, her frown deepening. "Am I missing something here? I thought this was a PR exercise?"

"Maybe it is," said Jamie. "At least partly. But I'm with Qiang. There's something going on here that we're not being told, and I'm sure it's got something to do with Lazarus."

"Why are you sure?" asked Ellison.

Jamie shrugged. "Matt Browning is pretty much the project's second-in-command, and I haven't seen him for over a week. Nobody has. And as far as I can tell, nobody has seen *anybody* from the project for three or four days, at least. And now the SOP gets changed. It might be nothing. But I don't think it is."

"Because you haven't seen your friend for a week?" said Ellison. "That's a bit of a reach, don't you think?"

"Maybe so," said Jamie. "But think about it. Why do we have to bring vamps back to the Loop with us? If this was just about PR, if it was the Director trying to show the world that we don't just kill indiscriminately, then the new SOP could just be a ban on lethal force. But it *specifically* tells us to bring vampires back alive."

The three Operators fell silent. The van's engine rumbled as it carried them towards their Patrol Respond grid in the north Lincoln suburbs. The fold-down screen glowed in the darkness, waiting for an alert from the Surveillance Division that would see them leap into action.

"It would be something, though, wouldn't it?" said Ellison, her voice low. "A cure, I mean. It would change everything."

"Yes," said Qiang.

"It could give us a real advantage," said Ellison. "Particularly if it could be weaponised, like into an aerosol that we could spray over a large area. We could take out dozens of vamps at a time. Hundreds, even."

"It would be huge," said Jamie. "Every vamp that doesn't want to be one could go back to normal. We could cut the numbers down to almost nothing."

"What about Dracula?" said Ellison. "Surely it would work on him if it worked on the others?"

Jamie shrugged. "Unless he's something different. He was the first, after all."

"Have you ever wondered about that?" asked Qiang. "About what turned Dracula in the first place?"

"I don't know," said Jamie. "I don't think anybody does, except for him. And I can't imagine he's going to tell us."

"You should give it a shot," said Ellison, and grinned. "Next time you see him, ask him if he's got a spare five minutes to explain it to you."

Jamie smiled. "I'll do that," he said. "Remind me when—"

An alarm tone rang out of the speakers as the screen changed to display an alert from the Surveillance Division.

ECHELON INTERCEPT REF. 97692/3BR
SOURCE. Emergency call (landline telephone 01522 983572)
TIME OF INTERCEPT. 22:07

TRANSCRIPT BEGINS.
OPERATOR: Emergency service operator, which service, please?
CALLER: I need the police and the fire brigade.
OPERATOR: What is the nature of the emergency?
CALLER: There's a bloody mob outside my house. They're trying to get into my neighbour's and they're shouting that they're going to burn them out. You have to come now.

OPERATOR: Please stay calm, sir. Tell me your address.

CALLER: It's 83 Lemington Close, Lincoln.

OPERATOR: Emergency services are on their way, sir. Are you in danger yourself?

CALLER: I don't know. I don't think so, unless they torch next door. They're vampires, my neighbours. They're vampires and people are trying to get to them. They've got cans of petrol and sticks and bloody bats. There's dozens of them.

OPERATOR: Stay in your home and lock the doors, sir. Help will be there very soon.

TRANSCRIPT ENDS.

INTERCEPT REFERENCE LOCATION. Lemington Close, Lincoln, Lincolnshire. 53.247426, -0.501337

RISK ASSESSMENT. Priority Level 1

"Jesus," said Ellison, her face pale. "How far?"

"Eight minutes," said their driver.

"Do it in five," said Jamie.

Four and a half minutes later the van hurtled into Lemington Close, a suburban cul-de-sac of small detached houses and neatly tended lawns.

The external cameras showed the three Operators a wide view of the street; halfway down it, gathered outside one of the houses on the left, was a surging crowd of people, screaming and shouting and waving lengths of wood and cricket bats in the air. It was at least twenty strong, perhaps even thirty or thirty-five.

"How close do you want to be, sir?" asked their driver.

"Right behind them," said Jamie. "Ellison, Qiang, Ready One as soon as we're clear of the van. I want this dispersed as quickly as possible. I don't care where they go, as long as it's away from here. Scare the shit out of them and send them running. Clear?"

"Yes, sir," said his squad mates, looks of calm determination on their faces.

The van's brakes squealed, rocking them in their seats as the vehicle shuddered to a halt. Jamie threw open the door, leapt down on to the road, and was sent crashing to the ground as something hard and heavy smashed into the back of his head.

The impact was huge; without the protective cushioning of his helmet, it would have shattered his skull into a thousand pieces. He slammed on to the tarmac, his eyes wide, his head ringing, and felt his vampire side come roaring forward; heat filled his eyes, his fangs slid down from his gums, and a wave of fury exploded through him as he leapt back to his feet and looked around for whoever had been stupid enough to hit him.

A baseball bat swung out of the darkness, directly towards his visor, but he was ready for it; he flung himself backwards, rising easily into the air and hovering above the tarmac. The man holding the bat overbalanced and staggered sideways; Jamie sped forward, his gloved hands curled like claws, and hurled him against the rear of the van. The man's head cracked against the metal and he folded to the ground, the bat tumbling from his grip. Behind him, Jamie's squad mates leapt out of the van as Ellison spoke directly into his ear.

"Jesus Christ, sir. Are you all right?"

"I'm fine," said Jamie, his voice little more than a growl. "Move out."

The three Operators stared at the chaos unfolding before them. Half the crowd were still focused on the house, screaming abuse through the windows and hammering on the door. The others had turned to face the new arrivals, their faces twisted with anger; there was a fleeting moment of stillness before they rushed forward, bellowing and swinging their fists and bats. Jamie shouted for his squad mates to spread out and push them back, but they were swallowed up by the rioting crowd before they had a chance to move. They were instantly separated as punches and blows rained down on them, and Jamie felt a flicker of fear in his stomach as he leapt backwards into the air, trying to regroup.

Never seen anything like this before, he thought. *Never seen so much anger.*

Qiang was driven back against the van, shielding himself from attacks with his arms, kicking out as the crowd surged against him. He rolled to his right, trying to create separation, and was pursued out into the middle of the road by a dozen of the feral men and women. In front of the house, Ellison had managed to get clear and was backing away across the lawn, her Glock pointing at the crowd; it flicked from side to side as she retreated from the baying mob. Jamie watched, hoping against hope that she didn't pull the trigger; if they shot one of the crowd, he suspected they would have to shoot many more to get out of the cul-de-sac alive.

Jamie bared his teeth behind his visor, and hurled himself into the men and women who had followed him away from the kerb, scattering them like bowling pins. They scrambled to their feet as he backed away again, straining his ears for the sounds of sirens; their presence had clearly inflamed the situation, and unless the police arrived soon he was increasingly sure this was going to end with someone dead.

There.

The approaching two-tone scream sent relief rushing through him. He spun in the air, saw a fire engine speed round the corner, and felt his heart sink.

We need police, not firemen. This crowd isn't going to be scared of firemen.

"Block it!" shouted a voice from near the house, as if reading his mind. "Block it out now!"

Jamie turned back towards the besieged house in time to see a middle-aged woman apply a lighter to a rag stuffed into a clear bottle, and hurl the Molotov cocktail through the big picture window at the front of the building. The glass shattered, before heat and flames exploded out of the empty space with a vast *whoosh*. Jamie recoiled as three men peeled away from the main crowd and sprinted to the kerb. They climbed into cars and screeched towards the approaching fire engine, smoke billowing from their tyres, then braked and turned the vehicles nose to nose, blocking the entire width of the road. The fire engine skidded to a halt, its horn blaring, but by the time the firemen were out of their cab and shouting for the cars to be moved, the drivers were already running back towards Jamie, who watched them, unsure of what to do; the situation was escalating so quickly, and it was like nothing he had ever had to deal with before.

Behind him, the burning living-room curtains billowed through the broken window, dripping lumps of flaming cloth on to the lawn beneath. Away to his left, Ellison was still retreating, her gun trained on her pursuers, and out in the middle of the road, Qiang was fighting for his life; he had managed to get hold of one of the crowd's baseball bats and was swinging it almost indiscriminately, keeping the advancing mob just about at bay. In front of the house, the remainder of the men and women had abandoned trying to get through the front door, and had backed away from the increasing heat of the fire; they were screaming up at the windows of the house, chanting "NO MORE VAMPS" over and over again. Everywhere Jamie looked was violence, and flames, and hatred; it was like a suburban scene from Hell.

Then he heard it.

From somewhere inside the house, over the screams and shouts of the crowd, over the roar as the fire took hold of the thin walls and cheap furniture and began to burn in earnest, came the distant sounds of two voices screaming for help, and something smaller, and much worse.

It was the high-pitched wail of a baby.

The noise galvanised Jamie; the heat in his eyes rose to a temperature that was close to agonising, and he rocketed through the air towards the fire engine. He dropped to the ground in the middle of the road, and shouted for the firemen gathered round the blockade to get out of the way. They did as they were told, backing away with wide eyes as Jamie took hold of the front bumper of one of the cars. He threw it up and over on to its roof, took a millisecond to marvel at his own strength, then did the same to another car, creating a gap that was wide enough for the fire engine.

"Get moving!" he yelled. "There are people on the first floor!"

He didn't waste time waiting for them; he leapt into the air and sped back towards the burning house. He spun to a halt above the lawn, dodged a volley of thrown stones and half-bricks, and assessed the situation. Qiang had moved almost thirty metres down the street, but a trail of groaning, semi-conscious men and women had been left in his wake, and he was now being pursued by only four.

He can handle them on his own, thought Jamie.

To his left, Ellison was still retreating from a crowd that was bigger than ever, now swollen by those who had lost interest in the burning house or lost their appetite for chasing Qiang. Her Glock was pointing steadily at them and, as Jamie watched, she twisted a dial on her belt.

"Get back now!" she shouted, her voice amplified and booming. "This is your last warning!"

A man at the front of the crowd, who was wearing a smart

shirt and trousers and looked like he should have been at home checking his stock portfolio, bellowed something incoherent and leapt forward. Ellison swung the Glock towards him, and pulled the trigger. The shot was deafening; the crowd screamed as the bullet took the man in the stomach and exited through his back with a huge gout of blood that splashed across the rest of the crowd. The man fell to the ground, his hands clutching at his belly, and began to scream.

Half of the crowd scattered, stumbling and running across the road, disappearing down the narrow alleys between the houses. Those that remained, most of them splashed with blood that wasn't theirs, stared down at the screaming man for a long moment, then turned on Ellison, their faces contorted with anger.

"Scum!" they screamed. "Dirty scum! Murdering bastards!"

But Ellison had not been remotely distracted by the wounded man; with the crowd's attention diverted, she had holstered her Glock and drawn her MP7. The submachine gun was now resting steadily against her shoulder, its barrel tracking slowly back and forth across the crowd.

"Stay where you are," she warned. "Nobody else needs to get hurt. Just stay right there until the police arrive."

Her mention of the police proved the final straw; the remainder of the once seemingly untameable crowd turned tail and fled, leaving only the man screaming and bleeding on the lawn and the trail of prone figures that Qiang had managed to incapacitate as he retreated. The Chinese Operator now ran back towards his squad mate, and Jamie knew that they could handle the situation without him; he rose through the air, shot forward, and smashed through the first-floor window at the front of the house.

He landed in a bedroom thick with acrid smoke. The filters in his helmet shielded him from the worst of it, but he instantly began to cough as he searched the room, checking that there was nobody hiding underneath the bed or in the cupboard. When he was sure that it was empty, he took a deep breath and kicked the door off its hinges. A roaring ball of fire burst into the room, but he ducked beneath it and forced his way out into an inferno.

Flames had charged up the stairs, setting the walls and ceiling ablaze. The heat was overpowering, despite his uniform's climate-control system, and for a terrible moment Jamie was transported back to another place, to a room full of burning petrol in which a man he had tried to help had been suspended, his guts spilled, his life ended at the point of a knife.

A fit of coughing cleared his mind, and he looked around the landing; there were three visible doors, one at the top of the stairs, and two more on the other side of the corridor. Jamie listened, trying to pick up the voices again, but could hear nothing over the roar of the fire; as he watched, it reached the carpet at the top of the stairs and began to spread. He flew forward, ducking his head as chunks of burning ceiling tiles rained down on him, and kicked open the first door he came to.

Screams rang out, and Jamie shoved his way into the room. The smoke inside seemed almost solid, so thick that he could not see more than a few centimetres beyond his visor. He dropped to his hands and knees, hacking and coughing, his chest wracked with pain, and crawled forward. The smoke was mercifully thinner near the floor, and in the corner of the room, seemingly as far away from the door as it was possible to be, he could make out two huddled figures clutching shapes wrapped in towels in their arms.

"Help!" cried one of the figures, its voice raw and choked. "Help us, please!"

Jamie crawled round the foot of a bed and along the wall towards them. When he was beneath the window, he held his breath, leapt up into the dense black cloud, and blindly smashed out the glass with his gloved hand. Smoke billowed out through the opening, but the change in pressure sucked flames into the room from the landing, and the two figures screamed again.

Jamie ducked back down and reached out towards them. "Come on!" he yelled. "Take my hand!"

A woman crawled forward, her eyes flickering with pale pink fire, her skin grey and pallid. She took hold of his hand and he pulled her towards him, the towel-wrapped object in her other hand.

"Where's the baby?" he yelled. "I heard a baby!"

"Here," croaked the woman, and nodded at the towel. "I've got her."

"Can you fly?" asked Jamie.

The woman nodded.

"OK," he said, and let go of her hand. "I'm going to boost you through the window. In front of the house are two people wearing the same uniform as me. Go straight to them, not to anyone else. Got it?"

She nodded again.

"All right," said Jamie. "Go!" He grabbed the woman beneath her armpits and pushed her up and through the empty window frame. She screamed and, for a terrible moment, he was sure she was going to plummet to the ground. But she righted herself, hovered unsteadily in the air for a brief second, and flew away from the burning house, her baby clutched tightly against her.

He dropped back to his hands and knees and crawled forward again. He reached the second figure, a man in his early thirties holding a cardboard box covered with a towel.

"We have to go!" shouted Jamie. "Put that down and come on!"

The man shook his head; his eyes were streaming with tears, but there was determination in them. "Take this," he said, and held out the box. "Be careful with it. I'll follow you."

222

Jamie wasted no time arguing. He took the box, felt it shake as something inside it moved, and got to his feet. The smoke was thicker than ever, and half the room was burning; flames were spreading over the walls and ceiling, and through the open door he could see nothing but fire. The man appeared beside him, coughing around the hand covering his mouth. Jamie threw himself backwards through the window, gripping the box tightly, and floated in the cool air, his gaze fixed on the inferno inside the house.

Nothing happened.

He waited, his heart thundering in his chest, and was about to dive back into the fire when the man appeared, half jumping and half falling through the window. Jamie darted forward and caught his hand; the man arrested his fall, and let himself be dragged over the burning roof of the house and down on to the lawn on the other side.

Jamie released the man; he staggered, but stayed upright, and went to the woman. She was sobbing, the baby in her arms, and the man pulled her against him and hugged her as his own tears began to flow. Beyond them, pairs of firemen were spraying huge jets of water into the house. Jamie watched as one of the emergency personnel made their way towards him.

"Anyone else in there?" he asked.

Jamie flipped his visor up and shook his head. "No," he said. "Just them."

The fireman let out a long sigh of relief, then clapped Jamie hard on the shoulder. "Good work, mate," he said. "Well bloody done."

More sirens screamed down the road, and Jamie turned to see three police cars pull to a halt beside their van, their lights spinning. Half a dozen officers climbed out and stared incredulously at the carnage around them: the burning house, the gut-shot man, the unconscious men and women scattered across the road, the sobbing vampires, and the three jet-black figures standing on the lawn. Jamie smiled behind his visor.

I bet the paperwork on this will be fun, he thought. *Rather you than me.*

The box in his hands rattled again. He crouched down, set it on the grass, and slowly pulled back the towel. Lying in the box, partly wrapped in a bright red blanket, was a black and white cat; its eyes were pink from the smoke, but its side was rising and falling steadily. Jamie reached a gloved hand into the box, scratched the cat behind its ear, and heard an appreciative purr. The blanket around her stomach was moving and he pulled it back, suddenly – *joyfully* – sure what he was going to see.

Five kittens were lined up in a neat row, suckling determinedly at their mother. They were tiny, barely more than a couple of weeks old at most, their heads mostly ears, their bodies balls of fluff, their eyes firmly shut. Two were jet-black, one was the same black and white as the mother, and two were brown and white tabbies, their backs already covered with beautiful markings that ran down to their stubby tails.

"Oh God," said Ellison. "That is genuinely the most adorable thing I've ever seen. I want one. Actually, scratch that. I want *all* of them."

Jamie looked around. His squad mates were standing behind him, their visors raised as they stared down at the box. Qiang was smiling, and Ellison looked like all her Christmases had come at once.

"Look after them," said Jamie, and stood up. "I need to talk to their owners."

Ellison crouched down in his place, and began stroking the cat as he walked towards the vampire couple. Their sobbing had ceased; they were standing with their arms round each other, their attention fixed entirely on the baby they were holding between them.

"How are we doing over here?" asked Jamie.

The man looked up, and gave him a look of such fierce gratitude that Jamie almost took a step back. "We're all right," he said, his voice barely more than a croak. "Are the cats OK?"

Jamie smiled. "They're fine."

"Thank you," said the woman, looking at him with eyes that were red and wet with tears. "I don't know what we would have done if you hadn't come."

"That's what I wanted to ask you," said Jamie. "Why didn't you leave when you had the chance?"

"We didn't think they'd actually do it," said the man. "We've had trouble before, knocks on the door late at night, things shouted through the windows, but we never thought they'd go this far. We never thought they'd try to kill us."

"Things are crazy at the moment," said Jamie. "I'm really sorry this happened to you, and I know it's a lot to take in, but when you're both ready I need you to come with me."

The woman frowned. "Come where?"

"Somewhere safe," said Jamie. "While we sort this all out."

"Somewhere safe," repeated the man. "You promise?"

"I promise," said Jamie, his gut twisting as he spoke. Out of the corner of his eye, he saw a policeman striding across the lawn towards him with wide eyes and a red face. "Excuse me for a moment," he said, and turned towards the new arrival.

"You're Blacklight, right?" said the policeman, stopping in front of him and drawing himself up to what Jamie assumed was his full height.

He nodded.

"Then maybe you can tell me what the hell went on here? Who shot that man?"

"My colleague did."

"On whose bloody authority?" asked the policeman, his face darkening.

"Mine," said Jamie. "The only authority she needed. Is he going to be all right?"

The policeman glanced over his shoulder to where paramedics were crouched round the bleeding man; his eyes were closed and he had stopped screaming, which was something.

"Apparently, he'll live."

"Good," said Jamie. "Then you can ask him what happened. We're leaving."

"Hold on a bloody minute," said the policeman. "You can't just leave. I've got a house burned half to the ground and a man with a bullet in his belly and half a dozen men and women laid out in the middle of the road. What the hell do you expect me to do with all this?"

"Sort it out," said Jamie. "Do your job."

He left the red-faced policeman spluttering on the lawn and led the man and woman, who had listened to the exchange with clear confusion on their faces, towards the open rear door of the van and helped them inside. Ellison handed the box of cats to the man, a look of profound unhappiness on her face, then stepped back as Jamie swung the door shut and faced his squad mates.

"Well done," he said. "That was an absolute nightmare, but we came through it in one piece, and so did they." He nodded towards the van. "There'll be a proper debrief after I write it up for the Director, but there's something I need to discuss with you first."

Qiang narrowed his eyes. "What is it?"

"I don't know for sure why we've been told to bring vampires back to the Loop," he said. "None of us do. But I think Qiang is right, and I'm not going to hand people over to be lab rats against their will. I won't do it."

"So what are you suggesting?" asked Ellison. She was frowning, but her eyes were clear, and her voice was steady.

"I'm going to ask them if they want to be cured," said Jamie.

"If they say yes, then great, we'll take them back. But if they say no, I'm letting them go. I understand that would mean breaking the new SOP about twelve hours after it was changed, but I don't care. Imprisoning innocent people isn't what we do. If you don't want any part of it, I'll understand, and I'll take full responsibility when we get back. But this is what's happening."

He looked at his squad mates. He dearly hoped they would agree, that they would back his decision, but he knew he couldn't blame them if they didn't; asking them to disobey a direct order on the basis of guesswork was hardly fair.

"I am with you," said Qiang.

"Me too," said Ellison. "Do it, Jamie."

He smiled widely. "Thank you," he said. He pulled the van door open again and looked in at the vampire couple. The woman was rocking their baby gently on her lap, and the man had one hand in the box, stroking the cat as she fed her kittens. They looked round at him, nervous expressions on their faces.

"I have a question for you," said Jamie. "I need you to answer it honestly, OK?"

"OK," said the woman.

The man nodded.

"Do you like being vampires?" said Jamie. "And by that I mean, if there was a way that you could go back to normal, is that what you would want, or are you happy as you are?"

The couple looked at each other.

"I know I speak for both of us," said the woman, "when I say that there is nothing in the world we'd like more than to be normal again."

"In which case," said Jamie, "I have a feeling this might just be your lucky day."

20

HUMAN TRIAL

NINETY MINUTES EARLIER

Matt looked down at the stretcher, his heart thumping in his chest.

Beside him were Paul Turner, Professor Karlsson and one of the doctors from the Loop's infirmary; the four of them were standing silently inside one of the Lazarus Project's sterile laboratories, wearing paper boiler suits that would be incinerated later. The lab was a long rectangle, with a row of stretchers standing in its centre. Machines and monitors stood either side of them, and the rear wall contained three large plastic windows, revealing small square rooms beyond.

The woman lying on one of the stretchers had already been sedated; her eyes were closed, her heartbeat showing as spikes on a running graph on one of the monitors, in perfect time with the slow beeps ringing out of the speakers. She was middle-aged, her hair dark, her skin pale; she looked peaceful, as though she was enjoying a well-deserved rest.

"I'm going to say this one more time," said Matt, without taking his eyes off her. "Are we absolutely sure we should do this?"

"She signed the release," said Turner. "We explained the risks. I say do it."

"I agree," said Karlsson.

Matt took a deep breath, and nodded. He walked across to a stainless-steel bench, opened the door of a small fridge sitting on its surface, and took out a plastic bag full of blue liquid with a label stuck to its side. What was printed on the label would have meant nothing to anyone outside the Lazarus Project; if the cure was cleared for release to the public, Matt was sure the tabloids and the TV news would give it a catchy name, but for now it was simply known as *Sample Formula 5204R56J*. Its blue colour was artificial, the result of a dye that was added to each active sample to provide an additional level of precaution; the rule of thumb inside the Lazarus Project was that anything blue should be handled with the utmost care.

Holding the bag gently in his gloved hand, Matt walked back across the lab and handed it to the doctor, who made a series of notes on his clipboard, attached the bag to an IV drip, and punctured the seal. The four men watched in silence as the blue liquid ran slowly down a plastic tube and disappeared through a needle into the woman's forearm.

"Let's move her," said the doctor. "Quickly."

Turner nodded. He took hold of the monitoring trolley as the doctor gripped the corners of the stretcher, and together they wheeled the woman and the machines connected to her towards the far end of the room. Matt walked ahead of them, as Professor Karlsson brought up the rear, and pressed the button on the wall beside the window on the left. It slid silently upwards; the Director and the doctor wheeled the woman beneath it and into the room. Turner pushed the trolley into the corner as the doctor clipped the stretcher to the rear wall of the room, locking it in place. The two men exited, and Matt pressed the button again, lowering the thick plastic window back into place. He joined his colleagues, shivering as though he had just got out of a cold shower.

"What will it mean if it doesn't work?" asked Turner, his eyes fixed on the unconscious woman.

"It might not mean anything," said Karlsson. "The dose might need adjusting, or the formula itself. We'll just have to wait and see."

"How long?" asked Turner. "How long until—"

The woman on the stretcher opened her eyes and let out a scream of such deafening volume and pitch that Matt physically recoiled; he staggered backwards, his eyes wide with shock. Her eyes boiled with red-black fire, so intense that her features were hidden from view by the roaring glow. She twisted on the stretcher, her scream seeming to go on forever.

"What the hell?" shouted Turner. "What's happening?"

"I don't know," said Karlsson, his voice low. "We have no model for an adult human reaction."

"We have to stop it," said Matt, raising his voice to make himself heard over the awful noise of the screaming.

"How?" asked Karlsson.

"She signed the release," said Turner.

"I don't care what she signed!" shouted Matt. "We have to stop it now!"

Turner took a half-step towards him. "I can't let you go in there, Matt. Please don't try it."

He stared at the Director, his face full of unbearable, shameful heat. Turner looked back at him with an expression that Matt had never seen before; it was almost as if the Director was silently pleading with him not to make things worse.

He wants to stop this too, he realised. *But he can't. He knows he can't.*

The bloodcurdling scream finally died away, leaving the woman twisting silently on the stretcher.

Maybe it's over, thought Matt, turning back to the window. *Maybe that's it.*

The woman burst up off the stretcher, so fast that she was little more than a blur, and slammed into the ceiling with an impact that Matt felt through the soles of his boots. She hung suspended in the air, screeching and clawing and gibbering, hammered into the ceiling again, then rocketed towards them, thudding into the plastic window; it looked like some huge, invisible hand was hurling her back and forth across the room. She crashed into the rear wall, sending the stretcher and the trolley of machinery flying; sparks and shards of metal exploded into the air, but the woman was already out of range, soaring up towards the ceiling before curving impossibly in mid-air and hitting the plastic window face first. There was a loud snap as her nose broke; bright crimson blood squirted against the plastic and ran towards the floor. Her screeches reached an inhuman pitch, and all four men retreated, holding their hands over their ears as she was flung around the room, leaving trails of blood on the white walls.

"Oh God," whispered Karlsson, beneath the deafening racket. "Oh Jesus. Oh God."

Matt ran forward, his only thought that he had to stop this, had to do something, *anything* to help the woman. He was reaching for the button on the wall when Turner tackled him, wrapping his arms round his waist and driving him to the ground. His teeth came together on his tongue with an audible *clunk* and Matt tasted blood. He howled, partly in pain and partly from dreadful, guilty misery.

"No!" shouted Turner. "It's not safe!"

"WE HAVE TO DO SOMETHING!" he screamed.

Matt was dragged to his feet. Arms wrapped round him from behind, pinning his own to his sides and holding him tightly in place.

"There's nothing we can do," said Turner, his voice low. "We just have to wait for it to end."

Matt stared through the window with tears in his eyes. The

woman was jerking back and forth, screeching and scratching at her skin, as though she was covered with bugs that only she could see. Her eyes were flaring crimson, and her fangs were sliding in and out, gleaming wetly under the fluorescent light. She spun into the rear wall, and Matt's stomach lurched as her arm broke with a thick crunch; her elbow was bent back the wrong way and pointed ends of bone were sticking through the skin.

The woman jerked back into the middle of the room and hung in the air, her incoherent ranting and raving stopping as suddenly as if someone had flicked a switch. The veins stood out in her neck, and her back arched alarmingly; any further, and Matt was sure her spine would break. Her throat convulsed, as her limbs vibrated in a blur and her eyes blazed black. A howl rose from the woman's mouth, a terrible cry that sounded like it was coming from the deepest depths of her soul. Then she went limp, and dropped to the ground like a stone.

"Open the door," said the doctor. "Open it now, for God's sake."

Karlsson looked round, his eyes wide and staring, but didn't move. Matt felt Turner's grip on him loosen; he broke free and hammered the button beside the door. The doctor ran under the rising plastic window and slid to his knees beside the woman, his fingers pressed against her neck. For a long moment, there was silence in the wide laboratory, full of the terrible prospect of tragedy.

"She's breathing," said the doctor.

Matt let out a gasp of relief. Beside him, Karlsson put his hands on his knees and bent over. Matt was suddenly sure his boss was going to throw up; he was visibly swaying, and his skin had turned pale green. But Karlsson took a series of deep breaths and straightened unsteadily back up, his face a mask of shock. The Professor was a scientist, a theorist, and Matt doubted he had ever seen anything remotely as horrible as the events of the last five minutes.

"I need to get her back on the stretcher," said the doctor. "Can one of you help me lift her?"

"Neither of you move," said Turner. "Doctor, come out of there. Now."

Matt turned to the Director, a deep frown on his face. Karlsson was still staring at the woman, seemingly paralysed by what he had seen.

"She needs to go to the infirmary," said the doctor. "I need to set her arm immediately."

"I understand that," said Turner. "But I want to make sure this is over, and I'd like to have that window between her and us if it isn't. So come out of there. That's an order."

The doctor stared at Turner, then got to his feet and walked out of the room. He pressed the button to lower the plastic barrier, and lined up beside his colleagues. Matt watched the woman's chest rising and falling, and was surprised at the intensity of the relief that was pulsing through him. He had been sure he could handle the test, that the scientist in him would be able to rationalise it away as being for the greater good, but the reality had been almost too much to bear.

"Was that what you were expecting?" asked Turner.

Professor Karlsson shook his head. "No," he said. "I don't think anybody was expecting that."

"So?" said Turner.

"So what?"

"Did it work?" asked the Director, turning to face the Professor.

"I have absolutely no idea," said Karlsson. "Doctor?"

The doctor shrugged. "Her pulse is steady," he said. "But if you're asking me if she's still a vampire, I won't know until she wakes up or I shine a UV light on her."

"Could you do that?" asked Turner.

The doctor narrowed his eyes. "I could," he said. "But I really hope you're not asking me to."

Matt was watching the exchange when something moved in the corner of his eye. He looked back in time to see the woman open her eyes and roll her head to the side. She stared directly at him, her eyes wide and unfocused.

"Hey," he said. "She's awake. Look."

Turner frowned. "Is that a good sign?" he asked.

"This was the first time this procedure was carried out on a human being, sir," said the doctor, with a noticeable edge in his voice. "None of us knows what's a good sign, or a bad sign, or anything in between. It doesn't matter how many times you ask."

Turner gave the doctor a brief, narrow-eyed stare, then stepped up to the window. "Can you hear me?" he asked, in a raised voice.

"Yes," said the woman, her voice hoarse and slightly slurred. "I can hear you."

"How do you feel?" asked the doctor.

The woman grimaced. "My arm hurts."

"I know," said the doctor. "Try not to move. We're going to fix that for you in a minute. How do you feel, apart from that?"

"I don't know," said the woman. "I don't…"

"Take your time," said the doctor.

The woman nodded. She lay on the floor, her body still, her breathing slow and deep, and closed her eyes. A long second later they flew open, and a smile of such staggering beauty broke across her face that it made Matt gasp out loud.

"It's gone," she said. "My God. I can't feel it any more. It's really gone."

Marie Carpenter's smile widened, and she burst into tears.

ZERO HOUR
PLUS 194 DAYS

21

NO GOING BACK

Jamie found himself distracted as he walked down the cellblock corridor, and as a result he didn't realise his mother's cell was empty as soon as he exited the airlock.

The reasons for his distraction were clear. For the entirety of his Blacklight career, the operational SOP had been to destroy vampires on sight, which meant that the cells on Level H were very rarely full. The fourth room on the right was occupied by Valentin, the last on the left by his mother, and that was usually all.

Now, the first room on the left contained a man lying asleep on a bed. Two cells down, a pair of middle-aged women were huddled together on plastic chairs, talking so quietly that even his supernatural hearing could barely make out their words. Halfway along the corridor on the right, a teenage boy stared petulantly at Jamie as he passed, his hands stuffed into the pockets of his jeans, his eyes full of faint red fire. And on the opposite side of the cellblock, three further cells along, he found the family he had rescued the night before.

The man was asleep on the bed, his body rolled towards the wall. The woman was sitting in a chair, gently rocking her daughter in her arms. She looked up as Jamie paused outside the cell's UV barrier, smiled, and raised a finger to her lips in a message that was abundantly clear.

Don't wake them up.

He smiled back, and nodded. He glanced round the rest of the cell and saw the box he had carried on the floor at the back; the cat's black and white head peered over the cardboard lip, and Jamie was pleased to see that someone had found her a bowl of water and a plate of what looked like offcuts of ham.

"Are you OK?" he mouthed.

The woman smiled, and gave him a thumbs up with her free hand.

"I'll come back later," he whispered. "When they're awake."

She nodded, and returned her attention to the sleeping baby. Jamie watched them for a moment, then walked on down the corridor, feeling pretty pleased with himself. His squad had safely extracted the family of vampires from a chaotic situation, and had managed to do so without any loss of life; he had woken to a message on his console informing him that the man Ellison shot would survive. All in all, it had been a pretty satisfactory night.

Jamie stopped outside the last cell on the left and looked through the purple barrier. When he didn't see his mother, his first thought, strangely, was that she must be hiding, so he crouched down to look under the bed, feeling slightly silly as he did so.

Nothing.

He frowned. His mother occasionally left her cell for medical and physical tests, but she hadn't mentioned anything about a new round having been scheduled.

Although, whispered a voice in the back of his head, *you didn't exactly part on good terms yesterday. Maybe she didn't feel like telling you.*

Jamie grimaced with guilt. He had not come down to the cellblock to apologise to his mother, as he didn't think he needed to be sorry for not automatically agreeing with her views on a potential cure, but *had* done so with the genuine desire to put things right between them. He didn't like arguing with his mum, and he hated the thought of her worrying about whether or not he was angry with her.

For long moments, Jamie stared into the empty cell. Then he turned on his heels and headed back along the corridor, far quicker than he had come. He stopped outside Valentin's cell; the youngest Rusmanov was in his usual position on his sofa, one ankle resting on the other knee, a newspaper open in his hands. It hid his face, but Jamie knew the ancient vampire would be entirely aware of his presence.

"Valentin?" he said.

The seated figure didn't move a muscle.

"Valentin?" he repeated, increasing his volume. "Don't ignore me."

The newspaper was lowered, and the vampire smiled at him with eyes that flickered red, sending a shiver up Jamie's spine.

"I wasn't ignoring you, Mr Carpenter," said Valentin. "I was attempting to decide whether I could be bothered to spend my precious time talking to you. I suggest you make this quick, while my decision remains unmade."

"Fine," said Jamie. He allowed heat to rise into the corners of his own eyes, hoping to show Valentin that he wasn't scared of him. "My mother isn't in her cell. Did you see her leave?"

"And what if I did?" asked the vampire.

"I hope you would tell me."

"Really?" asked Valentin. "Why would you hope that? Because you and I are such good friends, who converse with each other and confide in each other and keep no secrets from each other? Or because you are an Operator of Blacklight, and I am a prisoner who should do as he is told?"

"Whichever you prefer," said Jamie.

"I prefer neither," said Valentin. "Is there anything else I can help you with?"

"No," growled Jamie. "There's nothing else." He backed away

from the purple barrier, determined not to lose his temper and give the old vampire what he wanted, and headed for the airlock.

"You know," called Valentin, "I did see something last night that might be of interest to you. How silly of me to have forgotten."

Jamie turned and stared at the vampire. "Are you going to tell me what it was?"

"Of course," said Valentin, and smiled. "I'm not a monster, Mr Carpenter. As it transpires, I *do* remember seeing your mother last night."

Jamie's heart accelerated. "Where did you see her?"

"Right where you're standing now," said Valentin. "She walked past, accompanied by two of your colleagues. It was around ten thirty, maybe eleven o'clock, if I had to guess. And I haven't seen her since."

"Are you telling me the truth?" asked Jamie.

The vampire shrugged. "If you don't believe me, I see little point in trying to convince you. Have a lovely day, Mr Carpenter."

Valentin raised his newspaper again. Jamie stood frozen to the spot, a deep frown creasing his forehead.

Maybe there was some kind of problem, he thought. *Maybe she needed to talk to the Director, or ask him something. Maybe—*

His heart stopped in his chest.

No. They wouldn't. Surely they wouldn't do that to her.

The thought, sudden and terrible and all too plausible, charged his limbs with life. He flew along the corridor, dropped to the ground outside the cellblock guard post, and knocked on its thick plastic window. The Duty Operator jumped and spun round, a look of shock in her wide eyes.

"Lieutenant Carpenter," she said. "I'm sorry, I didn't hear—"

"Was my mother taken off the block last night?" he interrupted.

The Operator frowned. "I wasn't on duty last night," she said. "I can check the log—"

"Do it," growled Jamie, and felt heat flicker behind his eyes. "Quickly."

The Operator swallowed; she looked very pale as her fingers tapped her keyboard. A voice in the back of Jamie's head was yelling at him, reminding him that whatever had happened was not her fault, but he barely heard it; his mind was full of a possibility so awful that he could barely contemplate it.

"Ten fifty-two last night," said the Operator, looking up from her screen. "Marie Carpenter escorted off block by Captain Williams and Lieutenant Browning. No absence parameters."

"What the hell does that mean?" asked Jamie.

"It means they didn't list a time for when she's expected back, sir."

He stared at the Duty Operator, but he was no longer really looking at her, or anything else; the names she read out had hit him like a punch to the stomach.

Captain Williams and Lieutenant Browning. Jack and Matt.
My friends.

Everybody in the laboratory jumped when somebody hammered on its metal door.

It was a phenomenally rare occurrence; the Lazarus Project was off-limits to all but the most senior members of the Department, and unauthorised visitors were prohibited, especially now. But the noise that was echoing through the cavernous room was loud and relentless; it sounded like someone was very determined to gain entry to the lab.

"Matt?" asked Natalia. Her voice was low and tight, and she was looking over at him with wide eyes.

"Don't worry," he replied. He had spun his chair round and was staring at the door. "I'm sure everything's fine."

"What is going on out there?" asked Professor Karlsson. "Somebody check the cameras."

Matt sighed deeply and typed rapidly on his keyboard, his head thudding with stress and tiredness; he had been working all night, ever since Marie Carpenter had been taken to the infirmary, and he doubted that he was going to see the inside of his quarters any time soon. The modifications to the sealed rooms were now complete, the next three test subjects would be arriving in half an hour, and the pressure inside the Lazarus Project, which was crushing at the best of times, was only going to increase as the trial progressed.

The security grid appeared on his screen, and he opened the live feed from the corridor. It showed an Operator pounding on the metal door, their fists little more than a blur. Matt stared, concern twisting in his stomach, until the figure raised its head and looked directly into the camera with eyes full of dark red light.

"It's Jamie," he said. "What the hell is he playing at?"

"Are you expecting him?" asked Karlsson.

"No, sir," he said. "I don't know why he's out there."

"Should we let him in?" asked Natalia, her voice low.

"He's Zero Hour cleared," said Matt. "If we want to let him in, we can."

"He looks angry," said Natalia.

"He rarely doesn't," said Matt.

"I'm calling Security," said Karlsson. "This is completely inappropriate."

That might not be a bad idea, thought Matt, as the hammering intensified. *By the sound of things.*

"He can pull that door off its hinges if he decides to," he said. "I think I should talk to him."

"Be careful," said Natalia, and gave him a look of clear warning. "I do not like this at all."

Matt forced a smile. "It's OK," he said. "He's my friend."

He got up from his desk and walked towards the door. Behind him, Professor Karlsson was on his phone, asking the Security Division to urgently send a team down to assist them; Matt tried to ignore what that would mean, and pulled his ID card from his pocket. He raised it towards the control panel on the wall, hesitated for a split second, then took a deep breath and pressed his card against it. Machinery rumbled into life as a series of locks disengaged and rolled back. Matt reached for the handle, but before his fingers could close round it, the door crashed open and a blur of black and red exploded through it.

"Where is she?" demanded Jamie, his eyes blazing as he seized Matt by the throat. "Where's my mother? What the hell have you done with her?"

Matt's eyes bulged. Fingers constricted his throat as he felt himself lifted off the ground. He heard Natalia scream, heard shouted protests as his colleagues scrambled out of their seats and away from what was happening.

"What..." he croaked. "I don't... what?"

Glowing red eyes stared into his; fury was boiling out of his friend in an almost visible cloud. "You and Jack took her out of her cell last night," growled Jamie. "Where is she? Tell me right now."

"Jamie... she's in the infirmary... please, Jamie."

The grip on his neck tightened as he was jerked upwards and slammed into the ceiling. A bolt of pain raced through his head, and he saw stars.

"You couldn't wait?" shouted Jamie. "You couldn't wait eight hours for me to bring you vamps to do your tests on? You had to use my mother?"

In that moment, despite the dizziness swirling through him, Matt understood what his friend thought had happened, and real fear exploded through him; if he didn't make Jamie understand that he was wrong, and quickly, there was every chance that this ended with him being badly hurt.

Or worse, he thought.

"Jamie…" he gasped. "I didn't… we didn't. She volunteered… I promise you, Jamie… she volunteered. Please…"

A frown creased his friend's face, and Matt felt the grip on his throat loosen, ever so slightly. He sucked in a desperate, pressure-easing breath and looked down. Most of the Lazarus Project were huddled with Professor Karlsson at the far end of the room, their faces pale with terror, but Natalia was standing directly beneath him, her eyes fixed firmly on his own.

"She volunteered?" said Jamie. His voice had dropped, and the fire in his eyes had lost some of its fervour. "How?"

"She asked to see the Director," whispered Matt. "She asked him if you were right, if there really was a cure, because she wanted it if there was. The Director told her that we were just getting ready to begin testing it, and she volunteered. Turner gave her a release form and told her to think about it. She said she didn't need to, but Turner insisted. He sent Jack and me down an hour later to ask if she was still sure. She said she was, Jamie. She said she was sure. What was I supposed to do?"

Jamie's expression changed, his rage transforming before Matt's eyes into something that looked a lot like shame. "I'm sorry," he whispered. "I should have known you would never hurt her."

"It's OK," he said. "Honestly. Just put me down, all right?"

Jamie looked down. His eyes widened, as if he hadn't realised that they were nearer to the ceiling than the floor, and he immediately descended. Matt took a quick step backwards when their feet touched the ground and his friend let go of his neck, as Natalia appeared beside him and took hold of his hand; she was trembling with anger.

"How dare you?" she hissed. "What is wrong with you?"

Jamie winced. "I'm sorry," he said. "I'm really—"

The door swung open again and banged against the wall as the Security Division squad that Professor Karlsson had requested burst into the laboratory: six Operators in full uniform, MP7s raised to their shoulders.

"Everybody stay where they are!" bellowed the squad leader. "Hands on your head, Lieutenant Carpenter! Now!"

Jamie did as he was ordered. Matt watched, feeling an uneasy combination of sympathy and vicious relief; he could feel his neck starting to swell, and he was painfully aware that he had been attacked and humiliated in front of the entire Lazarus Project.

Four of the Operators trained their guns on Jamie as one took up a station by the door and the squad leader went to Professor Karlsson.

"Is anyone hurt?" he asked.

Karlsson shook his head, his face pale. "Ask Matt," he said. "It was him the vampire attacked."

The vampire, thought Matt. *That's how the rest of them see Jamie. As a vampire, nothing more.*

The squad leader strode back down the room and stopped in front of him.

"Are you hurt, Lieutenant Browning?" he asked.

"No," he said. "It's fine. It was—"

"It is *not* fine," said Natalia, giving him a furious look. "You were attacked for no reason. There is *nothing* fine about that."

"Natalia," he said. "Please."

She looked at him, her anger seeming to have temporarily

transferred to him. Then her expression softened, and he saw tears in her eyes.

"I'm sorry," repeated Jamie, his voice low. "I really am. I lost control. I have no excuse."

"No," said Paul Turner, striding into the laboratory. "You don't. Explain yourself, Lieutenant Carpenter. Quickly."

Matt saw the look on the Director's face and, in that moment, would not have traded places with Jamie for anything in the world.

"I can't, sir," said Jamie. "Not in front of these Operators. It's Zero Hour level."

Turner stared at him, then looked at the Security squad leader. "Stand down," he said. "Wait outside."

The Operators lowered their weapons and exited the room. Once the door had swung shut with a heavy thud, Turner nodded at Jamie.

"Speak," he said.

"My mother wasn't in her cell, sir," said Jamie. "I found out that Matt and Jack Williams escorted her out last night, and given the new SOP, I thought they were using her for testing. I lost it, sir. I'm sorry."

Turner stared at the vampire Operator for several long seconds, then turned to face Matt.

"Lieutenant Browning," he said. "Are you all right?"

"Yes, sir," he replied.

"Do you want to bring disciplinary proceedings against Lieutenant Carpenter?"

"No, sir."

Jamie gave him a look of such gratitude that Matt felt his heart lurch. Deep down, he knew that his friend hadn't meant to hurt him; he was very familiar with the uncontrollable animal side that vampires spent much of their time trying to suppress, and he knew that it was what had been in control when Jamie arrived at the lab.

"Very well," said Turner. "Lieutenant Carpenter, you are hereby prohibited from entering the Lazarus Project for any reason, unless accompanied by myself or by another senior Operator with my express authorisation. Is that clear?"

"Yes, sir," said Jamie.

"Does that suit you, Professor Karlsson?"

The Lazarus Director nodded. "I think that will be fine, sir."

"Good," said Turner. "Another incident like this, Lieutenant Carpenter, and you will find yourself in a cell. Is that absolutely clear to you?"

"It is, sir," said Jamie. "I really am sorry."

Turner nodded. "All right," he said. "Wait outside with the Security squad."

Jamie walked slowly across the lab, his head lowered, and stepped through the door without a backward glance. Turner waited for it to swing shut, then faced the Lazarus Project staff.

"Carry on," he said. "I apologise for the interruption."

Turner exited the lab. Matt stared after him, Natalia's hand still tightly entwined with his own.

"All right," said Karlsson. "You heard the Director. Back to work, everyone."

Jamie waited in the corridor, alongside the Security squad that had been called into action on his account. Their guns were lowered at their sides, but they were keeping a clear distance, as though they expected him to explode again at any moment.

Scared of me, he thought. *Larissa always tried to tell me what it felt like, how awful it was, but I never really got it. Until now.*

The Lazarus Project door opened and Paul Turner emerged. He looked at the Security squad.

"Dismissed," he said. "Return to your stations."

The Operators nodded, and marched away down the corridor. The Director waited until they were out of sight, then turned to face Jamie.

"Do I have to tell you how unbelievably stupid that was?" he asked.

"No, sir," said Jamie. "I know."

"I hope so," said Turner, his voice low. "Because I meant what I said. You put me in a position like this again and you're going downstairs for a long time."

Jamie nodded. His entire body was pulsing with guilt, and the only thing he wanted to do was the one thing he knew he couldn't, at least for now: apologise to Matt and beg his forgiveness.

I had my hand round his neck. Jesus. Round his throat.

"You know your mother volunteered to receive the cure?" said Turner. "Did Browning manage to tell you that while you were choking the life out of him?"

"He told me."

"So you understand that this was about your mother making a decision that had nothing to do with you?"

"I understand, sir," he said.

"Good," said Turner. "Then I suggest you go and see her in the infirmary. That's a far better use of your energy than attacking your friends."

"I will," said Jamie. "I'll go right now, sir."

Turner's expression softened, ever so slightly. "I understand this is hard for you, Jamie," he said. "I understand the concept of a vampire side, and that impulse control can be difficult. But you almost hurt someone you care about, and you caused an incident inside a

Department that is living on its very last nerve. That can't happen again."

"It won't, sir," said Jamie. "I promise."

"Fine. Go and see your mother. She's been asking for you."

Turner turned and strode away down the corridor. Jamie stared for a long moment, then called after him.

"Sir?"

The Director turned back. "What is it, Lieutenant?"

"It's real, then?" said Jamie. "The cure, I mean. It's really real?"

Turner smiled. "See for yourself," he said.

22

QUICKSAND

THE HUDSON RIVER VALLEY UPSTATE NEW YORK, USA

Larissa woke from a deep, empty sleep and saw 06:13 glowing on the clock on her bedside table.

She had only gone to bed four hours earlier – Haven was, unsurprisingly, a predominantly nocturnal community – but she had always been an early riser, and the morning was her favourite part of the day. She swung her legs out from beneath her duvet and floated towards the bathroom. As she showered and dressed, she ran through her mental to-do list.

It was Wednesday, which was shopping day. There was a twenty-four-hour supermarket a fifteen-minute drive south on Highway 9, and making the trip in the community's pick-up truck was a much sought-after responsibility; it offered the chance to interact with people from outside Haven, if only briefly, and the opportunity to make sure that the fridges were stocked with the kind of beer that you liked. Larissa was on the rota to go, but had already decided that she would trade her spot with somebody else; it was an easy way to make one of Haven's residents happy, and it was no loss to her. She felt no great desire to go to the supermarket, or into town, or anywhere else for that matter.

She had everything she needed here.

Apart from the shopping, there were trees to be felled and sawed, foundations to be dug for the new row of cabins behind the big house, roofs to be tarred, grass to be cut, cattle to be bled, and a hundred other things that kept Haven running smoothly. She smiled as she buttoned her shirt and twisted a band into her hair; it was going to be a good day, she could just feel it.

Larissa flew down the stairs and swooped round towards the kitchen. The house's windows were all covered with pale blinds that had been nailed and taped to the frames, but the light was still bright and warm. At this early hour, Haven was blissfully quiet; even with her supernaturally powerful hearing, all her ears could detect was the rustling of tree branches, the chirping of birds, and…

She smiled, and accelerated slightly; the scent that accompanied the gentle breathing she had heard was unmistakable.

"Morning," said Callum, as she flew into the kitchen. "Sleep well?"

The Texan vampire was leaning against the breakfast bar, tapping an iPad with one hand and holding a steaming mug in the other. As usual, he looked like he had just fallen out of bed; his checked shirt was crumpled, his jeans were spattered with paint and tar, his long hair was pushed back from his face, and his cheeks were covered with fine dark stubble.

"You're up early," she said.

Callum shrugged. "It's a beautiful day," he said, and smiled. "Sleeping seemed like a waste. There's coffee in the pot."

Larissa flew across to the counter and poured herself a mug. She put bread in the toaster and sipped her coffee as she waited for it.

"What are you up to today?" she asked.

"I think I'm done tarring roofs," said Callum, his smile widening. "At least for a day or two. The rota says I'm felling trees, which suits me pretty well. You?"

Larissa's toast popped up. She transferred the slices to a plate and buttered them quickly. "Not sure," she said. "I'm going to swap out of shopping, so I thought I might help dig the new foundations. But I'm going to take a walk before I do anything else. Fancy it?"

"Sure," said Callum. He stood up straight, and stretched his arms out above his head. His shirt rode up past his hips, exposing a strip of flat, toned stomach, and Larissa did her very best not to stare at it. He let his arms drop back to his sides and smiled at her. "Let's go."

The two vampires walked round the edge of the lawn, keeping themselves safely beneath the canopy. The morning sun was low, and the strip of shade was barely two metres wide; it forced them to walk closely side by side, and every few steps her fingers brushed against his, sending a tremble through her and forcing Larissa to confront a simple truth.

She was attracted to Callum.

It was no use pretending that she wasn't, or that the feeling wasn't mutual; the evidence was in the gentle half-smile he seemed to reserve only for her, in the twist of excitement she felt in her stomach every morning when she saw him for the first time that day. Nothing had happened between them; she was still in love with Jamie, and even though he was more than three thousand miles away and she had no idea whether she would ever see him again, giving in to her attraction to Callum would have felt like betraying him. But in the back of her mind, her vampire side, the strident, aggressive part of her that she disliked but had so often relied upon, whispered two words with ever increasing frequency.

Why not?

And if Larissa was completely honest with herself, she was finding it harder and harder to come up with a good answer to that question. Jamie had made his feelings perfectly clear, and she was unsure how long she was supposed to keep punishing herself for leaving. She might *never* entirely stop loving him, and what would that mean for the rest of her life? That she was supposed to spend it alone, a voluntary spinster who rejected every opportunity for human warmth and comfort?

"Penny for them?" said Callum.

She looked round, roused from her thoughts. "They're not worth a penny," she said. "I was just thinking about this place. I still sometimes have to pinch myself to see if it's real. You know?"

Callum nodded. "I know," he said. "But it's real, Larissa. You and me and the others built it with our bare hands."

"I know what we did," said Larissa, and smiled.

They had reached the corner of the lawn, near the first of the row of cabins that led down to the riverbank. They strolled in comfortable silence as the sun dragged itself higher and higher into the sky, covering Haven's wide expanses of green and brown with warm golden light.

Callum stopped. "You hear that?" he asked.

Larissa frowned. "Yeah," she said. "I did." It had been low and distant, but unmistakable; the sound of a number of voices crying out at the same time.

The door of one of the cabins flew open and Emily Belmont peered out, a look of alarm on her lined, weathered face. She had been at least sixty-five when she was turned, and had been a vampire for more decades than she could remember; she was the oldest resident of Haven, which made her a strong contender for the oldest person in the whole of North America.

"There's been another one," she said, fixing her small, beady eyes on Larissa and Callum. "Another video. It's all over the news."

Larissa felt a shiver race up her spine. "Dracula?"

Emily nodded.

"Come on," said Callum. "Let's get back to the house."

Larissa looked at Emily. "Come with us?"

"No need," said the old vampire. "I'll stay here."

Larissa turned and flew beneath the canopy towards the big house, Callum at her side, her mind racing. There had been no further word from Dracula since the release of his first video, more than six months earlier, and once the initial panic had died down, much of the media had seemed to convince themselves that it was over, that nothing more was coming. She had never believed that, not for a single moment; she was absolutely certain that, wherever he was, Dracula was making preparations and plans, and that it was only a matter of time until he resurfaced.

That time, apparently, had now come.

She flew up on to the veranda of the big house and strode through the door. Callum followed her into the kitchen, where she turned on the television that hung above the breakfast bar and tuned it to CNN. She waited impatiently for a millisecond or two as the screen warmed up, and then the news network studio appeared; the anchor was talking into the camera as researchers and producers scurried in the background.

The headline filling the lower portion of the screen comprised five words and made its point unequivocally: SECOND DRACULA VIDEO GOES VIRAL. Larissa turned up the volume and stood silently beside Callum as the anchor's voice emerged from the television's speakers.

"…no comment yet from any official sources, although we are expecting a statement from the Department of Homeland Security later today. The new video appears to have followed the same pattern as the first, with a coordinated release across multiple platforms just after 10am Eastern time. For those of you just joining us, let's take another look at what appears to be a second message from the vampire who calls himself Dracula, and which has already been viewed more than two million times in the last fifteen minutes."

The studio disappeared, replaced by a black screen that gave way to a shadowy shot of the vampire who, in what now felt like another life, Larissa and Valentin Rusmanov had once fought to a standstill. There was widespread public doubt about the identity of the vampire in the videos, and whether the threats he had made should be taken seriously, but she did not share it; she knew exactly who he was, and exactly what he was capable of.

"Time grows short," said Dracula, his molten eyes staring directly into the camera. "To each and every one of you, I say this: prepare yourself for what is coming. Those who kneel before me will be spared. Those who do not will die. The time to choose has come. My rise is now at hand. This will be my final communication."

The video faded back to black. There was a long, pregnant pause, until two familiar words appeared, ghostly grey rising to glowing white.

HE RISES

ONE WEEK LATER

ZERO HOUR
PLUS 201 DAYS

23

EMPIRICAL EVIDENCE

"Eighty-two," said Paul Turner. "Eighty-two successful tests. That's incredible."

"Yes, sir," replied Professor Karlsson. "The reactions have continued to be violent, but the new precautions have prevented injury, and all eighty-two subjects show no trace of the vampire virus. They're cured, sir."

Turner stared at the two men standing in front of his desk. He understood the Lazarus Director's words, but he could still not fully accept their meaning; it felt somehow nebulous, as though if he let himself believe that what he had been told meant what it *should* mean, it would somehow all fall apart and drift away.

"Eighty-two," he said. "Eighty-two vampires cured."

"Yes, sir," said Matt Browning. "The process appears to be stable."

Turner took a deep breath. "Would you recommend it for public release?"

Browning frowned. Karlsson glanced over at him and shook his head.

"Absolutely not, sir," said the Professor. "Under normal circumstances, I would recommend at least a further year of double-blind testing, and that parallel testing be carried out in a minimum of four other laboratories around the world."

"But these are not normal circumstances," said Turner. "As you yourself have often said."

"True," said Karlsson. "And there have been precedents, although obviously not for anything exactly like this. There was an outbreak of the Ebola virus in West Africa not that long ago, and the World Health Organisation authorised the public release of an American drug that was still in its testing phase. But that decision was taken in the light of Ebola's high mortality rate, as the infected had literally nothing to lose. I don't know if the same could be argued in this case, sir."

"What about voluntary consent?" asked Turner. "If those who wanted the cure signed releases stating they understood the risks?"

Karlsson shrugged. "It's a possibility," he said. "But this is uncharted territory, sir, for all of us. I do know one thing, however. An application for a WHO exemption couldn't come from us. It would have to come from the government."

"Let me worry about that," said Turner. "How quickly can you give me a report on the tests you've carried out so far?"

"We're keeping a running report, sir," said Browning. "I can put a top sheet on it and have it to you in an hour."

Turner nodded. "Excellent," he said. "Truly excellent work, gentlemen. I can't overstate my gratitude to you both, and all of your team. Professor Karlsson, I need to talk to Lieutenant Browning for a few minutes, so you can consider yourself dismissed."

The Lazarus Director narrowed his eyes, but nodded and headed for the door. Turner watched him step through it, then faced Matt as soon as it was closed behind the Professor.

"Do I need to tell you what this is about, Lieutenant?" he asked.

Matt shook his head. "PROMETHEUS," he said.

"That's right," said Turner. "It's time."

"Why me, sir?"

Turner frowned. "Why you what?"

"Why is PROMETHEUS something you want *me* to work on, sir?" said Matt. "There are people more qualified, and far more senior. Especially for something so important."

"Lieutenant Browning, you're the only person who is both a member of the Lazarus Project and a serving Blacklight Operator," he said. "Which means you're perfectly placed to develop PROMETHEUS. Karlsson could handle the science, but he would not understand the military need. I could give it to Angela Darcy, or Jack Williams, but the science would mean less than nothing to them. And more importantly than all of that? I trust you, Matt. This needs to remain classified at the very highest level until we're ready to begin implementation, and I trust you to do what needs to be done. Is that good enough for you?"

Matt smiled. "I appreciate your faith in me, sir."

"I'm glad," said Turner. "Don't make me regret it."

"Who do you want me to use, sir? With Larissa gone, we're down to two options."

The Director shrugged. "Use whoever the results suggest will be best," he said. "The infirmary and the cells are full of cured vampires, more than enough for you to thoroughly test them both. Get started straight away, and don't mention a word of this to anyone but me. That includes Jamie Carpenter and Kate Randall, and even Natalia Lenski. Is that clear, Lieutenant?"

Matt frowned. "What am I supposed to tell Jamie, sir? He's going to want an explanation."

"Tell him whatever you want," said Turner. "As long as it isn't the truth. I want to see results no more than five minutes after you do, no matter how preliminary they might be. I want you to bring them to me in this room, in person. Is that understood?"

Matt's face was pale, but he nodded.

"Understood, sir," he said.

The Blacklight Director allowed himself a brief moment after Browning was gone in an attempt to let his mind catch up. Things were moving so quickly that it was becoming a struggle just to keep all the information in his head, let alone process it and arrive at conclusions.

Decades of fighting, he thought. *Hundreds of lives lost, thousands, in every dark corner of the world, and the answer to it all is a blue liquid in a plastic bag. I wonder what the founders would have made of* that.

He suspected that Abraham Van Helsing, who had carried out the first research into vampires and vampirism, would wholeheartedly approve. What Harker and Holmwood and the others would think, he couldn't begin to imagine; they had lived in a world in which antibiotics were a distant dream, let alone genetically engineered viruses that could rewrite the very building blocks of a human being.

Turner wished he could tell Henry Seward about the cure; he was sure it would hearten the former Director to know that the Lazarus Project, which he had founded, had succeeded so spectacularly. But he knew he couldn't; Henry was recovering well from the tortures he had suffered inside Château Dauncy, under the strict, watchful eye of his wife, Emma, but was no longer a member of Blacklight. His retirement had been agreed several months earlier, and with the end of his military career had come expiry of the security clearances required for any kind of access to the Department.

Turner leant back in his chair and closed his eyes, relishing the sensation of an emotion that was rare and unfamiliar.

Hope.

He savoured the moment, then opened his eyes and tapped rapidly on the keyboard of his terminal, launching the communications application on the wall screen. He selected NEW, scrolled down to the Prime Minister's name, and clicked CALL. The system applied its series of checks, encryptions and security measures; after what seemed like an eternity, the call began to ring. There was a click as the connection was established, and then the politician's voice echoed from the speakers set into the walls.

"Major Turner," said the Prime Minister. "This is a surprise. I wasn't expecting to hear from you until our regular call on Friday."

"Yes, sir," said Turner. "But I think you'll be pleased when you hear what I have to tell you. I'm calling with good news. Very good news, in fact."

"That makes a change," said the Prime Minister. "What is it?"

Turner took a deep breath. "I need you to apply to the World Health Organisation, sir. For special exemption to release a new drug into the population."

"Why would I want to do that?" asked the Prime Minister.

"I'll explain, sir," said Turner. "But I suggest you sit down first."

24

COLLATERAL DAMAGE (II)

WADDINGTON, LINCOLNSHIRE, ENGLAND

Janet Delacourte stood in her garden and watched the Sentry descend towards the runway that stood barely half a mile beyond her fence, the familiar pain beginning to build in her ears.

The Boeing E-3 was unmistakable, even without eyes as sharp as hers. It was huge and fat-bodied, lumbering through the air without the grace of many of the other planes she had watched come and go over the decades, and on its back spun its distinctive radar dome, a saucer as wide as the plane itself that allowed it to scan thousands of miles of earth and sky. Its running lights blazed, and Janet felt the air swirl around her as it was whipped and churned by the approaching aircraft. It touched down with a deafening screech and hurtled past her, its engines howling, but she watched with a smile on her face. Over the course of a long life that had proved disappointing in so many ways, she had always been able to rely on her planes.

And, in truth, the E-3s were far from the loudest she had known. RAF Waddington was now home to the Intelligence, Surveillance, Target Acquisition and Reconnaissance programme, flying heavy Sentinels and RC-135s that were every bit as noisy as the Sentrys, and unmanned Reaper drones that were ominously quiet. Even now, after so many years, it was rare for Janet to sleep through a take-off, but on several occasions she had seen a Reaper return that she knew she had not seen depart.

Always at night, she thought. *They always take off at night.*

During the Cold War, before the RAF had begun to scale back its bomber fleet, Waddington had been home to three squadrons of Vulcans, the huge delta-shaped planes that had carried Britain's nuclear deterrent into the stratosphere, ready to lay waste to the USSR if the order came. When *they* landed, and particularly when they took off, the noise had been so monstrous that Janet had often been left with blood running from her ears and a ringing in her head that lasted for hours. The Wellingtons and Lancasters that had headed east during the Second World War, their bellies heavy with bombs destined for the Ruhr and the Rhineland, had been quieter, although no less capable of causing pain; she had counted each one out and each one back, her heart aching when, all too often, the numbers didn't match.

At least you don't have to worry about that any more, she reminded herself. *If nothing else.*

The noise of the Sentry had faded away, and it was again quiet in the garden, although it was never truly silent. There was always the distant rumble of the vehicles on the base and the steady, relentless thud of the radar tower as it revolved, but Janet was so used to such sounds that she barely heard them; she looked no older than forty-five, but she had been living in the small house on the edge of Waddington for almost eighty years.

Janet flew back through her garden and into her kitchen. She stirred the saucepan of soup that was simmering on the stove, and poured herself a glass of wine as her supernatural hearing picked up the sound of an engine out on the road. When she had bought the house, cars had been the preserve of only the most well off, and the road that now ran through the woods towards Lincoln had been a rutted track that reached a dead end half a mile to the east. It was still far from being a main thoroughfare, but the cars that *did* come along it tended to be going much too fast, and were usually driven by teenagers. There were dozens of turnings in the woods where they parked up to drink and smoke with their friends, and do *other things* with their boyfriends and girlfriends, things that Janet did not remotely approve of. She was sure that the modern generation would consider her ancient and out of touch, but that was perfectly fine with her; she was, after all, more than a hundred and twenty years old.

She gave her soup another stir, and was raising her glass to her lips when the lights in her house went out.

Janet swore heartily; for a self-confessed prude, she possessed a remarkably colourful vocabulary, acquired in a munitions factory during the war. One of the downsides of her home's remoteness was the unreliability of its utilities; the electricity was unpredictable, to say the least, and she rarely went an entire winter without the drains blocking or her phone and television being cut off. She marched across the kitchen and pulled open the door that led down to her cellar. Bolted to the wall on the landing was the fuse box that had been installed ten years earlier; she had rewired the entire house after noticing that one of the plugs in the living room was sparking and fizzing behind plastic that was visibly melting.

None of the fuses appeared to have blown. She flipped the main breaker to OFF, then back to ON, but the house remained as dark and silent as a mortuary. Janet swore again, and flew to the front door. The overhead electricity wires wound up the road from Waddington village, and regularly got snarled in the branches that loomed out over the road from the trees on both sides.

Let's hope it's that, she thought, as she pulled on her coat. *As long as it's not the bloody substation again. Last time that blew it was a week before they got everything sorted.*

Janet opened the front door and looked up at the telegraph pole that stood at the edge of the road. There was nothing obviously wrong, and she sighed as she trudged down the path; she was going to have to walk the two miles to Waddington, checking it as she went. The last time she rang the electricity company to report a fault the audibly bored operator had questioned why she hadn't already done so, and she had no intention of giving them the chance to be snippy with her again.

She unlatched the gate and set off down the road. She walked briskly, her supernaturally powerful eyes raised towards the sky as she followed the electricity wires. As a result, she almost didn't notice the van parked in the lay-by at the crest of the hill.

Janet's first thought was to keep walking. A stationary vehicle was not an unusual sight in this part of the world, where the woods and back roads afforded people the kind of privacy that had become all too rare in the modern world, and she had learnt through bitter experience that people who parked in the darkness were usually not keen on being disturbed.

But something about the van made her pause. Its internal lights were on, and she could still feel the heat of its engine, which meant it had not been stopped for long, but she could hear neither voices nor the sounds that accompanied *other things* that might be happening inside the vehicle. She stared at the van for a long moment, then flew slowly across the lay-by and peered through the driver's side window. The key was in the ignition, but she had been right; there was nobody in the van.

It was empty.

Janet frowned. It made no sense; poaching was still prevalent in the woods, as was trapping, and badger baiting, but if whoever owned the van was intent on illegal activity, why would they leave the key in the ignition?

Somewhere to her left a branch snapped.

She turned, surprised by the heat that had risen behind her eyes. The woods were full of noise, particularly to ears as sensitive as hers, but the sound had been different from the usual rustling and whispering; it had sounded more solid, more deliberate.

It had sounded *heavy*.

Janet stood in the lay-by, her eyes glowing softly, her senses heightened, her heart accelerating, and made a decision. She would turn back, and sort out the electricity tomorrow. She would walk the road to Waddington as soon as the sun set, and not a minute before. Because all of a sudden, she just wanted to get home. She wanted to get home as quickly as possible.

Snap.

She froze. This one had been further away than the last, she was sure of it, but she had heard something else, something that was unmistakably not natural.

Out in the darkness of the woods, she had heard a muffled laugh.

Fire roared into Janet's eyes. She didn't know why she was suddenly scared; she was old, and strong, and she knew this part of the world better than anyone else alive. But the fear was there, and it was real; it twisted in her stomach like an eel. She backed slowly away from the van, which now seemed somehow malevolent, hulking and dark and out of place. The gravel beneath her feet gave way to the smooth surface of the road, and she turned back the way she had come, towards home.

Snap.

Janet leapt into the air and flew along the road, her eyes darting left and right, searching the dark trees for whoever was moving between them. She would never usually display her *condition* so publicly, but in that moment, she didn't care; she wanted to be safe in her kitchen, lighting candles and laughing at herself for being so easily spooked.

Her house loomed into view. Janet rose higher into the air and flew straight towards it, ignoring the gate and the wall and the path to the front door. She sped round the house, her heart pounding, and wrenched open the back door. She dived through it, and flung it shut behind her. Before it slammed into its frame, she heard a noise that sounded close, *so close*.

Snap.

Janet hauled open the drawer beside the stove, and pulled out a handful of thick candles. She struck a match and lit them; each one took several tries, as her hand was trembling. She could see perfectly well in the dark, but the pale yellow light of the candles calmed her, ever so slightly, as she took the phone down from its cradle on the wall. She lifted the handset to her ear, ready to call the police, knowing it was silly but not caring in the slightest.

Nothing.

The line was dead.

Janet stared at the phone, frozen where she stood. In the distance, she heard a Sentinel rumbling down towards the runway, but for once she paid the approaching plane no attention. She didn't know what was happening outside her house, but she was now horribly sure that she was at the centre of it.

Footsteps crunched quietly down the path outside her front door as another branch snapped, so close that it must surely have been inside her garden. And there was something else: a low hissing noise, like gas escaping from a split pipe. Janet stared at the kitchen window, paralysed by terror, in the candlelit gloom.

Snap.

The sound unleashed something inside Janet; anger exploded through her, burning away the fear that had gripped her, and she strode through the house, her eyes blazing.

This is ridiculous, she told herself. *Cowering in your own home like a child. You should be ashamed of yourself. You march right out there and you make whoever is doing this regret it.*

She threw the front door open, a growl rising from her throat. The roar of the Sentinel's engines was rising behind the house, partially deafening her as she strode out on to the path, her glowing eyes searching the darkness.

"Who's there?" she shouted. "This is private property! Get away or you'll be sorry!"

Nothing moved. Beyond the gate, the road and the woods were silent and still. The Sentinel was almost down, its engines screaming, its landing lights casting bright, artificial daylight across the house and its gardens.

"No?" she bellowed, her voice barely audible over the thunder of the landing plane. "Not willing to show yourselves? I thought as much!"

Janet turned back towards her house and felt her heart stop dead in her chest. The door had swung shut as she shouted at nothing, and there was something there, something white and dripping. She took a half-step towards it, the fire in her eyes fading, the Sentinel shaking the ground beneath her.

It was a wolf's head, crudely sprayed on to the door with white paint.

A black-gloved hand pressed something soft and damp over her mouth and nose. Janet's eyes flared red as panic and a pungent chemical smell filled her; she tried to move, to free herself, but her limbs felt like they were made of lead. Her mouth worked silently against the cloth, screaming for whoever was holding her to let her go, and her head swam as the plane screeched down on to the runway and thundered away into the distance.

Then her panic disappeared, drifting back into the darkness it had come from, and Janet was suddenly warm and calm and tired, more tired than she had ever been, so tired that she could no longer keep her eyes open.

THREE DAYS LATER

ZERO HOUR
PLUS 204 DAYS

25

A NEW DAY

Paul Turner stared at the wall screen opposite his desk, and felt for a brief moment like he was going to burst into tears.

The Blacklight Director could count on the fingers of one hand the times he had cried as an adult; the most recent, and by far the worst, occasion had been when he had carried the dead body of his son into the Loop after Valeri Rusmanov had murdered him. Those had been tears of agony, of insatiable grief, that had risen up from the very depths of his soul; what were threatening to appear in the corners of his eyes now were tears of almost unbearable relief.

The screen was tuned to the BBC News channel. BREAKING NEWS filled the bottom quarter of the screen as a bright red and white ticker crawled slowly above the headline, six words scrolling from right to left in endless repetition:

PRIME MINISTER ANNOUNCES VAMPIRE CURE, AMNESTY

The centre of the screen showed a shot of the Prime Minister, as sombre and handsome and sharply dressed as always, standing behind a lectern on Downing Street. In front of him, a tightly packed scrum of journalists jostled behind a rope barrier, waving microphones and voice recorders in the air.

"For those of you just joining us," said the disembodied voice of the presenter, "let's listen again to the statement made by the Prime Minister less than half an hour ago."

The sound switched to the excited clamour of the parliamentary press corps, as the Prime Minister gave them a nod and smiled briefly at them.

"Ladies and gentlemen," he said. "I am pleased to announce to the people of the United Kingdom, and to everyone listening around the world, that Her Majesty's government has today received an exemption from the World Health Organisation for the public release of an unprecedented drug treatment. The treatment, which was developed by the security department most commonly referred to as Blacklight, is a genetically engineered virus designed to reverse the effects of the condition known throughout the world as vampirism. I am pleased to announce that, so far, it has proven one hundred per cent effective."

There was an explosion of noise as the journalists surged forward against the rope line, bellowing a thousand questions at once.

"What I am announcing this morning," continued the Prime Minister, "is that, beginning tonight, this new treatment will be made available on a voluntary basis to any and all sufferers of vampirism. It will be distributed at a number of major hospitals throughout the United Kingdom, under the supervision of qualified physicians and the protection of Blacklight. The names and locations of these hospitals will be released shortly. Following meetings of the Cabinet and COBRA, and discussions with the Attorney General and the Home Secretary, I am also announcing a legal amnesty for all men and women who voluntarily receive this treatment, covering any and all crimes committed while suffering the effects of the vampire virus. This amnesty has received cross-party backing in both houses of Parliament, and will provide a clean slate for those afflicted by this terrible condition, and a new beginning for us all. This is a momentous day."

The news channel cut back to the studio, where the presenter was staring into the camera with an expression of professional solemnity.

"We're going to leave Downing Street now and get some live reaction to this remarkable announcement," he said. "In the studio with me are—"

Turner muted the screen. He knew that footage of the statement would be playing endlessly on every TV channel in the world, and he wondered what reaction it was causing in the homes of vampires, in the halls of power, and in the canteen and Briefing Rooms of his own Department. If nothing else, it had, at least temporarily, put an end to the coverage of Dracula's second video, which was a great relief. He had been given the heads-up by the Prime Minister barely five minutes before the announcement was made; the message had been short, and to the point.

Turn a TV On And Pat Yourself
On The Back.

He had forwarded the message to Robert Karlsson and Matt Browning, then settled down to watch the world change forever.

A tone rang out as a comms window opened up on the screen. Turner read the name of the caller, smiled, and clicked ACCEPT.

"Good morning, Prime Minister," he said. "And well done, if you don't mind me saying so."

"Thank you, Major," said the politician. "The credit belongs entirely to you and your Department."

"How hard did you have to fight for the amnesty?" asked Turner. He had recommended it to the politician the morning after bringing him up to speed on the cure – it had been *the* key strategic recommendation of both the Security and Intelligence Divisions – and he was delighted to see it announced; he had not been at all confident that it would be.

"Quite hard," said the Prime Minister. "There was some… resistance, shall we say, from certain quarters."

"I can imagine, sir," said Turner.

"It was the right thing to do, though," said the Prime Minster. "This has been a very good day, Major Turner, for the entire country. For the entire *world*, no less. Now we need to get to work."

"Yes, sir," said Turner. "What do you need from me?"

"I'm going to be relying on your Operators to provide security at the hospitals," said the Prime Minister. "Can I count on your help?"

"Of course," said Turner.

"Good. We should have the location list within the hour."

"I'll have a plan drawn up as soon as I see it, sir."

There was a long silence.

"This really is an incredible achievement, Major," said the Prime Minister, eventually. "Your scientists have done a remarkable thing, and the people of this country are going to be immensely grateful to you all."

"Thank you, sir," he said. "I'll make sure the Lazarus staff know that."

"Good," said the Prime Minister. "Thank you, Major. I'll be in touch later today."

"Goodbye, sir."

"Goodbye."

There was a loud click as the connection was cut. For almost a minute, Paul Turner didn't move; his mind had been overwhelmed by a wave of emotions that had become unfamiliar in recent months and years.

Pride. Satisfaction. Optimism.

Happiness.

26

RAPID REACTIONS

Jamie stared through the window in the infirmary door with a lump in his throat and familiar anger in his stomach.

He knew that taking the cure had been his mother's choice, and he knew it was not one she would have made lightly, but the sight of her lying in a hospital bed still hurt his heart. The anger churning through him was due to another decision that had been made: to place the infirmary off-limits to everyone apart from the medical staff and members of the Lazarus Project. He understood the reasoning, but it was nonetheless a source of great frustration; when he had reached the long white room after his awful confrontation with Matt in the Lazarus laboratory, his mother had been sleeping off the surgery to repair her broken arm, and by the time he had tried to see her the next morning, the new order had been given. As a result, he had not been able to see her since she had been cured, more than a week ago.

The infirmary was now almost fully occupied by recipients of the cure, men and women sleeping and chatting in low voices. A great many more vampires had already recovered and been returned to the cells on Level H; a dozen or so had even been released from the Loop entirely, free to resume their normal lives with all trace of the supernatural gone. Those men and women had received their treatments *after* the first trial, when the doctors had known what to expect and had started administering the cure in thickly padded rooms, like the isolation areas in a secure hospital. None had suffered anything more than a pounding headache when they woke up.

Which is great for them, thought Jamie. *It doesn't help her, though. Doesn't help my mum.*

Through the small window, he could see the purple ridges beneath her eyes, the results of a nose so badly broken it had needed splinting, and the harness suspending her arm, which had been coated from shoulder to wrist in plaster. Jamie considered it a miracle, having read the report of her reaction to the cure, that she had not broken her neck or fractured her skull.

In barely thirty minutes, he – along with every single other member of the Department – was due in the Ops Room for a briefing by the Director. He knew there was nothing to be gained by standing helplessly outside the infirmary, that they were not going to suddenly change the rules and allow him in to talk to his mother, but he was still reluctant to leave. Because he *needed* to talk to her; to ask her why she had done what she did, why she had taken such an enormous risk.

I never knew how unhappy she was, he thought. *How much she hated being a vampire. I mean, I knew, but I never really knew. Because I didn't want to hear it. I had my own problems, and they were all so huge and important and she was safe down there in her cell so I just assumed she was OK because that made it easier for me.*

I let her down so badly.

Jamie stared at his mother, wishing he could tell her the two things that suddenly seemed like the most important in the world.

That he loved her.

And that he was sorry.

* * *

Pete Randall knocked on Greg Browning's office door and pushed it open.

"Are you watching this?" he asked. "It's crazy."

Greg nodded, his eyes fixed on the TV in the corner of the room. "I'm watching. The Prime Minister looks very pleased with himself."

"Are you surprised?"

His friend shrugged. "I suppose not," he said. "Probably too much to expect a politician to show a bit of humility."

"We need to call a meeting, Greg," said Pete. "We need to start working out what we're going to do about this."

Greg tore his eyes away from the screen and looked at him. "What are you talking about?"

"We need to amend the call guidelines, for a start," said Pete. "Give the hospital list to the operators so they can pass it on to the vamps who ask about the cure. And we should get a press release out, saying that we're ready to assist distribution of the cure in any way we can."

"Why would we do any of that, mate?"

He frowned. "Why *wouldn't* we?"

"This organisation was founded to help the victims of the supernatural," said Greg. "Right from the start, we said that would include vampires who are victims themselves. And you think the best way to do that is for us to announce that we think they're nothing more than a disease that needs curing?"

"Of course not," said Pete. "But like you said, most vampires are victims themselves. They never wanted to be turned. This gives them a chance to undo it."

"And help Blacklight in the process," said Greg. "Is that what you want? To do their dirty work for them?"

"This has nothing to do with Blacklight," said Pete. "This is about helping people, which is exactly what we founded SSL to do."

"I disagree, mate," said Greg. "But it doesn't really matter, in any case. The board has already told me there are to be no changes to policy or procedures."

Pete frowned. "You talked to the board without me?"

"I'm sorry," said Greg. "I didn't realise I needed your permission. I'll make sure I ask you next time."

Pete narrowed his eyes. "What's going on here, Greg? Why are you being like this?"

Colour rose into Greg's face. "Nothing's going on, mate," he said. "You suggested something, I disagreed, and so did the board. It doesn't have to be a big deal, but for right now, I'm done talking about this."

"This is the biggest thing that has—"

Greg slammed his hand down on the surface of his desk. His eyes were suddenly blazing, and Pete belatedly realised that his friend was absolutely furious.

"Didn't you hear me?" asked Greg, his voice low. "I'm done talking about this. So unless there's anything else, I suggest you go and do some work."

Pete stared at Greg, a deep frown on his face. Every other member of SSL had reacted to the announcement of the cure like it was Christmas come early, especially after the fear and panic the second Dracula video had caused.

It makes no sense, he thought. *Why is he acting like this?*

"Actually, there is something else," he said, hearing the icy chill in his own voice. "I finished my review of the call logs."

"And?"

"I found another Night Stalker victim."

"What are you talking about?" asked Greg.

"The old woman who got killed in Waddington last week," said Pete. "She was a regular. Eight calls in five weeks, the last one two days before she died."

"I'm not surprised," said Greg, the colour in his face fading slightly. "We're getting almost ten thousand calls a week now. I reckon every vamp in the country has probably rung us at least once."

"Probably," said Pete. "I just thought you'd want to know."

Julian Carpenter sat in the garden of his mother's cottage, listening to the BBC on an old portable radio. The Prime Minister's announcement was being replayed at fifteen-minute intervals, and a fierce debate was already underway in the television and radio studios of the country; the phone-in he was listening to was rapidly descending into a cacophony of shouted insults and threats.

One of the loudest voices belonged to a man who was furious not at the cure itself, but at the amnesty that had been announced alongside it; he was bellowing that his brother had been killed by a vampire, and that the government was now officially letting his murderer off the hook. One of the other callers *was* a vampire, and was trying to simultaneously sympathise with the man and explain that, without the incentive of the amnesty, the strength of the anti-vampire feeling surging through the country would mean that many vampires who desperately wanted the cure would be too scared to come forward. An Oxford philosophy professor was trying, largely unsuccessfully, to get a word in, and was arguing that the very existence of the cure was a human rights violation, an admission by the government that they viewed the vampire population of the United Kingdom as a disease that needed wiping out. In the midst of it all, the DJ was desperately trying to regain some semblance of control of the conversation.

Julian didn't care about the wider impact of a cure; he was pleased at the prospect of fewer vampires in the world and, although he empathised with the point the increasingly angry caller was making, he could also understand the reasons for issuing an amnesty.

What he *did* care about was what the cure meant for his family.

It was possible that his wife loved being a vampire. He doubted it, but the sad truth was that he simply didn't *know*; given what she had been through in the years since he had seen her, it was unrealistic to assume that the woman living in a cell in the bowels of the Loop was the same woman he had slept beside for two decades. But, either way, his greatest fear, that his wife was trapped in a nightmare from which she could never escape, had now been quashed; if she wanted to be cured, and he hoped with all his heart that she *did*, she was now in the best possible place for that to happen.

And so is Jamie, he thought. *Although he might think being a vampire is brilliant, for all I know.*

Julian tried not to think about what the future might hold for his wife and son; if he dwelt on the impotent reality of the situation he found himself in, his guilt quickly became unbearable. But the Prime Minister's statement had given him hope that his family might be able to change their situation, even if he wasn't able to do anything to help them himself.

He glanced at the tracking chip he had cut out of his arm so many months ago.

For now, at least.

Larissa Kinley perched on a stool in the kitchen of Haven's big house, watching the analysis of the discovery of the cure. Similar statements had now been issued by the governments of the United States, France, China, Germany, Brazil, Russia and more than a dozen others, although none of them had been able to match the Prime Minister's for sheer jaw-dropping impact.

It was almost four in the morning, but she, along with the majority of the residents of Haven, was still awake. She had been about to go to bed when the Prime Minister walked out into Downing Street, but sleep was now the furthest thing from her mind. It had been difficult to comprehend the sheer magnitude of the announcement, and for a community of vampires that had shunned the wider world in favour of peaceful isolation, it raised a number of questions that they were not going to find easy to answer. Larissa knew it would only be a matter of time until people started asking each other whether they were going to take the cure, and she wouldn't be able to blame them; it was the biggest thing to happen to the realm of the supernatural since Dracula had first been turned, more than five centuries earlier.

As the news coverage droned endlessly on and on, Larissa felt as uncertain as she had in the final weeks before she left Blacklight and began the process of founding Haven. The inner peace that the community had provided her with was gone, replaced by concern for the future and the realisation that she too had a decision to make.

If anyone had asked her seven months earlier whether she would be interested in taking a cure for vampirism, she would have answered yes without a moment's hesitation; she had said as much to Jamie and her friends on a number of occasions, and had not been lying to them.

Now, though? She was no longer sure.

During her years with Alexandru – and even after she joined Blacklight – her vampirism had been a miserable, isolating condition, one that filled her with shame and singled her out from her friends and colleagues. At Haven, surrounded by people who were the same as her – *biologically*, at least – it was different; she no longer saw herself as a freak, as something to be distrusted and whispered about. At Haven, she felt accepted, and welcomed, and she wasn't remotely sure she wanted that to change.

"Still awake?" said Callum, from behind her.

She turned, and smiled at the Texan vampire. "Still awake," she said. "There's coffee in the pot."

Callum nodded. Larissa returned her attention to the TV as he lifted a mug from the drying rack beside the sink and poured coffee and cream into it.

"This is crazy," she said. "Half the countries in the world have announced they're going to distribute the cure."

"Hardly surprising," said Callum. "This is the first bit of good news they've had in a long time. Can't blame them for making the most of it."

"The Prime Minister is making a *big* deal about it being developed by Blacklight. You would think he'd been putting in shifts in the Lazarus Project labs himself."

"Now *that* is crazy."

"The Prime Minister trying to take all the credit?"

Callum shook his head. "That your friend Matt is probably at least partly responsible for all this."

Larissa smiled widely. "If I know Matt," she said, "there won't be any 'partly' about it."

He nodded, and took a sip of his coffee. "You need a top-up?"

"I'm good," she said. "Have you thought about what you're going to do, Callum?"

"Can't think about anything else," he said. "You?"

"The same."

Callum put his mug down and looked at her. "And?"

Larissa shook her head. "I have absolutely no idea."

As he sat down beside Professor Karlsson in the Ops Room, Matt Browning reached the conclusion that he was more tired than he had ever been.

He doubted he had slept for more than two uninterrupted hours at any point in the last week; his brain felt as thick and slow as treacle, and his body trembled constantly from a combined excess of caffeine and adrenaline. The Lazarus Project, which was hardly a relaxed environment at the best of times, had shifted into overdrive, a relentless regime of testing and reporting and observing and checking and double and triple-checking. Matt, who was usually glad his work got him out of all but the most vital meetings, had been genuinely relieved when the order to attend the mandatory briefing that was about to begin had come through; for at least a few minutes, he could allow his brain to stop churning and ignore the relentless voice inside his head that told him he could, and *should*, be working.

He glanced round at his boss, who gave him a small, tired smile. Matt returned it, and realised how much he envied Karlsson, and the rest of his Lazarus colleagues. They were killing themselves to finalise and produce the cure they had been gathered together to find, but none of them were dealing with the extra pressure that he was, pressure that could be summed up by a single word he had already come to hate.

PROMETHEUS.

The project's origin lay in a throwaway remark he had made during a conversation with Cal Holmwood almost a year earlier, a conversation that he had been forbidden to discuss with anyone else at the time, and then forbidden from doing so again by Paul Turner after he had been promoted to Director and inherited his predecessor's notes. Since then, there had been three short meetings, in which the hypothetical details of PROMETHEUS had been hammered out, details which had made Matt increasingly uneasy. He had been able to console himself with the knowledge that the concept was unfeasible until the day came that there was a workable, reliable cure for vampirism.

Now, that day had arrived.

There was a rush of whispered voices as the Director strode through the door and up on to the low stage at the front of the Ops Room. He looked out over the massed ranks of the Department, his gaze settling momentarily on Matt, then called for attention. Instantly, the room fell silent.

"Ladies and gentlemen," said Turner. "I am assuming that you all know what this briefing is about, so I'll get straight to the point. For the last year, the Loop has been home to a handpicked team of the finest scientific minds on the planet, working together on what has been codenamed the Lazarus Project. I am aware that the project and its staff have been the subject of a great amount of speculation, the result of the strict conditions of secrecy in which they have been operating. As you will no doubt have inferred from the Prime Minister's announcement, they were gathered together with a single goal, to find a cure for the condition that we know as vampirism, and I am delighted to confirm that they have succeeded in their task."

A low murmur of excitement rippled through the Ops Room, and Matt jumped in his seat as a number of hands clapped him on the back; he turned round to see Operators he didn't know grinning at him.

"Before I go into what this means for the Department," said Turner, "and for the world outside, I would ask each and every member of the Lazarus Project to stand up."

Oh God, thought Matt.

Professor Karlsson immediately did as the Director had asked. Matt turned in his seat, saw the rest of his colleagues getting nervously to their feet, and realised he had no choice but to join them. Slowly, his cheeks burning with sudden heat, he stood up and glanced over to where Natalia was also standing, her face a bright shade of pink, a wide, embarrassed smile on her face.

"Men and women of the Lazarus Project," continued Turner. "What you have done is nothing short of miraculous, and everyone in this room, *every single person on this entire planet*, will be forever in your debt. My profound thanks to each and every one of you."

The applause that exploded through the crowded room was deafening, punctuated by shouts and cheers as the entire Department rose to their feet, clapping and yelling and grinning. The members of the Lazarus Project were swallowed up by the crowd, and as Matt's hand was pumped up and down, as praise filled his ears and he was jostled back and forth by the gloved hands of dozens of strangers, he was able, just for a moment, to almost forget about PROMETHEUS.

Almost.

27

PROMETHEUS

Matt scanned the crowd as the men and women of Blacklight filed towards the Ops Room door.

Paul Turner was standing in front of the stage, talking to James Van Thal and Dominique Saint-Jacques; the Director was smiling slightly, the result, Matt suspected, of having given his first briefing in a long time that had not made the majority of the audience want to kill themselves. On the other side of the room, he saw Natalia walking side by side with Kate Randall, and felt a surge of warmth in his stomach as he dragged his gaze away and continued his search for Jamie Carpenter. Matt had seen his friend when he had been ordered to his feet by the Director, smiling proudly at him from maybe ten rows back, but now he couldn't locate him; he was about to conclude that Jamie had already left the room, when a voice spoke into his ear.

"Hey."

Matt jumped, and whirled round. Jamie was standing in front of him, his face tight with worry, his skin pale.

"Jesus," said Matt. "Do you forget how quiet you are or do you just like sneaking up on people?"

"Sorry," said Jamie. "Can we talk?"

Matt nodded. "I was looking for you to suggest the same thing," he said. "Let's go to my quarters."

"All right," said Jamie, and forced a tiny smile. "Lead the way."

Matt closed the door of his quarters as Jamie sat down in the chair beside his desk. He opened his mouth to speak, but his friend beat him to it.

"I'm so sorry, Matt," he said. "About what happened in the lab. I should have known you would never do anything to hurt my mother. I just wasn't thinking straight."

Matt smiled. "It's all right," he said. "No harm done."

"It's *not* all right," said Jamie, fiercely. "Stop being so good about this. Shout at me, or call me a dick, or *something*. I deserve it."

Matt shrugged. "What good would that do?"

"It might make you feel better."

"Would it?" he asked. "Or would it just make *you* feel better?"

Jamie stared at him for a long moment, then grunted with laughter and looked down at the floor. "You're so bloody clever," he said. "You can see right through me, can't you?"

"What I can see is that you're having a hard time and you made a mistake and you want to beat yourself up for it," said Matt. "I can't stop you if that's what you want to do, but I don't think it's healthy, and I don't think it'll help. So I'm sorry if you need me to be angry with you, because I'm not. I don't have time to be."

Jamie raised his head. "There are people inside this Department who think I'm arrogant," he said, and smiled. "That I think I belong at the centre of everything. Were you aware of that?"

Matt smiled. "I may have heard a comment or two along those lines."

"Just one or two?"

"Maybe half a dozen," he said. "At the very most."

"Right," said Jamie, his smile widening. "I can see their point, in all honesty. The last couple of years have been defining ones for the Department, and for better or worse, whether by design or blind luck, I've been in the middle of most of it. Would you say that was fair?"

"I would," said Matt. "So what are you saying?"

"I'm saying that, for a while, I started to think I was the hero. It's embarrassing to say out loud, but I really thought everything depended on me, that whether or not we won or lost was always going to come down to me. But I was wrong. *You're* the hero, Matt."

He frowned. "What are you talking about, Jamie?"

"All the vampires that me and the other Operators have destroyed, all the fighting and chasing and all the people who've died. What has any of it really achieved? Valeri and Alexandru are dead, and that's good, that's genuinely, objectively good. But we didn't stop Dracula rising and now we can't even find him. We can't stop the country tearing itself apart, can't stop the awful things people are doing to each other. But a cure? This bloody miracle that you and Natalia and Karlsson and the rest of Lazarus have come up with? It saves lives, and it gives people back what they lost. It might even give us a chance to stop Dracula. It changes *everything*, and I'm so proud of you I barely know where to start."

Matt stared at his friend. A lump had risen suddenly in his throat, and he found himself incapable of forming a reply.

"My mother got what she wanted more than anything because of you," continued Jamie. "She hated being a vampire, so much more than I ever wanted to hear, and now she doesn't have to be one any more. The same goes for the couple I brought in last week, for everyone recovering in the infirmary right now, and for thousands of people around the world. Every single one of them gets a second chance. Do you understand what you've done, mate? I mean, do you really, truly understand the magnitude of it?"

"I get it," said Matt, his voice low. "Thank you. That means a lot."

His friend fixed him with a fierce smile. "You deserve it. You all do."

Matt leant back against his door; if the lump in his throat grew any larger, he feared he would not be able to breathe.

"Are we OK?" said Jamie. "I know you said you're not angry with me, but you need to know that it's all right if you are. What I did was unforgivable."

"We're OK," he said. "Honestly. Do I wish you hadn't done what you did? Yeah. I do. Was I angry with you afterwards? I was *furious*, and I'm not going to pretend I wasn't. But I knew, even while it was happening, that it wasn't really you, that you weren't in control of yourself. You hurt me, and you scared me, and it's important to me that you understand that. But it's done. Let's move on, all right?"

Jamie nodded. "All right."

Matt paused as a thought occurred to him, one that had been driven from his mind by his friend's outpouring; he walked across his quarters and dug through the piles of files and boxes that covered both the surface of his desk and a significant amount of the surrounding floor. He found what he was looking for, a white plastic box, and carried it over to his bed.

"What's that?" asked Jamie.

"This is why I was looking for you," he said. "It's a swab kit. I need to take a sample from you."

Jamie frowned. "A sample of what? Blood?"

Matt shook his head. "We're moving into a new research phase, and it's really hard to get reliable histories from vampires. Most don't know who turned them, and even if they do, they don't tend to know anything more about them. But *your* vampire history is clear, and it involves probably only the second vampire that ever existed. I need a sample of the plasma on your fangs, so we can start trying to draw some conclusions. Is that all right?"

Jamie nodded. "Of course," he said. "Whatever you need."

Matt smiled, outwardly at least. He didn't like lying to his friend, especially given the exceptionally kind things that Jamie had just said about him, but it was the only option; there was simply no way he could tell his friend the truth. He opened the kit, took out a small glass jar and a plastic scraper, and looked at Jamie.

"Thank you," he said. "This is probably going to feel a bit weird, but it'll be over quickly. Can you open your mouth and bring your fangs out?"

"OK," said Jamie. "Be careful, though. They're sharp, and a single drop is all it takes. I know we've got a cure now, but take it from me, you don't want to go through the turn unless it's absolutely necessary."

Believe me, thought Matt. *I understand that all too well.*

"I'll be careful," he said.

Jamie nodded. He didn't look completely convinced, but he tilted his head back and opened his mouth. As Matt leant in, fangs slid down from his friend's gums; they gleamed under the fluorescent ceiling light, as a faint flicker of red appeared in the corners of Jamie's eyes.

Working very slowly, Matt raised the glass jar and positioned it underneath the left fang, resting it against Jamie's lower lip. He drew the scraper gently down the tooth, pushing clear plasma towards the point until it dripped into the glass jar. He moved across to the other fang, and thirty seconds later, it was done; he withdrew the jar, dropped the scraper into it, and screwed its lid on tight as Jamie closed his mouth and rubbed his jaw.

"All done?"

"Done," said Matt. "Thanks. Sorry if that was unpleasant."

"You were right, it felt a bit weird," said Jamie. "But it's fine."

"I appreciate it," he said. "It should be very helpful."

Jamie smiled, and got to his feet. "Cool," he said. "What are you up to for the rest of the day? I assume you're going back to work?"

"I'm heading down to the labs now," lied Matt. "What about you?"

"Nothing for a few hours," said Jamie. "Then Patrol Respond."

"Good," he said. "Keep those test subjects coming."

Jamie smiled. "We'll do our best. It's been good to see you, Matt. I know we always say it, but we really don't see each other often enough. We need to try harder."

"I know," he said. "We really do."

Jamie stepped forward and gave him a brief, tight hug. Matt hugged him back, a smile rising on to his face, until his friend released his grip and walked out of the room. Matt waited two slow minutes, then followed him through the door and headed down the corridor towards the lift.

As he stepped through the open metal doors, his hand moved automatically towards the button marked F, the floor that was home to the Lazarus Project and where he had told Jamie he would be going. He paused, then pressed H and leant against the wall, his momentary good mood drifting rapidly away, replaced by an uneasiness that made his stomach squirm.

"Mr Browning," said Valentin, a broad smile on his face. "How lovely. Do come in."

Matt nodded, and walked slowly through the ultraviolet barrier. He did not like voluntarily entering Valentin's cell; he would happily admit, to anyone who asked, that the ancient vampire scared him, cure or no cure.

After all, he thought, as he crossed the cell and sat down in one of the plastic chairs. *There's no cure for having my head ripped off.*

"Tea?" asked Valentin. The vampire was floating a few centimetres off the ground, his mouth curved into a smile that Matt thought looked more hungry than friendly.

"No thanks," he said.

Valentin nodded. "No time for pleasantries," he said. "Understood. Let's get down to business then. What can I do for you?"

Matt took a deep breath. "You know that we've developed a cure for vampirism," he said. "For the second phase of the research, we need to analyse samples from older vampires, those that are the most powerful, so that we can try to reduce the formula's physical effects. I'm here on behalf of the Director to ask you to give us a sample of the plasma from your fangs, so that we can include it in the research. I've been ordered to tell you that it would be highly appreciated."

Valentin stared at him for a long moment, then burst out laughing; he rocked back and forth in the air, his hands holding his stomach, as pink light spilled into his eyes. Matt felt embarrassed heat rise into his face, as anger bloomed in his gut.

"What's so funny?" he asked.

"Oh, my dear Mr Browning," said Valentin, smiling gently at him. "I am sorry. That was unforgivably rude of me. But you just looked so very earnest and your little speech is so well practised that I'm afraid I could not help but laugh, despite the insult."

Matt frowned. "What insult?"

"The fact that you clearly believe I am extremely stupid."

"I don't understand."

"Your story is eminently plausible, Mr Browning," said Valentin. "And were we not having this conversation inside a secret military installation, I might have been inclined to believe it. But I have been waiting for somebody to come to me with this request since I first heard about the discovery of a cure. I know exactly what you are doing, Mr Browning, because, in all honesty, it would be ridiculous if you weren't."

"What am I doing?" asked Matt. "Since you apparently know everything?"

"You are planning to turn your Operator colleagues into vampires," said Valentin. "You have a cure, which means you can return them to normal after the battle with Dracula is fought, and an army of vampires will help you even the odds. But you want them to be as powerful as possible, and Miss Kinley's departure leaves you only two realistic options. So you intend to test Mr Carpenter and myself, to see whose version of the vampire virus will be more effective in terms of creating supernatural Operators. Am I broadly correct?"

Matt stared, his eyes wide. "Did someone talk to you?" he said. "You have to tell me if they did. This is beyond classified."

Valentin frowned, then shook his head. "Nobody talked to me, Mr Browning," he said. "I worked it out all on my own, remarkably enough."

"Then how did you know?" asked Matt. He could hear something close to panic in his voice. "How?"

"Because I would do exactly the same thing in your position," said Valentin. "I was a General for a great many years, Mr Browning. I led thousands of men into more battles than you can imagine, and I have forgotten more about military strategy and tactics than anyone in this building will ever know. It would be irresponsible for you not to at least try and use the discovery of a cure to your advantage."

"So you'll help us?" asked Matt.

Valentin smiled. "I will help you by saving you a great deal of time huddled over test tubes and computers. Jamie is powerful, remarkably so for one so young, and his strength and speed will only increase as the years pass, but I was turned more than five hundred years ago. There are only two men left on earth who could produce vampires more powerful than me, and I doubt either of them will be inclined to help you."

Dracula and the first victim, thought Matt. *He's right about that.*

"So that answers your question, Mr Browning," continued Valentin. "And leads us to another, which is far more important. The question of whether I am inclined to assist you."

Matt frowned. "Why wouldn't you?" he asked. "You clearly see the strategic value of what we're doing, and I know you don't want to see Dracula victorious. So what would it gain you not to help us?"

"What will it gain me if I do?" asked Valentin, his smile wide and shark-like.

"I don't have the authority to offer you anything," said Matt. "I'll have to talk to the Director."

"Of course you will," said the vampire. "And I am sure he will give you a list of trinkets and favours to tempt me with, so let me spare your legs the back and forth. I *will* help you, but my conditions for doing so are not open for negotiation. This is a take-it-or-leave-it offer, Mr Browning. Is that clear?"

Matt nodded. "I understand," he said. "Tell me what you want."

"I will not let you scrape the liquid from my fangs like a snake being milked for its venom," said Valentin. "I can think of nothing less dignified. I will turn as many of your Operators as you wish, but only if I am allowed to bite them myself. It has been far too long since I tasted human blood, so this will work out well for everyone."

Ice crackled up Matt's spine. The vampire's voice had deepened and thickened, and his easy-going charm was gone, replaced by a cruel, animal hunger.

"There's no way," he said, his voice trembling, "that the Director is going to agree to that."

Valentin smiled. "Then nothing will have been lost, Mr Browning," he said, his voice once again warm and friendly. "But I believe Major Turner possesses a far greater capacity to surprise than you might think."

28

CLOSE ENOUGH TO TOUCH

NOTTINGHAM, NOTTINGHAMSHIRE, ENGLAND
TEN HOURS LATER

Jamie stared down at the bloody puddle, cold fury burning in his chest. The white paint that had been sprayed over the remains had bled pink at its edges, but was still wet; he guessed it was no more than five minutes old.

"It is the same," said Qiang. "Night Stalkers."

Jamie nodded, his mind pulsing with a single thought.

Too late.

The Surveillance alert that had brought them to this bleak industrial estate on the outskirts of Nottingham had been the first of their Patrol Respond; it had appeared on their van's screen when they were twenty miles away, barely inside their allocated grid, and despite the heroic efforts of their driver, they had evidently not managed to cover the distance quickly enough.

A 999 call had been made by a security guard patrolling the roof of the warehouse that now rose above them, a giant red-brick cube plastered with signs warning would-be intruders of 24-HOUR CCTV MONITORING and GUARD DOGS ON PATROL. The man had seen a dark van pull into the vacant lot below, and three black-clad figures drag the limp shape of an elderly man out on to the cracked tarmac; he had rung the police as soon as he realised what he was witnessing.

Jamie looked around. There was no sign of the security guard, despite the amplified requests they had made for him to show himself; he had likely fled what had now become a murder scene. Ellison and Qiang were beside him, their visors raised, their faces pale; the three Operators had seen more horror than most, but there was something about the Night Stalker attacks that turned their stomachs. Jamie believed it was the calculated viciousness of the killings; traces of a powerful veterinary sedative had been found in the remains of every Night Stalker victim, and he had seen with his own eyes how the vampires met their end, executed in cold blood, on their knees and utterly helpless.

Five minutes, he thought. *Five miles if they were doing sixty. Probably half that, at most.*

Ellison looked at him. "What do you want—"

"Stay here," interrupted Jamie. "I need to check something."

She frowned. "Stay here? Where are you going?"

Jamie didn't answer; his feet left the ground and he rocketed directly upwards, leaving his squad mates far below. A bank of grey cloud hung above him, filling the sky for dozens of miles in every direction; he stopped before he reached it, and floated easily in the cold night air. The urban sprawl of Nottingham stretched out below, taller and brighter in the town centre to the west, but dark and quiet directly beneath him; the men and women who worked in the warehouses and factories that filled this corner of the city were long gone.

He scanned the dark landscape, searching for the rumble of a van engine or the red pinpricks of brake lights. He could hear the distant hissing and screeching as a pair of cats faced off, and the steady bass percussion rising from an underground nightclub. He stretched his senses to their limits, feeling the pressure build in his head, and heard something.

It was faint, and getting fainter, but it was there.

An engine.

He squinted in the direction of the sound, scanning the maze of narrow streets for movement. For long, painful seconds, he saw nothing; then, at the furthest reach of his supernatural eyesight, a black shape moved across an intersection, little more than a mobile section of darkness.

Without taking his eyes off the van – if that was even what it was – Jamie spun in the air and rocketed towards it. The wind howled around him and the cold chilled his bones as he raced forward; without the protection of his visor, his eyes would have been streaming with tears. As he soared above the flat rooftops and empty car parks, he twisted the comms dial on his belt and opened a line to his squad mates.

"I see the van!" he shouted. "Follow my locator signal! Fast as you can!"

"We're moving," replied Ellison. "We've got you."

Jamie left the line open, swooped lower, and felt a wave of savage excitement roll through him. Moving slowly along an access road below him, in what he guessed was an attempt to avoid drawing attention to itself, was a dark van.

I can see you, he thought.

He scanned the surrounding area and dropped lower. No more than two miles ahead, the access road merged on to a busy local thoroughfare, and beyond *that* his supernaturally sharp eyes picked out the wide illuminated lanes of a motorway.

Have to get them before they reach it.

Behind him, he heard the rumble of a second engine. He rotated in the air, and saw the van containing his squad mates hurtle round a corner and accelerate along the road beneath him. It was gaining quickly on the target vehicle, but, as he turned back, he realised that its driver had seen the new arrival too. Jamie swore heavily. He should have anticipated that, should have ordered his squad to centre on his position without using the main access road, but it was too late for that now; the Night Stalkers' van had leapt forward and was racing towards the distant intersection.

Jamie hung in the air, momentarily unsure of what to do. Then an idea came to him, one that would not be found in any of Blacklight's tactical instruction manuals, and he burst forward again, grinning behind his visor. He accelerated, descending towards the road that was now little more than a blur beneath him. The van was directly ahead, its brake lights acting like a homing beacon, its engine howling.

He pushed himself to fly even faster, and drew alongside the vehicle. The van's driver, his face hidden by a balaclava, glanced out of the window and saw him; their eyes locked for the briefest of moments, before Jamie hurled himself sideways and slammed into the metal side of the van.

The impact was agonising; it drove the air out of him as pain exploded through his head. He flipped up and over, his limbs flailing out of control, as the van tilted on to two wheels then crashed on its side with a shower of sparks and a deafening screech of metal, and as he hurtled helplessly towards a brick wall that looked horribly solid, Jamie's reeling mind formed a single thought.

This might not have been such a brilliant idea.

Jamie opened his eyes and saw Ellison and Qiang standing over him, a combination of concern and anger on their faces.

He lifted his head, felt a nauseating bolt of pain race up the back of his neck, and looked down at himself; he was lying at the base of the brick wall, his legs splayed, his shoulders flat on the pavement. One of his arms was folded beneath him, but the other...

Jamie's head swam. His right arm was broken at the elbow, snapped almost all the way back on itself. He felt no pain, but knew it was only a matter of time until it arrived. His arm looked so violently *wrong* that he felt his gorge rise, and he fought back the urge to vomit.

"Don't move," said Ellison.

She crouched down beside him and tipped blood into his mouth from a plastic bottle. He swallowed the liquid hungrily, feeling the pain and disorientation disappear as heat bloomed behind his eyes, and watched with horrified fascination as his arm slowly un-broke: it folded out until it was straight, then the angular points of shattered bone beneath the sleeve of his uniform flattened out and disappeared. He kept drinking until the arm felt like new, then groaned, and sat up.

Behind his squad mates, the Night Stalkers' van lay on its side, surrounded by a halo of spilled oil and shattered glass. Its passenger and rear doors were open, one of its back wheels was still spinning slowly, and Jamie realised he could not have been out for long. Probably no more than thirty seconds or so.

"Did you get them?" he asked. "Where are they?"

Qiang shook his head. "Gone."

Jamie frowned. "What do you mean, gone? Gone where?"

"They were out of the van by the time we got here," said Ellison. "They scattered when they saw us."

"Why didn't you go after them?" asked Jamie, his voice rising.

"I don't know, sir," said Ellison, her eyes narrowing. "Maybe because our squad leader was lying unconscious with a badly broken arm and a belt full of deadly weapons for the taking?"

"I'm fine," he said. "You *knew* I'd be fine. You should have gone after them." He got carefully to his feet, stretched his repaired arm, and faced his squad mates. "Get back in the van. I'll search from above. They can't have gone far."

Ellison took a step towards him. "Is this going to be a regular thing?" she asked, her eyes flashing with anger. "You doing stupid, reckless shit that means we have to put you back together afterwards? Because I'm already bored of it. Sir."

"I said I'm fine."

"You're a vampire, Jamie," said Ellison. "You're not indestructible. It's time you understood the difference."

"Noted," said Jamie. His squad mate's sudden disapproval had made him recoil, but his embarrassment at his telling-off and the knowledge that she was right were threatening to turn into anger. "Now are you going to help me find these scumbags or not?"

Ellison stared at him for a long moment, then rolled her eyes. "Of course we are," she said, and glanced at Qiang. "Come on."

Jamie's squad mates headed for their van, which was idling next to the vehicle that he had destroyed. He was about to rise back into the air and begin the search for whoever had been inside it when a loud chorus of beeps rang out.

He grabbed at his belt. "That's me," he said.

"It's all of us," said Ellison, pulling out her console as Qiang did the same behind her.

Jamie frowned. He thumbed his screen into life and read the message that appeared.

ACTIVE_ROSTER/L1/FULL_RECALL/RETURN_TO_
BASE/ASAP
ALL_CURRENT_OPERATIONAL_OBJECTIVES_
OVERRULED

"What the hell?" asked Ellison. "I've never heard of the active roster being recalled."

He shook his head. "Me neither."

"It must be serious," said Qiang.

Jamie grimaced. Whoever had been in the Night Stalker van could not have got far, especially if – as was likely considering the state of their vehicle – any or all of them were injured. He was sure they could find them, and was full of a burning desire to do so; he had come to hate the Night Stalkers with an anger that bordered on irrational, and now, when they were within his reach, he was being told to let them go and return to the Loop.

It was *infuriating.*

"Damn it!" he shouted. "What's going on that's so serious they can't handle it without us?"

29

DEATH FROM ABOVE, PART ONE

CARCASSONNE, SOUTHERN FRANCE
FORTY MINUTES EARLIER

The American watched as the waiter refilled his glass, disappointed to realise the emotion that had filled him for the last four years was still there.

Despite the quality of the wine in the bottle and the steak frites on his plate, the magical surroundings of the ancient walled city, and the bright, shining happiness the long-planned European trip was bringing Cynthia, it burned as strongly within him as it had on the first day after his retirement; a single emotion of profound clarity.

He missed the army.

And he was now certain that he always would.

Alan Foster had retired as Colonel after four decades of long and decorated service. In the chaos that followed what was now known as V-Day, when the vampire Gideon had appeared on British television and announced the existence of his kind, he had called his former CO at the Pentagon and offered to re-enlist. He could still be useful, he had insisted, could help them handle what was happening. His old boss had thanked him, and told him they had it under control. And as Alan looked at the liver spots on the back of the hand holding his refilled wine glass, he understood why.

Old, he told himself. *You're too damn old.*

"Honey?" asked Cynthia. "Are you all right?"

He smiled. "Sorry. I was miles away."

"Was I boring you?"

Alan searched his wife's beautiful, immaculately made-up face for the tiny downward curve of her mouth that would let him know she was genuinely annoyed; instead, he saw the deep laughter lines at the corners of her eyes that always betrayed her when she teased him.

"No more than usual," he said, his smile widening.

Cynthia let out a gasp of fake outrage, and threw an olive at him. He swatted it aside – he was still fast, despite his years – and raised his glass. She clinked hers against it, and smiled as the sound rang out across the brasserie's terrace. Alan left his glass raised for a second or two, then sat back in his chair, took a deep sip of wine, and let his gaze drift.

The walls of the fortified city curved above and below where they sat, thick fortifications that had been built and rebuilt in the centuries since the Romans had first realised the strategic importance of Carcassonne. Above the roofs of the shops and restaurants rose the high angular tower of the Basilica of St Nazaire and St Celse, the ancient church that had been the region's cathedral until 1801, when a new building had been erected beyond the walls of the original city.

Couples strolled through the cobbled square beyond the brasserie's terrace as families strode back and forth, the children clad in sweatshirts and baseball caps bearing images of Carcassonne, the parents laden down with bags of shopping. The air was cool, but alive with sound, conversation and laughter and the shouted entreaties of waiters as they tried to persuade the undecided that *their* establishment was unquestionably the very finest in the city. Alan watched them all, the army-shaped hole inside him temporarily filled by steak and wine and contentment.

Then something caught his eye, on the far side of the square: a momentary flash of glowing red.

His hand went instantly to his belt, where the butt of a pistol would usually have been. Back home in Houston, he carried the 45 Beretta that had been his retirement present from his staff every day, but here, far from home, he was unarmed. He cursed silently, and scanned the square. His eyes were still sharp, mercifully undimmed by age, and he had no reason to doubt what he had seen. But now he saw nothing.

"Al?" asked Cynthia, the levity gone from her voice. "Everything all right?"

He glanced at her, and smiled. "Fine," he said. "Nothing to worry about." But as he looked back out across the square, he wasn't sure that was true.

Standing in a doorway on the far side of the wide space was a young man, his face almost entirely hidden by the hood of his top. Tourists were flowing past, paying the man no attention whatsoever, but Alan stared at him for a long moment; he couldn't know for sure, but he was suddenly convinced that the eyes hidden by the shadow of the hood were fixed on his own.

"Alan?" asked Cynthia again.

"It's all right," he replied, without shifting his gaze. "If I tell you to move, don't ask any questions, OK? Just do what I say."

"Alan, you're scaring me."

"I know, and I'm sorry. Just do what I tell you. Please, Cynthia."

At the north-eastern corner of the square, where an ornate stone arch marked the start of a road that led down the hill, a woman had appeared. Her face was also hidden by a hood, and she stood as perfectly still as the man in the doorway. Moving his head as little as possible, Alan scanned the wide, bustling space, and felt his blood run cold.

Eight men and women were standing motionless in the square; the man in the doorway, one by each of the four corner exits, and three stood like statues in the midst of the crowd. Their faces were hidden, but the angles of their heads converged on a single point: the table where he and Cynthia were sitting.

They know, he realised. *They know I've seen them.*

Alan took a deep breath. "In ten seconds' time," he said, "we're going to get up and you're going to lead me into the kitchen. Walk quickly, but don't run. Don't stop if anyone asks what you're doing. Just keep moving and I'll be right behind you."

"OK," said Cynthia. Her voice was low, but full of determination.

"Good," he said. "I love you."

"I love you too, Alan."

"I know you do," he said, and gave his wife a fierce smile. "Now go."

Cynthia got to her feet and slung her bag over her shoulder. Alan pushed back his chair and stood up, trying to keep all eight of the stationary figures in sight as he did so. But as he lifted his coat off the back of his seat, his concentration was broken, and in that brief moment they moved; he searched the crowd frantically, looking for hoods, for deliberate movement.

There.

His eyes found one of the women as she threw back her hood, took hold of a man who had, until a millisecond earlier, been strolling through the square without a care in the world, and sank a pair of gleaming fangs into his face.

The man's scream was deafening, a piercing screech of pain and terror. Then the rest of the hooded figures tore into the crowd, and it was joined by a chorus of others. Blood sprayed into the air as panic descended over the square; people ran blindly in every direction, crying and screaming as footsteps thundered across the cobblestones. Alan watched, his heart stopped dead in his chest.

On the far side of the square, a female vampire swooped into a wide-eyed group of Japanese tourists, scattering them. They tumbled to the ground as the woman ripped at their necks, her eyes glowing, her face twisted into a vicious grin of delight. Blood began to run between the worn cobblestones, shimmering beneath the yellow street lights.

At the centre of the crowd, people collided with each other and tumbled beneath stampeding feet. Alan saw a woman fall on her shoulder, and heard the dull crack and scream of agony as it dislocated. She tried to sit up, her face ghostly pale, and was driven back down as one of the hooded vampires landed on her like a bird of prey. The man dug his fingers into her neck and tore out her throat with a casual flick of his wrist. Blood jetted above the heads of the running, panicking crowd; the vampire was moving again before it reached the ground, throwing himself into the chaos, hacking and slashing at anything that moved.

"What is this?" asked Cynthia, her voice low. "Alan?"

He barely heard her; he was transfixed by the savagery that had been unleashed around them. Their fellow diners appeared similarly frozen; they were watching the carnage with wide eyes, as though it was a piece of particularly challenging street theatre. Something whistled through the air and landed with a wet thud in the centre of the table to Alan's left. It was a human head, its eyes blinking rapidly, its mouth twitching as though still trying to form words.

"Alan?"

The occupants of the table screamed and pushed themselves back, upending their chairs and breaking the collective paralysis of their fellow patrons. The restaurant was suddenly full of movement and noise, as men and women flooded blindly out into the cobbled square that had become a slaughterhouse.

"ALAN!" screamed Cynthia.

He jumped, and turned to face his wife, his heart racing. Then he was moving, taking a tight hold of her hand and leading her against the flow of diners, towards the kitchen at the rear of the restaurant. He kicked open the swing door, and ran into a wide room full of metal and steam. Two chefs shouted their objections, but he ignored them, his eyes locked on an open door at the far end of the kitchen. Cynthia kept pace behind him, so much so that she thudded painfully into him when he skidded to a halt beside a low shelf near the back door.

"What is it?" she shouted. "What's wrong?"

Alan examined the shelf. Its edge was a row of hooks, from which hung blades of every shape and size. He grabbed a long carving knife and held it out to his wife, handle first. Cynthia took it without a word as he lifted down a thick, heavy cleaver, tested the weight in his hand, and grunted with approval. He was about to head for the door when something lying on a counter made him pause.

It was a meat-tenderising hammer, but it was unlike anything Alan had ever seen: almost a metre long, with a spiked head that made it look like it belonged in a medieval torture chamber rather than a kitchen. He transferred the cleaver to his left hand, hefted the hammer in his right, and ran through the back door, Cynthia close behind him. A shape loomed out of the shadows, and he raised the hammer, but the figure stepped into the light of the kitchen door before he swung it, revealing a waiter with tendrils of smoke curling out of his nostrils.

"Ce qu'il se passe?" asked the man.

Alan wasted no time replying. He pushed the waiter aside, ignored a rapid torrent of French insults, and led Cynthia down a metal staircase. They found themselves on a small road, one of the narrow arteries that wound through Carcassonne, hidden from the tourists upon whom the city depended. The road was on a slight incline, and Alan didn't waste a moment deciding which way to go.

Down, he thought. *All the ways out are down.*

Their feet clattered over the cobblestones as they ran. The volume of the screams from the square decreased as he led Cynthia round a corner at the bottom of the street, but they were still horribly audible, and seemingly endless.

A growling shape leapt from the shadows, two points of red glowing in the centre of its face, and Alan's military instincts took over; he swung the meat hammer in a flat arc, slamming it into the vampire's jaw. The studs ripped through the flesh of its cheek and the impact shuddered painfully up his arm. The vampire crashed to the ground, its head hitting the cobblestones with a sound like a breaking egg, and lay still. Alan didn't give it a second look; he sprinted forward, Cynthia at his side.

The street narrowed as it passed through a short stone tunnel, then widened as it curved away from the ancient walls and back into the centre of the city. Up ahead, a wide arch opened on to Rue du Grand Puits, one of the roads leading down to the medieval gate that served as Carcassonne's main entrance and exit. As they neared it, a dull roar reached Alan's ears: the thunder of footsteps as screaming, howling men and women ran headlong down the hill. He skidded to a halt beneath the arch, put an arm across his wife's chest, and stared at the flowing mass of humanity before them.

He had been in a number of deadly riots over the course of his career – in Mogadishu, Baghdad and Kosovo, to name just a few – but what was happening in front of him was every bit as terrifying as any of them. Men, women and children were running blindly

310

down the hill, many of them so badly injured that Alan assumed adrenaline was the only thing keeping them on their feet. Blood ran thickly between the cobblestones and pooled at the edges of the street. Motionless bodies lay on the ground, kicked and trodden on by the panicking mass; as Alan watched, a teenage boy tripped over a crumpled figure and fell to the ground, screaming in terror. He was swallowed up by the thundering crowd, trampled and driven to the cobbles, until he too lay still.

"Dear God," whispered Cynthia.

Within the reeling, pulsing crowd, vampires moved with supernatural speed, rending and tearing. There were now many more than the eight Alan had seen in the square, their eyes blazing with crimson, their faces twisted into grins of sheer joy. One of them grabbed a middle-aged man by his shoulders and hauled him kicking and screaming into the dark night sky; seconds later, bloody lumps of meat began to rain down on the running men and women below.

"What do we do, Alan?" asked Cynthia.

He looked at his wife. Her eyes were wide, her skin pale, but he saw no panic on her face.

"I don't know," he said. "I'm so sorry. I really don't know."

30

THE ART OF WAR

Kate Randall was sitting at her desk in the Security Division, her head and heart still pounding with the hope that Paul Turner's briefing had instilled, when she heard the beep.

She, along with most of her colleagues, had attended a number of sombre, painful meetings in the Ops Room; she had been there when the names of the men and women who died in Valeri's attack on the Loop had been displayed, and when the Director had explained, in the aftermath of Château Dauncy, that Dracula was lost and the prospects of finding him were now slim. Good news had been extremely hard to come by over the last year or so, as darkness had piled upon darkness until it seemed poised to swallow them all.

Now, there was a small, flickering light at the end of the tunnel. They still didn't know where Dracula was, or what he had planned, but the discovery of a cure represented a real chance to change things for the better, to release thousands of people from a condition the vast majority of them had never wanted, and to bring a halt to the violence that was currently sweeping, almost unchecked, throughout the country.

The beep was accompanied by the appearance of a new window on the screen of her computer. Kate enlarged it, and frowned. It was a message from the Surveillance Division, forwarding a classified alert that had been released ninety seconds earlier. She scanned the text, her frown deepening, then picked up her phone and pressed the button for her direct line to the Security Officer.

"Kate?" said Angela Darcy. "Everything OK?"

"I'm not sure," she said. "The Civil Aviation Authority just put an alert out. They've lost contact with a commercial flight off the west coast of Scotland."

"What flight?"

"Virgin Atlantic 025," she said. "An Airbus A340, travelling from London to New York. Four hundred and twelve passengers and crew."

Beep.

"Has there been a response from the RAF?" asked the Security Officer.

"It's just come through," said Kate, reading the new message. "They've scrambled two Typhoons from Coningsby. They should be at the last recorded position in twelve minutes."

"OK," said Angela. "Keep me updated."

"Yes, Captain," said Kate. She hung up the phone, opened a new window, and accessed the secure Intelligence Services network; it was crammed with chatter, as GCHQ and SIS discussed the missing plane. The cockpit transmissions were already being listened to, but the extremely preliminary conclusion was that they contained nothing unusual.

Beep.

Another message appeared. Kate read it, and felt incredulity rise on to her face. She grabbed the phone again, and dialled her commanding officer.

"Have they found it?" asked Angela.

"I don't know," said Kate. "But an alert just came through from the American FAA. They've lost contact with three commercial flights in the last five minutes. One that had just left Atlanta, one over the

313

California desert, and one over the Atlantic on approach to New York."

"Three planes?"

"That's what they're saying," she said.

Beep. Beep.

Kate's fingers flew across her keyboard, opening the new messages.

"This is crazy," she said. "I've just got two more. The French have lost an American Airlines 757 on Paris approach and the Italians have lost an Emirates 777 somewhere near Turin."

"I'm logged in," said Angela. "What the hell is this?"

Kate shook her head. "I've no idea," she said. "Could they be mistakes? Some kind of air-traffic control error?"

"The national systems are all independent," said Angela. "I can't imagine what it would take for all of them to go wrong at the same time."

Beep. Beep beep beep.

Four new windows opened on the screen. Kate stared at them, her heart racing, her eyes wide. "Four more," she said, her voice little more than a whisper. "Japan, China, the Bahamas, Mexico. Jesus. These can't all be right. Surely they can't be?"

"I don't know," said Angela.

"What do we do?" asked Kate.

"I'll brief the Director," said Angela. "He needs to know what's happening, even if it's nothing to do with us."

It is, though, thought Kate. *Neither of us wants to say it, but we both know it is.*

"All right," she said. "What do you want me—"

The door to Kate's office banged open. She spun round in her seat and glared at the Operator standing in the doorway. "I'm on the phone," she said. "Can you give me a—"

"Turn your TV on," interrupted the Operator. "Something's happened in Moscow."

"What?" asked Kate, but the Operator had already disappeared back through the door.

"Kate?" asked Angela. "What's going on?"

"Turn on your TV," said Kate. "I'm coming to you."

She hung up the phone, strode out of her office, and ran across the Division towards the room she had once spent almost as much time in as her own. She knocked on the door and pushed it open; Angela was sitting behind her desk, her face pale, her attention fixed on the screen on her wall, which was showing the BBC News channel.

"What's happening?" asked Kate.

Angela shook her head. Kate frowned, her heart pounding, and turned towards the screen, which was showing a shaky, grainy shot of a crowd of people clustered together on a wide street. Ambulances were arriving in droves, their lights flashing, and the sounds of crying and screaming echoed out of the screen's speakers.

"Terrible scenes in Moscow this evening," said a disembodied voice. "Details are still sketchy, but what we know for certain is that, some fifteen minutes ago now, an emergency call was made from the Kurskaya Metro station, and that the call made reference to a train having arrived 'full of blood'. As you can see from this exclusive footage, emergency services are now on the scene, as conflicting reports emerge from inside the Russian capital. We have heard claims that a train has derailed at Kurskaya, we have at least one account of a possible gunman on a train, and we have received a number of reports of vampire sightings across the Moscow Metro system."

Beep.

"Not another one?" asked Kate.

"Argentina," said the Security Officer, her voice low as she stared at her computer screen. "They've lost a 747 over Buenos Aires."

Kate just stared; she felt numb, as if her insides had been turned to ice. She couldn't process what was happening; the entire world seemed to have fallen into chaos in the last five minutes.

"Stand by for breaking news," said the news presenter. "We're getting… this is absolutely remarkable… but we're now getting reports of a number of explosions at subway stations in Beijing. We're working to get you more details as soon as we can, but…"

The footage of Moscow disappeared, revealing the presenter looking away from the camera, a deep frown on her face, one hand pressed against the microphone in her ear.

"Is this right?" she said. "Are you sure you want me to…"

There was a moment of silence, until the presenter finally looked back down the lens.

"Ladies and gentlemen," she said. "We are now receiving unconfirmed reports of vampire attacks on passengers on both the Paris Metro and the London Underground. The New York Transit Authority has ordered a complete closure of the New York subway system, presumably in response to these reported incidents. I don't… I just…"

Beep. Beep.

The screen changed to show an archive photograph of a walled city, one that looked like a sprawling medieval castle. The caption beneath the image read CARCASSONNE, FRANCE.

"What is this?" asked the Security Officer; it was clear from her face that she already knew the answer to her own question.

"It's Dracula," said Kate.

31

DEATH FROM ABOVE, PART TWO

CARCASSONNE, SOUTHERN FRANCE

The first vampire, the creature once known as Vlad Tepes but who now went by a name that struck fear into the hearts of men and women alike, floated anonymously through the screaming, panicking crowds like a theatre director making an impromptu check on a performance.

The tourists running for their lives paid him no attention, and the vampires knew his scent well enough to keep their distance. He did not join the attack; he was a General, and despite the longing in the pit of his stomach and the glorious scent of blood in his nostrils, violence was something he ordered, not something he carried out himself.

There was much that Dracula still did not understand about the modern world; he had lain dormant through a century in which humanity had advanced more rapidly than all the previous centuries combined, and many of those developments were still a mystery. What had become *abundantly* clear, however, during conversations with Valeri Rusmanov and the many dinners he had shared with Admiral Henry Seward, were the enormous advances that had been made in the field of murder.

He had tried to imagine rockets that could be fired from halfway around the globe to land on a single building, machines that flew to the edge of space to drop their payloads on to unsuspecting men and women below, and found he could not. But then he had seen, with his own eyes, the single bomb that had annihilated the thick stone walls and deep foundations of Château Dauncy, the helicopters that had swept his soldiers with deadly ultraviolet light, the armour that had allowed his enemies to survive blows that should have been instantly fatal. When he had still been a man, battles had been fought on foot and on horseback, with swords and spears and bows; on several occasions, Dracula had allowed himself to wonder how different his long campaigns against the Turks might have been if even one per cent of the modern world's weaponry had been at his disposal.

Around him, the fleeing crowds were beginning to thin. The first vampire checked his watch, and saw that fifteen minutes had passed since the assault had begun. Thus far, his followers were carrying out their orders perfectly; they had torn into the inhabitants of Carcassonne with great relish, rending and killing and driving those who managed to avoid their fangs and fingernails down the old streets and out of the city.

Dracula rose into the air and soared rapidly towards the high stone tower of the Basilica. In the cobbled square below the church's walls stood the Hôtel de la Cité, an elegant old building surrounded by pristine gardens that extended out over the steep edges of Carcassonne. There, if his orders had been competently followed, the next phase of Dracula's plan would be waiting for him.

The ancient vampire climbed high above the city, savouring the screams and sobs that were still floating through the air beneath him, and took a moment to look at the place he had chosen to be his new citadel. Although the architecture was somewhat different, it reminded him in many ways of Poenari Castle, his seat of power during his reigns as the Prince of Wallachia. Both occupied the highest ground for many miles, their walls and battlements draped across rising peaks and uneven hillsides, making them almost impregnable, at least from medieval means of attack. The destruction of Château Dauncy had made it clear that the thick stone of Carcassonne would be no match for contemporary weaponry, but that did not matter; Dracula was relying on something else staying the trigger fingers of his enemies.

Osvaldo, the Spanish vampire who was the closest thing to a confidant that he had allowed in the aftermath of the death of Valeri Rusmanov, had suggested that a more remote location might have been more suitable for his new base of operations – a Pacific island, perhaps, or a section of the south-western American desert – but Dracula had explained to him that remoteness is only an advantage when you are intending to hide. And hiding was the last thing on his mind.

The ancient vampire looked out across the slanted, unruly rooftops of the city, enjoying the cool evening air on his skin, then descended towards the square near the summit. As he reached the ground, he noted the vampires stationed at its four corners, guarding the ways in and out, and allowed himself a small smile.

They're not real soldiers. The least of my Wallachians was worth ten of them. But they are so very keen, and so very scared.

Dozens of his followers were milling about in the wide space in front of the hotel, hissing and growling, reliving the attack, but a respectful silence settled instantly over them as he touched down. He turned slowly, favouring the vampires with an expression that was not quite a smile but which contained no obvious reproach.

"Well done," he said. "All has gone according to plan, and now the real work begins. Do not let me down."

He saw flickers of glowing red in faces set with determined pride, held their gaze for a long moment, then turned and strode into the hotel. Osvaldo was waiting in the wood-panelled entrance hall; he bowed as his master approached.

"My lord," he said. "The police have arrived."

"As expected," said Dracula. "Where?"

"Most are tending to survivors outside the walls, my lord, where ambulances and fire vehicles have also arrived. However, a small squad of armed officers is making its way into the city."

"Kill them," he said. "Have their bodies brought up here. Intact."

"Of course, my lord. We should also expect to see helicopters shortly. The police will send them, and so will the television news, once word gets out."

"Bring down the first one that flies inside the border of our walls. That will make the others keep their distance."

"Yes, my lord," said Osvaldo, and flew quickly through the hotel's door. A second later Dracula heard him bark orders at the vampires waiting in the square, and smiled.

After the humbling, harrowing defeat at Château Dauncy, the first vampire had lain low for several months in a farmhouse in northern Italy owned by one of the tiny number of his followers that had also survived the battle. In the first weeks, he had refused to see anyone; he had shut himself away with his rage and disappointment and frustration. He had not been as strong as he needed to be, as strong as he *should* have been, and it had almost cost him his life; he had been arrogant, and stupid, and he had no intention of making the same mistake again.

When he emerged from his isolation, the survivors of the battle had been joined by almost fifty other vampires; it was a paltry amount in the grand scheme of things, but heartening nonetheless. The new arrivals had sought him out, pledging themselves to his vision of the future, a future in which vampires were the planet's dominant species and human beings were little more than cattle. He had welcomed them, thanked them for their loyalty, then ordered them to go out and recruit more men and women to their cause.

His followers had done as he commanded, delivering vampires to the farmhouse in steadily increasing numbers; one or two a day at first, then a dozen, then twenty, until they were arriving at the rate of more than a hundred a week. There was quickly no room for them all at the farmhouse, so the first vampire sent them away as they arrived, ordering them to lie low in one of his ever-expanding network of safe houses until they were needed.

Osvaldo had been in the farmhouse when Dracula at last emerged from his isolation. The Spaniard had no military experience – he had been an advertising executive in his former life – but he had already established himself as the de facto leader of Dracula's followers. He did not shout, or fight, or growl, nor did he manipulate or scheme; he simply possessed a natural air of authority, and when he suggested an idea or a plan, they invariably proved successful.

As a result, the first vampire had immediately considered killing him; he could not tolerate anything even approaching divided loyalties, and Osvaldo's death would have made that abundantly clear. What had stopped him was the look in the vampire's eyes as he bowed before his new master, a look that he recognised instantly: the boiling fervour of a true believer. By the end of their first conversation, Dracula knew that Osvaldo wanted nothing more than to help him burn the world down. And so it had proved.

The call had gone out twenty-four hours earlier.

The first vampire had sent a hundred vampires to board commercial flights around the world, a hundred more to the major underground railways in Europe, America and Asia. Each one of his followers had been given a detailed plan and a time of attack that was to be adhered to on literal pain of death; coordination was vital if his opening salvo was to have the desired impact.

The bulk of his new army, now almost seven hundred strong, had taken wing for Carcassonne.

Dracula walked through the entrance hall of the hotel, his boots clicking rapidly on the wooden floor. A low hum of noise could be heard from around the corner beyond the reception desk, where the corridor opened up into a large lobby full of sofas and tables, with an ornate wooden bar on one side and windows that looked out on to an immaculate garden. He stepped around the corner, enjoying the hush that fell as his presence was noted, and surveyed the wide space.

Huddled together in the middle were a group of men and women, their eyes brimming with fear. Many were bloodied, their clothes torn, but none had life-threatening injuries, just as he had ordered; injured hostages caused complications, which he did not have time for. There were perhaps a hundred of them: waiters and shopkeepers, tourists of every nationality, men and women, boys and girls, young and old.

In a shadowy corner on the far side of the lobby, Dracula saw Emery staring at the hostages with his dark, hollow eyes, and suppressed the urge to shudder with disgust. The quiet, softly spoken Englishman was the only one of his new followers who was not a vampire; what he *was*, was one of the most profoundly empty creatures Dracula had ever come across. He had appeared outside the farmhouse one morning, his clothes neat, his eyes like black holes behind the sensible glasses he wore at all times. He had carried no bags, and it had become rapidly clear that luggage was not all that he was lacking; he was also devoid of a conscience, a sense of right and wrong, and even the most basic empathy towards other living creatures.

Osvaldo had been obviously wary, and Dracula's first instinct had been to have the new arrival killed. But when he had summoned the man to his rooms, he had found himself instantly intrigued; Emery had shown no fear in his presence, no panic, nothing but calm, polite composure. He had looked into the man's eyes and seen darkness, the kind of inky absence of light that he had only seen once before, many centuries earlier; in that moment, he had made a decision, and told Emery that he was welcome to stay. The Englishman had thanked him by telling him the things that he would happily do if he was ordered to, and Dracula, who had forgotten more about cruelty and torture than most people would ever know, had felt his stomach turn with revolted admiration.

The hostages looked suitably terrified as the first vampire swept his gaze across them, which was good; he was searching for the set of a jaw or the narrowness of an eye that might suggest someone potentially capable of resistance. He saw nothing but fear, and smiled widely.

"My name is Count Dracula," he said, "and you are prisoners in a war that you could not have known was being waged. You should not blame yourselves for the situation in which you find yourselves, and should not take it as anything more than a stroke of misfortune. It is not my intention to kill you, as you are more valuable to me alive than dead, but that is the limit of my generosity. The punishment for resistance, for insubordination, for any refusal to do as you are told, will be death. Is that clear?"

Silence.

"You will not speak to me without permission," he continued. "If I address you, you will answer by referring to me as 'my lord' or 'master'. You will be fed and watered, and if you conduct yourselves with obedience and deference, your imprisonment may pass without incident. But I urge you not to misunderstand the reality of your situation, which is that you are no longer free. You are prisoners, and will remain so until I decide differently. The sooner you accept this, the better." He looked at his followers, who were watching him in silence. "Lock them in the rooms on the first and second floors. Give a list of their names and locations to Osvaldo."

"Yes, my lord," growled the vampires, and moved forward. Dracula watched the crowd of hostages shrink back in terror, then frowned as footsteps echoed along the entrance hall behind him. He turned to see one of his followers round the corner, pushing an older couple before him. The man's face was lined and his hair was grey, but his eyes were clear and full of anger. The woman looked more frightened, but she was walking under her own steam; every few seconds, she glanced over at the man, as if drawing strength from him.

"My lord," said the vampire, and bowed his head. "I found these two in the backstreets. Osvaldo told me to bring them to you."

Dracula nodded. The vampire bowed again, released the man and woman, and backed towards the entrance hall. The couple stood where they were, looking around at the crowd of people and vampires.

"What is this?" asked the man. "Just what the hell is going on here?"

Dracula smiled. Then he swept forward, far faster than any human eye could follow, and lifted the man into the air by his throat. Screams rang out as the woman made to move towards him, but one of his followers was there before she had the chance. The vampire pinned her arms tightly behind her back and held them in place as the man struggled in Dracula's immovable grip, his face reddening alarmingly. As it began to turn purple, the first vampire released him. The man fell to the floor, clutching at his neck, spluttering and gasping, as Dracula looked down at him.

"You will not speak unless you are spoken to," he said. "Stand up. Now."

The man got to his feet. There was shock in his eyes, and pain, but in the set of his jaw and the squareness of his shoulders was visible determination.

Military, thought Dracula. *I'd bet my life on it.*

"Tell me your name," he said.

"Colonel Alan Foster," said the man. "United States Army. Retired. Who the hell are you?"

"I am the person who will decide whether you live or die," said Dracula. "Would you like me to make that decision now?"

Foster didn't respond.

"I thought not," he said. "I assume this lady is your wife?"

"That's right," said Foster.

"Excellent," he said. "Emery? Come here."

The Englishman walked forward. He didn't hurry, the way the rest of Dracula's followers did when they were called for; he came at his own pace, as slow and deliberate as a spider approaching an insect caught in its web.

"My lord," he said, and dipped his head.

"Colonel Foster," said Dracula. "This is Emery. If you cause me so much as a moment's trouble, your wife will spend some time in his company, and the worst thing you ever saw in your military career will seem like a fairy tale in comparison. Do you understand?"

Foster stared at him for a long moment, then nodded.

"Good," said Dracula. "Join the others, and be glad you found me in a forgiving mood."

His follower pushed Foster roughly forward, dragging the man's wife behind him. Dracula turned away as they were manhandled towards the rest of the hostages, and walked back into the entrance hall, leaving Emery standing blankly where he was. As he exited the hotel, he heard the hostages being shepherded up the staircase and into the rooms where they would spend the foreseeable future.

There was no sign of Osvaldo in the square outside, and Dracula assumed he had personally taken a squad of vampires down to deal with the police; such attention to detail was characteristic of the Spaniard. He listened for the screams that would mean his order had been successfully carried out, straining his supernatural hearing, then growled as the thunder of a helicopter engine hammered into his ears, as suddenly as if it had materialised beside him. The acoustics of the old city were unpredictable, which he didn't like, but there was nothing to be done about that; it was a rabbit warren of old stone perched on a hilltop, and strange echoes and dead spots were only to be expected.

Dracula leapt easily into the air and rose above the rooftops, searching for the source of the noise. He turned south, towards the main gate and the modern city of Carcassonne that sprawled beyond the walls, and was engulfed in the blinding white beam of a spotlight. He howled in pain, and flung himself clear; the light was agonising to his supernaturally sharp eyes, and he felt crimson fire flood into them as anger roared through his body.

The fools, he thought, as black spots and points of light wheeled across his vision. *They have no idea what they bring upon themselves.*

His eyes cleared, and he immediately located the helicopter. It was painted blue and white with the word POLICE printed on its side, and was rising quickly over the distant ramparts to the southwest, its hateful searchlight sweeping back and forth across the sky. Dracula spun up and around, keeping a safe distance between him and the wide beam, silent and invisible in the darkening sky.

Gunfire rattled out, from somewhere near the bottom of the hill, punctuated by a terrible screech of pain. Dracula smiled as two more screams rang out, followed by an awful gagging noise, like the sound of someone trying to breathe underwater, and a second, final burst of gunfire.

He spun forward in the air until he was looking down into the square below; less than thirty seconds later four vampires flew in from the south-east corner, each one dragging two black shapes behind them. The bodies of the police officers were dumped in front of the entrance to the hotel, and Dracula permitted himself a moment of satisfaction; ability and experience were valuable traits, but obedience outranked them both, and on that front, his army were thus far proving acceptable.

He spun back upright, and sought out the helicopter again. If the order he had given to Osvaldo was not carried out quickly, he would fly down and deal with it himself. But as he located the helicopter, now flying low over the western walls, he saw that his intervention would not be needed.

A distant trio of dark shapes soared silently up from the narrow streets. They accelerated towards the unsuspecting helicopter from below, safely out of reach of its searchlight, and slammed into it with crippling force, driving its metal body up and over. The engine noise rose to a deafening howl and its rotors sent turbulent air billowing in every direction as the pilot tried to stabilise the aircraft. The three vampires, one of which he believed was Osvaldo himself, hammered the protesting helicopter back and forth, then began to haul it up and away from the walls. The engine screamed, the sound awful to Dracula's ears, then gave out in a shower of sparks and an explosion of shearing metal. Without power, the helicopter pitched forward and fell towards the ground. Osvaldo and his comrades held on, steadying it with its nose pointing directly down; across the clear, suddenly quiet night sky, Dracula could hear the muffled screams of the pilot and the thuds as he beat at his cockpit windscreen.

Then the helicopter was moving again, as his followers swung it out and up. They released their grip and sent it flying over the walls, flipping end over end until it dropped out of sight. A second later the sound of an explosion hammered into the air as a bright cloud of orange fire bloomed above the ancient battlements and screams and sirens filled Dracula's ears.

Now, he thought. *It's time.*

He sped over the city towards the thick stone wall that stood above the drawbridge. The old entrance was purely ceremonial, designed to make tourists feel that they were entering something old and dramatic, but that was just fine for his purposes. As he descended towards it, he got his first look at the scene beyond the walls. There was a long line of ambulances, standing in front of rows of police cars and fire engines, around which paramedics were frantically treating the men and women who had made it out of Carcassonne with their lives. Further down the hill, approaching along the wide streets of the new city, he could see a great many spinning blue lights.

The survivors of the attack he had ordered were wandering aimlessly or slumped on the grass, groaning and sobbing and begging for help. The paramedics were running back and forth between them, as the police looked on with apparent paralysis. Beyond them, Dracula could see a steady stream of people making their way up the hill; word that something was happening in the old city had clearly travelled fast.

He hovered in the air, searching for what Osvaldo had assured him he would see. He scanned the chaotic crowd, then settled his gaze on a man standing beside a white van who was holding what he was looking for: the wide glass lens of a television camera.

The walls of Carcassonne were ringed by powerful spotlights that illuminated the pale stone once the sun had set. Dracula dropped silently on to the top of the wall above the drawbridge, his clothes and hair fluttering in the night air, and looked down at the oblivious crowd. They looked so like ants, diligently going about lives that were insignificant at best. He took a deep breath, then spoke in a voice that rumbled the walls beneath the feet.

"Citizens of Carcassonne," he said. "I am Dracula, and I have taken possession of this city."

Shouts and screams rose from the crowd, and he smiled as several people turned and fled down the hill without a backward glance. The rest stayed where they were, frozen in place, their eyes fixed on him. He kept his own gaze on the camera, marvelling at the thought of how many people this modern technology was allowing him to speak directly to.

"I will keep this communication short," he continued. "To those of my kind who would submit themselves to my service, I say this: come, bow your heads, and make yourselves known to me. And to those humans who reside in Carcassonne: you have forty-eight hours to leave the city. Failure to do so will result in your deaths. This place is no longer your home."

ZERO HOUR
PLUS 205 DAYS

32

THE MORNING AFTER

CARCASSONNE, SOUTHERN FRANCE

The residents of Carcassonne woke to a display that had not been seen in Europe for more than five centuries. Staring down at them from poles driven into the high walls of the medieval city were the lifeless eyes of dozens of impaled men and women, their blood-caked bodies twisting slowly in the morning breeze.

Below, the modern city was significantly emptier than it had been as the sun set nine hours earlier. Thousands of people had already fled, piling belongings into their cars and driving away, many of them with no real idea of where they were going, or what they would do when they got there; all they cared about was not being inside Carcassonne when the forty-eight hours were up. The outskirts of the city had seen roads jammed with cars, horns blaring as men and women wove their way through the narrow streets.

The authorities had been just as unprepared for Dracula's sudden appearance as everyone else and although they were now scrambling to respond, there had been little progress overnight. As a result, hundreds of cars were parked in the empty fields beyond the city's borders, their owners wandering through the pale morning light, waiting for someone to tell them what to do. Fifty miles to the north, a convoy of trucks was rumbling south with large red crosses painted on their sides, carrying tents and food and water and blankets; everything that would be needed to begin the process of setting up a camp for the Carcassonne refugees.

Inside the city, queues had formed outside the supermarkets and boulangeries as those who had not already left prepared to do so. Despite the early hour, the streets were busy with scared, fractious men and women who did not really understand the horror that had befallen their quiet corner of the world. The police – or rather, those police who had not packed up and left in the night – were out on the streets in force, defusing the fights and arguments that were breaking out with increasing frequency as the shops began to run low on essentials like bread and bottled water. They had been assured that the military would arrive no later than noon to take charge of the situation, but, until then, they were on their own, and hopelessly outnumbered.

At the centre of the city, an enormous crowd swarmed round the railway station as residents without cars sought seats on the first train to anywhere; to Marseilles and Montpellier, to Bordeaux and La Rochelle, even all the way north to Paris. Mothers and fathers gripped their children tightly and dragged them towards the platforms, their faces pale and tight with the effort of attempting to appear calm for the sake of their kids. And from the shadows, unnoticed by anyone, Dracula watched them with a smile on his narrow face.

The first vampire had slipped out of the medieval city under cover of darkness, rising silently into the air and descending into the chaos below. He was wearing clothes that Osvaldo had brought him from one of the newly empty boutiques near the summit of the old city, clothes that felt ridiculous but which he had been assured would allow him to pass unnoticed. The Spaniard had actually attempted to persuade him against venturing down into the city to see what was happening for himself, as he considered it an unnecessary risk, but Dracula had reminded him that if he wanted his counsel, he would ask for it.

The shoes were the only part of his disguise that he was pleased with; they were made of wonderfully soft leather, a far cry from the heavy boots he had worn first as a man then during his first incarnation as Count Dracula. The rest of the clothes – the jeans, the thick woollen shirt, the hooded top and gloves – felt like the clothes a commoner would wear, apparel wholly unsuitable for a Prince who was about to become the ruler of an entire planet. But as he walked among the men and women of Carcassonne, taking care to keep his face, which was his only area of exposed skin, angled away from the sun, he saw that Osvaldo had been right about one thing: nobody gave him so much as a second glance.

On several occasions he had slipped unseen into cities his Wallachian armies had conquered, almost always over the protests of his advisers. He had known it was dangerous, perhaps even foolhardy, but he had not cared; there was nothing more thrilling than experiencing the terror of his enemies first hand, to bask in the knowledge that the same men and women who were ignoring him would soon be dead at his command.

This was different, in some ways, as it would no longer matter if anyone recognised him; in those days he had been human, whereas now he could have defended himself against the entire population of Carcassonne without breaking a sweat. But the fear, the sweet, palpable *fear*, was the same; he could see it in the wide eyes of every man and woman who hurried past with their meagre belongings in their arms, could *smell* it rising from their pores.

He had allowed his army a few hours to celebrate once the medieval city had been taken; vampires had filled the Hôtel de la Cité and the cobbled squares, drinking blood and alcohol, tormenting and torturing the last few tourists who had been flushed from their hiding places in the surrounding streets. The hostages, locked safely in their rooms, were off-limits, however; he had made that abundantly clear, along with the penalty that would befall anyone who disobeyed his orders. In the early hours, he had called the revelry to a halt, and ordered Emery to oversee the creation of the gruesome decorations that now adorned the walls of the city. They had finished their work as the first light crept over the eastern horizon, and he had allowed most of them to seek the cover of darkness and the emptiness of sleep; there would be work to do as soon as the sun set again. The rest were on a watch rota that Osvaldo had organised; they patrolled the empty streets and perched high above the low sprawl, waiting to see what form the human response would take.

Dracula was confident that it would not come for at least a day, whatever it was; in truth, he was counting on it. His enemies' best option would have been to send everything they had into Carcassonne, as quickly as they possibly could; his vampire army was loyal and enthusiastic, but it was also inexperienced and undisciplined, and he knew it could be routed if it was attacked with enough conviction. But to respond so quickly, with the overwhelming force a frontal assault would require, would have risked the deaths of thousands of innocent civilians, and he was certain that they would not entertain the prospect of such losses, especially given the carnage that his followers had unleashed around the world overnight.

Osvaldo had shown him the television coverage of the crashed planes and the blood-soaked underground stations, and he had felt a brief surge of pride; his followers had carried out their missions to the letter, and had provided an invaluable diversion. Dracula knew, probably better than anyone alive, that battles were won by the commander best able to focus solely on the destruction of the enemy; collateral damage, innocent victims, destruction of property, morality

336

and fairness were all distractions, and ultimately worthless. Victory was earned, more often than not, by sheer, bloody force of will.

His enemies' attention would be divided while they gathered forces from around the globe, analysed and overanalysed the terrain and resources and tactics they would employ, and reassured the relatives of the men and women on the list of hostages that Osvaldo had dropped on to the television crews gathered around the walls, all of which played directly into Dracula's hands; he was a medieval General, and a large-scale, winner-takes-all battle was not something he feared.

It was, in fact, exactly what he wanted.

Death or glory, he thought. *Win or lose. One battle to end them all.*

He walked away from the station, leaving the increasingly restless crowd to their desperation. The main street that ran up to the walled city was almost deserted; its clothes shops and mobile-phone kiosks and brasseries and cafés should by now have been getting ready to open, but their shutters were all down, and the pavements were empty. He turned south, heading out of the central commercial district and into the residential streets that encircled it.

The contrast was immediately striking; here, the narrow roads were full of activity, as civilians dragged their belongings out of their homes and forced them into overflowing car boots or on to groaning roof racks. There was a feverish sense of urgency rising from the residents, as if they were worried they might look at their watches and see that forty-eight hours had passed in an instant, or – perhaps more likely – that Dracula would not keep his word. The thought gave him great satisfaction; he intended to honour the two days he had promised, unless his position was attacked, but it pleased him to see that this was not being taken for granted.

There was nothing in the world he enjoyed more than proof that people were scared of him.

He strolled along one of the streets, ignored by everyone. Up ahead, in the small garden of a terraced house, a heavy-set man was bellowing up at an open window, demanding that his wife hurry up. The woman strode out of the house, her face crimson with anger, and shouted back at her husband, demanding to know exactly why he thought it was OK for him to just stand outside and order people around.

On the pavement outside the garden, a little girl in a pink coat sat on a three-wheeled bike, watching her parents scream at each other. She stared at them for a few moments, then turned away, clearly bored, and began pedalling her bike determinedly towards Dracula. He smiled at her, and she smiled back in the mischievous way of all children when an adult they don't know – a *stranger* – notices them. She pedalled faster, then turned her handlebars and darted between two parked cars, her eyes fixed on the pavement on the other side of the road. Dracula looked past her and saw a car approaching, moving far too fast. He registered the blank, panicked face of the driver, the screaming parents whose attention was still focused angrily on each other, the little girl on the bike who was about to emerge in the middle of the road, and realised what was going to happen.

Delicious, he thought. *How absolutely delicious.*

For a moment, he did nothing.

Then he sprinted forward, taking care not to leave the ground or let glowing heat enter his eyes, and out into the centre of the road. The car driver didn't see him; he was staring into the middle distance, seeing nothing but escape. Dracula accelerated, racing towards the parked cars from between which the bike would appear, any second now. There would be no chance for the car to stop; it would hit the little girl head-on, at killing speed.

He reached the parked cars as a small, determined blur of pink rattled out from between them. To his surprise, the car driver *did* see her, and then finally him. He braked, but far too late; the car kept coming, screeching across the tarmac towards them. The girl looked round and screamed as Dracula reached her; he lifted her off her bike with one hand, as though she weighed as little as a feather, and dived out of the way. He rolled across the bonnet of a parked car, the girl wrapped in his arms, as the car that had almost obliterated her skidded to a halt twenty metres down the road. For a long second there was silence, until the little girl began to shriek.

Her mother and father rushed out of their garden, their eyes wide, the colour drained from their faces, as he sat up and held the girl out towards them. The woman snatched her from his hands and held her tight, sobbing and shaking and whispering that it was all right, she was OK, she was all right. Dracula climbed off the bonnet, and was instantly grabbed into a crushing bear hug by the girl's father.

"*Merci*," he gasped. "*Merci, monsieur. Merci bien.*"

He grinned. This was all simply *too* delightful.

"*De rien,*" he said.

The father released him, and hauled his daughter out of his wife's arms. He started scolding her, telling her that she was lucky to be alive, that she knew she was never, *ever*, ever to ride her bike in the road. His wife looked with eyes that were wet with tears as the driver of the car appeared beside them, his face white with shock.

"I didn't see her," he said. "She rode right out. You all saw. I couldn't have seen her."

The woman threw herself at him, her face blazing with anger, and pounded his chest with her fists. The driver recoiled, raising his arms in self-defence as he was driven back against the garden wall by the fury of her assault.

"Slow down!" she screamed. "Slow down, you stupid shit!"

"I'm sorry!" shouted the driver, turning his body away from her blows. "I didn't see her! I'm sorry!"

Dracula watched the unfolding scene with happiness radiating through him. He looked down at the pavement and saw a stone at the bottom of the garden wall; it was about the size of a grapefruit, and smooth. He stepped round the yelling, flailing woman and picked it up.

Perfect, he thought, feeling its weight in his hand.

The driver had curled into a crouch, his head down, his hands over the back of his neck. Dracula caught one of his attacker's swinging fists and put the stone in it without a word.

The girl's mother didn't hesitate for even a single second; she brought the stone crashing down on the back of the driver's head. He let out a strangled grunt and slid to one knee, blood spurting from his scalp, bright red in the early morning light. The little girl screamed again. Her father pressed her tightly against his chest and covered her eyes with his hand, but made no attempt to stop his wife as she swung the heavy stone a second time. It connected with the driver's head with a sound like breaking crockery, and he slumped to the ground, his eyes rolling, his limbs twitching.

Dracula turned away as the woman knelt on the pavement, her face a mask of blind animal savagery, and walked back towards the main road as she brought the stone down again and again.

33

THE ELEPHANT IN THE ROOM

Jamie's stomach churned as he took a seat at the Ops Room table.

Even by the elevated standards of Blacklight, the last twenty-four hours had been remarkably chaotic; the acts of terrorism that had been unleashed across the world, acts that had cost tens of thousands of innocent lives and announced that Dracula had finally made his move, had sent shock waves through the Department. He had watched the coverage of the unfolding crisis in the officers' mess, standing silently as Dracula issued his proclamation from atop the walls of the medieval city, as planes tumbled from the sky and men and women were butchered without mercy in subway cars and shopping malls.

Nobody had said a word; Jamie doubted that anything would have been remotely adequate to describe what they were seeing. The first vampire in the flesh at last, the absent threat that had loomed over every Operator for months staring into a trembling camera and announcing the opening gambit of his campaign against the human world.

Unsurprisingly, nobody had talked about anything else for the rest of the night, and a single question had been asked over and over again.

What the hell do we do now?

Jamie glanced around the Ops Room table as Paul Turner got to his feet at its head. His colleagues were staring silently at the Director, their faces pale and tight.

"Zero Hour Task Force in session," said Turner. "All members present. There are three things that we need to discuss today, the first of which is no doubt extremely obvious. As you must all know by now, what this group was first brought together to prevent has now come to pass. The images from Carcassonne, and from around the world, leave no room for ambiguity. Dracula has finally made his move."

"Right," said Angela Darcy. "So what are we going to do about it?"

"I will tell you what's been discussed so far," said Turner. "I spoke to the Directors of the other Departments this morning, including the FTB, who are liaising directly with the French government. We have no reliable intelligence regarding what happens to Carcassonne once Dracula's deadline passes, but given the acts of terrorism that took place last night and the hostages that we know he's taken, the consensus is that we cannot afford to simply hope for the best. The residents of the city appear to agree, as early estimates suggest that as many as twenty per cent of them fled overnight, with a great many more preparing to leave this morning. The French government has officially requested assistance from NATO and the UN, who have agreed to send peace-keeping troops and disaster-relief resources into the area, although neither is expected to arrive for at least eighteen hours."

"Why so long?" asked Kate Randall.

Turner gave her a thin smile. "Global bureaucracy moves slowly at the best of times, Lieutenant. It moves even slower when most of the world's major countries are dealing with the aftermath of the worst acts of terrorism they've ever known. Thankfully, both the Red Cross and UNICEF have already arrived at the scene and begun the process of assisting the refugees of Carcassonne. They will be establishing a displaced persons camp outside the city, and Director Allen of NS9 is en route to set up a local command centre at the same location."

Frankenstein frowned. "Why is Bob Allen going?" he asked. "Why not someone from the FTB?"

"Because France has allowed NATO to assume authority over the situation," said Turner, "and the White House wanted an American commander on the ground."

"So what do we do?" asked Jack Williams. "Twiddle our thumbs?"

"We'll provide General Allen with any assistance or resources he requests," said Turner. "Right now, the priority is to clear Carcassonne as fully as possible before the deadline, so if we're needed to help with that, we will go. If the government asks us to go to London and help with the aftermath of the Tube attack, we will say yes. In the meantime, we will wait, and we will prepare ourselves, which is what the third point of this briefing will cover. Before then, I want to discuss something else."

Jamie took a deep breath. 'Wait and see' had not been what he wanted to hear, and the looks on the faces of his colleagues told him he was not alone in that opinion. He understood the situation the Directors found themselves in: until Dracula's plans became clear, the priority had to be to remove as many people from Carcassonne as possible, even though Jamie suspected that they were playing directly into the first vampire's hands by doing so. It seemed clear that the widespread attacks and the forty-eight-hour deadline had been specifically designed by Dracula to occupy the time and resources of his enemies, and prevent them from formulating a rapid response. But even if so, there was no real alternative; given the previous night's chaos and dreadful loss of life, the French government and the supernatural Departments simply could not be seen to be ignoring a credible threat to an entire city of innocent people.

"Second item," said Turner. "While I appreciate that everything else may now seem inconsequential, we cannot allow ourselves to be frozen in the headlights by Dracula. We have to carry on our work, no matter what's happening in France, and, as a result, tonight will see the first public release of the vampire cure developed by the Lazarus Project, at University College Hospital in London. We're expecting protests and demonstrations from both pro- and anti-vampire organisations, so we'll be sending Operational Squads to ensure the safety and security of those who volunteer to receive the treatment. Captain Williams, I'm putting you in charge of this."

Jack rolled his eyes. "Great," he said. "There's definitely nothing more important I could be doing right now than babysitting doctors while they give injections to vampires."

Turner stared at him. "Are you finished?"

Jack stared back for a brief moment, but crumbled under the weight of the Director's gaze. "I'm finished," he said. "Sorry, sir."

"Thank you," said Turner. "I want you to take two squads to London, and I expect you to treat this like the Priority Level 1 operation it is. Every single dose of the cure robs Dracula of a potential soldier, and tips the odds in our favour."

"Fractionally," said Angela Darcy.

"Maybe so," said Turner. "But perhaps we can shift them a bit further. For the third item on our agenda, I'm going to ask Lieutenant Browning to take over. Matt?"

Jamie frowned as his friend got to his feet.

What's this, Matt? he wondered. *What haven't you told me?*

"Thank you, sir," said Matt, and glanced nervously around the room. "I want to tell you about PROMETHEUS, a last-resort strategic programme that has been developed in secret over the last few months. It was a hypothetical exercise, pending the existence of a workable cure, but today sees its official launch. It will—"

"Hang on," said Jamie. "What do you mean, developed in secret?"

Matt looked over at Turner, who had sat down.

"Membership of this Task Force is not a VIP card, Lieutenant Carpenter," said the Director. "There are things that are classified above Zero Hour, and until now, PROMETHEUS was one of them."

Jamie felt anger threaten to bloom in his stomach, but forced it down; instead, he shifted his gaze back to Matt, his eyes narrowing.

"Like I was saying," said Matt, "PROMETHEUS depended on the discovery and production of a workable cure. It's a strategic application of the principles of what has become known as the Browning Theory, and an extrapolation of certain—"

"For God's sake, Matt," said Angela. "Just tell us what it is."

Matt blushed, and nodded. "Sorry," he said. "To prepare for the likely confrontation with Dracula, the active roster of the Department will be turned into vampires. That's what PROMETHEUS is."

There was a moment of stunned silence before the Ops Room burst into uproar. Jack Williams and Frankenstein were out of their seats, as the rest of the Task Force hurled questions back and forth across the table.

"This is a joke, right?" bellowed Jack Williams. "Please tell me this is a joke?"

The embarrassed colour in Matt's cheeks had darkened to crimson, but he did not back down from the reaction his words had caused; he looked straight at Jack, and shook his head. Jamie stared, too stunned to speak or even move; he never would have thought he would hear such a concept from the mouth of his gentle, nervous friend. Matt's relationship with Natalia and his increasing influence inside the Loop had changed him in recent months, seen him grow into himself, but Jamie suddenly felt as though he didn't know him at all any more.

I don't recognise this person, he thought, as his colleagues shouted and argued around him.

"What's the point?" demanded Kate. "If we turn Operators today, they'll still be weak when we fight Dracula. Or do you think it's going to be months until we have to deal with him?"

"They'll still be stronger than they are now," said Matt. "And we can give them the best possible chance. We have access to one of the most powerful vampires in the world."

A chill ran up Jamie's spine. "Valentin?" he said. "That's who you're going to use for this?"

Matt turned to him. "Yes, Jamie," he said. "Valentin has agreed to help us."

"And what's he getting in return?" asked Jamie.

"That's not something you need to concern yourself with, Lieutenant," said Paul Turner.

Jamie felt heat rise behind his eyes. "Why not use me?" he said. "If you're serious about this, why not use what covers my fangs?"

"Because research shows that vampires turned by Valentin will be a minimum of seventeen per cent more powerful than vampires turned by you," said Turner. "And that seventeen per cent might make all the difference."

"What research?" asked Jamie, frowning deeply. "When did you—"

Understanding hit him like a punch to the stomach. Cold spilled up his spine as he remembered the conversation with Matt in his quarters, the swab kit and the scraper.

"Jesus," he said, his voice low. "How could you lie to me like that, Matt?"

Kate frowned. "What are you talking about?"

"I'm sorry," said Matt, holding his gaze. "It was classified."

"Classified," said Jamie, and grunted with laughter. "No more secrets, right?"

Matt grimaced. "Please, Jamie," he said. "This isn't about you."

"So what is it about?" he asked. "Defeating Dracula? No matter what it takes to do so? No matter the—"

Paul Turner stood up. "Enough!" he shouted. "This is a Zero Hour Task Force briefing, not a debate. Is that clear?"

Jamie dropped his eyes to the table; he could no longer look at Matt.

"Nobody's going to agree to this," said Jack Williams, his voice low. "You're asking people to give up their humanity."

Matt narrowed his eyes and stared at Jack. "What about Jamie?" he said. "Do you no longer consider him human?"

Jamie recoiled. "What did you say?"

"Of course I consider him human," said Jack. "That's not what I'm saying. You know I—"

"PROMETHEUS will give us more than a hundred Operators with Jamie's speed and strength," said Matt. "By using a process that we now know is completely reversible."

"You're talking about our colleagues, Matt," said Kate, her eyes wide with shock. "About our *friends*."

Matt glanced at her, and said nothing.

"It doesn't matter," said Frankenstein, his voice a low rumble. "Jack's right. Nobody is going to agree to this."

"That's irrelevant, Colonel," said Paul Turner.

"What do you mean?" asked Jack.

"We will not be *asking* anyone to take part," said the Director. "We will be *ordering* them to. Participation in PROMETHEUS is mandatory."

The cold working its way up Jamie's spine spread through his body as he stared at the Director.

Everything's changed, he thought. *I don't know when it happened, or why I didn't notice, but it has. Whatever happens, whatever's to come, I don't know if there's any way back from this.*

We're at the end of the line.

34

A VISION OF THE FUTURE

Marie Carpenter stepped out of the airlock for the first time since she had volunteered to take the cure, and felt something other than the sense of desperation that usually filled her when she looked at the grey surroundings of the cellblock.

She could normally read the words on the warning sign at the far end of the corridor, more than a hundred metres away, and feel the tingling warmth of the purple walls of ultraviolet light. Now, all she could see in the distance were the white lines painted along the floor, the border that visitors to the cellblock were not supposed to cross, so as not to get too close to the prisoners.

Her arm throbbed with pain inside its cast, despite the painkillers she had taken before she left the infirmary, her eyes were still swollen almost shut, and she felt *exhausted*, felt mentally and physically worn out. All that notwithstanding, Marie was as happy as she could remember being; she felt like *herself*, for the first time since Alexandru Rusmanov had sunk his fangs into her neck, and arguably much longer than that.

She walked slowly down the corridor, relishing the aches in her back and the mild headache lurking at the back of her skull. For more than a year, she had felt almost nothing physical; her vampire side had masked all discomfort, and a sensation of overwhelming power and euphoria had been only the flex of a muscle away.

What she wanted now, more than anything, was to see her son. She knew he had visited her in the infirmary the morning after her arm had been repaired, when she had been sleeping off the surgery, and that a change in the rules had prevented him from returning; the doctors had explained it all to her when she had wondered aloud if he was ever going to come and see her. She had a suspicion that Jamie would be angry with her for not having told him what she was going to do before she did it, but she was confident she could make him see why she had not been able to wait.

"Hello, Marie."

She jumped, and spun round to see Valentin Rusmanov smiling at her. She had been so deep in thought that she had not realised she had reached his cell and, as ever in this type of situation, her first response was to be embarrassed; how *rude* it must have seemed as she just walked past without bothering to say hello.

"Hello, Valentin," she said. "Sorry, I was in a world of my own."

"That's quite all right," said the vampire. "I would imagine you have a good deal on your mind."

"You would imagine correctly," she said, and smiled. "How are you?"

"Unchanging," said Valentin, returning her smile. "Come on in, why don't you? I was about to make tea."

"Thank you," she said, and walked towards the cell. She paused at the ultraviolet barrier, even though she knew she no longer needed to worry about such things; the habit had become deeply ingrained. She took a deep breath and stepped through the purple light, feeling a warm tingle on her skin, and took a seat on the sofa as Valentin boiled the kettle and prepared two mugs; the look of disdain on his face as he placed teabags into them never failed to amuse her.

"So you did it?" he said, glancing over his shoulder at her. "You took the cure?"

She nodded. "I did it."

"Were you the first?"

"I'm not sure," she said. "I think so."

He looked at the cast on her arm, and smiled. "Risky."

"I suppose it was," she said. "One worth taking, though."

Valentin carried the steaming mugs across the cell, handed one to her, and sat down at the other end of the sofa.

"Did you really hate being a vampire that much?" he asked.

"I did," she said, and sipped her tea. "I really did."

"Why, if you don't mind me asking?"

"I don't mind at all," she said. "I didn't feel like myself. I saw the same face in the mirror, but I felt like I had become someone else. Or *something* else, at least. Don't you ever feel like that?"

Valentin smiled. "I was turned more than five hundred years ago," he said. "If I ever felt that way, I'm afraid I no longer remember it."

"So it's safe to say you won't be taking the cure then?"

"No," said Valentin. "I don't see that happening."

Marie nodded. "You love it, don't you?"

The old vampire narrowed his eyes, and smiled. "Love what?"

"Being powerful," said Marie. "Being older and wiser and stronger and faster than everyone else. It's what you live for."

Valentin's smile widened into a grin. "It *was*," he said. "It certainly was, for a long time. For more than a century, men and women flocked to my house in New York for the express purpose of showering me with their adoration. They would literally kill to spend time in my presence, and I'm afraid to say that I permitted them to do so. In truth, I encouraged them to."

Marie grimaced. "I wish you wouldn't talk like that," she said. "I don't like to think of you in such a way."

The vampire nodded. "I appreciate that," he said. "And I agree that it is hardly appropriate afternoon tea conversation. But I can no more change the past than you can. Mine lives inside me, as yours lives inside you. Although the reality of mine is far less blood-soaked than you have likely been led to believe."

"Really?" she asked. Despite his reputation, Valentin had only ever been polite to her, and kind, and she could hear the hope in her voice.

"Really," said the old vampire. "I know all too well the stories that circulate about me, the legends and myths, because I started many of them myself. If you ask Paul Turner, or any other man or woman inside this base, they will tell you that I have been something of a one-man genocide, an evil creature of extravagant cruelty and viciousness who has ended thousands of lives. The truth, my dear Marie, is markedly different. I doubt I have personally killed more than a hundred people in the last five centuries, which, when you are as notorious as I have been, when you are an endless target for vampires desperate to prove themselves, is really not very many. It is certainly far fewer than Valeri, and orders of magnitude fewer than Alexandru, who fitted the descriptions whispered about me far better than I ever have. I would never claim to be innocent. I have done terrible things, and been party to many more. But I am not the monster they would have you believe."

Marie realised she had been holding her breath as the ancient vampire spoke, and let it out in a long sigh. "Why haven't you told anyone this?" she asked.

Valentin smiled. "Because I take great satisfaction from people being scared of me," he said. "Getting what you want without having to use violence is true power. I was taught that many centuries ago, and it still holds true."

"By Dracula?" she asked.

"Indeed. He was a brilliant man, in many ways. A perfect creation of his time, possessed of endless determination and absolute ruthlessness, willing to do whatever was necessary to ensure victory. His time has long passed, however. He does not fit the world as it is."

"It seems he thinks otherwise," said Marie. "If what I saw on the news is anything to go by."

Valentin sighed. "I saw it too," he said. "Dracula is a creature of rage and vengeance. He would burn down the entire world rather than fail to impose his will upon it."

Marie grimaced. Her good mood had evaporated, replaced by unease about the future and, in particular, the part her son would be required to play in it.

"What will happen?" she asked. "If Dracula wins, I mean. What will the world look like then?"

Valentin shrugged. "I cannot say," he said. "The world he wanted to conquer when I served him was very different. But I would imagine that you will be very grateful that you have taken the cure. I don't think the long life of a vampire is going to be something to cherish if Dracula is victorious."

Marie stared at him for a long moment, then drained her mug and stood up.

"Thank you for the tea, Valentin," she said. "And the conversation. I'll miss talking to you when this is all over."

The old vampire smiled. "The feeling is mutual," he said. "You have been a beacon of grace and civility in this drab place, and I will always think of you most fondly."

Marie smiled, and turned away. She walked through the purple barrier without pausing, and almost crashed directly into Matt Browning. They leapt awkwardly out of each other's way, their faces reddening, embarrassed apologies spilling from their mouths.

"I'm so sorry, I didn't—"

"No, I'm sorry, that was my—"

"Please, I should have been—"

"Are you OK? Did I—"

Marie stopped talking, and smiled. Her son's friend did likewise, his cheeks pink, a nervous look on his face.

"Let's start again," she said. "Hello, Matt. It's nice to see you."

"You too, Mrs Carpenter," said Matt, nodding vigorously. "How are you doing?"

"Much better than I was," she said. "All thanks to you."

The colour in his face deepened, and she briefly wondered whether it was possible for a person to actually explode with embarrassment.

"That's good news," he said. "Really good."

"What about you?" she asked. As she looked more closely, she could see that the teenager's eyes were red and puffy and, with the exception of his crimson cheeks, his skin was ghostly pale. "Are you sure you're all right, Matt?"

He winced. "I'm fine," he said. "Just… I'm fine. Rough meeting."

Marie nodded. "If you're sure?"

"I'm sure," he said. "Thank you, though."

"You're welcome. Have you seen Jamie?" she asked.

Matt frowned. "Why?"

Marie smiled. "I'd like to see my son," she said. "If you see him, will you tell him I've been discharged? In case he doesn't know?"

"Right," said Matt, his frown not quite disappearing. "I mean, yes. Of course I will. If I see him."

There's something going on here, she thought. *Have he and Jamie had a fight? It feels like it.*

"Thank you," she said. "So what are you doing down here?"

Matt nodded towards the purple barrier. "I'm here to see Valentin."

Inside the cell, the vampire got to his feet.

"Is it time?" he asked.

"Yes," said Matt. "It's time."

35

INTERNATIONAL AID

OUTSKIRTS OF CARCASSONNE, SOUTHERN FRANCE

All activity inside the displaced persons camp stopped as the helicopters rumbled over the horizon.

They were Russian Mi-26s, the largest transport helicopters ever to fly, but there were no Russians inside their huge holds; they had been sent to Toulouse airport by the SPC to meet the plane that had brought General Bob Allen and his NS9 team across the Atlantic, and carry the Americans to their destination. It was a display of international teamwork that would have been unlikely as little as five years earlier; the thaw that followed the end of the Cold War had taken a long time to penetrate the highly secretive world of the supernatural Departments.

The helicopters landed with a series of deafening thuds. Their engines and rotors began to wind down, and a loud beeping noise echoed out across the fields as the loading ramps at their rears were lowered slowly to the ground. Bob Allen stopped halfway down one of them, and looked out across the fledgling camp.

Surrounding the landing site were a dozen large white tents, emblazoned with the logos of the Red Cross and UNICEF. Beyond them, parked neatly along one edge of the field, was a row of trucks and jeeps, and on the other side of a low hedge he could see hundreds and hundreds of parked cars; it looked like the outskirts of a music festival. To the north, there were at least two fields of grey and blue tents, all of them bearing the legend HUMANITARIAN AID. It was a sight General Allen had never expected to find in the countryside of a developed European country; it looked like the camps he had seen during his military days, in places like Rwanda and Sierra Leone.

Behind him, Danny Lawrence led four squads of Operators down on to the grass while the technical support team started unloading towering pallets of containers and flight cases from the second helicopter. Allen didn't waste time giving them the order to start assembling the command centre; he knew they would do their jobs without him needing to. He glanced round, saw Danny order the Operators to survey the camp and report back, and smiled; he had complete faith in his team, even in circumstances as strange and unprecedented as these.

"General Allen?"

He turned to see a French Army Captain standing in front of him.

"I'm Allen," he said.

"Captain Mathias Guérin," said the man, and extended his hand. "Welcome back to France, General. I am sorry it is not in better circumstances."

Allen took Guérin's hand and shook it. "Thank you, Captain," he said. "I take it the Germans aren't here yet?"

"We are expecting the FTB within the next two hours," said Guérin. "Although I understand you will remain in charge?"

"That's correct," said Allen. "I will act as Commanding Officer, under NATO authority. Can you give me a progress update?"

"Yes, sir," said Guérin. "More than eight thousand people have left the city so far, of which more than five thousand are here in this camp. Reconnaissance indicates—"

"What's the population of Carcassonne?" interrupted Allen.

"Forty-eight thousand permanent residents, sir," said Guérin. "Although there are likely to be at least three or four thousand tourists currently visiting the city."

"So more than fifty thousand people?" said Allen. "That's a hell of an evacuation."

"Yes, sir," said Guérin. "Reconnaissance indicates that a large number are preparing to leave later today, and we believe that many more will do so as the deadline approaches tomorrow."

"Believing so isn't good enough," said Allen. "We need to make sure they go. This is a mandatory evacuation."

"We are doing everything we can, sir," said Guérin. "Many of the city's police and emergency personnel appear to have already left, but those who are still here and still working have been deployed to keep the roads open and manage the crowds at the train station. SNCF has agreed to run extra rail services through the night, but are stopping them at noon tomorrow. The airport is closed to all non-military flights, and the Red Cross and UNICEF are going door to door inside the city, telling people that they are required to leave and assisting those who cannot do so on their own."

Allen nodded. "Dracula?"

Guérin's face paled, ever so slightly, but his voice remained calm and steady. "There have been no vampire sightings since last night," he said. "Satellite thermal imaging shows heat blooms all over the old city, but the stone is thick, and it is impossible to tell the vampires from the hostages."

"Tell me about them," he said.

"One hundred and eleven names on the list that was distributed to the TV crews," said Guérin. "Thirteen nationalities. French, German,

British, American, Chinese, Japanese, Swedish, Spanish, Korean, Canadian, Russian, Norwegian, Turkish. No demands as yet."

"There won't be any," said Allen. "They're not really hostages. They're a human shield."

Guérin nodded. "Has NATO decided on a response?"

"As of this moment, the priority remains evacuation. We get the city clear before the deadline, then reassess the situation."

"Has a tactical strike been ruled out?"

"For now," said Allen.

"I saw what was done to Château Dauncy," said Guérin. "Is a similar result not possible here?"

Allen smiled. "Château Dauncy was a unique situation, Captain," he said. "There was only a single non-vampire inside, and he was a serving member of Blacklight who was aware of the risks. Here we have more than a hundred civilians at the primary location, plus thousands more in the surrounding area. Neither NATO nor the government in Paris think our first response should be to flatten a city, and I can promise you that Beijing and Washington agree with them, at least for now."

"I understand," said Guérin.

"General?" shouted a voice.

Allen turned, and felt his smile widen into a grin. During the five minutes he had been talking to the French Captain, a large grey building had appeared in the centre of the field, seemingly out of nowhere. The woman who had shouted, a Technical Division Specialist named Luisa Ramirez, was standing in front of it.

"Yes, Operator?" he asked.

"We're up, sir," said Ramirez. "Ready for your inspection."

Allen nodded. The compound would eventually sprawl far beyond the single structure that had been erected so far, but getting the nerve centre up and running, less than ten minutes after landing, was outstanding.

"Excellent," he said, and turned back to face Guérin. "I'm going to ask you to be part of my command team, Captain. Can you handle that?"

"Yes, sir," said Guérin, and smiled proudly. "Thank you."

"All right," he said. "I'll keep you informed. Dismissed."

Guérin saluted, turned sharply on his heels, and strode away towards the white tents. Allen watched him go, then walked across to the grey building, and pushed open the door.

The majority of the wide room was piled high with boxes and cases and coils of wires, but a space at the far end was immaculately tidy. There, a wide bench had been bolted to the metal floor, upon which sat five networked terminals and a dozen screens showing satellite images of Carcassonne, rotating feeds from the city's CCTV network, French and American twenty-four-hour news channels, various comms windows, and the remote-access screen for the NS9 network.

"Everything's hot," said Ramirez, emerging from behind the bench with a soldering iron in her hand. "Secure lines in and out, radar and radio and satellite surveillance. All the comforts of home, sir."

Allen grinned. "Great work, Operator," he said. "Let me get settled in."

Ramirez nodded and exited, closing the door behind her.

Allen dragged a chair across to the bench, sat down, and cycled quickly through the CCTV feeds; he knew what he was going to see, but needed to check for himself. The screen showed a series of monochrome images of the shopping streets of Carcassonne, train and bus stations, bars and restaurants, then turned black for almost a minute. He noted the numbers of the cameras until the screen came back to life with a shot looking up the hill towards the medieval city, and checked their locations against the list that had been loaded on to his desktop.

As I expected, thought Allen. *All the cameras in the old city are down. He doesn't want us watching him.*

He looked back at the screen. The walls of medieval Carcassonne reared up, thick and wide and seemingly impenetrable, topped with impaled bodies that were even more gruesome in grainy black and white. Had it not been for the parked cars visible at the bottom of the frame, he could have easily believed he was looking at an image that was hundreds of years old; a medieval castle, bristling with ghastly trophies, ready to repel invaders.

The NS9 Director sat back in his chair and pulled his radio from his belt. He keyed in a frequency, pressed SEND, and held the handset to his ear.

"Sir?" said a voice, instantly.

"I need to see you in the command centre," he said. "Right away."

"On my way, sir."

Allen cut the line, and got up from his chair in time to see Danny Lawrence step through the door.

"Everything OK, sir?" asked the Operator.

"Fine," said Allen. "Did I see you send the squads to check the camp?"

"Yes, sir," said Danny. "I told them to report back at 1430."

Allen checked his watch. Forty-eight minutes from now.

"All right," he said. "I want a security perimeter in place as soon as possible, including a strict no-fly zone. News helicopters hovering overhead is the last thing we need. I doubt we can confiscate the cellphone of every resident of Carcassonne, but I want it made very clear to them that they are part of a military operation, whether they like it or not. I don't want to see any photos of Operators on Twitter. Is that clear?"

"Yes, sir," said Danny.

"Good," said Allen. "Bring me the compiled reconnaissance reports when you have them, then take a squad into the city and assess the situation on the ground. There are still four hours of daylight left, so don't go anywhere near the old city, just get a sense of what's happening in there. Clear?"

Danny nodded. "Yes, sir."

"Dismissed."

36

WILLING VICTIMS

"How are you feeling about this?" asked Valentin, as the lift doors closed.

"About what?" asked Matt.

"Lining up your friends and colleagues to let me bite them."

He grimaced. "How do you think I feel about it?"

The vampire shrugged. "I have no idea," he said. "I would assume that you find the concept unpleasant, but that you intend to stiffen your upper lip and bravely carry on in the name of the greater good. But you seem largely unperturbed."

"Of course I don't like it," he said, "but it's necessary."

"Necessary," repeated Valentin, and nodded. "That word has been the justification for many of the worst things that have ever happened."

"Can you just shut up?" he asked. "Please?"

Valentin mimed zipping his lips closed. Matt sighed, and stared at the wall of the lift, silently urging it to hurry. He hated spending time with the youngest of the Rusmanov brothers; it felt like walking a tightrope over quicksand, where one wrong step might cost him dearly. He was a scientist, a believer in facts and hypotheses, and the only certainty when it came to Valentin was that he could not trust a single word the vampire said.

Of course he didn't like PROMETHEUS; it bothered him greatly, far more than he would have admitted to anyone other than Natalia and Paul Turner. He really *did* believe it was necessary, that it might be the Department's only chance to face Dracula on anything like a level playing field, but he understood all too well the moral and ethical issues the project raised, especially the decision to make it mandatory. In the Zero Hour Task Force briefing that had just finished, he had refused to let Jack Williams back him down; he had stood his ground, as shock and disappointment rose on to the faces of his colleagues and friends, but the hail of shouted questions and protests had hurt him deeply. He would have had to be a monster for them not to.

He winced at the memory of the look on Jamie's face as he realised that Matt had deceived him. It had been disappointment, rather than anger, which had been far worse; the look of someone whose heart was hardening behind his eyes.

Can't think about that now, he told himself. *You can fix things with Jamie later, if he lets you. Right now, you need to focus.*

"Are you sure you're all right, Mr Browning?" asked Valentin.

Mercifully, the lift slowed to a halt on Level C, and Matt slid through the opening doors without responding. He walked down the corridor with Valentin flying easily at his side, and pushed open the double doors of the infirmary, which had been hurriedly emptied to make way for the launch of PROMETHEUS; testing of the cure had been suspended in the aftermath of Dracula's attack on Carcassonne, and those civilians who had been recovering inside the long white room had been moved up to empty quarters on Level B.

The infirmary was now crammed full of beds, eighteen along each wall, each enclosed by a white privacy curtain; the turn could be a horrible, undignified experience, even with abundant blood and medical professionals on hand. The plan was to turn the first thirty-six Operators whose names had been selected at random, then the next thirty-six, and so on until it was done. The projection was that it would take three and a half days, although there were very few certainties where the mechanics of vampirism were concerned.

At the back of the room stood a sombre line of men and women. Paul Turner was at its centre, with two of the Loop's medical staff on either side of him. To one side stood six Operators from the Security Division; they eyed Valentin with clear disdain as Matt led the vampire down the long room and stopped in front of the Director, who nodded.

"So," said Valentin, grinning widely. "Where do you want me?"

Matt watched with growing unease as Operators, a large number of whom he recognised, filed into the infirmary.

At the front of the queue was Angela Darcy, her face pale and determined. Five or six places behind her was Dominique Saint-Jacques, and near the back was Lizzy Ellison, whom Matt had never actually spoken to but felt like he knew from Jamie's many stories about her. All of a sudden, PROMETHEUS felt very *real*; something that had started out as a distant hypothetical was about to actually happen, and the thought churned his stomach, particularly if he glanced at the expression of hungry delight on Valentin's face.

Near the doors of the infirmary, one of the doctors was checking names off a list. When she was finished, she made her way down to the front of the room and spoke to Paul Turner in a low voice.

"Thirty-four, sir," she said. "Lester and McCluskey aren't here."

Turner nodded, then turned to the Security Operators. "Have them found."

The squad leader nodded, pulled his radio from his belt, and spoke rapidly into it.

"This is actually happening, then?" asked one of the queuing Operators. He stepped out of line and stared down the infirmary, his eyes narrow with anger. "It's not a joke? You actually expect me to let that piece of shit bite me?"

"Ouch," said Valentin, a smile on his narrow face. "That hurts my feelings."

"Your orders were clear, Lieutenant," said Turner, ignoring the vampire. "Get back in line and be quiet."

The Operator stepped forward, his face flushing red with fury. "You can't make me," he said. "This is bullshit. It's *inhuman*."

"Your concerns have been noted," said Turner. "Now get back into line. Don't make me tell you again."

"*My concerns have been noted?*" said the Operator. "Have they really? That's great. That's absolutely bloody *fantastic*. Why do I have to let him bite me, when everyone knows they turned the Broadmoor patients with injections? Why can't you at least do that?"

"That is not an option at this time," said Turner, his voice full of ice.

"Why not?" demanded the Operator, and pointed at Valentin. "Because he wouldn't agree to it? Because he *wants* to bite people and you're just going to let him?"

Valentin's smile widened into a grin as Turner visibly fought to control his temper. "You have two choices, Lieutenant," said the Director. "You can follow the order in hand, or you can go to the cells. Which is it going to be?"

Matt stared, his heart pounding. PROMETHEUS hadn't even started, and already it was going wrong.

The red-faced Operator walked slowly towards the Director, every pair of eyes in the room on him as he moved, and put his arms out before him, his wrists together.

"I'll take the cells," he said. "Better that than this. Much better."

"Fine," said Turner. "Have it your way."

He looked over at the Security squad, and nodded. Two of them stepped forward and zip-tied the Operator's wrists, then led him silently towards the infirmary doors. Matt watched them go, then looked at the remainder of the line, wondering who was going to be the next to protest; if they all made the same decision as their colleague, PROMETHEUS was going to be dead in the water.

"Anyone else?" shouted Turner, causing a number of the queuing Operators to jump. "Anyone else unable to follow a simple order? Before you make your decision, I would urge you to think about why this is happening. Do you think it's because we like putting you through something unpleasant? Or because we believe it gives us our best chance, perhaps our *only* chance, of defeating Dracula? I understand that it's unusual, that nothing like this has been done in the history of the Department, but you all know that we now have a working cure for vampirism, and your orders make it perfectly clear that PROMETHEUS is a temporary measure. But they *are* still orders, and I expect you to follow them. So raise your hand, right now, if you're unwilling to do so."

The colour had drained from a number of Operators' faces, but nobody moved, and Matt breathed a silent sigh of relief.

"Thank you," said Turner, and turned towards him. "Carry on, Lieutenant Browning."

Matt nodded, and looked at Valentin.

"Ready?" he asked.

"Of course," replied the vampire. "I'm positively salivating with anticipation."

Matt grimaced. "All right then," he said. "Let's get started."

Angela Darcy stepped forward, her eyes slightly narrowed. Matt, who had spent his first months at the Loop in the grip of an overpowering crush on the deadly former spy, swallowed hard and forced a small smile.

"What do you need me to do?" she asked.

"Open your collar, please," said Valentin. "And turn your head to one side."

Angela fixed him with a disgusted stare, then unfastened the collar of her uniform, lowered its zip past her collarbones, and tilted her head. There was no fear on her face as the vampire stepped towards her, just a clear desire for this to be over and done with as quickly as possible.

Valentin took hold of her waist with one hand, and placed the other against her cheek. Angela shuddered, but stayed still as the vampire leant slowly forward, his eyes smouldering red, and buried his face in her neck. Her eyes flew wide, and Matt saw her fists clench as an awful sucking sound filled the room; he stared, appalled by the reality unfolding before him, until out of the corner of his eye he saw the Director shoot him a quizzical look, and remembered himself.

"That's enough," he said.

Valentin didn't move. Over the vampire's shoulder, Angela met his eyes.

"That's enough, Valentin," Matt said, his voice rising, and grabbed the vampire's shoulder.

Valentin turned on him, his face a monstrous vision, and Matt felt his stomach turn to water. The vampire's fangs were huge and gleaming, his mouth smeared with blood and twisted into a snarl, his eyes roaring with swirling crimson-black as Matt stared into them, frozen solid with terror. Then the glowing fire died, as suddenly as if a switch had been flipped inside the vampire's head.

"I'm sorry," said Valentin, his voice low, and released his grip on the Security Officer. Angela's hand flew to her neck, but she didn't back away; she stared at the vampire with hatred twisting her face.

"I'm sorry," repeated Valentin. "It has been a long time since I tasted human blood. Especially human blood as sweet as that."

The vampire smiled at Angela, who gave him a wide smile in return, then stepped forward and spat in his face.

Oh shit, thought Matt, and looked desperately at the Director. Turner was watching with his usual impassive expression, but his hand had gone to the grip of his T-Bone.

A deep growl rumbled from the vampire's throat. Slowly – dreadfully, *ominously* slowly – he raised his hand and wiped the spit from his cheek, his eyes locked on Angela as red flickered in their corners.

"Valentin," said Turner, his voice low and full of warning.

The vampire and the Security Officer stared at each other for a seemingly endless moment, pregnant with the prospect of disaster. Then, with a casualness that was either genuine or a truly phenomenal piece of acting, Valentin broke their gaze and smiled at Matt.

"Next," he said.

A doctor appeared at Angela's side, pressed a bandage to her neck, and led her towards one of the beds. She looked back over her shoulder as she went, her eyes full of anger, until a curtain was drawn round the bed at the furthest end of the room, hiding her from view.

The second Operator in line stepped forward, a man in his early forties whom Matt didn't recognise. His face was ghostly pale, but his hands were steady as he unzipped his uniform and turned his head.

"Don't be ridiculous," said Valentin, smiling at the man. "Roll your sleeve up, for heaven's sake."

The man frowned, but did as he was told. Valentin raised the Operator's arm, gave the skin of the wrist the tiniest bite imaginable, and let him go.

"Next," said the vampire.

37

DOWN THE RABBIT HOLE

LINCOLN, LINCOLNSHIRE, ENGLAND
EIGHT HOURS LATER

Pete Randall put his car into gear and followed Greg Browning through the dark streets of Lincoln, keeping a safe distance between them.

He had tried to persuade himself that everything was fine, for mostly personal reasons; he was tired, and he wanted more than anything to believe in what they were doing at SSL, that it really was the force for good that Greg had pitched to him.

But he could no longer convince himself. His friend's behaviour following the announcement of the cure had been the final straw, the tipping point for concerns that had been growing steadily for some time, not least the unsettling coincidences he had found in the call logs, the incident with the security guard at the blood drive in Peterborough, and Greg's blatant lies afterwards.

Pete hoped there was nothing going on. He really, truly did. Nothing would give him greater pleasure than to have to admit to himself that he was simply a paranoid fool who had clearly lost the ability to trust people.

He just wasn't sure that was the case.

Two hundred metres ahead, Greg turned left at an intersection; he was strolling along, his hands in his pockets, headphones in his ears, his eyes fixed forward. Pete pulled over, counted thirty seconds in his head, then followed his friend round the corner.

Greg was gone.

The road stretching out in front of Pete was long and straight, but there was no sign of his friend on either pavement.

Lost him, he told himself. *Lost him after barely two minutes. What a bloody awful spy you'd have made.*

He slowed the car to a crawl, peering desperately out of the windows on both sides. As he passed a newsagent's, the shop door opened and Greg emerged, his attention focused on the chocolate bar he was unwrapping. Pete froze behind the wheel; there were less than ten metres between them, and if Greg looked up, they would be staring straight at each other. He fought back the urge to stamp his foot on to the accelerator; a revving engine and squeal of tyres would be guaranteed to draw his friend's attention. Instead, Pete forced himself to maintain his speed, hoping that a nondescript car passing by on a main road would not qualify as noteworthy. His heart thumped as he rolled forward, his eyes locked on the rear-view mirror, through which he could see Greg stuffing chocolate into his mouth as he resumed his stroll. Pete took the first left he came to, accelerated, took two more lefts, and turned back on to the main road, a safe distance behind his friend again.

He kept up his slow surveillance for the next fifteen minutes, during which his friend did nothing to suggest he was doing anything other than enjoying a walk in the cool evening air. As the shops and commercial buildings began to give way to suburban streets, Greg finally turned off the main road, and walked across the forecourt of a pub called The Red Lion.

What a waste of time this has been, thought Pete. *He's going for a bloody drink after work.*

But as he parked his car down the quiet street at the side of the pub, a question occurred to him.

Who with? Greg spends more time than anyone in the office, and he's never mentioned any friends in Lincoln. So unless he's come three miles away from his flat to have a drink on his own, who's he meeting in there?

Barely fifteen minutes later he got his answer.

Greg emerged from the pub at the centre of a group of men, laughing and jostling and pushing each other like teenagers on a night out. Pete watched them carefully, waiting for them to pass beneath the street light outside the pub, and drew in a sharp breath when they did.

There were eight of them, including Greg. He didn't recognise three of them, although he instantly didn't like the look of them; they looked like hard men, their heads shaved, their jaws square, their bodies thickly muscled. The other four he knew; three were SSL volunteers, all of them men in their twenties who had joined in the past month, as the charity had expanded as fast as it could. The final man, who was walking beside Greg and chatting to him like they were old friends, was Phil Baker, the security guard Pete had dismissed from the blood drive in Peterborough.

I knew there was something going on, he thought. *I bloody knew it.*

The men turned on to the road where Pete was parked, and a burst of panic raced through him. They were still fifty metres away, but were walking directly towards him; he didn't know whether Greg would recognise his car, but he was absolutely *certain* that he would recognise his friend sitting behind the wheel. He huddled low in his seat, ready to duck down and squeeze himself into the footwell, his eyes peering over the black plastic of the dashboard, his heart pounding.

Barely thirty metres away, Greg stopped and unlocked a car that

Pete had never seen before. Baker opened the doors of a jeep parked behind it, and the eight men folded themselves into the two vehicles; it looked like a tight squeeze, even from Pete's unorthodox vantage point. He watched as the two vehicles pulled away from the kerb, and sat up in his seat as the tension in his chest eased. He started his car, waited thirty seconds, then followed them back out on to the main road.

Twenty minutes later, Pete pulled to a halt behind a low-lying sprawl of industrial units on the outskirts of Lincoln.

The vehicles he was following had stopped outside a warehouse at the end of the road while one of the men got out and rolled up a wide metal door, then disappeared inside the building. Pete got out of his car, made his way slowly down the side street until he reached the corner, and peered round it.

The rolling door was still raised, and he could hear the noise of engines. He squinted into the dark warehouse, desperate to know what was going on, then shrank back as headlights blazed into life, seeming to point directly at him. He pressed himself against the wall, crept forward again, and looked back round the corner in time to see four black vans drive out of the warehouse and on to the road, one after the other. Three immediately accelerated away while the fourth stopped by the open warehouse door, its engine rumbling. Pete shielded his eyes against the glare of the headlights and saw Greg hop down from the driver's side. He lowered the metal door, locked it, and walked back to the van.

Pete's heart stopped dead.

Greg had changed clothes while he was inside the warehouse and was now wearing all black. But as he climbed back up into the van, Pete had clearly seen the crude white outline of a wolf's head on his friend's chest.

Night Stalker, he thought. *Oh, Greg. What the hell have you done?*

The van roared away from the warehouse. By the time Pete got back to his car, fired up the engine, and reached the main road, it was barely more than a black speck in the distance. He put his foot down, his insides churning with worry.

Even now, as he chased after the van, he did not believe that Greg Browning was a bad man. But he *was* easily led, and easily manipulated, and possessed of a wellspring of frustration and a rage that was never far below the surface. Pete had not known him before the darkness had reached into both their lives and laid waste to them, but he was sure that, knowingly or not, his friend had retrospectively idealised that time; to hear Greg tell it now, his had been a life of domestic bliss with a wife he adored and two kids who idolised him. What was undoubtedly real, however, was his bitterly held belief that the subsequent unravelling of his existence and estrangement from his family was due to vampires, to Blacklight, to bad luck and bad timing; in short, that it was everybody's fault apart from his own.

Pete had thought their ordeal at the hands of Albert Harker had softened his friend, had shown him that violence and intimidation were futile; he had believed that was what had led to the founding of SSL. But now, as he closed the gap on the van, he wondered whether the truth was exactly the opposite; that Greg's anger and hatred had been solidified by their experience, that his world view had been twisted far more radically than Pete had realised.

I have to do something, he thought. *I need to stop this before it's too late.*

He knew he should call the police; he should have taken out his phone and dialled 999 the second he saw his friend emerge from the warehouse with what was very clearly the Night Stalker logo emblazoned on his chest. But he hadn't, and until he knew *why*

Greg was doing it, until he could look him in the face and ask him to stop, he wasn't going to.

Part of him was thinking about SSL. If it got out that one of the charity's founders was also part of a vigilante group who were responsible for the murders of *at least* a dozen vampires, it would ruin them, and all the good they had done would be for nothing. But even though there could be no possible way to justify what Greg and his fellow Night Stalkers had done, a larger part of him simply wanted to give Greg the chance to explain himself; he felt he owed his friend that much.

On the edge of Lincoln, where the city bled into the countryside, the van turned down a narrow lane. Pete slowed, saw a postbox on a pole at the turning, and swore heavily. He had been hoping the road led to a village, but the lone postbox suggested that all that was down there was a single house; if that was the case, there was no way he could follow without giving himself away. He drove past the turning, looking for a place to pull over and wait for the van to re-emerge. After barely two hundred metres, his headlights picked out a lay-by; Pete pulled gratefully into it, turned off the car's engine, and got out.

For long minutes, he stood at the edge of the road, listening for the telltale growl of an engine over the chirping and rustling of the woods and the thudding of his heart. On two occasions, he thought he heard it, only for a car to sweep past him and disappear into the darkness, its headlights blinding. Eventually, as the tension threatened to overwhelm him, he heard a distant rumble. He froze, holding his breath and straining his hearing, until there could be absolutely no doubt.

The van was coming back.

Pete got into his car and waited to see which way the van would turn when it reached the main road. After thirty seconds, surely long enough for it to have come past him if it was going to, he pulled out, accelerated over a low rise, and saw brake lights disappearing round a bend in the distance. He put his foot down and followed Greg back towards the city, a frown etched on his face.

The van led him into Lincoln's grimy industrial district, until it finally came to a halt on a patch of waste ground beside the canal. Pete pulled into the shadowy car park of a factory half a street away and got out of his car.

Then everything began to happen very fast.

He crept along the road, sticking to the shadows and watching the ground for anything that might creak or crack underfoot. As he reached the corner of the last building, the spot that marked the limit of his cover, the van's rear door swung open, and Pete clamped a hand over his mouth so he didn't cry out.

A black figure – wearing a balaclava so he couldn't tell whether it was Greg or one of the others – jumped down from inside the vehicle and hauled an old man out on to the ground. The man's arms and legs were limp, his head lolling back as he was dragged away from the van, but his eyes were open, and Pete could see the naked fear that filled them. Near the edge of the canal, the Night Stalker lowered the old man and positioned him on his knees, like he was arranging a doll. The limp figure almost overbalanced, but the masked man grabbed his shoulders and set him upright.

"Sit still, you old fart," said the Night Stalker, and Pete felt his stomach churn as he recognised Greg's voice.

The driver's door opened and the second Night Stalker got out. The dim glow of security lights on the surrounding buildings illuminated them, and Pete realised that the two men were armed; guns hung from their belts, alongside ultraviolet torches. He stood in the shadows, terrified by what was happening in front of him, but equally terrified of revealing himself; he didn't think Greg would hurt him, but he wasn't sure enough to force his legs or his vocal cords into action.

"Jacob Hillman," said Greg. "Look at me."

For a long moment, nothing happened. Then the other Night Stalker stepped forward, and roughly pushed the old man's head back.

"That's better," said Greg. "You preyed on desperate and vulnerable boys and men for more than two decades. You confessed to your sins, and the time has come for you to be held accountable for your crimes. Do you have anything to say for yourself?"

The Night Stalker shook the old man's head from left to right, and the two black-clad figures laughed.

"Good," said Greg. "I've no time for excuses. Take a moment to make peace with whatever you believe in."

The second Night Stalker released the old man's head and let it flop forward. Greg drew a metal stake from his belt, and Pete felt himself move, his legs carrying him forward seemingly without any instruction from his conscious mind, his hands raised, his face ashen. The Night Stalkers didn't notice his approach; their attention was entirely focused on their victim.

"Greg," he said, his voice high and wavering. "Please stop this. Please."

The Night Stalkers jumped as though an electric current had been passed through them, then spun round, drawing their guns from their belts. They pointed them at Pete, who raised his arms even higher.

For long seconds, nobody moved. Then Greg reached up and pulled his balaclava over his head.

"Pete?" he said, an incredulous frown on his face. "What the hell are you doing here, mate?"

"I followed you."

"Why?"

Pete had no response; the circumstances seemed so insignificant now that he was faced with the reality he had discovered. He merely stared at his friend.

"Turn around and walk away, Pete," said Greg.

The other Night Stalker turned towards him. "What are you—"

"Shut up," said Greg. "I'm serious, Pete. Go home, right now, and keep your mouth shut. This doesn't have to change anything."

"I can't," said Pete, his voice trembling as he spoke. "You know I can't. What are you *doing*, Greg?"

His friend grimaced. "You wouldn't understand," he said. "That's why I didn't include you. I knew you wouldn't understand."

"Understand what?" asked Pete. "What in God's name is there to understand about this?"

"Don't worry about it, mate," said Greg, lowering his gun so it was no longer pointing at Pete's chest. "It's going to be all right. Come over here where I can see you."

Pete walked across the litter-strewn ground, aware that the second Night Stalker had not moved his weapon so much as a millimetre, and stopped beside the open rear doors of the van. From his knees, the old man looked up at him with tears brimming in his eyes.

"There's a war going on," said Greg. "*That's* what you don't understand, mate. The vamps we take out are scum. They're the worst of the worst, they say so themselves. They *brag* about it. This, what we do? They know it's what they deserve. They're glad when it comes."

An awful piece of the puzzle slotted into place, and, for a moment, Pete thought he was going to throw up.

"Oh God," he said, his voice thick with horror. "The SSL helpline. The vampires who call in and confess what they've done. You're using the helpline to pick your victims."

Greg shrugged, the faintest flicker of a smile on his face. "There's no room for morality in war," he said. "We do what needs doing. That's why the public backs us, because they get it. They know that every dead vamp means a world that's a little bit safer for them and their families. They *thank* us, mate."

"You're going to kill this man for things he confessed on the helpline?" said Pete. "How do you know he even did them? What if he was lying?"

"Maybe he was," said Greg. "It doesn't matter either way."

"So you're just going to execute him?" he asked, his voice rising as anger overwhelmed his fear. "No trial, no evidence? You're just going to put a stake through his heart?"

Greg didn't respond, but his eyes had narrowed, and he was staring at Pete with an expression that looked a lot like disappointment.

"Have you forgotten about Albert Harker, Greg?" he continued. "Have you forgotten how scared we were, how helpless we felt? How can you do the same thing to someone else?"

"I haven't forgotten anything," said Greg, his voice low and dangerous. "Not a bloody thing, mate. I remember exactly how it felt, and I'll die before I let anyone make me feel like that again. I don't care whether this piece of shit did the things he bragged about on the helpline or whether he made them up. He's a vamp. That's enough. If there were no vamps in the world, Matt and Kate would be safe at home right now."

You bastard, thought Pete. *Oh, you hateful bastard.*

"Don't you dare use my daughter to justify this," he said. "She'd be appalled by what you're doing, and so would Matt."

"Maybe," said Greg. "Maybe not. But we can't ask them, can we? And that's the point."

"So what's the plan then?" said Pete. "You and your friends kill every vampire on earth, one at a time?"

"No need," said Greg. "We're a lightning rod, mate. We show people that they don't need to be afraid, that they can take matters into their own hands. We lead, the rest follow."

"You're talking about a civil war," said Pete. "Humans versus vampires. Is that what you want? For thousands of people to die fighting each other?"

"*Want* has nothing to do with it," said Greg. "It's inevitable. Human beings can't share the world, mate, we've never been able to. It's obvious. We're at the top of the food chain, and when another species threatens us, we take them out. This is no different."

Realisation struck Pete like a bucket of cold water. "That's why you refused to help after the Prime Minister's announcement," he said. "You don't want them cured. You want them destroyed."

"Damn right," said Greg. "*An amnesty?* So animals like this can be let off the hook for everything they've ever done, and be allowed to be normal again? *To be like us?* Does that seem fair to you?"

"Yes," said Pete. "It does."

"Not to me," said Greg. "Not to the rest of us. And not to our backers."

"Backers?"

"You think I can afford all this on my SSL salary?" asked Greg, and laughed. "You sign the payroll every month, just like I do."

"So who's backing you?" asked Pete.

"Haven't you figured it out yet?" said Greg, a cruel smile on his face. "The same people who're backing you, mate. The SSL board."

Pete stared at his friend.

No, he thought, his mind reeling. *It can't be. It can't all have been about this.*

"Greg," said the other Night Stalker. "We've been out here for too long. Let's finish it."

"Shut up," said Greg, shooting a narrow-eyed glance in the masked man's direction, then looking back at his friend. "You shouldn't feel bad, Pete. You've done good work, you and the others. You really have. You just didn't know the whole story."

"What are you saying?" asked Pete. He could hear how thick his own voice sounded, how audibly on the verge of tears. "That SSL was never real? It was all just a cover for this?"

"I'm sorry," said Greg. "I really would've told you if I thought you could have handled it. I wanted to. We're making a new world, mate. A *better* world. I just wish you were going to be there to see it."

The gun came up so quickly and smoothly that Pete barely saw it move before it was pointing at his chest. Panic exploded through him, and he hurled himself to the left as Greg pulled the trigger.

The gunfire was deafening metallic thunder as he crashed to the ground beside the black van. He scrambled to his feet as he heard Greg bellow something incoherent behind him, and took off along the canal bank, sprinting for his life. Dust and shards of tarmac exploded around his feet as the night was shattered by a second burst of gunfire, but he kept running, not risking a look over his shoulder to see if they were coming, his mind empty of anything but the desperate, primal instinct to survive.

His feet pounded across the concrete as he accelerated; in the gloom ahead of him, a distant wrought-iron bridge led into the towering maze of buildings on the other side of the waterway, and he fixed his gaze on it. If he made it across, he might be able to lose them, double back to his car, and make it out of this alive.

Gunfire roared behind him for the third time, but he thought it sounded quieter, as though it was coming from ever so slightly further away. He still didn't risk a backward glance, but his heart surged with sudden, savage hope.

I'm getting away, he thought.

Something punched him in the shoulder, harder than he had

ever been hit by anything in his life. He spun round, saw blood fly in the dark air, blood that a distant, detached part of his brain understood was his own, and felt his balance fail him. His legs tangled, he pitched to his right, and tumbled over the low rail into the dark canal below.

The water was shockingly cold, and he sank instantly, his legs slamming painfully into the uneven bottom of the canal. For a terrible moment, one of his feet caught on something and wouldn't move; Pete thrashed, bubbles erupting from his mouth, and hauled for all he was worth. He hung, suspended below the surface, until slowly, agonisingly slowly, his foot came free, like a cork escaping from a champagne bottle. He dragged himself upwards, clawing at the water with one arm as the other hung uselessly at his side. He broke the surface, took a huge, gasping breath, then was sucked back under again as the current pulled at him, sending him tumbling downstream as his head began to pound and black and red spots swarmed at the edges of his vision.

He fought with everything he had left, reaching for the surface with his one working hand, his lungs screaming and spasming in his chest. He could see light above him, and knew there were only another thirty centimetres to go, another fifteen, another two, just *one more.*

Pete shoved himself up with all his strength, with everything he had left.

He didn't make it.

Darkness crowded in, and everything went black.

38

THE HOTTEST TICKET IN TOWN

EUSTON ROAD, LONDON, ENGLAND

The staff of University College Hospital were used to seeing things that were unusual; their accident and emergency department served a large section of Central London, and regularly received more than three hundred patients a day, with everything from broken fingers and infected insect bites to heart attacks and gunshot wounds. But none of the staff had ever seen anything quite as strange as the convoy of black vans that pulled up outside the hospital's side entrance, and the men and women who climbed out of them.

Jamie Carpenter stepped out of the second van, his visor down over his face. Qiang appeared beside him, followed by an Operator that neither of them were familiar with: an American in her early twenties by the name of Laura O'Malley, who had been temporarily added to their squad after Lizzy Ellison had been selected for the first round of PROMETHEUS. O'Malley had not said much on the drive down to London, but she seemed calm and composed, and the fact that Larissa had selected her from the ranks of NS9 meant that Jamie was not worried. If anything, he was more worried about his own mental state than hers; he had tried to push the Zero

Hour briefing out of his mind, to focus on the task at hand rather than replay his awful, awkward conversation with Matt over and over again, but was struggling to do so.

I still can't believe he would use me like that, or lie to my face so casually, or line his friends and colleagues up to be bitten by Valentin. I can't believe any of it.

He surveyed the scene as the other two vans discharged their passengers, ordering himself to concentrate. There would be time to deal with Matt later; right now, there was work to do.

The side street was long and narrow, running between the hospital and one of the many red-brick buildings that made up University College London. Ambulance bays were marked out on the ground in straight yellow lines, and a wide glass entrance was set back from the sloping kerb, beneath a wide canopy. Standing in front of the doors was a man in a white coat; he was holding a clipboard and looking at the vans with a mixture of curiosity and obvious unease.

From the lead van, Jamie saw three more Operators step down on to the road. One of them was Jack Williams, who was technically in charge of this Operation, and the others were the usual members of his squad; neither Ben Harris nor Kim Caldwell had been lucky – or *unlucky* – enough to be selected for PROMETHEUS.

A member of the Lazarus Project that Jamie didn't know climbed out of the third van, alongside the same member of the Loop's medical staff who had looked after him when he went through the turn himself. The man held a large plastic box in his hands, stamped on all sides with HAZARDOUS MATERIAL warnings; he carried it carefully across to where Jamie was standing, and forced a thin smile.

Jack Williams arrived beside them, raised his visor, and turned to the man standing in the hospital doorway.

"Doctor Walder?"

"That's right," said the man.

"Good to meet you," said Jack. "You'll pardon me if my colleagues and I don't introduce ourselves, but this is Doctor Bartholomew of our Department's medical team, and Professor Van Eich of our Science Division. He was part of the team that developed the cure."

"Pleased to meet you both," said Walder. "You can go inside."

"Thank you," said Bartholomew, and walked towards the entrance, holding the box out before him as though it might explode if not handled with the utmost care. Van Eich followed him, leaving Walder with a small, confused smile on his face.

"This is crazy," he said. "We've never done anything like this before."

"Nobody has," said Jack. "Do you have everything you need, Doctor?"

Walder nodded. "We've set up like we were told," he said. "We've padded three sealable rooms, we've got beds for a hundred and fifty vampires, and the eighth and ninth floors have been placed into isolation."

"Great," said Jack. "Both Bartholomew and Van Eich have radios. They have orders to call us if anything goes wrong."

"You'll be down here?"

"Correct," said Jack. "Our understanding is that this is where the action is likely to be."

Walder frowned momentarily, then smiled. "You haven't been to the front yet, have you?"

"Not yet," said Jack. "Why?"

"You'll see," said Walder. "We'll call if we need you. Be careful."

He strode into the hospital, leaving the six Operators standing on the tarmac.

"What did he mean, be careful?" asked Qiang.

"I don't know," said Jack. "Let's find out."

"OK," said Jamie. "I get it now."

The six Operators were standing on the steps in front of the hospital's main entrance. The area below them, a wide section of Euston Road, had been encircled and sectioned off by a perimeter of metal crowd-control barriers, which wound back and forth on themselves in long snaking lines. Every centimetre of space inside the barriers was full of vampires; the queue stretched along the front of the hospital, doubled back along its width eight times, and disappeared round the corner on to Gower Street. Qiang had done a rough headcount, and had told them there were at least four hundred men and women already waiting in line.

This is crazy, thought Jamie. *I never expected there to be anything like this many. And I know we only brought a hundred and fifty doses of the cure.*

Beyond the queuing vampires, penned inside a second grid of barriers and separated by a wall of uniformed Metropolitan police officers, two large crowds surged and shouted and sang. The smell of alcohol was thick in the air, and though the mood seemed to be largely jovial at present, there was an undercurrent of menace that Jamie didn't like. The police were clearly aware of it too; the aggression with which they were pushing people back from the barriers was visibly increasing.

The group on the left was waving signs and boards that made their position abundantly clear; Jamie could see one that read **VAMPIRES ARE NOT A DISEASE** and another announcing that **HUMAN BEINGS DON'T NEED TO BE CURED.** On the other side of the line of police, the signs sent a very different message; **NO AMNESTY FOR VAMP KILLERS** said one, **NO CURE**

FOR EVIL another. The two groups were chanting and screaming insults at each other; Jamie watched them with a tight knot of tension in his stomach, aware that the faces in both crowds of protesters were becoming angrier with each passing minute.

This is going to boil over, he thought. *This is going to end with somebody getting hurt.*

"What do you reckon?" asked Jack.

"I'm not sure," he said. "Let's see what happens when we start letting people in."

Jack nodded. "And when we start turning people away."

Jamie grimaced. "Shit. Right."

Jack turned to face the rest of the Operators. "Qiang, O'Malley, take position at the far end of the access road," he said. "Only ambulances come in and out, clear?"

The two Operators nodded, and jogged back towards the corner of the building.

"Harris, Caldwell, I want the two of you working the queue," continued Jack. "Make sure the police understand what they're dealing with. Jamie and I will monitor from up here. Remember that we're here to help this run smoothly, not exacerbate the situation. Understood?"

Jack's squad mates nodded. They walked down towards the queue and moved away along the line of vampires in opposite directions, their MP7s drawn but lowered at their sides.

Jamie watched them go. "I'm already wishing there were more than six of us," he said.

Jack gave him a tight smile. "Me too."

The doors of the hospital's main entrance slid open behind them, and Jamie turned to see Walder step through them. The doctor looked out across the crowd, then shouted for everyone's attention. The cacophony dropped, just a little, as every pair of eyes turned towards him.

"Thank you," he said. "My name is Doctor Andrew Walder. I'm the clinical director here at University College Hospital. We're going to start admitting patients now, but I can already tell you just from looking at this queue that not all of you are going to receive the cure this evening. We will treat as many people as is humanly possible, but you'll need to be patient, and we will shut the programme down at the first sign of any trouble out here. Am I making myself perfectly clear?"

There was a low rumble of grudging agreement.

"All right then," said Walder. "We'll take the first ten of you now."

The police officers at the front of the queue stepped aside. Ten men and women walked up the steps to a chorus of boos and pleading from the protesters on the left and a shouted volley of insults and accusations from those on the right. Jamie watched them; they walked with their heads up, and if they heard the abuse coming from behind them they gave no sign of it.

The vampires disappeared into the hospital as the protesters started up their songs and chants again. Jamie frowned behind his visor, and realised that his hand had gone to the butt of his MP7.

That's ten, he told himself. *Only a hundred and forty more to go.*

For the next two hours, Jamie watched group after group of vampires file through the doors to an ever more boisterous response from the crowds beyond the queue.

There had been a number of small scuffles between the protesters, and the police had dragged maybe half a dozen people into the vans that were lined up at the kerb, but the chaos he had feared would be inevitable when he had first looked out at the mass of vampires and protesters had not occurred. The pungent smell of alcohol was thicker than ever, and the shouted insults – particularly those from the anti-vampire side of the crowd – had become ever more unpleasant, but the police were doing a good job of keeping them separated. It would be stretching things slightly to say that the first distribution of the cure had gone smoothly, but it had happened, and it was nearly finished, and that was ultimately all that mattered.

Jack had moved halfway down the steps. Jamie joined him, and surveyed the crowds of protesters.

"All right?" he asked.

"Yeah," said Jack. "I'm starting to think we might get away with this."

"Don't get carried away," said Jamie. "Say that when we're in the vans on our way home."

The hospital doors opened again and Doctor Walder appeared, clipboard in hand.

"Here we go," said Jamie, quietly.

"We'll now be taking the final ten patients of the evening," said Walder. "Please can the rest—"

The doctor's voice was drowned out by an explosion of noise as the queuing vampires bellowed their objections. They surged against the metal barriers, their eyes filling with red, sending the police staggering backwards. Jamie raised his T-Bone and ran down the steps towards them, twisting the comms dial on his belt with his free hand.

"Calm down!" he shouted, his amplified voice causing the vampires to recoil with shock. "You were told that you wouldn't all be seen tonight, but we'll be running the programme at the same time tomorrow. So just calm down and go home."

The vampires swayed, eyes glowing in the darkness, growls and hisses rising from their throats. Jack appeared at Jamie's side, his own T-Bone set against his shoulder, as Caldwell and Harris trained their MP7s on the queue. Beyond the lines of vampires, both sets of protesters were screaming and yelling, galvanised by the prospect of trouble.

"We will not tell you again," said Jack, his voice booming out across the crowd. "Unless you are one of the next ten vampires in line, disperse and go home. Immediately."

The red glow faded, as did the rumble of discontent. The police at the head of the queue stepped aside once more, and let the last ten vampires through. They walked up the steps towards the hospital, looks of profound relief on their faces.

"That was close," said Jack. "For a moment, I—"

"Shut up," said Jamie, and turned his head as heat bloomed behind his eyes. Somewhere in the crowd, inaudible to anyone who did not share his supernatural senses, he could hear a male voice, thick with emotion.

"What is it?" asked Jack.

Jamie ignored him; he was scanning the crowd, trying to pinpoint the voice.

"Scum!" it was yelling. "You're all bloody scum! One of you killed my brother, you bastards! You should all be put down! Exterminate the lot of you!"

He found the shouting man's red, tear-streaked face as he whipped his arm forward. Something glittered under the yellow glare of the street lights as it soared through the air; it was an empty whisky bottle, and as Jamie opened his mouth to form the first syllable of a warning, it crashed into the head of a vampire woman about to walk through the glass doors into the hospital.

It shattered, sending fragments of glass raining down on to the steps, and the woman staggered, her eyes flaring with involuntary crimson as a plume of blood sprayed out from above her ear. For a long moment, there was silence, as she raised a trembling hand to her head, and stared at the blood dripping from her fingers. Then an animal growl rumbled from her throat and the fire in her eyes darkened almost to black; she took a single step forward, then leapt into the air and rocketed towards the crowd.

Oh shit, Jamie had time to think, before everything turned to chaos.

The woman hit the anti-vampire protesters like a missile, sending them flying as she tore into the middle of them. Seeing their chance, the pro-vampire group surged forward, taking the police line that had been separating them by surprise and breaking through it. Fighting instantly broke out as the two sets of protesters got their hands on each other; men and women fell to the ground, punching and kicking and clawing, as others backed away, clearly wanting no part of what the protest had suddenly become. The remaining vampires in the queue took to the air; many of them fled into the night, but almost as many followed the injured woman's lead, and hurtled into the mass of brawling, howling men and women beyond the police line. For a moment, Jamie just stared, frozen to the spot; in what seemed like no more than a second or two, a situation that had been largely under control had exploded into something very close to a full-blown riot.

Jack Williams sprinted down the stairs, shocking him out of his momentary paralysis. Jamie ran after his friend, holstering his T-Bone and twisting his comms dial as he moved.

"Qiang, O'Malley!" he shouted. "Front and centre, right now! Ready One!"

Over to his left he saw Jack's squad mates wade into the crowd, dragging men and women apart as the police, who now found themselves at the very centre of things, tried desperately to regroup and form a new line. As Jamie reached the crowd, his vampire side roared into life, hungry and gleeful. He hurled himself into the melee, punching and kicking as though his life depended on it.

The interior of the heaving, swaying crowd was utter bedlam:

a frantic landscape of swinging arms and legs accompanied by a cacophony of shouts of fury and screams of pain. Jamie ducked a punch, located the man who had thrown it, and kicked him sharply between the legs. The man folded silently to the ground, the colour draining from his face, and curled into a foetal position, his eyes squeezed shut with pain. Jamie left him where he fell and waded further into the crowd, searching for the woman whose assault had started all this; if she found the man who had thrown the bottle before he found her, he was absolutely sure they were going to have at least one death on their hands.

Through the comms plug in his ear, he heard disembodied shouts of pain and protest as Qiang and O'Malley joined the fight. A vampire lurched towards him, his eyes blazing with fury, a sign in his hand that he had presumably taken from one of the protesters – it read **VAMPIRES ARE A PLAGUE FROM GOD** – and swung the wooden board at Jamie. He ducked beneath it, took hold of the incredulous, off-balance vampire by his collar, and threw him up and out of the crowd; the man spun end over end, and tumbled from view on the other side of the wide road. Another man took the vampire's place, but made no move towards him; he was bleeding heavily from a wound in his forehead, and one of his eyes had been glued shut with blood. Jamie shoved the man in the direction of the hospital, then pushed forward again, scanning the crowd for the vampire who had been hit by the bottle.

There.

He lunged through the crowd, and reached her at the same moment as she grabbed the man that had thrown the bottle by the throat and lifted him effortlessly off the ground. The man's face was bright red, his eyes bulging with fear, his legs kicking uselessly above the pavement as she drew him close to her blood-splattered face. Jamie skidded to a halt, drawing his MP7 from his belt and raising it as he did so.

"Put him down!" he yelled.

The woman gave no indication of having heard him; her attention was entirely focused on the face she was holding in front of her own.

Jamie hesitated. He could shoot the vampire in the legs, without killing her or harming anyone else, but was surprised to realise how strongly he didn't want to; the woman had blood pouring out of her head, despite the fact that she had done absolutely nothing wrong, and he couldn't remotely blame her for being furious. Instead, he raised the MP7 towards the sky and let out a deafening burst of automatic gunfire.

The fighting stopped instantly, as men and women hurled themselves flat on the ground, their hands over their ears. The vampire woman looked round at him, surprise filling her glowing eyes.

"Put him down," repeated Jamie, and pointed the gun at her. "He isn't worth dying for."

"What would you know about it?" she growled. "You don't know what it's like to be hated for something that isn't your fault."

Jamie raised his visor. Boiling heat was filling his eyes and she recoiled, but did not let go of the struggling, spluttering man.

"I know," he said. "Believe me, I do. I get why you're here, why you wanted to be cured. And you still can be. Put him down and this can be over for you tonight."

She looked at the man, then back at Jamie, the light in her eyes fading, ever so slightly.

"Are you going to arrest him for throwing that bottle at me?" she asked. "Or doesn't it count, because I'm a vampire?"

"Put him down and I'll see to it that he spends at least tonight in jail," said Jamie. "I promise you."

The woman growled, but it sounded more full of uncertainty than anger.

"Fine," she said.

She lifted the man as high as she could reach, then released her grip. He fell like a dead weight to the pavement, and Jamie felt a savage surge of pleasure as his ankle broke with a loud, dry snap. The man's face turned bright white, before he threw back his head and screamed, the sound echoing over the crowd.

"Thank you," said Jamie. "Go and take your place inside."

The woman fixed him with a long stare, then nodded and walked slowly towards the hospital.

"Hang on a minute," said one of the police officers. "She just broke that bloke's ankle. You can't just let her go."

Jamie turned on the man, his eyes blazing, a thick growl bursting from his throat. The policeman took a step back, his eyes wide with fear.

"Get this piece of shit inside and arrest him the very second the doctors have splinted his ankle," said Jamie. "And if you so much as *speak* to that woman I will end your career. Is that absolutely clear?"

The policeman nodded vigorously.

"Good," said Jamie. He looked around at the still, silent crowd. "Those of you who are not vampires," he continued, raising his voice to a shout. "If you don't want to be arrested, you have thirty seconds to get out of my sight. Vampires, stay right where you are."

Nobody moved.

"Now!" he yelled. "Twenty-nine! Twenty-eight! Twenty-seven!"

The crowd scattered, leaving broken signs and empty bottles and pools of spilled blood behind it. Jamie waited until the running footsteps had faded from even his hearing, then turned to face the vampires that remained. There were at least sixty or seventy of them, men and women who had used the eruption of violence as a chance to either stand up for one of their own or gain some measure of release against people who openly hated them. Jamie could not condone their behaviour, but nor could he condemn it.

"We're finished for tonight," he said, "but we'll be back tomorrow. We probably shouldn't be, given what a bloody mess this turned into, but this is more important than a few broken bones and a bit of hurt pride. So I want you all to come back tomorrow evening, and queue up and wait your turn. Don't let anyone stop you from making this choice. Don't let them win. All right?"

There was a low murmur of agreement.

"Good," he said. "Get out of here."

The vampires dispersed, some through the air, some trudging across the ground. Jamie watched them go, as Jack Williams appeared beside him.

"It's going to be like this every time," said Jack. "Isn't it?"

"I hope not," he said. "But yeah. Probably."

Jack raised his visor and smiled. "It's a strange feeling," he said. "Protecting vampires from humans. They never really covered it in Blacklight training."

"I know," said Jamie. "Everything's changing. We just have to try and keep up."

"Deep," said Jack.

"Piss off," said Jamie, and grinned at his friend.

ZERO HOUR
PLUS 206 DAYS

39

COLLATERAL DAMAGE (III)

Kate Randall frowned as she read the message on her screen, and started pulling her uniform back on.

Her console had beeped when she walked back into her quarters from the shower block, as her brain was attempting to process a long, chaotic day in the Security Division. So far, there had been no official reports from inside PROMETHEUS, but word was spreading through the Loop like wildfire. Everyone now knew that at least one Operator had been imprisoned for refusing to take part, and everyone was aware that Angela Darcy had been the first person bitten by Valentin Rusmanov. Kate had known before everyone else: the Security Officer had sent her a message telling her that she was in charge until her commanding officer was discharged from the infirmary. And, although it was exactly what Kate wanted, it had proven a bad day to have her ambitions realised.

The first dispensation of the cure had descended into violent chaos, and the process was being expanded to three more hospitals tonight, all of which needed Operators to secure them, and all of whom had watched the footage from London and voiced their concerns. On top of that, the preparations were continuing in France as the clock ticked down towards Dracula's deadline, and

Kate was trying to deal with the personal fallout of the previous day's Zero Hour Task Force briefing. She had sent a number of messages to both Matt and Jamie, but had received no reply from either of them.

As a result, she groaned when she saw that the message was from the Director of the Department.

Come and see me immediately.

Kate tied her wet hair back and zipped up her uniform. She pulled on her boots, and a minute later she was exiting the lift on Level A and treading the well-worn path towards the Director's quarters.

The Security Operator stepped aside and waved her past. Kate nodded, and walked down to the door. She knocked on it, and heard Paul Turner's voice call out immediately.

"It's open," he called. "Come in, Kate."

She pushed open the heavy metal door, walked into the room, and frowned. The Director was in his usual position, sitting in the chair behind his desk, but he looked pale, almost ill; there were bags beneath his eyes, his skin was waxy, and he was looking at her with an expression she didn't like.

It looked like pity.

"Sir?" she said, as she stopped in front of the desk. "Is everything OK?"

Turner shook his head. "No, Kate," he said. "I'm afraid it's not."

She felt her heart accelerate. "What is it, sir?" she said. "What's going on?"

"It's your father, Kate," said Turner. "He's in hospital in Lincoln. In intensive care."

Cold spread through her; she felt it race down her spine and out to the tips of her fingers.

"What happened to him?" she heard herself ask.

The Director fixed his gaze on hers. "He was shot, Kate. Last night."

Her frown deepened with incredulity, and she fought back the sudden urge to laugh. "Shot?" she said. "What are you talking about?"

"We don't have any details yet. Two council workers pulled him out of the Lincoln canal and gave him CPR. They saved his life."

"But... you're sure he was shot?"

"Yes," said Turner.

"Why?"

"That's all we know, Kate. But SSL is controversial. It's possible they have enemies."

"I have to go to him," she said. The words formed automatically, seemingly without input from her brain; she was staring at the Director in a state of complete shock, her body and mind frozen solid.

Turner nodded. "Of course you do," he said. "There's a car waiting in the hangar."

An hour later, a black SUV pulled up outside Lincoln General Hospital.

Kate looked up at the tall concrete building, suddenly unable to move; she had spent the drive from the Loop ordering herself to stay calm, to assess the situation and put her personal feelings aside until she knew that her dad was OK, but as she stared at the hospital, all of her self-admonishments were forgotten.

"Lieutenant Randall?" asked her driver, peering round from the front seat. "This is it. We're here."

Kate stared helplessly back at him. Then Larissa's voice appeared in her head, warm but firm.

Snap out of it. You can do this. You have *to do this. You know you do.*

"All right," she said.

"I'll be two minutes away," said the driver. "Let me know when you need extraction."

She nodded, pushed open the car's door, and got out. For a moment, her legs trembled so violently beneath her that she was sure she was going to fall, but she steadied herself, took a deep breath, and walked towards the entrance of the hospital.

Kate stood in the doorway of a room on the third floor, staring at the occupant of its only bed.

She was not prone to unnecessary self-criticism; she knew that she was smart, and capable, and would have disagreed vehemently with anyone who suggested otherwise. But as she stared at her father, she felt, for the first time in many years, like the little girl she had been, small and weak and scared. She wished she was wearing her uniform; despite the Glock 17 tucked into her belt, her jeans and T shirt made her feel like a civilian, and added to her feeling of helplessness as she stared at the bed.

Her father looked like he was dead.

He wasn't – the steady beeping of the machines attached to his body were testament to that – but his skin was almost translucent, and had the dull, plastic sheen of a waxwork. His arms and chest were covered with needles and sensors, multicoloured wires rose from him in a tangled web, and a thick wad of bandages covered his left shoulder. She started to cry, furious with herself but entirely unable to stop her tears; it wasn't fair that her father was clinging to life in a hospital bed, for no other reason than trying to make the world a little bit better, to offer help to people who had seen the dark underbelly of the world. And in the back of her mind, a voice was whispering the painful, inarguable truth over and over again.

This is your fault. If you had said no to Blacklight, if you had just gone home when you had the chance, he wouldn't be here. He would never have been dragged into Albert Harker's crusade, and never would have founded SSL. None of this would have happened if you had just gone home.

Kate blinked her tears away and took a tentative step into the room. She had talked to the doctor in charge of her father's case at the nurse's station, who had confirmed that he had been shot once in the shoulder; the bullet had fractured his clavicle as it passed through, and exited just above his armpit, which was the good news. The *bad* news was that her dad had spent an unknown amount of time in cold, dirty water, long enough for him to have technically drowned. He had been revived by the council workers who had called the ambulance the night before, and there was no indication that he had stopped breathing for long enough to cause brain damage; there was no cranial swelling, and they had decided not to put him into an induced coma. But he was weak, and hypothermic, and an infection of the bullet wound was almost certain, given the canal water that had filled it when it was open and raw. He was on a precautionary antibiotic drip, and being monitored for any changes in his temperature or vital signs. The doctor's final assessment had been that her father had been very, very lucky indeed, a viewpoint that was hard for Kate to accept as she looked at him.

She took another step, and another, until she was standing beside the bed. She reached out, gave his hand a gentle squeeze, and realised with sudden, blinding clarity that she would do anything in return for him being OK. If he woke up and asked her to quit Blacklight and move back to Lindisfarne, if he made her promise to turn her back on her friends and the life she had made for herself, she would agree without hesitation.

Anything, as long as he was all right.

A low groan emerged from his lips. Kate let go of her dad's hand and stared at the monitoring screens, preparing to press the CALL button on the wall above his head if she saw even the slightest change in the readings. She watched for long, agonising seconds, until she was sure that nothing was happening, and turned back to look at him. His eyelids were fluttering, and as she leant in closer, they opened as slowly as the sliding doors of the Loop's hangar. His eyes rolled, then locked on her face.

"Dad?" she whispered. "Can you hear me, Dad?"

"Kate…"

Tears spilled from the corners of her eyes. "Yeah, Dad. It's me. I'm here."

"Where…"

"You're in hospital," she said. "You're fine, though, you're going to be absolutely fine. I promise."

He stared at her with apparent incomprehension. Then his eyes sharpened, and the ghost of a frown creased his forehead.

"Not here…" he whispered.

Kate leant in closer. "What do you mean, Dad? What's not here?"

"Not… safe… here…"

Her heart thudded in her chest. "From who, Dad?" she asked, trying to keep her voice calm and reassuring. "Not safe from who?"

His eyes closed, and for a long second she thought he had fallen back to sleep. Then they opened again, and there was far more of the man she loved in them; they looked like the eyes of her dad.

"Night Stalkers," he whispered. "Get me out… of here… not safe."

"Did the Night Stalkers do this to you?" she asked.

He nodded; the movement was almost imperceptible, but she saw it.

"Who are they?" she demanded. "Tell me, Dad."

His eyes closed again. She waited again, but after a long, silent minute, his breathing deepened, and she realised he was asleep. Kate stared at him for a long moment, then backed away from the bed, her heart racing.

She checked her Glock, and felt a rush of relief at the feel of its plastic grip; there was no way she could have lost it between the car and her father's room, but she suddenly had to be sure. Her system was flooded with adrenaline, as though she had been dropped without warning into a Priority Level 1 situation; her Operator side had asserted itself completely and was surveying the small room. There was a single door, which was good for access control, but bad for extraction if that became necessary; she had no idea why her dad was saying he wasn't safe, but she had to trust him and assume the worst. She had to assume the Night Stalkers were on their way to the hospital right now to finish him off.

Kate pulled her radio from her belt and keyed in the Blacklight emergency frequency. She pressed SEND and held the handset to the side of her head.

"Security," said a voice. "Code in."

"Randall, Lieutenant Kate, NS303, 78-J."

"Hold for authorisation."

There was a moment of agonising silence as her voiceprint was checked against the Department's database.

Come on! she shouted, silently. *Come on, for God's sake!*

"Authorised," said the voice. "What's your emergency, Lieutenant Randall?"

"I need an immediate civilian extraction," she said. "From Lincoln General Hospital to the Loop. Civilian's name is Pete Randall."

"Reason for transfer?"

"His life's in danger," said Kate. "He has information on the Night Stalkers that will be valuable to the Department."

"I'll take it to the Security Officer for approval."

"Do it quickly, please."

"Yes, Lieutenant," said the voice. "I'll call you right back."

"Good," said Kate, and pressed END. She backed into the corner of the room, her gaze alternating between her father and the door. The entire hospital suddenly felt threatening; every person that passed the window in the door seemed like a potential threat, every distant voice sounded dangerous.

The door opened and Kate jumped. Her hand flew to the Glock at the back of her jeans, her heart racing, as a nurse in a white uniform appeared.

"Everything all right in here?" she asked.

"Fine," said Kate. "Leave us alone, please."

The nurse rolled her eyes. "Sorry I spoke," she said, and backed out of the room.

Kate glanced at her sleeping dad, then darted to the door and checked the corridor in both directions. She saw nothing suspicious: doctors, nurses, men and women in civilian clothes, who were presumably visiting patients, as she was.

The radio buzzed into life.

"Randall," she said, holding it to her ear.

"The Security Officer has approved your transfer request, Lieutenant."

Kate closed her eyes.

Thank you, Angela, she thought. *Thank you.*

"Good," she said. "Do you have an ETA for the extraction team?"

"The current ETA is forty-eight minutes," said the Operator.

Jesus.

"That's the best they can do?" she asked.

"That's what I was told, Lieutenant."

"OK," she said. "That's fine."

"Are you with the civilian?" asked the Operator.

"Yes."

"Can you stay with him until extraction?"

"I'm not going anywhere," said Kate.

40

JURISDICTION

THIRTY-FIVE MINUTES LATER

Kate checked her watch for the thousandth time. She had never known time to pass so slowly; it was as though some kind of cruel temporal anomaly was occurring inside Lincoln General Hospital.

The nurse walked past the door again, peering through the window as she passed, her eyes narrow. It was the fourth time since Kate had ended her radio call with the Loop; it was clear that her continued presence on the intensive-care floor was beginning to attract attention.

She checked her watch again. Eleven minutes to go, providing the ETA hadn't changed. She checked the Glock. Still there.

What was worrying her most was not the potential arrival of the Night Stalkers; she did not really believe that vigilantes would attempt to kill a patient in a hospital in broad daylight and even if they did, she was confident she would be able to handle them. What *was* worrying her was her inability to be proactive until the extraction team arrived to help her. She was in plain clothes, and could not, under any circumstances, identify herself as a Blacklight Operator; to do so would break one of the most fundamental rules the Department had. And even if she did, if she decided to ignore the rule, she could not prove it; her ID card was in the pocket of her uniform. All she could do was wait.

Her radio buzzed and she raised it to her ear.

"Randall," she said.

"Extraction team ETA seven minutes," said the Security Operator. "Four minutes ahead of schedule. Hospital staff have been briefed to expect a patient transfer."

"What's the cover story?" asked Kate.

"Pete Randall is an undercover policeman working for the Lincolnshire narcotics unit," said the Security Operator. "He was shot by members of a drug gang, and needs to be moved to a secure location immediately."

"OK," said Kate. "That's good."

"Extraction will be via Lincoln General's rooftop helipad. Staff and security have been advised not to interfere."

"Understood," said Kate, and ended the call. She checked her father, saw his chest gently rising and falling, then opened the door a fraction, and peered out.

She froze.

Standing at the nurse's station were two uniformed police officers.

Kate stared at them, her eyes widening, then ducked back as the nurse pointed down the corridor, seemingly directly at her.

Shit, she thought. *Six minutes. Shit.*

Kate backed along the wall away from the door, drew her Glock, and waited. She fought to control her breathing, taking slow breaths in through her nose and out through her mouth, and counted in her head.

Ten.

Eleven.

Twelve.

The handle turned. She fought back a surge of adrenaline as the door opened slowly towards her, shielding the policemen from view. One stepped into the room, his attention on the bed and its occupant. If he looked to his left, he would see her, but he didn't. The second appeared next to his colleague, and Kate moved. She stepped to her right, kicked the door shut, and raised the Glock as the two policemen spun round, surprise on their faces that quickly turned to shock as their eyes found the pistol.

"Not a sound," she said. "Back up, both of you. Do it now."

The policemen raised their hands and retreated towards the corner of the room, their faces pale. When their shoulders touched the wall, she took a step forward.

"Pull those over," she said, nodding at a pair of plastic chairs beside her father's bed. "Only one of you move."

One of the men nodded, and slid slowly along the wall. He picked up the chairs, and carried them back to the corner.

"Put them against the wall and sit down," said Kate. "Hands beneath your legs."

The two men did as they were told, and stared at her as she stepped forward, and read the name badges on their uniforms. "Officers Sudbury and Woodford," she said. "Tell me why you're here. More importantly, tell me who sent you."

"What do you mean, who sent us?" asked Sudbury. "This man is the victim of a serious crime."

"What crime?" asked Kate.

"Attempted murder," said Woodford. "He was shot by suspected Night Stalkers, and we're the investigating officers. Who the hell are you?"

Kate felt a chill run through her. "How do you know it was the Night Stalkers?" she asked, ignoring his question. "This man was pulled out of the canal with a gunshot wound. He's the only one who knows who shot him."

The men glanced at each other, then Sudbury smiled at her. "Ever heard of CCTV?" he said. "We recorded a black van leaving the area within the likely timeframe, similar to one used in previous Night Stalker attacks. Our sergeant sent us to take a statement from the victim."

"What's your sergeant's name?" asked Kate.

A brief hesitation. "Parker."

"And your station?"

"Lincoln."

"Lincoln what? There must be more than one police station in—"

There was a click as the door opened behind Kate. She turned to see the nurse standing in the doorway, her eyes wide as she stared at the Glock.

"Get in here and shut the door," said Kate. She turned back to the men, suddenly aware that she had taken her eyes off them, but Sudbury was already halfway across the room, his face twisted into a smile, his fist hurtling towards her. She raised her arm to protect herself, but was far too slow; Sudbury's punch knocked it aside and slammed into her mouth, driving her back across the room as stars exploded across her vision and a single thought filled her mind.

Failed.

Kate was sitting on the floor when she came, to her back against the wall.

Her head was pounding, her mouth felt like someone had filled it with razor wire, and her throat was thick with liquid. She raised the back of her hand to her face, fought back a scream of pain, and felt her head swim as it came away soaked with red.

Bleeding, she thought, her mind thick and slow. *Why am I bleeding?*

Then she looked up, and adrenaline roared through her as she remembered where she was.

Woodford was standing beside her dad's bed. Sudbury – *if that's even his name*, she wondered – was standing over her, pointing her own gun at her chest. Behind him, in the corner, the nurse sat trembling on a chair.

"What's the plan?" asked Woodford.

"No witnesses," said Sudbury.

"All three of them? Randall was the order. These other two don't have anything to do with it."

Sudbury shrugged. "You know what an evolving situation is," he said. "Remember Helmand?"

"This isn't Afghan," said Woodford.

"It's a war," said Sudbury. "Different enemy, that's all."

"I don't like it," said Woodford. "This one's a nurse and we have no idea who the other one is. Why attract more heat by killing civilians?"

Sudbury sighed. "How many civilians have you met that pointed a Glock 17 at you?" he asked. "Anyway, don't you read the papers? Pete Randall's daughter is Blacklight. That's why he founded SSL in the first place. This must be her."

Woodford looked at her. "That right?" he asked. "You're Blacklight?"

Kate stared up at him, her mind blank.

"She's a soldier," said Sudbury. "I know one when I see one. So I'll make it quick. I'll do that much for her."

He raised the Glock until its barrel was pointing between her eyes. Kate saw not a flicker of doubt in the man's eyes; he had killed before, and she knew he wasn't afraid to do it again.

I'm going to die, she thought, her heart freezing in her chest. *I'm going to die, and that nurse is going to die, and then my dad is going to die.*

Sudbury's finger tightened on the trigger. "Say goodbye, Miss Randall," he said. "It's time to—"

The door crashed open, and Kate's heart thundered back to life as she spun round.

Two Operators in full uniform, purple visors over their faces, silenced MP7s at their shoulders, burst into the room. The Night Stalkers were fast – Sudbury's Glock rose in a blur as Woodford drew a Beretta from his belt with well-practised speed – but the Operators were used to facing vampires. The MP7s fired, the suppressors reducing the shots to low thuds, and the two men hit the ground, expressions of surprise on their faces and neat holes in their foreheads.

Kate got unsteadily to her feet and looked at the nurse. The woman was staring at the two bodies, her eyes and mouth comically wide, but she wasn't screaming, and Kate was grateful for that; screams would have attracted more attention, which this situation absolutely did not need.

"Are you all right?" asked one of the Operators, their voice cold and metallic through their helmet filters, and all of a sudden she understood how terrifying an encounter with Blacklight must be to a member of the public: the calm precision of the violence, the voices and faces hidden by technology.

"I'm OK," she said. "Did you have to kill them?"

"Better them than you," said the Operator.

Kate stared at the impenetrable purple visor; she could think of no response to such a blunt assessment.

The Operator took a step towards her. "Are you *sure* you're all right?"

"I think so," she said. "Yeah. I'm all right."

The Operator nodded. "OK. Medical team, the room is clear. Extraction is a go."

Two Blacklight medical staff, wearing full NBC suits and hoods, strode into the room, followed by two more Operators. Kate stepped aside as the doctors went to her father's bed and the Operators led the nurse towards the door. She went without protest, her face a mask of shock: Kate knew she would be given a copy of the Official Secrets Act to sign, then left with nothing but a memory that would give her nightmares for years to come.

Kate shut the door as the medical staff leant over her father and began removing the needles and monitoring patches from his body. When he was fully unhooked from the machines, which let out a horrible droning beep as his vital signs disappeared, they unfolded a plastic isolation tent and threw it over his bed, clipping it tightly to the frame.

"Ready," said one of the doctors.

The Operator nearest the door nodded, pulled it open, and followed the medical staff as they wheeled her father's bed through it. The other looked over at her.

"Coming?"

Kate stared. "Thank you," she said, her voice trembling with relief. "Thank you so much."

The Operator flipped up their visor and Dominique Saint-Jacques smiled at her.

"You're very welcome, Kate," he said. "Tell me one more time that you're OK."

"I'm OK," she said, a tiny smile rising on to her face.

"I believe you," said Dominique. "Now come on. I want your dad safely at the Loop before Dracula's deadline."

Kate frowned; she had thought about nothing else since Paul Turner had given her the news about her dad, and had completely lost track of time.

"How long have we got?"

"Just over an hour," said Dominique. "Then we'll see what we're dealing with."

"Yeah," said Kate. "I suppose we will."

41

THE SCOURING OF CARCASSONNE

CARCASSONNE, SOUTHERN FRANCE

Every clock in Carcassonne ticked over to 10.06pm as every resident of the city held their breath.

Silence.

In the displaced persons camp, at the Loop and Dreamland, in Washington and London, and in homes around the world, people waited, hearts in their mouths, for Dracula to make good on his promise.

Silence.

Watching through a pair of binoculars from his command centre, General Allen momentarily allowed himself to consider the prospect that the ancient vampire had been bluffing.

Perhaps he already has what he wanted. Perhaps he just wanted the city cleared. Perhaps—

The night sky burst a bright, blinding orange, illuminating the city with a vast, silent flash. A millisecond later the sound hit; a roaring explosion that rumbled the ground beneath Allen's feet and hammered into his skull. He staggered backwards, bellowing in pain, and turned to the monitor tuned permanently to a French news channel. It was showing helicopter footage of Carcassonne on a five-second delay; as he watched, enormous fireballs erupted into the sky as every petrol station within a five-mile radius of the medieval city exploded at the same moment.

Dracula smiled as shock waves thundered across the empty city, blowing his long hair back from his face. The sound that followed them was agony to his supernatural ears, but his smile didn't waver.

The first vampire was floating above the highest section of the ancient walls, as his army flooded down the hill below him to carry out the task they had been given. Blowing up the petrol stations had not been strictly necessary, but Dracula had always instinctively understood the need for theatre when it came to warfare, to consider not only the damage you could do to your enemies' body but also the effect you could have on their minds. Fear, as he had told the Rusmanov brothers on a great many occasions, was the greatest weapon any commander wielded; it was the one thing that could defeat an enemy before the fighting even began.

The fireballs had illuminated the countryside for miles around; what they left in their wake were more than a hundred burning buildings, flames roaring up from their roofs and walls. They were scattered around the city sprawl, blocks – *even miles* – apart, but, as he watched his vampire army fan out through the dark streets, Dracula knew they were about to spread.

Osvaldo led his master's followers along Carcassonne's main street, a snarling mass of glowing eyes and growls and wide smiles of excitement. Their orders were clear and unambiguous, and the Spanish vampire was determined to see them carried out as quickly and efficiently as possible.

Burn it down. Burn it all down.

He spun in the air and flew backwards, facing the army of vampires.

"Teams of three," he shouted. "Spread out and do as our lord has ordered."

A roar rose from the crowd, a huge noise that was somewhere between a cheer and a growl, before it scattered in every direction, a dark shadow rippling out across the city. The two vampires Osvaldo had selected – Carina, the young Italian girl who had turned up at the farmhouse when Dracula was still in seclusion, and Richie, the quiet, solid American who had arrived in Carcassonne barely two hours after they had sacked the old city – flew to his side, and followed him along the suddenly empty street. He dropped to the ground outside a mini-supermarket nestled between a clothes shop and a cinema and pointed towards the former. Carina and Richie flew across to it, ripped its metal security shutter up, and smashed their way inside.

A deafening alarm rang out, but Osvaldo paid it no attention; he knew there was nobody coming. Instead, he floated towards the supermarket, and kicked its shuttered door off its hinges. A second alarm blared as he flew through the broken doorway and towards the shelves of alcohol at the back of the store, carrying a shopping trolley easily in one hand.

Moving quickly, he filled the trolley with bottles of vodka and carried it back out to the street. Carina and Richie were already there, and had torn a pile of T-shirts into long strips. The three vampires got to work, twisting off the caps of the bottles, shoving rags into their necks, and soaking the trailing wicks with alcohol.

"First pitch is yours," said Richie.

Osvaldo nodded, a smile on his face. He lifted one of the bottles, took a cigarette lighter from his pocket, and applied its flame to the soaked strip of cloth. It flared blue and he hurled the bottle into the supermarket. It hit a shelf full of paperback books and exploded, spraying burning liquid in every direction. The books and shelves of produce caught immediately, and as the vampires moved away, the supermarket roared into an inferno.

Osvaldo threw another flaming bottle through the upstairs window of a tourist shop; its inventory of cheap T-shirts and flags and plastic souvenirs burst into flame like it had been soaked with petrol in advance. He led Carina and Richie down the street, setting fire to every second or third building, then ordered them away in opposite directions as they reached a wide junction; Carina flew in the direction of the train station as Richie carried an armful of bottles towards a tall office building, both vampires smiling savagely. Osvaldo carried on towards the edge of the commercial centre, then looked back, and felt a rush of pleasure at what he saw.

Carcassonne's main street was already burning wildly out of control, fire billowing from the shops and offices and sending great clouds of sparks up into the dark night sky.

Bob Allen stared incredulously at the monitor.

The fires were spreading quickly, and from the news helicopter's high vantage point it was clear that new ones were constantly bursting into life, so rapidly and across such a wide area that there was no doubt they were being started intentionally. A thick pall was spreading over Carcassonne, choking the air with acrid smoke that he could smell inside the command centre, more than ten miles away.

The door behind him swung open, and Jason Neves, the Red Cross site director, stepped into the room. His eyes were wide, his face tight and pale.

"Are you seeing this?" he asked. "It's crazy."

"I'm watching," said Allen. "Are all your people out?"

Neves shook his head. "I'm sorry, General," he said. "We've still got a team inside."

Allen narrowed his eyes. "You told me the city was clear."

"I thought it was," said Neves. "The last team stopped to check a social housing block. They were almost out when the petrol stations went up."

Allen groaned. "For Christ's sake," he said. "You knew the deadline. *Everyone in the world knew it.* Why didn't you make them leave?"

"What was I supposed to do?" asked Neves. "I told them to ignore the block and return to camp, but they refused. If I'd sent a team back in to get them, we'd just have more people stuck inside."

"Are there still residents in there?" asked Allen.

"I'm afraid that's a certainty," said Neves. "We evacuated as many as we could, but we couldn't check every single building in Carcassonne in forty-eight hours. We estimate we got ninety-five per cent."

"Goddamnit," said Allen. He sighed, forcing himself to stay calm. "Where are they? Your team?"

"They were coming out on the N113," said Neves. "We lost contact with them somewhere around Rue Claude Debussy."

Allen unfolded a map of the city of Carcassonne, spread it out on the table in the middle of the command centre, and traced a finger across it.

"Four miles from here," he said. "How many people?"

"Six," said Neves. "The team leader is Francisco Rodriguez."

"Tell me right now if there's anything else I need to know, Jason."

"There's nothing else, General," he said.

"All right," said Allen. "Get out and let me deal with this."

Neves nodded and backed out of the command centre. As the

door swung shut, Bob Allen tipped his head back and squeezed his eyes shut, gritting his teeth to prevent the scream of frustration building inside him from gaining release.

How much clearer could I have been about the deadline? How many times did I tell the goddamn Red Cross and goddamn UNICEF to be out of there at least an hour before? At least!

He took a long, deep breath, opened his eyes, and stared at the map; the location Neves had given was a residential neighbourhood straddling one of the main roads in and out of Carcassonne, and the ease of a rescue mission was going to depend on exactly where the Red Cross team were. If they had been able to stay on the N113, then it might, just *might*, be a straightforward extraction. But if the fires that were now burning wildly out of control had forced them into the suburban streets, there was no telling how tight the situation might have become.

Allen pulled his radio from his belt, typed a code into the keypad, and hit SEND. There was a burst of static, then Danny Lawrence spoke.

"Sir?"

"Priority Level 1, Danny," he said. "I need your squad in the air in ninety seconds. There's a Red Cross team inside the city."

"How many?"

Allen smiled with pride. Danny hadn't wasted time asking why there were still civilians inside Carcassonne; his only interest was in acquiring the intelligence he needed.

"Six," he said. "I'm sending the coordinates to you now, and I want you to keep a comms channel open throughout. You can expect to meet resistance."

"I'm on it, sir," said Danny.

"Good boy," said Allen. "Out."

He pressed END and clipped the radio back to his belt. He

walked back to the bench, opened a comms window on one of the monitors, and clicked CALL.

"Paul?" he asked. "Are you there?"

"I'm here, Bob," said Paul Turner, sitting forward in the chair behind his desk as the NS9 Director's voice emerged from the speakers in the walls of his quarters. "Do you know what the final evacuation figures are?"

"We don't have exact numbers," said Allen. "The Red Cross think we got ninety-five per cent out."

"That's good," said Turner. "It's miraculous, to be honest with you."

"Thanks," said Allen. "I don't think anyone who's still in there would agree with you, but we did the best we could."

"I'm guessing most of those that are still there decided not to go?"

"Or couldn't. Like I said, we don't really know."

"Did you get all your people clear?" asked Turner.

"We did," said Allen. "Though I've just had to send a squad back in to extract a Red Cross team that got caught inside."

"What are the emergency services doing?"

"Absolutely nothing," said Allen, with a grunt of laughter. "You can see the pictures, Paul. The whole damn city is on fire. Even if I believed for a second that Dracula would let anyone try to put the fires out, which I don't, there's nothing they could do. It's completely out of control."

Turner looked at the footage playing on his wall screen; the individual fires had merged into a vast, rapidly spreading inferno. He glanced over at Victor Frankenstein, who was standing beside his desk, an unreadable expression on his face as he watched the screen. Turner had always suspected that Dracula's move, when it finally came, would be terrible, but he had never even entertained the prospect of the first vampire burning a major European city to ash.

"Why is he doing this?" he asked. "Why claim a city then destroy it?"

"I have no idea," said Allen.

"He never wanted the whole city," said Frankenstein. "He wants the *old* city, the medieval city. You aren't thinking about this like he is."

"What do you mean, Colonel?" asked Allen.

"Dracula is a medieval General," said the monster. "I don't care what he's learnt about the modern world, or from the battle outside Château Dauncy. Carcassonne is a walled medieval city, high and easily defendable. It is exactly the kind of place he would have taken as his base five hundred years ago. It is his new castle."

"So what does burning down the rest of the city get him?" asked Allen.

"Apart from acting as a show of strength and scaring the hell out of everyone watching?" asked Frankenstein. "It will give him a perimeter, a ring of scorched earth that means nobody can get close without being seen. It's a no-man's-land, General. It's a battlefield."

The helicopter descended into the choking grey smoke, its running lights blazing, its engines howling.

Danny Lawrence sat in the hold, his visor down, his T-Bone resting on his lap, and stared at his squad mates. He had only been working with Anna Clement and José Arias since V-Day, when NS9 had reorganised its entire roster to spread its Operational experience as widely as possible, but he was already entirely comfortable with them. Clement had come from the Office of Naval Intelligence, and was every bit as calm and analytical as Danny would have expected, and Arias had been a Navy SEAL, the elite Special Forces regiment that had sent more men and women to NS9 than any other.

"Got them," shouted one of the pilots, over the intercom. "Directly below. Taking us down."

The helicopter lurched, sending Danny's stomach leaping into his throat as it descended rapidly. He raised his visor, and looked at his squad mates.

"In and out," he said. "Weapons free the second I open the door. We get them to the LZ and get the hell out of there. Clear?"

"Yes, sir," chorused Clement and Arias.

Danny nodded, and lowered his visor. He felt no nerves, no doubt, just the calm desire to carry out the orders he had been given and get his squad mates safely back to the camp.

The Black Hawk touched down with a heavy jolt. Danny was out of his seat instantly, unlocking the heavy access door and hauling it open. Smoke billowed into the hold, and he felt the heat of the fires through his climate-controlled uniform as he leapt down on to the tarmac. He checked his surroundings as his squad mates followed him out of the helicopter; the street was a long curve, with tightly packed rows of houses running parallel on either side. To the west, towards the N113, he could see nothing but fire, a thick wall of orange that had already engulfed the first half a dozen houses on both sides of the road. To the east, smoke filled the sky, lit from within by ominous flares of red.

There were still cars on the road, presumably abandoned by the former residents of the street as they fled; they were parked haphazardly, blocking driveways and paths. There was a tangle of crashed vehicles fifty metres east; the Red Cross Land Rover they were looking for was parked in front of this barricade of metal. Through the smoke, Danny could make out the dark shapes of six figures; they were standing beside the jeep, their arms waving frantically in his direction.

He twisted the comms dial on his belt and spoke directly into the ears of his squad mates.

"Target to the east," he shouted. "Fifty metres. All six visible. Arias, lead us in. Clement, with me."

Arias immediately crouched and ran forward, T-Bone in his hands, as Clement and Danny followed their colleague, keeping their eyes peeled for movement. The smoke swirled at head height, reducing visibility to a few metres, and the heat and noise of the burning city were overpowering; it was like trying to conduct an Operation in Hell. They reached the Land Rover, and Arias and Clement took up positions facing down the long road as Danny went to the men and women huddled beside it.

The volunteers had wrapped strips of clothing round their noses and mouths, but their eyes were red and streaming. One of them pointed to the helicopter.

"We go?" he asked, his voice a rasping croak.

"Is anyone hurt?" asked Danny.

The man shook his head. "I'm sorry," he said. "We didn't mean to—"

"Save it for when we're back at camp," interrupted Danny. "Follow me."

He raised a hand towards his squad mates, pointed at the helicopter, and clenched his fist. They dropped in behind the six coughing, wheezing volunteers as he led them forward, counting down the metres in his head.

Forty-five.

Forty.

Thirty-five.

Thirty.

Twenty-fi—

A dark shape burst out of the shadows on the south side of the street and streaked towards them, low and fast. Danny skidded to a halt, raised his T-Bone, and pulled the trigger. The stake rocketed out of the barrel, the bang of exploding gas silent amid the roaring cacophony of the burning city, and tore through the gloom.

The onrushing vampire raised its head at the worst possible moment. The stake plunged through its left eye and out the back of its skull, trailing blood and brain and metal wire; it fell to the ground in a thrashing heap, and Danny hit the button to wind his weapon back in as he sprinted across the road, drawing a stake from his belt as he ran. The T-Bone's projectile thudded back into the barrel at the same moment he reached the stricken vampire; its remaining eye was rolling wildly, its limbs drumming the concrete, and he thought it was almost a mercy to drive his stake into its chest. As the vampire exploded in a cloud of blood, gunfire rang out behind him and he spun round, searching for his squad mates through the smoke.

Fresh adrenaline burst through Danny as he saw Arias helping the Red Cross volunteers into the hold and Clement firing her MP7 at something he couldn't see on the other side of the road. He raised his T-Bone to his shoulder as he ran to her side.

"Where is it?" he shouted.

Clement shook her head. "Lost it," she said. "Definitely tagged it, though."

He scanned the empty street. The smoke was darkening and thickening, and visibility was almost down to zero. He twisted another dial on his belt, switching his visor's filter to infrared, but saw instantly that it was no use; the air around him was so hot that all he saw was a landscape of flat, featureless yellow.

"Load up!" he shouted, reverting to his normal view. "Let's get out of here."

Clement nodded and ran towards the Black Hawk. He backed up alongside her, his T-Bone at his shoulder, scanning the street for movement, until she leapt up into the hold and extended a gloved hand towards him. Danny grabbed it and climbed up into the helicopter.

"Everyone in?" he shouted.

"Yes, sir," said Arias.

The volunteers stared up at him; they looked terrified, exhausted by the heat and the smoke.

"Let's go!" shouted Danny.

The engines cycled up, the noise deafening, even over the noise of the inferno, as the Black Hawk hauled itself into the air. Danny leant over to slide the door shut, but as he took hold of the handle he looked down and saw something that froze his heart in his chest.

A vampire was rising through the smoke, a wild-eyed look on its face as it sped directly towards them. Danny released the handle and reached for his MP7, but there was no time; the vampire rocketed past the open door and slammed into the rotors above. There was an explosion of blood as it disintegrated, followed by a deafening bang as at least one of the rotor blades shattered and the helicopter lurched violently to the left. Danny saw the open doorway leap towards him, and flung his hands out, hoping to feel the metal edges of the frame beneath his gloves. His fingers closed on nothing, and he tumbled out of the helicopter, falling down towards the road.

He hit the tarmac at an angle and felt his left leg break. The pain was huge, red and full of teeth, and he screamed, the sound lost in the roar of the nightmare unfolding around him. The Black Hawk spun across his view, its stability compromised, its engines howling, its descent wildly out of control. He watched helplessly as it came down on one of the houses, destroying the roof and sinking into the building with a screech of shearing metal and a hail of shattered tiles and glass. There was a moment of stillness that seemed to last forever, until the helicopter's fuel tanks ignited, and the entire house exploded from within.

The noise struck Danny momentarily deaf as fire belched up into the sky and the front of the house blew up and out. He managed to get his arms over his head and roll on to his side as chunks of brick and metal hammered down all around him and fuel sprayed out of the remnants of the helicopter in flaming yellow plumes.

He pushed himself up on to his elbows, and looked at the devastated remains of the house. His ears were ringing with an agonising, high-pitched whine, but he ignored it; his mind was entirely full of the ten lives he knew had just been lost. There was simply no way anybody could have survived such a crash.

They're gone! shouted the part of his brain that had kept him alive through countless Operations. *You can't do anything for them now! Focus!*

Danny took a deep breath and surveyed the carnage, forcing himself to think analytically, despite the pain roaring through him. He knew there was no way he could stand on his leg; it was badly broken, the snapped bone visible through his uniform. But if he could drag himself to the Red Cross vehicle, maybe he could manage to drive it using only one leg.

Maybe.

The ringing in his ears faded, and was replaced by General Allen shouting for an update.

"Helicopter down," said Danny, his voice hoarse with smoke. "I'm the only one that made it out."

"Stay right where you are," shouted Allen. "Don't move. I'm sending help."

Danny looked down the street, to where the vast fire was burning unchecked, and felt a small smile rise on to his face as the tiny flicker of his hope was extinguished. Walking towards him, little more than black silhouettes against the orange inferno, were at least a dozen figures, their eyes glowing bright red.

"Negative," he said. "Do not send anyone. The situation is completely compromised."

"Cancel that shit!" roared General Allen. "Backup will be there in three minutes! Don't you give up on me, Danny!"

"I repeat, sir," he said, gritting his teeth against the pain, "do not send anyone. There's going to be nothing left for them to find."

The Director shouted something else, but Danny didn't hear it; he took his helmet off, put it down beside his shattered leg, and lifted his MP7 to his shoulder.

"Come on then!" he screamed at the advancing line of vampires. "Come on if you're coming!"

He squeezed the trigger, sending a volley of fire towards them. They parted like liquid, almost dancing round the bullets, then surged forward at supernatural speed, and Danny had time for one final thought before they were upon him.

Don't scream. Don't give them the satisfaction.

Three miles away, atop the walls of the medieval city of Carcassonne, Dracula watched the distant helicopter fall from the sky and smiled.

Welcome to the new world, he thought.

Paul Turner sat helplessly behind his desk, staring at Frankenstein's impassive face.

The two men had listened in impotent horror to Danny Lawrence's final transmission and Bob Allen's desperate demands for him to wait, to *damn well wait* for backup to arrive. Neither had spoken; they had both lost more colleagues than they cared to remember over the years, and they knew that there was nothing they could say that would mean anything to the American Director.

So much death, thought Turner. *So many lives lost already, and the worst is surely still to come.*

His radio buzzed, breaking the silence in the room. He left it lying on his desk and pressed SEND.

"Yes?" he asked.

"It's Darcy, sir," said the voice on the other end of the line.

"What is it, Captain?"

"We've confirmed extraction of Pete and Kate Randall from Lincoln General," said Angela. "They're on their way back now."

"Good," said Turner. "Let me know when they land."

"I will, sir," said Angela. "But there's something else."

"Yes?"

"Kate Randall was attacked by two men posing as police officers, sir. In her father's room."

"She's not—"

"She's fine, sir," said Angela. "The extraction team neutralised the threat."

"Good," he said. "Have cells prepped for them."

"Both men are dead, sir," said Angela. "They were about to execute Kate and a civilian nurse. Dominique authorised Ready One."

Turner sighed. "Night Stalkers?"

"We don't know, sir," said Angela. "But presumably so. Kate said her father told her he wasn't safe. She thinks they came to finish him off."

"Has he identified anyone?"

"No, sir. He's stable but unconscious."

"All right," said Turner. "Send Kate to me as soon as she arrives. And get a Security squad to Lincoln General for clean-up."

"Already done, sir."

"Fine. Let me know if anything else comes up." He cut the connection and looked up at Frankenstein. "Tell me something, Victor. Do you think there'll ever be a time when—"

The radio buzzed again.

Turner swore, and pressed SEND. "What is it now, Angela?"

"It's not Darcy, sir," said a familiar voice. "It's Captain Williams. I need you to come to the hangar."

He took a deep breath. "Now, Jack?"

"Right away, sir."

"Why?" he asked. "What's so damn important?"

"It's going to be easier just to show you, sir…"

42

ALL GOOD THINGS . . .

THE HUDSON RIVER VALLEY, UPSTATE NEW YORK, USA
FORTY MINUTES EARLIER

Larissa Kinley pulled on her Blacklight uniform as a loud voice in her head urged her to think again.

They don't need you! it insisted. *They can handle this without you! Why are you so arrogant that you don't think so? The people here need you! Why can't that be enough?*

She ignored the voice's increasingly frantic entreaties, clipped her console into the loop on her belt where it had hung so often, and felt a shiver of revulsion at how familiar its weight felt on her hip. She didn't turn the console on – she could not bring herself to do so, not yet – but she loaded her Glock before she slid it into its holster, and was glad she had left her MP5 and T-Bone behind when she left.

In the part of her mind that was committed to the decision she had made, a fantasy vision of her future stubbornly persisted; she would help Blacklight destroy Dracula, then return to Haven to quietly live out her days. In one version, she brought Jamie and Matt and Kate back with her. In another, she returned alone to find Callum waiting with that small, gentle smile on his face.

The first vampire's attack on Carcassonne had sent shock waves through Haven, which had already been reeling from the revelation that the condition that had brought its residents together could now be cured. The first forty-eight hours of the amnesty had seen almost half the community make the journey to New York or Boston to receive the bright blue liquid that had filled the front page of every newspaper around the world. But despite the potent effectiveness of the cure, which had stripped the vampire virus from their bodies in a chaotic, violent delirium that none of them could truly remember, barely a dozen of those who had taken it had actually left the community. They had come to Haven because they had nowhere else to go, nowhere they felt safe or accepted, and it had become their home; they had no intention of leaving it simply because they could now go out in the sun.

But the relief that followed the return of the majority of the cured had been diminished by the devastating attacks that had taken place on planes and subways around the world and by the news from France, the revelation that Dracula had finally, at long last, made his move. The prospect of terrible bloodshed, of outright war between the humans and the supernatural, now seemed depressingly possible, if not wholly inevitable.

Larissa's first instinct had been the same as most of her friends: to keep her head down and hope for the best. But she had quickly realised that she would not be able to live with herself if she did, no matter how much she might want to.

She had no idea what her friends in Blacklight now thought of her. It was more than possible that Jamie hated her, and she would not blame him if he did, Matt would likely be disappointed, if he had even looked up from his work long enough to notice she was gone, but she liked to believe that Kate would have stood up for her, would have understood her reasons and forgiven her.

If she was honest, Larissa knew there was a very good chance that nobody at the Loop would be pleased to see her return, and that was fine. In a way, it would be *better*, it would make it far easier to leave again once the issue of Dracula was settled. She was sure that Paul Turner would immediately reinstate her – she was far too powerful a weapon not to use – but part of her was hoping she was wrong, and that he would tell her the Department didn't need her; it would mean she could come home with a clear conscience.

She stood up straight, smoothed down her uniform, and looked at her reflection in the mirror inside her wardrobe door. The uniform fitted her like a glove, and looked so natural on her, so horribly *right*. Her eyes flared red and she closed them, suddenly full of an overwhelming desire to break the mirror, to smash the wardrobe into splinters, to overturn her bed and tear down the walls and burn the entire house to the ground. She took a deep breath, let it out, took another, and opened her eyes. She stared at the black-clad Operator she had flown halfway around the world to get away from, and felt a lump rise in her throat.

It's not fair, she thought. *I was happy here. I really was.*

So stay, whispered her vampire side, its tone unusually soft, almost kind. *Nobody will blame you. Stay here, where you belong.*

I can't, she thought. *I can't let them face this on their own.*

Her vampire side fell silent. Larissa took a long look in the mirror, then walked out of her bedroom and closed the door behind her.

She flew slowly along the corridor and down the stairs, savouring every last moment inside the house she had come to love, then turned towards the front door and found Callum standing in front of it.

"Ready?" he asked.

"No," she said, and gave him a tiny smile. "Not in the slightest."

He took a step towards her. "I know why you're doing this," he said. "And I understand. But I'm going to ask you one more time. Do you have to go?"

Larissa felt tears rise in her eyes. "Yes," she said. "I do."

He grimaced, but nodded. "I'm going to miss you."

"I'm going to miss you too," she said. "Look after everyone. Do that for me, OK?"

"Of course," said Callum. "You started something here, Larissa. I'll make sure it carries on."

"I'm coming back," she said, her voice suddenly full of fierce passion. "When this is all over, I'm coming back. I'm—"

Callum stepped forward, raised his hands, and gently took hold of her face; she could feel the calluses and rough ridges of his fingertips on her skin. He dipped his head, and planted the briefest, most chaste kiss of her entire life on her lips. She stared into his wide brown eyes, and smiled as he released her and stepped back.

"For luck," he said.

Larissa didn't respond; there was nothing left to say, nothing to do but carry out the decision she had made as quickly as possible, before her heart broke. She opened the front door of the big house, stepped through it, and froze.

The veranda blazed with light; its wooden boards and walls had been covered in candles, their yellow flames flickering in the late evening breeze. And out on the wide lawn, surrounded by what must have been thousands more candles, stood what looked like every single resident of Haven; they smiled at her as she stared, her eyes wide, a lump in her throat so huge that she could barely breathe around it.

Emily Belmont stepped out of the crowd, her lined face creased by a broad smile.

"You didn't think we were going to let you leave without saying goodbye, did you?" said the old vampire. "This is our home, the first that a great many of us have ever known, and we have you to thank for it. Haven has become a place where we can feel safe, a place that all of us have come to love, and you will never, ever know how grateful we are for everything you've done. I speak for all of us when I say we understand why you have to go, so we won't ask you to change your mind, even though we wish you would. Instead, we just ask that you stay safe, and that you come back to us if you can. We love you, Larissa."

Tears broke loose and spilled down Larissa's face. She made no attempt to wipe them away; instead, she forced herself to walk on legs that felt incapable of holding her up, trying to withstand the pain in her chest and the unbearable wave of desperate love rolling through it. She reached Emily Belmont and pulled her close; the old vampire came willingly, wrapping her arms round Larissa and shushing her softly, like a mother urging their child not to cry.

She broke the embrace, and walked into the crowd, her bag hanging forgotten at her side. Faces smiled at her from all sides as arms reached out to hug her and hands clapped her gently on the back. A low chorus of thank yous and goodbyes and good lucks echoed around her as she walked among the men and women with whom she had built a place she could still not really believe she was about to voluntarily leave. The emotion of the moment threatened to overwhelm her; the outpouring of love and gratitude from all sides was too much: it was impossible and wonderful and painful all at once.

She reached the edge of the crowd, and turned back.

I don't know if I can do this, she thought, as she looked at the smiling, tear-streaked faces of her friends. *Oh God, I didn't know it would be this hard. Maybe it's too hard.*

But then she thought about her other friends. She thought about Matt working day and night to develop the cure that had brought hope to a world that had seemed to be on the verge of tearing itself apart, she thought about Kate and Jamie putting on their uniforms and flying into the darkness to confront the greatest threat humanity had ever faced, and she knew she couldn't stay. She would stand with them at the last, or she would never be able to forgive herself.

"Thank you all so much," she said, her voice choked with emotion. "Look after each other. Be safe."

Larissa rose into the air and accelerated east without another word, the lights of Haven shrinking away below her.

She didn't stop crying until she was almost halfway across the Atlantic.

Her sides ached from wracking sobs, her face was red-raw from a combination of salty tears and punishing wind, and her heart felt like a lead weight. Haven had been a place – perhaps the *only* place she had ever known – where she could really, truly be herself, a place full of light and noise and laughter, and she was already dreading the grey functionality of the Loop, the stares and whispered comments and crushing, debilitating monotony.

She soared over the Irish Sea, still heading east. Her supernaturally sharp eyes picked out the lights of ships ploughing through the wide grey body of water below, as transatlantic airliners rumbled above her towards the airports of London, the running lights on their wings blinding, the air swirling in their wake.

Larissa flew lower as the landscape flattened out into seemingly endless fields of grey and brown. She accelerated, descending all the time, and then, in the distance, she saw it: the holographic canopy that hid the Loop from prying eyes.

It was a remarkable illusion, and it had fooled surveillance planes and spy satellites alike for many years. But to Larissa, who knew exactly what she was looking for, it was as clear as a neon WELCOME sign; from her low angle of approach, she saw the telltale shimmer where the projected trees met the real ones, saw the ridges and peaks that were merely a suspension of reflective particles, and headed directly towards it. As she sped over the trees and dropped through the hologram, she heard a cacophony of distant alarms burst into life, and smiled; her arrival constituted an unidentified breach of Blacklight's airspace, but she knew she would be standing in the hangar before the Security Operators that had been scrambled from the levels below appeared.

Larissa glided over the ultraviolet bombs that stood, armed and ready, at intervals across the wide grounds, dropped to the tarmac outside the low rise of the Loop's surface level, and walked towards the huge open doors. Her stomach was churning, and her vampire side was still trying, even at this late stage in the proceedings, to persuade her that this was *stupid*, it was a terrible mistake, and she should just turn round now and fly home, before it was too late.

She walked into the hangar, which appeared not to have changed at all in the months she had been gone, and stopped atop the wide panel that slid aside to allow the *Mina II*, the Department's supersonic jet, to rise up from below. She stood with her arms out from her sides, making sure it was clear that her hands were empty; she knew Security would be coming, and she didn't want to create a panic by making it seem as though the Loop was under attack. She felt heat rise behind her eyes as the scream of the general alarm pounded into her ears, and pushed it back; her eyes blazing with supernatural red would certainly not help her create a good first impression.

The doors at the rear of the hangar slammed open and six Operators rushed through, their T-Bones raised to their shoulders, their faces hidden behind visors.

"Don't move!" bellowed the figure at the front of the squad. "Hands in the air! Don't you—"

The Operator stopped dead, then reached up and slowly raised its visor. Larissa saw the pale face of Jack Williams, a frown of profound confusion contorting it, and smiled.

"*Larissa?*" asked Jack. "Is that you?"

"Hey, Jack," she replied. "It's good to see you."

"What the hell are you doing here?" asked Jack. "You can't just show up like this. Nobody's seen you for months."

"Sorry," she said. "You probably need to alert the Director, right?"

"Damn right I need to alert the Director," said Jack, his frown deepening.

"In which case, I should probably stay here," she said, her smile widening into a grin. "And not move a muscle unless someone tells me to."

Jack shook his head; for the briefest of moments, she saw the ghost of a smile flicker across his face.

"You do that," he said. "Stay right there while I call this in."

Larissa nodded as Jack twisted a dial on his belt, his gaze never leaving her.

"It's not Darcy, sir," he said, eventually. "It's Captain Williams. I need you to come to the hangar." There was a pause, in which she could hear the faint murmur of the voice on the other end of the line. "Right away, sir." Another pause. "It's going to be easier just to show you, sir. Yes, sir, I'll stay here. Out."

Larissa waited in silence as Jack put his radio back on his belt, an easy smile on her face despite the five T-Bones aimed at her heart. She did not like having weapons pointed at her, but she also had no wish to provoke the situation; if it was her intention to cause trouble, she knew – *and knew that Jack knew* – there would be very little they could do to stop her, but there was nothing to be gained by making that point clear.

*   *   *

Three minutes later the doors swung open again, but this time only a single figure strode through them.

Paul Turner was not wearing a helmet, and Larissa felt her heart lurch at the sight of him; he looked utterly exhausted, as though he could barely stand. Then his eyes settled on her; they widened hugely, and he took a step backwards, like he had seen a ghost.

"Hello, sir," she said. "You're looking well."

Turner rallied magnificently; she would have expected no less of the man. His face regained its usual impassive expression, and he walked towards her with an air of something close to nonchalance.

"Lieutenant Kinley," he said, stopping in front of her. "Welcome home."

Larissa smiled. "This isn't my home, sir," she said. "Not any more."

"Fair enough," said the Director, and returned her smile with a narrow one of his own. "How about welcome back?"

"That's fine, sir," she said. "Thank you."

"Are you staying?"

"For a while, sir," she said. "If that's all right with you?"

"That's fine," said Turner. "Your old quarters are still empty. I presume you remember the way?"

Her smile widened. "I think so, sir."

"Good," he said. "Go and get settled in. I'll tell the Security Officer to bring you up to speed."

Larissa nodded. "Can I make a request, sir?"

"Already?" asked Turner.

"Yes, sir," she said. "Please don't tell anyone I'm back. There are some conversations I'm not ready to have just yet."

"You have my word," said Turner. "But you won't be able to hide for very long. You're quite recognisable."

She nodded. "I'm very aware of that, sir," she said. "Believe me."

ZERO HOUR
PLUS 207 DAYS

43

THE MORNING AFTER

Paul Turner sat at his desk, watching news footage of the huge cloud of smoke that was now hanging over Carcassonne, trying to take in the magnitude of what he was seeing and somehow fit it into his increasingly overstretched mind.

The smoke was too thick for the cameras to penetrate, but it was clear that the devastation unleashed on the French city was going to be revealed to be vast; the fires had lit up the sky overnight for hundreds of miles and even though the flames had now been extinguished, the damage they had caused was surely going to be horrendous, the loss of life huge.

I need to tell Larissa and Matt about Danny Lawrence, he realised, and added it to the many other unpleasant tasks that filled his mental to-do list. *They both worked with him in America. Great news for them to wake up to.*

He continued to stare at the screen, but he was no longer watching it. It felt like his mind was being pulled in a thousand different directions – Carcassonne, the cure, Dracula, Kate, the Night Stalkers, Larissa – and he was struggling to decide what required his attention first.

His radio buzzed into life. He pressed the SEND button on the handset, and sat back in his chair.

"Turner," he said.

"Morning, sir," said Angela Darcy. "I know it's early, but Pete Randall is awake in the infirmary. I thought you'd want to know."

In his quarters on Level B, Jamie was roused from a thick, restless sleep by a heavy knock on his door. He swore, and swung his legs out of bed, and groaned. His head felt heavy and slow, and his limbs were aching, despite the litre of blood he had drunk before he fell into bed six hours earlier.

The second night of the distribution of the cure had gone slightly better than the first; there had been less panic, less frantic urgency among the queuing vampires, and no overt acts of violence. But it had still been long, had still taken careful management, and had left him in a state of exhaustion which was not entirely unwelcome; he had come back to the Loop and gone straight to sleep, where he could stop thinking about his friends, if only for a few hours.

Jamie hadn't spoken to anyone about anything other than professional matters for two days. He knew it was petulant, and self-indulgent, but the Zero Hour Task Force briefing had devastated him. He was still struggling to believe that PROMETHEUS was real, and that Matt not only approved of it but had been instrumental in its creation, but he could see the strategic argument for the programme, even if he didn't agree with it; what he could *not* reconcile with himself was that his friend had lied to his face, and had done so with the clear intention of using him if he saw fit to do so, in a way that he had never even been given the chance to agree to.

It was a betrayal that he simply did not know if he could get over. He had received almost a dozen messages from Kate since, entreaties for the three of them to talk, to sort things out, but he had ignored them all; for the time being at least, he didn't want to talk to anyone.

The knocking came again. He forced himself upright, floated above the cold floor, and unlocked the door, a single thought pulsing through his mind as he pulled it open.

This better be good.

His heart stopped dead in his chest.

Larissa Kinley was standing in the corridor.

For a long moment, neither of them moved. Jamie stared at her, his eyes wide, his body frozen to the spot. Larissa was wearing her Operator uniform and the only thought in his head, one that had burst unbidden from somewhere dark and unstable, was that the last six months or so had never happened; she hadn't left, she had been here the whole time, and it had all just been a particularly vivid nightmare.

Stillness.

Silence.

Jamie's body worked involuntarily, forcing his lungs to inhale, and he realised he had not been breathing as he looked at her. The breath broke his paralysis; he stepped forward, his arms reaching out towards her. She didn't protest as he wrapped them round her shoulders and pulled her tight against him, but her body was stiff in his arms, and he realised something with instant, awful certainty; he didn't know why she had returned, but it was not for this.

It was not for him.

The deep wound in his heart yawned open, releasing a wave of agony. He released her, stepped back, and forced a tiny smile.

"Come in," he said, and stood aside.

She nodded, and walked into his room. Jamie closed the door as she took a seat on the edge of the bed, her back straight, as though she was waiting to be called in for a job interview. He pulled his chair out from beneath his desk and sat down. She stared at him, her face pale and expressionless, and he suddenly wanted to scream at her, to call her every awful, terrible name he could think of, to rant and shriek and smash the room to splinters, to show her exactly what she had done to him when she left.

But he didn't.

"You just left," he said.

"I know."

"You didn't even say goodbye."

"I know, Jamie."

He searched her expression for something he could take comfort from, something that even *suggested* she still cared about him, but saw nothing; she was as beautiful as ever, if not even more so, but her face was pale and empty. It felt like a robot had replaced his ex-girlfriend.

"Where did you go?" he asked.

She winced, ever so slightly. "I'm not ready to talk about that."

"OK," he said.

Jamie had imagined the moment of Larissa's return so many times that he believed he had covered every possible scenario, from tearful joy to screaming hatred. But he had *not* allowed for the possibility that they would find themselves looking at each other, and talking to each other, like strangers; like people who had never even met before, let alone shared the experiences they had.

"I'm sorry," he said.

She narrowed her eyes. "For what?"

"For the night you left. The things I said."

"It's all right," she said.

"No," he said, and shook his head. "It's not all right. I blamed you for something that wasn't your fault, and I told you I didn't trust you. I can't blame you for leaving after that."

Her expression softened, just a fraction. "That wasn't the only reason I left, Jamie," she said. "I knew that was what you'd think, but I left because of a lot of things. That night was just the final straw."

"What things?" he asked.

"You knew I wasn't happy here," she said. "I mean, you *did* know that, right? You must have."

Jamie nodded. "I knew. I think I just tried not to think about it."

"So did I," said Larissa. "I tried really hard. But it got to the point where I couldn't look at myself in the mirror any more. More than anyone, you know what it takes to do this job, how you have to believe you're doing more good than harm. I just couldn't convince myself that was true any more, Jamie. What you said to me that night just finally tipped the balance."

He looked at her, his mind churning with a potent mix of emotions. There was relief that it hadn't all been his fault, but there was guilt too, and shame; how had he not realised how unhappy his girlfriend really was, until it was far too late? What kind of person did that make him?

Selfish, whispered a voice in the back of his head. *Arrogant. Self-involved.*

"So why are you here?" he heard himself ask.

Larissa shrugged. "I don't really know," she said. "I told myself that Dracula isn't my fight any more, if he ever was, but I couldn't just stand by and do nothing while people I care about put themselves in danger."

"The Director will definitely be glad you're back," said Jamie. "Although you aren't as unique as you were when you left."

She frowned. "What do you mean?"

"Ask Paul about PROMETHEUS next time you see him."

"All right," she said. "I will."

They stared at each other for a long moment. Larissa's frown remained in place, and Jamie recognised the expression with a burst of bittersweet nostalgia; it was the look she wore when there was something she wanted to say to him, but was still deciding whether or not she was going to say it.

"What about you?" she said, eventually.

"What about me?"

"Are you glad I'm back?" she asked, her voice low.

"I don't know what you want me to say," he said. "Am I pleased to see you? Like, right now, in this moment? Of course I am. But I don't believe you're really back, Larissa. Everything about you makes me think that if we manage to defeat Dracula then you'll disappear again. Am I right?"

"I don't know," said Larissa. "Maybe. Probably."

Jamie shrugged. "There you go then," he said. "There's not much point in me getting used to having you around again, is there?"

Silence settled over them once more. It was not as glacial as it had been when she first walked into his quarters, but it was still cold, still full of guilt and recrimination.

"I missed you, Jamie," she said.

Pain stabbed at his heart. "Don't say that," he said. "Please don't."

"I'm sorry," she said. "But it's the truth. I don't regret leaving, and I get that this isn't what you want to hear, but I really did miss you."

"I missed you too," he said. "For a long time."

"And then what happened?"

"I stopped," he lied.

44

SCORCHED EARTH

OUTSKIRTS OF CARCASSONNE, SOUTHERN FRANCE

Bob Allen stood at the edge of the displaced persons camp, staring at the cloud of dark smoke hanging over what was left of the city of Carcassonne. The fires had raged through the night, the sky pulsing orange, the heat uncomfortable even across miles of countryside.

Then, barely an hour before dawn, they had started to go out.

The satellites had been unable to pinpoint exactly what was happening – their cameras had recorded little more than bursts of movement in the darkness – but the inferno had rapidly begun to subside, as though it was being blown out by some vast celestial being. The new plumes of smoke from the dwindling fires had reduced visibility even further, leaving the men and women in the camp, along with the millions watching the unfolding disaster on televisions around the world, with no option other than to wait and see what remained when the sun finally rose over the eastern horizon.

Allen had waited with his colleagues and the charity directors, giving orders and discussing the unfolding situation at length, but his head and heart were somewhere else, although nobody he spoke to would have known that was the case; he was hugely experienced at hiding his true feelings from others.

Outwardly, he continued to appear the calm, highly capable American General whose leadership they could trust completely. Inwardly, he was wracked with pain at the death of Danny Lawrence.

There were many Operators back in Nevada more experienced than Danny had been, but Allen believed that none of them had been able to match the young Virginian for natural talent; the only one to come close had been Tim Albertsson, who had also died a violent death, many thousands of miles from home. Over the last year or so, Danny had been the Operator to whom Allen had entrusted the majority of NS9's highest priority missions, and never once had he let him down.

And now he was dead.

Allen had listened to Danny's final, shouted challenge to the vampires who killed him, his blood running cold, his body and mind frozen by helplessness.

Come on then! Come on then if you're coming!

It had been the reason he had not slept for a single minute of the long, burning night; Danny's last words had echoed endlessly through his head, bringing him to the verge of tears, particularly once he had gathered himself together enough to make the call he knew he had to make, to tell Danny's friends that he was gone.

Kara, Kelly, Aaron and Carlos had managed to maintain what his friend Paul Turner would have called a stiff upper lip, but there had been no hiding the shock and hurt in their eyes, even as they immediately asked whether there was anything they could do. Allen knew at least two other people who were going to be devastated by Danny's death, and had already asked the Blacklight Director to pass the news on to Matt Browning. He had no idea how to get in touch with Larissa Kinley; she had dropped off the radar months earlier, much to his professional and personal disappointment.

Across the wide fields to the east, he watched the morning sun attempting in vain to penetrate the acrid grey pall, trying his very hardest not to blame the Red Cross team for what had happened, despite their reckless disobedience of a direct order. He knew they had been trying to help men and women too scared or simply unable to leave the doomed city on their own; they had paid for their mistake with their lives, and there was nothing to be gained from speaking ill of the dead, although part of him wanted to.

Part of him really, *really* wanted to.

"Sir?"

Allen turned to see Luisa Ramirez standing a respectful distance away, her face pale.

"Is it time?" he asked.

"It is, sir," she replied. "They're waiting for you in the command centre."

"Thank you," he said, and nodded. "Tell them I'll be there in two minutes."

"Yes, sir," said Ramirez. She walked towards the middle of the camp as Allen turned back to face the smouldering ruins of Carcassonne. Less than five miles away, on a nondescript suburban street beneath the smoke and amid the ash and rubble, lay whatever remained of three of his Operators. And as he stared at the swirling cloud of black and grey, Allen couldn't shake the certainty that Danny Lawrence and his squad mates were merely going to be the first of many, many deaths to come.

Five minutes later, Allen pulled open the door of his now greatly enlarged command centre and stepped through it. He could hear a low hum of conversation as he walked towards the centre of the structure, where Captain Guérin and Director Karla Schmidt of the FTB were waiting for him.

"We said nine," said Schmidt, and looked at her watch. "It is almost quarter past."

The German team, consisting of more than sixty Operators and almost as many support staff, had been at the camp for two days, but Schmidt herself had only arrived six hours earlier; she had been in Paris, liaising with the French government, since the crisis had begun. She had immediately sent one of her Operators to the command centre with a request to see him, but it had been barely forty minutes after Danny's team were lost, and he had refused the request; he had been scarcely able to form a coherent thought, let alone bring another Director up to speed on a situation that was evolving faster than anyone could process. He had sent the FTB Operator away with a suggestion that Schmidt ask Guérin to brief her, a professional snub that he suspected he was paying for now.

"My apologies," said Allen. "Shall we get started? Captain Guérin?"

The French officer nodded. "Before we begin," he said, "I would like to say that I am very sorry for the loss of your Operators."

"The FTB also offers it condolences," said Schmidt. "I worked with Operator Lawrence on two occasions, and I thought very highly of him."

"Thank you both," said Allen. "It's appreciated."

Guérin nodded. "To business, then," he said. "Unsurprisingly, details are very hard to come by. The Red Cross has given a final evacuation estimate of ninety-one per cent. UNICEF believes the figure is eighty-seven. As a result, we can say for certain that the city was not empty when it burned, and fatalities are now inevitable."

"Perhaps as many as six or seven thousand," said Schmidt. "If UNICEF turns out to be correct."

Allen nodded. "An exact number is going to be difficult to come by."

Guérin frowned. "Why can we not send volunteers in to search for bodies?" he asked. "The sun will not set for another nine hours."

"Because it is not safe," said Schmidt. "Apart from the high temperatures and the risk of collapsed buildings, you need to understand that vampires *can* go out during the daytime, as long as they keep their skin out of direct sunlight. It is perhaps unlikely that Dracula will have vampires patrolling the ruins, but it cannot be ruled out. His deadline for the city to be empty was very clear."

"Then the bodies will stay where they are," said Guérin.

"Let them," said Allen. "There are more important things right now."

"Agreed," said Schmidt. "Do we have a damage assessment yet?"

Allen nodded. "I sent a drone under the smoke at first light," he said. "My tech team finished a composite image ten minutes ago."

"Have you looked at it?" asked Guérin.

Allen shook his head. "Not yet."

He walked across to the bank of monitors, opened a new message and dragged the attached file on to the wide screen at the centre of the array. It opened, and he felt his heart lurch as Guérin and Schmidt gasped behind him.

The composite was grainy, and had been digitally brightened, but there was no mistaking what it showed. At its centre, the pale, concentric lines of the medieval city stood perched on their high hill, surrounded by a narrow ring of colour: green grass on the low slopes of the hill, grey tarmac roads, white painted lines, the orange roofs of buildings. After that, there was nothing but devastation in every direction; a vast circle of blackened earth with a radius of more than five miles. The roads were scorched lines of black, tracing through the remnants of the city like veins, and where there had once been thousands of homes and shops and offices there was now only a featureless landscape of smoking ruins.

"So little is left," said Guérin, staring at the screen.

"The full assessment won't be ready for a few hours," said Allen. "But my tech team's estimate is that close to eighty per cent of the city is gone."

"*Scheisse*," said Schmidt, her eyes narrow. "So much?"

"It makes Dracula's strategy clear, if nothing else," said Allen. "Once the smoke clears, there's going to be no way to get anywhere near the old city without being seen. If we make an air approach, his vamps will knock us out of the sky, and he knows the hostages make it unlikely that we'll take it out long range. What's left is bad ground to fight on, and unless we think of something else, that's exactly what he's going to make us do."

"So what is the plan?" asked Guérin, smiling thinly. "Leave him in there and hope he doesn't do anything else?"

"Maybe," he said. "Although hopefully we'll be able to come up with something better than that."

"We?" asked Guérin. "Who is we?"

"I've called a meeting of the supernatural Directors for this afternoon," said Allen. "Two will be here in person, the rest joining us by video link. I will be attending both as the Director of NS9 and as the NATO Commanding Officer, so I would like you to attend as well, Captain."

"Of course, General," said Guérin, an expression of pride on his face.

"Who else is coming in person?" asked Schmidt. "Turner and Ovechkin?"

Allen nodded. "Correct," he said, and returned his gaze to the composite image. "And we need to come up with an implementable strategy ASAP. Because we all know it's only a matter of time until Dracula makes his next move, and the only question is whether it's going to be even worse than his first."

45

SINS OF THE FATHER

The lift doors slid open to reveal the Level C corridor, its grey walls indistinguishable from the rest of the Loop. Paul Turner walked until he reached the white double doors of the infirmary, and pushed them open.

The white room was full of beds surrounded by curtains, behind which Operators who had already taken part in PROMETHEUS were recovering. One bed was uncovered, halfway down the right-hand wall; lying in it, propped up against a mountain of pillows, was Pete Randall. He was connected by a maze of wires to a bank of machines, but his eyes were open; he looked up as the Director entered the room and gave him a small, nervous smile.

Turner walked over and stopped beside the bed.

"Mr Randall," he said, returning his smile. "I'm very pleased to see you looking so well. Welcome back to the Loop."

"Thank you, Major Turner," said Pete, his voice hoarse. "Where's my daughter?"

"She's safe," said Turner. "She was attacked in the process of extracting you from Lincoln General, but she's safe."

"*Attacked?*" said Pete, his eyes widening. "By who?"

"Two men posing as policemen."

"Night Stalkers?"

He nodded. "We're assuming so. I have photos, if you feel up to looking at them? I warn you, they're not pleasant."

"Show me," said Pete.

Turner nodded, drew his console from his belt, and loaded the photos of the men Dominique Saint-Jacques' squad had killed. They had been cleaned up for examination, but the neat black holes in their foreheads were clearly visible. He held the console out towards Pete, whose face paled as he looked.

"Jesus," he whispered.

"Do you recognise them, Mr Randall?" asked Turner.

Pete shook his head. "I'm sorry."

"It's all right," he said. "We should have identification soon, regardless. And as I said, Kate is perfectly safe."

Pete nodded, but he didn't look remotely convinced.

"I need to ask you about last night, Mr Randall," said Turner. "I'm sorry, but it's important. Did you recognise the men who shot you?"

Pete nodded. "Yes," he whispered. "It was Greg Browning."

Turner inhaled sharply. "Matt's father?"

"Yes," said Pete, tears appearing in the corners of his eyes. "He's the Night Stalker. Or one of them, at least. Did you know there's more than one?"

Turner nodded. "We knew."

"I knew something was going on," continued Pete. "Just little things, you know. Security guards I didn't recognise, coincidences, unnecessary lies. And Greg was adamant that we shouldn't help you distribute the cure. So last night I followed him after work. He met up with some other men, some of them from SSL, some of them I didn't recognise, and they split up and drove off in black vans. Greg and his partner abducted a vampire from a house on the edge of Lincoln, and were going to execute him on wasteland by the canal. I confronted him, until he raised a gun. Then I ran."

"I'm sorry," said Turner.

Pete nodded. "I ran down the canal," he said, his face creased with pain at the memory. "Until... you know..."

Turner nodded. "The bullet went through your shoulder."

"I suppose I was lucky then," said Pete. "I lost my balance and fell into the canal. To be honest, I don't really remember anything after that until I woke up in hospital and saw Kate."

"How many men did you see last night, Mr Randall?" he asked.

"Eight," said Pete. "There are four Night Stalker teams, at least. They use the SSL helpline to identify vampire targets, vampires who confess to violence. Then they kill them."

"Can you give me the names of the men you recognised?"

Pete nodded. "Greg Browning. John Bolton. Ben Maddox. Dan Bellamy. They all work at SSL. And a man who told me his name was Phil Baker. He works as a security guard, and he said he used to be a Marine."

"Thank you," said Turner. He pulled his radio from his belt, keyed in a frequency and held the handset to his ear. "Angela?" he said, after a tiny pause.

"Yes, sir?" said the Security Officer.

"I have five men I want brought in for immediate questioning. Greg Browning, John Bolton, Ben Maddox, Dan Bellamy, who are all employees of the SSL charity in Lincoln, and Phil Baker, who may be a former Royal Marine. Priority Level 1 for all of them. Is that clear?"

"Of course, sir," said Angela. "I'll let you know as soon as we have them."

"Thank you," he said. He pressed END, and kept the radio in his hand.

"Are you going to hurt them?" asked Pete.

He looked down at the man lying in the bed. "Do you want me to?"

"Yes," said Pete, then grimaced. "No."

"I'm not going to hurt them, Mr Randall," said Turner. "But I do need to make sure they don't hurt anyone else. That's my priority. This room is currently off-limits to everyone but the medical staff and myself, but I'll have you moved as soon as the doctors tell me it's safe, so Kate can come and see you. You have my word. In the meantime, focus on getting better. I'll let you know when we have any news about your colleagues."

Pete nodded. "Thank you."

"All right," he said. "Goodbye, Mr Randall."

He turned and walked back towards the infirmary doors, typing into the handset again as he pushed through them into the corridor. He raised it to his ear, waiting for the Intelligence Director's voice to come on the line.

"Yes, sir?" said Major Bennett.

"I want to know everything there is to know about SSL," said Turner. "Priority Level 1."

"We investigated them when they first appeared, sir," said Bennett. "What do you want to know?"

"Who finances them?"

"Private donors, in theory," said Bennett. "There's a limited company behind their charity number, but the trail goes offshore immediately. There's a holding company underneath about a dozen layers of shell companies and dummy LLCs."

"Based where?" asked Turner.

"Two guesses, sir."

"Bermuda?"

"No."

"Grand Cayman?"

"Bingo."

Turner grimaced. "Have you seen any other charities with a structure like that?"

"No, sir," said Bennett. "I haven't."

"I want the details of the holding company," said Turner. "I want to know who's been paying for all of this."

"I can request the information, sir. The Cayman finance ministry will tell me exactly where to go, but I can do it if you want me to."

"Is there any other way?" asked Turner.

"I can ask GCHQ to investigate."

"Anything else?"

"My division can hack into the Cayman register of companies in about five minutes, sir," said Bennett. "Although I never said so, and it goes without saying that you never asked me to."

Turner grinned. "Of course not."

46

THE WAITING GAME

CARCASSONNE, SOUTHERN FRANCE

Dracula looked out over the ruined sprawl of Carcassonne, a sense of profound satisfaction filling him.

The night had gone perfectly to plan; the fires had burned with beautiful fury until the first purple light had appeared below the eastern horizon, and his followers had descended the hill to put them out, drowning the flames with water that boiled into plumes of white steam and choking grey smoke.

The destruction of the city had served as a fine display of his power; now he needed his enemies to react to it as he was expecting them to. He *needed* them to come for him with everything they had, with every man and woman at their disposal and all guns blazing, so their defeat would be both total and undeniable, and the whole world would see that he, and he alone, was now the dominant force on the planet.

Dracula had not yet decided how many people would need to die once his rule was established. Some of the killing would happen naturally; once his enemies were ground beneath his feet, he expected that vampires who even now remained hidden would unleash a genocidal retribution against the humans who had forced them into the shadows. But that would not be sufficient; an uncoordinated wave of revenge killings would be hugely effective at terrorising the majority of the human population into submission, but would also, he knew from experience, fan the flames of rebellion, and killing those who stood up against him, as publicly and graphically as possible, would be his highest priority. Their deaths would undoubtedly make them martyrs, but with each example that was made, the subsequent resistance would shrink, until it was nothing more dangerous than muttered words of dissent in private homes.

It would be the one absolutely inviolate rule: anyone who publicly opposed Dracula, in any way, would die, and die badly.

Turning new vampires without explicit permission would again be forbidden, as he remade the world. He would allow a certain number of politicians to remain in their posts, for the purposes of administrating day-to-day matters, but he would place vampires he could trust above them all; his new empire would run on fear, which had always been the greatest motivator he knew. It would be hard at first, and brutal, but in the end a combination of terror and desperate relief would make those who had survived the early purges grateful for their lives.

Eventually, they would come to love him.

The eastern sky was lightening, but Dracula was not yet ready to go back inside; he wanted to watch the dying city breathe its last. The majority of his followers had fled gratefully for their beds when he dismissed them, but he had never felt more awake, more alive; he was standing on the precipice of something unprecedented, something he had always known was his destiny.

Footsteps echoed across the cobblestones behind him, and he smiled. There had never been any doubt that Osvaldo would remind him to take shelter from the rising sun; the Spanish vampire was unfailingly conscientious. Dracula turned to face him as he approached, his smile still in place.

"Osvaldo," he said. "Isn't it beautiful?"

"It is, my lord," said the vampire. "But it is time."

"I know," he said. "But I am reluctant to leave such a view."

"There will be finer sights than this, my lord."

Dracula's smile widened. "How right you are," he said. "Accompany me to the Basilica."

"Of course, my lord," said Osvaldo.

Dracula strode across the cobbled square, the Spanish vampire falling in beside him. Before him stood the Hôtel de la Cité, where the hostages were being kept in relative good health until their inevitable deaths, either at the hands of his enemies or of Dracula himself. Rising above its rooftops was the spire of the Basilique Saint-Nazaire, the ornate church that he had taken as his private quarters, and which few of his army were willing to enter: he had seen otherwise fearless vampires hiss and screech and spit at the mere thought of setting foot on its consecrated ground.

Children, he thought. *Heathens. They do not even understand themselves. The church can do them no harm.*

Unlike his followers, Dracula loved the Basilica. It was the grandest building in the medieval city, and therefore only fitting that he take it as his residence, but there was more to it than that; the interior of the old church was beautiful, with high walls and carved stone pillars interspersed with stained-glass windows, and it was cold, and empty. He had already decided that once the upcoming battle was won, and his dominion over the planet was absolute, it would be his throne room.

"What if they don't come, my lord?" asked Osvaldo, as they rounded the corner and walked up into the wide plaza in front of the Basilica.

"Then we will burn another city," said Dracula. "And another, and another, until they do. But that won't be necessary. They will come."

"If you say so, my lord," said Osvaldo. "I do not doubt you."

Dracula nodded.

Nor should you, he thought. *Not if you value your life.*

"Tell me of our new arrivals," he said. "I trust you are handling them?"

"I am, my lord," said Osvaldo. "Almost a thousand now since you spoke on the walls, and more arriving with each hour that passes. Many are cowards, seeking nothing more than your favour, but some are proving useful. There are true believers among them, my lord, men and women who will die at your command without a second thought."

"Excellent," said Dracula. "See that they are made good use of."

"Yes, my lord," said Osvaldo. "The only problem I can foresee is one of space. It will not be long until there is no more room in the city for your army."

Dracula smiled narrowly. "That problem will resolve itself," he said. "Providing that all goes to plan, a great many of them will soon be dead."

Osvaldo frowned. "You believe so, my lord?"

"Of course," he said. "Only a fool would believe that a battle could be won without casualties on both sides, and our enemies are fast, and strong, and resourceful. They are a worthy foe, and must be taken seriously. Those who fight with us and survive will live like kings for the rest of their days, while the rest will die with honour and glory. What finer possible fate could there be?"

"None, my lord," said Osvaldo, his voice thick with devoted fervour. "It is exactly as you say."

"Your agreement is unnecessary," said Dracula, as they reached the door of the Basilica. "What of the hostages?"

"Physically, they are fine, my lord," said Osvaldo. "They are scared, and they want to go home. Their fear keeps them well behaved."

Dracula pushed open the heavy wooden door and stepped into

the church, relishing the cold air and the scent of long-extinguished candles. The wooden pews had been piled against the walls, creating a wide empty space; he walked down the long aisle at the centre of the nave, his footsteps loud on the tiled floor, Osvaldo following a deferential distance behind him. A large wooden cross stood in an alcove on the left and an elevated stone chancel rose at the far end, beneath panels of bright multicoloured glass. A large chair had been placed at its centre; it faced down the cavernous building, and it was from where Dracula issued orders and dispensed judgements.

"Of course they want to go home," he said. "Make sure they continue to believe it is a possibility."

"Yes, my lord," said Osvaldo.

Dracula nodded, and floated up on to the chancel. "Leave me," he said.

The vampire bowed, and walked quickly towards the door.

"Osvaldo," said Dracula, just before he reached it.

"Yes, my lord?" said the vampire, turning instantly back to face his master.

"Have Emery torture one of the hostages when you return to the hotel. I do not want them becoming too comfortable."

Osvaldo nodded. "Of course, my lord. Any one in particular?"

"It makes not the slightest bit of difference to me," said Dracula. "Let Emery choose, but do not let him kill them. I want their suffering to serve as a warning."

Osvaldo nodded, and exited the Basilica, closing the door behind him. Dracula settled himself into his chair and allowed his mind to return to its most constant topic: exactly when his enemies would make their inevitable move against him.

Surely no more than two days, he thought. *Three at the very most. Any longer and I will have to give them fresh motivation.*

47

AFTERSHOCKS

There were few things in the world that Matt had less wanted to see when his console beeped in his pocket than a message summoning him to see the Director.

The influx of data from PROMETHEUS was overwhelming the Lazarus Project, and he was trying to find more than a stolen moment to spend with his girlfriend while also trying to ignore the part of his brain that was constantly telling him that he was a bad person, and a worse friend for what he had done to Jamie; he was stretched as thin as he thought he ever had been, and felt like he had no more capacity to absorb surprises or bad news, both of which were the likely result of a summons to see Major Turner.

He walked down the short corridor on Level A, pushed open the door, and froze.

The Director was in his usual position, in the chair behind his desk. But standing in front of him, her head turned to look at Matt with an expression that was entirely unreadable, was Larissa Kinley.

He merely stared at her; a jumble of emotions were jostling for position, momentarily paralysing him.

What else? he managed to wonder. *What else is there left to go wrong?*

"Shut the door and come in, Browning," said the Director. "You look like you've seen a ghost, for heaven's sake."

It feels like I have, thought Matt.

He forced his body into action, closed the door, and walked slowly across the room, his gaze fixed on Larissa.

"Hello, Matt," she said, and gave him a tiny smile.

"Hello, Larissa," he said, his voice unsteady. "So you're back?"

"I'm back," she said. "I got in last night and—"

"I'm sorry," interrupted Turner. "I know you probably have a lot of catching up to do, but I have to leave for France in thirty minutes and I have something I need to tell you both. I'm afraid it's bad news, but I didn't want you to hear it from someone else."

"I've been back twelve hours and you've already got bad news for me," said Larissa, her smile disappearing. "Nothing changes around here, does it?"

"I'm afraid not," said Turner. "You are both aware of what has taken place in Carcassonne over the last twelve hours?"

"Yes, sir," said Matt, as Larissa nodded her head.

"When the fires were started, a Red Cross team was trapped inside the city," said Turner. "General Allen sent a squad in to get them out, but they were ambushed by vampires and both the volunteers and the Operators were killed. The NS9 squad was led by Danny Lawrence."

For a long moment, neither Matt nor Larissa responded; they simply stared at the Director.

"Danny's dead?" said Larissa, eventually.

Turner nodded. "I'm truly sorry. I know you both knew him."

"Yeah," said Larissa. "He was my friend."

Matt felt anger, sharp and cold and painful, trickle through him. It wasn't fair that Danny was dead; he had been good, and brave, and kind, and it *just wasn't fair*.

"What happened?" he heard himself ask. "Do we know?"

"Vamps brought their helicopter down," said Turner. "Danny

survived the crash, but he was badly injured. General Allen scrambled another squad to go in after him, but Danny told him not to send them. He said it was too late."

"Oh God," whispered Larissa, her eyes glistening with tears.

"He didn't want anyone to risk their lives trying to save him," said Matt. "Did he?"

Turner shook his head.

Of course he didn't, thought Matt, a lump lodged in his throat. *So brave. Right to the end.*

"General Allen asked me to tell you, Matt," said Turner. "He doesn't know you're here, Larissa, but he said you'd both want to know."

Larissa nodded, then grimaced as the tears brimming in her eyes spilled down her cheeks. Matt didn't respond; he didn't know how to.

"Danny Lawrence was a fine Operator," said Turner. "And he'll be missed by everyone who knew him. I wish I could spend more time discussing this, but I'm due in a meeting in France that simply will not wait, for anything. If you want to talk to me when I get back, send me a message and I promise I'll find some time. But right now, I'm afraid you're both dismissed."

Matt nodded, and turned towards the door. Larissa didn't move; she was staring at the ground, her cheeks wet with tears, her face crumpled in an expression of profound misery.

"Larissa," said Matt, gently. "Come on."

She looked round at him, and slowly nodded. He made for the door again, and this time she followed him. They walked in silence past the Security Operator and out into the main Level A corridor, where they stopped and faced each other.

"Does Jamie know you're back?" he asked. "I'm sorry to ask, but, well, you know…"

Larissa wiped her eyes with the back of her hand and nodded.

"He knows," she said, her voice thick with emotion. "I saw him this morning. We talked."

"OK," said Matt.

"Do you want to come to the canteen with me?" asked Larissa. "I'd really like to talk about Danny with somebody who knew him. If you've got time?"

Matt grimaced. "I can't," he said. "I have to get back to work."

Larissa nodded and gave him a small smile that didn't reach her eyes. "Of course," she said. "I understand."

"I'm sorry," said Matt. "I really am. I just... I just can't."

He turned and fled down the corridor, almost breaking into a run, so desperate was he for the safety and security of the Lazarus Project lab, where he could throw himself into work and not think about anything else, not Danny or Larissa or Jamie or the pain and misery that seemed to be crowding in on him from all sides.

Turner watched the door close, then grabbed his radio as it buzzed on his desk.

His heart ached for his two Lieutenants as he pressed SEND; they had seen more death and misery than most people would experience in a lifetime, and although they bore it with tremendous resilience, Turner knew there was only so much anyone could take before their souls sustained permanent damage.

He had debated long and hard with himself over whether to tell Matt that Pete Randall had identified his father as a Night Stalker, but, in the end, he had decided against it. He didn't doubt Kate's father's account of what had happened to him, but it was still *technically* an unsubstantiated accusation; he couldn't think of any reason Pete would have to lie, but he would feel a lot better when they had proof, and preferably when they had Greg Browning safely in custody. Then he would be in a position to answer at least some of the many questions Matt was bound to have when he was told the truth about his father.

"Sir?" asked the Security Officer.

"Go ahead, Angela."

"The medical staff have moved Pete Randall into a room in the Science Division, sir. Do you want me to let Kate know she can go and see him?"

"No," said Turner. "I'll do it. Thank you, Angela. Out."

48

DIRECTORS' GUILD

OUTSKIRTS OF CARCASSONNE, SOUTHERN FRANCE
NINETY MINUTES LATER

"I'm going to go ahead and call this meeting to order," said Bob Allen. "All Directors in attendance. Also present is Captain Guérin of the French Army, who is acting as NATO liaison in this matter. Any objections?"

Paul Turner looked round the table in the middle of the command centre that had been erected in Field 1 of the displaced persons camp. Bob Allen, Karla Schmidt, Aleksandr Ovechkin and Captain Guérin looked back at him; it was not only the first time in his relatively short tenure in charge of Blacklight that four Directors had been in the same place at the same time, it was also something he doubted had ever happened more than once or twice. The other seven Directors – the heads of the Chinese, Japanese, Indian, Egyptian, Canadian, South African and Brazilian Departments – were watching from screens at the end of the room.

"Any objections?" repeated Allen.

Nobody spoke.

The NS9 Director nodded. "All right then," he said. "Let's get started. You've all been receiving my progress reports from here in

France, but I'll very quickly summarise them again, starting with the obvious. The destruction of the modern city of Carcassonne is almost total. We're still relying on long-range reconnaissance, as we're not currently allowing anyone to enter the city, but as the smoke clears, the picture is getting clearer and clearer. I'm sure you've all seen the footage and the composite images."

There was a murmur of agreement.

"We have no accurate casualty numbers," continued Allen, "but we can safely assume that we're talking about hundreds dead, probably thousands. We evacuated at least eighty-five per cent of the city's residents, but I'm afraid that leaves as many as six thousand people currently unaccounted for. We have no updates on the hostages being held inside the medieval city, and, as you know, there has been no further communication from Dracula. So I'm going to move straight on to the only item on this meeting's agenda: what the hell are we going to do about all this?"

"The answer did not require a meeting," said Colonel Ovechkin. "There is only one option."

"Which is?" asked General Tán. The Chinese Director was younger than his counterparts, but he had earned a reputation as a calm diplomat and brilliant strategist in the five years since he'd taken over PBS6. Turner had never met him, but he had impressed Bob Allen during a visit to Nevada three months earlier, and that was more than enough reason to give him the benefit of the doubt.

"We stop him now," said Ovechkin, fixing his grey eyes on Tán's screen. "Or we do not stop him at all. It is that simple."

Silence fell over the room. The eleven Directors eyed each other, seemingly daring one another to be the first to respond. Eventually, it was Bob Allen who did so.

"Does anyone disagree with Aleksandr's assessment of the situation?"

"I do not necessarily disagree," said Colonel Maroun, the Director of Egypt's Section G. He was a large man, with sharp, piercing eyes and a thick black beard. "But I do have a question. What is the involvement of the regular military and emergency services going to be?"

"I can only speak for my country and for NATO," said Allen. "But I can tell you now that neither will be sending regular forces to assist us."

"Why not?" asked Maroun.

"Because they'll be needed for domestic duties if we fail to defeat Dracula," said Allen.

"That is hardly a vote of confidence," said Tán, smiling narrowly.

"It does not matter," said Ovechkin. "Regular soldiers will only get in the way. This is *our* business, not theirs."

"I agree," said Schmidt.

Turner stared at Bob Allen, who was looking at his colleagues with a tight expression.

What aren't you telling us, Bob? he thought. *Out with it. There's no time left for secrets.*

The NS9 Director didn't make him wait.

"I also agree," said Allen. "But for the sake of full disclosure I should tell you all that, despite official objections from NATO, the French government has refused to rule out the nuclear option."

There was an explosion of noise in the room, a deafening cacophony of protest and accusation. Turner stared at his American counterpart, incredulous; he could not believe what he had heard. General Allen had turned towards Captain Guérin, whose eyes had widened like a rabbit caught in headlights.

"That is completely ridiculous," said Schmidt. "A detonation on mainland Europe would violate every nuclear treaty that has ever been signed."

"I am sorry," said Tán. "Are you telling us that the French are prepared to drop a nuclear missile on one of their own cities?"

"Guérin?" said Allen.

The French Captain swallowed hard. "Carcassonne is already dead," he said, his voice low. "It is not the preferred option in Paris, but General Allen is correct. It has not been ruled out."

"In what circumstances would it *become* the preferred option?" asked Turner. "Given that we have no idea whether a nuclear detonation would actually kill Dracula, at least as far as I'm aware. Or whether or not we could even hit him. The first vampire is faster than any creature on earth, and I would back him to be able to get clear of the blast radius in the time between launch and detonation."

"What would you like me to say, Major?" asked Guérin. "I have told you that it remains an option. Whether you agree with it or not does not seem particularly important to me at this moment."

"We're getting sidetracked," said Allen, shooting them both a warning glance. "We don't need to be worrying about what happens if we fail. We need to focus on making sure that we *don't* fail."

"Correct," said Ovechkin. "We have already wasted too much time."

"You are so impatient, Aleksandr," said Schmidt. "What would you have had us do? Storm the city as soon as dawn broke?"

"That would have been better," said Ovechkin, glaring at the German Director. "While we talk, Dracula fortifies his position and plans his next move. We are playing into his hands by taking so long to respond. We have already allowed him to change the battlefield to his liking. What else will he do while we sit here debating with each other?"

"Why don't you tell us all what we should do, Colonel?" said Tán. "You seem very sure."

"With pleasure," said Ovechkin. "Although before I do, I

would like Major Turner to update us on the programme his Department has recently undertaken. PROMETHEUS, I believe you have called it?"

Turner nodded. "We have turned fifty-five per cent of our active roster," he said, "and have recorded no adverse effects so far."

"It is remarkable to me that you were able to find so many volunteers," said Maroun. "I do not believe my people would have been so enthusiastic."

"My understanding is that the Blacklight Operators were not given any choice in the matter," said Tán, and smiled. "Isn't that right, Major?"

Turner stared at the Chinese Director, his grey eyes narrowing. "You are correct, Colonel Tán," he said. "PROMETHEUS was mandatory. And if the rest of you had followed my lead we'd be in a better position than we are now."

"What you have done is an abomination," said Maroun, his voice a low rumble. "It is a disgrace."

"Fine," said Turner. "In which case, I will order my vampire Operators to stand down and let your Department take the lead. How does that sound?"

Maroun scowled at him, but did not respond.

"Enough bickering," said Allen. "Aleksandr, are you going to tell us your plan or not?"

Ovechkin nodded. "It is very simple," he said. "A frontal assault that engages Dracula's army while a small strike team enters the medieval city to take out the first vampire himself. I asked Major Turner for an update because I would propose selecting the strike team from Blacklight's vampire Operators."

"How large a force are you referring to?" asked Schmidt. "For the main assault?"

"Everyone," said Ovechkin. "All of us, all at once. I do not believe we will get a second chance, and I therefore see no point in keeping Operators in reserve."

"Major Turner?" asked Tân. "What do you think?"

"I completely agree with Aleksandr," he said. "I think it represents our best chance of success. And I think we need to do it quickly."

"How quickly?" asked Allen.

"Forty-eight hours from now," said Turner. "Sunset, the day after tomorrow. I think sooner would be better, but I don't think gathering our forces together any quicker is realistic."

"Sunset?" asked Guérin. "Why not send everyone we have into the city now, when we have the advantage of daylight?"

"Because Aleksandr's plan relies on drawing Dracula's followers out into open ground," said Schmidt. "Inside the old city, in the narrow streets where the sunlight does not reach the ground, they'd swarm all over us."

"What about the hostages?" asked Guérin. "Have we forgotten about them?"

"Of course not," said Allen. "As far as the public is concerned, their safety remains our highest priority. But their best chance for survival is for us to kill the vampires holding them captive, because I don't believe Dracula has any intention of ever letting them go. Do any of you?"

Silence.

"All right," said Allen. "In which case, let's—"

Turner's console beeped into life. He snatched it up from his belt and thumbed it open as the NS9 Director stared at him, his eyes narrowing.

"I'm sorry, Paul," said Allen. "Are we distracting you from something important?"

"My apologies," said Turner. "I left a Priority Level 1 investigation in progress." He opened the message that had arrived and quickly scanned it.

FROM: Bennett, Major Alison (NS303, 47-E)
TO: Turner, Major Paul (NS303, 36-A)
SSL terminates at Rusmanov Holdings Limited. Registered in Grand Cayman in 1982. Sole listed director Valeri Rusmanov.

Turner stared at the screen.

Jesus Christ, he thought. *How deep does this go?*

"Can I have your attention for a moment?" he said, raising his eyes and looking around the table.

"Go ahead, Paul," said Bob Allen.

"Are you aware of a vigilante group that has been operating in Blacklight jurisdiction known as the Night Stalkers?" he said.

There was a low chorus of agreement and a series of nods from his fellow Directors.

"There have been more than a dozen vampire murders in the last three months," he continued. "The British press has been all over the story, and public opinion has been split down the middle. Half the populace believe the Night Stalkers are criminals, while the other half seem to think they're heroes. There have been protests and counter-protests. Violence. Rioting."

"We get the picture, Paul," said Allen. "Most of us have similar groups operating in our territories. What's your point?"

"Sorry," said Turner. "I have a man who survived a Night Stalker attack in the Loop's infirmary right now, a man who was able to identify his assailants. Several of them worked for a recently founded UK charity called SSL, the Supernatural Survivors League. It operates a helpline for vampires and their victims, which the Night Stalkers used to identify their targets."

"That is horrible," said Schmidt. "But I do not see what it has to do with what we are discussing."

"I ordered my Intelligence Division to investigate SSL," said Turner. "I wanted to know who was financing it and, presumably, bankrolling the Night Stalkers. They've just informed me that the charity's financial trail ends in the Cayman Islands, with a limited company called Rusmanov Holdings. The company has a single director listed. Valeri Rusmanov."

There was a long moment of silence, before everyone started to talk and shout at once.

"Why?" asked Schmidt. "Why would Valeri do this?"

"It is not Valeri," said Ovechkin. "Valeri is dead. This is Dracula, or someone acting for him."

"Why, though?" demanded Schmidt.

"To create fear?" said Tán. "And unrest? To distract Blacklight?"

"But this group was killing vampires," said Schmidt. "He was financing the murder of his own kind."

"That should come as no surprise," said Turner. "Dracula wouldn't think twice about killing a million vampires if their deaths served his ambitions. The lives of others mean nothing to him."

"The attacks as he took Carcassonne," said Allen, his voice low. "The planes and the massacres on the subways, attacks that must have taken months of planning. The videos. And now this. What the hell else has he got in store for us? What else don't we know?"

"I have no idea," said Turner. "But if the rest of you really do have similar groups in your own countries, I'd suggest you investigate them immediately. Because I don't see any reason why Dracula would only try to destabilise the UK."

"No," said Ovechkin, his voice low. "Nor do I."

Silence descended over the table. Turner raised his console, tapped REPLY, and typed rapidly on its screen.

FROM: Turner, Major Paul (NS303, 36-A)
TO: Bennett, Major Alison (NS303, 47-E)
Leak this to the press immediately. Be unequivocal about the link between SSL and Dracula. Hopefully it will flush Greg Browning out.

"All right," said Allen. "Thank you, Paul. I'm sure we now all have calls we want to make, so let's talk about the implementation of Aleksandr's plan. Thoughts? Problems?"

"I will not bring my entire Department," said Tán, immediately. "I know without even asking that Beijing will not sanction it. But I will commit seventy-five per cent of my Operators, which, I should remind you all, is more fighting men and women than any two of your Departments combined."

"Excellent," said Allen. "Thank you. What about the rest of you?"

"I will match Colonel Tán's contribution," said Maroun. "Seventy-five per cent of my Department. I will not leave my homeland entirely undefended, as I'm sure you can all understand."

"Of course," said Allen. "Who else?"

The other Directors quickly gave their figures: seventy-five per cent from Canada, India and Brazil, eighty-five from Japan and South Africa. Turner listened, greatly heartened by the response; he had been bracing himself for at least one of his counterparts to either refuse to endorse Ovechkin's plan or claim geographical isolation, that what was happening in southern France was not their problem. The look of profound relief on Bob Allen's face suggested he had been expecting the same thing.

Ovechkin looked over at him. "Major Turner?"

476

He held the Russian's gaze. "Everyone," he said. "My entire active roster."

Allen gave him a fierce smile, then turned to the FTB Director. "Colonel Schmidt?"

"The same," said Schmidt. "Unless we win, there will be nothing left to defend."

"I agree," said Ovechkin. "I will bring the entire SPC. General Allen?"

"Everyone," said Allen, instantly.

Turner smiled as the eleven Directors looked at each other.

Eighty-five per cent of all the Operators in the world, he thought. *Maybe even ninety. More than I dared to hope for. Please, please let it be enough.*

49

ENEMY AT THE GATES

FIVE HOURS LATER

Paul Turner stepped down on to the tarmac outside the Loop's hangar and stretched his aching arms above his head.

He was absolutely exhausted.

After the Directors' meeting had concluded – and after Ovechkin, Schmidt and Allen had ordered their respective Departments to immediately investigate all vigilante activity in their territories – Turner had boarded the helicopter that would take him home, but had found himself unable to take advantage of the brief opportunity for rest the flight provided; his mind had been whirring endlessly with possibilities and outcomes.

He had no idea what was going to happen; the numbers they were going to be able to bring to bear were hugely encouraging, but for all their experience and training and equipment, the overwhelming majority of the Multinational Force would still be human. Dracula's army, on the other hand, was composed entirely of vampires and, if recent reports were accurate, growing with each hour that passed.

Turner was sure they would still have the numerical advantage when the fighting began, but he suspected it might be smaller in forty-eight hours' time than it was now, or had been yesterday. And in a battle between humans and vampires that was remotely close to even, there would only be one outcome in the end. Everything was going to depend on the strike team they sent into the old city to hunt for Dracula himself, and who it should consist of had been one of the subjects occupying his thoughts as the helicopter flew north-west.

He walked through the hangar doors, took the lift down to Level A, and headed along the corridor towards his quarters. Turner nodded to the Security Operator on duty, unlocked the door, and settled into the chair behind his desk with a long, deep sigh. For a moment he merely stared at the piles of files and folders that required his attention, then took a deep breath, lifted the first one down, and opened it.

When the intercom buzzed, the Director opened his eyes and saw that fifteen minutes had passed. He had not intended to sleep, but his body had clearly hijacked the decision-making process.

He pressed TALK. "Yes?"

"Kate Randall is here to see you, sir," said Operator Gregg. "She came three times while you were in France. She says it's urgent."

"Send her in," he said, rubbing his eyes with the palms of his hands. The door swung open and Kate stepped through it, her face pale.

"Hello, Kate," he said. "Are you all right?"

She stopped in front of his desk and nodded. "I'm fine, sir. How was France?"

"Tiring. You got my message then?"

"I did, sir. Thanks for moving him."

"You're welcome," he said. "How was he when you saw him?"

"Pleased to see me," she said, and smiled. "Which was nice. And safe, which is the main thing. He told me the two of you talked."

"Did he tell you who shot him?" he asked.

Kate nodded. "This is going to absolutely *destroy* Matt."

Turner nodded. "That's why we need to find Greg Browning and bring him in," he said. "Before anyone else gets hurt."

"I just can't believe he would do that to my dad," said Kate. "They were friends."

"I know," he said. "Maybe the Albert Harker business affected him more than we thought. Maybe it was a mistake to let him go home."

"You couldn't have known this would happen," said Kate. "Nobody could."

"Maybe," said Turner. "But this goes a lot deeper than we thought."

Kate frowned. "What do you mean?"

"After I talked to your father, I ordered the Intelligence Division to investigate SSL. They traced the charity's finance to a company in the Cayman Islands. It's called Rusmanov Holdings."

Kate stared at him. "Valeri," she said, her voice low.

"Either him, or Dracula, or someone working for him," he said. "It's starting to look like SSL was just a front, a way to gather intelligence for the Night Stalkers."

"Why, for God's sake?" asked Kate.

Turner shrugged. "To cause trouble?" he said. "To frighten people? To distract us? Take your pick."

"Jesus," said Kate. "Dracula hasn't just been recovering from Château Dauncy, has he? He's been planning all this for months."

"It looks that way," he said. "What we don't know is—"

The radio on his desk buzzed into life. Turner stared at it, suddenly full of a desire to smash the plastic handset to pieces, then pressed SEND and raised it to his ear.

"Yes."

Angela Darcy spoke for several seconds. Turner listened, his heart accelerating in his chest.

Oh God, he thought.

"Understood," he said. "I'll be right there."

He pressed END and clipped the radio to his belt.

"Everything OK, sir?" asked Kate.

"No," he said. "There's a situation at the authorisation gate. A car was crashed into it, and the driver is threatening protesters with a gun. Apparently he's demanding to see his son."

Kate followed the Director through the access door at the end of the authorisation tunnel, her Glock drawn, and emerged into a nightmare.

To her left, wedged against the towering gate, was a white car, steam billowing from beneath a bonnet that was crumpled in on itself. In the distance, huddled among the trees and the tents of the protest camp that was now a permanent fixture outside the gates, were dozens of men and women, their faces full of fear. The signs they usually waved at Blacklight vehicles as they came and went were absent, as was the steady drone of music that usually filled the camp. The protesters were keeping their distance, for reasons that were obvious.

Arranged in a wide semicircle, from directly in front of the gate to the edges of the forest on either side of the road, were more than a dozen Security Operators, their weapons raised to their shoulders and pointing at the middle of the road.

At Greg Browning.

Kate recognised him as soon as she stepped out of the tunnel, and felt a wave of horror race through her as she took in the reality of what she was seeing.

Oh God, she thought. *Oh dear God, what a mess this is.*

Matt's dad was pacing back and forth in the road, dripping with clear liquid. Beside him, kneeling on the tarmac, were a woman in her thirties and a man who looked barely out of his teens; both were also soaking wet and looked terrified out of their minds. In one of Greg's hands was a black MP5, and in the other he held a silver cigarette lighter. The smell of petrol was overpowering, and the look on Matt's father's face filled her with dread; it was the wild, disconnected expression of someone who has lost their mind.

"Jesus," said Kate, her voice low.

Turner glanced round at her and grimaced.

"I want to see my son!" bellowed Greg. "I'll burn us all, I swear to God I'll do it! I want to see my boy!"

Kate stared at him, her heart pounding in her chest. She had no idea how to handle this situation; it was so far out of her sphere of experience that she felt an enormous wave of relief roll through her when Paul Turner stepped forward.

"Put them down, Mr Browning," said the Director. "Then we can talk. You don't want to do this."

"I'll burn them!" screamed Greg. He waved the cigarette lighter, as the kneeling protesters sobbed with terror. "I'll burn them so you'd better take me seriously, Goddamnit! Do you hear me? I want to see my son!"

"Put the lighter down," said Turner. "Please. You don't want to hurt them."

Greg stared at the Director, his face running with tears and twisted with bright, burning hatred. "Why did you have to take him?" he asked, his voice trembling. "Everything would have been fine if you hadn't taken him. What did I ever do to you? Why did you ruin my life?"

Kate stepped forward. "Matt wanted to be part of Blacklight, Mr Browning," she said. "He volunteered."

Greg shook his head furiously. "That's a lie," he said. "That's a filthy lie."

"I promise you it isn't," she said, forcing as much calm and warmth into her voice as she possibly could. "He wanted to help people. He wanted to do something good, like you did with SSL, like I'm sure you thought you were doing with the Night Stalkers. He wouldn't want to see you like this."

Greg stopped pacing and stared directly at her.

"I shot your dad," he said. "Did you know that?"

"Take it easy," whispered Turner.

"Yeah," said Kate, meeting the man's gaze. "I know you did."

"I was trying to kill him," said Greg. "I *wanted* to kill him. Everything would've been OK if he'd just died like he was supposed to. Now it's all ruined."

Kate felt anger boil in the pit of her stomach. She tightened her grip on her Glock, and forced herself to lower her aim from the centre of Greg's chest; she was suddenly less confident of her ability not to pull the trigger.

"Put the lighter down, Mr Browning," said Turner. "It doesn't have to end like this. You still have the power to change it."

"I can't do anything!" screamed Greg. "Everything I've tried to do, you've spoilt! You ruin everything! You're monsters!"

"We didn't do anything," said Turner, his voice low and calm. "Your choices are your own. It's nobody else's fault that you keep making them so badly."

"I tried!" shouted Greg, his voice suddenly hoarse. "I *tried* to do good! Nobody would let me!"

"That's right," said Kate, forcing her anger down. "I know you tried, Mr Browning. I don't think you're a bad person, and we know the Night Stalkers weren't your idea."

Greg began to cry, huge sobs that wracked his body as tears

streamed down his face and thick ribbons of snot hung from his nose. The protesters stared up at him, struck dumb by fear.

"I didn't know," said Greg, his voice wavering. "I swear I didn't know, until I saw the news this morning. A man came to me, and he talked to me, and he told me what I could do, and he was right. There's no room for us and the vamps. This is a war. It's a *war*."

"Who was it?" pressed Kate. "Who told you to start the Night Stalkers?"

Greg looked at her. "*I don't know*," he said. "I never saw him again. But it was his idea. SSL, all of it. Get the vamps to confess and punish them, like an inquisition. He told me we were the same. I didn't know who he was working for."

He broke down sobbing again. The realisation that his crusade against vampires had been started and funded by the very worst of them appeared to have unravelled him completely.

"I want to see my son," he whispered.

"We can talk about that," said Turner. "But only if you put the lighter and the gun down."

"Please," said Kate. "You don't want to do this, Mr Browning. I know you don't."

Greg threw back his head and howled. To Kate's ears, it sounded barely human: it was the broken, wounded cry of an animal. He lowered his head and fixed her with eyes that were full of pain.

"Get my son," he said. "Please. Just get him. GET MY SON RIGHT NOW!"

"I can't," said Turner. "I'm sorry. Not until you put everything down."

Greg stared at them for a long moment, then placed the muzzle of the MP5 against his temple.

"Don't," said Turner, his voice suddenly full of urgency. "Please. It doesn't have to end like this, Greg."

Matt's dad grunted with laughter, his tears shining in the early evening gloom. Kate stared at him and made a decision; she could not watch her friend's father kill himself, at least not unless she had tried absolutely everything to stop it. She took a step towards him, put her Glock on the ground, and raised her empty hands.

Greg pointed the MP5 at her. "Don't come any closer."

"You're not going to shoot me," said Kate, with far more conviction than she felt. "We both know that. Put the gun down."

"Kate," said Turner, his voice low and full of warning. "Step back. Now."

"Why do you want to see Matt?" she asked, ignoring the Director. "What will you say to him if we let you see him? Tell me."

The hand holding the MP5 began to shake, and Kate tried not to look at the finger curled round the submachine gun's trigger. She took another step forward.

"Come on, Mr Browning," she said. "Tell me what you want to say to your son."

Greg grimaced, and for the briefest of moments he looked down at the ground. Kate's muscles tightened, but before she could leap forward and take the gun away from him, his eyes were back on her, huge and wide and wet with tears.

"I need him to know that I'm sorry," he whispered. "For everything. Will you tell him for me? Please?"

"Tell him yourself," said Kate. "That's the least he deserves. Put the gun and the lighter down and we can go to him right now."

Greg shook his head. "I can't," he said. "You have to tell him for me. You have to."

Kate took another step.

"Put the gun down," she said. "Please, Mr Browning."

"Don't come any closer."

Kate raised her hands higher. "Just put it down."

"DON'T COME ANY CLOSER!" screamed Greg, the gun trembling wildly in his hand.

"You're not going to shoot me," said Kate. She drew in a deep breath, and stepped—

Bang.

ZERO HOUR PLUS 208 DAYS

50

JUST WHEN YOU THINK . . .

Matt Browning stepped out of the elevator on Level H, turned away from the airlock door, and walked along the corridor towards the non-supernatural cellblock, his brain aching with exhaustion.

Tiredness was a constant inside the Loop, particularly within the Lazarus Project, and was not normally worth commenting on, or complaining about; this morning, however, was different. After the awful news about Danny Lawrence and his awkward, halting encounter with Larissa, Matt had gone back to his desk and thrown himself into his work with an enthusiasm that bordered on manic, trying to replace everything in his head with figures and formulas and reports. He had collapsed into bed just after 4.30am, his mind finally cleansed by exhaustion, and had instantly fallen into an unconsciousness so deep and impenetrable he was not sure it could accurately be called sleep.

What had woken him two and a half hours later was the piercing, hateful beep of a message arriving on his console.

He had fumbled on his bedside table for the plastic rectangle, his eyelids feeling like they weighed several tons each, and held it up in front of his face. It had taken several jabs of his finger until the screen finally awoke, revealing four lines of glowing text.

FROM: Turner, Major Paul (NS303, 36-A)
TO: Browning, Lieutenant Matthew (NS303, 83-C)
Meet me in non-supernatural containment in fifteen minutes.
Don't speak to anyone or access any overnight reports.

Matt rounded the corner and saw the Director standing at the entrance to the cellblock, his face as pale and expressionless as ever. He walked towards him, trying not to let the nervousness that was beginning to spread through him show.

"Lieutenant Browning," said Turner. "Have you been to sleep?"

"I got a couple of hours, sir," said Matt, stopping in front of the Director. "Is everything all right?"

Turner shook his head. "No," he said. "I'm afraid it's not. There's no easy way to say this, so I'm just going to come out with it. Kate Randall is in a critical condition in the Lazarus Project, and your father is in Cell D."

Matt narrowed his eyes and studied the Director's face, looking for some suggestion that this was a phenomenally out-of-character joke, but seeing only deadly seriousness.

"What are you talking about, sir?" he asked.

Turner looked steadily into his eyes. "This is going to be hard for you to hear," he said, "but you're a grown man, and I see nothing to be gained by shielding you from the truth. So here it is. Your father has been murdering vampires as part of the vigilante organisation known as the Night Stalkers. SSL itself appears to have been little more than a front, a way for the Night Stalkers to acquire their targets, set up on Dracula's behalf and funded by a company that belonged to Valeri Rusmanov. Two nights ago your father and another man attempted to kill Pete Randall, but failed. Randall was brought here after life-saving treatment, and identified your father as his attacker. A warrant was issued for his arrest, but last night he arrived outside the authorisation tunnel, demanding to see you and threatening to kill both himself and two protesters from the camp. Kate tried to talk him down and he shot her in the neck. I shot him twice in the leg, and we were able to subdue him and bring him in. I'm very sorry."

Matt stared, his mind empty of everything but a rising incredulity. There was just simply no way that what Turner had just told him could be true. It was absolutely ridiculous, surely nothing more than yet another joke at his expense in a lifetime full of them, this one perhaps the cruellest of all. It was so mean, and vicious, and unfair, but when he opened his mouth to tell the Director so, what came out was something entirely different.

"Kate got shot?" he asked, his voice a barely audible whisper. "Is she all right?"

Turner shook his head. "No," he said. "I'm afraid she's not. The bullet cut her carotid artery. They've stabilised her, but her condition is critical."

Matt felt tears rise in his eyes. "Does her dad know?" he said. "Do Jamie and Larissa?"

"Not yet," said Turner. "I'm telling them shortly."

Matt nodded. He could barely breathe; his chest was locked tight with what he was distantly aware was the early stages of shock.

"You shot my dad?"

"Yes," said Turner, and there was an audible tremor in his voice. "After he shot Kate, he turned the gun on himself, but I fired before he could pull the trigger again."

"Why?" Matt managed. "Why did he do these things? Why did he kill those vampires?"

"Someone approached him," said Turner. "We don't know who it was, but they came to him and told him that vampires and humans were at war, and offered him a way to do something about it."

Matt was pretty sure he nodded, even though he had barely heard the Director's words and his mind was somewhere else. He was wondering how it was possible to go to sleep in one world and wake up in another, a world of vigilantes and attempted murders and botched suicides with his dad at the heart of it all.

"Can I see him?" he asked.

Turner nodded. "Five minutes."

Tears sprang instantly into Matt's eyes as he stepped into Cell D.

The standard metal bed had been removed to make room for the hospital bed that was now in the centre of the small concrete room. His dad was lying on it, his wrist handcuffed to its frame, his left leg wrapped in layers of white bandages. A trolley of monitoring equipment stood next to the bed, from the top of which a video camera was pointing directly at the bed; it was presumably how the medical staff were monitoring him.

His dad turned his head towards him as he walked slowly into the cell; he looked pale, and tired, and *old*. As Matt reached the side of the bed, the man lying on it began to cry.

"I'm sorry," said Greg, the words cracking between low sobs. "I'm so sorry, son, I'm so sorry for everything. I always screw everything up. Couldn't even kill myself properly and spare you the shame of having me as your dad."

Matt stared. He had wondered, during the short walk down the cellblock, what he was going to feel when he saw his dad; now he was standing over him, it had become abundantly clear.

It was raw, blinding fury.

"Shut up," he growled. "Shut up, just *shut up*. You don't get to feel sorry for yourself, not after what you've done. You just can't help yourself, can you? SSL was bad enough but this? What the hell am I supposed to think about all of this?"

His dad stared up at him, but didn't respond; his skin was ashen, and his eyes were wide with shock, but Matt was in no mood to let him off the hook.

"Did Kate's dad know that SSL was just a front for the Night Stalkers?" he asked. "Tell me the truth."

"No," said Greg, his voice a hoarse croak. "Pete never knew anything."

"Why didn't you tell him? Because you knew he wouldn't have gone along with it? Because you knew he would have tried to stop you?"

His dad grimaced, but nodded.

"Is that why you tried to kill him?" asked Matt.

"I wouldn't have if he hadn't followed us," said Greg. "If he hadn't—"

"I don't care," he interrupted. "Did you try to kill him because he tried to stop you doing what you were doing?"

Another almost imperceptible nod.

"You disgust me," said Matt, his voice hard and thick with anger. "I can barely even look at you. You tried to kill the only friend you've got, the one person who's stood by you since Mum left and tried to help you, because some stupid crusade means more to you than a real person's life. Kate is one of my best friends in the world, and you tried to kill her too. *You tried to murder her.* You pathetic, selfish bastard."

"I didn't mean to hurt your friend," whispered his dad. "I told her not to come any closer, I told her so many times, and the gun just went off. I didn't mean it."

"I don't believe you," said Matt. "Not for a single second."

His dad didn't respond. Deep in his eyes, Matt saw a flicker of the anger that had scared him so badly when he was young, but it was faint, crushed down by guilt and failure. He squeezed his eyes shut, as the adrenaline left his system and exhaustion flooded back in, then looked down at the bed.

"It's over, Dad," he said. "You understand that, don't you? There's nothing I can do to help you this time. They're going to lock you up and throw away the key, and you know what? I'm glad. You don't deserve anything else."

"You're right," croaked Greg "About everything. I know you hate me, son, and I don't blame you. I hate myself more than you ever could, and I know I let everyone down. I just wish there was something I could do to make amends."

"So do I," said Matt. "But it's too late for that. Far too late. Goodbye, Dad."

He walked out of the cell without so much as a backwards glance.

Paul Turner walked through the main Lazarus Project laboratory and pressed his ID card against one of the doors in the rear wall, silently cursing the world's apparent determination to make his life harder and more complicated.

We lock the infirmary for PROMETHEUS and within three days we get a critically injured Operator, her recovering father, and a wanted criminal with two bullet holes in his leg, he thought. *We've got wounded men and women all over the bloody place. We're going to be stacking them in the corridors if this continues.*

He stepped through the door into a smaller room that had been built as a containment lab, a place where sterile experimentation could be carried out. It had been hurriedly converted into an individual infirmary, filled with state-of-the-art equipment from the main facility on Level C and permanently staffed by rotating members of the Loop's medical team, all for the purposes of looking after the teenage girl lying unconscious on the bed in the centre of the room.

The doctor currently on duty was sitting behind a desk in the corner, and looked up as the Director entered.

"There have been no developments, sir," she said. "I would have alerted you immediately."

"So the prognosis hasn't changed?" he asked.

"No, sir," said the doctor. "She's stable, but she lost a huge amount of blood and she's extremely weak. We've harvested vampire plasma from the first round of PROMETHEUS Operators so we'll turn her as soon as she's strong enough, and hope for the best."

"You can't do it now?" asked Turner.

"I could," said the doctor. "But I won't. I don't believe she'd survive the process, sir."

Turner grimaced. "Fine," he said. "Give me a minute, please."

The doctor got up and left the room. When the door had closed behind her, Turner walked over and looked down at the bed.

Kate Randall was lying on her back, her eyes closed, her skin ghostly pale. Wires ran from pads on her arms and chest to machines standing beside the bed, and a huge wad of bandages covered the left side of her neck, where Greg Browning's bullet had sliced through it. Her pulse showed on a monitor, slow, rhythmic spikes of glowing green accompanied by low beeps.

She's alive, he told himself. *It could have been worse. At least she's alive.*

Rage burst through him like wildfire, burning everything in its path. He was suddenly full of the desperate, fervent desire to go back to the detention level, open the door of Cell D, draw his Glock, and put a bullet through Greg Browning's stupid, hateful head. It would be nothing less than he deserved, unlike the girl he had almost killed; Kate had done nothing to warrant lying unconscious on a hospital bed, her body too weak to wake up, her mind adrift in the darkness.

Calm. Stay calm. STAY CALM.

But he couldn't.

The sight of Kate collapsing to the ground with blood spurting from her neck had been the second worst thing he had ever seen, outdone only by the sight of the lifeless body of his son lying on the landing area outside the hangar. Greg Browning had raised his MP5 towards his own head as Kate fell, and Turner was grateful that his soldier's instinct had taken over as the human part of him reeled in horror; he had shot Matt's father twice in the leg, dropping him screaming to the ground, and had run to Kate as the Security Operators had gone to secure Browning. The rest had been a blur of blood and screams and stretchers and desperate, repeated demands for the teenage girl not to die, to not even dare *think* about dying.

He stared down at her.

Wake up! he shouted, silently. *Wake up, Goddamnit!*

He squeezed his eyes shut for several seconds, then opened them. Nothing.

I'm going to have to tell Jamie, he realised. *And Matt and Larissa. And her father, her poor father. I don't know if I can do it. This might be the end of him.*

Pull yourself together, ordered a voice in the back of his head; it was cold, and hard, the voice that had kept him alive for so many years. *You'll do what needs to be done. That's all you can do.*

Turner nodded to himself, and looked down at the teenage girl in the bed.

"Wake up," he whispered. "Just wake up, OK? Do you hear me, Kate? You do *not* have permission to die."

He stared at her for a long moment, then headed back towards the door, pulling his radio from his belt as he walked.

51

... IT CAN'T GET ANY WORSE

Matt walked slowly towards the canteen on Level G, his heart pounding with misery so great it was threatening to drag him under.

He had made it out of the cellblock on the level below before the tears had come, great sobs that shook his body and hurt his chest. He had crouched beside the lift for a long time, his arms wrapped round his stomach, his head lowered, unable to do anything but cry: for Kate, for both their fathers, for himself. He could not even begin to process what his dad had done; it was so monstrous, so *evil*, that he simply could not reconcile it with the man who had raised him. Matt had always been scared of his dad, but he had never really, truly believed that he was a bad person. Unkind? Regularly. Cruel? At times.

But not *bad.*

What had eventually broken the paralysis of his grief had been the beeping of his console. He had fumbled it from his belt, woken up its screen, and read the message that had arrived on it.

FROM: Carpenter, Lieutenant Jamie (NS303, 67-J)
TO: Browning, Lieutenant Matthew (NS303, 83-C)
Just heard about Kate. Breakfast in the canteen. Ten minutes.
No excuses.

Matt pushed open the canteen door and scanned the wide, bustling space for his friend, if that was even what Jamie still was. In the far corner of the room, a black-clad arm shot up into the air and waved at him; he acknowledged it with a nod of his head, then crossed to the food counters and filled a plate with two huge bacon rolls and a scoop of hash browns. He put the plate on a tray along with two large mugs of steaming coffee, and pushed his way through a crowd of Operators gathered round one of the large screens on the walls. Jamie was looking up at him from a table in the corner, a measured expression on his face.

"Morning," said Jamie. "You got my message?"

Matt narrowed his eyes and sat down. "No," he said. "Me being here at this particular moment is a complete coincidence."

Jamie blinked. "OK, I deserved that."

Matt sighed. "No," he said. "You didn't. I'm sorry."

For long moments, the two teenagers looked silently at each other.

I don't know, thought Matt. *I don't know if we can fix this.* He stared at Jamie, grief and pain coursing through him, and came to a realisation.

We have to try, though. Because otherwise what's the point of any of this?

"I betrayed you," he said, his voice low. "I let you down, and I'm sorry."

Jamie grimaced. "Don't, Matt," he said. "It's all right. You did what you had to do."

"That's right," he said. "But I could have told you why I was doing it. I *should* have told you."

"Maybe," said Jamie. "Or maybe there are things going on right now that are more important than keeping secrets from your friends. I overreacted, in the briefing. I was hurt, and I felt like you used me, and I overreacted."

"So did I," said Matt. "I felt like everyone was blaming me for a decision that the Director made. PROMETHEUS was a direct order, and I *did* protest when Major Turner gave it to me, whether you believe that or not. But I'm the only member of Lazarus who is also technically an Operator, so it was given to me."

"It's the right thing to do," said Jamie. "It really is. I don't like it, because I know what the people in the infirmary are going through, but it makes sense. And if we beat Dracula because we turned our Operators then cured them afterwards, nobody's going to remember that PROMETHEUS was controversial. Nobody's going to care."

"As long as we beat him," said Matt, his voice low.

Jamie nodded.

"Beat who?" asked a familiar voice.

Matt looked round, and saw Larissa standing beside the table; she was watching them with a curious expression on her face.

"Hey," said Jamie. "I'm glad you came."

"Your message said no excuses," said Larissa, and smiled. "What choice did I have? Morning, Matt."

"Morning," he replied. "It's good to see you. I'm sorry about yesterday."

Larissa's smile faded. "It's all right," she said. "It was a bad moment."

Jamie frowned. "What happened yesterday?"

"We found out that someone we knew had died," said Larissa. "Danny Lawrence. He was NS9. I don't think you knew him."

"I didn't," said Jamie. "Shit. I'm sorry to hear that."

"It's all right," said Larissa, and sat down. "I mean, it isn't, at all, but thank you."

Matt took a sip of his coffee and looked at his two friends. There was no obvious animosity between them, but the atmosphere at the table was strange; it felt guarded, like they were three people getting to know each other and still deciding how much of themselves to reveal, rather than three friends who knew they could rely on each other.

Not really a surprise, he thought. *I don't know how they bridge a gap that wide. Even though it seems so unimportant this morning.*

The grief that had momentarily receded as he talked to Jamie flooded back into him, sharp and raw.

"So you heard about Kate?" he said.

Jamie and Larissa nodded.

"I'm sorry," he said, hearing the tremor in his voice. "I'm really sorry."

Jamie frowned. "Hey," he said. "You didn't do this, Matt. None of this is your fault."

"Really?" said Matt. "Because it sort of feels like it."

"Jamie's right," said Larissa, firmly. "You're not responsible for what your dad did."

Apart from being the reason he started hating vampires in the first place, he thought. *Apart from making Mum leave him and starting him down the road that led to the Night Stalkers.*

"Right," he said. "Sure."

"Do we know anything new?" asked Larissa. "Is she going to be all right?"

"No change," said Jamie. "I talked to the Director fifteen minutes ago. She's stable, and they're going to turn her as soon as they think she's strong enough, but she's not there yet. There's no timetable."

"They're going to turn her?" asked Larissa, her eyes narrowing. "Why?"

"If they can successfully turn her, enough blood will fix her injuries, no matter how bad they are," said Matt. "But it's an enormous strain on a person's system."

Jamie nodded. "She lost a huge amount of blood," he said. "They transfused her in the hangar, but if it hadn't happened right outside the gates she would've died. That's what Paul told me, anyway."

"So we just have to wait?" asked Larissa. "Until they think she's strong enough to survive the turn?"

Matt nodded, his stomach churning with grief and guilt. "That's all we can do."

"She's in the best place she could possibly be," said Jamie. "She'll be all right. I know she will. She has to be."

"I haven't even seen her," said Larissa. "I looked for her yesterday, after Major Turner told us about Danny, but I couldn't find her."

"So she doesn't even know you're back?" asked Jamie.

"I don't know," said Larissa. "I suppose someone else might have told her, but I think she would have sent me a message in that case."

"I would think so," said Jamie. "She'd have been pleased to see you."

Silence settled over the table, full of a curious mixture of sympathy and unspoken recrimination.

"I missed the whole Night Stalker thing," said Larissa, eventually. "They were vigilantes killing vampires? Is that right?"

"Basically, yes," said Matt. "They used the charity helpline that Pete Randall and my dad founded to identify vampires who confessed to having killed people, then executed them."

"I met them," said Jamie, his voice low. "Twice."

Matt frowned. "You never mentioned that."

Jamie shrugged. "I didn't know it was important at the time," he said.

"What were they like?" asked Larissa.

Jamie took a sip from a mug of tea. "I don't know if I met the same people both times, and I don't know whether any of them were Matt's dad. But the first time we intercepted a 999 call and found a house with their wolf head painted on the door. We tracked a van, and found two of them about to kill a vampire. He was on his knees."

"Jesus," said Larissa.

Jamie nodded. "I shouted for them to stop, but they staked the vamp anyway. I went after them, but one of them drew an MP5 and emptied it into my chest. My uniform stopped most of the bullets, but a few got through, and they got away from Qiang and Ellison. The second time we didn't get there until the vamp was already dead, but we located their van and I took it out. We were about to go after them on foot when Carcassonne happened, and everyone got called back to the Loop."

Matt listened, his heart pounding. Hearing what his dad had been a part of described so bluntly was awful; he could not imagine what the vampire victims of the Night Stalkers had gone through, the terror as they were dragged from their homes to be murdered in cold blood.

"How much do you know about what happened two nights ago?" he asked, his voice low. "With Kate's dad?"

"Paul brought me up to speed," said Jamie.

"All I got told was that Kate was hurt," said Larissa. "I'd like to know how."

Matt took a deep breath, and began to talk. When he was finished, Larissa grimaced.

"I'm sorry, Matt," she said. "I'm so sorry."

"Thanks," he replied. "It's not me you should feel sorry for, though. It's Kate, and her dad, and all the innocent people my dad hurt. I can't even begin to understand it, to be honest with you. I don't even know how to start trying. The only thing I really know is that I'm done with him. I can't forgive him for this."

"As long as you know it's not your fault," said Jamie. "The Harker thing, and everything afterwards. None of it is on you."

Matt nodded. "I know exactly whose fault it is," he said. "It's his. But he's never going to get the chance to hurt anyone else. He's never going to get out of that cell."

Tears rose in the corners of his eyes, and he blinked them away.

"All right," said Jamie, a frown of concern on his face. "Let's talk about something else. How's PROMETHEUS going?"

Matt grunted with laughter. "Way to lighten the mood, Jamie."

Jamie smiled. "No problem," he said. "Well?"

"The Director suspended the programme overnight," he said. "Jack Williams was the last one."

I bet he was pleased about that, thought Jamie, *after what he said in the briefing.*

"How far through did we get?" he asked.

"Seventy-two Operators have been turned so far," said Matt. "Just over forty-five per cent of the active roster, and twenty-four of them are recovering in the infirmary. They should be discharged this afternoon."

"Why is it on hold?" asked Larissa.

"I'm sorry," said Jamie. "I didn't think. Do you even know about PROMETHEUS?"

Larissa nodded. "I know about it. Angela briefed me yesterday on what's been happening while I was away."

"OK," said Jamie.

"So why is it on hold?" repeated Larissa.

Matt shrugged. "I don't know."

"I think it means we're going to France," said Jamie. "Soon. That's the only reason I can think of to suspend the programme, so we don't have any Operators halfway through the process when we ship out."

"I've heard the same suggestion inside Lazarus," said Matt. "But I genuinely don't know. I'd tell you if I did."

"No more secrets," whispered Larissa.

Jamie shot a glance in her direction, his expression unreadable, then looked back at Matt. "Have you tested the Operators who've been turned?"

Matt nodded. "There's no baseline for vampire power, no growth chart, for want of a better description, but testing indicates that their strength and speed are comparable to the Broadmoor patients. They'd be extremely powerful if we could wait a year before we needed to use them."

Jamie smiled. "Wouldn't that be great?" he said. "But it's still better than nothing."

The memory of watching Valentin Rusmanov bite Operator after Operator hit Matt like a punch in the stomach. He shuddered, and nodded at his friend.

"It worked," he said. "If nothing else, it definitely worked."

Larissa's eyes had narrowed. "I still can't believe the Director authorised it," she said. "What happened if people didn't want to be turned?"

"Nobody was forced," he said.

"Did anyone refuse?"

"Six."

"And where are they now?" asked Larissa.

"In cells on Level H," said Matt.

Glowing red flashed momentarily into Larissa's eyes. "They were locked up because they wouldn't let the Department turn them?"

"That's right," he said, aware of the look of unease that had appeared on Jamie's face.

"And you're OK with that?" said Larissa, her voice little more than a growl.

Matt sighed. "No," he said. "I'm not. But I'm tired of defending PROMETHEUS, Larissa. Like I said to Jamie before you got here,

I didn't give the order, I didn't make it mandatory, and I certainly didn't decide the punishment for those who refused to take part. All I did was help create the science that made it possible. And to be perfectly honest with you, given that we now have a working cure, I really don't see what the big deal is."

Larissa smiled narrowly, crimson still flickering in the corners of her eyes. "You're the only non-vampire sitting at this table," she said. "I don't know how qualified you are to make that statement."

"All right," said Jamie, frowning at her. "Take it easy."

"It's fine," said Matt. "If you want to take it up with the Director, Larissa, then be my guest. But I'm not going to fight with you about this, and I'm not exactly sure why you think you get to just stroll back in here and start criticising. Are you even still an Operator? Have you told anyone where you've been for the last six months?"

Larissa stared at him; he held her gaze as Jamie looked back and forth between them, his eyes wide with worry. After a long, silent moment, the glow in her eyes faded away, and she nodded.

"You're right," she said. "That was crappy of me. I'm sorry."

"Me too," said Matt, instantly. "I really don't want to fight."

Larissa nodded, and sat back in her chair. Matt took a nervous sip of coffee and looked at Jamie, silently willing him to break the tension. Thankfully, his friend did not let him down.

"Speaking of the cure," said Jamie, "I assume you heard about what the last couple of nights have been like in London?"

Matt nodded, grateful for the slight change of subject. "I read the reports," he said. "It sounds like the first one was crazy."

"The first what?" asked Larissa.

"The first distribution of the cure," said Jamie. "We're releasing it in eight hospitals around the country, and it's all going pretty smoothly now, but the first night it was just one, UCH in London, and it was pretty hairy."

"You were there?" asked Larissa.

Jamie nodded. "Mine and Jack's squads were the security. About four hundred vampires turned up, trying to get the cure, and we had anti-vampire protesters, anti-cure protesters, and about a hundred police trying to keep them apart."

"What happened?" asked Matt. "I read there was some violence."

"There was," said Jamie. "Although it wasn't as bad as it could have been. The vampires kicked off when we had to announce that we were only taking ten more of them, and then the protesters broke the police line and someone threw a bottle that hit one of the vamps in the head. So *she* went mental, and we had to go in and calm it all down."

"Jesus," said Matt.

Jamie shrugged. "It was all right in the end," he said. "I went back to London two nights ago and it was better, and the reports from last night were better still. I think we're on top of it."

"*Still* speaking of the cure," said Larissa. "How's your mum, Jamie?"

Jamie grimaced. "I haven't seen her," he said. "They locked the infirmary down when they started testing the cure, and then the last two days have been crazy."

Larissa frowned. "You haven't had five minutes to go down and see if she's all right?"

"No," said Jamie, his eyes narrowing. "What with people coming back out of the blue and Dracula starting the end of the world, I've had a lot to deal with."

Larissa stared at her ex-boyfriend; he held her gaze for a long moment.

"I saw her," said Matt, softly.

Jamie frowned. "Saw who?"

"Your mum," he said. "I saw her in the cellblock, when I went to get Valentin for the start of PROMETHEUS."

"Was she all right?"

Matt nodded. "She seemed fine," he said. "Happy. She was talking to Valentin. She said she was looking forward to seeing you."

Jamie grimaced. "You didn't tell me."

"I meant to," said Matt. "But like you said, it's been crazy."

"You knew she'd been discharged," said Larissa. "You shouldn't need Matt to tell you that your mother would like to see her son."

Red flashed into the corners of Jamie's eyes, but died as quickly as it had arrived. His grimace deepened, and he nodded.

"You're right," he said. "I'll fix it. For now, let's talk about something more cheerful, shall we?"

"What've you got in mind?" asked Larissa.

"Carcassonne."

Matt burst out laughing, spraying coffee across the table. Jamie and Larissa recoiled, wide grins on their faces.

"Sorry," he said. "Are there any updates from France?"

"Only what we've seen on the news and what we were told in the Zero Hour briefing," said Jamie. "But things are happening. The Director was in Carcassonne yesterday, and I really think the suspension of PROMETHEUS is telling."

"What don't I know?" asked Larissa. "Angela brought me up to speed, but I don't think she told me everything."

"Has your Zero Hour classification been reinstated?" asked Jamie.

"I don't know," said Larissa.

"Did you know your friend General Allen is running things on the ground?"

"No," said Larissa.

Jamie nodded. "He's taken charge on behalf of NATO and the

FTB is taking the lead on behalf of the Departments. I think everything else is public knowledge."

Larissa nodded. "All right," she said. "That's a smart move. Bob Allen will do a good job."

"So what do you think our response is actually going to be?" asked Matt.

"I don't know," said Jamie, and shook his head. "Paul will tell us as soon as they finalise a plan, but if you ask me, I think we need to move as soon as possible. If we don't, Carcassonne will just be the start."

"Level with me," said Matt. "And I mean *level with me*. If we go in after Dracula, what are the chances we make it out alive?"

Jamie shrugged. "I honestly don't know," he said. "Probably not all that good. Larissa?"

"Not good," she said, and nodded. "Valentin and I fought Dracula together and didn't beat him, and that was more than six months ago. He'll be stronger now than he was then, probably *a lot* stronger."

"It doesn't make any sense, does it?" said Matt. "The end of the world, I mean. It's just something people say, that doesn't really mean anything. But we might be about to watch it happen."

They fell silent. The loud buzz of the canteen continued around them, but for a long moment, the three teenagers merely stared at each other.

Matt was suddenly full of desperate love for his friends, the two sitting with him and the one who was lying unconscious one floor above them. There were problems between them, problems that were sticky and hard to solve and had opened wounds that he knew ran deep, but they were all still here, still breathing in and out, still mostly intact, on the outside at least. For how much longer, nobody knew, but for *right now* they were still alive, and they would fight with everything they had until the end.

"America," said Larissa, suddenly.

Jamie frowned. "What?"

"That's where I went," she said, her eyes fixed on her ex-boyfriend.

Matt looked at his friend. Jamie's face had paled, but he saw neither the anger nor the hostility he was expecting; what he saw instead was something that looked a lot like resignation, or even acceptance.

"To Nevada?" asked Jamie.

Larissa shook her head. "Upstate New York," she said. "I built something there, on the banks of the Hudson River, a community for vampires. We called it Haven."

"Like Valhalla?" said Matt.

"Exactly like that," said Larissa, and gave him a small smile. "For vampires who didn't want to hurt anyone, and were willing to swear an oath that they wouldn't. That's where I was, until the day before yesterday."

"What did Valentin have to do with it?" asked Jamie.

"Didn't he tell you?" asked Larissa.

"No," said Jamie. "He's always refused to tell anyone what you and he talked about the night you left."

Larissa nodded. "I asked him not to tell anyone where I was going," she said. "I just sort of assumed he wouldn't keep his word."

"So he did know where you were?"

"Of course," said Larissa. "Haven is built on an estate that belongs to him."

"Why did he help you?" asked Matt. "It doesn't seem like something he'd do."

Larissa shrugged. "I don't know. He didn't ask for anything in return. I suppose he probably enjoyed the thought of damaging the Department, and I'm absolutely sure he loved refusing to tell you where I was."

Jamie stared at her, and said nothing.

"Would you ever have come back?" asked Matt. He knew this was extremely dangerous ground, but he wanted as many cards on the table as possible. "If it wasn't for Dracula, would you be here?"

Larissa looked at him for a long moment, then shook her head. "No," she said. "Haven is my home."

Jamie winced, but nodded; he had clearly expected nothing else. Matt's heart went out to him, but he did not regret asking the question; it was better for everyone to know where they stood.

A deafening rattle of noise broke the silence, as the console of every Operator in the canteen beeped in unison. The room was suddenly full of movement as men and women, including the three friends sitting at the table in the corner, reached as one for their belts.

FROM: Turner, Major Paul (NS303, 36-A)
TO: Active_Roster
ALL/MANDATORY_BRIEFING/PRIORITY_LEVEL_1/
OR/1230

Matt checked his watch as a cold ball of unease settled into his stomach.

Twelve thirty, he thought. *Ninety minutes from now.*

Jamie set his console down on the table and smiled at his friends. "What did I tell you?" he said. "This is it. It's time."

52

INSERTION POINT

CAISTER-ON-SEA, NORFOLK, ENGLAND

Julian Carpenter folded the letter, slid it into an envelope, and sealed it shut. He placed it carefully in the inside pocket of his black holdall, set the bag on the floor beside his green duffel, and walked out of the kitchen of his mother's cottage.

He stopped in the narrow hallway, breathing in the familiar smell of the old house; it went right to the heart of him, to the place where nostalgia and loss and regret gathered, and he let the sensations mingle, savouring them for what he was sure would be the last time. He hoped he was wrong; despite the painful unravelling of his life over the last few years, he had no wish to die. But he *did* have to be realistic, and what he was about to do was unquestionably fraught with risk; he was consoling himself with the hope that – if the worst was to happen – the letter he had just written would go some way to explaining why he had hurt the people he loved so badly.

Julian stepped into the lounge and did a slow circuit of the room, turning off the electricity outlets and drawing the curtains. He had *hated* being confined in this place – a prison that was comfortable and familiar was somehow far worse than a concrete box in the bowels of the Loop – but as he made his final preparations to leave it, he nonetheless felt a small, bitter stab of sadness. His family had spent happy days and weeks in the old cottage, and there had been a time when he had believed there would be many more to come. But such a prospect was now long dead, and the reality was very different.

His wife was beyond his reach, his son had made it very clear that he never wanted to see him again, and his only other friend in the world, the one to whom he owed more than anyone else, had also cut ties with him. He had received an email a week after his ill-fated reunion with Jamie, containing three short sentences. It had been sent from an address he didn't recognise, but there had been absolutely no doubt from whom it had come.

> I did what you asked, even though I knew it would cost
> me dearly. Consider the oath I swore paid in full.
> Do not contact me again.

He couldn't blame Frankenstein for his decision.

Julian had known that if the monster did him the favour that he had requested, if he brought his son to see him, it would expose his part in the deception the two of them had perpetrated, and he had known that the fallout, particularly from Jamie, would likely be awful. He had known, and he had asked Frankenstein anyway, playing on the monster's loyalty, and on the oath he had sworn to protect the Carpenter family. He had not been surprised by the email, and the cold, painful rebuke it contained; he knew he deserved it.

Julian strode back into the kitchen, hefted the bags on to his shoulders, and headed for the front door. Through its frosted glass, he could see the blurred silhouette of Ben waiting for him; the teenager, who lived half a mile down the road towards Caister, was on time, which was at least something. He stepped through the door, locked it behind him, and walked down the path.

"Morning, Ben," he said. "All right?"

The teenager grunted.

"Great," said Julian. "You understand what I need you to do?"

Another grunt.

"You're sure?"

Ben rolled his eyes and nodded.

"OK," he said. He rolled up his sleeve, pulled the elastic band with the locator chip tied to it off his wrist, and held it out. Ben reached for it, and Julian gripped his hand tightly.

"Eight hours," he said. "*At least.* Stay in the countryside, away from anywhere there might be a CCTV camera. Got it?"

Ben stared at him, his expression one of insolent boredom. "Got it."

"Good," said Julian. He released the teenager's hand and fished a fifty-pound note out of his pocket. "Here you go."

Ben took the money, snapped the elastic band on to his wrist, and turned away without a word. He strolled down the path, through the gate, and set off along the dirt road towards the fields, the same route that Julian ran every morning. He watched until the teenager was out of sight, then walked out of the garden, and turned towards the village, where the Ford he had bought the year before, the one that, unlike his mother's old Mercedes, was *not* equipped with a tracking device, was waiting for him.

Ten minutes later he was driving south, his past shrinking into the distance behind him.

The sun was high overhead as Julian turned down a small road marked by a sign that showed the outline of a white aeroplane against a red background.

The airfield appeared to be an airfield in name alone. There were no permanent buildings, just a row of mobile trailers facing a runway of heavily rolled grass and a large tarpaulin suspended over a line of light aeroplanes. A car was parked next to the trailers, a dirty red Peugeot, and a plane on the runway with its engine idling; both presumably belonged to the man he was here to meet, a man he had only spoken to once on a burner mobile phone.

He parked next to the Peugeot and checked his watch. Four hours and thirteen minutes had passed since he had given his locator chip to Ben and, providing the teenager followed his instructions, it would be almost four more hours until he dropped the elastic band through the letterbox of Julian's mother's cottage. He was not wholly confident that Ben *would* walk for the eight hours that had been agreed; it had been pretty obvious that Julian was not coming back any time soon, and he would not be surprised if the teenager had got bored and quit, confident that he would not be made to answer for doing so. But if that was the case, there was nothing Julian could do about it now. He would have to rely on Blacklight having more important things to do right now than checking on his movements.

If someone in the Surveillance Division decided to take a look, they would see – or *think* they were seeing – the only car they knew he owned sitting idle in the cottage's drive while he walked the nearby countryside, where they would not be able to get visual confirmation. If they wanted to be absolutely sure of his whereabouts, they would have to send someone out to check in person, and even if they did so, and found Ben wearing his chip, the teenager had no idea where Julian had gone. He didn't *think* there was any way they could find him, but he refused to be complacent: Blacklight's resourcefulness was something he understood better than most.

Julian got out of the car and pulled his bags from the boot as a man emerged from one of the trailers and strolled towards him;

he was perhaps fifty, his face deeply tanned and lined, a blue cap perched atop his head.

"Mr Frank?"

"That's me," said Julian.

"Pat Landon," said the man, and extended his hand. "We spoke on the phone."

"We did," said Julian, shaking the offered hand. "Are we all set?"

"She's fuelled up and ready to go," said Landon.

"All right," said Julian. He put the green duffel bag on the Ford's bonnet, unzipped it, and pulled out a brown envelope. "Here you go."

Landon took the envelope and peered inside.

"You can count it," said Julian.

Landon appeared to consider this for a moment. "No need," he said.

Julian smiled at him. "We only just met," he said. "Count it."

Landon shrugged, and pulled a thick sheaf of notes out of the envelope. He licked the tip of his finger and quickly counted them. "Ten thousand."

"So we're good?" said Julian.

"We're good," said Landon. "I can't take you all the way to Carcassonne, but I guess you knew that?"

"I knew," he said. "The airspace is closed, right?"

Landon nodded. "All the way out as far as Toulouse," he said. "The closest I can get you is a place called Fumel-Montayral. It's a local aerodrome about two hours' drive to the north. I've arranged for someone to meet us there and take you into town. You should be able to get a car there."

"That's fine," said Julian.

"Good," said Landon. "All right. Let's do it."

The two men walked across the grass towards the plane. It was a white and blue Cessna 172, which suited Julian perfectly; the little four-seater was one of the most common planes in the world, and could almost have been hand-selected to not attract attention.

Landon unlocked the plane's passenger door and held it open. Julian threw the duffel bag on to the seat, then unzipped the black holdall and checked that the letter was still where he had put it. He knew it was stupid – there was no possible way that it could have disappeared during his drive to the airfield – but he couldn't help himself. Some things simply went beyond the rational.

His fingers closed on the rectangular shape, and he pulled it out of the pocket far enough to see the five words he had written barely five hours earlier.

To my wife and son

Fingers tapped his shoulder, causing him to jump. Julian pushed the envelope back into the pocket, zipped the holdall, and turned to find Landon looking at him with a curious expression on his face.

"Ten thousand in cash is a lot for this trip," said the pilot, and nodded at the holdall. "I don't make a habit of involving myself in other people's business, but is there anything in that bag that's going to get me into trouble?"

Julian smiled. "Do you really want to know?"

Landon stared at him for a long moment, then grunted with laughter and shook his head.

"No," he said. "Get in."

53

COME TOGETHER

Paul Turner paced back and forth in his quarters.

In less than five minutes he would brief his Department on their response to a situation that was nothing less than a threat to the entire world as they knew it, but his mind was somewhere else entirely; it was with a teenage girl lying unconscious five floors below him.

A small part of him was furious with Kate. Greg Browning had been broken, sobbing and screaming with rage and disappointment, and she should have known better than to think he could be reasoned with and approach him unarmed. Turner had ordered her to step back, but she had ignored him, and now she was fighting for her life. They would never know for certain whether Matt's father had meant to shoot her, but it didn't matter; the gun had fired and the damage was done.

The rest of him was churning with pain, his heart aching for the girl he had come to love like a daughter, and for whom he had more affection than anyone else in the Department. He could not imagine a world without her in it. He had lost his son, and that had almost destroyed him; to lose her as well was unthinkable.

Turner took a deep breath and tried to clear his mind, to focus on the extremely pressing matter at hand; there was nothing he could do for Kate, and he would not be honouring her by allowing his pain to distract him from what he needed to do. He could clearly picture the Ops Room; by now, it would be full to bursting with every man and woman who called the Loop home, as they waited to be told what was happening. It would be his job to make them believe they were going to survive what was coming, that they would be in safe hands as he led them into battle.

They deserved nothing less.

And he would not let them down.

Jamie sat in the middle of the fifth row of seats, his foot tapping with impatience.

The Ops Room was packed; every seat was occupied, and people were standing two and three deep along the curving walls. Beside Jamie sat Larissa, her eyes fixed on the lectern behind which Paul Turner would shortly appear. The tight seating forced them into a proximity that his ex-girlfriend was clearly uncomfortable with, but thankfully not *so* uncomfortable that she had refused to sit next to him; such a rejection would have been extremely awkward for both of them.

On her other side sat Matt, and beyond him Natalia. The Russian girl was staring at exactly the same spot as Larissa, her back straight, her hands resting on her thighs, but Jamie couldn't help but notice, out of the corner of his supernaturally sharp eye, that every thirty seconds or so she stretched out the little finger of her left hand to touch Matt's leg. The tiny gesture of affection made him smile inwardly, even though it drew into sharp focus exactly what he had lost.

What he was increasingly sure he could not get back.

The Ops Room door opened and Paul Turner walked through it. The low hum of conversation filling the wide space immediately gave way to silence as the Director stepped up on to the stage and looked out across the massed ranks of his Department. Jamie felt tension twist in his stomach as Turner cleared his throat, took a sip of water, and began to speak.

"Men and women of Blacklight," he said. "I stand before you now not only as your Director, but as a husband, a father, a colleague, and as a human being who will not stand by and let darkness overwhelm us. Because the moment of reckoning has arrived. We've known it was coming for many months, no matter how hard we may have tried to convince ourselves otherwise, and now it's here. So make no mistake: this is the fight of our lives. Of *all* our lives."

The Director surveyed the room, as Jamie felt heat threaten to rise into his eyes.

"If we, and our friends from around the globe, do not stop Dracula now, he will never be stopped," continued Turner. "And Carcassonne will only have been the beginning. He has made his vision of the future perfectly clear: anyone who does not submit to him will be killed, and any force that tries to stand against him will be destroyed. Vampires are flocking to his side, and soon he will have an army capable of tearing through cities like a tornado, of unleashing chaos and violence on a scale that will make Château Dauncy look like a playground squabble. I do not want anyone to be under any illusions about the stakes of the battle that will soon be fought. We are the only people who can push him back. *We* are all that stands between the world and Armageddon."

The atmosphere in the Ops Room was so thick you could have cut it with a knife. Jamie felt like an electric current was being passed through him as a narrow smile rose onto the Director's face.

"But there is something I want you all to remember," said Turner. "Despite the legends, despite the horror stories and tales of terror, and despite the power we have seen with our own eyes, *Dracula is still just a vampire*. He is flesh and blood, and a single, well-placed T-Bone shot will end him just as surely as the rest of his kind. He is not a demon, he is not the Devil, and we will *not* fear him. Is that clear?"

A rumble of affirmation shook the Ops Room; it was as though the entire Department was speaking with one voice.

"At this very moment, across the Channel," said Turner, "the largest force in the long history of the supernatural Departments is being mobilised. More than three-quarters of all the Operators in the world are being brought together for a single purpose: to stop Dracula now, while there's still time. And tomorrow evening, as the sun sets on Carcassonne, we will make our stand. Detailed briefings and orders will follow throughout today and tomorrow, but the bulk of our combined forces will engage Dracula's followers in the ruins of Carcassonne, while a small strike team is sent into the medieval city to take out the first vampire himself. It won't be easy, and we will suffer losses, but I do not have the slightest doubt that we will be victorious."

The Director stared out from behind the lectern, his face so pale and full of determination that it looked like it had been carved out of marble.

"We will stand together and face the creatures that inhabit the darkness," he said, his voice low. "We will stand together and kill vampire after vampire until they surrender or until none are left alive to do so. And when the dust settles, there will be no doubt as to who has dominion over this planet. We will show the world once and for all that the future is full of hope, not fear; of light, not darkness. We will stand together, and we will win."

Jamie looked around at his colleagues. Nobody clapped, and nobody cheered, but he saw faces full of resolve, full of calm.

Celebrating can wait, he told himself. *We can clap and cheer when we get back. When this is over.*

When we've won.

54

SOME CORNER OF A FOREIGN FIELD

OUTSKIRTS OF CARCASSONNE, SOUTHERN FRANCE
ONE HOUR LATER

Bob Allen watched the activity taking place around him with a small smile on his face and hope flickering faintly in his chest.

The SPC had arrived forty minutes ago, descending out of the bright noon sky in a fleet of enormous helicopters, and hundreds of black-clad Russian Operators and staff had immediately got to work, unloading vehicles and case after case of weapons and equipment, erecting tents and canopies and field buildings. What had started out as a displaced persons camp filling three fields on the edge of Carcassonne was now beginning to resemble Camp Bastion in Afghanistan: a huge forward operating base covering more than three square miles of French countryside.

And more than half of the Departments aren't even here yet, he told himself. *We're going to need to expand the perimeter again. By a long way.*

The six fields of Red Cross and UNICEF tents that housed the men and women who had fled their homes were now surrounded by eight that were entirely military; the camp now contained a fully equipped field hospital with more than a hundred beds and three state-of-the-art surgical theatres, a long motor pool full of jeeps and mobile armour, a temporary hangar containing two dozen helicopters, a command centre comprising more than twenty rooms, dormitories for two thousand Operators, a mess hall and canteen the size of a small shopping mall, and mile after mile of barbed-wire fencing equipped with motion sensors and ultraviolet lights.

Precisely controlled chaos had filled the camp since just before dawn, when Military Detachment Alpha had confirmed they were on their way from Toulouse airport. The South Africans had barely touched down, however, when Allen had received a call from Colonel Maroun, informing him that Egypt's Section G were only fifteen minutes away themselves. Since then, it had been all hands to the pumps.

Allen watched as Russian Operators swung the metal sides of a supply hut into place and began bolting it together, then turned and headed for his command centre. In the pit of his stomach, a knot of excitement and anticipation was already squirming, but alongside it was an unfamiliar sensation of camaraderie. He had no doubt that if they defeated Dracula, relations between the Departments would return to their usual state of slightly frosty distrust, but for the time being, for this short period of hours, everyone was resolutely on the same side.

As he strode into Field 1, Allen saw Guérin making his way towards him. He had officially confirmed the French Captain as his NATO second-in-command, and was already pleased with his decision to do so; Guérin was smart and capable, and possessed local knowledge that had already proven valuable. He also provided access to the conversations taking place in Paris, which was absolutely vital; Allen was not remotely convinced the French government was thinking clearly, and was far from alone in that suspicion.

"Captain," he said. "Everything all right?"

"Yes, sir," said Guérin. "The Russians know what they are doing."

"Let them get on with it," said Allen. "We'll have the Chinese here before nightfall, so the more the SPC gets done before then, the better."

"I think they will be set up in an hour," said Guérin. "Maybe two, at the most."

"Fine," said Allen. "Have you talked to Paris this morning?"

"Yes, sir."

"What news?"

"The nuclear option remains in play," said Guérin. "I am sorry, General. I communicated your concerns, and NATO has made a formal objection, but the government is not prepared to rule it out. A fifty-mile exclusion zone has been drawn up around Carcassonne and an evacuation order has been prepared for those living inside it."

"Which will cause absolute panic if it's given," said Allen. "What the hell are they playing at, Guérin? What's your take on this?"

"I cannot say for certain, sir," said Guérin. "But I can give you my personal opinion, if it is of interest?"

"It is."

"This is a way for Paris to assert some control over the situation," said Guérin. "The entire world is watching a crisis take place in France, while everyone *apart from the French* appears to be dealing with it. You have sent the news helicopters away, but everyone knows that an American is in charge, and everyone can see Germans and South Africans and Russians arriving. If we fail tomorrow, I do not think the government wants to be seen to have stood by and done nothing while Dracula started his war on their soil."

"I understand that," said Allen. "I honestly do. What I *don't* understand is why their fallback plan is to blow a big chunk of their own country off the map."

Guérin shrugged. "They are scared, sir," he said. "Everyone is scared. *I* am scared, and I do not mind admitting it."

"There's only one thing for us to do, then," said Allen.

"What is that, General?"

"Make sure we don't fail tomorrow."

Half a mile away, a Red Cross volunteer waved Julian Carpenter forward as he nosed his car through the gates at the entrance to the camp.

A man wearing a French Army uniform stepped out from a guard post and motioned for him to stop. Julian braked, and took a deep breath. This was the moment he had been dreading; if the soldier searched the black holdall in the car's boot, then his journey from the UK would all have been for nothing.

The flight itself had been uneventful.

Landon had made a couple of attempts at starting conversation as the Cessna climbed towards the Channel, but Julian's perfunctory answers had quickly seen the pilot give up and merely fly the plane.

The landing at Fumel-Montayral had been equally straightforward. Landon had guided the Cessna expertly down on to a tarmac strip surrounded by woods and farmland, and brought the plane to a halt beside a row of buildings that looked fractionally sturdier than those at the airfield they had left behind in England. Parked beside the buildings was an ancient-looking red van with a man leaning on its bonnet; he raised a hand and waved as the plane rolled past. Landon acknowledged it, and turned the Cessna in a wide loop that brought it to a halt in front of the van.

"This is where we say goodbye," he said.

Julian nodded. "Thank you."

"No problem," said Landon. "Look after yourself."

"I'll try," said Julian, and gave the pilot a brief smile.

He opened the plane door, pulled his bags across the seats, and stepped down on to the grass as Landon immediately taxied the Cessna back towards the runway. He watched the plane climb back into the air, then turned to face the man who was clearly there to meet him. He was in his late thirties, with the kind of deep tan that only comes from spending most of your life outdoors, and a tiny hand-rolled cigarette burning between his fingers. He smiled at Julian and stuck out a hand.

"*Bonjour*," said Julian, taking the hand and giving it a brisk shake. "Henry Frank."

"*Bonjour*," said the man, and nodded. "Laurent Lefèvre. *Ça va?*"

"*Oui, ça va bien, merci*," said Julian, exhausting the last of his conversational French.

Lefèvre smiled. "You need a car?"

"*Oui*," said Julian. "Thank you."

"*De rien*," said Lefèvre, and gestured towards the van. "Please."

Julian climbed into the passenger seat, the green duffel bag at his feet, the black holdall on his lap. Lefèvre settled behind the wheel and guided the rattling, spluttering van out on to the roads of rural France. The two men sat in silence until Lefèvre pulled to a halt outside a Renault garage on the outskirts of Villeneuve-sur-Lot, almost half an hour later.

"We are here," said Lefèvre.

Julian peered through the window. The garage was a square concrete building with two cars raised on platforms and men working beneath them. Tyres and mudguards and body panels were piled round puddles of water gleaming with spilled oil. Next to the garage, enclosed by a sagging chain-link fence, sat a small cluster of battered Renaults, with prices scrawled on their windscreens.

"Perfect," he said. "*Merci.*"

He took a fifty-euro note from his wallet, held it out, then pulled it away as Lefèvre reached for it. "You have not seen me," he said. "Yes?"

Lefèvre smiled. "Seen who?"

He nodded, and let the man take the money. Julian climbed out of the van as Lefèvre pocketed the note and drove away without a wave or a backward glance.

Twenty minutes later, he was driving south in a Peugeot 205 that was older than his son and registered in the name of a man who didn't exist.

The French soldier tapped on the car window. Julian rolled it down and gave the man a thin smile.

"*Bonjour*," said the soldier. "*Habitez-vous Carcassonne?*"

"My name is Henry Frank," said Julian. "I lived in Carcassonne."

"What was your address?" asked the soldier, slipping into perfect English.

"1376 Rue Baudelaire," said Julian. "I was renting it from the owner."

The soldier nodded. "Where have you been?"

"Avignon," said Julian. "I don't know what I'm supposed to do now. Is there someone here who can help me?"

"You need to talk to the Red Cross," said the soldier. "You can park in Field 12."

He stepped back and waved his hand. Julian breathed a long sigh of relief as he drove slowly past the guard post and into the main camp. Printed signs had been nailed to wooden posts, giving directions to the various fields, and he brought the car to a halt as he reached the first of them.

Someone's been busy, he thought, as he looked at the sprawling camp. *Very busy indeed.*

A sign marked **Fields 8–16** pointed to the north, where Julian could see the roofs of hundreds of cars and the silver tops of seemingly endless rows of tents. A second sign, announcing **Fields 1–4 (RESTRICTED)**, pointed south, towards what he was looking for: a large complex of metal buildings and grey tents.

Command centre, he told himself. *All right then. Here we go.*

He got back in the car and followed the signs to the entrance of Field 12, where a pair of Red Cross volunteers got up from behind a folding table and told him to come and see them once he was settled. He told them he would, and drove on, searching for a remote space where what he was about to do would hopefully go unnoticed. At the northern corner of the field, at the junction of two thick hedges and beneath an overhanging tree, he parked, got out, and took a long, careful look around.

In the centre of the field, Julian could see men and women standing around the silver tents as children ran back and forth, laughing and chasing. Near the Red Cross table, two cars had blocked each other, and he could hear the distant sound of raised voices.

Nobody was anywhere near him.

Nobody was paying any attention to him at all.

Julian opened the Renault's boot, lifted out the black holdall, and set it on the bonnet. The pungent scent of gun oil filled his nostrils as he opened it, but he pushed the Glock and the MP5 aside; what he needed now was folded neatly beneath them. He took a last glance around, positioned himself between the car and the hedge, and shook out the Blacklight uniform.

Working quickly, he stripped off his jeans and shirt and pulled the black material into place. He zipped it up and fastened it at his neck, as a feeling of nostalgia so strong he thought it might make him cry flooded through him; it was as though the last three years had been a bad dream, and he was now finally awake, and back where he belonged.

He tied the laces of his boots, then strapped on his belt and quickly began to fill it. The MP5 and Glock went into slots on the left, alongside the console that was his biggest concern; there was a good chance the regulation device had been upgraded in the years since he had stashed a spare underneath his shed, and he suspected it would be obvious to any eagle-eyed Operator that he was carrying obsolete equipment.

A pair of ultraviolet grenades slotted into pouches on the right, beside the thick loop that held his T-Bone, and a UV beam gun completed his arsenal of weapons and equipment. Julian stood up, enjoying the feel of the uniform against his skin, pulled a pair of gloves out of the holdall, and put them on. Finally, he lifted out the shiny black helmet and carefully placed it over his head. He connected its wires into a socket at the back of his neck, and felt a shiver of excitement as the systems booted up with a low rumble. He put the empty holdall back into the boot, locked the car, then swung the green duffel bag over his shoulder and set off towards the distant entrance to Field 12.

By the time he passed the Red Cross table, all the nervousness that had filled him as he entered the camp had disappeared; he was an Operator again, his mind clear and calm. The volunteers didn't so much as glance at him as he walked past them, his gaze fixed on the command centre looming in the distance; he strode purposefully towards it, a man who, for the first time in years, was once again at peace with himself.

55

THE TIP OF THE SPEAR

TWO HOURS LATER

Jamie's heart sank as he walked into Paul Turner's quarters and saw Frankenstein staring squarely at him.

He had been standing in the officers' mess when the Director's message arrived. Around him, Operators had already started to receive orders and briefing schedules, but what had appeared on his console had been an immediate summons to Paul Turner's quarters, with no detail whatsoever. Excitement had instantly burst through him, as he had allowed himself to consider the possibility that he had tried his hardest not to take for granted: that he would be part of the strike team sent to take down Dracula.

After all, it would make sense; he and Larissa were the most powerful Operators in the Department, and had direct experience of confronting the first vampire. He assumed that Angela Darcy would lead the team, given that she was the Security Officer and had been the first person turned by PROMETHEUS.

What he had *not* considered was that Frankenstein might be chosen too.

"Lieutenant Carpenter," said Paul Turner from behind his desk. "Come in."

Jamie narrowed his eyes and walked slowly into the room, towards where Angela, Larissa and Frankenstein were standing. He nodded, trying to somehow silently convey a greeting to the two women, but *not* to the monster, and stopped beside the Security Officer.

"We're waiting for one more of you," said Turner. "Then we'll get started."

Despite his disappointment at the presence of Frankenstein, Jamie felt his excitement return. There could surely be no doubt now: this was going to be the strike team, and he was part of it. His thoughts turned immediately to who the final member might be – the newly turned Jack Williams, perhaps, or Dominique Saint-Jacques, or even Lizzy Ellison from his own squad. All would be good. He would happily fight alongside any one of them.

Footsteps echoed down the corridor outside the room, and he frowned as he turned towards the door; there were two sets of feet thudding rhythmically across the ground.

Paul said we were only waiting for one, he thought. *What's going on?*

A familiar scent entered his nostrils. Jamie's eyes glowed with crimson fire and a growl rolled from his throat as Valentin Rusmanov stepped into the room, a Security Operator at his side.

"Well," said the ancient vampire, looking round the room with a smile on his face. "Here we all are. How terribly exciting."

"Come in and shut up, Valentin," said Turner. "I haven't got time for jokes this afternoon."

"Of course, my dear Major Turner," said Valentin. The ancient vampire walked across the room, stopped next to Jamie, and gave him a broad grin.

He stared at the youngest Rusmanov's pale, handsome face.

Him? he shouted silently. *A mass murderer who helped Larissa leave and took great pleasure in biting our Operators? We're really going to trust him with something so important?*

"This is ridiculous," rumbled Frankenstein, as though he could read Jamie's mind. "Are you briefing a mission or a farce?"

"You can shut up too, Victor," said Turner, fixing the monster with a cold stare. "In fact, that goes for all of you. Until further notice, I am the only person in this room who has permission to speak. Is that clear?"

An uncomfortable silence settled over the room. Jamie tore his gaze away from Valentin and focused his attention on the Director.

"All right," said Turner. "I'm going to credit you all with enough intelligence to know why you're here, but in case I'm being too kind, let me spell it out. The five of you have been selected for the strike team that we will be sending into Carcassonne tomorrow, while the majority of the Multinational Force engages Dracula's army. You will have a single objective: to destroy the first vampire himself. If any of you don't understand the importance of this mission, leave now."

Nobody moved. Jamie stared at the Director, excitement crawling up his spine; it was out in the open now, in black and white.

They were being sent to kill Dracula.

He was being sent to kill Dracula.

Heat pulsed behind his eyes as his fangs itched for release inside his gums.

Calm, he told himself. *Stay calm.*

"The five of you were selected by me, in consultation with the other Directors," said Turner. "I am fully aware that there is negative history between several of you, and I know it's unlikely that any of you would have selected this specific group of people. But the simple truth is that you are the five most powerful men and women the Department has at its disposal, and three of you are among the most powerful vampires in the world. We are sending you after *the* most powerful, so nothing else matters. You don't like each other? Fine. Would prefer not to work with each other? I couldn't care less. This is bigger than any of you, and all I'm interested in is whether or not you can follow the orders I'm about to give you. If you don't think you can put your personal shit aside for the sake of the most important mission in the history of this Department, speak up now."

Jamie glanced at his colleagues. Their faces were set with determination, and nobody said a word.

"Last chance," said Turner, eyeing each of them in turn. "No? Good. Direct your attention to the screen behind you."

The newly appointed strike team turned as one. There was a rattle of keys and the wall screen lit up, displaying an overhead photograph of Carcassonne's medieval city.

"Intelligence regarding the locations and numbers of Dracula's vampires is extremely limited," said Turner. "The buildings of Carcassonne are old, with thick walls, and vampires are arriving each night. We may not have a clear picture until tomorrow, when Dracula's army moves out to meet us."

"What if he's with them?" asked Angela Darcy. "This whole operation relies on him staying inside the city. What if that doesn't happen?"

"In such a scenario, your objective would remain the same," said Turner. "The difference will be that you'd go after him on the battlefield rather than in the city. The advantages and disadvantages of such a scenario will be covered before we ship out, but we're going to move forward on the assumption that he'll stay put. He was a General, and our belief is that he'll remain removed from the actual fighting unless it becomes absolutely necessary for him to intervene."

"That is exactly what he will do," said Valentin. "He will restrain himself unless the battle turns. He will want to fight, but he will not consider it appropriate."

You should know, thought Jamie. *You fought for him often enough.*

"Thank you, Valentin," said Turner. "Our expectation is that he'll watch from above the city."

"Out in the open," said Frankenstein. "What will stop him fleeing if things go our way?"

"Pride," said Valentin, his voice low, his eyes fixed on the screen. "Arrogance. Call it whatever you want. He will not run."

"What about the hostages?" asked Angela.

"They are not a mission priority," said Turner. "Their best chance lies in you completing your objective."

"Not a mission priority," repeated Angela. "One hundred and eleven innocent people."

"I am aware of the numbers, Captain," said Turner. "I suggest you reread the Intelligence Division's projection of how many lives will be lost if Dracula asserts his authority over the entire world. It may help soothe your conscience."

Angela gave the Director a long, cold look. He met her gaze for several tense seconds, until the Security Officer slowly turned to look back at the screen.

"So we don't know how many vampires the main force are going to face," said Jamie. "We don't know whether Dracula will fight with them, and if he doesn't, we don't know exactly where he'll be located. We're taking a lot on faith here, sir."

"Yes," said Turner, simply. "We are. General Allen and I will be in constant contact with the five of you, and I promise that you will know everything we know. We'll just have to hope it's enough."

"So what exactly is this plan of yours?" asked Valentin. "We fly into the city, tap Dracula on the shoulder, stake him, and be back home in time for dinner?"

"That would be ideal," said Turner. "But you should probably expect to face a little bit more resistance than that. We're assuming he'll keep a cadre of vampires close to him for protection. Does that tally with your experience?"

"Yes," said Valentin. "When I fought with him, he kept his

Wallachian Guards at his side. Every one would have happily died for him."

"So we kill them and then we kill him," said Frankenstein.

"That's the plan," said Turner.

Ninety minutes later, the Director watched the door swing shut behind the five people on whose shoulders he had just placed the future of humanity, and let out a deep sigh.

He knew what his reputation had always been among the men and women of Blacklight: cold, robotic, precise, a man you would definitely want beside you in a fight but would not necessarily want to be friends with. It had never been the whole truth, but it had suited Turner to let people believe it – it had made them keen to impress him and scared to let him down – and he had needed it for the meeting that had just ended.

On a personal level, he was very fond of the five men and women who had been selected for the strike team, even Valentin, in a very particular and somewhat strange way, and he knew the feeling was largely mutual. But he was asking them to do something astonishing, to go against enormous odds and save the world, and he knew there was every chance that any or all of them might not survive. They had not needed him to be their friend, to pat them on the back and tell them everything was going to be fine; what they had needed was for him to be their Director.

The intercom on his desk beeped and Turner pressed the TALK button.

"Yes?"

"Lieutenant Browning is here, sir," said the disembodied voice of Tom Gregg. "As requested."

"Send him in," he said, and smiled. *This* situation required precisely the opposite approach to the one he had just been considering.

The door opened – it occurred to Turner that he might as well just have it taken off its hinges, such was the frequency of his visitors in recent days – and Matt Browning stepped through it.

"At ease, Lieutenant," he said. "Everything all right?"

Matt winced, but nodded. "I'm OK, sir."

"Your father?"

"Yes, sir," said Matt. "And Kate. And Jamie and Larissa. And about a million other things."

I know exactly what you mean, thought Turner.

"There's a remarkable amount happening at the moment," he said, "so I'll get straight to the point. We've spoken before about your unique status inside the Lazarus Project."

Matt nodded. "Yes, sir."

"You were removed from the active roster when Lazarus was founded, but you *are* still an Operator," said Turner. "And every Operator in the Department is going to France tomorrow to fight Dracula."

The Director watched Matt closely as he spoke. He prided himself on his ability to read people, but the teenager's reaction required none of his skill to interpret; the colour drained from his face as an expression of profound terror rose on to it.

"Lieutenant Browning?" he said. "Is there anything you want to say?"

This was the key test, as far as he was concerned. He had no intention of forcing the brilliant, gentle teenager to fight, but he would only excuse him if Browning *didn't ask him to*. If Matt showed the bravery expected of every member of his Department, Turner would show him the mercy he unquestionably deserved for everything he had done; if he showed cowardice, his Director would not be so lenient.

Browning was staring at him, his eyes wide, his face almost translucent.

"Matt?" he said. "I asked you a question. Is there anything you want to say to me?"

The teenager swallowed hard, and shook his head. "No, sir," he said. "When will I receive my orders?"

Good boy, thought Turner.

"You won't," he said, and sat back in his chair. "Public distribution of the cure will continue regardless of what's taking place in Carcassonne, so you will not be allowed to go to France. I'm sure this will be disappointing, but I'm afraid my decision is final."

The expression of relief that appeared on Matt Browning's face was one of the most heart-warming things Paul Turner had ever seen.

"If you say so, sir," said the teenager.

"I do," said Turner. "Get back to work, Lieutenant. Dismissed."

Matt walked stiffly along Level A until he reached the lift at the far end. He stepped through the doors, pressed the button marked F, and slumped against the metal wall, his head lowered as he fought back tears of relief.

He could not have accurately articulated what he was feeling; the jumble of emotions was too strong, too varied. As awful a prospect as it was, if he had been ordered to go to France, he would have gone, and tried not to embarrass himself or get anyone else hurt. But he would have been afraid.

So very, very afraid.

As the lift slowed, he said a silent thank you. He knew the Director had lied to him; distribution of the cure did not require his supervision, and was no reason for him to be excused from the battle that would begin in barely twenty-four hours. What Paul Turner had done was show him mercy in the guise of orders.

Thank you, sir. Thank you.

Matt exited the lift and walked the familiar route towards the Lazarus Project. As he extended his ID card towards the black panel on the wall outside the door, guilt slammed into him, hot and sharp. What kind of person would accept a Get Out Of Jail Free card when his friends were getting ready to risk their lives? What did it say about him? Was it the action of the man he had started to believe he was becoming?

I wouldn't be any use, he told himself. *I'd just get in the way, and I'd only make everything worse.*

That isn't the reason, whispered a voice in the back of his head. *Be honest with yourself, if nobody else.*

Matt grimaced.

Fine. If I went to France, I would die. And I don't want to die.

He pressed his ID to the panel and opened the door. A few of his colleagues smiled at him and returned to their work; the majority of them didn't so much as look round. Only a single pair of eyes stayed fixed on him: the beautiful grey gaze of Natalia Lenski. He gave her a tight smile, and nodded towards the corner of the laboratory. She immediately got up from her desk and made her way over; he walked along the edge of the room to meet her.

"Are you all right?" she whispered. "What did Major Turner want?"

"I'm fine," said Matt. "He wanted to tell me that I'm not allowed to go to France, even though I'm technically still an Operator. I have to stay here."

Natalia grabbed his hand and squeezed it. "That is good news," she said. "That is very good news."

"I suppose so," he said. "I was relieved, though, Natalia. I was *so relieved*. Maybe I'm just a coward."

Natalia frowned at him. "That is stupid," she said. "There are many ways of fighting. What we have done here, what *you* have done, has changed the battle before it even starts. Without PROMETHEUS, it would be much harder for Jamie and Larissa and the others. So, what? You should go and die, in France, just to prove that you are brave?"

Matt blinked. "I…"

"Turner ordered you to stay here because you are not a soldier. Do you want to be a soldier?"

"No."

"Then it is good," said Natalia, and smiled at him. "OK?"

Matt looked at her. The guilt still lurked in the pit of his stomach, squirming and pulsing; he knew it would not disappear until the people he cared about returned home safely, which he understood was far from a certainty. But at the same time, he knew Natalia was right.

He nodded. "OK."

"Are you sure?" she asked.

Matt nodded again, more convincingly.

"I'm sure," he said. "But if I'm not going to France, I want to do something useful. If we defeat Dracula, we're going to see a lot more vampires come forward for the cure, not to mention the Operators who've been turned for PROMETHEUS. I want to see if we can improve the formula, make it quicker and less painful. They shouldn't have to be cured in padded rooms."

Natalia smiled at him. "That sounds like a much better use of your talents," she said. "So back to work, then?"

Matt returned her smile and nodded. "Back to work."

ZERO HOUR
PLUS 209 DAYS

56

A PROMISE IS A PROMISE

Victor Frankenstein woke with a heavy heart, wondering if this was going to be the last morning he saw.

He knew it was a possibility; he had long been someone who believed there was nothing to be gained by lying to himself. His previous stubborn refusal to accept reality, regarding certain situations and people, had caused much of the trouble that had befallen him in the first two centuries of his life; it was one of many things that had changed on the snowy New York night he had sworn his oath to John Carpenter, altering the trajectory of his life forever.

The monster lifted his uneven arms above his head, stretched his recycled muscles until they creaked, then set about making coffee. His head felt thick and fuzzy, like it had on so many mornings in Paris and Istanbul and Rome, like it had during the dark, whisky-soaked months after he had regained his memory and been brought home to the Loop. He had not touched a single drop the night before, however; this was something deeper than a hangover, a tiredness that seemed to radiate from inside his bones. Frankenstein pulled on his uniform as the kettle rattled, then poured himself a mug of coffee so dark and threatening it looked like it was made of antimatter. He took a sip, grimaced, then drained the mug and poured another.

For the last six months or so, the monster had felt like a ghost. His *condition* put him out of commission for three days of every month, leaving him squarely on the sidelines as the country went into meltdown before their eyes and the Department tried frantically to keep its head above water. He had watched as the boy he had sworn to protect had first been turned into a vampire, then rejected him utterly for a betrayal the teenager could not forgive. Frankenstein understood now that he had made a terrible mistake by not telling Jamie that his father was still alive; he had prioritised the Carpenter that was broken – the one that had been his closest friend – over the one who had really needed him, and he would always regret it. But if he *was* going to die today, he was not going to do so without trying one final time to fix the only thing left that mattered.

Frankenstein stepped out of the lift on Level B and strode along the curved corridor until he reached the door of Jamie's quarters. He took a deep breath, collected himself, and knocked sharply on it.

A faint groan rang out from inside the room, followed by scuffling sounds and the heavy thuds of disengaging locks. The door swung open, and Jamie appeared. His eyes were red and bleary with tiredness, until they settled on the monster, and sprang open wide.

"What do you want?" asked Jamie.

"To talk to you," said Frankenstein.

"Not interested," said the teenager, and swung the door shut.

The monster jammed a boot inside the frame. "Five minutes," he said.

Jamie glanced down; when he raised his head, red fire was flickering in his eyes. "Move your foot."

"No."

"Move it or I'll move you."

Frankenstein met the teenager's gaze. For a long moment, neither man moved; they stood in silence that was thick with tension. Eventually, after an unknowable amount of time, Jamie sighed.

"Five minutes," said the teenager, and backed into his quarters.

Frankenstein nodded, and followed him inside. Jamie strode across the room, flopped down into his chair, and folded his arms across his chest, an impatient look on his face. Frankenstein shut the door and faced him.

"Well?" said Jamie. "Talk."

Stay calm, he told himself. *Don't let his petulance get to you.*

"In a few hours, we'll be in France," said Frankenstein. "And you know as well as I do that a lot of people are going to die."

"You're absolutely right," said Jamie. "I do know that."

Calm.

"Fine," he said. "I know you'd prefer it if I wasn't part of the strike team, and I understand that, but Paul's right. We're going to have to work together, whether you like it or not. Personal feelings have to be put aside."

"I'm totally fine," said Jamie. "You should worry about yourself."

"You're totally fine?"

"Isn't that what I just said?"

"It is," said Frankenstein. "I just don't believe you."

Jamie's eyes flashed red. "I stopped giving a shit about what you believe a long time ago."

"I know," said Frankenstein. "When you found out your father was still alive. And that I hadn't told you."

"I don't want to talk about him," growled Jamie.

"Are you sure?"

The teenager stared, his face darkening with anger. "Why are you here?" he said, eventually. "Do you want me to forgive you? Because that's not going to happen."

Frankenstein shook his head. "No," he said. "I don't want you to forgive me. I want you to forgive *yourself*."

"I'm sorry?"

"I should have told you your father was alive," he said, and took a step forward. "I thought my loyalty to him took precedence over my loyalty to you, and I made a decision that I will always regret. I can't blame you for believing I let you down, and I'm not going to tell you that you're wrong to do so. But *what I am* going to tell you is that you are not your father, no matter how much you may fear that you are. You took the truth about him out on Larissa, and she left you, just like Julian did. You couldn't bring yourself to tell her you needed her, just like Julian was too proud to ask for help when Alexandru Rusmanov was moving against him, and you ended up alone. But you're strong, Jamie, far stronger than he was when he was your age, so you get up every morning and put one foot in front of the other, because you've convinced yourself that your mother needs you, that your friends need you, that the entire Department needs you. And you're right, they do. But I don't think you've ever dealt with what your father being alive really meant."

Jamie didn't say a word. The colour had drained from his face, leaving it ghostly pale.

"I know you grieved for him," continued Frankenstein, "and I know that what happened that night has come to define you, to provide you with the fuel that keeps you going. So if you can't see why you pushed everyone away as soon as you knew he was still alive, why you've been taking so many risks and putting yourself in so many dangerous situations, then you're either not as clever as I think you are or you simply don't want to see the truth."

Jamie stared at him. The red fire in his eyes was gone, replaced by a glistening shimmer.

Say something, thought Frankenstein. *Anything.*

"That's the most I've ever heard you say," said Jamie, his voice low.

"It needed saying," said Frankenstein. "I might not get another chance."

"Is that why you said it? Because we're going to France in a few hours?"

He shook his head. "I know you'll do your job, whatever you might think of me," he said. "And I will always try to protect you, whether you like it or not. I said it because I care about you a great deal, Jamie, and if the worst should happen, I want to know I tried everything I could to make you see that. Because I don't want anything left unsaid."

"I know you care about me," said Jamie, his face creasing with pain. "I never doubted that. That wasn't the problem."

Frankenstein didn't respond; it felt like a crack had appeared in the high walls the teenager had put up around himself, and he didn't want to do or say anything that stopped it from widening.

"I mourned him," said Jamie, his voice little more than a whisper. "My dad. We buried him, and we mourned him, and for a long time I was lost. Then you saved me from Alexandru, and brought me here, and I found a place where I felt like I belonged. I didn't think I'd ever trust anyone again, but I trusted you, and I trusted Henry Seward, and Cal Holmwood. Paul Turner. Even Valentin, for God's sake. But then you disappeared, and Henry was taken, and Cal died. I got you back, but for a long time you weren't the same. You know that, right?"

Frankenstein nodded. "I know."

"My dad turning out to be alive wasn't the problem. It really wasn't. What killed me was finding out that you and Larissa had known about it. I was so angry with you both, so angry that I could barely speak, could barely be around anyone, but what did it get me? I lost you both. That's all. I couldn't apologise to Larissa because she was gone, and I couldn't bring myself to apologise to you, even though I knew I should. I just couldn't bear the thought of being let down again. Can you understand that?"

Frankenstein's heart thudded with pain. "Yes," he said. "Better than you know, Jamie. I understand hating yourself, and I understand putting walls up so you can't be hurt. But it was your grandfather who showed me that living like that isn't really living. Yes, other people *can* hurt you, and sometimes they do, whether they mean to or not. But you can't exist alone."

"Kate's hurt," said Jamie. "Larissa is back, but she isn't really. If we survive Carcassonne, she'll go, and it will be only a matter of time until Matt goes too. My mum is all I've got left."

Frankenstein took another step forward. "That's not true," he said. "Not unless you want it to be. I'm here, and so are Ellison and Qiang, and Paul, and Angela Darcy, and Jack Williams, and dozens of other people who care about you. *You're not alone.* Maybe you've convinced yourself that it would be easier if you were, but you're not. After today, you're going to have to start accepting that."

Jamie grunted. "If we're still alive."

"That's right," said Frankenstein. "I've told you everything I came here to tell you, Jamie. Is there anything you want to say?"

Jamie smiled. "See you in the hangar?"

Frankenstein grunted with laughter. "Indeed you will."

He turned towards the door. As he took hold of the handle, Jamie said his name, and he turned back to see the teenager looking at him with an expression of affection that momentarily warmed his heart.

"Yes?"

"Thank you," said Jamie.

"For what?"

"Caring enough to say what you said."

Frankenstein smiled.

"It's all right, son," he said, his voice a low rumble. "It's going to be all right."

A wry smile rose on to Jamie's face. "I don't believe you," he said. "But that's OK."

57

CLEAN SLATES

I don't want anything left unsaid, thought Jamie. *Absolutely right.*

He was still sitting in his chair, staring at the door that Frankenstein had exited through five minutes earlier, trying to process what had just happened. The sight of the monster when he opened the door had filled him with a bitter cocktail of anger and disappointment, the same emotions he had felt whenever he had seen him in the last six months or so. Now, barely fifteen minutes later, what he was feeling was an overwhelming sense of relief, as though a huge weight had finally been removed from his shoulders and set aside.

Both Kate and Matt had asked him many times whether he missed Frankenstein, and he had never lied to them by saying no. He had told them that he did, *of course he did*, but that he could not forgive the monster for what he had done, and didn't think he would ever be able to. But now, staring around his empty quarters, he realised how wrong he had been; in the end, he had forgiven him as easily and completely as if Frankenstein had borrowed a pen and forgotten to give it back.

He got to his feet, walked across the room and opened the door, and was halfway down the corridor towards the lift before it had even swung shut behind him.

Jamie strode down the cellblock, bracing himself to see his mother for the first time since she had been cured.

It had almost come as a surprise to him when Larissa had asked how his mother was and he had admitted that he hadn't seen her since she had been discharged from the infirmary; the last seventy-two hours had been so utterly hectic – even by the standards of Blacklight – that he had simply forgotten about her.

It hurt his heart to admit it, but it was the truth.

As a result, he was bracing himself for anger or – *at the very least* – disappointment, neither of which he would be able to blame her for. He took a deep breath, and walked out in front of the now redundant UV barrier that formed the front wall of his mother's cell.

"Hi, Mum," he said.

She looked up from her seat on the sofa and smiled so widely at him that he thought for a brief moment that he was going to burst into tears.

"Hello, love," she said. "I think that's the first time you've ever been down here and I didn't hear you coming. Come in, come in."

He smiled, and pressed his ID card against the panel on the wall. He was pretty sure he could move through the purple light fast enough to avoid being hurt, but this was not the day to try and discover he was wrong. The UV wall disappeared and he walked into the cell; his mother met him in the middle of the square room and wrapped him in a one-armed hug that squeezed the air out of him, even though her supernatural strength was now a thing of the past.

"Hey," he whispered. "It's all right, Mum. It's all right."

She released him and stepped back. Her left arm was still wrapped in plaster, her eyes were bruised black and brimming with tears, but her smile was wide and full of happiness. "Tea?" she asked.

He grinned. "Sure. Thanks, Mum."

His mother nodded, and set about filling the kettle and putting teabags into mugs. He watched her work through a task so familiar it was almost second nature, even with only one working arm, feeling his heart throb in his chest.

How could you leave her down here on her own? How could you not even take five minutes to come and see her? What the hell is wrong with you?

"I'm sorry, Mum," he said, his voice low. "For not coming till now. I'm really sorry. It's just that—"

She looked at him, and shook her head sharply. "Don't, Jamie," she said. "Valentin told me what's happening upstairs. I understand."

"Still," he said. "That's no excuse. I just—"

"Please, Jamie," she said. "It's all right. I know you tried to see me when I was in the infirmary. I know you were worried about me, and I knew you cared. It's all right, honestly it is."

She handed him a mug of tea. He took it from her, scarcely able to believe that that was it, that the anger he had been expecting, that part of him had almost been looking forward to, was nowhere to be found, but she was either telling him the truth or had somehow become a far better and more convincing liar than he had ever known her to be.

"How are you feeling?" he asked.

"My arm hurts," said his mother, settling back on to the sofa and raising her cast towards him. "And my nose is never going to be quite the same shape again. But it's strange. I'd got used to being a vampire. I mean, I never *got used to it*, but I got used to the power that came with it, and now it's gone. The second day I was in the infirmary, I got a cold. Nothing serious, just a sore throat and a blocked nose, but I'd forgotten what it felt like to be ill, and

I got really angry about it. I hated feeling weak and tired. But it passed, and I felt better. I *feel* better. I feel like myself again."

"You were the first vampire ever to be cured," he said. "I read the report. It sounded like it was rough."

"I think it was," she said, and sipped her tea. "I can't remember it, to be honest with you. I remember lying on a stretcher and the doctor telling me they were going to sedate me, then the next thing I knew I was awake and my arm was broken and my nose hurt. But I knew, straight away. I knew it was gone the second I woke up."

Jamie grimaced. "I did something stupid," he said. "After they cured you."

His mother frowned. "What did you do?"

"I attacked Matt," he said, his stomach churning at the memory. "The morning after. I found out you were gone, and I thought they'd used you as a test subject, and I went up to the Lazarus Project lab and I lost it."

"Did you hurt him?"

"No," he said. "Not really. But I scared him, Mum. I didn't mean to, but I was so angry, I just lost control."

Her frown deepened as her eyes narrowed. "You listen to me, Jamie," she said. "Taking the cure was my choice, and mine alone. Is that clear? I volunteered. If anything, Matt and Paul Turner tried to talk me out of it."

"I know," he said. "Paul told me once I'd calmed down. I'm sorry, Mum."

"You should be," she said. "I'll never be able to explain to Matt and his colleagues exactly how grateful I am for what they did. They gave me the chance to undo the worst thing that ever happened to me."

"I didn't mean sorry for that," he said. "I mean, I *am* sorry for what I did to Matt, but we sorted it out. I'm sorry for never really getting how much you hated being a vampire."

She smiled, ever so slightly. "I told you often enough, Jamie."

He nodded. "I know you did," he said. "I just didn't listen. I understand that you couldn't wait once the cure existed, that you had to take it, even if it was risky. I get it now."

"Thank you," she said, her smile widening, and finished her tea. She got up and poured herself a second mug. "How are you, love? Are you OK?"

"I'm all right," he said. "What did Valentin tell you?"

"About Carcassonne," said his mother. "And about the planes, and the subways, and the hostages. About Dracula."

Jamie nodded. The ancient vampire shouldn't have told her anything – she was a civilian, and everything related to Dracula was Zero Hour classified – but he found himself glad; even though he had no doubt that she would find the reality of the situation in France upsetting, he was also sure she would rather know than remain in the dark. He had debated how much he was going to tell her, but now he decided to follow Valentin's lead.

"We're going to France this afternoon," he said. "We go into Carcassonne at sunset. Everything will be settled tonight, one way or the other."

"Who's going?" she asked.

"Everyone," said Jamie. "All of Blacklight, plus all the Departments around the world."

"Is Matt going?"

"No, Mum," he said. "We need him here."

"Kate?"

Jamie winced. "Yes," he lied. "Kate's going."

"Valentin told me Larissa had come back," said his mother. "Is that true?"

"It's true," he said. "She came back to help us fight Dracula."

"Is that really why?"

"Yes," he said, firmly. "She's going back to America as soon as this is over."

"Oh."

"It's all right," he said. "There are more important things right now."

"Do you have to go?" she asked.

"To France?"

"Yes."

He frowned. "Of course I do, Mum," he said.

She looked at him and said nothing.

"The chances of killing Dracula are better with me there," he continued, trying not to meet his mother's gaze. "But even if they weren't, I couldn't just stand by while everyone else risked their lives. You know I couldn't. Please don't be angry with me."

Her face creased with pain, then lit up with a smile so full of love that he almost physically recoiled from it.

"I'm not angry with you, Jamie," she said. "Don't think that, not ever. I'm so proud of you I could burst."

He blinked back sudden tears. "I love—"

"Don't," she interrupted. "You can tell me tomorrow. When you're home safely."

"OK," he said, his voice suddenly thick. "I have to go, Mum."

She got up from the sofa and hugged him again, far more gently this time.

"Be careful," she whispered.

He squeezed her tightly, taking care not to so much as brush against her broken arm, then let her go. They stared at each other, until Jamie turned away and walked out of the cell; all that was left to say was goodbye, and he could not bring himself to form the word.

OK, he thought, as he stepped into the airlock. *Two down. One to go.*

* * *

Five minutes later, Jamie knocked on a door on Level B and waited.

After a long moment, it opened to reveal a dishevelled Larissa Kinley. She was wearing a vest and shorts, her hair piled up loosely on her head, her eyes barely open, but Jamie felt his heart race; as far as he was concerned, she had never looked more beautiful.

"Jamie," she said, and rubbed her eyes. "Everything OK?"

He nodded. "I think so. Can I come in?"

The faintest hint of a frown crossed her face, but she stepped aside. He walked into the room and stood by the bed as she closed the door.

"What's up?" she said. "And don't say nothing, Jamie. I know you too well."

"You used to," he said, and instantly regretted it.

Larissa narrowed her eyes. "That's a cheap shot."

"I'm sorry," he said. "I'm really sorry. Frankenstein came to see me and it got me thinking about a lot of stuff."

Larissa sat down on the edge of her bed. "What stuff?"

"My dad," he said. "Me and him. Me and you."

"Jamie…"

He shook his head. "I don't mean me and you like *me and you*. I mean before you left, before I screwed everything up. Frankenstein thinks I pushed you both away because it was easier for me to be on my own after what happened with my dad. After *both* things that happened, me thinking he was dead *and* him turning out to be alive. If I kept everyone at a distance, then nobody could let me down, and I couldn't get hurt. Do you think he's right?"

"Yes," said Larissa, instantly.

"Was I that transparent?"

"Sometimes," she said. "There were times you were so like a closed book that I wanted to scream and shake you until whatever was going on inside your head fell out so I could see it. But as far as this goes, yeah."

"Shit," said Jamie, and rubbed his face with his hands. "I'm such a mess."

"Oh, please," said Larissa. "Self-pity doesn't suit you, Jamie. At all. What happened with your dad was incredibly traumatic, and it left you with some serious abandonment issues, but don't start thinking you're special. The circumstances might have been, but you're not."

Jamie rolled his eyes. "Thanks," he said. "That means a lot."

"You're welcome," said Larissa, clearly refusing to indulge him. "Look around you, Jamie. Look where you are. Everyone in this place has seen things they wish they could forget, and far too many of them have lost someone they care about. What matters is getting up every day and putting it all behind you and carrying on, which is what you've managed to do. Be proud of yourself for that."

"OK," he said. "I'll try."

Larissa nodded. "So did you and Frankenstein sort everything out?"

"Sort of," said Jamie. "He apologised for not telling me my dad was still alive, that he was torn between his loyalty to him and his loyalty to me and made the wrong decision. I can believe that. So we're OK, I think."

"That's good," said Larissa. "I couldn't believe it when Angela told me the two of you hadn't spoken the whole time I was gone. I don't know which of you is more stubborn."

Jamie smiled. "I'm so glad you're back, Larissa," he said. "There was a real shortage of people to insult me without you here."

"Get over it," she said, and smiled at him. "So is that why you're here? To tell me that you and Frankenstein are reconciled?"

"Yes," he said. "No. I don't know."

"Spit it out, Jamie," she said. "Whatever it is."

"Frankenstein came to see me because we might not make it back from France," he said. "And he said he didn't want anything left unsaid."

"OK," said Larissa. "That makes sense."

"I thought so," he said. "So I went straight down to see my mum, like I should have done three days ago."

"Good."

"It just made me think," he said. "About all the things I haven't said to people because there wasn't a right time, or because I just assumed they knew. I don't want to leave things like that with you."

She tilted her head to one side. "All right," she said. "But if you're—"

"I loved you," he said, interrupting her. "I really did. I'm sorry if I gave you reason to doubt that, and I'll never be able to apologise enough for how it ended between us, but I want you to know that I really did love you."

She stared at him for a long moment, until a small, delicate smile appeared on her face. "I know that, stupid," she said. "I loved you too. I still do. You mean the world to me."

Jamie felt his chest constrict. "You still love me?"

She narrowed her eyes, but her smile remained in place. "Don't get any ideas," she said. "Things are different now. But yes, I still love you."

"Things are different *now*?" he asked. "Or they're just different?"

"I don't know," said Larissa. "Why don't we just focus on trying to survive today and worry about that later?"

"Fair enough," he said, slightly more encouraged than he had expected to be as he planned the conversation in his head on his way up from the cellblock. "Do you think we're going to make it? I don't mean just *us*. Do you think anyone is coming back from France?"

"I want to."

"But you don't?"

"No," she said, her voice low. "I don't think so. What about you?"

"I think we'll be dead before the end of the day," he said, and forced a small smile. "I think we've left it too late."

"We might as well not go, then," said Larissa. "Let's just tell Paul we don't think we should bother."

"Good idea," said Jamie. "Let's do it now. I'll be right behind you."

Larissa made as if to get up, then shuffled back across the bed so her back was against the wall. Jamie laughed, and shook his head.

"Coward," he said.

She grinned, and stuck her tongue out at him.

"Charming," he said.

"I aim to please," she said. "So let's say we're wrong. Let's say everything goes to plan and we're back here tomorrow morning with Dracula dead and everyone safe. What are you going to do then?"

Jamie shrugged. "I have no idea," he said. "You'll go back to America, right?"

"I will," she said. "Maybe not tomorrow, but yeah. Haven is my home."

I could come with you, he thought. *We could start again, away from everyone and everything. We could have a clean slate.*

"Tell me about it," he said. "The place you made."

"Not now," said Larissa. "Maybe later. If there is one."

Jamie nodded. "What about Kate and Matt? What do you think they'll do?"

"If we win?" said Larissa.

"Yeah."

"And if Kate survives?"

Jamie grimaced. "Yeah."

"I don't know," said Larissa. "Kate could do whatever she wants. Don't you think so?"

"Yes," said Jamie, firmly. "I do."

"The same goes for Matt," said Larissa. "He's not built for this place, no matter how hard he worked to get here. The Lazarus Project, sure, but not the Department. Not in the long term. I'd have thought it's only a matter of time until him and Natalia go to Oxford or Cambridge and work on black holes or cure cancer and have a bunch of genius kids."

"He wants to go to university," said Jamie. "I know he does. Natalia has already been, crazily enough, but I know Matt was looking forward to it before all this happened. It was going to be his escape from a life he didn't like."

"Then I hope he goes," said Larissa. "And given that he was instrumental in the biggest scientific breakthrough in living memory, I don't think he'll have a lot of trouble getting in wherever he wants."

Jamie smiled. "You don't think he's going to need the right predicted grades?"

"I suspect not," she said, and grinned at him.

Jamie could see it clearly: Matt surrounded by eager students, teaching them something he would never understand in a million years before going home to Natalia and a house full of books and ideas and conversation. It was a happy vision, a future that seemed so essentially *right* that it would be a crime if it did not come to pass, and it filled Jamie with sudden, fervent determination.

We won't lose, he told himself. *We won't let it end today. Not if I have anything to do with it.*

"What time is it?" asked Larissa.

Jamie cleared his mind and checked his watch. "Nine twenty-seven."

"Ninety-three minutes until we're due in the hangar," she said. "What are we going to do between now and then?"

"I can think of something," said Jamie.

Larissa's eyes narrowed. "Don't make me punch you, Jamie."

"Breakfast," he said, rolling his eyes and smiling at her. "I was talking about *breakfast*. You need to drag your mind out of the gutter."

She smiled at him. "Don't make me punch you *hard*, Jamie."

"I'm sorry," he said. "Breakfast?"

She hopped up off the bed. "Breakfast," she said. "Let's go."

58

DULCE ET DECORUM EST

TWO HOURS LATER

The helicopters flew south-east like a swarm of hornets, rattling and buzzing and bristling with threat.

There were eight of them, six big AgustaWestland Merlins and two super-heavy transports that had been built especially for Blacklight from prototypes that the RAF had decided not to put into production; inside their holds they carried the Department's entire active roster, fifty technical and support staff, six jeeps, two armoured cars, and more than twenty crates of weaponry and equipment.

Paul Turner sat in the cockpit of the lead helicopter, his face impassive as ever, his gaze fixed on the bright horizon. He had spoken to Bob Allen before he ordered his men and women to load up, and had been pleased to hear both that the Chinese had arrived overnight and the clear incredulity in the NS9 Director's voice as he described the scene that was waiting for them outside Carcassonne.

More than three thousand Operators. A hundred aircraft, two hundred ground vehicles. A base camp covering four square miles.

An army readying itself for war.

"We should be over the Channel in ninety seconds, sir," said the pilot sitting beside Turner. "ETA forty-seven minutes."

It's almost time, he thought. *One way or the other, we settle this today.*

Eight storeys beneath the wide grounds of the Loop, Marie Carpenter sat on the edge of her sofa, trying to convince her racing heart to slow down.

She had told her son the truth; she understood he had to go, and she really, *really* didn't blame him for doing so. She was so proud of Jamie that it was physically painful; it was a constant vibration of her insides, relentless waves of pride shot through with terror as her brain tormented her with visions of the hundreds of ways he could be hurt, or worse.

The long cellblock was now empty apart from her and the Operator who had been left behind to man the guard post by the entrance. There had been an influx of vampires into the cells in recent weeks as men and women waited to be given the cure, although few of them had stayed for more than twenty-four hours, forty-eight at most, before they were gone. For the last few days, since she had been discharged from the infirmary and the Department had shifted its attention entirely to what was happening in France, it had been just her and Valentin, but now he was gone too.

She was alone.

Marie got up from the sofa, crossed the square room, and started making tea. She didn't *want* tea, but she needed to do something to occupy herself, even if only for a minute or two. She knew she was not going to be able to think about anything else until Jamie walked back through the airlock in one piece, a prospect she knew was many hours away, if it happened at all. She poured water into the teapot, filled a mug, and selected a biscuit from the small tin on the table. She carried them back to the sofa, her heart sick with worry, her head full of her son, and settled down to wait.

Her vigil had begun.

Seventy miles away, Marie's son was sitting in the hold of the helicopter that had been designated Falcon 3, his helmet between his feet, his T-Bone and MP7 lying on his knees, trying his hardest not to treat this mission differently from all the others.

Focus, he told himself. *Your objectives, your surroundings, your squad mates. Ignore the stakes, ignore the fact that it's Dracula. Just do your job.*

Objectively – which was how he was attempting to view it – the Operation was extremely straightforward. His colleagues, and the Operators of the other Departments waiting for them in France, had a far more complicated situation waiting for them: a large-scale battle with an enemy of unknown numbers and competence fought on unfamiliar and unreliable territory. The five members of the strike team had been tasked with destroying a single vampire.

That doesn't really cover it, though, does it? whispered a voice in his head. *You can't really refer to Dracula as just 'a single vampire'.*

But he could. And not only *could*, but *had to*.

If he allowed Dracula's legend, the first vampire's prodigious power and viciousness, to loom in his mind, then fear would begin to creep in, and fear was something Jamie could not allow. He would respect their target, and treat him with appropriate caution, but that was all; if they did their job properly, he would die like any other vampire.

He looked around the dark hold. No more than one of the strike team had been permitted in any single vehicle, in case the fleet of helicopters was attacked before they reached Carcassonne, but he was still surrounded by his friends. Jack Williams was opposite him, his eyes closed, his face pale, and sitting next to Jack was Lizzy Ellison; her eyes were open, and fixed squarely on him.

Jamie smiled at his squad mate. He didn't speak; he didn't want to disturb the thirty or so Operators sitting around them who were currently in worlds of their own, preparing however they saw fit for what was coming. Many had their eyes closed like Jack, but others were staring straight ahead, up at the ceiling, or down at the floor. Most were gripping weapons as though their lives depended on them, which they soon would.

Ellison didn't smile back at him. Her expression was calm and determined, its unspoken message clear.

You can do this. We can do this.

In his makeshift quarters at the centre of Field 1, Aleksandr Ovechkin got down on his knees and prayed for the first time in more than three decades.

He had been raised Russian Orthodox in the barren expanses of Chukotka, but his faith, inasmuch as it had ever existed, had been largely ground out of him by the Red Army instructors who had moulded his wide-eyed, seventeen-year-old self into a soldier. Whatever had remained had not survived his long career, first with the KGB – as it had still been known – and then with the SPC; reconciling the existence of God with the horrors he had seen perpetrated on innocent men and women, by the supernatural and by his fellow human beings, had proved impossible.

Nonetheless, he prayed.

Not for victory, however. He would not insult the Operators of the Multinational Force by suggesting the battle would be won or lost at the whim of something as ethereal as God's favour; it would be won or lost as a result of their skill, and bravery, and heart. Instead, he prayed for those who would not survive the fighting that was about to begin, for the unknowing men and women whose lives could now be measured in hours and minutes. He prayed they would find peace in the darkness, that the universe might allow them to take some echo of pride with them at having fought well, on the side of good.

Ovechkin clasped his hands together and closed his eyes.

Our Father, he began. *Who art in heaven. Hallowed be thy name…*

In the hold of Falcon 4, Larissa thought about what she had told Callum before she left Haven.

I'm coming back, she had said. *When this is all over, I'm coming back.*

She had meant it then, and was almost surprised to realise that she meant it even more determinedly now. Her return to Blacklight had brought forth the uneasy cocktail of emotions she had expected, not least nostalgia at the intense familiarity of the Loop itself. There had been guarded happiness at the prospect of seeing Kate and Matt, mainly because she hadn't known whether they hated her for leaving or not, and palpable *dread* at the thought of seeing Jamie, even though the desperate, naïve part of herself that had believed all along that it would be OK had turned out to be right, more or less. There was a deep wellspring of anger inside her ex-boyfriend, and it was horribly obvious that at least *some of it* was directed at her, but Jamie was clearly working hard to contain it and at least attempt to understand why she had done what she did.

But even though the thing she had worried about most had not turned out to be as bad as she had feared, the endless corridors of the Loop, the black uniforms, and even the very faces of the people who had been her friends and colleagues, still transported her back to a place and time where she had felt trapped and alone and as if she had become a person she didn't know, or like.

All of which meant that her motivations for the mission they were about to undertake differed slightly from the rest of the Operators in the hold of Falcon 4. On a macro level, she wanted Dracula stopped; she knew the fate of the world was largely resting with the Multinational Force, and she *liked* the world as it was. But when it was all over, if they were victorious, the survivors would go back to bases around the world and resume their careers inside the supernatural Departments.

She, on the other hand, would go back to Haven. It was the prospect that was keeping her focused on the task at hand, because if there was *anything* she was certain of, it was that she *wanted to go home*.

And Dracula was standing in her way.

In the command centre of the displaced persons camp, Bob Allen waited for Blacklight to arrive, his mind teeming with the dead.

When he had been promoted to Major, what seemed like a lifetime ago now, the NS9 Director at the time, a formidable former CIA spook named Alan Mathis, had invited him to his quarters to raise a celebratory glass. Over Scotch that was older than them, they had talked about the life they had committed themselves to, about the horrors they had seen and those that, inevitably, were still to come. Emboldened by whisky, Allen had eventually asked the Director how he dealt with it when those under his command were killed; Mathis had been legendarily cold, and there had been a widespread perception that the deaths of NS9 Operators didn't affect him at all. The Director had drained his glass, set it down, and stared directly into Allen's eyes.

"I'm glad that's what they think," he said. "Each and every death tears a piece from my heart, but what would be the good of me showing them that? Would they respect me more if I wailed and howled at every coffin? Would they follow my orders more faithfully if I existed in a state of perpetual mourning? Of course they wouldn't. There is no time for grief, Major. My job is to take the blows, deal with them, and move forward. That is the burden of command, and you'll come to understand it all too well."

And Allen had. Oh God, *he had.*

Men had died, and women had died, and he carried on, his heart accumulating layer after layer of scar tissue. He carried on because that was what was needed; there was no time to stop the clocks, no time for parades and medals and eulogies. He absorbed the pain, and then he gave new orders, sending Operators on missions every bit as dangerous as those that had cost their colleagues their lives, because that was what had to happen.

That was his burden, and it had never felt heavier than it did right now.

Allen pushed the image of Danny's smiling face aside, and checked his watch.

Forty-five minutes till Paul gets here, he thought. *Forty-five minutes until we're ready. Then God help us.*

High above the English Channel, Falcon 2 roared south-east. In its hold, the fifth vampire that had ever existed smiled to himself.

It had been more than a year since Valentin Rusmanov had surrendered to Jamie Carpenter and become a voluntary prisoner inside the Loop, so he was heartened by the looks of nervousness that still crossed the faces of the Operators sitting around him when they glanced in his direction; he had assumed that time and familiarity would have dulled his ability to inspire fear, but it did not appear so.

Most of them are still expecting me to betray them, he thought. *They're wondering how far I'm going to take this before I show my true colours.*

The thought was delicious; there were few things that had pleased

Valentin more over the long course of his life than generating unease and whispered gossip. It had sustained him through much of the seemingly endless twentieth century, as he had gradually been forced to accept that there was little left in the world that he had not experienced: nowhere he hadn't been, nothing he hadn't done. As technology and science had accelerated forward, the only thing that had kept his interest was the apparently unchanging nature of people. No matter the circumstances, human desires and emotions were constant; people wanted proximity to power and glamour, fought jealously for position, and would do awful, unthinkable things if properly motivated.

And motivation had been Valentin's speciality.

The ancient vampire sat back and gave a friendly nod to an Operator who was staring at him with a furrowed brow and narrowed eyes. Valentin knew that some inside the Department would never accept that he was genuinely on their side, and he had never made any secret of the fact that all they could truly rely on was for him to do exactly what was in his own best interests. But those interests were currently firmly aligned with Blacklight's, and, although he enjoyed the trepidation of his temporary colleagues, he had no intention of turning on them, at least for now.

His original impetus to side with the Department had been a desire to prevent the rise of his former master. Valentin had known that Dracula would seek him out and demand a return to his service, and that was something he had no intention of doing, under any circumstances; it was no exaggeration to say that he would rather die.

But now, after the Battle of Château Dauncy, Valentin had a more personal motivation; he wanted revenge for what Dracula had done to him in that field in southern France, for injuries that were by far the closest any had ever come to proving fatal. Had it not been for Larissa Kinley, the darkness that had enveloped him as Dracula's sword sliced him in half would have been permanent, and for that, he was in debt to them both; he owed the vampire girl his eternal gratitude, and he owed his former master an agonising death.

The helicopter rumbled towards Carcassonne, as Valentin allowed his head to fill with the bitter prospect of vengeance, and the sickly sweet promise of spilled blood.

In the Basilique Saint-Nazaire, Dracula sat with his legs stretched out before him, his head lowered in silent contemplation.

In the old days, when he had still been only a man, he had taken private time before battle in a tent surrounded by the dark silhouettes of his Wallachian Guards; the grand, ornate interior of the Basilica was far more to his liking.

He had sent Osvaldo away ten minutes earlier to make final checks of his army and hostages, but the Spanish vampire was as efficient as he was loyal, and it would not be long before he returned with his report; in the meantime, Dracula savoured the silence and stillness of the old church, and allowed his thoughts to drift towards the battle that was now imminent. The first vampire had no intention of joining the fight unless it was absolutely necessary – it would not be fitting for the world that was soon to belong to him to witness him brawling like a common soldier – but an ever-growing part of him was hoping that became the case; he had scores that he would greatly prefer to settle in person.

The traitor Valentin, for one.

The vampire girl who had almost beaten him, for another.

The door to the Basilica swung open, and Dracula sighed inwardly as Osvaldo stepped through it and bowed his head. He could not chastise his most fervent follower for being too efficient, but he would have preferred to be alone for as much time as possible between now and when the battle began.

"Deliver your report," he said, when the vampire was barely halfway down the aisle at the centre of the nave. "Do it quickly."

"My lord," said Osvaldo. "Eight more helicopters have arrived, but everything is exactly as you have commanded. We are ready."

"Good," said Dracula. "Find Emery and send him to me. If all goes well, there will be work for him. Then return when you see movement from our enemies."

Osvaldo bowed again, and backed out of the church without a word. Dracula waited until the door thudded shut behind the vampire, then closed his eyes.

We are ready, he told himself. *It is almost time.*

59

IN FADING LIGHT

OUTSKIRTS OF CARCASSONNE, SOUTHERN FRANCE
THREE HOURS LATER

There was silence throughout the displaced persons camp as the sun dropped below the western horizon.

Electricity crackled through the wide fields. Men and women whose homes had been destroyed by Dracula's savage assault on their city stopped what they were doing; many crossed themselves as they stared at the darkening sky. Charity volunteers came out of their tents, support staff exited the temporary buildings, as, beyond the exclusion perimeter, journalists and camera operators fell silent.

The Operators that made up the Multinational Force did not see the sun set; they had already boarded the helicopters that would transport them the short distance to the battlefield, and were checking their weapons and equipment as they came to terms with the reality that was about to envelop them.

For long moments, nothing and nobody moved. The tension was palpable, causing hearts to race and skin to break out in gooseflesh. Rotor blades spun in blurs, engines rumbling beneath them. A column of trucks and armour sat motionless at the camp's main gate, their exhausts belching blue smoke into the sky. Paul Turner sat beside Bob Allen in the back of an open-topped jeep, his skin tingling with anticipation as he surveyed the suddenly still camp. Eventually, after what felt like hours, the NS9 Director raised his radio to his lips and spoke two simple words.

"Move out."

They rolled into Carcassonne in silence.

The trucks and armoured vehicles led the convoy between the shells of cars and fallen rubble that littered the roads. Around them, on every flat surface that remained – every fragment of standing wall and expanse of unbroken road and pavement – three words had been painted over and over, in every imaginable size and colour; three words that made the skin of every Operator crawl.

HE IS RISEN

In the distance, across the flattened landscape, the medieval city perched atop its hill, the highest point for miles in any direction. Turner looked back as they approached it through what had been the city's commercial district and felt his heart surge in his chest; the sky behind the column of vehicles was full of helicopters, a wide black line flying low and slow. Inside them sat more than three thousand Operators, each one armed to the teeth, each one ready to fight, and kill.

The lead truck drew to a halt a mile before the foot of the hill. The rest of the column peeled to the left and right and stopped, creating a long line of vehicles with fifty metres between them. The roar of the helicopter engines increased as they descended; they touched down a safe distance behind the line. The doors of the holds slid open and a tide of black-clad figures disembarked and jogged between the vehicles to their rally points. Turner watched as

Blacklight's vampire Operators moved to the front of the rapidly filling line; they would lead the army into battle, their supernatural power put straight to use.

The helicopters immediately rose back into the air and hovered half a mile behind the army they had carried in their bellies, their weapons systems trained on the wide space between the black line and the foot of the hill.

No-man's-land, thought Turner.

"Initial deployment complete," said a voice in his ear, over the command frequency that he and the rest of the Directors had tuned their comms systems to.

"Copy that," said Bob Allen. "Ready One. Wait for my go."

"This is it," said Turner, his voice low.

Allen gave him a hard, thin smile. "It looks like it," he said. "Scared?"

"Of course I am."

"Me too," said Allen. "Wouldn't be human if we weren't, right?"

Turner shook his head, and looked out across the line of Operators. It was an astonishing display of strength, particularly given the speed with which it had been assembled, but, even as he looked at it, he knew that the space in front of the army was not where the battle was going to be won or lost; their ultimate fate rested in the hands of five men and women who were still six miles behind their colleagues. He twisted the comms dial on his belt and spoke into his helmet's microphone.

"Strike team," he said. "Do you copy?"

"Copy, sir," said Angela Darcy. "Standing by."

"We're in position," said the Director. "Wait for my go."

"Yes, sir."

"Out."

* * *

The Security Officer looked round at her squad mates. "Everyone get that?"

Jamie nodded, as the rest of the strike team murmured in agreement.

"Good," said Angela. "Stay calm. They'll let us know when they need us."

They were standing in a secure room at the middle of the camp's command centre, watching an array of screens showing live feeds of the battlefield from satellites and vehicle-mounted cameras; the army of Operators was clearly visible, still and silent as it waited. Ellison and Qiang and Jack Williams and Dominique Saint-Jacques and dozens more of Jamie's friends were among them, and he felt pride flood through him as he stared at the screen.

Nobody could have asked us for more than we've given, he thought. *Nobody can ever say we didn't do everything we could.*

Seventy miles away, in the waters off the town of Perpignan, Commander Alain Masson ordered the *Terrible* up to launch depth.

The submarine was the lead boat of the *Triomphant* class, the cornerstone of France's nuclear deterrent. There were four, with at least one at sea at all times, ready to do the unthinkable if the unthinkable was ever required. In hardened tubes that ran the length of her foredeck, sixteen M51 missiles waited silently, each containing ten independently targeting nuclear warheads capable of delivering a hundred times as much firepower as the bomb that had destroyed Hiroshima.

Command of the *Terrible* was the highest honour the French Navy could bestow, and Masson did not take it remotely lightly. His crew were their country's last line of defence, a devastating deterrent lurking silent and unseen beneath the waves, and if the time came for him to give a launch order, Masson knew they would do their duty, regardless of the consequences.

"Launch depth, sir," said the diving officer.

"Good," said Masson. "Commence hover."

"Hovering, sir."

He nodded, and checked the communications screen where new orders would appear if they were issued, orders that he could still scarcely contemplate.

The screen was dark.

For now.

Turner stared up at the medieval city, his heart full of unexpected joy.

Deep down, the Blacklight Director did not expect to survive the coming battle; he believed the remainder of his life could likely now be measured in minutes rather than years. But as he stared, he found that the prospect didn't fill him with fear; he was proud of the life he had lived, a life of thrills and marvels and danger, and if it was really about to end in these blasted ruins, then so be it.

He would meet death head-on, without regrets.

Purple and orange blazed across the horizon to the west, reflecting against low banks of clouds to create a breathtaking vista of light. Turner smiled; it was as though the universe had decided to provide their army with a glorious final reminder of what they would soon be fighting for, of the beauty and wonder of the world they were trying to protect.

The air changed.

He felt it before he heard it, in his teeth and his bones; a thick humming vibration, rising rapidly. Turner frowned and looked along the line of Operators. His vampires had felt it too, whatever it was; they were growling and hissing, several of them holding the sides of their helmets.

What the hell? he had time to wonder, before the noise rose to a deafening, pulverising scream, and coherent thought left his mind.

The sound tore through him, making his insides feel like they were going to be shaken to pieces; it was otherworldly, impossibly loud and terrifyingly high-pitched. Vampire Operators collapsed to the ground and thrashed in the ash and mud as their Director fell to his knees, his head boiling with pain, distantly aware that the sound would be even louder without the dampeners and filters in his helmet, a prospect he could not begin to imagine. Beside him, Bob Allen lurched to his right and tumbled out of the back of the jeep on to the ground; Turner could do nothing but watch.

The pitch rose and rose as he screamed silently behind his visor. On his belt, the lens and bulb of his ultraviolet torch shattered, sending broken glass tumbling to the ground. He saw the same happen to the weapons of the line of Operators, and managed to twist round on his knees in time to see the windscreens of the vehicles and the lights of the helicopters explode, their glass unable to withstand the aural onslaught that had been unleashed from God only knew where. The windscreens of the helicopters were bulletproof plastic, and didn't break, but he saw several lurch alarmingly as their flight crews reeled against the noise.

Turner looked down as the agony inside his head reached a blistering crescendo, saw the broken shards of his UV beam gun, and slumped to the floor of the jeep's bed as understanding hammered into him.

Sonic-disruption weapon. Destroy our UV lights. Disorient our vampires. Dear God, what else is there? What more has he planned that we haven't seen coming?

Then, as suddenly as it had arrived, the sound disappeared.

Turner lay flat on his back, his eyes squeezed shut, trying to clear his mind. He reached a trembling hand inside his helmet and clicked his fingers beside his right ear, praying that he would hear

575

the snap. It was distant, low and muddy, but it was there, and he breathed a sigh of relief.

Not deaf. Thank God.

He climbed back to his feet, and was relieved to see Bob Allen standing unsteadily beside the jeep before he checked their army. The Multinational Force's line was ragged and broken, and he could see blood running down the necks of a number of the Operators, but, as he watched, the ones who had fallen to the ground dragged themselves up and started to regroup.

Movement.

It started near the summit of the hill, by the tall towers of the Basilique Saint-Nazaire, and gathered pace as it descended. By the time it reached the battlements and spilled through the gate and over the walls, it had become a flood, a vast torrent of vampires, thousands of them, maybe as many as there were Operators waiting for them. They stopped barely half a mile away and formed an uneven line, jostling and clawing and snarling at each other, their eyes casting a thick crimson glow in the gathering darkness. Turner magnified the view through his visor – which, mercifully, was made of plastic, and had survived – and scanned the old city of Carcassonne. In the distance, floating above the highest walls, he saw the dark silhouette of a single figure.

This is it, he thought.

"Darcy?" he said, his voice low.

"Yes, sir?" said his Security Officer.

"Are you OK?"

"We're OK, sir," she said. "What the hell was that?"

"It doesn't matter now," said Turner. "Are you ready?"

"Yes, sir."

"Go."

There was no further reply; he knew the strike team would be gathering their equipment and preparing to carry out their part in what was about to unfold.

Bob Allen climbed back into the jeep and glanced in his direction. The American's face was white with pain, but his gaze was solid and determined; Turner met it with his own, and nodded.

The NS9 Director raised his radio.

"Go."

Immediately, as though operated by remote control, the wide line of Operators moved forward; several of them staggered their first few steps, but not a single one hesitated. The howling din from Dracula's followers increased as a number of them rose into the air, their burning eyes fixed on the approaching army. In the jeeps either side of the one Turner and Allen were standing in, the other Directors watched their men and women march away. Out of the corner of his eye, Turner saw Aleksandr Ovechkin cross himself and momentarily lower his head; when he raised it again, the Russian's eyes were cold and clear.

The crunching rhythm of footsteps across the broken ground increased as the Operators quickened their pace. The vampires began to move forward, darting and snapping and hissing; through his visor, Turner could see savage grins, and the fervent anticipation of violence.

"Ready One!" bellowed Allen. "Kill them! Kill them all!"

60

DEATH'S GREY LAND, PART ONE

CARCASSONNE, SOUTHERN FRANCE

Larissa followed the rest of the strike team out of the command centre, her spine tingling with excitement.

The waiting had been almost unbearable; now the battle was actually beginning, they would finally know whether they were going to savour victory or suffer defeat. In the distance, the first crackle of gunfire and the first screams of pain reached her supernatural ears. She shivered with a mixture of unease and anticipation, and looked at her squad mates.

"Shall we?" asked Valentin, a smile on his pale, handsome face.

"By all means," said Angela. "Let's do it."

Jamie nodded, took hold of Frankenstein beneath his arms, and rose into the air. The monster grimaced at the indignity, but said nothing. Larissa followed suit, relishing – as she always did – the moment when her feet left the ground. Valentin and Angela joined them, and for a silent moment, the five men and women floated in the air, staring at each other. Larissa's heart was pounding in her chest, but her mind was clear; she enjoyed the sensation of clarity, knowing from long experience that it would soon be replaced by the rampaging bloodlust of her vampire side.

"Follow me," said Angela.

Ellison felt power surge through her as she stepped into the air and, for the briefest of moments, found herself completely overwhelmed.

She had been using her supernatural abilities constantly for the three days since she had been turned, and had believed she was starting to understand them; she could control her eyes and her fangs, was managing to cope with the sensory overload of her dramatically improved sight and hearing, and was able to fly in a straight line, more or less. But nothing she had experienced in the Playground had remotely prepared her for what she was feeling now; her vampire side had sent fire coursing through her nerve endings, coating her skin with electricity and bulldozing everything from her conscious mind beyond the need to fight and kill and drown in blood.

Ahead of her, the vampire army spread out for what seemed like miles, but Ellison didn't care; she accelerated through the air with her eyes blazing and a wide grin on her face, and as she drew the stake from her belt, her mind was full of an urgent question.

How can I go back from this? How can I possibly let this power go?

There was an explosion of noise as she and her vampire colleagues thundered into Dracula's followers, sending them flying in all directions. Behind her, the unturned Operators charged in, the noise of their guns deafening. The scent of blood filled her nostrils as screams and crunching thuds rang out from all sides, and Ellison felt savage satisfaction as she buried her stake into the chest of a vampire who looked like he was suddenly, belatedly unsure exactly what he had got himself into. The man burst with a thunderclap of blood, but she was already past him, pushing on into the blurred, screeching line of the enemy. She plunged her stake between the shoulders of a vampire whose face she never saw, felt its point puncture the heart, and leapt forward without even wasting time to look back and see the woman explode.

A vampire dropped out of a sky that was suddenly full of blood and movement, an expression of desperate hunger on his face, and swung an axe at her head. Ellison moved without thinking, sliding beneath the axe's wicked arc, her knees skidding through the black ash of the battlefield. The swing dragged the vampire off balance; she rose like a shark from the depths and slammed her stake up through the soft flesh beneath his chin. The metal point burst out of the vampire's mouth, shattering his teeth into enamel splinters, and his eyes widened comically as he screamed around the metal filling his mouth. She wrenched the stake out, and drove it into his chest. The man stared at her with a momentary expression of disbelief before he exploded, his blood drenching her uniform and splattering to the burnt ground like crimson rain.

Ellison shook liquid and flesh off the stake, and threw herself into the battle, her head full of the urge to commit violence, her vampire side in total, gleeful control.

High above the burnt, bloody ground, in the still air around the Basilique Saint-Nazaire, Dracula watched the opening moments of the battle unfold.

His eyes had flared red-black as the smell of blood floated up into his supernaturally sharp nostrils, and it had taken every bit of his self-control not to dive through the air and hurl himself into the fray, to merely watch and wait instead. He did not believe the battle would be lost; he was sure his enemies would not have anticipated the surprises he had in store for them, or be able to counter them when they were sprung. But a growing part of him hoped that he was wrong, that the men and women in black would somehow overcome the odds stacked against them, and that the fighting would reach the point where it required his personal intervention.

Until then, he would restrain himself.

At the centre of the second line of the Multinational Force, with only the vampire Operators between him and Dracula's followers, Julian Carpenter sprinted forward.

For what felt like as long as he could remember, he had been spinning aimlessly, seemingly unable to assert any control over the chaos his life had become. His family, career, friends, even his *liberty*: all had either been compromised or taken from him entirely, leaving him a spectator in the limbo that had become his reality. But some part of himself had returned as he flew to France in direct disobedience of the order Cal Holmwood had given him, and had grown once he reached the displaced persons camp and found himself surrounded by Operators and technicians and guns and T-Bones and helicopters. Now, as he drew his MP5 from his belt and trained it on the snarling, charging line of vampires, a profound sense of peace settled over him.

I'm home, he thought, and squeezed the trigger.

Fire licked from the end of the submachine gun's barrel as the deafening rattle of gunfire filled his ears and the smell of cordite filled his nostrils. The vampires he had aimed at scattered in all directions, hurling themselves into the air and swooping away as the two armies collided, but Julian ignored the ones his bullets had missed and focused on those they hadn't. Through the raging, fighting mass, he saw a vampire with ragged holes where his knees should have been trying to crawl back the way he had come, churning the ground with his elbows as he dragged himself across it. Julian sprinted forward, letting his MP5 swing down on its strap as he drew his T-Bone, and skidded to a halt. He raised the launcher in a smooth arc, and as he levelled it and sighted down the barrel, his chest tightened with nostalgia so profound that it momentarily threatened to send him to his knees.

Jesus.

He shook it off, and pulled the trigger. The T-Bone fired with a bang of exploding gas and a screech of unspooling wire, and the metal stake punctured the crawling vampire's back; the man burst in a shower of steaming blood. The stake wound back towards the T-Bone's barrel as Julian stalked forward, searching the chaos for the other victims of his bullets.

Movement.

On his right.

He spun, bringing the T-Bone round, and was hit in the face by what seemed like a bucket of blood. It splashed across the visor of his helmet, soaking the shoulders and chest of his uniform, and Julian staggered backwards, recoiling with horror. He wiped frantically at his visor with his gloved hands, and felt his stomach lurch as he saw the source of the blood: a Blacklight Operator, her helmet gone, her throat sliced to the bone, her eyes wide and staring as she sank to her knees and toppled over on to her side. For a long moment, he merely stared; despite the hours spent lost in his memories, his endless daydreams of reinstatement, and his desperate need to *do* something, to *be* something again, he had forgotten the raw reality of this life. It was death, and pain, and blood.

In the end, it always came down to blood.

Julian balled a fist and punched the side of his helmet. His head cleared, in time for him to duck beneath a severed arm hurled from somewhere inside the pulsing, thundering crowd, take a deep breath, and wade back into the fight.

Floating above the drawbridge that had once controlled access to the medieval city of Carcassonne, Osvaldo watched with an impassive expression as vampires began to die in their hundreds.

He felt a tiny pang of sorrow as men and women whose company he had enjoyed were staked and shot, their blood spilling on to the ground, their lives ending in sudden violence, but their deaths were ultimately irrelevant, and unavoidable. The first few minutes of the battle had always been destined to be chaos; both armies were fresh, and the initial exchanges would favour the experienced soldiers and their guns and stakes. From his high vantage point, he saw the two long lines envelop each other, creating a seething mass of humans and vampires, tearing and clawing and firing and flying.

Screams began to echo across the darkening expanse of the battlefield as the battle began in earnest. Osvaldo knew this was when his master's army would assert themselves: once the fighting became close and messy, and their speed and savagery would begin to tell.

And it wouldn't matter in the slightest if every single one of them died, he reminded himself. *This is merely the opening act of the play.*

PROLOGUE, REDUX

CARCASSONNE, SOUTHERN FRANCE
NOW

Jamie Carpenter soared over the battlefield, carrying Frankenstein effortlessly beneath him, marvelling at the scale of the fighting taking place below.

His view of it was fleeting, such was the speed he and the rest of the strike team were travelling, but it was enough to make quite an impression; the battle was already spread out across more than a mile of blasted landscape, the air full of movement and gunfire and screaming, the ground littered with bodies and soaked with vampire remains. Jamie tore his gaze away and focused on the looming shape of the medieval city, its pale stone darkening in the fading light, and, as he rose over the outer walls, his squad mates close behind him, he saw a distant figure floating near the summit of the hill, high above the raging battle.

Dracula, he thought, his heart leaping in his chest. *Right where they said he would be.*

This is going to be too easy.

Jamie swooped over the walls, rising above the wide cobbled street that led up through the city. He accelerated, the evening air cool as it rushed over his uniformed body, the rooftops passing below him in a blur, and allowed a smile to rise on to his face. As he soared over a wide square, he heard something above him, something that sounded like a flock of birds, and rolled to the side so he could look up and see what it was.

The sky above him was full of vampires.

They dropped silently out of the clouds, a vast dark swarm, and ripped into the strike team like a bolt of lightning, sending them spinning towards the ground. Something connected with the side of his helmet and he saw stars, his vision greying at the edges as his grip on Frankenstein loosened and gave way; the monster slipped from his grasp and fell towards the ancient city. Jamie lunged after him, but was hammered from all sides by heavy blows that drove him back and forth, bellowing with pain. He fought back furiously, but might as well have been trying to punch the wind; there seemed to be vampires all around him, as insubstantial as smoke, apart from when they struck. He ducked under a swinging fist and looked desperately around for his squad mates, but it was like trying to see through a colony of bats that had taken wing at the same time; all around him was darkness and churning movement.

A boot slammed into his stomach. Jamie folded in the air, the breath driven out of him, and sank towards the ground, barely able to even slow his fall. Cobblestones rose up to meet him, and he hit them hard enough to drive his teeth together on his tongue, spilling warm coppery liquid into his mouth. Pain raced through him, before being driven away by the heady taste of his own blood.

He leapt to his feet and scanned the narrow street he had landed in. There was no sign of his squad mates, or the vampires that had attacked them. He looked up, expecting to see them hurtling down towards him, but the sky was clear and empty; it was as though they had never been there at all.

Stupid, he told himself, and felt his eyes blaze with heat. *Arrogant. Stupid.*

Jamie leapt into the air, determined to locate the rest of the strike team and get their mission back on track.

A hand closed round his ankle and whipped him downwards.

Surprise filled him so completely that he didn't get his hands up until it was too late; his helmet thudded against the ground, and everything went black.

61

DEATH'S GREY LAND, PART TWO

CARCASSONNE, SOUTHERN FRANCE

Everything fell away.

The politics, the bureaucracy, the endless meetings and briefings and red tape, everything that went with being the Director of Blacklight was suddenly gone, leaving Paul Turner with a simple, cold reality: himself, an enemy and the chance to do what he had always been so horribly good at. He could have stayed standing in the jeep, removed from the battle like Dracula and the rest of his fellow Directors, and he knew nobody would have blamed him.

But *this* was where he belonged.

Turner raised his T-Bone and fired it through the stomach of a vampire leaping towards the back of an NS9 Operator. The woman wasted no time acknowledging the reprieve; she threw herself straight back into the carnage without so much as a glance. Turner ran forward, his T-Bone's motor winding furiously, plunged his stake into the stricken vampire's chest, then leapt back and swung his MP7 into his hands. The vampire burst, and Turner fired his submachine gun through the resulting gout of crimson, the bullets spraying the gore in every direction and filling the air with the bitter smell of burning blood.

A chorus of screams rang out as the remains of the vampire splashed to the ground. Turner's bullets had ripped through a group of Dracula's followers who had foolishly turned to see what had befallen their comrade; they fell to the ground, screaming, the faces that had not been destroyed by the volley of gunfire twisted with pain and red-eyed confusion.

Turner holstered his MP7 and his T-Bone, raised his stake, and ran towards them, a man doing what he had been born to do.

High above the city, Dracula smiled as his personal guard dropped from the clouds and sent the black-clad figures plummeting into the narrow streets below.

Had his enemies really believed he would float in plain sight without protection? Or that he would not expect them to send an assassination squad in the hopes of ending the battle before it had even really begun? If so, then they were stupider than he had even allowed himself to hope, and deserved no mercy.

I know everything they are going to do before they do it, he thought. *I highly doubt the reverse is true.*

Valentin ducked a punch, gave the vampire who had thrown it a look of outright contempt, then tore his head off with a sound like ripping cardboard.

Blood spurted from the stump, bright arterial red under the pale street lights of Carcassonne. The decapitated body took a faltering step forward, its hands clenching and unclenching reflexively, before it overbalanced and toppled to the ground. Valentin strode across the cobblestones and stamped his foot through the vampire's chest; the heart gave way beneath his heel, and the man burst with a wet thud across the cobbled street.

Valentin heard a low growl behind him, and turned slowly towards it. Three vampires, two women and a man, were floating up the street, their eyes glowing, their fangs gleaming. He narrowed his eyes, taken aback by the strength of the emotion coursing through him; it was rare that his opulent and privileged life gave him reason for anger, but he was angrier than he could remember being in decades, angrier even than when he had discovered the desecration of his home in New York and beaten one of the culprits to death with his bare hands.

He was absolutely *incandescent* with rage.

The three vampires were smiling, and it was their expressions that had triggered his fury; the thought that these *nobodies* had the nerve to approach him was absolutely outrageous.

It was *offensive*.

Valentin strode towards them, meeting their smiles with a wide, warm grin. He had lost his helmet in his fall from the sky, but he gave it no thought; he had hated wearing it, and was happy it was gone. One of the women leapt towards him, and he fought back the urge to laugh at her pitiful lack of speed. He slid to his left, a blur in the evening gloom, and grabbed her throat with his gloved hand; her eyes widened with shock as he drew his arm back and hurled her at the stone wall on the opposite side of the road. She hit it with an impact that cracked the stone in a wide spiderweb and a crunch of breaking bones that echoed up and down the street. The vampire slid down the wall and landed in a crumpled heap on the ground; there was a long second of silence, before she began to howl in hoarse, broken agony.

The two remaining vampires took a step backwards, their easy arrogance faltering, but Valentin was upon them before they could flee. His fist shot out like a piston and crashed against the man's sternum; it broke with a dry snap, and the vampire screeched as he folded to the ground. Valentin leapt over him, and buried his fangs in the female vampire's face. Blood sprayed down his throat, and he drank deeply as she screamed into his mouth. He released her, and spat out a lump of her flesh as she scrambled backwards, her hands clutching her face, her screams so loud and desperate it was as if the world was ending around her.

Which, in truth, it was.

She stumbled into the air, seeking escape, but Valentin was much too fast. He grabbed her hair as she babbled apologies and pleas for mercy, hurled her down on to the cobblestones, and plunged his stake into her stomach. She stared at him with an expression of profound surprise as he shoved the metal stake up through her torso and into her heart. She exploded in a thunderclap of steaming blood, but Valentin was already on his way back up the road, the dripping stake in his hand. He didn't hurry; he *wanted* the two broken vampires to see him coming, to have time to process what was about to happen to them, and for delicious expressions of terror to rise on to their faces.

He staked the male vampire without slowing, a dismissive crouch and flick of his wrist that put an end to the man's tortured howling, and advanced on the tangled woman. Her face was bright white, her mouth open. He looked down at her shattered body and felt nothing; no sadness, no pity, no mercy. He crouched down, pressed the tip of the stake against her chest, and paused.

"Look at me," he said.

The vampire's eyes rolled in their sockets and settled unsteadily on him. A wheezing sound was coming from her throat, and Valentin realised she was still trying to scream; either her vocal cords had torn, or something was so badly broken inside her that she could no longer make them work.

He held her gaze, then pushed the stake forward. Her eyes widened as the thick muscle of her heart was pierced, then they burst, along with the rest of her. Blood splashed across Valentin, but he made no effort to avoid it; it was a spoil of war, the only one that really mattered.

Don't even think about it, Bob Allen told himself. *You're too damn old. Just stay right where you are.*

The NS9 Director was still standing in the back of the jeep, although he was now its only occupant; Paul Turner had managed to restrain himself for barely more than thirty seconds before he had leapt to the ground and joined the fight. Allen was theoretically in charge of directing the battle, but the fighting had immediately taken on a life of its own, just as he had known it would, rendering the team colours and squad designations he and his fellow Directors had worked out all but irrelevant; what would carry the day would be the strength and will of the Operators fighting and dying in front of him. His headphones carried a jumble of voices directly into his ear; he could have tuned them out, could have twisted the comms dial on his belt back to the command frequency, but he didn't. The noise of the battle roused something primal inside him, something that was straining for release.

Don't even think about it, he repeated to himself.

Allen looked along the line of jeeps parked safely behind the row of Operators who had been tasked with staying back to protect their Directors. His counterparts watched silently, their eyes fixed forward; they looked like the conductors of an orchestra. The need to do something surged relentlessly inside him, and he grimaced behind his visor at the dilemma; if he joined the battle and was killed, the consequences for his Operators could be dire. But if he stood by while they fought for their lives, how would he ever be able to face them again?

Then, in the jeep to his right, Aleksandr Ovechkin moved.

The SPC Director drew his Daybreaker, swung himself down to the ground, and strode towards the chaos, his greatcoat billowing out behind him. Allen watched him for a long moment, then unholstered his T-Bone and went after his friend.

He caught up as Ovechkin cut left round a pile of burnt wood that looked like it had once been a street trader's stall. The Russian spun round, his eyes flaring, then smiled.

"You too?" he grunted.

"Yeah," said Allen, and smiled back at him. "Me too."

They walked forward side by side, their weapons drawn and raised. The battle spread out before them, the noise increasing with each step they took, but Allen was breathing easily. His body and mind were at peace now that he had decided to involve himself, even though that decision had dramatically increased the likelihood that he would not live to see another dawn.

So be it, he thought, as his boots crunched across the black landscape. *If this is the end, then so damn well be it.*

"Wait!"

The voice came from behind them, and both Directors turned to see who it belonged to. General Tán was running towards them, holding a weapon that Allen didn't recognise. The PBS6 Director stopped in front of them, and gave them a tight smile.

"Three is better than two," he said. "Don't you agree?"

Larissa tumbled towards a narrow alley hung with washing lines and full of rubbish bins, managed to rotate herself in the air as the cobblestones rushed up towards her, and hit the ground on her back with a thud.

The impact sent pain coursing through her; heat exploded into her eyes, and a thick growl rose from her throat as she got to her feet and looked around. The alleyway was tight and winding, one of the hidden arteries that had served the people who had actually lived and worked in the city, as opposed to the tourists they relied on. There was no sign of her squad mates, or of the vampires who had ambushed them from above.

Stupid, she thought. *Should have seen that coming.*

They had assumed that Dracula would have kept a cadre of vampires within the city to protect him, but they had been expecting them to rise from the streets below, rather than attack them from above. Now they were scattered throughout the city, their mission in tatters; they needed to regroup, and do so very, very quickly.

"Strike team," she said into her helmet's microphone. "Come in."

Silence.

"Come in, strike team. Come in."

Nothing.

Larissa strode along the alley, preparing to leap back into the air and get a better vantage point from which to search for her squad mates, then stopped. From the other side of a tall stone wall, she could hear noise: footsteps, heavy breathing, low growls.

Vampires.

She drew her stake from her belt and floated silently up the face of the wall. She hovered as she reached the top, forcing the glowing red out of her eyes, and peered down into the cobbled street on the other side. Two vampires were approaching the doorway of a toyshop, in which was lying the unconscious form of Frankenstein; their eyes were blazing, and the smiles on their faces were hungry.

She settled herself silently on top of the wall, drew her T-Bone, sighted down its long barrel, and pulled the trigger. The bang of exploding gas was deafeningly loud in the quiet streets; the vampires jumped, and whirled towards her. As a result, the stake that would have pierced the rightmost vampire's heart ripped through his stomach, punching a hole the size of a grapefruit and spilling the man's guts on to the cobblestones. For a second he only stared at her, his eyes bulging in their sockets, then he threw back his head and screamed.

Larissa was already moving, dropping the T-Bone and swooping down from the wall. She drove the second vampire against the wall, drew her stake, and brought it up in a short, hard jab. She leapt back as the man burst, spraying the wall with dripping crimson, and darted across to the disembowelled vampire; he was standing motionless in the middle of the street, staring down at a steaming pile of his own innards. She shoved the stake through his back, and the look on his face as he exploded suggested that ending him had been a kindness. The T-Bone's metal wire fell to the bloody ground as she crossed to the unconscious figure in the shop doorway and crouched beside him.

"Colonel," she said, raising her voice as far as she dared. "*Colonel.*"

Frankenstein stirred, but didn't open his eyes. Larissa checked him, searching for severe injury, and found none; there was a lump the size of an egg above his left eye, but his chest was rising and falling steadily, and his limbs were straight and unbroken, at least as far as she could tell.

"*Colonel Frankenstein,*" she hissed. "Wake up, sir."

No response.

She swore under her breath, and looked through the window of the toyshop. Inside the door stood a fridge full of bottles of water and cans of Coke; the power was off, but that made no difference for what she had in mind.

Larissa stood up and pushed open the door; it was locked, but it took only a fraction of her supernatural strength to pop it out of its frame. She grabbed two bottles of water from the fridge, unscrewed the first, and splashed half of it into Frankenstein's face. His eyes flew open and he sat up, coughing and spluttering and wiping water from his skin.

"What the hell are you playing at?" he growled.

"Saving your life," said Larissa, and gestured at the two smears of blood that had been living, breathing vampires thirty seconds earlier. "You're welcome."

Amid the charred ruins of Carcassonne, at the heart of the raging battle, Qiang wound his T-Bone back in and ran for cover.

The battle was completely unprecedented, both in its scale and ferocity. Thousands and thousands of Operators and vampires were raging across a space more than a mile wide and half a mile deep as a constant rattle of gunfire and a pall of grey smoke filled the air.

The Chinese Operator was not a vampire – PROMETHEUS had been suspended before his name had been called – but he was causing as much damage to Dracula's army as any of his turned colleagues; he had destroyed nine in the first five minutes, his T-Bone and MP7 working in perfect harmony, his situational awareness almost supernatural in itself. A vampire loomed in front of him, and he shot him in the heart with his T-Bone without so much as a second thought; the man exploded with a confused look on his face, and as the stake wound back in again, Qiang checked his position and considered his options.

They could keep killing vampires one at a time, but there were no guarantees they could outlast Dracula's followers. The ultimate result of the battle lay in the hands of Jamie and Angela and the rest of the strike team, but that didn't mean there was nothing that could be done on the ground to help tip the odds in their favour. The vampire army was a seething mass, seemingly obeying no set plan or implementing any identifiable strategy, but as Qiang surveyed the battlefield, it was clear that there *was* a hierarchy at work; behind the hacking and slashing lines of men and women, above the drawbridge that controlled ground access to the walled city, a small group of vampires surrounded a single man.

He is important, he thought. *Whoever he is. He is in command.*

Qiang checked his surroundings, then bolted from cover. He ran away from the battle in a low crouch, circling up and round the side of the hill, past the half-burnt ruins of a hotel, and down into what had once been Carcassonne's moat. He crept forward across the grass, keeping to the deep shadows at the base of the towering walls, and looked up at the drawbridge; the vampire commander's attention was focused entirely on the battle, and, as Qiang got nearer, he spoke to one of the vampires surrounding him in rapid Spanish.

The Chinese Operator stopped and raised his T-Bone, steadying the vampire's chest in the centre of its sights.

He took a deep breath, and pulled the trigger.

62

DEATH'S GREY LAND, PART THREE

CARCASSONNE, SOUTHERN FRANCE

Osvaldo was so focused on the battle that when he heard a bang and saw something hurtling towards him out of the corner of his eye, he was almost fatally slow to react.

His eyes flared as he turned his head away, his hand coming up automatically to protect himself. Something hot and sharp splattered the hand to pieces, sending severed fingers flying into the dark night air, and tore along the side of his head. His right ear was ripped off and spun away in front of him, before a metal stake followed it, trailing a gleaming wire and taking most of his cheek with it. Blood sprayed into the air as his intact hand flailed for the speeding wire and took hold of it. He yanked the wire with all his strength as the pain hit him; he tipped back his head and screamed, his eyes blazing with crimson fire. From down in the moat, a dark shape was jerked into the air, its limbs flailing, and crashed down on to the wooden boards of the drawbridge.

The soldier's helmet flew off as he hit the ground, and Osvaldo saw an infuriating lack of fear in the man's eyes; he saw determination, and something close to resignation, but that was all. Osvaldo's head was full of fire, and his hand felt like it had been soaked in acid; he raised it to his face, saw the spurting stumps where his fingers had been, and felt bright, savage rage. As his guards, who had been unforgivably slow to respond to the attack, turned towards him with wide eyes, he leapt on the soldier and took hold of his head. The man kicked and fought, until Osvaldo hammered his head down on the wooden planks with a sound like a cracking egg, and the man's eyes rolled white. He slammed it down again, and again, a howl of pain and fury erupting from his mouth, until all he was holding in his one good hand was blood and limp flesh. He staggered to his feet, his guards staring at him, and licked the blood from his hand; the pain receded, and he looked hungrily down at the mess that was left of the soldier.

No, he told himself. *It would not be proper. Control yourself.*

"Blood," he growled. "Bring me blood. Now."

One of the guards nodded, and raced away into the city. Osvaldo took a deep breath, and turned his gaze back to the raging battle; the blackened ground was now so littered with corpses and soaked with blood that it was rapidly becoming a swamp. He took a deep breath, lifted his radio from his belt, and pressed the SEND button.

"Now, my lord?" he asked.

"No," came Dracula's voice. "Not yet. I will tell you when it is time."

Julian ducked as a vampire soared over his head, reloaded his MP5, and ran forward with the submachine gun set against his shoulder.

The battle around him was raging chaos, but he felt no fear. His professional instincts, which he had feared lost during his years of inaction, had burst to the fore and taken over; to Julian, it suddenly felt like the time since his false death – the awful, *wasted* time – had passed in a heartbeat.

He sighted down the MP5's barrel and fired into a cluster of vampires descending from the dark sky. They scattered, snarling and hissing, but one wasn't fast enough; a bullet took him above his left eye and ripped off the top of his head. The glow in the vampire's eyes disappeared as he fell to the ground, blood and brain oozing from the gaping crater in his skull. Julian drew his stake, and was about to plunge it into the stricken man's heart when a dark figure raced across the blasted landscape and beat him to it. The vampire burst, and the Operator turned towards him, visor raised, a wild grin on his face, his eyes glowing with red fire.

Julian stopped dead, panic rushing through him.

It was Jack Williams, one of the many men and women who had joined Blacklight during the period in which Julian had been one of the Department's senior Operators, and one of the relatively small number of combatants who would undoubtedly recognise him. His gloved hand rose involuntarily to his visor, checking that his face was still hidden, and touched smooth plastic.

"Good shooting!" shouted Jack. "Come on."

Julian nodded, and followed his former colleague down into a broken concrete trench. They scrambled up a pile of rubble at the other end of the valley, and emerged behind a trio of vampires backing away from an advancing line of Operators. Jack's stake was still in his hand, and Julian drew his own.

In the moment before they leapt forward and plunged their stakes into the backs of the retreating vampires, his mind turned to his son, who was even younger than Jack, and even more inexperienced, despite the astonishing things he had done in his brief Blacklight career.

Please let him be OK, thought Julian. *That's all I ask. Just let him be OK.*

Jamie's eyes opened as a boot stamped down towards his chest.

His head was spinning and his limbs felt like lead, but he managed to bring a hand up and deflect the foot; it crunched against his shoulder, sending a bolt of agony through his body. The pain galvanised him, and as the vampire stumbled, his balance momentarily compromised, Jamie rolled to the side and pushed the man's leg as hard as he could. The vampire toppled to the ground as Jamie got to his feet, a low growl rumbling from his throat. The vampire stood up and stared at him, his glowing eyes flicking to the weapons on his belt. Jamie took a step forward, letting his hand go to the grip of his T-Bone, hoping that the threat appeared convincing; his legs felt unsteady beneath him, and he thought he might be about to throw up.

The vampire hissed, and took a step backwards. The road they were standing in was narrow, and Jamie moved to one side, trying to show his enemy an escape route: a crossroads barely ten metres behind him, wreathed in deep shadow. The vampire backed further away, his eyes smouldering. Jamie took another step, willing the man to retreat; after a long, still moment, the man took his chance and raced away along the road. Jamie waited until he disappeared round the corner before he let out the breath he had been holding; he felt dizzy and shaky, and was genuinely unsure what would have happened if the vampire had attacked him.

A thick grunt echoed against the high stone walls that surrounded him. Jamie drew his T-Bone, and pointed it unsteadily in the direction the vampire had fled, where the sound had come from. For several long seconds, nothing happened. Then something came flying out of the shadows at the crossroads, something that bounced and rolled across the cobblestones and came to rest at his feet. Jamie looked down, and felt his stomach revolve.

It was the vampire's head.

The man's eyes rolled as his mouth worked furiously, as though he was still trying to speak. Jamie stared, then took a staggering step backwards, his T-Bone raised, his eyes flaring red behind his visor.

"Who's there?" he shouted. "Show yourself!"

A figure walked round the shadowy corner, dragging something behind it. Jamie's finger tightened on the trigger as the shape moved into the light, then relaxed as he breathed out with relief.

"Don't shoot," said Valentin, a broad smile on his pale face, and threw the decapitated body of the vampire to the ground beside its head.

Jamie lowered the T-Bone. "Jesus," he said. "Are you all right? Have you seen any of the others?"

"I'm fine," said Valentin. "And no, I haven't. You?"

"No," said Jamie. He twisted the comms dial on his belt. "Strike team, come in. Larissa? Angela? Is anyone there?"

"I'm here," replied Larissa, and Jamie felt relief spread through his chest. "I'm with Colonel Frankenstein. Are you all right?"

"Yes," he said. "I'm with Valentin and we're both OK. Have you seen Angela?"

"No."

"Shit," he said. "All right. Fly straight up."

"Why?" asked Larissa.

"So I can see where you are," he said, and glanced at Valentin. "Stay here."

The ancient vampire nodded. Jamie rose slowly into the air, scanning the sky for the vampires that had ambushed them. He saw no movement until Larissa appeared in the distance, maybe two hundred metres away across the rooftops.

"Got you," he said. "Stay there. We'll come to you."

"OK," replied Larissa.

"Valentin," said Jamie, looking down to the street below him. "Get up here."

The youngest Rusmanov appeared at his side, and the two vampires flew towards Larissa; as they passed above the maze of streets and yards and alleyways, Jamie kept his gaze fixed downwards, searching for any sign of Angela, but seeing nothing. They reached their squad mate, and followed her down to where Frankenstein was waiting for them, outside a toyshop on a narrow road.

"Everyone in one piece?" asked Jamie.

The members of the strike team nodded.

"What about Angela?" asked Larissa.

"We'll find her," said Jamie. "Until we do, she can look after herself."

"So what's the plan?" asked Frankenstein.

"Same as it was," said Jamie, and felt heat rise back into his eyes. "Kill Dracula."

Before she opened her eyes, Angela was aware of the pain.

It filled her, radiating from her hands and feet and coursing through her body, hot and sharp. She grimaced, and as she forced her eyelids open, she tried to move.

Nothing happened.

Fear flooded her system with adrenaline. She was suspended above the ground, over a jumbled pile of wooden benches, and as her eyes adjusted to the gloom, she saw that she was inside a church; carved stone pillars rose up towards an ornate ceiling, with great panels of stained glass between them. There was something hard and flat behind her; she tried to move forward, to push against it, but remained still. She could remember nothing since the vampires had swooped out of the clouds above them; she had no idea how much time had passed since the attack, or what had happened to her in that time.

Then Angela turned her head, and saw.

Her arms were stretched straight out against a plank of wood, parallel to the floor below, and nails had been hammered through the palms of her hands. Her eyes widened, her stomach churning; she looked down, straining her neck as far as she was able, and saw metal sticking out of her feet.

Crucified, she realised, her mind teetering on the edge of shock. *I've been crucified. Oh God. Oh God.*

The pain intensified, surging through her like a wave of acid. She flexed her muscles, trying to thrash against whatever she was pinned to – *a cross, it's a cross, oh God* – but didn't move a millimetre; she tried to bring the fire into her eyes, to force her vampire side to the surface, but felt nothing but pain and emptiness. She tried to think around the pain, to push it aside, but it was so big, so *huge*, that she could barely form a rational thought; she had never felt so weak, so drained of energy.

She looked down again, and saw blood. It was pooled at the base of the cross, running freely down her legs from somewhere inside her uniform, and Angela understood what had been done to her; she had been bled, to make sure she was too weak to resist.

Panic overcame her, and she screamed in the silent stillness of the church, an animal howl of terror and pain. Her head swam, and she fought against the shock that was threatening to drag her down into unconsciousness, even though she had never felt so tired, so exhausted, so utterly *helpless*.

Footsteps.

She forced her eyes to focus and saw a figure walk slowly down the centre of the nave. It was a man in his forties, with precisely parted hair and neat, ironed clothes; had it not been for the dripping hammer in his hand, he could easily have passed for an accountant, or an estate agent. He stopped below her and looked up into her eyes with an expression so blank and empty that Angela thought for an awful second that she was going to burst into tears.

"Tell me," he said. "Tell me how much it hurts."

She stared at him, her eyes wide and wet, bile churning in her stomach. Then shock and pain finally overwhelmed her, and she sank into welcome oblivion.

63

DEATH'S GREY LAND, PART FOUR

CARCASSONNE, SOUTHERN FRANCE

Less than a hundred metres away, on the second floor of the Hôtel de la Cité, Alan Foster felt the knot of nerves in his stomach tighten as the door of the room adjacent to theirs opened.

He and Cynthia had been imprisoned in Room 31 for almost a week, and although Foster would have been forced to admit that it was unusually luxurious, it was still a cell. They had been wearing the same clothes for six days, washing them each night in the bath and drying them on the radiator, and eating only what their vampire captors thought to bring them; mostly potato crisps and an occasional bag of sweets or chocolate bar.

Minibar food, thought Foster, as he picked up the result of two hours' careful work and tested its weight in his hand.

The window beside the bed only opened a few centimetres at the top. It was barely enough to provide the warm, stuffy room with even the slightest breeze, but more than enough to allow the distant rattle of gunfire – a sound Foster was more than familiar with – into the room. He didn't know exactly what, but it was clear that *something* was happening. Their vampire captors had checked on them every three hours since they had first been locked inside the room, but almost twelve had passed since the last visit, leaving Foster sure that the time to make a move had come; he believed this was the best chance he was going to get.

The club was as ugly a weapon as he had carried in his long military career. For several days, he had been working at the screws that held the metal towel bar to the bathroom wall, chipping away long-dried paint with the corkscrew he had found in their fridge and working at the screws themselves with the back of the safe key. It had been slow work, but Foster was by nature proactive, a man who hated sitting aimlessly around, and he had been pleased to have something tangible to do. That morning, shortly after the last time they had been checked on, the bar had come away from the wall with a small shower of plaster dust and flaked paint. It was almost a metre long, and although it was hollow, and therefore not as heavy as he would have liked, it was solid enough.

"So you've got it," Cynthia had said. "What now?"

"I'm going to use it," he had replied, giving her a tight smile.

Working quickly, he had wrapped a small hand towel round one end of the bar, looping it over and over and tying it off as tightly as he could. It was not perfect – if he swung it with enough force, the towel might simply fly off – but it was the best he could do under the circumstances. Their luggage was in a hotel bedroom outside the medieval walls, providing it had not been burned to ashes, along with seemingly the rest of modern Carcassonne, but Cynthia had kept hold of her handbag when they were seized by Dracula's followers, and for that he would be eternally grateful. He wrapped the two water glasses from the bathroom in another towel, stamped on them, and carried the towel over to the desk in the corner. He popped the cap off the can of hairspray his wife always carried in her bag, without fail, and sprayed the towel-covered end of the metal bar. While it was still wet and sticky, he pressed pieces of broken glass into the towel, pointing the sharp edges outwards as much as possible; once the head of the club was coated in glass, he emptied the rest of the hairspray on to it, coating it on all sides. Fifteen minutes later, it had dried as hard as resin.

The door on the other side of the wall slammed shut, and Foster listened as footsteps stopped outside their room. He moved silently into position behind the door as Cynthia lay on the bed, flicking through channels on the TV with apparent nonchalance. A key turned, and the door swung slowly open. Foster held his breath, and waited. The vampire stepped into the room, barely more than a boy, twenty-one at most, with a bored look on his face and a gun in his hands.

"Where's your—"

Foster brought the club down with all his strength. It hit the vampire behind his right ear, slicing open a wide flap of scalp and driving him down on to one knee. The gun tumbled to the carpet and red bloomed momentarily in the vampire's eyes until Foster hit him again, and he slid unconscious to the floor.

Foster kicked the door shut, his heart beating rapidly in his chest. Cynthia was on her feet, staring down at the stricken figure with a look of outright disgust.

"Get the gun," he said. "Don't look. I don't want you to see this."

Cynthia nodded, picked up the gun, and stepped into the bathroom. As soon as she was out of sight, Foster brought the club down again, and again, and again, until all that remained of the vampire's head was a lumpen smear on the carpet. He knew it wasn't dead, but it would neither be able to follow them or raise the alarm, and that was good enough for now.

"OK," he said.

Cynthia reappeared, glanced down at the crimson mess, then fixed him with a look of icy determination. She held the gun out towards him, grip first, and in that moment, he had never been more proud of her, had never loved her more.

He checked the weapon. It was a SIG-Sauer MPX with a full magazine. He nodded appreciatively.

Could be worse, he thought. *Could be a lot worse.*

Across the thundering field of battle, Paul Turner watched Allen, Ovechkin and Tán join the fight and smiled.

No second chances, he thought. *Everything on the line.*

Turner was near the western edge of the battlefield, having fought his way right into the middle, and allowed the flow of the chaos to take him to his left. He wasn't keeping score of the vampires he had destroyed, but he knew it was already half a dozen, probably more; one or two had escaped the speeding stake of his T-Bone, but there was no time for him to be overly hard on himself.

The black-burnt remains of a shopping mall loomed in the darkness before him. He had chased a retreating trio of vampires, who had clearly reached the conclusion that their loyalty to Dracula was not infinite, towards the ruined building; they had disappeared inside, and Turner was taking a moment to compose himself before he went in after them. The Director part of his brain was telling him not to do so, that their nerve had clearly failed them and it was better to simply let them escape, but the part of him that would always be an Operator rejected that idea outright; the only way he would know for certain that they were no longer a threat was when they were dead.

There was a flash of movement, and one of his Department's vampires dropped out of the sky beside him, flipped their visor up and smiled; it was Dominique Saint-Jacques, one of Turner's most trusted Operators.

"Mind if I join you, sir?" he said.

Turner smiled. "Not at all, Captain," he said. "Let's go."

The two men ran into the half-collapsed building, and immediately saw that the inside was even more badly damaged than the outside; the walls and ceiling were black, the floor tiles scorched and cracked, the shops and stalls annihilated so completely that it was impossible to even guess what they had once sold.

Dominique growled, then shot into the air like a bullet from a gun and disappeared in the gloom near the creaking, broken roof as Turner drew his stake. There was a heavy thud, then something fell down towards him like a meteor. One of the vampires he had been chasing hit the ground with a bone-cracking crunch, his eyes swivelling, one side of his face already swelling where – he assumed – Dominique had punched him. He darted forward and staked the twitching vampire, leapt out of the way of the ensuing explosion of blood, and moved deeper into the mall, scanning the dark corners for the two remaining vamps and the blackened ceiling for his colleague.

Another thud, from somewhere high above.

A second later, a female vampire tumbled limply out of the sky. She landed head first on the cracked tiles, and her neck broke as her skull flattened grotesquely on one side. Turner staked her as her eyes rolled and spun, then looked up in time to see Dominique land beside him.

"The third one is still here," growled the French Operator. "I can smell him."

"All right," said Turner. "Let's find him."

They pressed ahead, into a section of the mall that was slightly more intact; the roof was less full of holes, the walls deep brown rather than sooty black. As they approached the exit at the far end of the building, Turner wondered for a moment if the third vampire had somehow slipped past them, or squeezed itself out through a hole and made good its escape. Then a low growl emerged from the corner of the wide space, and he saw what had happened.

The third vampire had backed himself into a corner from which there was no way out; the walls around him were still standing and the ceiling above was still solid, creating a concrete box that the vampire was pressing itself against the back of, his eyes glowing red, his face a mask of profound panic as he shook his head.

"Please," he whispered. "Please don't—"

Turner raised his T-Bone and shot the vampire through the heart.

It exploded with a dull *whump*, spraying the walls and floor with blood that gleamed almost black. He wound the stake back into the T-Bone's barrel and faced his colleague.

"Good work," he said. "Let's get back out there."

"Yes, sir," said Dominique. "How are we doing?"

Turner shrugged. "Right now, I'd say we have the upper hand. But that's not going to matter in the slightest if the strike team fails."

Atop the medieval city, above the Basilique Saint-Nazaire, Dracula forced himself to ignore the delicious screams of pain and terror echoing from inside the church, and focus on the battle as it moved into its second phase.

The initial charge had decimated both armies, entirely as planned. Now the fighting was spread out across the wide landscape, as soldiers and vampires stalked and tracked each other through the ruins; he estimated that there were still more than three thousand men and women fighting for their lives below him. His enemies had done well in the early exchanges, as he had known they would, and it could have been argued that, at this moment, they had the advantage.

Which meant it was time to change the odds.

He drew his radio from his belt and pressed SEND.

"Yes, my lord?" said Osvaldo.

"Now," said Dracula.

64

DEATH'S GREY LAND, PART FIVE

CARCASSONNE, SOUTHERN FRANCE

Captain Guérin was walking through the Field 1 gate when he heard something in the distance.

He was still disappointed at having been left behind when the Multinational Force moved out; he understood that he was not a member of a supernatural Department, and grudgingly accepted General Allen's reasoning that *somebody* had to stay at the camp, but he wished he could have been out there, fighting alongside the Operators who had gathered from every corner of the globe. He had just conducted a patrol of the perimeter and was about to head back into the command centre to get the latest information from the battlefield, but now he paused.

The noise had been soft, as low and distant as the wind moving through the trees surrounding the sprawling camp, and the rational part of his brain assured him that was all it was. The primal part of his brain disagreed.

He turned slowly, straining his ears. The camp was quiet; most of its residents were gathered round fires and in tents, huddled over radios and mobile phones, listening for any update on what was taking place less than five miles away. The technical staff and the small security squad that had been left behind were inside the mess hall, silently watching civilian news channels on wall screens. From the far distance, the occasional crackle of gunfire floated into the camp on the evening breeze.

Guérin listened, suddenly aware that his heart was racing, and scanned the dark horizon until his eyes hurt.

He could see nothing. He could hear nothing.

There's nothing there, he told himself.

But he was wrong.

The noise came again, louder this time, and recognition flooded through him; it was the muffled sound of voices.

No, he thought, as he spun round and froze to the spot. *Not voices. It's laughter.*

The vampires appeared over the trees to the north, a dark cloud rolling towards the camp at impossible speed, so many that Guérin could not even hope to count them; the distant points of glowing red light seemed to number in the hundreds, or even the thousands. They reached the treeline and swooped towards the ground; in another few seconds, they would surge over the fence and into Field 11, one of the resident camping fields.

Thousands of men and women, entirely unaware of what was coming.

Unarmed.

Unprepared.

The thought broke Guérin's paralysis. He grabbed his radio as he ran back through the Field 1 gate, bellowing into the handset to anyone who could hear him.

"Vampires! Run! Run for your lives!"

Bob Allen fired his T-Bone into the heart of a vampire, then was thrown to the ground as a deafening blast rang out behind him.

He scrambled across the blood-soaked ash, his heart pounding, and got to his feet in time to see the flaming remains of one of the helicopters that had carried the Multinational Force to the battlefield spin into its neighbour, sending it tumbling out of the sky. It hit the ground and exploded, sending a mushroom cloud of fire blooming into the air and thousands of razor-sharp pieces of metal over the battlefield in a deadly hail. The rest of the helicopter fleet, more than twenty of them, began to rise and bank, pulling themselves up and away from the fire that had suddenly appeared beneath them.

Allen stared, wondering what the hell had happened behind them as they had been fighting. Then he saw three distant plumes of smoke rise from the blasted suburban landscape, and understood.

Shoulder-fired rockets slammed into the underbellies of three more helicopters, blowing them to pieces and triggering a terrible, unstoppable domino effect. The explosions took down four more of the closest helicopters, which spun through the rest, shattering rotor blades and destroying engines. As Allen watched, dumbstruck, the entire fleet sank to the ground in an apocalypse of fire and noise that paused the entire battle. Flames and thick black smoke billowed up into the air as twisted fuselages settled against each other, creating a wall of fire along the northern edge of the battlefield. The NS9 Director desperately searched the sky for parachutes, but saw none.

Nobody is getting out of that, thought Allen. *Nobody.*

Something moved at the centre of the inferno, and for a brief moment Allen hoped he was about to be proved wrong. A dark figure stepped through the flames, followed by another, and another, until a vast group of shadows filled the horizon, all moving forward with red light where their eyes should have been.

Jesus, thought Allen. *Oh Jesus Christ. We're dead.*

We're all dead.

The line of vampires was at least as large as the army that had lined up against them, possibly even larger. It came across the ruined landscape without hurrying, stretching out in both directions as far as Allen could see, and for a long moment he just stared at it; the Multinational Force was now vastly outnumbered and surrounded, its air support was burning in a huge twisted pyre, and he didn't have the slightest idea what to do.

Dead. All dead.

Guérin's voice burst into his ears. "Vampires!" he shouted. "Run! Run for your lives!"

Reserves of adrenaline that Allen would not have believed he possessed surged through him, clearing his head. He twisted the comms dial on his belt and shouted directly into the ear of every Operator still alive on the battlefield.

"Battalion Three, return to camp immediately! Battalions Four through Six! Regroup at rally point, on the double! New hostiles to the north!"

In his office at the top of the Direction Générale de la Sécurité Intérieure's anonymous building in Paris's seventeenth arrondissement, Central Director Jean Vallens watched a live satellite feed of the helicopters crashing to the ground in flames.

He stared, incredulous, as fire roared into the sky. He had listened to the NATO briefings inside the displaced persons camp, and had been heartened by the confidence of General Allen and his fellow Directors; their faith in a positive outcome had at least allowed him to hope, if not fully *believe*. Now, as the fires burned and men and women dropped like flies, he realised their faith had been misplaced.

Movement filled the screen, as hundreds and hundreds of vampires made their way towards the burning helicopters and the remnants of the Multinational Force beyond. For a second, Vallens thought his eyes must be playing tricks on him; the vampires seemed to be appearing out of thin air. Then he saw a cluster of dark figures emerge from the ruined shell of a suburban house, and realised what he was seeing; the vampires were swarming up out of the cellars and basements of the buildings that had burned down. They must have been hiding in them since the fires had been put out, when the vast cloud of grey smoke had hidden the city from view; the Multinational Force had quite literally driven and flown over their heads.

Such patience, he thought. *To stay underground for three days, just waiting. Such careful planning. Incredible.*

Vallens watched as the second vampire front moved in from the north, cutting off the primary route of retreat and surrounding the surviving Operators.

"Are you seeing this?" he asked. He was alone in his office, but the speakerphone on his desk was connected to a conference call with Alain Ducroix, the French Army's Chief of Staff, and Pascal Desjardins, the Minister of Defence; the three men comprised the central brain trust of their country's domestic and military intelligence. "Are you watching?"

"I am watching," said Desjardins. "What do we do, Alain?"

"I'll update NATO," said Ducroix. "Jean, talk to Captain Guérin and get us an update on the grand. Then you're going to have to brief the President."

Four-fifths of the strike team made their way up the medieval city's main thoroughfare, towards the high towers of the Basilica at the summit.

The low angle hid Dracula from view, but Frankenstein had no doubt the first vampire was still there, floating in the darkness and overseeing the destruction and chaos he had unleashed far below.

"So quiet," said Larissa.

"Spooky, isn't it?" said Valentin, smiling happily.

"Don't you take anything seriously?" asked Larissa. "Are you just incapable? Our friends are dying down there, and one of our squad mates is missing."

The ancient vampire's smile disappeared. "I have taken few things in my life more seriously than this, my dear Lieutenant Kinley. I'm sorry if my small joke was so terribly offensive."

"Shut up, both of you," said Jamie. "We don't have time for bickering. We need to—"

The explosion was huge, even across the distance between the northern edge of the battlefield and the old city. Frankenstein turned with his squad mates and saw orange flames light up the landscape as the Multinational Force's helicopters sank out of the sky in a tangle of metal and smoke and fire.

"Holy shit," said Jamie, the glow in his eyes darkening.

"Do we go back?" asked Larissa.

"No," said Valentin, instantly. "Absolutely not. Helicopters don't matter."

"What about the people in them?" asked Jamie.

"Valentin is right," said Frankenstein, the words tasting foul in his mouth. "We can't do anything for them. The only way we can help is by doing what we were sent to do."

Silence descended over the strike team.

They know I'm right, thought the monster. *If we fail, burning helicopters and dead pilots and Operators will mean less than nothing.*

"All right," said Jamie, tearing his gaze away from the fires and looking at his squad mates. "We go on."

The young Lieutenant strode up the steep, cobbled road. Frankenstein followed him with Valentin and Larissa at his sides, their footsteps echoing in the warm evening air. They passed empty cafés and looted shops, their stock scattered across the pavements outside broken windows and missing doors; chocolates and wine and tiny plastic reproductions of the city itself lay discarded on the ground.

The road curved to the right as it rose. Jamie led the strike team round the bend, his T-Bone drawn and raised, then stopped dead in his tracks.

On the eastern side of the battlefield, fighting resumed with even greater ferocity. Ellison had stopped along with everybody else to watch the destruction of the helicopters, but had quickly realised there was nothing she could do and decided instead to take advantage of the situation; she had staked three distracted vampires before any of them had time to realise what was happening.

General Allen had bellowed into her ear as the chaos burst back into life, ordering three Battalions towards the new vampires approaching from the north; instantly, hundreds of Operators disengaged from the battle and sprinted back the way they had come. The order didn't apply to her – she, along with the rest of the vampire Operators, was part of Battalion One – so she watched them go, cursing silently at how easily their force had been split, even though she had been expecting something similar; she had never really believed that Dracula would simply put his entire army front and centre and let the Multinational Force take them on.

A chorus of low growls rang out, and Ellison grimaced behind her visor; by letting her focus drift for just a split second, she had allowed herself to become surrounded by vampires. There were four of them, three women and a man, all of them soaked with blood and staring at her with hungry crimson eyes. She took a deep breath, formulating what she was going to do in her mind, then moved, a black blur in the deepening gloom.

She leapt at the closest vampire, taking her by surprise, and plunged her stake into the woman's heart before she had time to so much as raise her hands in defence. The vampire exploded in Ellison's face, soaking her uniform and coating her visor with gore. She kept moving forward, creating separation as she flipped the visor up; there was no time to clear it.

A hand clawed the air, missing her eyes by millimetres. She leant backwards and jabbed the stake at the trailing arm; it found the inside of an elbow, tore through the skin and split the joint entirely. The arm folded back the wrong way and its owner, a woman with dark hair and bright, burning eyes, screamed in sudden agony. Ellison yanked the stake out and swung it into the side of the woman's head, sending her sprawling, then turned to face the two remaining vampires.

The third woman growled, and took a step backwards. Her eyes were blazing with hatred, but Ellison was pleased to see a flicker of fear in them too; the speed and savagery with which her comrades had been despatched had clearly left her uncertain. The male vampire leapt forward, his arms outstretched, his fingers curled into claws, but Ellison easily sidestepped his lunge and punched her stake into his neck as he careered past. Blood sprayed out in a shocking, high-pressure torrent as the man crashed to the ground, clutching at his gushing throat. With two lightning-quick movements, she staked both the man and the unconscious woman; they exploded as she turned back to face the final vampire, a smile on her blood-splattered face.

The woman stared at her for a long moment, her skin ghostly pale, then leapt into the air and fled. Ellison watched her go, satisfaction coursing through her, then turned back to the battle, her bloody stake in her hand, her visor still up, and saw a vampire with a long knife in its hand swooping towards the back of an Operator. Acting on pure instinct, she drew back her arm and threw the stake as hard as she possibly could.

It streaked through the air, glinting wickedly in the light of the burning helicopters, and struck the vampire just below its ribcage. The man tumbled screaming to the ground, as the Operator who had been about to receive a knife between the shoulder blades spun round. The dark figure staked the screeching man, then turned towards Ellison and raised its visor.

"Thanks," said Jack Williams. "I owe you one."

"Don't mention it," she said. "Are you OK?"

"Surviving," said Jack, and smiled. "For now, at least. Do you want to kill some vampires with me?"

Ellison smiled at him. "I'd be delighted."

Emery stared up at the crucified woman, trying to decide whether to wake her up so he could hurt her again.

He knew – had *always* known – that the way he saw the world wasn't how everyone else saw it, and, although he had always refused to do so for the many psychiatrists and psychologists who had asked him over the years, he was quite capable of explaining the difference; he was simply unable to attach any importance to other people, to their feelings, their wants and desires, and – ultimately – their lives. He knew they were *real*, in the sense that they *physically existed*, but beyond that, they meant nothing to him; they were like ghosts, like grey shadows moving through the world. There was no reason to respect them, or consider them.

No reason not to hurt them.

No reason at all.

The woman groaned as her eyelids fluttered. Emery understood enough to know she would be considered attarctive by the other ghosts, but such things were of no interest to him. To him, she was merely a plaything.

Soft, fragile meat, and nothing more.

"Wake up," he whispered.

The woman stirred again, and opened one eye. Emery held up a screwdriver, let her see it, and felt familiar warmth in his stomach as the eye widened with fear.

"I'm sorry," he lied. "This is really going to hurt."

"Be straight with me," said the French President. "Is the battle lost?"

"No, sir," said Minister Desjardins. "But the situation is precarious. That cannot be denied."

"Do the rest of you agree with that assessment?" asked the President.

"Yes, sir," said Chief of Staff Ducroix.

"Yes, sir," said Vallens, in his empty office. "I agree."

"So be it," said the President. "General Ducroix, I want you to release my Presidential launch codes. Transmit them to Mont Verdun and tell them to order the *Terrible* to arm their missiles and load the target package. There is to be no launch unless I personally give the order. Is that clear?"

"It is clear, sir," said Ducroix. "Although I urge you to give the Multinational Force more time."

"As do I," said Vallens.

"I will give them every chance to complete their mission," said the President. "But if they fail, I will not hesitate to do what is necessary. If that is a problem for any of you, let me know now so I can relieve you of duty."

Jesus, thought Vallens. *This is real. This is actually happening.*

"That won't be necessary, sir," said Ducroix. "I will transmit the codes and your order to Mont Verdun."

"Good," said the President. "Do it now."

65

DEATH'S GREY LAND, PART SIX

CARCASSONNE, SOUTHERN FRANCE

Jamie stared at the twelve vampires standing in the middle of the road, his eyes burning with heat.

For a long moment, nobody moved a muscle. Then, as if responding to a silent shout of 'Charge', the strike team sprinted up the street, Jamie taking the lead. He and his colleagues were outnumbered three to one, but the fight was still nothing short of a mismatch; it was over in thirty bloody, brutal seconds.

He accelerated towards the closest vampire like a human wrecking ball. The man swung a punch that would have annihilated most people, but which seemed to Jamie like it was moving in slow motion; he slipped past it and hammered a gloved fist on to the point of the vampire's chin. The man was sent flying, his eyes rolling back white, his limbs limp, and collided with the stone wall above the door of a café with a bone-cracking impact, before sliding to the ground in a heap.

Beside him, Frankenstein crouched low and swung one of his tree-trunk arms into the stomach of a female vampire with blonde hair down to her waist and crimson hatred in her eyes; the breath exited her lungs with a sound like a bursting balloon, and she folded to the ground, her eyes bulging in their sockets. The monster plunged a stake into her heart as Jamie did the same to the vampire he had punched.

Two down, he thought, grinning savagely behind his visor.

Larissa tore into the vampires, her stake glinting under the remaining street lights. She plunged it through the heart of one, reversed it, and brought it around in a backhand sweep that was little more than a gleaming blur. Two vampires burst with thunderclaps of blood, but she gave no sign of even having noticed; she advanced on a third, who staggered backwards, a look of outright terror on his face. She leapt through the air, as fast as a striking cobra, and slammed the sole of her boot into the vampire's neck; his face turned instantly purple as the red glow died in his eyes. He made a hoarse gasping noise, followed by a thick grunt as her stake broke through his sternum and a loud pop as he exploded across the cobblestones.

That's five, thought Jamie.

One of the vampires leapt on to his back, but he threw it over his shoulder without so much as flinching. The woman spun up into the air, a look of immense surprise on her face, then shrieked in pain as he drove her down on to the street shoulder first. The bone broke, and her arm collapsed uselessly across the cobbles. The shriek reached an ungodly pitch and volume, and the vampire looked almost relieved when Jamie staked her.

Six.

"Catch," said Valentin.

Jamie turned towards the old vampire, plucked something red and dripping out of the air as it flew towards him, and looked at it; it was a human heart, still beating in his gloved hand.

"Jesus, Valentin," he shouted, and dropped the organ. He stamped it flat, and jumped as a man sprawled on the other side of the street burst into strings of gore. Valentin ran through the steaming mess, lifted two of the remaining vampires into the air by their throats, hammered their heads together with a sound like breaking glass, and hurled them down the road. They fell in a tangled heap at Frankenstein's feet; the monster shook his head, then crouched down and staked them quickly in turn.

Nine.

One of the final three vampires, a man in his early sixties with a mane of silver-grey hair, rushed towards Jamie. He hammered his stake up through the man's ribs, lifting him off the ground and splitting his heart in two; he saw no value in prolonging the man's suffering. The vampire burst, drenching him with blood. Jamie gagged behind his visor; the smell of the steaming liquid was overpoweringly strong.

Ten. Time to finish this.

Jamie drew his T-Bone and fired it through the back of a vampire woman as she retreated from Larissa, her hands raised in surrender. He hit the button that wound the metal stake back in before the woman had even exploded; it sped back through a cloud of blood and lodged in the barrel. He turned and fired the weapon again, sending the dripping stake through the armpit of the last of the vampires, a man who was staring around at the carnage that had befallen his colleagues with wide-eyed incredulity. The man burst with a wet thunderclap; the stake wound back in as silence descended over the cobbled street.

Twelve.

Jamie flipped his visor up and looked at his squad mates. There were small smiles on all their faces, the thrill of the fight combined with the pride of overwhelming victory. Jamie opened his mouth to congratulate them, then frowned as gunfire echoed down the narrow street, from somewhere near the summit of the medieval city.

There are no Operators up there, he thought. *What the hell is going on?*

On the bridge of the *Terrible*, Commander Masson felt a shiver race up his spine as the command screen lit up.

A printer rattled instantly to life, spitting out the order that arrived from the Central Military Command facility at Mont Verdun. Masson tore off the sheet of paper and read the short paragraph.

"Sir?" asked Clément, the *Terrible*'s executive officer. "Is it a launch order?"

"No," he said, and shook his head. "Give me weapons control."

Clément nodded, and opened a line to the small station one deck below where the weapons officer sat hunched in front of a dozen screens and terminals. Masson lifted down his comms handset and held it to the side of his face.

"Weapons control?"

"Yes, sir."

"Load targeting package 0193/3475. Arm missiles five through eight and await further orders."

"Yes, sir."

Masson placed the handset back in its cradle.

"Is this happening, sir?" asked Clément, his face pale.

"I don't know," said Masson. "Not yet, at least. I want an immediate ship-readiness report. If we are ordered to launch, I want the protocols followed to the letter."

"Yes, sir," said Clément. "Right away."

"And tell the crew to stay calm," said Masson. "This might still come to nothing."

"Do you really think so, sir?"

"No," said Masson. "But I live in hope."

*　　*　　*

Guérin ran towards Field 1, his uniform soaked in blood that wasn't his.

He had raised the alarm as loudly and widely as he could, but it had not been enough; the killing had already started as the security squad and tech staff and charity workers emerged from the mess hall, frowns of concern on their faces. The first screams had come from Field 11, but had quickly spread throughout the entire camp, which now resembled a scene from Hell; fires were burning in every field, filling the sky with an orange glow, and everywhere he looked were vampires, trailing glowing streaks of red light as they chased panicking men and women in all directions.

The gunfire that had briefly rung out as the security Operators attempted to repel the invaders had all but fallen silent; Guérin had no idea if any of them were still alive, or whether they had tried to flee with everyone else, and as he sprinted through the Field 1 gate, he realised it made little difference.

The command centre loomed before him, an angular sprawl of tents and buildings. He had been in Field 5, firing his MP5 at vampires that seemed as insubstantial as smoke, when Central Director Vallens' voice had sounded in his ear, demanding an update on the situation on the ground. He had screamed something incoherent, his attention entirely focused on the massacre unfolding around him; he had temporarily forgotten the potential consequences of Paris believing the battle was lost, but now they filled his mind, huge and unimaginable.

A vampire dropped silently out of the dark sky in front of him, and he shot it in the face without breaking stride. The vampire crashed to the ground, rolling and screaming. Guerin knew it wasn't dead, but didn't care as long as he was not stopped before he reached the command centre and spoke to Vallens; what happened after that didn't matter. He raced forward, as men and women on all sides were plucked into the air and came back down in pieces, then staggered as a huge explosion hammered the air to his right; he guessed it was the vehicle fuel store going up. He glanced over at the rising cloud of fire, steadied himself and ran on.

The security door slammed shut and locked behind him as Guérin sprinted into the command centre. The entire building shook as something hit it with a deafening thud, followed by another, and another. The lights above his head flickered but he ignored them, as he ignored the sound of the outer tents being ripped apart as the vampires sought a way into the command centre. There were several centimetres of reinforced steel around its nerve centre, but he had no idea how long it would withstand their efforts; he would just have to hope it was long enough.

The main screen above the comms bench was displaying a high-resolution satellite feed of the battle, and Guérin felt his blood run cold as he stared at it. The Multinational Force was still fighting, and still numbered in the many hundreds, at least, but was about to be encircled by the second front of vampires approaching from the north, from in front of the vast fire caused by the destruction of the helicopters. He scrolled through the secure comms list, selected Central Director Vallens' name, and paused.

Maybe you shouldn't try to stop them, whispered a voice in the back of his head. *Maybe they're right. Maybe it's the only way to save this situation.*

He stared for a long moment, then clicked CALL. He could not allow a nuclear launch on French soil without at least being able to say he had done all he could to stop it.

"Guérin?" said Vallens.

"Sir," he said. "The camp is overrun, and I don't know how long I can stay on the line. But you can't let them do this, sir. You have to give the Operators more time. You have to—"

"Captain," interrupted Vallens. "There's nothing more I can do. It's out of my hands."

"What do you mean?"

"The codes have been transmitted to Mont Verdun," said Vallens. "The decision now rests solely with our President."

"Has he given the launch order?" asked Guerin.

"Not yet," said Vallens. "But if he decides to, there's nothing I can do to stop him."

Guérin stared at the satellite feed, unable to think of a remotely appropriate response to what the DGSI Director was saying.

"Are you still there, Captain?" asked Vallens. "Can you get out?"

He grimaced. "I don't think so, sir."

"I'm sorry."

"It's not your fault, sir," he said. "I'll hold them off as long as I can."

"I'm sure you will," said Vallens, his voice low. "Good luck, Captain."

"Thank you, sir," said Guérin. "Out."

He clicked END, and checked the magazine of his MP5.

Seven rounds, he thought. *It could be worse. Could be a lot better, though.*

There were thousands of full clips in the armoury, barely a hundred metres from where he was standing, but he knew without checking the camp's CCTV monitors that there was no possible way he could reach them. The command centre door thudded again, and Guérin saw a large dent appear at its centre. The sounds of movement around the secure room intensified, until it sounded like he was standing at the centre of a hurricane. From somewhere beyond the reinforced inner walls came the shriek of rending metal, and he checked the magazine again before he loaded it back into the MP5.

Seven rounds.
Six for them.
One for me, if it comes to it.

Alan Foster ran along the hotel corridor with the vampire guard's keys in his hand, opening door after door and whispering to his fellow hostages to follow him.

Several refused to move, shaking their heads with faces full of shame and fear, and two men told him to stop what he was doing, that he was going to get everyone into trouble. Foster ignored them; he had never believed for a single moment that the vampires were ever going to let them go, and if he was going to die then he was damn well going to do it on his feet rather than cowering behind a door.

By the time he reached the end of the corridor, Cynthia moving silently at his side, there were almost thirty people following him: men and women of at least a dozen nationalities and a range of ages, their faces pale but determined. Foster paused in the atrium at the end of the first floor, from where a wide staircase curved down to the lobby below, and darted his head round the corner of the wall.

"One by the entrance hallway," he whispered, turning back to face the freed hostages. "Two directly below."

"Only three?" asked a Japanese woman. "That is not many."

Foster nodded. She was right; three was *not* many. He had been expecting to find the lobby crawling with vampires; if he was entirely honest, he had been expecting his escape to end in a Butch and Sundance charge, in which he would kill as many vampires as possible before he died a glorious death. But three? *Three might actually be possible.*

"We do this now," he said. "So if you aren't sure, this is your last chance to go back to your rooms. I promise that nobody will think any less of you."

Not a single person moved; the hostages stared at him with clear eyes.

"All right," he said, and pointed at a door on the opposite side of the atrium. "I want you all to go down the service stairs, as quietly as you can. When you hear shots, rush the lobby. There'll be two guns lying on the ground. Take them, and meet me at the bottom of the staircase."

"I'm staying with you," said Cynthia.

Foster shook his head. "No," he said. "You're not. I need you to go with the others."

His wife stared at him, then nodded.

"All right," he said. "Wait till you hear the shots. Now go."

Cynthia led the hostages across the atrium, opened the door, and disappeared through it. The others followed her, as Foster risked a second glance down into the lobby.

The vampires hadn't moved. The two below him were chatting to each other, as the one by the entrance hall stared out of the window, his fingers tapping its wooden frame with obvious boredom.

OK, he told himself. *Let's do this.*

Foster took a deep breath and inched round the corner, the SIG raised to his shoulder. He settled his shoulder against the wall at the top of the staircase, then sighted along the submachine gun's barrel, aiming at the head of one of the vampires standing below him.

Everything slowed down.

The years fell away as Foster's heart beat steadily in his chest; it was as though he had never retired, had never been forced to waste his final years behind a desk.

It was like he was young again.

He took another deep breath, held it, and pulled the trigger.

The vampire's head exploded in a shower of bone and brain, but Foster was already swinging the gun to the right, targeting the second vampire who was now soaked in his partner's blood, his face a perfect expression of wide-eyed shock. Foster shot him above the ear, blowing off the top of his head, and brought the gun round again, searching for the vampire by the reception desk on the far side of the lobby. The man had spun round at the sound of the shots, his eyes blazing red, but either surprise or indecision – *or both* – froze him to the spot; Foster sighted a third time, and shot him in the mouth. The vampire's teeth erupted in a hail of blood, and he sank to his knees, clutching at his ruined face. Foster shot him again and the vampire folded to the ground, limbs twitching.

Below him, a door banged open, followed by the thunder of running footsteps.

Five seconds, he thought, pride flooding through him, as he ran towards the staircase. *Three targets down. Not bad for an old man.*

At the centre of the raging, relentless battle, Bob Allen surveyed the scene, and could no longer reject the truth that had been racing through him since the helicopters had burst into flames.

We're going to lose.

Around him, Operators were fighting with everything they had, with astonishing dedication to a visibly fading hope. The ground was soaked with the remains of dead vampires, reducing wide areas to swamps of ash and blood, but there was no denying the reality. They were killing at a prodigious rate, but the Multinational Force was losing too many of their own; it was only a matter of time until simple mathematics decided the outcome, and, with each minute that passed without word from the strike team, that time was becoming increasingly short.

Allen raised his T-Bone and skewered a vampire soaring above the battlefield like a vulture. As the woman was dragged screaming to the ground, Allen ran towards her, drawing his stake as he did so, a silent plea tumbling through his mind.

Please. Don't let it end like this. Give us a miracle. Please.

Foster sprinted down the stairs as two of the hostages picked up the vampires' guns from where they had fallen. He met them at the bottom as the two large windows at the front of the hotel exploded in a blizzard of flying glass, and vampires poured through them.

"Drive them back!" he yelled.

He dropped to one knee, and started firing. The SIG's bullets sliced through a vampire as she leapt through one of the windows; she crashed against the frame, stuck in a dozen places by broken glass, and hung there. Vampires piled up behind her, and Foster sent bullets into their heads and necks. Behind him, the other two guns roared into life, and although he saw a number of holes appear in the walls and ceiling, plenty of bullets hit home. Blood flew in the air as screams echoed through the lobby and the vampires scrambled backwards, trying to escape the killing zone.

"Cynthia!" he shouted. His wife appeared at his side, and he pointed towards the offices at the rear of the lobby. "Check them! Look for more weapons!"

She ran towards the doors as Foster returned his attention to the wide front of the hotel. The flood of vampires had slowed to a trickle; he shot a woman peering through a window in the head, and heard a gratifying chorus of hisses and growls from outside in the square.

They're nervous, he thought. *They're not sure what to do now.*

"Come out," shouted a voice. "There's no need for any of this. Come out and you can all just leave."

Foster stood up, the SIG still trained on the windows.

"Nothing," said Cynthia, arriving back at his side. "No weapons."

"OK," he said.

"What do we do?" asked one of the hostages. "Do we go?"

"Don't be stupid," said another. "There's no way we can trust them. We should stay here."

"And do what?" asked Foster. "We've got three guns between us. When whatever is happening outside the city is over, the vampires will all come back here and there'll be no way to hold them off. If we stay, we're dead."

"We should have stayed in our rooms," said a woman, staring at him accusingly. "We were safe there."

"For how long?" asked Foster, his voice rising with anger. "If you really believe that they were going to let us go when whatever this is is done, then go back to your room. You can tell them you had nothing to do with it."

"It's too late," hissed the woman. "They'll kill us all now as punishment."

"Then we don't have much of a choice, do we?" he said. "We have to keep going."

"And do what?" she asked.

"Fight," said Foster, simply. "It's our only chance. Maybe some of us will get away."

"*Some of us?*" said the woman. "What about the rest?"

Foster stared at her, and didn't respond.

"Oh my God," she whispered. "We're dead. We're all dead."

"That's enough," said Cynthia. "Nobody made you leave your room."

The woman narrowed her eyes in the direction of Foster's wife, but fell silent. The American Colonel nodded, and faced the rest of the hostages.

"We go straight out the front door, fire our guns empty, and scatter," he said. "Keep running, no matter what you hear, or what happens to anyone else. Is everybody totally clear on that?"

There was a low murmur of agreement.

"All right," said Foster. "Follow me."

He walked across the lobby, his gaze fixed on the windows, alert to a second assault if it came. On the floor near the reception desk, beside the body of the vampire he had shot in the mouth, lay a snub-nosed Uzi machine pistol; he picked it up and held it out to Cynthia, who took it without a word.

Foster reached the door, took a deep breath, and stepped through it. Part of him was expecting to be killed instantly, his throat torn out by a vampire hiding in the shadows outside the entrance, but nothing happened; he stepped on to the cobblestones, his wife beside him, the rest of the hostages behind, and looked at what was waiting for them.

The square was full of vampires.

There had to be at least a hundred of them; they were standing silently in the darkness, with glowing eyes and smiles on their faces. At their centre, regarding him with an expression of open loathing, was the vampire who had caught him and Cynthia as they tried to escape from the carnage that had been unleashed in the city.

"You," growled the man. "Of course it's you. I should have killed you when I set eyes on you."

"You're right," said Foster. "You probably should have."

"At least I get the chance to put that mistake right," said the vampire, his eyes blazing. "Any final words?"

"Go to hell," said Foster.

"You first," said the vampire. "I'll see you there."

Here it comes, he told himself. *This is it. This is the end.*

The crowd of vampires swayed and pulsed in the darkness. Foster silently gave thanks for the life he had lived, for the woman he had been privileged to share it with. Then he wrapped his finger round the SIG's trigger, and prepared to die.

"They are overrun," said the President. "It is time. Order the launch."

Vallens felt ice crawl up his spine. The President's conclusion was inarguable, given the images being relayed from the satellites over Carcassonne and Captain Guérin's description of the situation, but he still could not truly believe what was about to happen.

"Sir, I…" began Ducroix, but the President spoke over him.

"That is a direct order, General. Order the launch."

"Yes, sir," said Ducroix, his voice low and hoarse.

Here we go, thought Vallens. *God help us. And may our children forgive us.*

66

DEATH'S GREY LAND, PART SEVEN

CARCASSONNE, SOUTHERN FRANCE

When Angela swam back into consciousness, she was once again alone inside the church.

The pain seemed less; whether that was because her body had gone into shock, or because she was now so dangerously low on blood that signals were no longer being effectively transmitted to her brain, she didn't know. All she knew was that she could think slightly more clearly, and that if she was going to do anything about her situation, she was going to have to do it now.

She focused all her concentration on her right hand, trying to make it move, even just a millimetre. She gritted her teeth, her head pounding with rising pressure, and pressed as hard as she could; after a long, agonising moment in which nothing happened, her hand began to tremble. She bore down with every bit of strength she had left, her body screaming with pain, and saw her palm slide along the nail that had been pounded through it. Her hand had moved less than a centimetre, but it *had* moved; she relaxed her muscles, and tried her hardest not to burst into tears of relief.

Angela took a deep breath and focused again, working her hand back and forth, faster and faster.

Larissa flew round the curve in the road and stopped dead beside Jamie.

Before them was a beautiful cobbled square, with small, neat shops and cafés on three sides and the façade of a grand hotel on the fourth, its pale stone carved and rising to soaring roofs and ramparts. Standing in front of it, filling the square with a pulsating red glow, were vampires.

Dozens and dozens of vampires.

Their attention was fixed on the stone archway of the hotel entrance, where Larissa could see a small cluster of men and women, several of whom were holding guns.

Who the hell are they? she thought. *The hostages?*

But as she wondered, her heart racing in her chest, the vampires turned, seemingly as one, and looked at the strike team.

A hundred of them, she thought. *At least. And four of us.*

She had been in fights with worse odds, although none of them were experiences she was keen to relive. But there was nothing to be done; there was no backup they could call, no strategy or surprise they could deploy. All they could do was fight, until they could do so no more.

A low growl rose from Jamie's throat. She glanced round, saw the crimson glow below his raised visor and complete absence of fear on her ex-boyfriend's face, and felt her heart surge. It was not in Jamie's nature to back down from anything, a quality that was often maddeningly frustrating, but which, in circumstances like these, was also one of his greatest strengths.

The air crackled with tension, with the prospect of imminent violence, as the vampires stared at them, and Larissa felt the heat in her eyes rise to a temperature that was almost unbearable.

Come on then! she silently screamed. *Come on!*

Out of the corner of her eye, she saw movement. Up by the highest towers of the ancient church, she saw a black silhouette floating in the darkness and two glowing pinpricks of red light as Dracula stared down at them.

You're next, you old monster, she thought. *As soon as we're done here, we're coming for you.*

The tension in the square became unbearable, as though the air itself was alive with electricity. A vampire near the centre of the crowd opened his mouth, his fangs gleaming, presumably to give the order to attack, and Larissa took a deep breath. But before the vampire was able to form the first syllable, a silver-haired man at the front of the small crowd in the hotel entrance raised a submachine gun in hands that were visibly steady, and pulled its trigger.

The gunfire was deafening in the enclosed square. The bullets ripped into the crowd, who had all made the mistake of turning their backs on the man. Screams rang out and blood flew as three more of the – *hostages?* – men and women opened fire; bodies crashed to the ground, blood pouring from them, as the rest of the vampires leapt into the air; panic overwhelmed them as they dodged the deadly streams of lead, all thoughts of attack forgotten, their only focus suddenly on defending themselves.

Jamie saw their chance, as Larissa knew he would.

"Go!" he bellowed, and raced towards the crowd, his MP7 raised. She followed him, a huge smile on her face, her mind blazing with violence.

*　　*　　*

Floating beside the Basilique Saint-Nazaire, Dracula watched as the four soldiers joined the fight in the square below.

They had fought their way up through the medieval city, which deserved a modicum of his respect. If they made it past the remainder of his guard, it would increase, right up until the moment he killed them himself.

We are entering the final act, he thought. *Now we'll see whether I will be required to bloody my hands.*

The command screen on the bridge of the *Terrible* glowed into life again. Commander Masson grabbed the order as it emerged from the printer, and felt his chest tighten.

"What is it, sir?" asked Clément.

Masson passed the page to his executive officer, and watched the man's face pale as he read it.

"I do not understand," said Clément. "How can this be necessary, sir?"

"This order means the battle at Carcassonne is lost," said Masson. "That is the only explanation. Would you have Dracula and his army sweep across the entire country unopposed?"

The executive officer stared at him, but didn't respond.

"Give me weapons control," he said.

Clément grimaced, but opened the comms line. Masson lifted the handset, and waited for the voice on the other end of the line to speak.

"Weapons control."

"This is the Captain," said Masson. "The President of the Republic has ordered the launch of missile six on target package 0193/3475. Please confirm that you understand your order."

"I understand, sir."

"Carry it out immediately."

"Yes, sir."

"Confirm the launch," said Masson.

There was a moment of silence that seemed to stretch out forever, until the entire submarine rumbled beneath his feet and the steady beep of an alarm rang out across the bridge.

"Missile away, sir," said weapons control. "Altitude seven hundred metres, speed two hundred kilometres, both rising. Time to target six point one minutes."

"Very good," said Masson. "Give me thirty-second updates."

"Yes, sir."

Clément stared at him. "What do we do now, sir?" he asked.

"Pray," said Masson. "We pray."

"For them or for us?"

"Both."

Frankenstein raised his M4 to his shoulder and fired the assault rifle point-blank into a panicking group of vampires.

The heavy bullets punched gaping holes in their bodies, shattered bones and severed limbs, and sent them screaming to the ground. The monster checked behind him, and backed up to the edge of the square; he looked to his right, and saw the men and women in the hotel entrance driving back a wave of vampires, kicking and punching and firing guns they had taken from the vampires that were falling all around them. A number of them were lying still on the cobblestones, but the older man, the one with the silver hair who had unleashed the chaos that had quickly engulfed the square, was calmly directing the survivors with quick, clear gestures that left Frankenstein in no doubt whatsoever as to what the man was.

A soldier, he thought, as he laid down a burst of suppressing fire and moved along the front of the hotel. *A soldier if ever I've seen one.*

The square was a frenzy of movement, as the remaining vampires desperately attacked both the Operators who had appeared behind them and the hostages who were now fighting back with such determination; howls and hisses rang out above the constant thunder of gunfire. Vampires were strewn across the ground, bleeding and screaming. The strike team were disabling as many of them as possible as quickly as possible; there would be time to stake them all once the fight was won. Frankenstein could see his squad mates darting back and forth through the crowd in a series of black blurs; despite the thousands of fights he had survived in his long life, they moved with such incredible speed and precision that watching them made him feel like a ham-fisted amateur. Jamie's helmet was gone, and blood was running freely from Larissa's nose, but that appeared to be the extent of the setbacks they had sustained.

The monster sidestepped along the front of the hotel, reloading the M4 as he moved, and arrived at the entrance. The silver-haired man glanced round at him, and nodded; if he was surprised to see such a huge figure dressed all in black, he gave no sign of it.

"NS9?"

"Blacklight," said Frankenstein. "Is this all of you?"

The man fired his SIG, and shook his head. "There's more inside," he said. "They didn't want to come."

Cowards, thought Frankenstein, then silently chastised himself. Fear and torture were incredibly powerful weapons, and he had no idea what the other hostages might have been through since Dracula had taken the old city.

"Thanks for the assist," said the man. "Thought we were done for till you guys showed up."

"No problem," said Frankenstein. He sighted down the M4's barrel and sent a bullet through the ear of a vampire on the other side of the square. "Military?"

"Army," said the man. "Retired. Alan Foster."

"Good to meet you."

"Don't you have a name?"

"Not one I can tell you," said Frankenstein.

Foster grunted with laughter. "Fair enough," he said. "On your left, stranger."

The monster spun, and saw a vampire dragging himself across the cobblestones towards him. His left leg was gone below the knee, his right arm missing entirely, but his face was alive with hate, and his eyes still burned red. Frankenstein shot the vampire between the eyes, and turned back to Alan Foster's side. He raised the M4, and was about to pull its trigger again when Bob Allen's voice burst into his ear.

Captain Guérin watched the missile appear on the radar screen inside the command centre, his eyes wide and staring.

The red dot appeared off the coast of Perpignan and began to move steadily north-west as alarms and alerts and a hundred incredulous conversations burst into life; the radio surveillance screen was instantly overwhelmed as seemingly the entire global intelligence community asked what the hell was happening at the same time. A dozen calls appeared on the comms screens, all of them marked urgent, but Guérin ignored them. There was nothing he could do to stop what was happening; all he could do was watch, along with everyone else.

The noise had increased to a relentless scream around him and the muffled voices of the vampires trying to get to him were much closer; he knew it was only a matter of time before they got in, but as he watched the red dot move across the radar map, he was strangely comforted by the realisation that it would soon not matter in the slightest. He stared at the screen for a long moment, then reached out and opened a comms line to General Allen.

He deserves to know what's coming, thought Gúerin. *Even if there's nothing he can do about it. I owe him that much.*

Julian Carpenter waded through ankle-deep blood, his eyes locked on the drawbridge above him, his stomach churning.

He was a veteran of a great many conflicts, and he knew better than most that the battle would not be won – if it *was* won – on the ground, in the thick of the killing; it would be won by cutting off the enemy's head, not by hacking at its body. He could do nothing about Dracula himself – he had gathered from overheard discussion in the displaced persons camp mess that a team had been sent into the city with the sole aim of destroying the first vampire – but as he looked up at the entrance to the old city, he realised he might be able to do the next best thing.

A vampire holding a radio was floating above the drawbridge, his eyes locked on the battle raging below. Julian had watched him as he fought his way across the blasted landscape, trying not to lose sight of him as he staked vampire after vampire. He was now far from a hundred per cent – he had taken a crunching blow that had broken at least three of his ribs, and he had a deep gouge across his neck where a vampire had come within millimetres of tearing out his throat – and he was exhausted, running almost entirely on adrenaline, but he was far from done; his heart was still beating, and his eyes were shining with determination.

There had been a dozen vampires surrounding his target when the battle began. Julian had seen several of them fly into the walled city, and at least two had been taken out by long-range gunfire; now, after God only knew how much time had passed, there were only four left. They surrounded his target, their glowing eyes scanning the landscape on all sides, but a plan had formulated in Julian's mind as he battled his way towards them; a plan he was now ready to put into action.

A vampire crawled across the blood-soaked ground in front of him, its arms and upper chest riddled with bullet holes. He strode forward, grabbed the man by his bleeding shoulder, and pulled him to his feet; the vampire hissed in protest, then grunted with shock as Julian jammed his stake into its back. The vampire went limp, the fire in its eyes fading to a low glow as he leant it back against him. Then he dipped his head and pushed the stricken vampire up the hill, hiding himself behind it as its blood soaked into his uniform.

He was within ten metres of the drawbridge when the vampires surrounding his target noticed the shambling approach of the vampire he was holding before him like a shield, and bellowed for him to stop. Julian did as he was told, then ripped the stake up through the vampire's body and pierced its heart.

The man burst in a huge spray of blood, as Julian drew his MP5 and fired through the gore. The vampires – *guards, that's what they are, they're guards* – went down, blood pumping out from dozens of wounds, but the man holding the radio shot up into the air like a launching missile, twisting away from the gunfire. Julian raised his gun, trying to sight him as he sped through the air, but was nowhere near fast enough; the vampire rocketed down out of the sky and threw a punch like a piledriver into the side of his helmet. A bolt of pain sliced through Julian's head as he was sent sprawling back down the hill, his vision greying at the edges. He hit the ground on his shoulders, hard, and for an awful second he thought the MP5 was going to spill from his hands; he held on to it tightly as he skidded to a halt, and looked up, searching the sky for his attacker.

The vampire was charging down the hill, a look of incredulous anger on his face as Julian raised the MP5 and pulled the trigger again. The man darted to his left, but one of the bullets found its target, punching a hole in his arm and spinning him to the ground.

He got up, screamed with primal fury, and advanced towards Julian again, his eyes full of homicidal fire.

Bob Allen raced across the battlefield, leaving Ovechkin and Tán behind as he chased a vampire towards the remnants of a hotel at the bottom of the steep hill. He found solid footing, brought his T-Bone up, and was about to pull the trigger when Guérin's voice sounded in his ear.

"General Allen?"

"Damn it!" he shouted, lowering his weapon. "What is it, Guérin?"

"I'm sorry, sir," said the French Captain, and something in his voice made Allen pay attention; it sounded like the man was on the verge of tears. "I really am. There was nothing I could do."

"About what, Guérin?" asked Allen. "What's going on?"

"The President gave the order, sir. The missile is in the air."

For several seconds, Allen couldn't speak; shock had momentarily paralysed him. "When?" he managed. "How long have we got?"

"Five minutes," said Guérin. "The safe distance is eight miles. I am so sorry."

Allen stared out across the battlefield. Thousands of men and women were surging back and forth across the wide space, running and thrashing and fighting and dying.

There's not a chance, he thought. *No way we can disengage and get to the safe distance in five minutes. Not a chance in hell.*

"It's not your fault," he heard himself say, as if someone else was using his vocal cords; his mind was reeling from the enormity of what was on its way towards his army. "I'm sure you did everything you could, so don't do anything stupid, OK? Do you hear me? Stay where you are. Stay safe."

"I do not think that is an option, sir," said Guérin. "But thank you."

The connection was cut, but for a long moment Allen didn't move. He was still staring at the battlefield, his mind trying to process the reality he had been presented with.

Everyone I can see, vampires and Operators alike, is going to die. Every single one of them. There won't be anything left but radioactive ash.

He twisted the comms dial on his belt and opened a line to the strike team.

"Listen to me very carefully," he said. "There isn't much time."

67

DEATH'S GREY LAND, PART EIGHT

CARCASSONNE, SOUTHERN FRANCE

Jamie slammed his stake into a vampire's chest and leapt back, a deep frown on his face.

"Say again, sir?" he shouted, trying to make himself heard over the chaos. "The French have done what?"

"They've given the order," shouted General Allen, directly into his ear. Jamie's helmet was gone, lost somewhere in the frenzy of battle, but his earpiece was still in place, and the backup microphone on his collar was doing its job.

"What order, sir?"

"The *nuclear* order!"

Cold spilled down Jamie's spine. "They can't do that."

"It's done!" shouted Allen. "The missile is in the air. It'll be here in five minutes."

"What do we do, sir?" he asked.

"I don't know," said Allen, his voice full of what sounded dangerously close to resignation. "I honestly don't. Whatever you can. I'm sorry."

The line went dead.

Jamie looked around the square, panic rising through him in a steady wave; vampires still flew back and forth, but most were now on the ground, broken and bleeding. In the hotel entrance, Frankenstein and the man with silver hair had been sniping them out of the air like two friends on a Sunday morning duck hunt, but the monster was now staring straight at him, his M4 lowered, his eyes wide with shock.

"Sub launch," said Valentin, appearing at Jamie's side as suddenly as if he had teleported. "It has to be."

"Where's the nearest coastline?" asked Larissa, joining them in a blur of black and glowing red.

"To the south-east," said Valentin. "I'll take care of it."

"*Take care of it?*" repeated Jamie, incredulously. "What are you talking about? What are you going to do?"

Valentin smiled. "I have absolutely no idea," he said. "But don't worry. I've always been very resourceful."

The ancient vampire leapt into the air, and disappeared over the rooftops.

"What do we do, Jamie?" asked Larissa, her voice low.

He shook his head. "We carry on," he said. "If Valentin manages to do something, then brilliant. If he doesn't, I don't think being at ground zero of a nuclear explosion will hurt very much."

Larissa smiled at him. "Probably not," she said. "Let's finish this."

Valentin accelerated almost vertically, searching the expanding horizon for the missile.

The absurdity of the situation struck the ancient vampire as he climbed, and he fought back the sudden urge to laugh. The fate of thousands of men and women now rested solely in his hands; unless he was able to do something, they – along with several square miles of the French countryside – would be vaporised by nuclear fire. But if he *was* able to stop the missile, to somehow divert or defuse it, and they then failed to kill Dracula, he was going to be essentially responsible for the end of the world.

A voice in his head was screaming for him to just get to a safe distance, hover in the warm air, and watch the blast obliterate Carcassonne; it was the sensible thing to do, and inarguably in his own best interests. But as he soared upwards, he found himself unable to do so. He had happily broken his word on many occasions when it suited him, but he had made a promise to Paul Turner, and told Jamie and the rest of the strike team that they could trust him; for reasons he didn't fully understand, he was unwilling to let them down.

Besides, a nuclear blast would make it impossible to know for absolutely certain that Dracula was dead. And that could not be tolerated.

In the distance, streaking across the darkening sky, he saw the missile's vapour trail, and growled with anger. It was far higher than he had expected; as he tracked the trail across the sky, he saw that it was already past him. He swore, and hurtled after it, pushing his body as fast as he could through air that was increasingly cold and thin.

Less than thirty seconds later, Valentin pulled alongside the missile and marvelled at the sheer size of it.

The cylinder of grey metal was more than twelve metres long, with a long trail of fire and heat blasting out from its rear. He looped round it, trying to concentrate through the deafening roar of the rocket, momentarily transfixed by the astonishing destructive power hidden beneath the innocuous-looking panels of grey metal.

Do something, he told himself. *Anything. It's not like you can make it worse.*

Valentin matched the missile's speed and floated beside it. He ran his gloved hands along its smooth surface, feeling the slight depressions at the edge of the metal panels; in his mind, he was picturing a cross-section of a missile that he knew was almost certainly inaccurate, but was all he had to go on. In his mental image, the rear of the cylinder contained the engine, the middle contained the fuel, and the front section and nose contained what he was interested in: the nuclear warhead itself, and the computers that controlled the guidance and firing systems. The missile was cold beneath his hands as he slid towards the front, and stopped. He dug his fingers into the ridges at the sides of a wide panel, took a deep breath, and ripped it out.

Nothing happened.

Valentin breathed out with relief, and tore at the second layer of metal, dragging out panel after panel, exposing the interior of the missile. The noise of the rocket was so loud that he could barely think straight, but he risked a glance to the west, and forced himself to concentrate.

On the distant horizon, probably no more than thirty miles away, his supernaturally sharp eyes could see the medieval city of Carcassonne.

The target.

Larissa raced across the cobbled square, staking stricken vampire after stricken vampire without slowing.

Jamie and Frankenstein were doing the same, finishing off the dozens of men and women who had fallen under their guns and swinging fists. The surviving vampires, no more than ten of them in total, had fled up the hill towards the Basilica, but the strike team had not given chase; it would only take a few litres of blood to revive the vampires lying on the cobblestones and turn them back into threats.

Larissa's heart was pounding; she had no idea whether there was still any point to what they were doing, whether they and the hostages standing in front of the hotel were all about to be vaporised, but all she could do was carry on. There were only three of them left now, probably not enough to stop Dracula if they even got close enough to try, but turning back, when they were so close, was not an option.

"Clear," shouted Jamie. "Let's move."

He was standing in front of the hotel with Frankenstein and the hostages, who were staring at the blood-drenched square with obvious disgust. She flew across to join them.

"Where to?" asked the monster.

"Up," said Jamie. "Until there's nowhere left to go."

"What about them?" Larissa asked, nodding at the hostages.

Jamie turned to face them. "Get as far away from the city as you can, as fast as you can," he said. "Don't go through the main exits if you can help it. Is that clear?"

Most of the men and women nodded, their eyes bright with fear. The silver-haired man, whom Frankenstein had been beside as the fighting raged, narrowed his eyes.

"Are you going after Dracula?" he asked.

"Yes," said Jamie.

"Good," said the man. "I'm Colonel Alan Foster. I'm coming with you."

"I'm not going to stop you," said Jamie. "And I don't have time to argue. But we won't be able to look after you."

"That's fine," said Foster, and smiled. "I can take care of myself."

I bet you can, thought Larissa.

A woman stepped forward and took hold of Foster's arm.

"Alan?" she said. "Do you have to?"

"You know I do," said Foster, and gave her cheek a gentle kiss. "I'll be all right. Help the others, OK?"

The woman nodded, her face pale but tight with determination.

"All right," said Jamie. "Follow me."

He turned towards the narrow road that led up to the summit of Carcassonne, where death or victory awaited them.

The wind howled around Valentin as he wrenched out a plastic screen, exposing a mass of wires. As he stared at them, the missile shifted as its nose began to tilt towards the distant ground.

All right, he told himself. *It's all right. There's still time.*

He drew in a deep breath, and took hold of two handfuls of the wires. He was suddenly aware that what he was about to do might be the last thing he ever did; no amount of blood was going to help if a nuclear missile went off in his hands, because he was pretty sure there would be no remains to revive. He glanced down and saw that the ground was already closer.

Much closer.

Valentin shut his eyes, and permitted himself an indulgent moment to consider the life he had lived, a life almost unparalleled in human history, full of light and dark and every shade of grey between.

Then he breathed out, and tore the bundle of wires in half.

Osvaldo strode across the blood-soaked ground with the hunting knife that had been his father's in his hand, his body physically vibrating with anger.

He knew he should just return to his post on the drawbridge, revive his guards, and send one of them down the hill to finish the man off, but his mind was coursing with a simple, unstoppable desire: he wanted to kill the soldier so very badly.

The destruction of the helicopter fleet and the reveal of their second front meant that the battle was now indisputably going their way, but it was still far too early for complacency. Until each and every one of their enemies lay dead on the ground and his master descended from the Basilica to begin his reign, he would assume nothing.

The soldier got to his feet at the same moment Osvaldo reached him and plunged the hunting knife into his gut. The man's eyes widened; he let out a thick grunt and slumped forward as Osvaldo hauled the knife upwards, slicing flesh and muscle until a thick ridge of bone stopped the blade. He yanked out the knife, and shoved the soldier backwards; the man spun limply through the air, his insides trailing, and slid across the blackened ground. For a long moment, Osvaldo considered going after him and finishing him off, but the bloodlust that had gripped him so urgently was already fading, and he could see there was no need.

The man was done.

I'm hurt, thought Julian, as shock flooded through him. *Oh God, that hurts so much.*

The vampire was staring down at him with a cold expression on his face. Julian tried to move, but couldn't; his mind was horribly clear, but his body would simply not obey its commands. His insides felt like they were on fire, like someone had scooped his organs out and replaced them with burning coals, and his hands were cold beneath his gloves, so cold that he could suddenly no longer feel his fingers. He tried to raise his head, and felt liquid gush up his throat and into his mouth; he gagged and spat, blood running down his face and neck in warm rivers.

The vampire was still staring at him, its eyes smouldering red in the darkness.

Come on then! he wanted to shout. *Come on and finish me!*

But he couldn't form the words. All he could do was stare back, and hope the fear pulsing through him was not visible in his eyes.

The vampire frowned.

His eyes flared crimson and he looked up at the sky, a millisecond before fifty-two tonnes of intercontinental ballistic missile obliterated him completely. It hammered into the ground and exploded with a belch of fire, a noise that struck Julian momentarily deaf, and a storm of flying shrapnel.

Julian stared at the fireball billowing up into the air, dimly aware that the missile had not detonated, that only its fuel tank had blown; the heat was overpowering, and he could smell cordite and blood and burning metal, but he wanted to throw back his head and scream with joyous laughter. If the frown on the vampire's face before the sky quite literally fell on him was the last thing he ever saw, he could think of a great many worse sights.

Despite the protective material of his uniform, the heat on his skin began to rise to an unbearable level. He couldn't move himself away from the burning wreckage of the missile, but he knew it didn't matter. The pain the vampire's knife had caused was gone, replaced by shivering cold and a sensation of profound exhaustion; the ground beneath him was soaked, and he was starting to feel light-headed.

It's all right, he told himself. *It's really all right. Just let go.*

A dark shape dropped out of the sky, landed heavily, and staggered backwards down the slope. The figure was wearing a Blacklight uniform, but it spun round as it threw its arms out to keep its balance, and Julian saw red eyes glowing at the centre of a face that was strangely familiar.

His first thought was that it was Alexandru Rusmanov standing before him, but he knew that wasn't possible; Alexandru was dead, destroyed on Lindisfarne by Julian's son. Valeri was dead too, which left only one explanation.

Valentin, he thought. *It has to be Valentin.*

The vampire frowned at him, and took a series of quick steps down the hill.

"I recognise you," it said, its voice low. "Why do I recognise you? What's your name?"

"My name is Julian Carpenter," he replied, each word requiring tremendous effort. "We've never met, but I recognise you too, Valentin."

The vampire smiled. "You are Jamie's father. The traitor."

Julian grimaced. "I betrayed nobody."

Valentin narrowed his eyes, then nodded. "I believe you," he said. "What are you doing here, Mr Carpenter? I don't believe you are still a member of Blacklight."

Julian opened his mouth to answer, but a wave of pain rolled through his body; he gritted his teeth and squeezed his eyes shut until it passed. When it finally did so, he found Valentin looking at him with open curiosity.

"You're dying, Mr Carpenter," said the vampire.

Julian grunted, and forced a thin smile. "I'm well aware of that."

"I could bite you," said Valentin. "I can tell by looking at you that it won't help, that you won't live long enough for the turn to begin. But I will try if you want me to."

"Why would you do that for me?"

"Because I liked your father a great deal, Mr Carpenter," said Valentin. "And because I am very fond of your son."

He frowned. "You know Jamie?"

"I do."

Julian felt his throat fill with liquid, bitter and horribly warm. He spat out blood so dark it was almost black, and looked up at the old vampire.

"I don't want you to bite me," he said, his voice low and thick. "Even if there was time for it to work, I wouldn't want you to."

Valentin nodded. "I understand," he said. "The chance to choose how you meet your end is not something many men are lucky enough to have."

Lucky, thought Julian, and smiled again. *Right. I'm really lucky.*

"There is something you can do for me," he said. He reached

a shaking hand inside his uniform and pulled out the envelope he had carried with him from his mother's cottage; it was now smeared with his blood, and he would just have to hope that the letter inside was still legible. He held it out towards the vampire. "You can give this to my son."

Valentin frowned, and took the letter from his fingers.

"Will you?" asked Julian, his voice urgent. "Will you give it to him? Please?"

The old vampire stared at the envelope for a long moment, then raised his head and nodded. Julian smiled, despite the pain and cold spreading through him.

"Thank you," he whispered.

Valentin slid the envelope into his uniform. Then he turned and rocketed towards the summit of Carcassonne, so quickly it was as though he had simply disappeared, and Julian let his head sink back to the ground; it was suddenly so heavy that he could barely lift it.

An image of his wife rose into his mind, her smile wide, her hair fluttering around her beautiful face. He wished he could have seen her again, just one last time, to tell her he loved her and say goodbye, but maybe it was for the best; she and Jamie lived in his memories, where they were perfect, where they would always be happy, where reality had never intruded on their lives. He thought about his son, not the man he had become who was out there somewhere in the darkness, but the boy he had been, his hair messy, his knees scraped, his eyes so bright and full of hope.

I loved you, he thought. *I loved you both so much.*

A peaceful smile rose on to Julian's face.

Then his eyes closed, and he died.

68

DEATH'S GREY LAND, PART NINE

CARCASSONNE, SOUTHERN FRANCE

Dracula strode towards the heavy doors of the Basilica, then turned back to address the remnants of his personal guard.

Barely a dozen had survived the massacre in the square below, a ragtag group of bloodied vampires with glowing eyes and faces full of fear. Their cowardice disgusted him, and the first vampire fought back the urge to kill them himself and be done with it.

"You will stay out here," he said. "You will fight with everything you have left, and you will die with honour. If you run, I will personally make you understand the true meaning of pain. Is that clear?"

The vampires growled in agreement, their eyes locked on their master. He stared at them for a long moment, then turned and swept into the old church, slamming the doors shut behind him.

He strode down the centre of the nave, his heart pounding with anticipation. In the alcove on the left, the soldier hung limply from the cross, and Dracula smiled; he was sure the assassination team would try to save her when they arrived, a human weakness he had every intention of exploiting. Emery appeared from behind one of the carved pillars and bowed his head deeply.

"My lord," he said. "Should I leave you?"

"No," said Dracula, without slowing. "Watch her, and stay out of the way."

"Yes, my lord," said Emery, and backed towards the crucified soldier, his gaze fixed on the floor.

The first vampire floated up on to the chancel, and settled into in his chair to wait. He knew the vampires he had left outside would likely do nothing more than slow the approaching assassins, but there was always the slight chance that one of them might strike a lucky blow and injure a member of the squad sent to kill him. Either way, it was now almost time for the meaningful battle to begin; the roaring chaos at the bottom of the hill was ultimately a sideshow, and both sides knew it.

The real victory would be won inside the church.

Paul Turner stopped fighting as Guérin spoke a single word into his ear.

"Incoming."

The Blacklight Director stood statue-still at the pulsing centre of the battle, his T-Bone in his hands, and scanned the darkening sky, his heart beating steadily in his chest. His greatest fear had always been that he would die because he made a mistake, that his death would be something that could have been avoided; being vaporised by a nuclear explosion did not qualify.

Out of the corner of his eye, Turner saw his fellow Directors also stop and raise their heads. The moment seemed to stretch out forever, full of awful inevitability, the certainty of utter hopelessness. The battle continued around them, as men and women who had no idea what was about to happen fought on with grim determination, and for a brief moment, Turner envied them. They would never know what hit them; he doubted they would even see the flash before they died.

"There," said Tán, and pointed.

Turner followed the Chinese Director's finger and saw a faint grey shape dropping out of the sky above the medieval city. It streaked down in front of the pale stone walls and he closed his eyes as it reached the ground.

An explosion rang out, but he instantly knew it was not the world-ending roar he had been expecting; it sounded like little more than the blast of a rocket-propelled grenade.

He opened his eyes. On the low slope beneath the wide drawbridge, a shallow crater had been blown in the hill; it was surrounded by twisted hunks of metal, and ringed with small, flickering fires.

"Holy shit," whispered Bob Allen, his eyes wide.

"It didn't fire," said Tán.

"I don't understand," said Turner.

"Neither do I," said Ovechkin, and hefted his Daybreaker. "But we can worry about it later. There is still work to do."

Turner nodded, his heart racing, then raised his T-Bone as the four Directors hurled themselves back into the fight.

"Stand by," said General Ducroix.

Central Director Vallens stood motionless, hunched in front of the screen in his empty office. The seconds seemed to stretch out for hours, days, even years; his chest felt as though someone had fastened a belt round it, and his hands were trembling on the surface of his desk.

"No detonation," said Ducroix. "I repeat, we have no detonation."

For a long moment, Vallens just stared; he was so overwhelmed with relief that for a brief second he was sure he was going to faint.

"What happened?" he managed. "Did the missile fail?"

"I don't know," said Ducroix. "I'm trying to get hold of—"

"Order a second launch," interrupted the President. "Immediately."

"No, sir," said Ducroix. "I will not."

"Then you are relieved of duty," said the President. "I'll do it myself."

"No, you won't, sir," said Ducroix, his voice steady. "I've cut the line to Mont Verdun. I don't think you are thinking clearly. Central Director Vallens, Minister Desjardins, do you agree with my assessment?"

"Yes," said Vallens, instantly.

"Yes," said Desjardins. "I'm sorry, sir. We need to give the Multinational Force more time. While they are still fighting, there is a chance."

"There is no chance!" shouted the President. "Do as I say before it is too late for us all!"

"No," said Ducroix. "Sir."

Silence.

"Think carefully about what you are doing, gentlemen," said the President, his voice low and as cold as ice. "This is treason."

"Yes," said General Ducroix. "It is."

Ellison raced above the battlefield, Jack Williams beside her.

There were far fewer Operators fighting than there had been when the battle began, and there still seemed to be so, *so* many vampires, but in that precise moment, she didn't care; she would kill every single one of them herself if she had to.

Four vampires appeared in their path, retreating from the onslaught of bullets fired by a group of Operators as they advanced across the blood-soaked landscape. Ellison leapt forward, a silent shadow in the darkness, and drove her stake through the back of one of the unsuspecting vampires. The man exploded in a crimson cloud as Jack descended on one of the others, spinning her round and staking her in a single smooth motion.

The remaining two vampires spun round, their mouths open with shock, their eyes boiling red, but Ellison was already moving, far too fast for them to react. She kicked one of them in the stomach, doubling her over and sending her staggering towards Jack, who obliterated her with a quick jab of his stake. The other leapt into the air, presumably intending to flee, but Ellison rose with him and slammed her stake into his chest. His remains pattered to the ground in a thick, steaming rain as Ellison landed, and smiled broadly at Jack.

"Nice work," he said, returning her smile with a grin of his own. "Four more down."

Ellison nodded. Her mind was suddenly full of Jamie Carpenter; she now understood the reckless abandon he had displayed once he had been turned, and wondered what her squad leader was doing at that exact moment.

"Do you think the strike team have a chance?" asked Jack, as though he could read her mind.

"Yes," she replied, instantly. "I absolutely do."

Six miles away, inside the command centre of the displaced persons camp, Captain Guérin lowered his head, his eyes brimming with tears of relief. He had no idea what had happened to the missile, and he genuinely didn't care; all that mattered was that it had not fired, and they were still there.

Over the noise surrounding the sealed room, a deafening screech echoed round the metal walls. Guérin leapt to his feet and spun towards it, raising his MP5 to his shoulder. A section of the reinforced wall had been peeled back like the lid of a tin can, and through the jagged hole he saw movement, and glowing red light.

A vampire's head appeared, eyes full of hunger, fangs gleaming. Guérin shot it in the eye, and it slumped backwards, blood spurting into the air.

One bullet.

The stricken vampire was dragged aside, and a second figure leapt through the hole and into the room. It howled, the rising roar of a wild animal, and launched itself at Guérin. He pulled the trigger, but the bullet went wide as the vampire danced to its left. He brought the gun round, crouched down as it reached him, and sent a bullet up through the flesh beneath its jaw, tearing away part of its face and revealing a bloody patch of skull. It crashed to the ground, screaming and clawing at its ruined face. Guerin staked it, and backed up, his gun again at the ready.

Two.

Three.

A pair of vampires leapt through the hole together, their faces twisted with hatred. They raced forward through the narrow room, and Guerin forced himself to stand his ground; there was nowhere for him to go, and he had known it would come to this.

He fired the MP5, taking one of the vampires in the throat and sending it backwards, blood erupting from its butchered neck. His second bullet caught the other vampire in the shoulder; it spun round like a ballerina, but kept coming. He fired again, and took the man's head off above his eyebrows in a shower of blood and bone.

Four.

Five.

Six.

Guérin took a deep breath, his gaze locked on the hole. Movement swirled inside it, and for the briefest of seconds, he wondered whether he had successfully made them think twice. Then vampires poured through, dozens of them, their eyes glowing in the dim light of the room as they hissed and growled, and he smiled with resignation.

He allowed himself a millisecond to say a silent goodbye to his family as the vampires thundered towards him, then raised the gun to his temple.

Seven.

Jamie watched the missile explode in a tiny ball of fire and turned to his remaining squad mates, his eyes blazing with heat.

"He did it," he said. "I don't believe it. Valentin did it."

"Did what?" asked Larissa.

"I don't know," he said, and shook his head. "Something. It was enough, whatever it was. So let's go."

He led the two Operators and the American Colonel up the steep path towards the church, his T-Bone drawn and raised. They crested the hill, and emerged in front of the grand façade of the Basilica – the stained glass, the carved stone, the huge wooden doors – and the ragged line of vampires standing before them; the space between them and the survivors of the massacre in the square was no more than five metres.

Jamie stared at the vampires. He saw no fight in their flickering red eyes; all he saw was fear, and something close to despair.

"Any of you who don't want to die, leave now," he said.

Half instantly fled; they simply leapt into the air and disappeared over the turreted walls of the city without a backward glance. The six that remained growled as they looked at each other with obvious unease, the light in their eyes darkening.

"Last chance," said Jamie.

The volume of the growling increased, but none of the vampires moved.

Jamie sighed. "Fine. Have it your way."

The three remaining members of the strike team fired their T-Bones at the same time. The metal stakes screamed through the air and crunched into the chests of three of the vampires, exploding them. Three huge splashes of blood soaked the surviving vampires, who shrieked and hissed as the stakes wound back into the barrels of the weapons. They stared at each other, drenched in blood from head to toe, the fear on their faces turning into open terror.

"What about now?" he asked.

Without a single word, the three bloody vampires rocketed into the sky. Jamie breathed a sigh of relief, lowered his T-Bone, and walked across to the doors of the Basilica. He leant his head against the old wood, and heard three distant heartbeats; one was dangerously slow, one sounded like that of a regular human, while the other was the loud, steady drumbeat of a vampire.

A *powerful* vampire.

"Is he in there?" asked Larissa.

Jamie nodded.

"Then this is it," said Frankenstein.

"This is it," he said, and reached for the ornate door handles.

"Don't you dare go in there without me," said a voice from behind them, and Jamie smiled as he turned towards it.

Valentin was sitting casually atop the high rampart wall opposite the church; he looked like a tourist posing for a photograph.

"Oh, for God's sake," said Larissa, and smiled. "There really is just no getting rid of you, is there?"

Angela let her chin rest against her chest and tried not to move as Dracula walked through the nave of the church.

The man who had done this to her, the man with the empty eyes, bowed at the first vampire as he passed, then backed towards where she had been hung, and looked up at her with an expression so devoid of humanity it made her want to vomit.

"Please," she whispered. "Please…"

The man smiled, and took a step towards her. He gently took

hold of her chin, the sensation of his skin on hers so intolerable that it took all her resolve not to scream in horror, and lifted her head.

"What is it?" he whispered. "Does it hurt?"

Angela muttered something under her breath. The man took another step and tilted his ear towards her.

"It's all right," he said. "You can tell me. Does it hurt?"

Angela smiled as her fangs slid out of her gums and red light exploded into her eyes. The man recoiled, but before he could stagger out of range, she yanked her right hand forward with all her remaining strength; it ripped free of the cross, the nail still sticking through the palm, and she clenched it into a tight fist. She swung it up under the man's chin, lifting him into the air as the nail pierced his flesh. His eyes flew open, and he gagged as blood gushed into his mouth and down her arm. She bore down, hauling him up and towards her, bringing his throat within range of her fangs.

"You tell me," she growled. "Does it?"

69

DEATH'S GREY LAND, PART TEN

CARCASSONNE, SOUTHERN FRANCE

The man stared at Angela, disbelief filling his eyes, until she tore out his throat with her fangs, and drank the blood that spurted into her mouth.

Power surged through her. She let the hateful man drop to the ground, and shattered the giant cross with a single flex of the muscles in her back. It exploded into splinters, and she floated in the air for a long moment, breathing deeply, her mind blanked by fury and the desire for revenge. Then she yanked the nails out of her hands and feet, threw them aside, and flew out into the centre of the nave as the doors of the church creaked open behind her.

The rest of the strike team walked into the Basilique Saint-Nazaire, their footsteps echoing on its tiled floor. Larissa's skin was tingling with anticipation; after so much time, so much bloodshed and death, it was simple.

Them and Dracula, to the end.

Her eyes immediately found the far end of the church, where the first vampire was sitting in a grand chair that was almost a throne, a narrow smile on his face as he stared at them. Then a black shape darted out from one of the alcoves on the left, and she found herself looking at the pale, furious face of Angela Darcy.

Larissa's heart leapt as relief burst through her. She sprinted forward and grabbed her friend's shoulders, her squad mates close behind her.

"Angela!" she said. "What happened? Are you all right?"

"No," said Angela, her voice trembling. "I'm not remotely all right. But I'll tell you about it later." She looked down the aisle, and growled. "Once we're done with him."

Dracula floated down on to the floor of the Basilica, and drew the giant broadsword that he had carried into battle more times than he could remember.

He let its point rest on the tiles and stared at the six men and women, his heart steady, his mind clear. That his trophy had managed to kill Emery and escape from her cross was annoying – he had been looking forward to her distracting her colleagues – but in the end, it would make no difference.

They would all still die.

"So," he said, as the assassination team walked towards him. "You are the ones sent to kill me."

He looked first at Valentin – the hateful, *despicable* traitor – then at the vampire girl who had made him believe, for a terrible moment more than six months earlier, that he might actually be about to die, and allowed crimson-black fire to fill his eyes.

"I owe debts to two of you," he said. "Debts that I have long looked forward to settling. As for the rest of you, when you are lying on the ground with your life ebbing away, console yourself with the belief that you did the best you could, and the knowledge that you never had a chance. There is no shame in—"

Valentin yawned extravagantly, and shook his head. "How long have you been planning this speech?" asked the former servant. "Six months? Longer? And this is the best you could come up with?"

The heat in Dracula's eyes rose to an unbearable level as rage boiled through him. "So be it, traitor," he said, his voice so low it shook the walls of the old church. "No more talk. Come to me, and embrace your destiny."

Valentin grinned, and strode towards his former master.

Chasing the missile through the night sky had been exhausting, but euphoria at having prevented a nuclear apocalypse was coursing through him, and he felt as strong, as *powerful*, as he ever had. Dracula walked to meet him, until, as if responding to some unspoken command, the two ancient vampires began to run, their feet pounding the tiled floor of the church.

They met halfway down the central aisle with an impact that shook the Basilica to its foundations. Valentin swung a huge, devastating punch, intending to crush his former master's head like a watermelon, but struck only thin air. Dracula's fist, so fast it was merely a blur, collided with his chin like a wrecking ball, arresting his momentum and sending him back through the air, his limbs trailing limply, his mind reeling.

Never been hit so hard, he managed to think. *By anyone, or anything. Nothing like that hard.*

He crashed to the ground, cracking the tiles beneath him, and felt blood spray into his mouth as his fangs snapped shut on his tongue. He slid backwards, unable to stop himself, and skidded to a halt in front of his squad mates.

Jamie looked down at him, his face full of concern; Valentin tried to smile, to show him he was all right, but could not make his muscles obey his command.

* * *

Alan Foster felt Dracula's punch through the soles of his feet.

The retired Colonel was astonished by the display of power, but as he raised the SIG to his shoulder he felt more alive than he had in many years. It was as though the universe had seen fit to bestow one last mission on him, and not just *any* mission; one that had more riding on it than any during his long and decorated military career.

He sighted the submachine gun on Dracula's chest and pulled the trigger. Fire licked from the barrel as the bullets raced through the air, but by the time they reached their target, the ancient vampire was no longer there. Dracula leapt to his left, a streak of black and glowing red, and picked up one of the church pews as though it was a matchstick. He threw it with an almost nonchalant flick of his arm, and Foster was barely able to raise a protective arm before it hit him.

The heavy wooden bench broke as it drove him backwards in a shower of splinters. He tumbled to the floor of the church, the SIG spilling from his grip as he slid across it, and hit the stone wall head first.

There was a sharp crunch, like the sound of a hard-boiled egg being cracked open, and everything went black.

Jamie watched the American slump unconscious against the wall, glanced down at Valentin lying bleeding at his feet, and felt his eyes blaze red.

He had known that Dracula would be strong, and fast, but he felt no fear as he stared at the ancient vampire; Gregor, the first victim, who had turned him, had been as strong and fast, or so close that it made no difference, and Jamie had seen nothing in the opening seconds of the fight to challenge his belief that they could beat Dracula.

That they were *going to* beat him.

He leapt into the air, drawing his MP7 as he flew towards the left-hand wall of the church. He pointed the gun down at Dracula, who was staring up at him with a contemptuous look on his face, and pulled the trigger. The ancient vampire easily slid out of the way of the stream of bullets, but that was fine; it was what Jamie had been counting on. He swung the barrel, firing constant short bursts and driving Dracula away from the chancel and into the air above where the pews had once stood, where the faithful had listened to sermons on peace and forgiveness.

Below him, Larissa's eyes flared with understanding, and she and Angela separated, crouching low and racing across the tiled floor in opposite directions. Dracula spun back and forth, trying to keep an eye on all three of them at the same time, his face twisting into a frown. Jamie fired over his head, drawing his attention and forcing him to swoop back towards the ground. Angela and Larissa opened fire, driving him backwards towards the doors; the first vampire moved like oil, growling and hissing, his face twisted into a dismissive smile that seemed to ask a simple question.

Is that the best you can do?

The smile on Dracula's face faltered as he was suddenly enveloped in a wide shadow.

Got you, thought Jamie.

The first vampire spun round, directly into one of the most devastating punches ever thrown. Frankenstein had swung the haymaker with every ounce of his strength, and his fist slammed into Dracula's face with a noise like a detonating bomb; blood and teeth exploded from his mouth as he was sent hurtling through the air, his body limp, the black fire in his eyes fading.

Angela felt a shock wave push her backwards through the air when the monster's punch connected, and felt the heat in her eyes rise as a scream of primal fury ripped from her mouth and echoed against the walls of the church.

She swooped forward, ready to leap down on to Dracula when his spinning body reached the ground, to look into his eyes before she killed him.

Frankenstein ran forward, savage pleasure flooding his huge, misshapen body.

The punch had rendered his right hand and arm numb, but it had felt good; it had felt really, *really* good. He moved while Dracula was still in the air, eager to hit the ancient vampire again, and again, and again. Out of the corners of his eyes he saw Angela and Larissa fly forward, but paid them no attention; his mind was focused solely on their enemy, who crashed to the floor in a heap barely five metres ahead of him and slid along the central aisle of the nave. The monster's huge strides carried him forward, ungainly but lethally fast, and he was already swinging back his fist again when the first vampire moved.

Dracula flipped upwards, in seeming defiance of the laws of physics, and landed on his feet, his face covered in blood, his eyes burning with unholy fire. Momentum was still carrying him backwards, but he dug his heels into the floor, shattering the tiles and gouging long grooves in the stone beneath. His broadsword was still in his hand, and he held it out before him like a lance.

Frankenstein realised, perhaps no more than a millisecond too late, what was going to happen, but he was too close.

There was nothing he could do.

Everything seemed to slow down.

He was carried helplessly forward, as though caught in a current. He threw his arms out behind him, but they felt like they were weightless, and did nothing to arrest his momentum. From somewhere above him, he heard Jamie scream his name, scream for him to *look out*, but it was too late.

The huge blade of Dracula's sword slid into Frankenstein's stomach as though his flesh was as insubstantial as smoke, and exited through his back with a gout of blood that splashed across the tiled floor of the church.

DEATH'S GREY LAND, PART ELEVEN

CARCASSONNE, SOUTHERN FRANCE

For a long moment, nobody moved.

Dracula was gripping the hilt of the sword, Frankenstein was staring down at the blade, and everyone else was motionless inside the silent church. The monster felt no pain, just a sensation of awful *wrongness*. His mind remained clear, remarkably so, and he saw there was still a chance to do something.

He reached out, took hold of the huge broadsword's cross guard, and pulled himself forward, the blade sliding deeper into him. A frown crossed Dracula's face, and the first vampire growled as he tried unsuccessfully to pull the sword free; the huge punch had clearly weakened him, and Frankenstein was holding on with all his remaining strength. He hauled himself along the blade, feeling it slice through his insides, inching closer and closer to Dracula, who was staring at him with blazing incredulity; the vampire pulled at the sword again, clearly unwilling to let it go, but he held firm, his mind full of the prospect of vengeance.

Frankenstein dragged himself forward a final time as the pain finally arrived, a torrent of agony that ripped through him as blood spilled out of his stomach in a dark river. He reached out, momentarily blinded by pain, and his huge grey-green hand found the first vampire's face; he ground his thumb into the vampire's eye, as hard as his suddenly failing strength would allow. Dracula screamed and released the hilt; he leapt back, thrashing and clutching at his head like he was surrounded by a swarm of bees.

With the vampire's grip on the sword gone, Frankenstein toppled backwards. The pain pounded through him, turning everything red, and the sword blade snapped beneath him as he crashed down on to the tiled floor, and lay still.

Jamie watched the monster fall, his heart frozen in his chest, a silent scream splitting his head.

Dracula let go of his face, spat blood on to the floor, and growled. The first vampire's left eye was almost closed, but his mouth curled into a smile of cruel satisfaction as he looked at the prone monster, and it was this smile that caused Jamie to temporarily lose his mind.

He threw himself across the church, a rage more powerful than anything he had ever known flooding through him. He tore into Dracula, punching and kicking and clawing, wanting to rip the ancient vampire's life from his body with his bare hands. The first vampire reeled, caught off guard by the ferocity of Jamie's onslaught, and was driven backwards, his arms raised to defend himself from the blizzard of blows.

Somewhere in the distance, Larissa screamed for Jamie to move, to give her a clear shot, but he could not have stopped himself even if he wanted to; he pounded at Dracula, hammering him with blows that would have knocked down walls, his rational side entirely gone, his vampire side baying for blood. His gloved knuckles laid the first vampire's cheek open to the bone, spraying blood into the cool, still air of the church, and Dracula screeched with pain. Jamie didn't let up, his arms and legs little more than black blurs as he drove the hateful old vampire along the central aisle of the church, his eyes glowing the colour of lava.

Dracula leapt back, creating separation, then surged forward, his face burning with outraged fury.

"Enough!" he bellowed, and swung a fist in a wide arc. It hit the side of Jamie's head with a noise like a clap of thunder and sent him flying across the church. He thudded painfully into the stone wall, slid down to the floor, and leapt back to his feet as a thick growl rose from his throat, the anger in his head so hot and sharp that it was physically painful.

At the centre of the cavernous space, Dracula drew himself up to his full height. His face was a bloody mess, and his left eye was swollen shut, but the right one roiled with black fire, and he stared at Jamie with monstrous hatred. At the other end of the central aisle, Valentin got to his feet, his mouth pouring with blood but twisted into a gruesome smile. Jamie flew across to him as Larissa and Angela dropped down to join them, and what was left of the strike team advanced on Dracula together. The first vampire backed into the wide space before the chancel, and spread his arms wide, inviting them forward with a smile on his face.

The four squad mates moved in a blur of black and red. Larissa fired her T-Bone, sending its stake rocketing towards Dracula's heart, Jamie dropped to one knee and emptied his MP7 at the snarling vampire, as Angela and Valentin leapt towards him, their arms outstretched, their hands curled into claws.

Dracula reacted with terrifying, impossible speed. He slid out of the way of Larissa's T-Bone stake, spun up and over Jamie's stream of bullets, grabbed Angela out of the air by her throat and threw her like a javelin; she flew across the wide space, her arms spinning as she futilely tried to arrest her momentum, and collided with Larissa, sending both of them head first into the wall. A pair of loud cracks echoed through the church, and they fell still, their eyes rolled back in their heads.

Jamie hurled himself at their enemy, his stake in his hand. Dracula spun back round, searching out the next attack, then doubled over as Valentin landed a crunching kick to his stomach. Jamie soared above him, his searching fingers passing through the space where the first vampire's throat had been barely a millisecond earlier.

Dracula exploded upwards like a shark from the depths, and slammed a fist into his stomach as he rocketed overhead; Jamie convulsed in mid-air, his equilibrium disappearing along with all the air in his lungs, and he curled into a foetal ball as he tumbled to the floor. He rolled over to see two of the oldest vampires in the world staring at each other, growls rising from their throats, the thrill of violence in their eyes.

Jamie got to his feet, took a staggering step, and collapsed back to the floor. His chest was constricted, and he was unable to drag air into his lungs. He tried to calm down, to breathe normally, and surveyed the church. Alan Foster was unconscious at the base of the far wall near the door, Angela and Larissa were lying slumped on the other side, although both appeared to be stirring, and in the centre of the huge space was the motionless shape of Frankenstein, the long hilt of the broadsword rising out of his gut; Jamie dragged his eyes away from the dreadful sight in time to see Valentin launch himself at Dracula.

The ancient vampires attacked each other with blows that shook the Basilica, swooping and darting back and forth almost too quickly for his eyes to follow. Punches and kicks connected with deafening impacts, but neither gave so much as an inch; they were fuelled by over five hundred years of history, five centuries of anger and betrayal, and blows that would have killed a normal man were dismissed as though they were nothing more than mosquito bites.

Dracula leapt forward, grabbing for Valentin's neck, but the youngest Rusmanov slipped beneath his former master's outstretched hands and hammered an elbow into his throat. The first vampire was driven backwards, but surged forward again immediately, ducking a punch that would have decapitated him and unleashing a kick like a piledriver into Valentin's side. The two vampires backed away from each other, growling like animals, then leapt forward again, a hurricane of crunching violence.

Out of the corner of his eye, Jamie saw Angela stagger to her feet, sight down the barrel of Larissa's T-Bone, and pull the trigger. The weapon fired with a bang of exploding gas, and the metal stake screeched through the air towards Dracula's chest. At the last millisecond, at the point when it seemed impossible that the metal projectile would not find its target, Dracula ducked under Valentin's arms, grabbed his waist, and spun his former servant into the stake's path. It plunged through Valentin's left eye with a sound like a slamming door and exited the back of his head, trailing blood and brains behind it.

Dracula let the twitching body crash to the ground, blazing triumph on his narrow face, and seized the metal wire as it sped past him. He yanked it forward, hauling Angela off her feet. She spun through the air, her eyes wide with shock, and into the first vampire's waiting arms. Her fists pounded at him as he took hold of her head and twisted it sharply to the right. Her neck broke with a loud snap, and she dropped limply to the floor beside Valentin.

Just like that, thought Jamie. *Just as fast as that.*

He forced his reeling body into action and stood up, his legs unsteady beneath him.

Dracula stared at him, a wide smile of pure arrogance on his face. Jamie stared back, trying not to let shock and exhaustion show on his face; the sounds of the stake punching through Valentin's eye and the breaking bones in Angela's neck would stay with him for a long time, if there was such a thing left. He walked into the central aisle, a dreadful sense of inevitability sweeping through him; somehow, he had always known it would come down to this, and now the moment had arrived.

"You are strong," said Dracula. "And fast. Who birthed you?"

"I was turned by the first person you ever drank from," he said. Talking to the old monster felt obscene with his friends lying broken around him, but every extra second allowed his muscles to recover a fraction of their strength.

Dracula frowned, then smiled again, more widely than ever. "The gypsy," he said. "I should have made sure he was dead, but I was not myself at that moment. Although it matters not. Shall we finish this?"

Jamie was terrified, more scared than he had ever been in his life, but he knew he could not refuse; there was nobody to take his place, nobody left to stand with him. He gripped the metal stake tightly in his hand, and walked down the aisle as the first vampire strode to meet him.

Dracula threw a punch, long and lazy but still fizzing with power. Jamie slipped under it, stepped in, and slammed the blunt end of the stake into the side of his head. The first vampire recoiled, took a step backwards, and grinned.

"Strong," he growled. "As I said. But not strong enough."

Dracula burst forward, so fast that even Jamie's supernatural eyes could barely follow him, and unleashed an overwhelming series of punches, like tree trunks being swung against his arms. He was forced backwards, the brutality of the attack completely irresistible;

the first vampire's eyes burned with savage cruelty as his fists came down over and over again. Jamie's right arm fell, no longer able to withstand the onslaught, and he followed it, ducking low and sliding to his right, then drove his foot into the ancient vampire's ribs, drawing a thick grunt and sending him back a step.

Dracula let out a deep growl, and came again. Jamie thrust out the stake, sending it on a direct line towards the old monster's heart, but the first vampire darted left and sent his fist crashing into Jamie's chin, knocking him flat. He leapt back up, his eyes full of fire, and drew his Glock from his belt as he ducked beneath a vast haymaker. He fired the pistol point-blank into Dracula's back, the bullets punching ragged holes in his flesh; blood sprayed out in dark bursts, and the vampire howled with pain. He spun and swung a fist out behind him, a blind punch that connected with Jamie's shoulder and sent the Glock spinning away into the distance. He reached for his T-Bone, but found only an empty loop and his shattered UV beam gun; his stake was all he had left.

The first vampire leapt forward, his face twisted with pleasure, even as he bled from half a dozen bullet wounds that would have ended a normal man. Jamie jabbed the stake out again, sinking it into the flesh of the vampire's arm, but Dracula kept coming as though he hadn't even felt it; he swung his fist into Jamie's stomach, driving what little breath he had managed to recover back out of him with a sound like a bursting balloon. The stake flew from his hand as he staggered backwards, the light in his eyes fading, until Dracula kicked him dismissively in the chest, sending him sprawling to the ground.

Can't beat him, Jamie thought, panic spreading through him. *Can't even breathe. Nothing I can do. Nothing.*

Dracula flew forward, his expression almost sympathetic.

"You tried," he said. "You did your best, and it was admirable. Let that console you in the next life."

Jamie pushed himself backwards, dragging a wheezing stream of air into his lungs, and kicked out weakly as the ancient vampire reached him. Dracula's expression changed to one of disgust; he swooped easily over the outstretched leg, and hammered the toe of his boot into Jamie's ribs. At least two of them broke, audibly, and he shrieked in pain. Dracula kicked him again, a sickening blow that shuddered through his bones, and again, and again. Jamie heard himself screaming as he was driven backwards, but there was no escape to be had; panic had overwhelmed him, turning his limbs to lead and his stomach to water.

Failed, he thought, his mind pulsing with terror. *Never had a chance. Failed. I'm sorry. So sorry.*

Dracula dug his foot under Jamie's side and flipped him over on to his front. He kept crawling, even though it was pointless, even though there was nowhere to go. Ahead of him, lying in the aisle, he saw the motionless shape of Frankenstein, the sword hilt sticking out of his body, and dragged himself towards it, acting almost entirely on instinct.

The first vampire walked alongside him, raining punishing kicks on his back and ribs. When Jamie was almost within reach of the monster, Dracula stamped on the back of his right calf with an impact that felt like a car had been dropped on it. Jamie heard the bones break, and a millisecond later the pain hit; it rolled up his body as a great grey wave of nauseating agony, churning his stomach and wiping his mind clear. He didn't scream; instead, he let out a terrible howl of pain and misery, his head thrown back, his body reeling at the damage done to it. He dragged himself forward a final time, and reached out a trembling hand for the sword hilt.

His gloved fingers closed on nothing but air.

Over, he realised. *It's all over.*

Jamie slumped to the ground, and saw something among the broken tiles in front of him, something small and angular. He reached out and closed his fingers round it; it was a wooden crucifix, small and plain and rough.

Hands that felt like vices took hold of his shoulders and turned him over on to his back. He stared up at the face of the first vampire, the cross gripped tightly in his hand. Dracula settled over him, his knees either side of his waist, and looked down at him with dreadful finality.

Jamie stared back, lost in the swirling crimson-black of the ancient vampire's eyes, and found himself looking past the narrow face looming over him; in the molten darkness, he saw his mother smiling at him with the pride and love that always filled her eyes, saw the faces of Larissa and Kate and Matt, of Henry Seward, of John Morton and Lizzy Ellison and Paul Turner, of Frankenstein and his grandfather and the ancestors he had never known. His heart swelled in his chest, tapping some distant reserve, and he raised the crucifix towards Dracula.

The first vampire's eyes narrowed for a brief moment, before he burst out laughing.

"You stupid boy," he said, his voice dripping with contempt. "You poor fool. Your death is at hand and you clutch at fairy tales. Surely you know that crosses don't work?"

Jamie didn't respond; he let the hand holding the crucifix fall to the floor at his side and stared into the old monster's swirling eyes.

Dracula lunged, black fire trailing from his eyes. His mouth yawned open as his face descended towards Jamie's neck, his fangs huge and gleaming.

As if acting on its own, his hand flew up and pushed the wooden cross forward with every last iota of strength he had left. It plunged into Dracula's throat, ripping through skin and muscle and burying itself in the hard knots of the first vampire's spine.

Blood exploded into the air and gushed down on to Jamie's face. The power that had momentarily filled him had already disappeared, but some of the old monster's blood sprayed into his mouth, giving him the strength to sit up. He did so, in time to see Dracula reel backwards, his eyes wide, his throat erupting in a crimson geyser.

Jamie forced himself to his feet, half standing and half floating on his shattered leg, and pulled the broken sword out of Frankenstein's stomach. When he turned back, Dracula had sunk to his knees, his eyes huge and staring, his hands tight round the crucifix lodged in his throat, his blood escaping in a seemingly endless torrent.

"Crosses don't work," said Jamie, in a trembling voice. "Are you sure about that?"

Dracula's eyes widened even further, and he leapt forward a final time, a shambling, blood-drenched monstrosity with hands that reached out towards Jamie.

Gunfire echoed through the Basilica.

Bullets slammed into the first vampire, driving him back to his knees and tearing his jaw clean off. Dracula's eyes swivelled, staring at seemingly everything and nothing as a mangled scream issued from his ruined mouth. Jamie risked a glance in the direction the bullets had come from, and saw Larissa slumped against the wall, her Glock smoking in her lap; she met his eyes, and gave him a small, exhausted smile.

He nodded, and returned his attention to the slumped form in front of him.

"Look at me," he said.

Dracula did so. Their gazes locked for a long moment, and Jamie saw what he wanted to see: bright, shining fear in the old vampire's eyes.

He raised the broken sword and drove it into Dracula's chest, burying it up to the silver cross guard.

The first vampire pitched backwards on to the floor, his arms and legs drumming violently on the tiles. Jamie glanced round as Larissa got to her feet and made her way towards him; she stopped at his side, and they watched in silence as Dracula's death throes began.

The ancient vampire's body became first a rattling blur, then suddenly as still as a statue. Black liquid began to bubble from the wound, spilling out around the sword's wide blade and spreading rapidly across his chest. Jamie's stomach churned; the liquid wasn't blood, it was slick and shimmering like oil, and it moved unnaturally, as though it was somehow alive. It covered Dracula's chest and began to swirl like it was caught inside a tornado, faster and faster, until it exploded up and out with a sound like the end of the world.

The liquid surged upwards in a thick column and blasted through the roof of the Basilica; stone and glass came crashing down around Jamie and Larissa, smashing floor tiles and hammering pews to splinters. The impossible column of liquid spun, in defiance of all that was natural, and in its shimmering surface Jamie saw things that he would never describe to anyone, things that would haunt his dreams for the rest of his life.

The spinning liquid gathered speed, and Jamie backed away from it; he didn't know why, not exactly, he just grabbed Larissa's hand and pulled her back. The sound inside the church was deafening, a howl of white noise that made Jamie want to tear off his ears and rip his skin to ribbons. When it reached a volume that was almost unbearable, when the column of liquid was spinning faster than even supernatural eyes could follow, a great rumbling rose beneath it all, shaking the church to its foundations.

The column exploded in a great belch of black fire and a shock wave that sent Jamie and Larissa flying through the air. The walls of the church cracked from floor to ceiling, and the beautiful windows shattered in a twinkling storm of stained glass. Jamie hit the ground, his head ringing, and forced himself back to his feet in time to see the vast mass of black liquid sink back into Dracula's body and spread out beneath him in a wide, perfect circle.

Screams and shouts of alarm rang out across the wide battlefield as black fire billowed from the summit of Carcassonne.

Everyone, Operator and vampire alike, stopped fighting and turned towards the distant, unnatural explosion. Paul Turner stared up at it, his eyes wide behind his visor, his heart pounding, trying not to let himself believe what he hoped it meant.

The shock wave that had devastated the Basilica rolled down the hill and thundered across the blasted landscape, knocking Operators off their feet and sending Dracula's surviving followers screeching into the air, their eyes flaming, their mouths wide as they howled in pain and fear. They scattered in every direction, racing away into the darkness without a backward glance, as though they were flying for their lives.

Turner clambered to his feet, and stared around the suddenly abandoned battlefield. Ovechkin and Allen joined him, their eyes wide, their weapons hanging seemingly forgotten at their sides. The NS9 Director looked at him, his face a mask of confusion, and all Turner could do was shrug and shake his head.

Jamie staggered back along the central aisle of the nave, Larissa close behind him, and stopped at the edge of the wide pool of black liquid. He had no idea what he was seeing, no idea whether it was even *real*, but he knew that someone had to bear witness to what was happening.

In the centre of the oily circle, Dracula sat up slowly. He looked down at the sword hilt sticking out of his chest, at the shifting black liquid, then up at the two black-clad figures watching him. The damage to his face and throat was gone, as was the blood that had coated them; his skin was pale, and his expression was one of profound confusion.

"What devilment is this?" he whispered.

The black liquid slid back and forth, as though responding to his voice. Then it began to rise in thick, glistening pillars that formed into clawed hands and took hold of Dracula's arms and legs. They began to pull him down, as if the liquid was as deep as a swimming pool, rather than a millimetre or two lying on a tiled floor; Dracula screamed and thrashed back and forth, but the black hands were implacable; he sank slowly, his resistance utterly futile.

"Jesus," said Larissa, her voice low and hoarse.

Jamie didn't respond; he was transfixed with horror. Dracula's legs had disappeared beneath the oily surface, but still he fought, his arms pounding and dragging at the oil, his head thrown back as he screamed for mercy. His waist sank into the liquid as the clawed hands gripped his shoulders and arms, and one slid round his neck, reducing his screams to strangled croaks. As he was dragged relentlessly down, Dracula's eyes met Jamie's.

"Help me," he whispered. "Please."

Jamie held his gaze, ordering himself not to look away. For a long, seemingly endless moment, the first vampire hung suspended, half in and half out of the swirling, glistening liquid. Then the oily hands pulled a final time, and Dracula disappeared beneath the surface.

Instantly, the black circle began to shrink, drawing in before Jamie's eyes until it was little more than a black dot, then disappearing completely. The air felt alive, thick and crawling with greasy, crackling power; he could feel every hair on his body standing on end, could feel pain in his teeth and bones. A pulse of energy shuddered through him as the Basilica seemed to *flex*, as though it had suddenly expanded and contracted back to its normal dimensions.

Then the air was cold and clear and silent once more; whatever had been there, whatever had flowed out of Dracula's body and taken him, was gone.

Jamie simply stared for a long moment, his mind struggling to begin the process of understanding what he had just witnessed. Then his eyes widened as reality came crashing back, and he raced across to where Frankenstein's body was lying on the cold tiled floor. He slid to his knees beside the monster, and waved Larissa away as she made to follow him.

"Find blood," he said. "For the others."

She nodded, and sped towards the church doors, leaving him alone with the monster. Frankenstein was still alive, but the pool of blood beneath him was huge and dark; his grey-green skin was almost translucent, and his chest was barely moving. He spluttered, blood running from the corners of his mouth, and fixed his eyes on Jamie's.

"It's going to be OK," whispered Jamie, his voice thick and choked. "We'll get help. You're going to be fine."

Frankenstein's face slowly twisted into a wide, bloody smile. "You're not much of a liar," he said, his voice a low croak. "We both know this is where my path ends."

"Don't say that," Jamie said, fiercely. "Don't you—"

The monster's hand closed over his and squeezed it. "It's all right," he whispered. "It's all right, Jamie."

He stared at Frankenstein, his throat sealed shut by the lump that had risen in it. The monster stared back at him, then something changed; one moment the wide, misshapen eyes were locked with his own, the next they were staring at nothing, the light fading from them as Jamie watched.

No. Oh, please, please no.

He placed a shaking hand on Frankenstein's huge chest, willing it to move, willing the monster's old, battered heart to beat again, and felt nothing.

Footsteps raced along the aisle and Larissa slid to her knees beside him, a plastic bag filled with bottles of blood in her hand. She dropped them on the tiles, and pulled him against her. He went willingly, his eyes squeezing shut as his face reached her shoulder, and began to cry, great wracking sobs that he could no more have stopped than he could the sun rising in the morning.

They stayed like that for a long time.

71

AFTER THE FIRE

CARCASSONNE, SOUTHERN FRANCE

Paul Turner stared impatiently at his NS9 counterpart.

"I'm not waiting any longer, Bob," he said. "Are you coming with me or not?"

Allen held up a finger as he spoke into his helmet's microphone. "Understood," he said. "Get me a report as soon as possible. Out." He cut the connection and turned towards Turner. "All right, Paul. Let's go."

"About time," he said, and strode up on to the drawbridge.

The Blacklight Director understood that Allen, as NATO Commanding Officer on the ground, had a great many things on his mind at this particular moment, but Turner had only one: he wanted to enter the old city, discover what had happened to bring the battle to its sudden conclusion, and find his strike team. Allen joined him on the drawbridge, Ovechkin and Tán and a dozen Operators behind him, and together they walked beneath the towering stone arch and on to the steep cobbled street that ran all the way up to Carcassonne's summit.

"I've sent a security team back to the camp," said Allen. "Your vampire Operators are taking the wounded there too."

"Good," said Turner, and nodded. He couldn't allow himself to think about the losses they had suffered on the ruined landscape at the foot of the hill; there would be more than enough time to dwell on them later. His raised his eyes to the distant Basilica, perched atop the city like a gargoyle, and felt a shiver crawl up his spine.

What the hell was all that? The black fire, the shock wave. What happened up there?

They walked up the street in silence, past looted shops and cafés that had been smashed to pieces, over cobblestones strewn with glass and stained with blood. Turner had tried to reach the strike team as soon as it had become clear that the main battle had been won, but had not been able to raise them; as a result, they were walking into the unknown.

Then, from somewhere up ahead, came the echo of footsteps.

Turner stopped dead, as Operators raised T-Bones and MP7s behind him. Bob Allen was stationary beside him, his face tight with unease; the two Directors stared in the same direction, waiting for whatever was about to round the corner. If it was vampires, or – *even worse* – Dracula himself, he doubted whether the remnants of the Multinational Force had strength enough to fight on.

Dark shapes appeared in the distance, moving steadily down the hill. Turner's heart pounded in his chest, then almost burst with relief as the first of the figures passed beneath one of the surviving street lights. It was Larissa Kinley; her face was pale, her eyes dark and empty, but her head was up and she was walking under her own steam.

Thank God, he thought. *Oh, thank God.*

Behind her came Valentin Rusmanov, the gentle smile on his face giving him the appearance of a man taking nothing more than a pleasant evening stroll, Angela Darcy, and a man with grey hair that Turner didn't recognise.

That's three of them, he thought. *Now where are the other two?*

Less than a second later, he had his answer.

Jamie Carpenter rounded the corner, his eyes smouldering with red fire, and walked slowly down the road, holding something large and bulky before him.

Oh no.

The members of the strike team noticed the cluster of Operators below them, and raised their hands in gestures of tired recognition. Turner gave no response; he was staring at Jamie Carpenter, at the teenage boy carrying the limp shape of Frankenstein in his arms, as carefully as if the monster's body was the most precious thing in the world.

The Blacklight Director walked up the hill to meet his Operators, his footsteps echoing in the night air until the two groups stopped and faced each other. Turner found himself unable to form a single word; whatever had happened up there in the darkness, four of them had lived to walk back down the hill. If nothing else, that was a remarkable achievement.

"What happened, Operators?" asked Bob Allen. "Did you get him? Is it over?"

Jamie glanced at his squad mates, then looked directly at Paul Turner.

"Yes," he said. "It's over."

Lizzy Ellison joined the growing crowd of Operators below the drawbridge with Jack Williams at her side and a mixture of surprise and confusion filling her mind.

She had been about to plunge her stake into the chest of a vampire when something had burst across the blackened battlefield, an invisible wall of energy that had slammed into her like razor wire, sending pain coursing through her body and filling her head with agonising white noise. The vampire had leapt into the air, screeching and howling and tearing at its skin, then bolted for the horizon, along with seemingly every single one of Dracula's followers. Ellison had been overcome by the desire to do the same; the feeling had been so awful, so horribly, painfully *wrong*, that she hadn't believed she could bear it.

Then, as quickly as it had come, it had disappeared.

Ellison had found herself momentarily incapable of standing and had sunk to her knees, her eyes flaring as she looked round the battlefield. The chaos of movement and noise that had surrounded her for what seemed like longer than she could remember was all gone, leaving behind an eerie silence and the silhouettes of hundreds of Operators as they looked around at each other, clearly unable to understand what had just happened.

Now, those same men and women were gathered in a deep semicircle below the entrance to the old city. Ellison was heartened by their number, but there was no escaping the reality of their losses; bodies were strewn across the battlefield as far as the eye could see. The crowd of survivors was silent, every pair of eyes trained on the drawbridge, through which Paul Turner and three of his fellow Directors had led a team less than five minutes earlier. Ellison had a hundred questions – the same ones, she was sure, as everyone else who had made it through the roaring nightmare of the battle – and she was trying to stay calm, stay patient, although it was hard; she had no idea where Jamie was or whether he was all right, and she had not seen Qiang since the earliest minutes of the fighting.

They'll be fine, she told herself. *I'm sure they'll both be fine.*

A low murmur spread through the crowd as figures began to emerge on to the drawbridge. Ellison held her breath, without realising she was doing so, as a squad of Operators walked quickly across and joined their colleagues in the crowd below. Behind them came the Directors from Blacklight, NS9, PBS6 and the SPC; they stopped near the edge and surveyed the dark, silent mass of Operators, their expressions unreadable. Finally, as the pressure in her chest began to build to painful levels, five men and women walked slowly out of the medieval city.

Ellison's eyes found Jamie Carpenter, and she felt her heart swell so rapidly with pride that she wondered whether it might burst; then she saw what he was carrying in his arms, saw the grey-green skin of the fallen monster, and pride was instantly replaced by sorrow.

"Operators," said General Allen. "I do not have the words to do justice to what I'm about to tell you, so you'll have to settle for the simple facts. The mission has been a success. Dracula is dead."

There was no elation in the American's voice; as Ellison watched, his gaze moved beyond the crowd of survivors to the scattered bodies of those who had not been so lucky. For a long moment, nobody moved or made a sound, until Jack Williams silently raised a fist in the air and held it there.

A second fist rose, far over on the other side of the crowd, then another, and another, until everyone, Ellison included, was holding a clenched hand above their head, a gesture of triumph but also of tribute to the dead. She remained that way for a long time, in silent solidarity with her colleagues, but her attention stayed fixed on the members of the strike team.

Valentin was grinning widely, Larissa and Angela Darcy and a grey-haired man she didn't recognise were smiling awkwardly, but Jamie Carpenter was merely staring into the distance, his face pale, the limp body of Frankenstein resting in his arms.

Sometime later, Jamie sat in the back of one of the convoy of trucks that were slowly returning to the displaced persons camp.

It had taken a great many minutes, combined with the gentle entreaties of more than half a dozen of his colleagues, to persuade him to let go of Frankenstein's body; an irrational part of Jamie's brain had been insisting that it wasn't final, it wasn't really *real*, until he released his hold on his late protector, that time could somehow be wound back if he simply refused to acknowledge what had happened. In the end, he had allowed Jack Williams and Dominique Saint-Jacques, both of whom had accompanied him to Paris to rescue the monster, so long ago now that it felt like it had happened to other people, and four other Operators to carefully carry Frankenstein's body to one of the jeeps, where they had laid it gently in the vehicle's bed.

In the back of the truck, nobody spoke.

Out of the corner of his eye, Jamie saw Paul Turner staring at him with unmistakable pride, but was unable to meet his Director's gaze. His heart was cleaved in two by grief, and his mind was still reeling from the horror he had witnessed in the Basilica; he wanted nothing more than to regain the strength to fly back to the Loop and sleep for a week while everybody else dealt with the fallout of the battle.

After he had finally been persuaded to let go of Frankenstein, he had been hugged half to death by Ellison. Over her shoulder, as he hung unprotestingly in her arms, he had seen Alan Foster and his wife cry tears of joy as they were reunited, had seen Larissa and Angela sitting together in the back of one of the jeeps, their heads lowered as people kept a respectful distance, and had watched Operators who had previously been mortally afraid of Valentin approach the ancient vampire and shake his hand. He had managed to gather himself for long enough to ask Ellison if she had seen Qiang, but his squad mate had shaken her head; there were hundreds of survivors, hundreds of wounded, and many hundreds of bodies lying on the battlefield, and it was going to take a painfully long time to identify them all.

A thought occurred to him, one that made him feel guilty for it having taken so long to do so, and he looked up.

"Please can someone send a message to the Loop for me?" he asked. "To let my mother know I'm OK?"

General Allen nodded. "Of course, son."

"Thank you," said Jamie, and lowered his head again.

Bob Allen watched as Operators filed out of the trucks and dropped silently from the sky.

The displaced persons camp was a hive of activity; men and women were being ferried to the hospital and staggering into the mess hall as exhausted Operators patrolled the perimeter and the surviving citizens of Carcassonne milled round their tents, too excited or simply too frightened to go back inside. The early estimate was that around eight hundred men and women had been killed during the vampire attack on the camp; it was another awful number in a day full of pain and loss, but it would have been much worse had the massacre not been ended by whatever had happened inside the Basilica. The trucks and jeeps immediately drove back out to continue the grisly task of collecting the bodies from the battlefield, covered by the handful of helicopters that had not taken part in the original deployment, and had therefore not been blown out of the sky.

Allen turned to Paul Turner. "When can we get a report from the strike team, Paul?"

The Blacklight Director shrugged. "When they're ready," he said. "I'm not going to rush them."

Allen nodded. He wanted to know what had happened, was *desperate* to know, but he would not push the issue unless it became necessary; the Operators who had made it back down after their showdown with the first vampire deserved at least a few minutes to gather themselves.

The assessment team he had despatched to the Basilique Saint-Nazaire had already delivered a preliminary report from inside the old church; blood was everywhere, outside the building and in, the walls and floors were broken, the windows were smashed to pieces, and there was no sign of Dracula or what had caused the explosion of black fire and the devastating shock wave. They had so far found no sign of any vampires inside the medieval city; the only living beings they had encountered had been the last of Dracula's hostages, who were now being escorted back to the camp.

Allen had no idea how many of his Operators were lying out there on the battlefield, their eyes staring at nothing, their blood soaking the ground. He knew it was wrong to think of his Department's losses as separate from those suffered by the others, but he couldn't help it; he would mourn all the dead, regardless of their nationality, but the lost men and women of NS9 would stay with him always.

Larissa Kinley appeared, managed a momentary smile in his direction, and asked to speak to Paul Turner in private. The Blacklight Director nodded his head, and Allen watched as they stepped out of earshot.

"I want to go back," said Larissa.

Turner frowned. "Back where?"

"To the Loop," she said. "I know there must be a thousand things that need doing here, but I'm asking for your permission to leave, sir."

"Why are you in such a hurry?"

"It's private, sir," she said. "But I'm sure you can guess."

Turner smiled. "Yes," he said. "I suspect I can."

"So?"

"You can go," he said. "I would tell you to fly back here when you've done what you need to do, but that's not going to be an option, is it?"

"No, sir," she said, and smiled at him. "Thank you, sir."

"Fine," said Turner. "Don't leave again before the rest of us get back."

"I won't, sir."

"All right. Dismissed."

Larissa nodded, backed up a few steps, and rose easily into the air. She surveyed the sprawling camp as she climbed, the wide fields full of light and noise and movement, then accelerated north-west, the cold air raising gooseflesh on her arms despite her uniform.

There was no way for her to process what had occurred inside the Basilica, what she and her colleagues had done; it was too big, too huge, and she suspected it would take days, if not months or even years, to come to terms with. On a rational level, she understood that they had won – Dracula was gone, his vampire army scattered to the winds – but the scale of the carnage, the sheer number of men and women who had lost their lives made it hard to feel triumphant. Instead, she focused her mind on a single manageable thing, a long-held hope that could now become reality.

She accelerated over the French coast, pushing herself ever faster, trying to let her brain find neutral, to let the sight of Dracula being pulled down into an unnatural, impossible pit drift away, but the black, oily hands would not leave her mind; she wondered how often she would see them again in her nightmares.

Quite often, I suspect, she thought. *For a while, at least.*

Barely twenty minutes later, she descended towards the anonymous-looking patch of forest that hid the Loop from prying eyes. She touched down in the hangar, and strode towards the double doors at its rear, wondering what it must have been like to be here while the battle raged, to be able to do nothing more than watch, and wait for victory or defeat.

The hangar had been empty, but the Level 0 corridor was both busy and noisy. Men and women were wandering in and out of the open door of the Ops Room, incredulous expressions on their faces as they talked in low voices, clearly barely able to believe the news that was arriving from France. Several of them congratulated her as she passed, shaking her hand and hugging her and asking dozens of questions; she merely smiled, and nodded, and pressed forward towards the lift at the end of the corridor.

Larissa got out when the doors slid open on Level C and flew down the corridor, more aware of her supernatural abilities than she had been in a long time, full of something that was close to pre-emptive nostalgia as she pushed open the doors of the infirmary.

One of the medical staff instantly appeared, concern on his face. "Lieutenant Kinley," he said. "Are you OK? Are you hurt?"

"No," she said, and shook her head. "I'm not hurt."

"OK," said the doctor, frowning slightly. "Then what can I do for you?"

She smiled. "You can cure me," she said. "Right now, please."

ZERO HOUR
PLUS 210 DAYS

72

THE END (1)

The active roster of Department 19 descended out of the darkening sky.

Blacklight's own helicopters had been destroyed as the Battle of Carcassonne had turned brutally and seemingly irrevocably against them; their remains were still lying, twisted and blackened, in the ruins of the city, being picked over by the forensic teams that would be investigating the details of the battle for many months to come. As a result, the helicopters lowering themselves towards the wide landing area outside the Loop's hangar belonged to the RAF, and had been sent to France hours earlier specifically to bring the Operators of Blacklight home; it had seemed, to both the Prime Minister and the Chief of the General Staff, like the least the country could do for the men and women who had saved the world.

Not all of the survivors were crammed into the helicopter holds, however. More than fifty Operators were still lying in beds inside the displaced persons camp hospital, although none were now listed as critical; they would be shipped home as soon as they were deemed fit to travel, and discharged.

Doors slid open in the sides of the helicopters as they touched down on the tarmac, and a flood of black-clad figures began to spill out, their arms laden with bags and helmets, their faces pale with exhaustion but full of relief at having made it home in one piece.

Inside the hangar, those members of the Department who had stayed behind were waiting for those who had fought and survived. As the Operators walked into the cavernous space, there were no cheers, and no applause; just an atmosphere of tangible pride, and a low rumble of noise as their friends and colleagues welcomed them home.

Jamie walked into the hangar with his colleagues, barely able to keep his head up and his eyes open.

He had spent the last twenty-four hours alternately trying to sleep for more than half an hour without waking up in a cold sweat with a scream rising in his throat, convinced that oily black liquid was creeping across his body, and going endlessly over what had happened in the Basilica; he had been required to tell the story over and over, to what had started to feel like an endless succession of audiences, each with their own list of questions at the ready. Paul Turner had eventually taken pity and sent him to the camp's command centre with a stenographer who had transcribed his account of the death of Dracula, producing a detailed document to which all enquiries were now being referred. Not for the first time, he had found himself immensely grateful to his Director.

Jamie had eventually received the news that Qiang had not survived the battle; by then he had been expecting it, but expectation had not diminished the cold pain of the reality. He knew it was not his fault – his selection for the strike team had rendered him unable to protect either of his squad mates – and he knew, with absolute certainty, that Qiang would have fought as hard as he could, for as long as he could. But that ultimately meant nothing, as did his relief that Ellison had survived, along with Jack Williams and Dominique Saint-Jacques and Paul Turner and dozens of other men and women he cared about; his squad mate was dead, and no amount of soul-searching or self-justification was going to change that unrelenting truth.

Qiang was dead, and Frankenstein was dead, and Dracula was dead.

At the macro level, he understood that the loss of two of his friends, along with all the others who had fallen outside Carcassonne, would be considered a price worth paying for the destruction of the first vampire. Jamie didn't believe that he would ever be able to feel the same way.

Matt pushed through the throng in the hangar towards him, Natalia close behind, a huge smile on his face. He launched himself at Jamie, almost knocking him over, and wrapped his arms tightly round him; Jamie hugged his friend back, a smile rising unstoppably on to his face, as Natalia looked on with eyes that brimmed with tears.

"You did it," whispered Matt, fiercely. "You and Larissa and the rest of them. You bloody did it."

Jamie gently extricated himself from his friend's grip. "Thank you," he said. "It's good to see you too."

"It is good," said Matt. "It really, *really* is. I'm so pleased you're OK. I heard... well, I know a lot of people... aren't."

Jamie grimaced, and nodded.

"Welcome back, Jamie," said Natalia. "You have done so well."

His smile returned; it was small, and it was bittersweet, but it was genuine.

"Thank you, Natalia," he said. "Have either of you seen Larissa?"

Matt frowned. "Isn't she with the rest of you?"

Jamie shook his head. "She flew back on her own yesterday."

"I haven't seen her," said Matt, and turned to Natalia. "Have you?"

The Russian girl shook her head. "But I am sure it is OK," she said. "I am sure she is fine."

Jamie nodded, but he didn't remotely share Natalia's certainty; he was sure he knew why Larissa had come back, and what she would likely already have done.

"I'm sure you're right," he said. "How's Kate? Is there any news?"

Matt frowned. "Didn't anyone tell you?"

Jamie's heart lurched. "Tell me what?" he asked. "Is she dead? Don't lie to me, Matt. Tell me the truth."

Matt shook his head, and smiled. "She's not dead, Jamie," he said. "She's awake."

Jamie stepped out of the airlock on Level H and walked quickly along the cellblock, his footsteps echoing, his heart heavy in his chest.

For several long minutes after leaving Matt and Natalia in the hangar, he had stood outside the Level 0 lift, unable to decide what he should do. The news that Kate was awake was wonderful, almost wonderful enough to pierce the grief that had settled over him so completely that he had already begun to wonder whether it was a permanent fixture, and a huge part of him had wanted to go straight to her room at the back of the Lazarus Project lab and hug her and tell her how glad he was that she was OK. But he was not quite able to convince himself that she should be his priority at this particular moment in time.

Despite everything that had happened since her unexpected return, not least her blunt, crushing admission that she had *not* come back for him, it had still taken all of Jamie's strength not to go and find Larissa. He had never doubted that her oft-stated desire not to be a vampire had been genuine, but if he was right about why she had come back on her own from France at the earliest possible opportunity, then it was one of the many things he was now realising he had not taken as seriously as he should have. Before she left, it would never have occurred to him to be anywhere other than at her side if, as he suspected, she was in the infirmary, but things were different now.

It's none of your business, a voice in his head had whispered. *You're just assuming that she'll want to see you. What if you're wrong?*

Jamie had listened to the voice, and made his decision. Both Larissa and Kate could wait; there was one person in the Loop who he knew, with absolute certainty, wanted to see him more than anybody else in the world.

He stepped out in front of the purple wall of his mother's cell. With her supernatural senses now a thing of the past, she was as unaware of her surroundings as any other human; as a result, the expression on her face when she looked round was a perfect mask of shock.

"Hello, Mum," he said.

She got slowly to her feet, a hand pressed over her mouth, her eyes wide and instantly full of tears.

"It's OK," he said. "I'm OK, Mum. Honestly."

She walked across the cell and stepped through the ultraviolet barrier into the corridor. Jamie stared at her, a lump rising in his throat, his mind blanked by exhaustion.

His mother reached out and placed her hand on his shoulder, as though she didn't trust her own eyes, and was checking to see whether he was genuinely real.

"Say something, Mum," he managed. "Please say something."

She didn't. Instead, she stepped forward and wrapped her arms round him as she began to cry, great sobs of relief that reverberated through him as he held her.

Larissa shut the door of her quarters behind her, unzipped her uniform, and let it fall to the floor. She had hated having to put it back on when the doctor had told her she was being discharged from the infirmary, but she had hated the idea of walking through the Loop wearing only a hospital gown even more.

She opened the bag that she had twice carried across the Atlantic

Ocean and pulled out a T-shirt and a pair of jeans. She put them on, slid her feet into shoes that felt like velvet compared to the standard-issue Blacklight boots, tied her hair back in a loose knot, and examined herself in the mirror above her desk. She didn't think she looked any different, a prospect that had entered her mind as the doctor brought the plastic bag of bright blue liquid; she had momentarily wondered whether the five years in which she had aged almost imperceptibly slowly would suddenly present themselves in her face, changing the reflection she was used to seeing. But she *looked* the same, at least as far as she could tell.

How she *felt* was something else entirely.

The last eighteen hours had been a blur; she had drifted in and out of consciousness as the cure worked its way through her system, her thoughts scattered and insubstantial, until she had sunk down into unconsciousness so deep and absolute that not even dreams could penetrate it. Now, eight hours after she had woken up a fundamentally different person, what she mostly felt was weak.

Some of it, she knew, was the aftermath of the cure's radical transformation of her body, but most of it was simply the weakness that came with once again being human; she had forgotten how many aches and pains you just got used to, how easily tired you were, how dangerously vulnerable to heat and cold and hunger. Her life had changed beyond all measure since she had last experienced such things – she had been a teenager with horizons that stretched no further than the small town she had been born and raised in – and the feeling was unsettling, to say the least; her adult self had never really encountered anything like it.

There were also practical considerations that she had never really thought through; she had become accustomed to a freedom that was now gone, to the ability to live her life without any real limitations beyond the need to stay out of direct sunlight. Now, if she went back to Haven – *when*, she told herself, *not if*, when *you go back* – she would have to buy a flight to New York and sit in a plane for seven hours and wait in line at airport security and hire a car and drive up the Hudson River Valley and hope the traffic wasn't too bad, rather than simply glide across the ocean and land on the veranda of the big house.

She could no longer fly.

She could be hurt.

She would grow old, and one day she would die.

But she would never again need to drink blood, she could walk freely in the sun, and she could create a life that would have meaning, *real* meaning.

She could be a human being again.

And that was all that mattered.

Almost, she told herself. *Almost all that matters.*

She picked her uniform up off the floor, pulled the console from its belt, and started typing a message on its screen.

The door to Larissa's quarters swung open before Jamie had even finished knocking on it, and he smiled as soon as she appeared.

"So you did it then?" he said.

She nodded, and smiled back at him. "Did someone tell you or can you tell?"

"I can tell," he said. "You smell different. Not worse or anything, just… different."

"Different."

He nodded. "Your message said you needed to see me. Can I come in?"

"Of course," said Larissa, and stepped aside. "Sorry. I'm a bit out of it."

"Understandable," he said, and walked into her room. "Did you hear about Kate?"

"I did," she said. "I tried to go and see her when they discharged me, but the doctor looking after her told me I have to go back in the morning."

"That saves me a trip then," he said. "I'll go tomorrow. Does she know you're back?"

"I don't know. I don't think so."

"I guess you'll find out tomorrow."

Larissa nodded. "We can go together, if you want," she said. "It might be better for Kate to have all her visitors at once."

Jamie nodded. "Sounds good."

"Have you seen your mum?"

"I was just there," he said.

"How pleased was she to see you?" asked Larissa. "On a scale of one to ten?"

"About twenty-five," said Jamie, and grinned. "I asked them to let her know I was all right before we left Carcassonne, and someone *had* told her, but I don't think she believed them."

"She probably needed to see you with her own eyes."

Jamie nodded. "I guess so," he said. "So what did you need to see me about?"

Larissa looked at him for a long moment, the expression he knew all too well on her face, the one that meant she had something serious to talk to him about. Then it disappeared, replaced by a smile so beautiful it momentarily took his breath away.

"It can wait," she said. "You should go and get some sleep. We can talk after we see Kate."

Jamie frowned, but nodded. "If you're sure?"

"I'm sure."

"All right," he said. "Nine o'clock tomorrow?"

"Nine sounds good," said Larissa. "See you in the morning."

ZERO HOUR
PLUS 211 DAYS

73

THE END (II)

Kate Randall lay in her bed, watching the BBC news channel she had been glued to since she had woken up twenty-four hours earlier.

Details of what was already being referred to as 'The Victory Over Dracula' were still sketchy; most of what was being reported was anecdotal, second- and third-hand stories allegedly told by Operators who had taken part in the battle to residents of the displaced persons camp, which they had passed on to the reporters swarming in ever greater numbers outside the gates. There had been no official statement from any of the governments who had sent their supernatural Departments to Carcassonne, or from NATO, but there did seem to be a consensus of opinion on one thing, at least.

Dracula had been defeated, and humanity had won.

Kate had woken up the previous morning with a pounding headache and without the slightest clue where she was. She had looked around the sparse room, taking in the machinery beside her bed and the tubes and wires in her arms, and had locked eyes with one of the Loop's medical staff, who had almost jumped out of his skin before rushing to her side and summoning an army of his colleagues. As he had examined her and asked her questions, what had happened to her had come flooding back: the hospital, her father, the smell of petrol, the gun trembling in Greg Browning's hand.

"My dad…" she had said.

"He's fine," replied the doctor. "He's recovering well. He's going to be fine."

Her waking up had clearly been a surprise to the Blacklight doctors; they had told her since that their intention had been to allow her body to recover enough strength for them to safely turn her, and let her new vampire side repair her injuries. For long hours, they examined printout after printout of test results, before concluding that what had happened was simple: while they waited, she had healed and woken up. Then most of the medical staff had left in a hurry, leaving just one doctor behind to monitor her, and she had asked where they were all going.

"They're heading back this evening," said the doctor. "We need to be ready."

"Who's heading back?"

"Everyone," said the doctor, his eyes widening. "Oh God. Of course. You don't know."

"Don't know what?"

He had turned a monitor towards her, and tuned it to BBC News.

"It's over," said the doctor. "They did it. We won."

Less than ten minutes later – the exact amount of time, she suspected, that it had taken for the medical staff to tell him she had woken up – the doctor had passed her a message from Paul Turner, welcoming her back to life and telling her that Jamie had survived the Battle of Carcassonne, and she had closed her eyes for a long time as tears of relief rolled down her face. When the lump in her throat had subsided, she had started to watch the news coverage, and had done little else since. Matt and Natalia had kept her company for a few hours, but although it had been lovely to see them, and to see their clear relief at her recovery, they knew little more than she did about what had happened in France; they were all in the dark together.

The door of her room opened, making her jump. She turned towards it, and felt her heart swell in her chest as she saw Jamie standing in the doorway. Then he stepped into the room, and she froze as she saw who was with him.

"Hey, Kate," said Larissa, a fierce smile on her face.

For a long moment, she could form no words; she merely stared at her friend.

"Hey, Larissa," she managed, eventually, her voice little more than a whisper.

"How are you feeling?" asked Jamie.

She stared at them for a long moment, then smiled. "Close the door and get in here," she said. "I want to know absolutely *everything*."

"Are you going to take the cure, Jamie?" asked Larissa.

Jamie grimaced. They were standing in the corridor outside the Lazarus Project, having finally managed to persuade Kate that there was no detail of what had taken place in Carcassonne that she did not now know about, and that she should take her doctor's repeated advice and get some rest. It had taken a cast-iron promise that they would come back and see her that afternoon before she let them leave.

"Is this what you wanted to see me about yesterday?" he asked.

Larissa nodded.

"I'm not sure about the cure," he said. "Not yet, at least. I don't know."

She nodded. "Fair enough. You need to do what you think is best."

"I'm not ruling it out," he said. "I just… don't know."

"I get it, Jamie. It's OK."

He stared at her. She *looked* the same as she always had, but, even without his supernatural senses, he would have known that something was different; it was in the way she carried herself, in the set of her shoulders and the straightness of her neck. It looked like a great weight had been removed from her.

His console beeped on his belt. He swore silently, marvelling at the little plastic rectangle's almost unfailing lack of tact, and checked the screen.

"What is it?" asked Larissa.

"It's Paul," he said. "He wants to see me."

She nodded again. "You should go."

"Yeah," he said, and narrowed his eyes. "Do you actually feel better, Larissa? You know, now that you've done it?"

"No," she said. "I don't feel better. But that's sort of the point."

He nodded.

She stepped forward and kissed his cheek, a chaste brush of her lips. "I hope you work it out," she said. "Come and find me when you do."

Three hundred miles away, Bob Allen stood on the tarmac at Toulouse-Blagnac Airport, watching his Department load itself back into the two huge cargo planes that had brought them from Nevada.

The clean-up at Carcassonne would likely continue for months, but he wasn't sticking around for it; the French government was handling the aftermath of the battle, under the watchful eye of NATO, and Allen had been quite happy to be removed from command. He had handed over to General Ducroix of the French military and Central Director Vallens of the DGSI in the command centre the previous evening, and was confident the situation was in good hands.

He was just happy to be going home.

The huge hangars beside the runway were full of activity, as weapons and vehicles and equipment were broken down and packed and loaded. Hundreds of Operators and support staff were milling around, clearly as eager as he was to be on their way. Allen watched them, a mixture of emotions filling him. He was proud of what they had done, *immensely proud*, but also profoundly sad; a heartbreaking number of good men and women were going back to America, back on to the planes in bags, including Danny Lawrence.

He believed – would *always* believe – in what they had achieved in Carcassonne, in the battle they had fought with such bravery and determination, but oh God, the cost had been so high.

So very, very high.

Paul Turner was in his usual position behind his desk when his intercom buzzed into life and the Security Operator outside his quarters informed him that Lieutenant Carpenter was there to see him.

"Send him in," he said, and sat back in his chair.

In an act of almost unprecedented self-interest, the Blacklight Director had left the Loop less than ten minutes after the helicopters touched down from France the previous evening, and gone home.

A night's sleep in his own bed, beside the woman he loved more than anything else in the world, had done him more good than he could possibly have imagined; he felt like a new man, as if his depleted batteries had somehow been fully charged, filling him with energy and banishing the exhaustion that had become his constant companion in recent months.

When his driver had picked him up two hours ago to bring him back to the Loop, he had promised Caroline that he would spend more nights at home in the coming weeks and months. The smile that had appeared on her face was worth every sacrifice that had been required of him.

He had returned to find a mountain of new paper on his desk. On the top was a letter bearing the legend OFFICE OF THE PRIME MINISTER, congratulating him on his Department's efforts in Carcassonne and asking him to call Downing Street at his earliest convenience; the Prime Minister was apparently eager to hear his personal account of what had taken place. Turner had put the letter aside, and found similar notes of praise and thanks from the President of the United States, the Prime Minister of Japan, the President of Russia and a huge number of other world leaders and dignitaries. He had leafed quickly through them, until he reached a report from the Surveillance Division, stamped with a reference number he recognised. He had read it, read it again, and immediately summoned Jamie Carpenter.

The young Lieutenant pushed open the door and walked into the room.

"Good morning, Jamie," he said.

"Good morning, sir," said Jamie. "You wanted to see me?"

"Yes," he said. "I have to tell you something that came up yesterday. I don't know if it's good news or bad, to be entirely honest with you."

"OK, sir," said Jamie. "What is it?"

"It's your father," he said. "He's missing."

Jamie frowned. "Missing?"

Turner nodded. "The Surveillance Division noted some discrepancies in their monitoring while we were in France," he said. "They sent Norfolk police to check on him yesterday, but they reported no sign of him in your grandmother's cottage. What they *did* find in the same village was a teenager wearing your father's locator chip on a rubber band round his wrist."

Jamie grunted with laughter. "So he's gone?"

Turner nodded. "It looks that way."

"Do we have any idea where, sir?"

"No," said Turner. "A priority investigation has been opened, but I'd be extremely surprised if your dad left anything for them to find."

"So would I," said Jamie, and nodded. "He's an expert at disappearing."

"The likeliest result of this development is that Julian will eventually try to contact you," he said. "I'm not going to tell you what to do if that happens."

"Thank you, sir," said Jamie. "And thanks for telling me."

Turner nodded. "There's something else," he said. "Can I assume that you haven't taken the cure because other Operators got there first and you have to wait until a bed becomes available?"

Jamie didn't respond.

"You understand that the cure is mandatory for all members of the Department?" he asked.

"Yes, sir."

"And you understand that when something is mandatory, that means it applies to you?"

"Yes, sir," said Jamie, and grinned. "I understand that."

Turner nodded, and smiled at his young Lieutenant. "Good," he said. "I just wanted to check, given some of the conversations you and I have had in the past. Dismissed."

Matt and Natalia stood outside the door of the Loop's infirmary, watching through the window as dozens of Operators recovered from the cure they had helped to make a reality.

The programme of undoing PROMETHEUS had begun as soon as the men and women of the active roster arrived back from Carcassonne, but whereas the turn had been orchestrated on a random basis, the cure was being administered first come first served. Matt had been heartened to see that, despite the exhaustion that every Operator must surely be feeling, there was no shortage of volunteers. During one of their many conversations about PROMETHEUS, the Director had considered the idea of keeping a small number of vampire Operational Squads, an idea that Matt, who had devoted every minute of his waking life for many months to finding a cure, had been profoundly uncomfortable with; he was deeply relieved to see that the Director appeared to have abandoned the notion.

"Let's go," said Natalia.

Matt nodded, and they fell into step as they walked back towards the lift.

"It is good to see," said Natalia. "Everything is very good."

Matt smiled. "It is."

"So what happens now?"

"What do you mean?" he asked.

"Soon there will be no more Lazarus Project," said Natalia. "What then?"

"I don't know," he said, and pressed the CALL button as they reached the lift. "Do you think you'll go back to Russia when the project officially ends?"

"No," said Natalia, instantly, and Matt felt relief flood his system. "I do not want to go back."

"That's great," he said, and blushed at the enthusiasm in his own voice. "I mean, you shouldn't go if you don't want to."

She smiled at him, her face pale and beautiful, her eyes sparkling under the fluorescent lights. The doors of the lift slid open, and they stepped through them.

"What about you?" she asked, as he pressed the button marked B.

"I don't know," he said, and shrugged. "I'll still be a member of Blacklight when Lazarus is over. I expect they'll move me to the Science Division."

"I do not think Major Turner will make you stay unless you want to," said Natalia. "So what would you *like* to do?"

Matt smiled. "I'd like to go to university," he said. "If things had been different, I would have been going in a couple of months. I'd been looking forward to it since I was a little boy."

"University is a good thing," said Natalia.

"You should know," he said, his smile widening. "You graduated from one when you were fourteen."

She smiled, as delicate pale pink rose into her cheeks. "There is still a lot I would like to learn," she said. "Where would you go? I do not think you will have a shortage of options."

"I always liked the sound of Cambridge," he said, as the lift slowed.

"I am told Cambridge is nice," said Natalia, and smiled at him.

Matt smiled back, and took her hand as they walked down the corridor towards his quarters.

Jamie sat on the edge of his bed, turning what Paul Turner had told him over and over in his mind.

On the one hand, the thought of his father being on the loose was unsettling; knowing where he was, and that restrictions were in place to keep him there, had provided a welcome certainty to the situation. But on the other, it made the dilemma he had been struggling with for months – whether or not to tell his mother that her husband was still alive – an awful lot easier to resolve. There was now absolutely nothing to be gained by telling her the truth; if anything, telling her his dad was alive without any idea of where he was would be infinitely crueller than not telling her.

She's been through enough, he thought. *God knows she has.*

Jamie got up, exited his quarters, and headed for the lift at the end of Level B. As it descended towards the cellblock, he replayed the conversation he and his mother had managed the previous day once they finally stopped crying on each other's shoulders.

He had disabled the ultraviolet wall of her cell and flopped down on the sofa as his mother set about making tea. The relief and love on her face had disarmed him completely, and made him realise how much of the determination that had kept him fighting in Carcassonne had come from a desire not to let his mother down, not to put her through the unimaginable misery of losing her son less than five years after her husband.

"I don't want to know what happened in France," she said, as she tipped water into the pot. "I've had more than enough darkness to last me a lifetime, so I don't want to know any of the details. Just tell me one thing. Is all of this over and done with?"

"I think so," he said. "I hope so."

"Good," said his mother, and handed him a mug of tea. "I'm very pleased to hear it."

"So what are you going to do, Mum?" he said. "Now that you're free to go?"

She settled down on the sofa beside him, and sighed. "Oh, I don't know. I like the idea of sitting in the sun, so I suppose I might go away for a little while. France, maybe, or Italy." She looked at him, a small, hopeful smile on her face. "You could come with me, you know. I'm sure you deserve some time off."

Jamie smiled at her. "I think I probably do," he said. "Maybe I'll ask Major Turner for a holiday."

"Maybe you should," she said.

Silence settled over the cell as they drank their tea. Jamie knew his mother wouldn't push it, that she likely already believed that he wouldn't be accompanying her on whatever trip she decided to take, and he didn't have the heart to tell her that she was probably right.

"So what now?" she asked, eventually.

"I don't know," he said, and shrugged. "It will take months to put the Department back together, and I don't even know for certain whether they're going to. They might decide that—"

"That's not what I meant, Jamie," she said, gently. "I meant what now *for you*? Are you going to take the cure?"

He grimaced. "Not now, Mum," he said. "Please. I've barely had a second to think since we got back from Carcassonne."

"What is there to think about?" she asked. "You either want to be a vampire or you don't."

"It's not that simple," he said. "The official policy is for everyone who was turned to take the cure, without exception, but I'm not even sure whether I want to be an Operator any more, never mind whether or not I want to take the cure."

"What about Larissa?" said his mother. "What does she think?"

Jamie grunted with laughter. "She's already cured," he said. "She never wanted to be a vampire, so she took it the second she got back to the Loop. But she'll be going home to America any day, so it doesn't really matter what she thinks. She didn't come back for me."

His mother put down her mug and gave him a gentle smile. "You have to do what you think is right, love," she said. "That's all you can do."

What you think is right, thought Jamie, as he got out of the lift and stepped into the airlock. *That's great. But what if you don't know what that is?*

Ellison floated a centimetre above a deep leather armchair in the officers' mess with a bottle of beer in her hand, and waited for her friends to join her. It was barely lunchtime, early to start drinking, but every Operator who had gone to France had been given forty-eight hours off, and she saw no point in wasting them.

She had gone to the infirmary when she woke up, but had been told that she would have to wait until tomorrow at the earliest to receive the cure. In truth, she had not been *entirely* disappointed; she didn't want to spend the rest of her life as a vampire, but she would be lying to herself if she tried to claim that she would not miss the remarkable power that came with being one. The feeling of floating in the air, completely unshackled from gravity, was utterly intoxicating.

She had spent much of the last thirty-six hours grieving for Qiang. She did not have the slightest doubt that he had died doing his duty, but she couldn't help but wonder whether things would have been different if PROMETHEUS had not been suspended before it was complete. If Qiang had been turned, would he still be alive? And if she had *not* been, would she be dead? There was no way for her to know, but she doubted she would ever stop asking herself the questions.

The door of the mess swung open, and she managed a smile as Jack Williams and Dominique Saint-Jacques walked through it. It was instantly obvious to her that Dominique was still a vampire, whereas Jack had taken the cure. They smelled different, but there was more to it than that; there was something indescribable, something she could only perceive on an instinctive level that she could not have explained. Dominique seemed somehow *brighter* than Jack, as though he was simply more alive.

"Mind if we join you?" asked Jack, as they arrived beside her table.

"I suppose not," she said, and smiled at him. "I'm supposed to be meeting a handsome stranger, but the two of you will do until he gets here."

"What an honour," said Dominique, but he was grinning as he lowered himself into one of the empty chairs.

"Who else is coming?" asked Ellison.

"Angela," said Jack. "Laura O'Malley, Ben Harris, Tom Johnson and a bunch of others. Almost everyone who isn't in the infirmary."

"All right," said Ellison. "Get a drink, you two, quickly."

Jack nodded, and strode towards the bar. Ellison and Dominique waited in easy silence until he returned with an armful of beers. He set the bottles down on the table, and settled into his chair.

"OK," said Ellison, and lifted a bottle. "Before anyone else arrives. To Qiang, and your brother Patrick, and Frankenstein, and everyone else we've lost. To fallen friends."

Dominique and Jack sat forward and raised bottles of their own. "Fallen friends," they repeated.

Kate looked round as the door to her room opened again, an impatient expression on her face. She was still tired, and weak, but she was already bored of lying in bed, and had been silently counting down the minutes until Jamie and Larissa came back to see her again.

"It's about time," she said, as the door swung open. "I was starting to think you weren't—"

The words died in her throat.

Standing in the doorway, being supported by one of the Loop's doctors, was her father. His face was pale, and he looked older than he ever had, but his eyes were bright, and the smile on his face was wide and shining with love.

For a long moment, they simply stared at each other. In the end, it was her dad who found his voice first.

"Hello, love," he said. "I can't tell you how pleased I am to see you."

Jamie stopped outside the square room that had been home to Valentin Rusmanov for almost a year and looked through the ultraviolet wall.

The ancient vampire was sitting on his sofa. He lowered the

newspaper he was reading, and smiled. "Good afternoon, Jamie," he said. "Come to say goodbye?"

He frowned. "Are you going somewhere?"

"Not right this minute," said Valentin. "Tomorrow, in all likelihood. Come in, by all means."

Jamie entered his override code into the panel on the wall and walked into the cell.

"Tea?" asked Valentin, getting to his feet.

Jamie smiled. "No more tea," he said. "I've drunk enough to last a lifetime."

"That's a physical impossibility," said Valentin. "But as you wish. Do sit down."

Jamie nodded, took a seat in one of the plastic chairs, and looked at what was now the second oldest vampire in the world.

"What's the plan?" he asked. "Are you going back to New York?"

"Eventually," said Valentin. "But there's no hurry. All this time spent inside a concrete box has given me quite the wanderlust."

Jamie smiled. "I can imagine it would. I presume you won't be taking the cure then?"

"I suspect not," said Valentin, and smiled. "I have been a vampire for more than five hundred years. I don't know how to be anything else."

"You could learn?"

"No," said Valentin. "I don't think I could."

"Fair enough," said Jamie. "It's your life."

Valentin nodded, then narrowed his eyes. "What about you, Jamie? Have you made a decision?"

"I don't know," he said. "I really don't know."

"It's a simple choice," said Valentin. "Human or vampire. You've been both. So pick one."

"If it's so simple, then you choose for me," said Jamie, heat flickering behind his eyes. "Tell me what I should do."

Valentin looked at him with clear sympathy. "I'm not your father, Jamie," he said. "You're a grown man, and you need to do what feels right to you. But if you *did* want a small piece of advice, it would be this. There is a beauty to living a real life, with its phases and stages, in which you change and you grow. To live like I have is unnatural. Fun? Yes. Exciting? Yes. But in the end, it is not really living."

Jamie stared at the old vampire for a long moment, then got up, walked across the cell, and wrapped his arms round him. Valentin frowned, his eyes flaring with momentary red, then hugged him back, his mouth curling into a small smile.

"You did well, Jamie," he said, his voice little more than a whisper. "Make sure you find a moment or two to be proud of yourself. It was an honour to fight alongside you."

Jamie felt his heart swell, and released his grip. He stepped back and met the ancient vampire's gaze, refusing to be embarrassed by his display of affection.

"I have something for you," said Valentin, his voice still low. "I've thought long and hard about whether I should give it to you, whether it would be better just to destroy it, but I can't convince myself to do so. So I will do what was asked of me, and let you decide how to proceed."

Jamie frowned. "What are you talking about?"

The old vampire flew across the cell, withdrew something from the pile of books that covered his desk, and held it out; it was an envelope, creased and tattered and stained with patches of dark red. Jamie took it, frowning with confusion, then felt his heart stop dead.

He recognised the handwriting instantly; he had seen it thousands of times, in Christmas and birthday cards, on notes stuck to the fridge door and scribbled all over the crossword page in the Sunday paper.

To my wife and son, he read.

"What is this?" he asked, his voice low and suddenly hoarse.

"I saw your father," said Valentin. "Outside Carcassonne, after I defused the missile. He was terribly wounded, but we spoke, and he asked me to give that to you."

"He was there?" asked Jamie, forcing himself to tear his gaze from the envelope and look at the old vampire. "He was fighting at Carcassonne?"

Valentin nodded.

"Did he make it?" he asked, his throat tightening. "Did he survive?"

The old vampire met his gaze, then shook his head.

Jamie stared. "How did he die?" he managed.

"Well," said Valentin. "With honour."

Jamie grimaced, his face screwing up involuntarily as a cocktail of emotions threatened to overwhelm him; there was grief there, a wide, bitter streak of it, but there was pride too, in the fact that his father had clearly decided to try and do *something* rather than sit idly by as the end of the world approached. He turned the envelope over, took a deep breath, and ripped it open.

"Don't," said Valentin.

Jamie looked up. "What?"

"Don't read it here, Jamie. It's a private matter between you and him. I don't want any part of it."

He hesitated, then nodded and put the envelope in his pocket. "Thank you for bringing this to me," he said. "I appreciate it, probably more than you know."

"You're welcome," said Valentin. "I hope it brings you peace."

Jamie nodded again, and walked towards the open front of the cell. When he reached the border of the small room, he turned back. "Goodbye, Valentin," he said. "Look after yourself."

The old vampire smiled. "I have never done anything else," he said. "Goodbye, Jamie."

Ten minutes later, Jamie slid the sheet of paper out of the envelope and put it face down on his bed.

A large part of him didn't want to read it, wanted to rip it to shreds and burn the pieces and leave his dad where it had taken months to put him: in the past, where he could do no more harm.

But he knew he couldn't.

If he destroyed it, he would never stop wondering what it had said.

He took a deep breath, turned over the sheet of paper, and began to read the handwritten lines. When he was finished, he put the letter carefully back into the envelope, lowered his head, and squeezed his eyes shut. The final line danced endlessly through his mind: three simple words, one simple request that cut to the very centre of his being.

Jamie opened his eyes.

"I already have, Dad," he whispered. "I already have."

ZERO HOUR
PLUS 213 DAYS

74

THE BEGINNING

Jamie looked out through the huge double doors of the hangar and saw Larissa standing in the distance, at the point on the wide grounds where the early morning sunlight overwhelmed the shade.

He walked slowly across the tarmac of the landing area and the runway, and on to the soft grass. His head was thick with tiredness, his body weak, but the air around him was cool and invigorating. He stopped beside Larissa, and looked down at the line of shadow as it moved, almost imperceptibly slowly, towards them.

"You did it then," she said, without lifting her eyes from the ground.

Jamie nodded. "Yes."

"Why?"

"I don't know," he said. "It felt like the right thing to do."

"As long as you didn't do it for me," said Larissa. "You know that—"

"I know you're going back to America," he said.

They stood in silence for long, still moments. In the distance, Jamie heard the rumble of an engine as one of the black SUVs emerged from the authorisation tunnel; he strained his ears, and realised that it was all he *could* hear. Twenty-four hours ago, he would have been able to hear the humming and fizzing of the electrified fences at the Loop's perimeter, the birds and animals in the forest beyond, and the heartbeat of the girl standing beside him.

Now, he was once again the same as everybody else.

He pulled his father's letter from his pocket and held it out towards Larissa. She narrowed her eyes, took it from his fingers without a word, and began to read. Jamie watched, waiting silently for her to finish.

She lowered the sheet of paper, and looked at him with tears in her eyes. "Where did this come from?"

"He was at Carcassonne," he said. "Fighting with the others. He gave this to Valentin to give to me. Before he died."

"Oh, Jamie," said Larissa. "I'm so sorry."

"Thank you," he said, and nodded. "It's all right. I'm all right."

"Have you shown it to your mum?"

"No," said Jamie. "Not yet."

"Are you going to?"

"I honestly don't know," he said.

She stared at him for a long moment, then returned her gaze to the line of sunlight that was slowly creeping closer and closer to their toes.

"You could come with me," she said.

Jamie frowned. "What?"

"To Haven," she said. "You could come with me."

"I don't know," he heard himself say. "There's so much to do here, so much to sort out. There are vampires that want the cure, and ones who don't that need tracking down."

"I know," said Larissa.

"The Department needs rebuilding again. Kate's only just woken up, and Matt and Natalia and my mum are all going to go, probably sooner rather than later. Frankenstein's gone and Valentin's gone and you're going to go and it's all just—"

"I know," she said. "I get it, Jamie. I really do."

He nodded. "So what happens now?"

She shrugged. "I have absolutely no idea."

"So what do we do?" he asked.

Larissa raised her head and smiled at him, a beautiful, brilliant smile, full of life. "Take my hand, Jamie," she said.

He reached out, and watched her fingers close over his. Then she squeezed his hand and led him forward, into the light.

ACKNOWLEDGEMENTS

My love and thanks to Charlie, Nick, Sarah, Mum, Peter, and everyone else who helped turn a dream into a reality. You know who you are.

My eternal gratitude to everyone who has picked up a copy of a *Department 19* novel in a bookshop or a library, or downloaded an ebook. The idea that something I wrote is out there in the world, being read by people who could be doing literally anything else with their time, never ceases to be amazing, and humbling.

Lux E Tenebris.